Portraits of Murder

Alfred Hitchcock

Portraits of Murder

Galahad Books　　　　　　　　　　**New York**

Copyright © 1988 by Davis Publications, Inc.

Published in 1988 by
Galahad Books, a division of LDAP, Inc.
166 Fifth Avenue
New York, NY 10010

By arrangement with Davis Publications, Inc.

Library of Congress Catalog Card Number: 88-80837

ISBN: 0-88365-727-9

Printed in the United States of America

ACKNOWLEDGMENTS

Grateful acknowledgment is made to the following for permission to reprint their copyrighted material:

Quiet Backwater by Stanley Abbot, copyright © 1964 by H.S.D. Publications, Inc., reprinted by permission of Scott Meredith Literary Agency, Inc.;

To Kill An Angel by William Bankier, copyright © 1976 by Davis Publications, Inc., reprinted by permission of Curtis Brown Ltd.;

When This Man Dies and *The Most Unusual Snatch* by Lawrence Block, copyright © 1964, 1967 by H.S.D. Publications, Inc., reprinted by permission of the author;

The Healer by George C. Chesbro, copyright © 1974 by H.S.D. Publications, Inc., reprinted by permission of the author;

Who? by Michael Collins, copyright © 1972 by H.S.D. Publications, Inc., reprinted by permission of the author;

The Girl in Gold by Jonathan Craig, copyright © 1970 by H.S.D. Publications, Inc., reprinted by permission of Scott Meredith Literary Agency, Inc.;

Murder, Anyone? by Phil Davis, copyright © 1972 by H.S.D. Publications, Inc., reprinted by permission of Ann Elmo Agency, Inc.;

The House Guest by Babs H. Deal, copyright © 1967 by H.S.D. Publications, Inc., reprinted by permission of the author;

The Big Bajoor by Borden Deal, copyright © 1962 by H.S.D. Publications, Inc., reprinted by permission of the author's Estate;

Public Office by Elijah Ellis, copyright © 1964 by H.S.D. Publications, Inc., reprinted by permission of Scott Meredith Literary Agency, Inc.;

Room To Let by Hal Ellson, copyright © 1962 by H.S.D. Publications, Inc., reprinted by permission of the author;

Variations of an Episode by Fletcher Flora, copyright © 1967 by H.S.D. Publications, Inc., reprinted by permission of Scott Meredith Literary Agency, Inc.;

Murder in Mind by C. B. Gilford, copyright © 1971 by H.S.D. Publications, Inc., reprinted by permission of Scott Meredith Literary Agency, Inc.;

The Lure and the Clue by Edwin P. Hicks, copyright © 1963 by H.S.D. Publications, Inc., reprinted by permission of the author;

Shattered Rainbow and *Arbiter of Uncertainties* by Edward D. Hoch, copyright © 1963, 1969 by H.S.D. Publications, Inc., reprinted by permission of the author;

Wonderful, Wonderful Violence and *Minutes of Terror* by Donald Honig, copyright © 1959, 1974 by Donald Honig, reprinted by permission of Raines & Raines;

Money to Burn and *The Keeper* by Clark Howard, copyright © 1962, 1971 by H.S.D. Publications, Inc., reprinted by permission of the author;

The Island by William Jeffrey, copyright © 1972 by H.S.D. Publications, Inc., reprinted by permission of the author;

The Volunteers by Reynold Junker, copyright © 1966 by H.S.D. Publications, Inc., reprinted by permission;

CONTENTS

EDWARD D. HOCH

Shattered Rainbow

O'Bannion quit his job at three o'clock on a sunny Friday afternoon in April. It happened suddenly, though certainly he had considered the possibility many times in the past. It happened with words, a pounding fist, and then the decision that could not be recalled. It happened, oddly enough, on the same day that a man called Green robbed and killed an armed messenger for the Jewelers' Exchange.

O'Bannion, who had never heard of Green, spent the rest of the afternoon cleaning out his desk, separating the few personal possessions into a home-bound pile. When his secretary returned with her afternoon coffee she asked him what he was doing, though it must have been obvious.

"I finally did it, Shirl," he told her. "I walked out on the old man."

She sat down hard, the coffee forgotten. "You mean you quit?" she asked, still not quite able to grasp it.

"I quit. Walked out while he was still swearing at me. Now if I can just pack my briefcase and make it to the elevator before he comes after me, I really will have quit."

"What will you do?"

"I'm sure I won't sit around the house feeling sorry for myself. This is the best thing that could have happened to me." It sounded properly convincing, even to him.

He zipped shut the briefcase and told her goodbye. There was no sense being emotional about it at that point. "Goodbye, Mr. O'Bannion," she called after him. "Let me know when you get settled."

"Sure. Sure I will."

He rode down in the elevator with an afternoon's assortment of secretaries bound for coffee and businessmen bound for martinis, but he no longer felt a part of them. The cut-off had been too clean, too certain. He was a man without a job, and he wondered how he would tell his wife.

Kate and the kids were still out shopping when he reached home just before five o'clock. He hung his raincoat carefully in the closet and mixed himself a drink. It was the first time he'd drunk before dinner in years, but he felt as if he needed one.

Kate came in as he was pouring the second.

"Dave. What are you doing home so early?"

"I quit my job. Finally walked out on the old guy."

"Oh, Dave—"

"Don't worry, honey. I'll have another one by Monday morning. I've still got a few contacts around town."

"Who? Harry Rider?"

"I might call Harry."

"I wish you hadn't done it. That temper of yours, Dave—"

"We'll make out. We always have." Then, because he'd only just thought of them, "Where are the kids?"

"Outside playing."

"We won't tell them for a few days. They needn't know over the weekend, at least."

"All right, Dave."

"Want a drink?"

"I want you to tell me about it, how it happened."

He told her about it. They talked for the better part of an hour, until the two boys came running in for supper. Then they ate as if nothing at all had happened, as if it were a Friday night just like any other. But it wasn't, and he noticed toward the end of the meal that he was speaking more kindly to the children than he usually did. Perhaps he was beginning to feel a bit guilty.

After supper, when the boys were being tucked into bed by Kate, he phoned Harry Rider.

"Harry? How are you, boy? This is Dave O'Bannion."

The voice that answered him was sleepy with uncertainty. He'd forgotten that Harry Rider always napped after dinner. "Yes, Dave? How've you been?"

"Pretty good. Look, Harry—"

"Yes?"

"Harry, I quit my job this afternoon."

"Oh? Kind of sudden, wasn't it?"

"I'd been thinking about it for a while. Anyway, I'm looking, if you know of anything around town."

There was a moment of silence on the other end of the line. Then Harry Rider said, "Gosh, fella, I don't think I could help you right now. Maybe something will turn up though."

"Well, if you hear of anything, Harry—"

"Sure. I'll keep you in mind. Glad you called."

After he hung up, O'Bannion sat for some moments smoking a cigarette. When Kate came back downstairs, he was ready for the expected questioning look. "I heard you talking."

"I phoned Rider."

"Why?"

"Why not? He's got a lot of contacts around this town."

"All the wrong kind."

"Maybe in a few weeks I won't be so fussy."

"Can't you get unemployment insurance or something?"

"Not right away. I wasn't fired, remember. I walked out."

"But Harry Rider! He never did a favor for anybody in his life that didn't have a dozen strings attached."

"You didn't used to think he was so bad, back before we were married."

"That was before we were married. A lot of things were different then, Dave."

He lit a cigarette and started pacing the floor. "Anyway, you don't have to worry. He didn't have anything for me."

She shook her head as if to clear it. "Oh, I'm sorry. I guess the whole thing is just too much for me all at once."

"Just stop worrying. I'll have a job by the end of next week and a better one than I left. You can bet on it!"

She smiled at his words, even though neither of them felt quite that optimistic. They both knew it would be a long weekend.

Monday morning was warm and rainy, with a west wind blowing the drops of rain against the front windows with disturbing force. O'Bannion gazed out at it unhappily. It would not be a pleasant day to be trudging the streets of the city in search of a job. The kids, not yet old enough to attend school, were cross with the prospect of a day indoors, and he could see that Kate was already tense.

"Cheer up, honey. I'll phone you after lunch."

"Where are you going to try?"

"Oh, there are a few offices around town that might have openings, especially for someone who walked out on the old man. I'll hit those today and tomorrow, and if the scent is cold I can always try an employment agency."

He went off in the car because Kate wouldn't be needing it and he wasn't quite up to facing the ride in on the same old commuters' train. It was still too early in the day, and there would be people he knew, people he wasn't yet in the mood to chat with. In the city, he parked the car at the ramp garage he occasionally used, nodding silently in reply to the attendant's cheerful morning greeting.

The first place he tried was an engineering firm where he had contacts. He thought. They listened in friendly agreement to everything he said, and one of them even offered to buy him lunch. But there was no job available and he wasn't yet ready to accept charity. He thanked them and went and bought his lunch from a white-coated sidewalk vendor who sold dry ham sandwiches wrapped in wax paper. He found an empty bench in the park and ate among the damp trees, thankful at least that the rain had stopped and the wind had died to a gentle breeze.

The job he'd left, O'Bannion was beginning to realize, had done little to prepare him for the necessity of stepping quickly into something else. He'd never had any opportunity to build upon some sketchy engineering courses he'd left unfinished at college. The job, for all its nine-thousand-a-year salary, had been little more than an arduous managership of an office full of unmarried and just-married girls more intent on dates and marriage than work.

He called on two other places that afternoon, and the best he came up with was a promise of something "maybe in a month or two." That wasn't good enough. He was already more depressed than he cared to admit to Kate.

Tuesday was much the same, and Wednesday. That afternoon, he swallowed his pride and called the familiar number of his old office. He got by the switchboard operator without being recognized and in a moment he was talking to Shirl.

"This is Dave. How are you?"

"Mr. O'Bannion! I'm fine, how are you? Everyone's been asking about you."

"I'll bet. Who are you working for now?"

"They have me in the pool till they get someone to replace you. Have you found anything yet?"

"Not yet. I've got a couple of leads. What I called for—has there been any mail for me? Anything personal?"

"Just the usual junk, Mr. O'Bannion. Except this morning a letter came for you from California. Los Angeles. It looks as if it might be personal."

"It is." He had some friends in Los Angeles who often misplaced his home address and wrote him at the office.

"Should I forward it?"

"I suppose so," he said, and then had a second thought. "Say, would you like to meet me for a drink after work? I could get the letter from you and you could tell me what's been going on."

She hesitated a moment, but finally agreed. "All right. I guess I'd have time for one."

"Fine. I'll see you at five—a bit after five—over at the Nightcap." He hung up and then phoned Kate to tell her he'd be a bit late for dinner.

By the flickering candlelight of the Nightcap, a quiet little place where it seemed always to be the cocktail hour, he really looked at Shirl Webster for the first time. She'd been his secretary for the better part of the past year, but in that dubious manner of modern business he'd tended to take her mostly for granted. She was nothing more than an impersonal machine to take his letters and dictation, answer his phone, and perhaps suggest a birthday present for his wife. He'd never really thought of Shirl Webster as a woman, though he was aware now that she was surely a woman, and a striking one at that.

"I'm sorry it all happened," she said, seeming to mean it. "I liked working for you."

He noticed for the first time that her eyes were blue, a very light blue in sharp contrast to the dark of her hair. She was a tall girl, perhaps nearing thirty with a certain regal grace about her. "I'm glad of that, at least," he said with a chuckle. "There were days when I thought the whole place was in league against me, including you."

She shook her head. "Not at all. I was kept busy all day Monday explaining what had happened to you. All the girls miss you."

"Makes me sound like a bluebeard or something." He sipped the martini in front of him. "Do you have that letter?"

She nodded and handed over a flat envelope with a Los Angeles postmark. He pardoned himself and slit it open, just to make sure the news was nothing more urgent than weather and kids and when-are-you-coming-to-visit-us. Then he folded it away in his inside pocket.

"Nothing important?" she asked.

"The usual stuff. They're old friends. I'll have to write them, tell them about my new status."

"Do these leads of yours sound good, Mr. O'Bannion?"

"I'm not your boss any more. Call me Dave."

"All right—Dave."

"To answer your question, no—the leads don't sound good."

"Maybe the old man would take you back. He's having a hard time replacing you."

"I have a little pride left, unfortunately. Want another drink?"

For a moment he thought she'd agree, but then she shook her head reluctantly. "I have to get home."

He realized that in almost a year he'd never even thought where home might be. "Got a boy friend, Shirl?"

She blinked at him. "I'm too old to call them boy friends any more."

"Oh, come on! How old are you—twenty-five?" He'd knocked a few years off his real guess.

"You're sweet. Now I really have to go. But keep in touch, let me know how you're doing."

"I will."

He watched her walk to the door, hips tight against the contoured fabric of her skirt, and he wondered why he'd never noticed that walk before.

Thursday was too nice a day to be out of work. It was fine to walk along Main Street on your lunch hour and moan about having to return to a desk on such a beautiful day, but O'Bannion quickly discovered it was only frustrating to be job-hunting on such a day. The trees in the park were already blossoming with spring, and the people he passed were smiling. He would have felt happier in a thunderstorm.

Friday was more of the same. An offer of a job at a thousand dollars a year less than he'd been making, a promise of something "maybe in the summer," a regret for a position just filled. It all added up to a big zero.

On Saturday morning he went to see Harry Rider. He knew the man would be at work on a Saturday because the tracks were racing. Harry's main source of income demanded a six-day week. He was a big man, with a face and hairline that made it difficult for O'Bannion to remember him as Kate's one-time suitor. The years had changed them all, but none more so than Harry Rider.

"What can I do for you, Dave?" he asked, not bothering to rise from behind the wide desk strewn with typewritten sheets, racing forms, and three telephones.

O'Bannion stared at the thinning hair, the wrinkles of tired skin around deep, calculating brown eyes, and said, "I phoned you last week. Maybe you forgot."

"Oh! Sure, I remember now. You're out of a job."

"That's it. I've got some good leads in town, but you know how it is when you just walk out on something. No two weeks' pay or anything like that."

"Need ten bucks?" Harry Rider was already reaching for his pocket. The words, coupled with the motion, made O'Bannion suddenly ill. He was sorry he'd come.

"No, no—nothing like that. I was wondering if you knew of anything around here. Even something temporary. You said once you had a lot of influence in the right places and just to come see you."

"Sure. I can get you a job cleaning out the stables up at Yonkers. How's that?"

O'Bannion's face froze. "I didn't come here for that sort of talk, Rider."

"Just kidding. Never take me serious! Ask Kate. She never took me serious."

"We weren't discussing Kate."

"Sure, sure. She know you came to see me?"

"No."

"Just as well."

"I intend to tell her when I get home. I have no secrets from her."

Harry Rider chuckled. "Maybe it's time you started having a few."

He could see he was getting nowhere with the man. There was no job in the offing, only this opportunity for ridicule. "I'm sorry to take up your time," he told Rider, rising from the chair.

"Wait a minute! Maybe I'll hear of something in your line."

"Thanks. Don't trouble yourself."

He was going out the door when Rider called after him, "I'll be in touch with you, Dave."

O'Bannion didn't bother to answer.

On Sunday he went to church for the first time in a year. Listening to the minister rant about the evils of overabundance, he wondered why he'd bothered. The previous evening he'd told Kate about his visit to Harry Rider. She reacted about as he expected and there had been an unpleasant scene. She hadn't accompanied him to church on Sunday, and when he returned to the house he found her mood had not improved.

"It's a nice day," he said, to make conversation.

"Just great."

"Still upset because I went to Rider?"

"Why shouldn't I be? Dave, there are employment agencies, friends, relatives—why go to Harry Rider for a job?"

"I didn't know you felt that strongly about it."

"You knew—you knew darned well. I have a little pride left, even if you haven't."

Anger growing within him, he spun around and started from the room. Then he paused to face her once more. "Do you happen to know how much we have in the bank? I figure it's just about enough to keep us going for another three weeks. Then we either stop eating or stop paying on the house and car."

Her lips were a thin line of —what? It almost could have been contempt. "Maybe you should have thought about the money before you quit your job," she snapped.

"Sure, sure! Maybe I—" The ringing of the telephone cut into any retort he would have made. He decided it was probably just as well and went to answer it.

"Is this Mr. Dave O'Bannion?" a strange voice asked. Male, perhaps a bit muffled.

"Yes."

"Mr. O'Bannion, I understand you are presently at liberty. I have a position available, temporary work, which I'd like to discuss with you."

"Sure. Who is this calling?"

"My name is Green. Could you meet me tomorrow to talk it over?"

"Certainly. Where are you located?"

"I'll be in Room 344 at the Ames Hotel, anytime after ten. It must be tomorrow, though, as I'm leaving for Canada on Tuesday."

O'Bannion assured him it would be tomorrow. Even this mysterious temporary sort of job was worth looking into. But when Kate questioned him about the call he implied it was from someone he knew, someone he'd contacted the previous week. He had a growing feeling in the pit of his stomach that the strange Mr. Green in his hotel-room office would prove somehow to be an associate of Harry Rider.

Green, if that was really his name, proved to be a tall man in his mid-thirties. He didn't really belong in the hotel room. He seemed more like a man made for the outdoors, a man who might venture inside only for a drink or necessary food. He was obviously ill at ease in the surroundings of impersonal luxury such as one found at the Ames.

"You're O'Bannion?" he asked, frowning as if he might have expected someone older.

"That's right." He held out his hand and Green shook it. Then they both sat down and O'Bannion added, "You have a job open?"

Green leaned back in his chair. "A temporary position. It would involve a trip to Canada."

"For how long a period? I wouldn't want to be away from my family." He said the words because they sounded right. Just at the moment Kate and the boys were far from his thoughts.

"Only a day or two. And the pay would be good."

"How good?"

The man shrugged. "Perhaps five thousand dollars."

His worst fears realized, O'Bannion got suddenly to his feet. "I guess you'd better tell Mr. Rider I'm not interested."

"Who?"

Why had he gone? Why had he gone to Rider when he'd known all along that this would be the only sort of job the man could offer? Across the border for five thousand dollars.

"Harry Rider. I believe that's a name you know."

Green was blocking him at the door, holding him back. "Wait, wait. Look, there's no risk, if that's what's worrying you. It's safe."

"Sure."

"I'll give you something to take with you. All you do is deliver it to an address in Toronto and you'll be paid the money."

"Five thousand dollars for no risk? Why don't you take it yourself?"

Green was nervous now, unsure of himself. "All right," he decided suddenly. "I guess I got the wrong guy. Go!"

O'Bannion went.

The remainder of the day he spent in a sort of twilight, wandering from office to office, filling out applications for jobs he neither wanted nor qualified for, existing in a world of mere minutes adding up slowly to hours. Again and again his thoughts returned to the man in the hotel room, to the five thousand dollars he'd offered for the flight to Canada.

O'Bannion tried to guess what would have been involved. Harry Rider's interests were mainly gambling, horse racing, and the like, although he occasionally dabbled in politics. Perhaps it was nothing more than transporting betting slips or some political material.

The afternoon was sunny, even now when it was almost ended, even with its twilight rays filtered through the blossoming branches of the park trees. He walked with a lengthened, broken shadow behind him, destination undetermined. Then, the random thought just crossing his mind, he started down the street toward his old office. They'd be leaving now, not a minute too early because the old man was always watching, but not a minute too late either. He stood in the shadow of a building, watching faces and figures already receding from memory after only a week's time. Then he saw Shirl Webster, walking very quickly along the curb, head down against the sunset.

O'Bannion crossed the street and intercepted her at the next stoplight. "Hello, Shirl," he called from a few paces behind her.

"Dave! I mean—"

"I told you Dave was all right. How are you?"

"Fine. I was just this minute thinking about you, wondering how you were coming along."

"Got time for a drink?" he asked, and as the words left his mouth he wondered just how accidental this meeting had been. Didn't he subconsciously seek her out rather than return home to Kate?

"Just one. I have to meet my boy friend."

He chuckled. "I thought you were too old to call them that."

"On days like this I feel younger. We going to the Nightcap again?"

"Why not?"

Over a drink, with the candle flickering on the table between them, he suddenly found himself telling her about his interview with Green in the hotel room. It was an odd sort of feeling she gave him and he wondered how he could have worked with her all those months without being affected by the sensuality of her presence.

"So you walked out on him," she summed up, making it a simple statement.

"I walked out on him. Wouldn't you?"

She toyed with the plastic stirring rod from her scotch-and-water. "I don't know. Five thousand dollars is more money than I make in a whole year. I don't know what I'd have done."

"It's obviously something crooked, with Rider involved."

She frowned into the glass. "The Rider you mention—if he *is* such a shady character, why did you go to him in the first place?"

Why? It was the sort of question Kate had asked too. *Why?* Was it purely a spirit of revolt against his wife's wishes, or was there more to it than that? "I don't know why," he answered finally. "Not really."

He lit her cigarette and watched while she settled back in her chair. "I think you're like me, Dave. I think you're sick of working your life away for someone like the old man, who doesn't care about anything but the profit and the overhead."

"You think I should have done it? What Green wanted me to do?"

"I don't know. I think you should have asked a few more questions, thought about it a little more."

"I don't know. I just don't know." He signaled the waiter for another drink.

"Are you going to discuss it with your wife?"

"How can I? She's already barely speaking to me because I went to Rider. Am I going to tell her now that she was right all along about him being a crook?"

"Are you asking me what you should do, Dave?"

He wasn't really. Until that moment he'd been convinced that he'd followed the right course of action. Now she had planted a doubt. "You'd have asked more questions."

"Go back and see him again, Dave. Why not?"

"He's gone. On his way to Canada."

"Maybe not. He might be looking for someone else to make the trip."

"I'm sure he wouldn't be sitting in that hotel room still. How'd he know I wouldn't come back with the police?"

"What could you tell the police? What do you know to tell them?"

"Nothing," he admitted glumly.

"Let me call the hotel for you, see if he's still there."

"I don't know. I'm getting in so deep—"

"It's a great deal of money, Dave. Enough to carry you over till you can find a really good job."

"Well, I suppose you could call. I know he won't be there."

She rose from her chair. "You said it was the Ames Hotel?"

"Yes."

She stepped into a phone booth near the door and he watched her dialing the number. She spoke a few words and then motioned quickly to him. When he joined her at the booth door she covered the receiver with her hand and said, "He's still there. I've got him on the line. You want to go over?"

"I—" He felt suddenly weak in the knees.

"Mr. Green," she said, returning to the phone. "I'm calling for Dave O'Bannion. He was up to see you this morning. Yes—Yes. Well, he'd like to reconsider your offer."

O'Bannion started to protest and then changed his mind. Well, why not? It was five thousand dollars, wasn't it?

He took the phone from her and heard the familiar voice of Green in his ear. "I'm glad you've reconsidered."

"Yes."

"You just caught me as I was checking out."

O'Bannion grunted.

"Can we meet someplace else? How about the park behind the library?"

"All right. What time?"

"It's almost six-thirty now. Make it seven o'clock."

"Fine. I'll be there."

"Alone."

"All right," O'Bannion agreed without hesitation. He hadn't even thought about taking Shirl with him.

He hung up and joined her back at the table. "All set, Dave?"

"All set. But he wants me to come alone."

"Oh." She seemed disappointed.

"I could meet you back here after if you'd like."

His words brought a smile to her lips. "I'd like."

"What about that boy friend?"

"I'll call him."

He tossed a couple of bills on the table. "Get yourself something to eat. I'll be back in an hour or so. Maybe sooner."

He left her and walked across the street to another bar. There he had a quick drink and phoned Kate at home, making some excuse about a possible job that sounded phoney even to his own ears. Then he started for the little park behind the library, his heart beating with growing excitement. He didn't know whether the excitement was caused by Green or Shirl or both. He only knew that Kate had no part in it.

The park was almost dark by seven, lit only by the random lamps in standards twined by ivy. It was a lunchtime spot for summer secretaries, a strolling place for evening couples, a clubhouse for after-dark drifters. Though he was only a hundred feet from the street O'Bannion still had a sense of fear.

He found Green lounging on a bird-specked bench deep in shadow, his eyes caught by a necking couple across the path. "Look at that," he said to O'Bannion. "At seven o'clock."

"Yeah."

"Cigarette?"

"I've got my own, thanks."

"Who was the girl?"

"My secretary."

"I thought you were out of a job."

"She used to be my secretary."

"Oh."

"Now what about this deal?"

Green was grinning in the flare of his match. "You're ready?"

"I'm ready."

"All right. I have a plane ticket here, round trip to Toronto, leaving tomorrow night at six."

"That's pretty short notice. How long will I have to be away?"

"A day. You can fly back Wednesday night if you want."

O'Bannion ground out his cigarette and lit a fresh one. The couple on the opposite bench had unclinched and she was repairing her lipstick. "What's the catch? What do I have to do? What's the deal?"

"Take a box of candy to a friend of mine."

O'Bannion's hands were steady. "What else?"

"That's all. I'll be there myself to pay you the five thousand."

"If you're going up too, why not take the candy yourself?"

Green smiled slightly and in the dim light he looked suddenly younger—no older perhaps than O'Bannion. "We don't need to kid each other. I've had trouble with the police. They might stop me at the border. I'm going up on the Thruway and crossing at Niagara Falls. I don't want them to find anything on me."

"What is it?"

Green looked vague. "That would be telling. You only get the money if the box is delivered intact."

It was now or never. This was the moment to back out, to go no further. But instead he simply asked, "As long as it's not narcotics. I don't want any part of something like that. O.K.?"

"No narcotics. What do you take me for anyway?"

"When do I get the box of candy?"

"Tomorrow afternoon, four o'clock. Right here."

"That doesn't give me much time to catch the plane."

"I don't want you to have much time. The man will be waiting for you at the airport in Toronto. You give him the candy and then get a room for the night. I'll probably pull in Wednesday morning and pay you off."

"How about part of it now?"

Green frowned. "I don't have it. The money's in Toronto. And there's no money unless you produce the box, unopened."

"Why don't you just mail it to him?"

"He's had police trouble too. They might be watching for something in the mails."

"All right," O'Bannion agreed at last. "I'll see you here at four."

Green left first, walking away fast. O'Bannion watched him go, watched him as in a dream, and wondered what he was getting into. He felt, in that moment, like a man trapped in a muddy bog. There was only Kate to save him, Kate and the children, and they were a world away. Then he remembered Shirl Webster waiting back at the bar and his spirits lifted.

"Why don't you come with me?" O'Bannion asked after he'd finished telling Shirl about his conversation with Green.

"What? Go *with* you! That's crazy, Dave. What would people say?"

"Who needs to know?"

It was crazy, but he began to think it might not be too crazy. He'd always been faithful to Kate in the nine years of their marriage—always, that is, except once in Boston with a girl he met in a bar. But now something had changed, something in him, or in Kate, or just in the times.

They talked, debated, argued for the rest of the evening, but he already knew she'd be on the plane with him.

His excuses to Kate in the morning were vague and uncertain. He would be away overnight, up in—Boston seeing about a job, a really good one right in his line. It was a damp, almost rainy day and the hours dragged till four and he met a trenchcoated Green in the park.

"Think the planes will be flying?" he asked.

Green handed over the candy, a great flat box with a ribbon tied around it. "Of course the planes'll be flying. A little rain never stopped them."

"This man will be at the airport?"

"He'll be there."

"How will I know him?"

Green thought for a moment. "His name is Dufaus. He has a little mustache and he's always carrying a briefcase. Looks like a government bigwig."

"All right. What about you?"

"I'll see you sometime before noon. I plan to drive all night. There's a little motel near the airport. Wait there for me."

"How do I know you'll show up?"

Green turned away. "Don't worry. I'm trusting you, you can trust me."

"Will Rider be there too?" O'Bannion asked on an impulse.

"Don't you worry about Rider. He takes care of himself."

Overhead, an unseen jet could be heard through the clouds. The planes were flying.

They held hands all the way.

It reminded O'Bannion of a youthful night on a hayride when he'd dated the most popular girl in the senior class for the first time. He'd held hands that night too, thinking and plotting all the way about how he'd work up to that first kiss, that first hand around her shoulders, on her knee. That night had ended disastrously, with the girl going home in a quarterback's car while O'Bannion sat alone behind the barn and cried for the first time in years. A year later, in college, he'd met Kate and there'd never been anyone else. Not really.

The weather was cooler when they landed, a clear coolness you didn't really mind. Above them the sky was full of stars and ahead he could see the flashing red-neoned MOTEL. The letters fuzzed and flickered irregularly as if the sign were tired. There to meet them at the airport was the mustached man with the briefcase, Mr. Dufaus.

He waited until they'd cleared customs and then he came up smiling. "Ah! O'Bannion?"

"That's right. You must be Dufaus."

"Correct. Quite correct. I have a car waiting. This way."

They followed him to a black foreign-built automobile with low, expensive lines. He motioned O'Bannion into the front seat with him but made no effort to start the car. Instead, he held out his hand. "The candy, please."

"No," O'Bannion said, halfway into the car.

"What?"

"No."

"What do you mean?"

"No candy until I get my money." O'Bannion hadn't really planned it that way, but suddenly he had spoken the words and there was no recalling them.

"You'll get the money tomorrow. Didn't he tell you?"

"He told me. You'll get the candy tomorrow."

Through all of this Shirl had stood behind him on the sidewalk. Now she tried to pull him from the car. "Dave, be careful."

O'Bannion backed out of the car, still clutching the candy box. "I'll be at the motel," he told Dufaus. "See you in the morning."

The man with the mustache was visibly upset. "The money cannot possibly be ready until I've had time to inspect the merchandise."

"Too bad. I'm sure we can work it out in the morning."

O'Bannion slammed the car door and walked quickly away, half pulling Shirl along with him. Dufaus made no attempt to follow.

"Dave, why did you do that? What's the matter with you all of a sudden?"

"Nothing. I just realized that I haven't decided about this thing yet, not really. I want more time to think. A few hours ago we were in New York, a few days ago I was still an honest man, and a few weeks ago I still had a job. Things are moving too fast for me. Too fast."

"Life is fast. We live and die before we know it, much too fast."

"Not by tomorrow morning. It's not over that fast. Let Dufaus sweat about it overnight. If this thing I'm carrying is so valuable, maybe I want to keep it a while."

They'd reached the motel, a low, long building of concrete that seemed about to crumble. The manager gave barely a flicker when they checked into a double room.

"What now?" she asked when they were alone.

"First things first. I'm going to check this candy. They didn't give me a chance before. I suppose that's why Dufaus risked meeting me at the airport— to get the candy before I had an opportunity to exercise my curiosity."

He removed the garish ribbon and lifted the lid, to disclose the regular designs of foil-wrapped chocolates. "Nothing but candy," Shirl observed over his shoulder.

"Maybe."

He unwrapped a piece and studied it. He squeezed with his fingers and broke it open. Inside, darkened and coated by the butterscotch filling, was something sharp and glittering in the light. "It's a—a jewel. Looks like a diamond. Still in its setting." He tried another piece of candy and it yielded up the red of a ruby.

"Dave, what is it?"

After the third one he answered, "It looks like part of a necklace of some sort. It's been broken at the links and separated into individual pieces so it could be hidden in the candy. Come on, help me look inside the others."

Ten minutes later, with all forty-eight pieces of candy broken open on the bed, they had a rainbow-colored collection of gems, each set in a glistening ring of platinum. "Who'd want to wear a thing like that?" Shirl asked, wide-eyed.

O'Bannion half remembered something he'd heard or read. "It's not for wearing, really. It's a necklace called the Rainbow and its gems are supposed to be worth a quarter of a million dollars. It was stolen a week ago from an armed messenger."

"You're sure?"

He nodded. "The messenger was killed. I'm into this a little deeper than I figured." He ran his palm across a forehead suddenly damp with sweat.

Later, sometime in the hours between midnight and dawn, when the only sound to be heard was the gentle buzz of the electric clock on the far wall Shirl said, "Do you think they'll come for us or something? Because you didn't give them the candy?"

He laughed and tried to sound amused. "You've been seeing too many movies, gal. Nothing's going to happen."

"They killed one man. You said so."

"Maybe I was wrong. Maybe these jewels are something else."

"You're not wrong, Dave. If you don't think anything's going to happen, why don't you come to bed?"

He laughed and lit a cigarette. "I don't know, maybe I'm shy." Then, after a moment's silence, "Tell me about this boy friend of yours, Shirl."

"He's just a guy."

"You like him? Well enough to marry him?"

"Would I be here with you if I did?"

"I don't know." He blew smoke in the direction of the window, watching it as it crossed the single bar of dimly filtered light from outside. "What are you going to tell him when you get back?"

"I'll think of something," she said. "More to the point, what are you going to tell Green and Dufaus in the morning?"

He thought about it for a long time before answering. "I think I'll go to the police, Shirl," he said finally.

"The police! But—but *why?*"

"This is murder. If I don't get out of it now, it may be too late."

"But what about *us?* What about your wife? Do you want it spread all over the newspapers that we were up here together?"

"No, of course not. But what else can I do?"

"Give them their foolish jewels and be done with it. Take the money and just forget about it. That's what you planned to do originally, isn't it?"

"I suppose so, but things have changed." Suddenly he ground out his cigarette. "All right, let's get out of here then. We'll get the jewels to the police somehow without implicating ourselves and be back in the States by noon."

But she held him back with her hand. "No, Dave. I'm afraid to go out there. I'm afraid they'll be waiting for us."

"I'll take a look around," he said and slipped into his jacket.

Outside, the world was a pale dark landscape sleeping in the full moon's glow. A car was parked at the head of the driveway. A cigarette-tip glowed like a far-off star. O'Bannion sighed and went back inside.

"What is it, Dave?"

"You were right. He's got somebody watching the place." He looked out the back window, but decided against risking it with Shirl. There was a twenty-foot drop to the highway. They could hardly make it without a twisted ankle or worse.

"So?"

"So we stay till morning and see what happens."

The sun was back in the morning, already high in the sky by the time the car drew up outside. O'Bannion had been watching out the window. He saw Dufaus and Green join the man who had been watching the motel throughout the night.

"Here they come," he told Shirl without looking at her. "Green's with them."

She came up to the window and stood just behind O'Bannion, watching. "Give them the jewels, Dave. We don't want trouble."

Then they were at the door, knocking. He opened it and looked into Green's expectant eyes. "Well! I was worried when Mr. Dufaus told me about his troubles. Let's get this settled now."

The two of them crowded into the small room, leaving the third man to wait outside. Green said, "The candy. Where's the candy?"

"We were hungry. We ate it," O'Bannion told them.

Green's mouth twisted into an odd sort of grin. "Look, cut out the wise talk. You'll get your money as soon as Dufaus inspects the candy and gives me the O.K."

"I didn't know I was getting involved in a murder," O'Bannion said. "That wasn't part of the deal."

Dufaus was suddenly agitated. "He knows too much!"

Green's hand dropped to his pocket. "All right, we're finished fooling, O'Bannion. I didn't let you bring this stuff five hundred miles across the border just so you could double-cross me."

His hand was coming out of the pocket when O'Bannion hit him, a glancing blow to the side of the head that tumbled him onto the bed.

Against the wall, Dufaus uttered a gasp of dismay. "No violence—please! I only want to purchase the gems!"

O'Bannion moved again, but this time Green was faster. The gun—a small .32—was out of his pocket, pointed at O'Bannion's middle. "We're through fooling," he growled. "Shirl, where did he hide the stuff?"

Behind him, as in a nightmare, O'Bannion heard her reply, "In the toilet tank. I'll get them." And then, almost as an afterthought, "I'm sorry, Dave. Really I am."

He sat on the bed, unfeeling, as Green and Dufaus counted the gems. And when she came to sit next to him it was as if a stranger had entered, a perplexing intruder.

"In the beginning I thought I was doing you a favor," she said quietly. "You needed the money and my boy friend—how I hate that expression—he needed someone to fly to Canada with the necklace. I talked him into calling you. I never thought it would come to this. I should have risked bringing the thing over myself."

"It wasn't Harry Rider," he said. That was all he could say.

"Not Rider, no. It was me. When you thought I was calling the hotel Monday night I was really calling Greeny's apartment. I was afraid you'd notice that I dialed the number without looking it up. I was afraid you'd notice Dufaus wasn't surprised to see me at the airport."

"I guess I didn't notice anything. Not a thing."

Green came over to the bed. "Dufaus is satisfied. Let's roll."

"A quarter of a million?" She breathed it, like a prayer.

"Not even half, but I can't stay to argue. It'll get us a long way."

"What about him?" Dufaus asked from the door, pointing at O'Bannion.

"That's five grand I saved myself," Green said. He brought the gun into view once more.

Shirl stepped quickly in front of him. "No, Greeny. No more killing." She held her position.

"I leave him here to tell the cops everything he knows?"

But Shirl stood firm. "He can't tell them anything without implicating himself, with the police, and with his wife. I don't think he wants to do that. Come on, let's get out of here."

Green faced him with the gun for another moment, uncertain, and then pocketed it as he turned away. "All right, we'll leave him."

She came over to O'Bannion one last time. "Dave?"

"What?"

Her voice dropped to a whisper. "When he gives me my cut I'll see you get something. A thousand or so anyway."

"Don't bother," he said, turning away.

"Dave—"

"Go on. Go!"

He heard them drive away, listened to the sound of traffic reaching him through the still-open door.

After a time he went out and walked until he found the motel manager, who was watering a spring garden by the highway. He asked where there was a telephone he could use and when he found it he dialed the number of the local police.

It would be a long journey back to Kate, and he wondered if he would make it.

DONALD HONIG

Wonderful, Wonderful Violence

What made it all so ludicrous was the fact that Angus Monroe was the most unlikely person in the bank to be caught up in so harrowing and dramatic a situation. He was the most ordinary and inconspicuous sort of person imaginable—just above fifty, short, portly, grey, immaculate, wordless. He was a shy bachelor without friends who lived in two rooms on the other side of town.

But beneath that veneer of reticence and anonymity there beat a sullen and resentful heart. Angus had the feeling that the world had cruelly passed him by, that he had never participated. There were, as a consequence, no grand and gaudy memories to sustain his loneliness.

He appeared at the bank's front door with predictable punctilio at five to nine every morning, materializing there like a ghost, neat, indisputable, inevitable, his hat balanced on his small head, his small eyes staring blinkless and persistent behind their silver-rimmed lenses. The assistant manager opened the door and greeted him with a curt nod to which Angus responded with just as curt a nod and a brisk "Good morning," and in his heart chanting with bitterness the same refrain, You pompous owl. He marched with short steps past the other employees, each of whom rendered him an assembly-line nod of greeting, to the employees' room where he hung away his hat and coat and poked his arms into his tan-colored working jacket, buttoned it primly, and went out and took his place as teller behind the third window just as the nine o'clock bell rang and with great pomp and dignity the assistant manager swept the doors back with a grand and benign baring of white teeth whether customers were there or not. You'd think the King of England himself was coming through, Angus thought darkly to himself.

The routine never varied. At the next window stood Mr. Carlisle, tall, good-looking, unctuous, with a smooth and clever word for every attractive feminine patron. All of that grated intolerably on Angus' nerves as he stood and listened to Carlisle say all the things he himself would like to say. It all made him clench his thin lips until they turned white.

And then one morning, a little before ten o'clock, the routine varied, violently. Angus had just left the cage to get a cup of water and was walking across the floor when two men moved through the door, letting the doors swing back behind them. They strode imperiously, their faces set, their long, taut-belted trenchcoats flapping tersely with each step. Angus stared at them curiously, feeling an odd intuitive snap inside of himself, finding himself wishing these men really were what he felt them to be. Their mere entrance seemed to generate something in the staid and placid air, a stirring, an uneasiness. They would do something, Angus hoped. They would hold up the tellers, throw bombs, fire bullets through the nerveless infuriating clock; they would do something.

And they did.

One of the men, the taller, slid his hand into his coat and snapped out a gun. There was instant pandemonium even before he uttered a word. A woman teller screamed. The assistant manager sprung up at his desk—and in the face of a mighty .45 automatic sat right down. The tall man was snapping orders, moving along the windows, his gun prominently in the faces of everyone. The smaller man was taking charge of the several patrons, herding them together against a wall which was obscured from outside eyes. The tall man, his fedora pulled forward almost covering his eyes, was collecting money in a large canvas bag. It was all happening swiftly, uncannily, almost dreamlike, the excitement poised and bristling in the startled air.

"You too!" Suddenly Angus heard the words directed at him, realized that this was the second time the small man had spoken to him. The portly teller was standing alone in the middle of the floor watching everything like a spectator, reserving all judgment. He realized everyone was looking at him as if expecting him to take some action.

The small man came menacingly toward him, holding his .45 automatic low, the black barrel glaring up at Angus.

"Get over there!" the small man ordered.

"I—heard you," Angus said, but still unable to move, rooted to the spot, not afraid but fascinated, almost like a child, watching it all with that blank speechless fascination of the child.

"Come on!" the tall man called. He was moving away from the tellers' cages, holding the large canvas bag, the top of which slacked over but which still showed considerable content. "Take him," the tall man said.

The small man shot a quizzical glance over his shoulder, then, turning back to Angus, drove the .45 up into his soft yielding stomach, making Angus gasp.

"Move out, Maxie," the small man said to Angus. "Slow and careful." He moved around behind Angus.

The tall man was at the door, addressing the line of frozen-faced people.

"Anybody says anything before fifteen minutes—" and he indicated the approaching Angus "—and he gets flowers and regrets." Then, with a bold and confident gesture, he swung open the doors and went out, followed by a hesitant, doubtful Angus and the small man whose eyes, as cold and as rigid as steel, swept meaningfully over the people.

There was a car parked up the block. As they approached it Angus could hear the motor trembling under the hood.

The tall man appeared casual, but his words and his gestures were brisk, cold, calculated.

"Shove the guy in front with us," he said, talking, moving, all in one smooth practiced breath, opening the door, the canvas bag disappearing into the back.

"All right, Maxie," the small man said, pushing Angus with his body. Angus slid across the front seat's cold smooth plastic seatcover. In a moment the two men were around him and the car had started.

Angus, still not fully emerged from his dream, from the shock of imagination ceasing and reality beginning, stared straight ahead through the wide curve of windshield, feeling an importance, a significance that he had never known before, a tingling of great excitement. Suddenly before his inward eye flashed the scene that must be occurring back at the bank. He saw them all darting around like people hurled and juggled, babbling and exclaiming and telling each other what had happened and what they thought and how awful it had been. And preeminent above it all would be his name, their concern for him, Angus Monroe, who had been abducted by thieves, thrust into the hands of potential killers, whose life was suddenly a heroic and dreadful thing. If only they could see how calm and composed he was, how easily he was facing it.

He began to sidle glances at the men. The tall man, guiding the wheel, sat aloof, his profile slightly raised, watching the road with a disinterest and impatience as though he had covered it a thousand uneventful times in his life and would a thousand times more. The other sat in a slouch, his arms crossed, a wryly pleased expression on his face. Angus could fairly feel him whirling the money about in his warped and corrupted brain.

But soon the captive began to feel a slight trickling of fear and apprehension. He felt it quavering in his knees, wallowing in his stomach. The excitement had worn away, the glory beginning to become dubious. But he endeavored to suppress the fear, to resist it, master it. He cleared his throat. This seemed to arouse the small man.

"Y'know, Maxie's all right," the small man said, shifting about in his seat. The tall man said nothing.

"No fuss, no yelling," the small man said.

"Nobody argues with a revolver," Angus said dryly, and was immediately pleased with himself. He thought it a singularly apt and clever statement. (Certainly, the obnoxious Carlisle would never have had the composure and alertness of mind in this situation to say such a thing.)

"Maxie," the small man said genially, grinning with small, rotted teeth that only half showed, "you're acquainted with a basic law of survival."

"My name is not Maxie," Angus said, still in that dry, almost bored tone. "My name is—" and he could not say Angus. That was suddenly a most ridiculous and unfortunate and unmanly name, hardly a name to invoke respect."—Floyd," he said, making a spontaneous choice, pleased with it.

"Maxie," the small man retorted promptly. "Your name is Maxie. Isn't that right, Champ?" he asked the tall man.

"His name is Blank for all I care," Champ said.

"His name will be Blank if he doesn't behave himself," the small man said.

"I know which side my bread is buttered on," Angus said, tossing it off with a casualness that astonished him.

"He'll behave," Champ said.

"You know why we call him Champ?" the small man asked. "That's because that's what he is. He's the champ of them all. Right, Champ?"

The tall man grinned tersely, his eyes still watching the road as if he expected it to break into pieces. "You could say that," he said.

They were outside of town now, speeding past neat little cottages, past great fields of barley, past the high school, heading out toward the country. The grass was very green, the trees rich in leaves and scent. The small man rolled down the window and the warm breeze poured into the car.

Angus was desperately anxious to ask where they were going but he knew such a question would be curtly repulsed. He was grimly determined not to behave like a "victim" so he sat as stolid and as noncommittal as if he were a legitimate part of the whole thing.

"You got a family, Maxie?" the small man asked, apropos of nothing.

"No," Angus said.

"That's good," the small man said.

It made the fear begin to tremble again. It sped the realities skidding into Angus' mind. He was utterly helpless here between these two men. He knew their faces now, even the name of one of them. He knew their car, the direction they had taken. They were being too casual with him, as if they could trust him never to speak of what had happened. It made him wish he had never come to work this morning, or that he had not stopped and stood so fearless and prominent in the middle of the floor for them to take him out. What was he going to gain from being a hero?

"I'm a man with a weak heart," he suddenly said, improvising.

"Hear that, Champ?" the small man said, leaning over to talk to the tall man. "Maxie's got a bad clock. Don't scare him."

"Wouldn't think of it," Champ said.

Soon they were deep in the country. They drove for miles without passing a house or a person or even another car. The tar road was dark with languorous shadows that kept clipping and bounding over the hood and fleeing up the windshield.

If Angus had been hoping for them to be stopped by state troopers or to encounter a road block somewhere, that hope was soon dissipated. They turned off the main road into a narrow dirt road, the car grinding over the rocks and ruts, a vague cloud of dust lifting around it, floating behind the windless air. They slashed through some brush and then came to a halt before a small, lifeless cabin. The halt, the sudden silence, was a relief.

The two men slid out of the car. The small man waited for Angus. The gun had reappeared, steady and menacing below the tight-smiling face. The tall man had reached in and hauled out the bag of money. They followed him into the cabin.

There was nothing inside except a table and several chairs. A small low cot stood against a wall. There was one window, the shade pulled down before it, muffling the sunlight that fell dimly to the floor. Their feet clumped on the pine-board floor.

Champ swung the bag onto the table.

"Get the rope," he said, his voice quiet, sharp, as if talking to no one in particular but knowing that someone would be there to hear, and obey.

They're going to hang me, Angus thought feverishly. Wild schemes filled him with furious desperation. His eyes glazed.

The small man went out and in a moment returned with a length of rope. He was whistling.

"Tie him up," Champ said, his voice still sharp and confident, his eyes hard upon the bag of money.

With relief, Angus gave himself to be bound. The small man sat him down in one of the chairs and with maddening efficiency tied him to it, binding his hands behind with the heavy scratchy rope. Angus sat there, as helpless and forlorn as a child. He watched the two men hold the bag upside down and the money empty onto the table. Champ was looking at him, smiling across the table at him.

"How much do you reckon it is?" Champ asked.

With his practiced eye, Angus regarded the money, his underlip pushing out.

"Ten thousand," he said after a moment.

"Maxie should know," the small man said.

"We'll see," Champ said. Slowly, tediously, he began to count the money, thumbing the edges of the packets, sliding the loose bills from hand to hand.

"Eleven thousand five," he said, finally.

There was a moment of reverence.

"Maxie was close," the small man said.

"What are you going to do to me?" Angus, unable to hold back any longer, blurted out.

"Let it be a surprise," Champ said.

"Yeah," the small man said. "Do you like surprises, Maxie?"

"Only pleasant ones," Angus said dimly.

His captors sat down then and lit cigarettes. They smoked quietly, placidly. For a while they seemed oblivious of Angus' presence. They seemed to be inhaling their wealth, accustoming themselves to it. They were quite at their ease.

Angus began to feel the indignity of himself sitting there bound and helpless, as miserable as a creature in a cage. He stared at them, his mounting indignation—as well as their oblivious serenity—making him want to shout at them. And then his thoughts began to drift back to the bank again, to all the furor and excitement that must have occurred there, most of which would have subsided by now. Everyone would be expressing concern for Mr. Monroe.

He imagined them envisioning his plight, shaking their heads, talking about what a fine old person he was. He wanted to snarl at them. He thought then, inexplicably, of the application form he had filled out twenty years ago when he had first applied for a job at the bank, of the line which read, "In case of emergency notify" and of the blank space he had left below it. Poor Mr. Monroe. That would go around the bank too. He would be a lonely heroic figure. Life would be changed for a while when he got back, when he took his place behind the teller's window again. He would be a more formidable person then, but only for a little while, gradually fading back into obscurity—if he got back.

They stuffed the money into the bag and took it out with them. He heard them putting it in the car. Then Champ came back and lay down on the cot that was behind Angus. Soon he was sleeping. The small man lounged in the doorway. He had shed his trenchcoat. His .45 bulged in his belt.

"What are you going to do?" Angus asked quietly.

"Nothing much, Maxie," the small man said. He was smoking, staring into the forest, the smoke weaving lazily on the dry windless air, rolling off into the forest.

"Are you going to leave me here?"

"Maybe. When it gets dark we're taking off."

"They'll be looking for your car."

"But not around here. They'll have us pegged as being a long way out by tonight."

"Clever," Angus said.

"We sure do hope so, Maxie," the small man said, flicking his cigarette into the air, expelling a final stream of smoke into the sunlight, sighing.

It was beginning to grow dark. The two holdup men were sitting outside in the car. Angus could hear the murmur of their voices. They had been sitting out there for almost two hours, ever since Champ had risen from his sleep. And all that while Angus had been wriggling and straining his hands, gradually loosening his bonds. It excited him greatly when he realized that his hands were almost free, that with a few more jerks and twists they would be free. What would happen then he didn't know. He gazed hopefully at the window, but it was right next to the car; it would hardly be the place from which to escape. There was a brief vision of himself leaping upon and subduing the two men, and an even more glorious one of him dragging them in by their collars, the bag of money tucked under his arm. They'd give me five dollars and an afternoon off for that, he thought.

The two men appeared in the doorway. They were staring at him. He knew now that they had been discussing his fate.

"We could leave him here," the small man said.

"They wouldn't find him for months," Champ said, his eyes regarding Angus thoughtfully, as if measuring him for an ordeal.

"It wouldn't really be murder either."

Angus stared back at the tall man, trying to read his eyes, which were small and inscrutable below the dark line of his hat brim.

"We'll decide when I get back," Champ said. "You watch him."

The tall man buttoned and belted his trenchcoat as carefully as if it was a uniform and left the cabin. They heard his feet scuffling softly, the sounds becoming more and more distant, then inaudible.

"Where's he going?" Angus asked.

"Just down the road to have a look," the small man said. He wandered about the cabin. He was still coatless, the gun still thrust into his belt.

Angus began to whirl desperate ideas through his mind. He was perspiring freely. If they left him there he would be all right; he would be able to get up and walk away after they left. But—he had seen the thought in Champ's eyes— he knew them, could identify them. Would they take the risk of leaving him when he could possibly extricate himself and incriminate them?

The small man stepped out of the cabin and went to the car. Instantly, purely on impulse, Angus shook the loosened bonds around his wrists to the floor and tried to leap up, his heart hammering, his body hot, wet, but the chair to which he was still tied hobbled him. He swung his arms, and by trying with all his strength to lurch free of the chair he toppled it over. Rickety to begin with, his weight plus the force of the fall wrenched the chair apart and he was soon up on his feet, freeing himself of the rope and the chair's fragments. His sudden freedom was almost unendurable, it called for swift and desperate action, action he was too terrified even to contemplate.

He heard the slam of a car door. He picked up a chair and pressed himself against the wall next to the door, lifting the chair higher and higher. He saw the small man's shadow roll across the threshold, and then his body, his face—his face startled for the instant and then furious as Angus hurled down the chair, giving him a vicious and intricate smash with it, crumbling him, the small man trying to catch himself in the doorway but missing, collapsing, and the thought burning like static fire in Angus' mind that the small man was merely dazed, not unconscious, and so Angus reached down for the gun, jerking it free as the small man began to turn in protest. Angus drew back, holding the gun on him.

And the small man gave him no choice. In the face of the loaded, weighty gun he began to rise, his bruised and snarling face brooking no fears, no threats. Angus fired, once. He was amazed that the gun worked, amazed at the roar, at the commotion it caused in his hand, almost causing him to drop it. And amazed as the small man, halfway to his feet, was hurled back against the doorway, his white shirt suddenly flowing with blood as he rolled over and flung a ghastly sightless face up to the pale moon that had risen over the trees.

Angus began to tremble. He jumped over the body and ran out into the woods. He almost expected the grotesque moon-cast forest to lunge and thrust at him, but it held back, still, attentive, the stars gathered round the peeping moon like dazzled eyes.

He suddenly became aware of the fast sounds down the road, the sounds of running feet rapping the dark road. He crouched behind the car, holding the immense gun in both hands now, training it on the spot in the dark from where Champ would emerge.

The running became louder, more urgent. A figure began to loom, floating out of the dark. The tall man came across the grass.

"Lou!" he shouted, seeing the small man's stretched and lifeless body in front of the door.

Angus stood up, holding the gun in both hands, not more than five feet from the moving figure that was now cautiously drawing a gun. Angus fired. Champ was sprawled across the ground. It seemed that he hadn't even fallen, that merely the roar, the smoke had driven him there. Angus peered down, his eyes wide, speculative.

A great hush descended. The forest crooned softly, interminably . . .

Angus Monroe sat in the police station, neat, shy, pale.

The chief of police was nodding. "You have our deepest sympathy, Mr. Monroe," he was saying. "It must have been a nightmare."

Angus nodded.

"You're lucky you're alive," the bank president said.

"You say you have no idea where they went?" the chief asked.

"No," Angus said, proceeding to repeat his story. "They knocked me out in the car and the next thing I knew I woke up in the bushes. I do know that they were going to meet someone else, in a cabin somewhere in the woods I believe they said, and, from what I gathered, someone they didn't trust very much. From the way they spoke they were anticipating trouble."

"Thieves always fall out," the bank president said righteously.

Angus nodded. But his mind was thinking ahead. Everyone would understand when he resigned his position. The ordeal had been too great. He would go away, far away. He would have everyone's compassion, as well as eleven thousand five.

LAWRENCE BLOCK

The Most Unusual Snatch

They grabbed Carole Butler a few minutes before midnight just a block and a half from her own front door. It never would have happened if her father had let her take the car. But she was six months shy of eighteen, and the law said you had to be eighteen to drive at night, and her father was a great believer in the law. So she had taken the bus, got off two blocks from her house, and walked half a block before a tall thin man with his hat down over his eyes appeared suddenly and asked her the time.

She was about to tell him to go buy his own watch when an arm came around her from behind and a damp cloth fastened over her mouth and nose. It smelled like a hospital room.

She heard voices, faintly, as if from far away. "Not too long, you don't want to kill her."

"What's the difference? Kill her now or kill her later, she's just as dead."

"You kill her now and she can't make the phone call."

There was more, but she didn't hear it. The chloroform did its work and she sagged, limp, unconscious.

At first, when she came to, groggy and weak and sick to her stomach, she thought she had been taken to a hospital. Then she realized it was just the smell of the chloroform. Her head seemed awash in the stuff. She breathed steadily, in and out, in and out, stayed where she was and didn't open her eyes.

She heard the same two voices she had heard before. One was assuring the other that everything would go right on schedule, that they couldn't miss. "Seventy-five thou," he said several times. "Wait another hour, let him sweat a little. Then call him and tell him it'll cost him seventy-five thou to see his darling daughter again. That's all we tell him, just that we got her, and the price. Then we let him stew in it for another two hours."

"Why drag it out?"

"Because it has to drag until morning anyway. He's not going to have that kind of bread around the house. He'll have to go on the send for it, and that means nine o'clock when the banks open. Give him the whole message right away and he'll have too much time to get nervous and call copper. But space it out just right and we'll have him on the string until morning, and then he can go straight to the bank and get the money ready."

Carole opened her eyes slowly, carefully. The one who was doing most of the talking was the same tall thin man who had asked her the time. He was less than beautiful, she noticed. His nose was lopsided, angling off to the left as though it had been broken and improperly reset. His chin was scarcely there at all. He ought to wear a goatee, she thought. He would still be no thing of beauty, but it might help.

The other one was shorter, heavier, and younger, no more than ten years older than Carole. He had wide shoulders, close-set eyes, and a generally stupid face, but he wasn't altogether bad-looking. Not bad at all she told herself. Between the two of them, they seemed to have kidnapped her. She wanted to laugh out loud.

"Better cool it," the younger one said. "Looks like she's coming out of it."

She picked up her cue, making a great show of blinking her eyes vacantly and yawning and stretching. Stretching was difficult, as she seemed to be tied to a chair. It was an odd sensation. She had never been tied up before, and she didn't care for it.

"Hey," she said, "where am I?"

She could have answered the question herself. She was, to judge from appearances, in an especially squalid shack. The shack itself was fairly close to a highway, judging from the traffic noises. If she had to guess, she would place the location somewhere below the southern edge of the city, probably a few hundred yards off Highway 130 near the river. There were plenty of empty fishing shacks there, she remembered, and it was a fair bet that this was one of them.

"Now just take it easy, Carole," the thin man said. "You take it easy and nothing's going to happen to you."

"You kidnapped me."

"You just take it easy and—"

She squealed with joy. "This is too much! You've actually kidnapped me. Oh, this is wild! Did you call my old man yet?"

"No."

"Will you let me listen when you do?" She started to giggle. "I'd give anything to see his face when you tell him. He'll split. He'll just fall apart."

They were both staring at her, open-mouthed. The younger man said, "You sound happy about it."

"Happy? Of course I'm happy. This is the most exciting thing that ever happened to me!"

"But your father—"

"I hope you gouge him good," she went on. "He's the cheapest old man on earth. He wouldn't pay a nickel to see a man go over the Falls. How much are you going to ask?"

"Never mind," the thin man said.

"I just hope it's enough. He can afford plenty."

The thin man grinned. "How does seventy-five thousand dollars strike you?"

"Not enough. He can afford more than that," she said. "He's very rich, but you wouldn't know it the way he hangs onto his money."

"Seventy-five thou is pretty rich."

She shook her head. "Not for him. He could afford plenty more."

"It's not what he can afford, it's what he can raise in a hurry. We don't want to drag this out for days. We want it over by morning."

She thought for a minute. "Well, it's your funeral," she said pertly.

The shorter man approached her. "What do you mean by that?"

"Forget it, Ray," his partner said.

"No, I want to find out. What did you mean by that, honey?"

She looked up at them. "Well, I don't want to tell you your business," she said slowly. "I mean, you're the kidnappers. You're the ones who are taking all the chances. I mean, if you get caught they can really give you a hard time, can't they?"

"The chair," the thin man said.

"That's what I thought, so I don't want to tell you how to do all this, but there *was* something that occurred to me."

"Let's hear it."

"Well, first of all, I don't think it's a good idea to wait for morning. You wouldn't know it, of course, but he doesn't have to wait until the banks open. He's a doctor, and I know he gets paid in cash a lot of the time, cash that never goes to the bank, never gets entered in the books. It goes straight into the safe in the basement and stays there."

"Taxes—"

"Something like that. Anyway, I heard him telling somebody that he never has less than a hundred thousand dollars in that safe. So you wouldn't have to wait until the banks open, and you wouldn't have to settle for seventy-five thousand either. You could ask for an even hundred thousand and get it easy."

The two kidnappers looked at her, at each other, then at her again.

"I mean," she said, "I'm only trying to be helpful."

"You must hate him something awful, kid."

"Now you're catching on."

"Doesn't he treat you right?"

"All his money," she said, "and I don't even get my own car. I had to take the bus tonight; otherwise you wouldn't have got me the way you did, so it's his fault I was kidnapped. Why shouldn't he pay a bundle?"

"This is some kid, Howie," the younger man said.

Howie nodded. "You sure about the hundred thousand?"

"He'll probably try to stall, tell us he needs time to raise the dough."

"So tell him you know about the safe."

"Maybe he—"

"And that way he won't call the police," she went on. "Because of not paying taxes on the money and all that. He won't want that to come out into the open, so he'll pay."

"It's like you planned this job yourself, baby," Ray said.

"I almost did."

"Huh?"

"I used to think what a gas it would be if I got kidnapped. What a fit the old man would throw and everything." She giggled. "But I never really thought it would happen. It's too perfect."

"I think I'll make that call now," Howie said. "I'll be back in maybe half an hour. Ray here'll take good care of you, kitten." He nodded and was gone.

She had expected that Howie would make the call and was glad it had turned out that way. Ray seemed to be the easier of the two to get along with. It wasn't just that he was younger and better-looking. He was also, as far as she could tell, more good-natured and a whole lot less intelligent.

"Who would have figured it?" he said now. "I mean, you go and pull a snatch, you don't expect anybody to be so cooperative."

"Have you ever done this before, Ray?"

"No."

"It must be scary."

"Aw, I guess it's easy enough. More money than a bank job and a whole lot less risk. The only hard part is when the mark—your old man, that is—delivers the money. You have to get the dough without being spotted. Outside of that, it's no sweat at all."

"And afterward?"

"Huh?"

The palms of her hands were moist with sweat. She said, "What happens afterward? Will you let me go, Ray?"

"Oh, sure."

"You won't kill me?"

"Oh, don't be silly," he said.

She knew exactly what he meant. He meant, Let's not talk about it, doll, but of course we'll kill you. What else?

"I'm more fun when I'm alive," she said.

"I'll bet you are."

"You better believe it."

He came closer to her. She straightened her shoulders to emphasize her youthful curves and watched his eyes move over her body.

"That's a pretty sweater," he said. "You look real good in a sweater. I'll bet a guy could have a whole lot of fun with you, baby."

"I'm more fun," she said, "when I'm not tied up. Howie won't be back for a half hour. But I don't guess that would worry you."

"Not a bit."

She sat perfectly still while he untied her. Then she got slowly to her feet. Her legs were cramped and her fingers tingled a little from the limited circulation. Ray took her in his arms and kissed her, then took a black automatic from his pocket and placed it on the table.

"Now don't get any idea about making a grab for the gun," he said. "You'd only get hurt, you know."

Later he insisted on tying her up again.

"But I won't try anything," she protested. "Honest, Ray. You know I wouldn't try anything. I want everything to go off just right."

"Howie wouldn't like it," he said doggedly and that was all there was to it.

"But don't make it too tight," she begged. "It hurts."

He didn't make it too tight.

When Howie came back he was smiling broadly. He closed the door and locked it and lit a cigarette. "Like a charm," he said through a cloud of smoke. "Went like a charm. You're O.K., honey girl."

"What did he say?"

"Got hysterical first of all. Kept telling me not to hurt you, that he'd pay if only we'd release you. He kept saying how much he loved you and all."

She started to laugh. "Oh, beautiful!"

"And you were right about the safe. He started to blubber that he couldn't possibly raise a hundred thousand on short notice. Then I hit him with the safe, said I knew he kept plenty of dough right there in his own basement, and that really got to him. He went all to pieces. I think you could have knocked him over with a lettuce leaf when he heard that."

"And he'll pay up?"

"No trouble at all, and if it's all cash he's been salting away that's the best news yet: no serial numbers copied down, no big bills, no runs of new bills in sequence. That means we don't have to wholesale the kidnap dough to one of the Eastern mobs for forty cents on the dollar. We wind up with a hundred thousand, and we wind up clean."

"And he'll be scared to go to the police afterward," Carole put in. "Did you set up the delivery of the money?"

"No. I said I'd call in an hour. I may cut it to a half hour though. I think we've got him where we want him. This is going so smooth it scares me. I want it over and done with, nice and easy."

She was silent for a moment. Howie wanted it over and done with, undoubtedly wanted no loose ends. Inevitably he was going to think of her, Carole Butler, as an obvious loose end, which meant that he would probably want to tie her off, and the black automatic on the table was just the thing to do the job. She stared at the gun, imagined the sound of it, the impact of the bullet in her flesh. She was terrified, but she made sure none of this showed in her face or in her voice.

Casually she asked, "About the money—how are you going to pick it up?"

"That's the only part that worries me."

"I don't think he'll call the police. Not my old man. Frankly, I don't think he'd have the guts. But if he did, that would be the time when they'd try to catch you, wouldn't it?"

"That's the general idea."

She thought for a moment. "If we were anywhere near the south end of town, I know a perfect spot—but I suppose we're miles from there."

"What's the spot?"

She told him about it—the overpass on Route 130 at the approach to the turnpike. They could have her father drive onto the pike, toss the money over the side of the overpass when he reached it, and they could be waiting down below to pick it up. Any cops who were with him would be stuck up there on the turnpike and they could get away clean.

"It's not bad," Ray said.

"It's perfect," Howie added. "You thought that up all by yourself?"

"Well, I got the idea from a really super-duper movie—"

"I think it's worth doing it that way." Howie sighed. "I was going to get fancy, have him walk to a garbage can, stick it inside, then cut out. Then we go in and get it out of the can. But suppose the cops had the whole place staked out?" He smiled. "You've got a good head on your shoulders, kitten. It's a shame—"

"What's a shame?"

"That you're not part of the gang, the way your mind works. You'd be real good at it."

That, she knew, was not really what he'd meant. It's a shame we have to kill you anyway, he meant. You're a smart kid, and even a pretty kid, but all the same you're going to get a bullet between the eyes, and it's a shame.

She pictured her father, waiting by the telephone. If he called the police, she knew it would be all over for her, and he might very well call them. But if she could stop him, if she could make sure that he let the delivery of the ransom money go according to plan, then maybe she would have a chance. It wouldn't be the best chance in the world, but anything was better than nothing at all.

When Howie said he was going to make the second phone call she asked him to take her along. "Let me talk to him," she begged. "I want to hear his voice. I want to hear him in a panic. He's always so cool about everything, so smug and superior. I want to see what he sounds like when he gets in a sweat."

"I don't know—"

"I'll convince him that you're desperate and dangerous," she continued. "I'll tell him—" she managed to giggle "—that I know you'll kill me if he doesn't cooperate, but that I'm sure you'll let me go straight home just as soon as the ransom is paid as long as he keeps the police out of it."

"Well, I don't know. It sounds good, but—"

"It's a good idea, Howie," Ray said. "That way he knows we've got her and he knows she's still alive. I think the kid knows what she's talking about."

It took a little talking, but finally Howie was convinced of the wisdom of the move. Ray untied her and the three of them got into Howie's car and drove down the road to a pay phone. Howie made the call and talked for a few minutes, explaining how and where the ransom was to be delivered. Then he gave the phone to Carole.

"Oh, Daddy," she sobbed. "Oh, Daddy, I'm scared! Daddy, do just what they tell you. There are four of them and they're desperate, and I'm scared of them. Please pay them, Daddy. The woman said if the police were brought in she'd cut my throat with a knife. She said she'd cut me and kill me, Daddy, and I'm so scared of them—"

Back in the cabin, as Howie tied her in the chair, he asked, "What was all that gas about four of us? And the bit about the woman?"

"I just thought it sounded dramatic."

"It was dramatic as a nine-alarm fire, but why bother?"

"Well," she said, "the bigger the gang is, the more dangerous it sounds, and if he reports it later, let the police go looking for three men and a woman. That way you'll have even less trouble getting away clear. And of course I'll give them four phony descriptions, just to make it easier for you."

She hoped that would soak in. She could only give the phony descriptions if she were left alive, and she hoped that much penetrated.

It was around three-thirty in the morning when Howie left for the ransom. "I should be about an hour," he said. "If I'm not back in that time, then things are bad. Then we've got trouble."

"What do I do then?" Ray asked.

"You know what to do."

"I mean, how do I get out of here? We've only got the one car, and you'll be in it."

"So beat it on foot, or stay right where you are. You don't have to worry about me cracking. The only way they'll get me is dead, and if I'm dead you won't have to worry about them finding out where we've got her tucked away. Just take care of the chick and get out on foot."

"Nothing's going to go wrong."

"I think you're right. I think this is smooth as silk, but anything to be sure. You got your gun?"

"On the table."

"Ought to keep it on you."

"Well, maybe."

"Remember," Howie said, "you can figure on me getting back in an hour at the outside. Probably be no more than half of that, but an hour is tops. So long."

"Good luck," Carole called after him.

Howie stopped and looked at her. He had a very strange expression on his face. "Yeah," he said finally. "Luck. Sure, thanks."

When Howie was gone, Ray said, "You never should have made the phone call. I mean, I think it was a good idea and all, but that way Howie tied you up, see, and he tied you tight. Me, I would have tied you loose, see, but he doesn't think the same way." He considered things. "In a way," he went on, "Howie is what you might call a funny guy. Everything has to go just right, know what I mean? He doesn't like to leave a thing to chance."

"Could you untie me?"

"Well, I don't know if I should."

"At least make this looser? It's got my fingers numb already. It hurts pretty bad, Ray. Please?"

"Well, I suppose so." He untied her. As soon as she was loose he moved to the table, scooped up the gun, wedged it beneath the waistband of his trousers.

He likes me, she thought. He even wants me to be comfortable and he doesn't particularly want to kill me, but he doesn't trust me. He's too nervous to trust anybody.

"Could I have a cigarette?" she asked.

"Huh? Oh, sure." He gave her one, lit it for her. They smoked together for several minutes in silence. It isn't going to work, she thought, not the way things are going. She had him believing her, but that didn't seem to be enough. Howie was the brains and the boss, and what Howie said went, and Howie would say to kill her. She wondered which one of them would use the gun on her.

"Uh, Carole—"

"What?"

"Oh, nothing. Just forget it."

He wanted her to bring it up, she knew. So she said, "Listen, Ray, let me tell you something. I like you a lot, but to tell you the truth I'm scared of Howie."

"You are?"

"I've been playing it straight with you, and I think you've been straight with me. Ray, you've got the brains to realize you'll be much better off if you let me go." He doesn't, she thought, have any brains at all, but flattery never hurt. "But Howie is different from you and me. He's not—well, normal. I know he wants to kill me."

"Oh, now—"

"I mean it, Ray." She clutched his arm. "If I live, Dad won't report it. He can't afford to. But if you kill me—"

"Yeah, I know."

"Suppose you let me go."

"Afterward?"

She shook her head. "No, now, before Howie comes back. He won't care by then, he'll have the money. You can just let me go, and then the two of you will take the money and get out of town. Nobody will ever know a thing. I'll tell Dad the two of you released me and he'll be so glad to get me back and so scared of the tax men he'll never say a word. You could let me go, Ray, couldn't you? Before Howie gets back?"

He thought it over for a long time, and she could see he wanted to. But he said, "I don't know, Howie would take me apart—"

"Say I grabbed something and hit you, and managed to knock you out. Tell him he tied the ropes wrong and I slipped loose and got you from behind. He'll be mad, maybe, but what will he care? As long as you have the money—"

"He won't believe you hit me."

"Suppose I *did* hit you? Not hard, but enough to leave a mark so you could point to it for proof."

He grinned suddenly. "Sure, Carole, you've been good to me. The first time, when he made that first phone call, you were real good. I'll tell you something, the idea of killing you bothers me. And you're right about Howie. Here, belt me one behind the ear. Make it a good one, but not too hard, O.K.?" And he handed her the gun.

He looked completely astonished when she shot him. He just didn't believe it. She reversed the gun in her hand, curled her index finger around the trigger, and pointed the gun straight at his heart. His eyes bugged out and his mouth dropped open, and he just stared at her, not saying anything at all. She shot him twice in the center of the chest and watched him fall slowly, incredibly, to the floor, dead.

When Howie's car pulled up she was ready. She crouched by the doorway, gun in hand, waiting. The car door flew open and she heard his footsteps on the gravel path. He pulled the door open, calling out jubilantly that it had gone like clockwork, just like clockwork, then he caught sight of Ray's corpse on the floor and did a fantastic double-take. When he saw her and the gun, he started to say something, but she emptied the gun into him, four bullets, one after the other, and all of them hit him and they worked; he fell; he died.

She got the bag of money out of his hand before he could bleed on it.

The rest wasn't too difficult. She took the rope with which she'd been tied and rubbed it back and forth on the chair leg until it finally frayed through. Behind the cabin she found a toolshed. She used a shovel, dug a shallow pit, dropped the money into it, filled in the hole. She carried the gun down to the water's edge, wiped it free of fingerprints, and heaved it into the creek.

Finally, when just the right amount of time had passed, she walked out to the highway and kept going until she found a telephone, a highway emergency booth.

"Just stay right where you are," her father said. "Don't call the police. I'll come for you."

"Hurry. Daddy. I'm so scared."

He picked her up. She was shaking, and he held her in his arms and soothed her.

"I was so frightened," she said. "And then when the one man came back with the ransom money, the other man took out a gun and shot him and the third man, and then the man who did the shooting, he and the woman ran away in their other car. I was sure they were going to kill me but the man said not to bother, the gun was empty and it didn't matter now. The woman wanted to kill me with the knife but she didn't. I was sure she would. Oh, Daddy—"

"It's all right now," he said. "Everything's going to be all right."

She showed him the cabin and the two dead men and the rope. "It took me forever to get out of it," she said. "But I saw in the movies how you can work your way out, and I wasn't tied too tight, so I managed to do it."

"You're a brave girl, Carole."

On the way home he said, "I'm not going to call the police, Carole. I don't want to subject you to a lot of horrible questioning. Sooner or later they'll find those two in the cabin, but that was nothing to do with us. They'll just find two dead criminals, and the world's better off without them." He thought for a moment. "Besides," he added, "I'm sure I'd have a hard time explaining where I got that money."

"Did they get very much?"

"Only ten thousand dollars," he said.

"I thought they asked for more."

"Well, after I explained that I didn't have anything like that around the house they listened to reason."

"I see," she said.

You old liar, she thought, it was a hundred thousand dollars, and I know it. And it's mine now. Mine.

"Ten thousand dollars is a lot of money," she said. "I mean, it's a lot for you to lose."

"It doesn't matter."

"If you called the police, maybe they could get it back."

He shuddered visibly, and she held back laughter. "It doesn't matter," he said. "All that matters is that we got you back safe and sound. That's more important than all the money in the world."

"Oh, Daddy," she said, hugging him, "oh, I love you, I love you so much!"

NEDRA TYRE

A Murder Is Arranged

Mary must murder her husband. There was nothing else to do. She hadn't the slightest doubt about it.

She had forgiven John everything except for his actions these last few weeks.

No, that wasn't putting it accurately. She hadn't forgiven him anything. Until recently, there had been nothing to forgive, no matter what people might have thought.

John was the ideal mate for her. What would her life have been without him? When she thought of the husbands of her friends—those dull, earnest, aspiring types—she shuddered. How blessed she had been to have John instead of one of them.

John was exactly right for her.

Her mother, her sisters, aunts, cousins, and friends had said she was too good for John—though, mind you, they admitted he was fascinating, a real charmer, the best company in the world. What they deplored was that John wrapped her around his little finger. That was what they all harped upon. She did what he wanted, she danced to his tune.

They twitted her that no matter what she thought, John didn't put the sun in the sky. They were wrong—John had put the sun in her sky, he *was* the sun in her sky.

If only they could have realized what had happened. She was no longer dancing to John's tune. She wasn't being twisted around his little finger.

She was about to murder him.

The only hindrance was that she had no idea how to murder John. Exactly how did a self-respecting woman go about killing her husband?

Why hadn't she learned how to shoot from her father and brothers? Marksmen all, they could so easily have taught her how to reach John's heart with one bullet—but there would be an awful noise and no doubt a great deal of blood. Besides, if she shot John her relatives and friends would no doubt say that John had got his just desserts at last. Nor did she have any intention of being tried for John's murder—that would defeat her purpose. John's death must be made to look either natural or accidental.

It had been foolish for people to insist she was too good for John and she didn't intend that anyone should crow or gloat over John's death. Because, for all his infidelities, he was everything she wanted. When they were together at dinners and parties his eyes didn't wander. Of course he greeted other women, exchanged pleasantries with them, complimented them on their clothes and appearance, but his arm embraced Mary all the while.

In contrast, how inexcusable was the behavior of the other husbands. At dances at the club, at cocktail parties in private homes, those other men began to make passes with the first whiff of Scotch, while John was beside Mary feeding her cream-cheese-and-chives dip and asking if she wanted more ice in her drink. His lapses might have been many, but they were all done with finesse while she was out of sight. He was careful to see that she lost no face. There was no flaunting of any of his encounters. Whenever he had been away with someone else he had acted like a dutiful son, sending flowers to Mama, writing cards and letters, assuring her that his love for her was deep and eternal. For a brief time he was, figuratively, only a jaunty dog gamboling down the street for a short trot and would return soon; and when he did return his arms were loaded with lavish presents.

Well, if people called that being twisted around John's little finger she preferred it to the sordid, sneaky liaisons indulged in by other men in their social group.

All this mulling was getting her no closer to dispatching John. She must murder him in a quiet, unobtrusive way. She much preferred that there be no blood.

What about suffocating him?

No, that wouldn't do. The poor man would gasp and turn purple and John was much too handsome to spend his last moments in such an agitated manner. Besides, she doubted that she had sufficient strength to strangle or suffocate him.

How sad that it had come to this—that her love for him, her devotion, infatuation, commitment, whatever it was, anyway her total absorption in him had been ruined.

His character, attitude and persona had altered entirely. He had become messy and slovenly. The impeccable, faultlessly groomed John had disappeared altogether, and he had begun to act like a satyr. When he accompanied her on shopping trips he would stop in the middle of a sidewalk to ogle a young girl. At the checkout counter he would make a pass at the clerk. John had always drunk well. He could drink for hours and not show it. Now his speech was often slurred. He even walked unsteadily.

His manners had become boorish. He didn't compliment Mary any longer on her cooking, but would scrape the food to one side of the plate as if it were beneath his contempt.

He had begun to speak harshly to her. *Dear, darling, beloved*, all those endearments with which he had addressed her had been deleted from his conversation as if they were obscene. Formerly he had hung upon every word she uttered. Now he often pretended he hadn't heard what she said. Twice he had told her to shut up—this from John who had never raised his voice in speaking to her! Now he had become a bully and a ruffian.

She was chagrined and mortified.

But how on earth was she to murder him?

There were no long flights of stairs down which she could send him spinning.
There was no swimming pool in which she might conveniently drown him.

More than anything, his new grossness disgusted her. How had he contrived
that leer? When had she ever refused him? When hadn't she welcomed him with
open arms? How dare he use those earthy, demeaning approaches when he
wanted to make love? When had she ever been coy? Love was an open,
defenseless plain upon which lovers met without reservation or pretense and he
was behaving now as if their passion were vulgar and degrading. He made her
feel cheap.

For the first time ever he had forgotten her birthday, and on their wedding
anniversary instead of taking her to the customary champagne dinner and
showering her with dozens of roses and carnations and an exquisite chiffon
nightgown, he had yawned and said he was much too tired to go out—a ham
sandwich and a bottle of beer in the kitchen were all he wanted. Then he had
said in an offhand but cutting manner that there had been enough celebrations
of an event so long in the past and he was sure she was as weary of them as he
was.

Finally, what set a limit to his few remaining days on earth was his cruel
reference to their having no children. "It's damned bleak, isn't it, not to have
any children? Nothing but the two of us."

He really was a brute. Just the two of them was what he had insisted upon!
He had said he didn't want children who would only come between them and
their happiness. They were complete in themselves. They needed nothing and
no one else.

John must die immediately for rejecting that premise on which so much of
their joy had been based. She must get this caricature that her husband had
become into the ground immediately.

Yet she owed him something for the happiness that they had shared and so,
to honor that debt, she would murder him decently and quietly by giving him
an overdose of sleeping pills.

Why had it taken her so long to think of the one perfect method? It seemed
stupid of her not to have arrived at it long before, but perhaps she had needed
to be goaded by that final insult of not having borne him any children.

John knew he hadn't deserved Mary, but he had made her happy. He
believed in love and rapture, and he had loved her completely. He was a
romantic. Men were the romantics of this world and women were the practical
ones.

There had been many women in his life, but Mary had come first and she
knew it. He went out of his way to show her. Not that he had exploited the
others. He had reason to think he had made them happy too. Mary, though,
was his life. His flirtations had never brought shame to Mary or made her feel
neglected. They had been minor skirmishes and only added piquancy to the

passion he felt for Mary. He wished he could have given her the world, but he had no knack for business, and he was grateful to his grandfather who had set up a trust fund for him shortly before he and Mary were married, and had then promptly and conveniently died. Also, Mary had her own tidy annuities gleaned from several rich and thrifty great-aunts and some cousins twice removed. He was grateful to them all. He loved women, no matter how old or young they were so long as they were pleasant.

He had a gift for love and dalliance.

But he had no courage and he could not endure pain and he could not abide sympathy. Illness robbed a man of everything. He could not confront agony and anguish. Perhaps that was why he had punished himself when he was younger by doing volunteer hospital work in the wards filled with the hopelessly ill. He had seen so many die hideous deaths of what he now had—but he refused to accept that painful, lingering death for himself. Perhaps he had thought that he could trick life into giving him an easy death if he helped others in pain. Well, life couldn't be manipulated; fate wouldn't oblige.

Mary, however, could be manipulated.

All those relatives and friends had joked over the years that John could twist Mary around his finger. It was true. He could have, but he hadn't. Yet now that he needed to manipulate her he knew that he could.

John might have taken his own life, but that would have been cowardly. It would have been an affront to Mary, who had made him completely happy—the life she had given him was more than happy, it had been blissful. To the world his suicide would have negated their perfect years together, and it would have placed upon Mary a terrible, unendurable burden of guilt. Mary must be made to give him death. An easy one. A quick one.

He knew her so well and was precisely aware of how she responded to him and what there was about him that attracted her. It would be a matter of only a few weeks until he could make her take his life.

The days had gone as he had predicted and Mary's disgust had flourished. He knew the exact moment when she had accumulated enough sleeping pills, and the next morning he pushed himself across the bed and nudged her—she had taken to sleeping as far away from him as the width of the large bed allowed. His voice was sharp and demanding, "I want a large glass of orange juice and I want it immediately."

Mary sprang out of bed and grabbed her robe and hurried to the kitchen. She was gone only a little while and John saw her hand quiver as she set a small tray holding the orange juice on the bedside table. He rudely jerked the glass from the tray and gulped the juice.

Only then could he trust himself to smile at her. "Thank you, darling," he said, but she had already left the room and did not hear him.

HENRY SLESAR

The Poisoned Pawn

If it weren't for the state of his own health (his stomach felt lined with broken green bottle glass), Milo Bloom would have giggled at the sight of his roommate in the six-bed ward on the third floor of Misericordia Hospital. Both of his arms were in casts, giving them the appearance of two chubby white sausages; the left arm dangled from a pulley in a complex traction arrangement that somehow included his left leg. Later, he learned that his companion (Dietz was his name), had fallen from a loading platform. Milo's hospital admittance record told a far more dramatic story. He had been poisoned.

"And I'll tell you something," Milo said, shaking his head sadly and making the broken glass jiggle, " I learned a lesson from it. I was lying under my own dining table, and my whole life flashed in front of my eyes, and you know what it looked like? One long chess game. I saw myself born on QB4, a white pawn wrapped in a baby blanket, and here I was, dying, caught in a *zugzwang* and about to be checkmated . . ."

Of course, Milo was still under sedation and wasn't expected to talk coherently. An hour later, however, he was able to express himself more clearly.

"Never again," he said solemnly. "Never, never again will I play another game of chess. I'll never touch another piece, never read another chess column. You say the name 'Bobby Fischer' to me, I'll put my hands over my ears. For thirty years I was a prisoner of that miserable board, but now I'm through. You call that a game? That's an obsession! And look where it got me. Just look!"

What he really meant, of course, was "listen," which is what Dietz, who had no other plans that day, was perfectly willing to do.

My father cared very little about chess. When he proudly displayed me to the membership of the Greenpoint Chess Club, and mockingly promoted a match with Kupperman, its champion, it wasn't for love of the game; just hate for Kupperman. I was eleven years old, Kupperman was forty-five. The thought of my tiny hands strangling Kupperman's King filled him with ecstasy.

I sat opposite Kupperman's hulking body and ignored the heavy-jowled sneer that had terrified other opponents, confident that I was a prodigy, whose ability Kupperman would underestimate. Then zip! wham! thud! the pieces came together in the center of the board. Bang! Kupperman's Queen lashed out in an unorthodox early attack. *Whoosh!* came his black Knights in a double assault that made me whimper. Then *crash!* my defense crumpled and my King was running for his life, only to fall dead ignobly at the feet of a Rook Pawn. Unbelievable. In seventeen moves, most of them textbook-defying, Kupperman had crushed me. Guess who didn't get ice cream that night?

Of course, I was humiliated by Kupperman's victory. I had bested every opponent in my peer group, and thought I was ready for prodigy-type encounters. I didn't realize at the time how very good Kupperman was. The fact that he was Number One in a small Brooklyn chess club gave no real measure of the man's talent, his extraordinary, Petrosian-like play.

I learned a great deal more about that talent in the next two decades, because that wasn't the last Bloom-Kupperman match; it was only the first of many.

Kupperman refused to play me again until four years later, when I was not only a ripe fifteen, but had already proved my worth by winning the Junior Championship of Brooklyn. I was bristling with self-confidence then, but when I faced the 49-year-old Kupperman across the table, and once again witnessed the strange, slashing style, the wild romping of his Knights, the long-delayed castling, the baffling retreat of well-developed pieces, surprising *zwischenzuge*—in-between moves with no apparent purpose—and most disturbing of all, little stabbing moves of his Pawns, pinpricks from both sides of the board, nibbling at my presumably solid center, panic set in and my brain fogged over, to say nothing of my glasses from the steam of my own accelerated breathing. Yes, I lost that game, too; but it wasn't to be my last loss to Kupperman, even though he abruptly decided to leave not only the Greenpoint Chess Club, but the East Coast itself.

I never knew for certain why Kupperman decided to leave. My father theorized that he was an asthma victim who had been advised to bask in the drying sunshine of Arizona or some other western state. Actually, the first postmark I saw from a Kupperman correspondence was a town called Kenton, Illinois. He had sent a letter to the Greenpoint Chess Club, offering to play its current champion by mail. I suppose he was homesick for Brooklyn. Now, guess who was current champion? Milo Bloom.

I was twenty-two then, past the age of prodigy, but smug in my dominance of the neighborhood *potzers*, and pantingly eager to face the Kupperman unorthodoxy again, certain that nobody could break so many rules and still come out on top consistently. I replied to Kupperman at once, special delivery no less, and told him with becoming modesty of my ascension in the club and my gracious willingness to play him by mail.

A week later, I received his reply, a written scowl is what it was, and an opening move—N-KB3! Obviously, Kupperman hadn't changed too much in the intervening seven years.

Well, I might as well get it over with and admit that Kupperman defeated me in that game and, if anything, the defeat was more shattering than the head-to-head encounters of the past. Incredibly, Kupperman posted most of his pieces on the back rank. Then came a Knight sacrifice, a pinned Queen, and a neatly-executed check.

Foreseeing the slaughter ahead, I resigned, despite the fact that I was actually ahead by one Pawn.

Obviously, my early resignation didn't fully satisfy Kupperman (I could just visualize him, his unshaven cheeks quivering in a fleshy frown, as he tore open my letter and growled in chagrin at my reply). Almost the next day, I received a letter asking me why I hadn't sent my White opening for the next game.

I finally did: P-Q4. He replied with N-KB3. I moved my own Knight. He responded by moving his Pawn to the Queen's third square. I moved my Knight to the Bishop's third square, and he promptly pinned it with *his* Bishop, contrary to all common sense. Then he proceeded to let me have both Bishops and bring up my Queen. I should have known that I was doomed then and there. He smothered my Bishops, made an aggressive castling move, and needled me with Pawns until my position was hopeless.

A month went by before Kupperman sent me the next opening move (this time, his letter was postmarked Tyler, Kansas) and we were launched into the third game of what was to become a lifetime of humiliating encounters.

Yes, that's correct. *I never won a game from Kupperman.* Yet, despite my continuing chagrin and, one might think, despite Kupperman's boredom, our games-by-mail were played for a period of *nineteen years.* The only real variations were in Kupperman's postmarks; he seemed to change his residence monthly. Otherwise the pattern remained the same: Kupperman's unorthodox, Petrosian-like style invariably bested my solid, self-righteous, textbook game. As you can imagine, beating Kupperman became the primary challenge, then, of my life.

Then he sent me The Letter.

It was the first time Kupperman's correspondence consisted of anything but chess notations. It was postmarked from New Mexico, and the handwriting looked as if it had been scrawled out with a screwdriver dipped in axle grease.

"*Dear Grandmaster,*" it said, with heavy irony. "Please be advised that the present score is 97 games to nothing. Please be advised that upon my hundredth victory, we play no more. Yours respectfully, A. Kupperman."

I don't know how to describe the effect of that letter upon me. I couldn't have been more staggered if my family doctor had diagnosed a terminal illness. Yes, I knew full well that the score was 97-to-0, although I hadn't realized that Kupperman kept such scrupulous records; but the humiliation that lay ahead of me, the hundredth defeat, the *final* defeat, was almost too much for me to bear. Suddenly, I knew that if I didn't beat Kupperman at least *once* before that deadline, my life would be lived out in shame and total frustration.

It was no use returning to the textbooks; I had studied thousands of games (*all* of Petrosian's, until I knew each move by rote) without finding the secret of overcoming Kupperman's singular style. If anything, his use of Knights and Pawns was even wilder and more distinctive than Petrosian's. It was no use hoping for a sudden failure of Kupperman's play; not with only three games left. In fact, it was no use believing in miracles of any kind.

I walked about in a daze, unable to decide whether to send Kupperman the opening move of the 98th game. My employer (the accounting firm of Bernard & Yerkes) began to complain bitterly about frequent errors in my work. The young woman I had been dating for almost two years took personal affront at my attitude and she severed our relationship.

Then, one day, the solution to my problem appeared almost magically before my eyes.

Strangely enough, I had seen the very same advertisement in *Chess Review* for almost a dozen years, and it never assumed the significance it did that evening.

The advertisement read: "*Grandmaster willing to play for small fee, by mail. Guaranteed credentials. Fee returned in case of draw or mate. Yankovich, Box 87.*"

I had never been tempted to clash with any other player by mail except Kupperman; I had certainly never been willing to lose money in such encounters.

I stared at the small print of the advertisement, and my brain seemed flooded with brilliant light. It was as if a voice, a basso profundo voice, was speaking to me and saying: Why not let someone *else* beat Kupperman?

The simple beauty of the idea thrilled me, and completely obliterated all ethical doubts. Who said chess was a game of ethics, anyway? Chess players are notorious for their killer instincts. Half the sport lay in rattling your opponent. Who can deny the malevolent effects of Fischer's gamesmanship on Boris Spassky? Yes, this would be different; this would be a blatant falsehood. If I gained a victory, it would be a false one; but if I could beat Kupperman, even a phantom victory would do.

That night I addressed a letter to the grandmaster's box number, and within two days received a reply. Yankovich's fee was a mere twenty-five dollars, he wrote. He required the money in advance, but promised to return it after the conclusion of the game, in the event of a draw or a defeat. He wished me luck, and on the assumption that I would be interested, sent me his opening move: P-Q4.

With a feeling of rising excitement, I sent off two letters that day. One to Yankovich, Box 87, and one to A. Kupperman in New Mexico. The letter to Yankovich contained twenty-five dollars, and a brief note explaining that I would send my countermove by return mail. The letter to Kupperman was briefer. It merely said: "*P-Q4.*"

Within two days, I had Kupperman's reply: "*N-KB3.*"

I wasted no time in writing to Yankovich. "*N-KB3,*" my letter said.

Yankovich was equally prompt. "*N-KB3,*" he said.

I wrote Kupperman. "*N-KB3.*"

Kupperman replied: "*P-B4.*"

I wrote Yankovich. "*P-B4.*"

By the sixth move, Yankovich-Bloom's Bishop had captured Kupperman's Knight, and Kupperman's King's Pawn took possession of our Bishop. (I had begun to think of the White forces as *ours*.) True to form, Kupperman *didn't* capture toward the center. This fact seemed to give Yankovich pause, because his next letter arrived two days later than usual. He responded with a Pawn move, as did Kupperman, who then gave up a Pawn. I felt a momentary sense of triumph, which was diminished a dozen moves later when I realized that Kupperman, once again poising his pieces on the *back* rank, was up to his old tricks. I fervently hoped that Grandmaster Yankovich wouldn't be as bemused by this tactic as I was.

Unfortunately, he was. It took Kupperman forty moves to beat him into submission, but after battering at Yankovich-Bloom's King's side, he suddenly switched his attack to the Queen's, and . . . *we* had to resign.

Believe me, I took no pleasure in the letter Yankovich sent me, congratulating me on my victory and returning my twenty-five dollars.

Nor was there much pleasure in the grudging note that Kupperman penned in his screwdriver style to the bottom of his next missive, which read: "*Good game. P-K4.*"

I decided, however, that the experiment was worth continuing. Perhaps Yankovich had simply been unprepared for so unorthodox a style as Kupperman's. Surely, in the next round he would be much warier. So I returned the twenty-five dollars to Box 87, and sent Yankovich my opening move: "*P-K4.*"

Yankovich took an extra day to respond with P-K3.

I don't know how to describe the rest of that game. Some chess games almost defy description. Their sweep and grandeur can only be compared to symphonies, or epic novels. Yes, that would be more appropriate to describe my 99th game with Kupperman. (By the fourteenth move, I stopped calling it Yankovich-Bloom, and simply thought of it as "mine.")

The game was full of plots and counterplots, much like the famous Bogoljubow-Alekhine match at Hastings in 1922. As we passed the fortieth move, with neither side boasting a clear advantage, I began to recognize that even if my next-to-last game with Kupperman might not be a victory, it would be no less than a Draw.

Finally, on the fifty-first move, an obviously admiring Yankovich offered the Draw to Kupperman-Bloom. In turn, I offered it to Kupperman, and waited anxiously for his rejection or acceptance.

Kupperman wrote back: "*Draw accepted.*" He added, in a greasy postscript, "*Send opening move to new address—Box 991, General Post Office, Chicago, Ill.*"

My heart was pounding when I addressed my next letter to Yankovich, asking him to retain the twenty-five dollars, and to send me *his* White move for what was to be my final match—with Yankovich, with Kupperman, or with anyone else.

Yankovich replied with a P-K4.

I wrote to Kupperman, and across the top of the page I inscribed the words: "*Match No. 100-P-K4.*"

Kupperman answered with an identical move, and the Last Battle was joined.

Then a strange thing happened. Despite the fact that I was still the intermediary, the shadow player, the very existence of Yankovich began to recede in my mind. Yes, the letters continued to arrive from Box 87, and it was Yankovich's hand still inscribing the White moves, but now each move seemed to emanate from my own brain, and Yankovich seemed as insubstantial as thought itself. In the Chess Journal of my mind, this one-hundredth match would be recorded as Bloom vs. Kupperman, win, lose or draw.

If the previous match had been a masterpiece, this one was a monument.

I won't claim it was the greatest chess game ever played, but for its sheer wild inventiveness, its incredible twists and turns, it was unmatched in either my experience or my reading.

If anything, Kupperman was out-Petrosianing Petrosian in the daring mystery of his maneuvers. Like a Petrosian-Spassky game I particularly admired, it was impossible to see a truly decisive series of moves until thirty plays had been made, and suddenly, two glorious armies seemed opposed to each other on the crest of a mountain. With each letter in my mailbox, the rhythm of my heartbeats accelerated, until I began to wonder how I could bear so much suspense—suspense *doubled* by virtue of receiving both sides of the game from the two battling champions, one of whom I had completely identified as myself. Impatiently, I waited to see how I was going to respond to Kupperman's latest castling, how I was going to defend against his romping Knights, how I was going to withstand the pinpricks of his Pawns.

Then it happened.

With explosive suddenness, there were four captures of major pieces, and only Pawns and Rooks and Kings remained in action. Then, my King moved against both Kupperman's Rook and Pawn, and Kupperman saw the inevitable. He resigned.

Yes, you can imagine my sense of joy and triumph and fulfillment. I was so elated that I neglected to send my own resignation to Yankovich; not that he required formal notification. Yankovich, however, was gracious to his defeated foe, not realizing that my defeat was actually victory. He wrote me a letter, congratulating me on the extraordinary game I had played against him, and while he could not return the twenty-five dollar fee according to the rules of our agreement, he *could* send me a fine bottle of wine to thank me for a most rewarding experience.

The wine was magnificent. It was a Chateau Latour, '59. I drank it all down with a fine dinner-for-one in my apartment, not willing to share this moment with anyone. I recall toasting my invisible chess player across the table, and that was the last thing I recalled. The next thing I saw was the tube of a stomach pump.

No, there wasn't any way I could help the police locate Yankovich. He was as phantomlike as I had been myself. The name was a pseudonym, the box number was abandoned after the wine had been dispatched to me, and the review could provide no clues to the identity of the box holder. The reason for his poisoning attempt was made clear only when Kupperman himself read that I was hospitalized, and wrote me a brief letter of explanation.

Yankovich's real name was Schlagel, Kupperman said. Forty years ago, Schlagel and Kupperman (his name, too, was an alias) had been cell mates in a Siberian prison. They had made five years pass more swiftly by playing more than two thousand games of chess. Schlagel had the advantage when the series ended with Kupperman's release.

Kupperman then took a different kind of advantage. Schlagel had charged him with seeking out the beautiful young wife Schlagel had left behind. Kupperman found her, and gave her Schlagel's best. He also gave her Kupperman's best. Six months later, she and Kupperman headed for the United States.

Like so many romances, the ending was tragicomic. Schlagel's wife developed into a fat shrew who finally died of overweight. No matter; Schlagel still wanted revenge, and came to the States to seek it after his release. He knew Kupperman would have changed his name, of course, but he wouldn't change his chess style.

Consequently, year after year, Schlagel-Yankovich ran his advertisement in the chess journals, hoping to find the player whose method Schlagel would recognize in an instant . . .

"Well, that's what happened," Milo Bloom told his roommate at Misericordia Hospital. "Believe me, if I didn't have a nosy landlady, I would be dead now. Luckily, she called the ambulance in time.

"Sure, it was a terrible thing to happen to anybody. But at least I've learned my lesson. Life wasn't meant to be spent pushing funnylooking pieces around a checkered board. But maybe you've never even tried the game . . ."

The man in traction mumbled something.

"What was that?" Milo asked.

"I play," Dietz said. "I play chess. I've even got a pocket set with me."

Milo, merely curious to see what the set looked like, eased himself out of bed and removed it from the bedside table. It was a nice little one, all leather and ivory.

"It's not a bad way to pass the time," Dietz said cautiously. "I mean, I know you said you'd never play anymore, but—if you wanted to try just *one* game . . ."

Milo looked at his casts, and said, "Even if I wanted to play—how could *you*?"

Dietz smiled shyly, and showed him. He picked up the pieces with his teeth. In the face of a dedication matching his own, how could Milo refuse? He moved the Pawn to P-K4.

DON TOTHE

The Lifesaver

Benny's Cottage was a cocktail lounge few unescorted women would venture into, especially on a Saturday night. Eleanor Matthews was one of the few. Five minutes had passed since Danny, alone in his green sportscar, had watched her saunter through the front door. Five more minutes would be just about right, just long enough not to arouse her suspicion when he "accidentally" bumped into her. If he waited much longer than that, he might find her already occupied with some other man. Too, the faster he could get her out of the bar the less risk of anyone later remembering his face, even though that part of it wasn't too much of a worry. He'd watched her go home with four different strangers in a week.

She was alone at the bar when Danny, wearing T-shirt, denims, and sneakers walked up beside her. He ordered a beer, then casually turned toward her. Her heavily painted lips parted slightly in a smile.

Danny feigned a thoughtful frown. "Don't I know you?" He knew her all right, knew enough about her to—

She stared directly into his blue eyes. "With your looks, honey, you don't need a line."

He snapped his fingers. "I remember now." He reminded her about the beach. She remembered too, and insisted on buying him a drink. It was the least she could do, she told him, after what had happened.

Later, in her living room, as he lowered the glass from his lips, the bourbon set fire to his tonsils, almost bringing tears to his eyes. He hoped she hadn't noticed. She herself swallowed her whiskey like a Little Leaguer gulps cherry-flavored soda after a hot ball game.

She seemed barely awake now, her head against his broad shoulder, her legs drawn up almost under her. A bottle on the coffee table in front of them showed less than two fingers of whiskey. She sat up with a start.

"Booze almost gone," she announced, thick-tongued but concerned, her mouth twisted in a grotesque smirk.

She picked up the bottle, her hand wrapped around the neck of it like a sailor hugging a cold beer, and put it to her mouth. Dropping her head back, she tipped the bottle upright. The liquor disappeared. Her arm dropped numbly. Whiskey trickled down her chin. She smiled drunkenly, then without opening her eyes she said, "Hey, forgot your name again."

"Ed," he lied. It would do no harm, really, to tell her his real name, because— But then, unnecessary chances were foolish.

"Eddie! Yeah, thass right. Remember now." She sank back on the couch.

He knew she was twenty-six. She looked thirty-five or forty. Her face was thin, wrinkled, her cheeks sunken. With her face filled out, she might have been attractive, even beautiful. Now, with her eye makeup running and her powder thick and splotchy, she looked dissipated, prematurely aged, a discarded piece of human rubbish. She was useless to herself or to anyone else. She wouldn't be missed.

The phone rang and Danny's hand involuntarily shot toward it, but he stopped himself in time. It rang again, demanding attention. The shock of the sound to him was the shock of diving into a cold ocean after sitting under a hot sun for several hours. His hand trembled and he was suddenly, acutely aware of how much on edge he had been the whole night. When it came right down to it like this, he was always a little nervous.

Eleanor Matthews didn't seem to hear the phone, not until the fourth ring. She'd fallen asleep, a drunkard's deep, sudden sleep. Now she stirred, tried to focus bleary eyes, glancing at Danny as if to ask why he wasn't doing something about that annoying sound and reached for the phone.

"Hello," she said, then waited. Danny heard a man's voice, the words too muffled to understand. Her nose wrinkled in anger—or disgust—Danny wasn't certain which.

"I told you! Leave me alone! We're through!" she closed her eyes a moment, listening, then shook her head. "We've had it, Carl. No! No! No! I don't want to try again. No, I can't see you. I don't want to talk about it." She slammed down the receiver.

The exchange had sobered her somewhat. Then she seemed to remember where she was and who she was with—a boy almost—somebody to occupy her mind, to make her forget. She took a cigarette from a bowl on the table and worked the lighter between trembling hands. Danny offered her no help. She took a deep drag and exhaled a thick billow of smoke. "Don't worry—we're separated. He's filing for a divorce. They all do sooner or later."

She looked around. "Be a sweet boy and get more booze for Ellie from the kitchen, will you?"

"Don't you think you've had enough?"

She slammed her hand on the table, losing her cigarette. "You too? A perfect stranger! Why is it everybody has to try to reform me? Look, honey, I *want* to drink. I *like* to drink. I'm a lush. I'm gonna die young! That's *my* business. Right?" She broke down, sobbing, her face buried in her hands.

Danny reached down and picked up her cigarette. He put it in the ashtray and stood up. Not yet twenty-one, he was tall, broad-shouldered, darkly tanned. His biceps bulged against the sleeves of his T-shirt. His blond hair, sun-bleached, was crewcut. His features bore a strange mixture of male handsomeness and feminine delicacy. His eyes were deep ocean-blue, his cheekbones pronounced above a broad jaw. "Excuse me." He turned and softly walked away from her.

She watched him move across the living room. "Hey! The kitchen's that way—the booze is in there."

He stopped and looked back over his shoulder. "I'm going to the bathroom."

"Oh." She giggled and put her hand to her mouth.

In the bathroom he used his handkerchief to turn on the tub faucets. Deliberately, he adjusted the hot and cold water. The tub began to fill. He hadn't closed the door behind him. By the sound of her steps, he knew she was staggering across the living room, and he turned as she appeared in the doorway.

"What are you doing?"

"Running bath water," he answered simply, smiling. Dimples cut into his cheeks, but his eyes studied her with an icy coldness. "I thought you might— like a bath." His manner changed. "I just thought—" he felt giddy, detached "—it would feel good."

"Me take a bath?" She looked from him to the tub and back to his face. "Are you nuts?"

Something flashed in his mind, and he moved forward, bringing his hands toward her throat. She staggered back. He stopped, fought to control himself.

"You're tired." He breathed deeply. "I thought soaking in a hot tub would feel good. Besides," he told her, putting his hands on her shoulders, "I could wash your back."

She relaxed, and laughed nervously. "Well, this is one I never heard. But I like it, I like it." She kissed him on the lips, her breath stinging his nostrils. "What happens then? Do you tuck me into a nice warm bed?"

"Why don't we wait and see?" He smiled. "I might just do that."

"O.K., surprise me." She unbuttoned her dress and pulled it over her head. Slip, panties, and bra followed. Naked, she stood before him without modesty. He hadn't made a move toward her. She sat down in the tub and let herself slide down into the warm water. "Hmmm, it does feel good."

He picked up a bar of soap and a washcloth. Muscles jumped along his wrists and forearms as he began sudsing the cloth. Silently, he soaped her shoulders, gently massaging her skin with his fingers. His hands moved closer to her neck.

She closed her eyes. "Hey, this is service."

"Give me your hands." He spread the washcloth open on his palm and she placed both hands in it. His fingers tightened like steel bands, choking off the circulation of blood in her fingers. He read the terror in her eyes. Holding both her hands in his hand, he moved them to her stomach, and drove his fist into her midsection.

She struggled against the pain. He grabbed a towel from the rack at his side. She was wide awake now, terrified.

She opened her mouth to scream, but he shoved the towel against her teeth and pushed her head down into the water. She kicked and thrashed, trying to break loose from his grip. Roughly, he jabbed her hands into her own stomach, knocking the wind out of her. The strength to fight left her. Her struggles weakened. She tried to shake her head free from his hand, but he held her down, moving the towel away from her mouth before it was too late.

She must not suffocate. She had to drown. That was important. She had to die that way, and that way only.

He looked straight ahead at the black tile squares. Then he closed his eyes, and still held her down. He started counting slowly—one—two—He couldn't tell when it was that she stopped moving. At the count of twenty, he stopped, and looked down at her body.

Water was running from the faucet too rapidly for the overflow drain to handle it and spilled over the rim of the tub. He was kneeling on the floor and his white denims darkened wetly from the knees down.

When he stood up water covered the bathroom floor. Carefully, he wrapped the towel around her head. He used his handkerchief again to turn off the faucets. With the water off, the house became very still.

Before leaving the room, he paused to be certain he hadn't touched anything that would hold a fingerprint. He took his time in the living room too, wiping the glass he had used and the whiskey bottle. He polished clean the knob on the front door as he stepped out into the night.

The L.A. night was damp and cold, permeated with a light misty fog. It was past twelve o'clock when Andy eased the unmarked squad car over to the curb. Stu Blake ambled out of the nearest apartment house, one of the plain grey square kind that looks like a prison building.

Andy Ettinger smiled to himself as he watched the lumbering gait of the large young man hurrying toward the car. His latest partner must be cursing the day, not many years ago, that he decided to be a police detective. A kid thinks of all the glamour, never gives much thought to the prospect of being rousted out of a warm bed to hurry out into a cold night to look at an often colder body. A kid doesn't think about that end of it, not until he's had to go through it a few times. If Andy had a buck for every night it had happened to him in twenty-three years, he could afford to tell the department to keep his pension.

Andy reached across the car and jerked back the door handle to let the door swing open. Stu got in and closed the door without slamming it.

"That's a good boy."

Stu looked at him with sleeping eyes. "Oh. Sure. Why wake everybody else up? Just because we're a couple of nuts who don't know when it's time to be home in bed."

Andy was tempted to make a crack about Stu's bride of six months. Instead he remarked, "You want regular hours? So you should have been a dentist."

"That's what my old man always said." Stu frowned. "In fact, Sally was saying that just the other day."

"Already?"

"What do you mean—already? We've been married almost seven months."

"Sorry, kid, I forgot you were an old married man."

"Another bathtub deal?" Stu yawned.

Andy nodded. "Over in the Wilshire District this time. Andrews phoned me soon as it came in. A woman. Husband found her dead, floating in the tub around—" he glanced at his watch "—twenty minutes ago."

"Sound like the others?"

"Andrews thought so. That's why he called me."

"How come nobody ever gets murdered in the daytime, at a decent hour?"

"Same reason babies are always born at three in the morning."

Stu grunted. "Ask a stupid question and—"

"When's the big day?"

"Doctor says between Christmas and New Year's."

"Maybe you'll get a haircut to celebrate, huh?" Andy looked at the young man beside him. Stu was twenty-five, an ex-football player, ruggedly handsome, with a head of thick brown hair that refused to be controlled. Andy had been ribbing him about it for the month they'd been working together.

"I know. It's tickling my ears. So who has time to go to a barber?"

"You're complaining? I wish I had a reason to go to a barber." Andy brushed his hand across his own bald head. They both laughed.

Thirty minutes later they stopped before a white Spanish-style stucco house with iron bars on the windows and red clay tiles on the roof. A patrol car was parked in the driveway.

A red-faced police officer opened the front door for them. "Hi, Andy."

Andy nodded, and looked past the policeman's shoulder to see a man sitting on a couch. "Matthews?"

"Yes, sir." He spoke softly. "Been sitting there, just sort of moaning and crying the whole time."

"Just you and he here?"

"Yes, sir. The lab boys are on their way."

Andy walked over to the couch and introduced himself and his partner. Matthews, a middle-aged man wearing a well-tailored dark-blue suit, stood up to shake hands with them.

"You discovered your wife's body, Mr. Matthews?"

Matthews nodded abruptly. He opened his mouth to answer, but a sob choked off his words.

Andy looked around the room. Besides the front door, there were two other doors, one leading to the kitchen and one leading to a hallway. Two sets of wet footprints on the rug pointed to the hallway door. Andy took a closer look.

"I'll take the bathroom. You can ask Mr. Matthews a few questions when he's up to it."

Stu nodded. "Right."

When Andy was on a case he was the first man into the murder room, and he went in alone. Nobody else entered until he said so. A few rookies had found it difficult to understand, but Stu hadn't given him any trouble. Walking close to the wall, Andy made a wide track around the wet imprints.

The floor of the bathroom was wet. The water in the tub was level with the bottom of the overflow outlet. The woman in the tub, a towel wrapped around her head and covering her face, appeared at first to be taking a beauty bath. A closer inspection showed she wasn't breathing. Andy left her exactly as he'd found her, leaving even the towel untouched. A bar of white soap was floating against her leg. Andy noted it had a thick softened outer layer, the way soap gets when it's left in the water. No chance for prints. Except for the wet floor and the woman in the tub he saw nothing unusual—no signs of a struggle, nothing remiss. As he studied the room, he heard Stu questioning Matthews in the next room.

Matthews said, "I rang the doorbell three times. She didn't answer. Her car was out front. She never walked anywhere. It was late. I was sure she was home. The lights were on. I was afraid something was wrong."

"Why should you think that, Mr. Matthews?"

"You see, Eleanor—my wife—she, well, she ran around. She was—was always meeting fellows in bars and bringing them home. She did it whenever I was out of town. She didn't think I knew." After a painful pause he continued, "Anyway, I waited. Then I let myself in. I still have a key to the house."

"You *still* have one?"

Andy smiled. The kid was turning out to be a good interrogator. It took a good man to catch the subtle but important remarks in a suspect's story.

"We've been separated for two months. That's why I came over—to try to patch things up."

If the woman had died any other way, or if Matthews hadn't struck him as such a decent sort, Andy would have jumped him right then. He could write a book just about the homicide cases he'd handled where a husband trying for a reconciliation had ended up by killing his wife, usually along with the boy friend with whom he found her.

"Go on," Stu said.

"I let myself in. I called her name. No answer, so I looked around the house. That's when I found her."

"You touched nothing?"

"Only the telephone, when I called the police."

"When was the last time you saw her alive?"

Silence a moment. "That would be about a week ago. That's why I had to see her tonight. I couldn't stand being away from her. I had to see her—even though she told me not to come."

"When did she tell you that?"

"I phoned her around nine o'clock. She—she hung up on me," he stammered.

Andy came back in the living room. "Did she seem upset?"

"No, not any more than usual. Not so much that I'd ever dream she'd kill herself."

"Kill herself?" Andy and Stu said it at the same time. Stu let Andy go ahead. "You think she committed suicide?"

"Of course. Didn't she? I've always been afraid of something like this."

Andy shook his head. "I hardly think so, Mr. Matthews. It's practically impossible for a person to drown himself."

"An accident then? Maybe she hit her head. Maybe she—passed out."

"The coroner can tell us more about that." Andy was convinced Matthews wasn't implicated. "That's all for tonight, Mr. Matthews. I know it's Sunday, but I'd like to ask you to come down to my office tomorrow—I mean today. It's important."

Matthews used his handkerchief to dry his face, then he blew his nose. "I've got to work. I don't know how I'll do it, but I have to. I'm a missile engineer. We're on a crash program, and if I don't get done what has to be done by Monday morning we'll have two hundred people sitting idle."

"Sometimes it's better to bury yourself in work." Andy spoke from experience. The day after his wife had been killed in a smashup on the freeway, he was investigating an ax murder in East Los Angeles.

"I'll be through around four o'clock. I'll come down then."

"I wouldn't ask you, but it is important. I doubt very much that your wife's death was an accident. Someone murdered her. Is there anything you can think of now that might help us find out who did it?"

Matthews shook his head in bewilderment. "No! Eleanor drank a lot, but she had no enemies. Everyone who knew her liked her, and tried to help her."

"O.K., we'll talk about it tomorrow. You can go now."

Matthews mumbled, "Thank you," then got up slowly and moved toward the door, pausing to glance once at the bathroom in disbelief.

The experts, two of them, got there right after Matthews left. The rug was thick and just absorbent enough to hold the shape of the imprints. They sprinkled plaster of Paris on the deepest indentations.

The shoe print was Andy's second clue in five cases. Several blond hairs, an inch or so long—barely long enough for the victim to grab but she had managed it in her struggle—had been found at the scene of the second killing.

"We have a lot to go on, sir—the color of his hair and the size of his shoe." Stu wasn't too encouraged.

"More'n a lot of cases I've seen. We've got the top and the bottom. All we have to do is fill in the middle."

The medical examiner wasn't much help. "Can't say for sure just yet, but my guess is she was just plain drowned. No signs of strangulation, no bruises or abrasions. No wounds that I can see. We'll know better after the autopsy."

"How long has she been dead?" Andy asked.

"Being in that hot water complicates things, but I'd guess three or four hours."

"You do a lot of guessing, don't you?" Stu said.

The coroner looked at Andy. "'Nother fresh one, huh?"

"Yeah, they stuck me with another one." Andy shrugged, and winked at Stu when the coroner wasn't looking. He figured rookies had a hard enough time of it.

Playa del Rey, a beach town almost directly west of L.A., lies on the coast between Laguna Beach and Malibu. Playa's beach is less crowded during the summer than most of the adjacent beaches. There's a lot of sand but no place to park a car. It's a wide beach, with a long walk to the water from anyplace you're lucky enough to find for your car.

It was late in the season, with one of the last good Sunday crowds. Danny always hated to see the end of summer, the deserted beaches. The usual heavy afternoon breeze was building up and the surf was getting choppy. It had been a slow day. He'd pulled a middle-aged businessman, a teenaged girl, and two surfers out of rip tides.

He sat on his chair-tower, his eyes taking a swinging glance at the water every few minutes. He read the bodies in the surf as easily as words on a page; a swimmer in trouble was as obvious as a word printed upside down. The most obvious potential rescue was a swimmer away from the crowd, out too far.

He was aware of her presence before he looked down. He felt her eyes on him.

"Hi, Danny." There she was looking up at him. She was eighteen or nineteen, with long blonde hair blowing loose. She smiled and he couldn't help but smile back. Her solid one-piece blue suit wasn't skimpy by modern standards, but she managed to look sexier in it than most girls do in bikinis. Her young body would look good in a baggy potato sack.

"Hi, Maggie."

"You saved another one, I saw the whole thing." Her eyes sparkled. Her hair bounced about her shoulders as she tilted her head and shaded her eyes against the sun. Every day she told him the same things about how wonderful he was. He could never be sure just how much his saving her life had to do with it— he'd pulled her out a week ago—but he didn't really care. She embarrassed him with her open hero worship, but he liked it and he liked her.

He made his way down the ladder from the chair to the sand.

"How many's that for today?"

"How many what?"

"You know, silly. How many people did you save?"

"You mean how many did I help out of the water?"

"Come on, Danny, how many?"

"Only four. Look, Maggie, probably none of them would have drowned. I just keep them from getting tired out there."

"Yeah, sure." She got serious. "Danny? Is there something wrong with me?"

"What do you mean?"

"Am I ugly or what? It's been a whole week. You haven't even asked me for my phone number."

"Well, we're not supposed to do that. Besides, how do you know I didn't look it up? I've got your name and address. Remember that card we filled out?"

"Why haven't you called then?"

"I've been busy. I'm shy too."

"You're fooling again, Danny. I don't have a phone. My father had it taken out."

"He sounds strict. What would he think of you talking to a strange boy on the beach?"

"You're *not* a strange boy—you saved my life. He wants to meet you, to thank you. How about it?"

"O.K. You doing anything tonight?"

She bit her lower lip excitedly. "No."

"Would you like to go to dinner and take in a movie?"

"Danny, I'd love to. Come by around six?"

Carl Matthews stepped into the office at four-thirty.

"Thanks for coming, Mr. Matthews." Andy shook his hand. "I'll try to make this as brief as possible."

Andy informed him of his constitutional rights and asked for his permission to tape the interview. Matthews insisted that he needed no attorney to be present. "I've nothing to hide. I don't need a lawyer to help me tell you the truth. I'm here to help you find the killer, not to figure out ways to prevent implicating myself. I suppose a lawyer would tell me not to say anything. We'd never get anywhere that way."

Andy admired the man's sincerity, but he'd seen a lot of innocent men become entangled in a bushel of trouble by not having an attorney with them. However, Andy wasn't going to press the point.

"I want you to start at the beginning, from the time you met Mrs. Matthews until—well, until now. Don't leave out anything. Tell me everything that comes into your mind."

Carl Matthews had known Eleanor for a year and a half. They had met at a party, fallen in love, and married two months later. She wasn't drinking then. She had tried to tell him that she'd once been an alcoholic, but he hadn't been able to believe her. She'd been married twice before. She wanted children badly, but neither of her first two husbands had been able to give her children. Matthews told Andy how she had started to drink after about a year, how he had realized when it was too late that she was turning to drink because of a feeling of inadequacy.

It was toward the end of the interview when Matthews said, "I really thought she had committed suicide when I found her in the bathroom. She spoke many times of trying it. In fact, I really think she was trying to kill herself, drown herself, in the ocean just a few weeks ago. The lifeguard got to her just in time. There was a heavy undertow—down at Playa del Rey. She—"

"Playa del Rey?"

"Yes, we went to the beach every chance we had."

Butterflies brushed their wings against the lining of Andy's stomach. Andy claimed he got butterflies in his stomach when the pieces begin to fit together. Some oldtimers claimed their feet itched, or their ears burned, or their mouths got dry, like a boxer when he's got that feeling the next punch is going to do it. This was one of the times.

Andy stood up.

"Mr. Matthews, I'm not going to keep you any longer. You've been very helpful."

"That's all you want to ask me?"

Andy had a good feeling about Matthews. "That's all for now. Just keep yourself available in case I need you."

"All right, I'll do that."

As soon as Matthews left, Andy dug out the files on the other bathtub cases. It was in the third case, the Johnson fellow, that he thought it had come up. He was right. He found it there in the interview with Johnson's wife. He read the transcription:

"Detective Ettinger: Is there anything else you can tell us?

Mrs. Johnson: It seems so funny that just a week ago, poor Leonard almost drowned in the ocean—right down at Playa del Rey—and now this in the —in his own bathroom."

It required seven phone calls and an hour for Andy to check out his hunch.

The pieces fit together. All five victims had been pulled from the surf at Playa del Rey during the past four months.

Andy dialed Stu's number. "I'm down at the office. Be here in fifteen minutes. We've got work to do."

By the time Stu arrived Andy had arranged to meet Paul Langly, the captain of the Playa del Rey beach-guard crew, at Langly's office.

Langly was waiting for them when they got there. A husky redhead with freckles, Langly failed to understand why they wanted a list of all the beach guards who worked Playa del Rey during the summer. When they told him what they had in mind, he came up with something better—the file of rescues. The guards must fill out a white card for each rescue, showing name, age, and address of the victim. There they were, all five names, and all with the same name at the bottom—Danny Gruen. Gruen lived in nearby El Segundo. They headed over there on the double.

A silver-haired woman answered their ring. Andy told her who they were. "We're looking for a Mr. Dan Gruen, ma'am."

"That's my son." Her eyes clouded. "Why are you—Danny hasn't done anything wrong. He's a good boy. He's *never* done anything wrong—"

"Is he home?"

"No, he's out on a date with a girl—a nice girl, he told me."

"Do you know the girl?"

"No, Danny didn't tell me her name. He doesn't always tell me who—"

Andy interrupted. "That's not important, Mrs. Gruen. This is an emergency. We'll have to search Danny's room."

"But I don't think you—" she started to object.

"Did your son bring a package home from work today?" Andy glanced at Stu and caught the look of puzzlement on his face.

"I don't know. I didn't see him come in."

"A clock—a small clock. It was left at your son's lifeguard station as a prank. It's really a bomb and we don't know when it's set to go off." Andy ignored Stu's cough. Sometimes you had to stretch the rules a little.

"Who would—"

"We don't have time to explain, Mrs. Gruen." Andy's tone was urgent. "Your son may have left it in his room. I think you'd better leave the house while we search for it."

"Are you sure—"

"Yes, ma'am. Some nutty kid at the beach was jealous because his girl kept flirting with your son." He turned to Stu. "It could blow any minute, Stu. You'd better help Mrs. Gruen outside. I'll have a look. No use both of us taking a chance."

Stu nodded, and took a firm grip on the woman's arm. Andy waited until they were outside.

He found the boy's room. It was in good condition—for a college kid's room. The bed wasn't made, several men's magazines were scattered near the bed, pajamas were draped over a chair, pennants took up half the wall space. All in all, it looked like a normal, growing young man's pad. Andy looked under the mattress. He searched the closet. A pair of tennis shoes lay in the corner—they were damp. On the floor was a discarded cardboard container. Andy traced the outline of both shoes on the cardboard, folded it, and put it in his coat pocket. If he tried to walk out with the shoes, it might look phoney. Besides, without a search warrant, the shoes might not be admissible as evidence.

He found what he was looking for in the bottom drawer of the dresser, a small notebook with names in it, pages and pages of names. Most of the names had lines through them. Some had crosses. Andy recognized the five that had been crossed out.

Four names were still open. He took a deep breath as he tucked the book into his pocket.

He was about to leave when he remembered one more thing. He went to the bathroom. There was a hairbrush, the kind men use on short haircuts, on the basin. He picked several hairs from it and dropped them into a small envelope he always carried.

"Nothing in there," he told Mrs. Gruen and Stu when he got outside. "Your son has a car, hasn't he, ma'am?"

She told them what kind of a car her son owned and found the license number on a gas credit-card bill.

They told Mrs. Gruen not to worry about her son's safety, that they would be sure to find him before anything happened.

Back in the car, Stu wasn't so sure they had done the right thing. "You didn't have to do that. You scared the daylights out of her."

Andy handed him the little black book. "I had to save time. That girl is in trouble."

Andy radioed for a car to be sent to Danny's house while Stu looked through the names.

"I see what you mean. Looks like four names are still open, three of them women."

"Yeah" was all Andy said. He was thinking about that nice girl Danny Gruen's mother had been talking about.

As they drove along Sepulveda the fog began to roll in from the ocean.

"Your folks are nice, Maggie." Danny meant it.

"Thank you. They like you too."

"How can you tell?"

"Oh, Papa didn't make a big deal about my deadline. When he doesn't like my date he makes a big deal about getting in by twelve-thirty."

"He watches you pretty close. Not many parents do these days."

"I don't mind." She smiled. "Papa's fair about it. Some girls' folks don't care what they do, where they go, who they go with. I don't think I'd like that."

Danny glanced at her. "How come so far away? Come on, scoot over so I don't have to yell."

"I thought you were shy." She slid over on the seat, moving closer to him without crowding him. "Where are we going to eat?"

"Like I told your father, Redondo Beach. You like fish, I hope."

"Love it."

Andy and Stu found phone numbers listed for two of the three women. Andy phoned one, Stu the other. Andy's was a Torrance woman, at home with her husband. Andy explained the situation to the man without going into detail and told him to keep his wife home until they heard from the police. The other gal was an S.C. coed. Stu talked to her father, who agreed to bring her home from her sorority house until things cleared up. The third girl, Maggie Randolph, wasn't listed in the phone book.

The two detectives headed for Maggie's house.

They got to the house an hour after the girl had left with "such a fine-looking young man," as Maggie's father put it. Andy figured there was no sense in overly alarming them. He told them they wanted Danny for questioning— routine questioning. "Did they say anything about their plans for the night?" Stu asked. "Where they were going?"

"We always know where our girl is going," Mr. Randolph answered. "They're going to have dinner in Redondo Beach, then they're going to see one of those Elvis movies."

"Did they say where for dinner?"

Mrs. Randolph volunteered, "No, but Danny said he knew a fine place for a fish dinner."

"How about the show?"

They both shook their heads.

"I think we have enough to go on," Andy told Stu. They gave the Randolphs a number to use just as soon as their girl got home. They didn't tell them they would have a car sent to the house to wait.

By the time they reached the Redondo Beach city limits the fog was so thick they had slowed down to five to seven miles an hour. Storefronts were barely visible from the street.

"Fog picked a great night," Stu moaned.

"Yeah, it's going to be rough."

Maggie blotted her lips and set aside her napkin.

"Good?" Danny needn't have asked. Her plate was clean except for a few fish bones.

"Lousy. I only ate it to be polite," she answered, then laughed at the shocked expression on his face.

He smiled. Maggie had an infectious warmth that reached out to him. He'd been relieved a week ago when he'd decided, without a doubt, that she had a place on this earth. She'd been worth saving.

"Why did you wait so long, Danny, to ask me out? I had to flirt with you every day for a week. I almost died waiting."

"I don't go out much. Like I told you, I'm shy."

"Am I the first one you've rescued and taken out on a date?"

He hesitated before answering. "Yes, as a matter of fact."

She stared into his eyes. "It must be wonderful to be able to save lives."

"That's what I'm trained for."

"I mean, it must *feel* wonderful. I bet you've saved a hundred lives."

"In three summers, at least a hundred, I guess."

"Well, doesn't it make you feel—Oh, I don't know how to say it."

"It makes me feel like I'm doing my job. That's what they pay me for. I don't like to talk about it." This kind of talk made him nervous. He wanted to drop the subject.

The mild outburst had surprised her. She nodded without saying anything, and they finished their dessert quickly and in silence.

When they stepped outside he asked, "You sure you want to go to a movie?"

"Why? Do you want to take me home? I made you angry."

"No, of course not. You're the first person I've met in a long time that I can talk to. I'd just like to talk. There's something I've got to tell somebody. We could walk out on the pier."

"In this fog?"

"Sure, it's fun."

She hesitated only a moment. "O.K., let's go."

The pier was a couple of blocks from the restaurant. They left his car in the parking lot and started through the fog. She held onto his arm tightly. "Don't let go of me," she told him. "Boy, I've never seen it this thick."

A foghorn broke the air.

Maggie hesitated. "I'm scared."

"Of what? You're with me, what's there to be scared of?"

"It's just so weird not being able to see anything in front of your face."

The shops had closed early. They walked along one side of the pier with Danny guiding himself by the rail and Maggie walking on the inside. It was like being blind.

When they had been walking for five minutes Maggie said, "You wanted to tell me something."

"I don't know if I should."

"Why not? Is it something wrong?"

"No, I don't think so—not really wrong. That is, I'm not sure. I just have to tell someone." He stopped. "Can I trust you? Can I really trust you? You promise not to tell anyone?"

"Sure, I promise, Danny. What is it?"

He knew he could trust this girl. He could tell her everything.

Andy and Stu had made their plans in the Redondo Beach Police Station. Captain Josephson was anxious to help.

The town force had been alerted. Each car was assigned to check all restaurants in its cruising area. Andy figured if Danny had told the truth, the couple might still be in one of the local eating places. The first step was to check the parking lots for Danny's green car. The fog was so thick the lots had to be checked on foot. Squad cars moved around the city at five miles an hour.

Andy and Stu, unfamiliar with the area, had chosen the three-block section where most of the restaurants were concentrated. They moved on foot.

Near the end of the last block they found the car, in the parking lot of Otto's Grotto. They checked their guns and entered the seafood restaurant. Stu phoned the station to let them know where they were while Andy questioned the girl cashier. The place was empty.

"Yeah, I remember him. Tall, blond, good-looking. He had a sweet-looking girl with him. They left an hour ago."

"You sure?"

"They're the only customers we had tonight, Mac."

"His car's out in back."

The girl shrugged. "Maybe they went for a walk. Maybe they went out on the pier."

Stu heard the remark as he walked up. The two men exchanged glances as Andy said, "Out on the pier. Phone Josephson. Tell him to send some men to the pier. Tell him to alert the Coast Guard too. We might need them."

"Right." Stu nodded and hurried back to the phone.

"What's the quickest way to the pier?"

"Straight down the street one block, then over a block. You can't miss it— when it's not so foggy."

At the end of the deserted pier Danny was telling Maggie what had happened at the beginning of summer. "It was a week after I saved his life that I saw his picture in the papers, all over the front page. He'd picked up this little girl, just six years old. He told her that her mommy was hurt. Then he took her for a ride, strangled her, left the poor little thing out in the bushes."

"How could a man do that, Danny?"

"Not a man—a monster. I've seen things like that in the papers before, but this time it was different. Here was a man who was alive only because I'd saved his life. If I hadn't pulled him out of the ocean he would have drowned. He would have been dead. And that little girl would still be alive. That's all I could think about for weeks."

"You can't blame yourself for that. It's fate."

He felt good telling her about it. He knew he could trust her now. He could tell her everything. She'd understand.

"I thought a lot about that little girl. I'd stay awake at night. Was she really meant to die like that? Was that monster really meant to be saved so he could live long enough to do a terrible thing like that? Or should he have died? And I interfered!" His last words were harsh, angry. "I helped kill her. If it weren't for me she'd be alive now, and I was responsible."

"Danny, you—you can't do this."

"I have the picture." He took out his wallet and opened it for her. "I cut it out of the paper. Such a tiny, pretty thing, with big brown eyes and pigtails." The tears came to his eyes as he thought about it.

"He's going to the gas chamber, Danny."

"That's right, he's going to die—but he should have died in the ocean." A hardness entered his voice. "I've got a secret to tell you. It's about one of the fellows I work with. He thinks that maybe some of the people we save are meant to die—not all of them, but maybe some of them. So after he saves them he checks into their lives. He follows them. He finds out whether they were worth saving or not."

"I don't understand, Danny. What good does that do?"

Danny waited a moment. He looked her straight in the eyes, trying to predict her reaction. Then he told her, "He kills them."

"That's crazy! That's murder!"

"No, no, not murder." How could he explain it so she'd understand? "The ones he kills are the ones who should have died." Something was wrong. Why was she backing away from him? "He saved their lives. He has the right to take them away, destroy them."

"He told you all this?"

"Yes. Because I was the one who got him started, when I saved that madman's life. That's what started him to thinking."

"We have to tell the police. Danny, don't you see? He's as crazy as the man who killed the little girl."

"What?" He grabbed her by the shoulders. "Don't say that!"

"You're hurting me."

"Say he's not crazy!"

"Danny, stop!"

"Say it! Say he's not crazy!" He turned her around until her back was against the low wooden railing.

The fog cleared for a moment. Their eyes met and he knew now that nobody would ever understand. He'd been a fool to think she would. "You know, don't you?"

"No, Danny, no."

"You lie. You're going to tell the police about me."

"Gruen. Danny Gruen." At the sound of his name echoing through the fog he stopped and listened. Maggie opened her mouth to scream. He caught her as she took a deep breath and clamped his hand over her mouth, forcing her back over the railing.

"I swear I heard voices out there," Stu insisted.

"Me too." Andy squinted, tried to penetrate the fog. It was no use. You couldn't see your own hand in front of your face. The flashlights had turned out to be useless.

"Let's hold hands and make a human bridge across the pier," Stu said. "That way he won't slip past us."

"It's worth a try. O.K., boys, let's make like ring-around-the-rosie." Andy was at the right end of the line, using the railing as a guide. He could hear the waves crashing below as they advanced.

"Let's go easy. We're not sure it's our man. Besides, if it is, he has a girl with him."

They hadn't gone far when they heard a girl's frightened scream. They stopped.

One of the Redondo men said, "I think she was falling."

"Let's go, on the double," Andy ordered. They started to trot, still holding onto each other.

Somebody ran into Andy, head-on. He fell on his back, a heavy body on top of him, fingers working at his throat. His grip with Stu had been broken.

"Andy, you O.K.?" It was Stu, yelling almost into his ear.

Andy gurgled, thrashed out with his arms. The grip suddenly loosened and he felt the weight lifted from him.

"Andy, is this you? Talk, man!"

"I'm down here," Andy blurted out, rubbing his throat. He could faintly make out two outlines struggling, punching at each other, next to the railing. There was a loud grunt, then one figure disappeared.

"Stu?" Andy asked cautiously, taking his gun from its shoulder holster.

"It's me. I'm all right. Our friend is in the water. Think I got him in the throat. I doubt if he'll make it. He's—"

"Help! Help!" The girl's cries, barely loud enough to reach them, were weak.

"Come on," Andy shouted as he moved along the railing. "She's farther out."

"Keep yelling so we can find you." Stu's deep voice carried through the fog.

They ran toward the voice, and stopped when it began to die away.

"We passed her." Andy turned and bumped into Stu. "Back up."

They walked, slowing, homing in on the voice.

"I think she's right below us now." Stu's voice was firm, confident. "I'm going in."

"Wait! You can't jump—you can't see anything down there."

Stu laughed nervously. "All the better—I'm chicken about heights. If you don't hear from me, keep talking to her."

Andy tried to grab his partner's arm as Stu climbed over the railing, but he was too late. Stu jumped into the fog and disappeared.

The Coast Guard made it in thirty minutes. Stu and Maggie had hugged a barnacle-laden piling. They were scratched, tired, and half frozen, but they were all right.

As the boat made its way to shore, Andy poured two cups of hot coffee and handed them to Stu and the girl, huddled under blankets. "Didn't anyone tell you we're supposed to be brains, not heroes?"

"No, sir," Stu answered innocently. "Nobody ever mentioned that, and it's not in the book. One of us had to go. I figured I had the best chance, so I just jumped."

Andy straightened up. "Hey, wait a minute. I'm not that old."

"I didn't mean it that way. I just meant that I figured I had enough hair on my head to keep my brain from freezing up in that cold water. But you, well—"

Andy laughed and slapped him on the back. "O.K., say no more, Tarzan."

The boat dropped the couple off and went back to search for Danny Gruen. They found him two hours later, floating face down. Andy assumed that Stu's karate blow had paralyzed the killer enough so that he hadn't been able to help himself after he hit the water. Andy wanted to believe he had drowned. It didn't help the other five, but it made a little sense.

JACK RITCHIE

What Frightened You, Fred?

The warden shook his head sadly as he looked me over. "You're not real bright, Fred. You are out not even forty-eight hours and now we got you back with us again. It was hardly worth the trouble filling out your parole papers."

Dr. Cullen sat at one end of the warden's desk. He took off his heavy shell-rimmed glasses and polished them with a handkerchief. "How old are you, Fred?"

"Fifty-five, sir," I said.

Warden Bragan puffed his cigar. "Just plain stupid."

Dr. Cullen smiled slightly. "Perhaps not, Warden." He turned back to me. "Did the big buildings frighten you, Fred? The people, the cars, and the loud noises?"

I wondered whether all psychiatrists wore bow ties and tweed jackets. Perhaps it was their uniform. "We had movies in here every Wednesday night, sir," I said. "I've seen big buildings and cars and people before."

"Ah," Dr. Cullen said. "But that's not the same as actually seeing them in real life, now is it, Fred?"

"No, sir," I said.

Dr. Cullen put the glasses back on his nose. "You've been in prison off and on for twenty-five years of your life?"

"I guess so, sir," I said. "If that's what the record shows."

Bragan grinned. "Well, anyway I'm glad to have you back, Fred. You're the best typist and file clerk I ever had."

"Thank you, sir," I said. I cleared my throat. "Will I have to put in any time in the laundry first?"

Bragan chewed on his cigar and thought about it. He was a big, heavy man, and he was going to run for governor. That's what the prison radio announced four days ago. It didn't mean anything to us in here, but I knew that some people outside wouldn't like Bragan to be governor.

He decided to do me a favor. "I should say not," he said. "I need you in the office. As far as I'm concerned, you haven't been gone at all."

Bragan's eyes went over me again. "You'd think that some people would learn to behave on the outside. But I guess nobody can teach you. Not even with a hammer."

Dr. Cullen folded his hands. "In a sense you are right about Fred. But I believe there's more to his case than that." He turned to me. "What was it like outside? Was it cold?"

"Yes, sir," I said. "I believe the temperature was around forty-five or even a little lower."

He smiled patiently. "That's not what I mean, Fred."

It had been gusty with the smell of winter hanging in the air when I walked out the pedestrian section of the big gates.

There wasn't anybody waiting for me in the graveled parking lot. I hadn't really expected anyone to be. I just had the small hope that Tony Wando might have remembered to send a car for old times' sake. He could have been keeping track of the time I spent inside the walls.

I made myself a cigarette and waited for the shuttle bus to come along.

The driver was only vaguely interested in me. He'd made pickups here before. At the railway station I bought a ticket and boarded the train.

When I got off two hours later, I passed up the taxi stands and walked. I had eighty-six dollars in my pocket, but that represented four years of sweat and I couldn't see spending any part of it for a ride. Not that money.

Big Mike Kowalski was in front of his place watching a delivery man wheel cases of beer into his bar. Mike had put on some weight since I'd seen him last, but he had the build that wasn't troubled by extra pounds.

I stopped next to him. "Hello, Mike."

He nodded and looked down at the suitcase. "You going someplace?"

"I've been Mike," I said. "Four years."

He remembered. "That's right. Hardly noticed that you were gone."

I smiled. "People don't."

He stifled a yawn. "When did you get out?"

"Just now. A few hours ago, as a matter of fact."

He put the cigar back in his mouth. "Let's go inside and get warmed up. I'll set up a round for old times' sake."

I shook my head. "Can't do that, Mike. I'm on parole."

He shrugged. "Can't see why anybody'd make a fuss about a few beers." His eyes went over me. "Did they get you a job?"

"I'm supposed to report to a warehouse on the north side Monday morning. It's office work, they tell me."

The wind swirled dust in the gutters and Mike shivered slightly behind his big white apron.

I changed the suitcase to my left hand. "I guess I'd better get going before you get pneumonia. I'll try to get a room in my old place. Let people know that I'm out, will you, Mike?"

He grinned. "Who'd want to know?" He asked that because he couldn't think of anybody right then and there.

"You never know, Mike," I said. "I could be important to somebody."

I began walking and after a while when it began to drizzle I turned up my coat collar.

I stopped in front of a small café and looked at the wall clock. Right about now we'd be filing into the big mess hall. It was Thursday and we'd be having beef stew, bread, and coffee.

I went inside the café. There was beef stew on the menu, but it didn't taste just right. Not so filling either, I thought.

"What did you do on the outside, Fred?" Dr. Cullen asked. "During those few hours?"

The warden snorted. "The fool got drunk and busted a tavern window."

"Yes, sir," I said. "That's what I did."

Dr. Cullen smiled. "Why didn't you run away after you did that, Fred? Why did you wait for the police to arrive?"

"I guess I had too much to drink, sir," I said. "I wasn't thinking clear."

Bragan showed large uneven teeth. "You sure weren't. You violated your parole and that's going to cost you another two years."

"Fourteen months, sir," I said respectfully.

Dr. Cullen consulted the papers on his lap. "You don't have any living relatives, do you?"

"No, sir."

"Did you get any mail while you were in here? Or write to anyone?"

"No, sir."

"Do you have any close friends on the outside? People you could go to?"

"No, sir."

He leaned forward. "But you do have friends here in this prison, don't you?"

"Yes, sir," I said. "I think I have a few."

He sat back, satisfied. "You were in trouble here only once. Isn't that right, Fred?"

"I don't remember, sir."

Bragan laughed. "He got caught in a shakedown inspection a couple of years ago. We found a knife in his mattress." He looked at me. "What would you want with a knife, Fred?"

It was the one I was going to use on Ed Reilly, for the way he shoved me around in the yard. But Ed had more enemies than me and somebody else got to him while I was in solitary.

"I don't really remember, sir," I said.

Dr. Cullen made a bridge with the tips of his fingers. "Fred came back here not because he was careless or stupid. He wanted to be back."

Bragan grinned, waiting for more.

"It's quite common, Warden," Dr. Cullen said. "Especially with those men who've spent a large portion of their lives in prison. It's called institutionalization. These men are actually ill-at-ease and even frightened by the outside world."

Bragan didn't go along with that. "Don't give me that malarky. Nobody likes to be told when to get up and when to go to bed, what to wear and when and how to wear it, when to eat, when to work, and when to stop. Isn't that right, Fred?"

I thought he had done a good job of describing the lives of almost anybody, inside or out. "I'm afraid I don't understand, sir," I said.

Dr. Cullen was patient. "Freedom means responsibility. It means decision and worry. That's why so many people actually reject it—without consciously knowing they're rejecting it, of course."

"Yes, sir," I said. "The whole world's a prison."

There was a trace of annoyance in the doctor's voice. "I am referring specifically to this place."

"Yes, sir," I said.

Bragan laughed. "You're up the wrong creek, Doc. Fred can't stand this place any more than I can."

Dr. Cullen became slightly stiff. "I know what I am speaking about. I have had training for my job, Mr. Bragan."

Bragan grinned. "Meaning that I haven't? I'm just a political appointee?"

Dr. Cullen said nothing.

Bragan kept grinning. "I don't need any training. This job is just a stepping stone for me. I've been here five years and I feel like I've been serving time myself."

Dr. Cullen turned to me. "The world outside must be a lonely place for you. Isn't that right, Fred?"

I didn't know exactly why I wanted to go back to my old rooming house. Maybe it was just because it was one of the few places where I was remembered.

Mrs. Carr answered the doorbell. She was a massive woman with suspicion permanent in her watery blue eyes.

"It's me," I said. "Remember? Fred Riordan."

She squinted until recognition came.

"I'd like a room," I said. "My old one, if that's vacant?"

Her voice was cold. "I don't have no rooms left."

I smiled. "That's not what the sign in the window says."

She stood immovable, a silhouette against the dim lights of the hallway.

"I've never made any trouble for you," I said. "I'll pay in advance. Two weeks."

She hesitated.

"I'm on parole," I said. "I have to be good."

She made up her mind. "Fourteen dollars."

I followed her up the balustraded stairway. The railing was damp with furniture oil. "Is Jake Miller still here?"

She stopped in front of my old room. "He died a couple of years ago. Nobody's here now that you'd know."

She opened the door of my room. Inside was the remembered bareness. A brass bedstead, a chest of drawers, a plain wooden chair. There'd probably be a half dozen wire hangers in the closet.

"No smoking in bed," Mrs. Carr said. "And I don't want trouble of any kind." Her eyes went over me. "You don't look too bad. Older, but well fed and rested."

"People live longer in prisons," I said. "It's the regular hours that do it."

When she was gone, I opened the paper-lined drawers of the chest until I found an ashtray. I sat on the bed and smoked a cigarette. When I was through I turned off the overhead light. I took off my shoes and lay down on the bed.

After a while the cold began to seep into my bones. The cold was something I'd forgotten. I'd have to get used to it again.

I pulled the quilt up to my chin.

I listened to the footsteps of the other roomers as they came up the creaking stairs and I heard the closing and opening of doors and the voices of strangers.

After a few hours there was nothing but the occasional hiss of auto tires on the wet streets down below.

There were no hundred men making their individual sleep-sounds. There were no echo-tinged footsteps of the guards walking the tiers.

"People get into habits of living," Dr. Cullen said. "When their routine is disturbed they become confused. They are lost."

I thought I could use a cigarette, but I knew that the warden wouldn't let me smoke one here. "Yes, sir," I said. "The bookkeeper looks forward to retirement all his life, but when it comes he doesn't know what to do with himself. He's unhappy."

Dr. Cullen forced a smile. "I'm afraid you still don't understand, Fred." He rubbed his temples. "What were you sent up here for, Fred?"

It was all there in the papers on his lap. "For armed robbery, sir."

Bragan lolled in his swivel chair. "Fred held up a filling station. He was picked up less than a half hour later. He don't seem to have much luck with his jobs."

Dr. Cullen tamped the record sheets to neat squareness and put them back into the folder. "He doesn't really want luck, Warden. He may not even realize it consciously, but this is his home. Here are the only friends he knows. Here it is warm. Here all his decisions are made for him. He has a bed and food and the work isn't too hard. He has absolutely nothing to worry about."

Bragan waited for the door to close behind the doctor and then turned to me. He grinned. "You're back here because you're plain stupid. Isn't that right, Fred?"

Mrs. Carr knocked at my door at noon the next day. "Telephone for you."

I went downstairs to the wall phone. It was Tony Wando and he wanted to see me right away, on the double.

Tony's high-ceilinged apartment was on the top floor of the Sheldon Building and he could look down at and down *on* the city he almost owned.

He mixed two drinks and handed one to me. "What's the matter, Fred? You like the big house?"

"No," I said. "I sweat when I even think about it."

He smiled slightly. "Then why did you keep fooling around with the little things, Fred? Filling stations, delicatessens, drugstores. You always got caught."

I sipped my drink. "You paid me good when I worked, Tony, but I got a job from you maybe once every two or three years. I couldn't live on that."

He thought it over and shrugged. "I guess you're right. I don't have much of your kind of business."

He finished his drink and then he told me what he wanted me to do.

I wiped my forehead with a handkerchief. "I don't want it, Tony. Get somebody else."

He shook his head. "This has got to look natural. Like one of the things that just happen when a man has a job like he has. If there's any smell that it's a syndicate killing we'll be knee-deep in investigations."

He stopped pacing, "You're perfect for the setup, Fred. You'll be near him and you can find the right time. You're good with a knife, Fred, and you can make it look like any one of a thousand could have done it."

He came closer. "It's got to be done. He's getting independent ideas, Fred. He don't wait until I tell him any more. He talks back. If he ever gets in the state capital he'll make his own organization." Tony's eyes were dark. "I can't have that, Fred. Bragan was nothing when I picked him up, but now he's biting my hand."

He watched me. "I know that it means another fourteen months back there for you, but you'll get a thousand for every month. It's that important to me."

After I left Tony, I went out and got drunk. Then I smashed a tavern window and waited for the cops to pick me up.

I had a job to do inside the walls.

HAROLD Q. MASUR

Doctor's Dilemma

As soon as we reached the courthouse corridor Papa's face convulsed like a baby's in torment. "I'm dying," he moaned. "I'm bleeding to death."

"You're fine, Papa," I said. "You'll outlive us all."

"Ten grand." A sob caught in his throat. "I posted bail for that lunatic client on your say-so, Counselor. 'Don't worry,' you told me. 'There's no risk.' So where is he? Why didn't he show up in court?"

Papa was Nick Papadopolous, bald, swarthy, barrel-shaped, with capillaries tracing a ruby pattern across his ample nose. "You're a bail bondsman," I said. "There are risks in every business. You win some, you lose some."

It wrung a groan of anguish from his throat. "You have to find him, Counselor. You owe it to me. I trusted you. You heard what the judge said. Have him in court by ten o'clock tomorrow morning or forfeit bail. If he took off, so help me, Jordan, I'll finish you with every bondsman in town. You'll never be able to raise another nickel."

"He'll be here, Papa. I'll have him in court tomorrow morning if I have to carry him. Jaffee isn't a bail jumper. He has too much at stake."

I believed it. Would a trained physician, a hospital intern, risk his career and his future by jumping bail and holing up somewhere because he's charged with felonious assault? Not likely. Dr. Allan Jaffee, a splendid physical specimen, young, handsome, studious, ambitious, seemed to have everything—except will power. He was an obsessive gambler; poker, craps, roulette, sporting events, anything. He had already run through a sizeable inheritance and now, with no liquid assets, he was in the hole to his bookie for four thousand dollars. So he stalled. So the bookie had dispatched some muscle to pressure the doctor, which turned out to be a mistake. Young Jaffee, a former collegiate welterweight champ, had inflicted upon the collector a bent nose, the need for extensive dental work, and various multiple abrasions, contusions, and traumas.

Because it was a noisy affair, someone had called the law. The cops shipped the collector off in an ambulance and promptly processed Jaffee into the slammer.

At the preliminary hearing, despite my plea of self-defense, the judge agreed with the Assistant D.A. that high bail was appropriate under the circumstances. He sternly labeled the fists of a trained boxer as dangerous weapons, and set the trial date.

So at 10:00 this morning, the clerk had bawled: "The People of the State of New York versus Allan Jaffee." The judge was on the bench, the jury was in the box, the prosecutor was ready, defense counsel was ready, everybody on tap—except the defendant. He hadn't shown.

"Your Honor," I said, "the accused is a medical doctor training at Manhattan General. It is possible that he was detained by an emergency. So it seems we have a problem—"

"No, Counselor. *We* have no problem. *You* have a problem. And you have twenty minutes to solve it." He called a recess.

So I had sprinted out of the courtroom, down the corridor to a booth, and got on the horn to the hospital, but they had no knowledge of Jaffee's whereabouts. I tried his apartment. The line was busy. Apparently he hadn't even left yet.

When the twenty minutes were gone, I approached the bench and said to the glaring judge, "If it please Your Honor, I would beg the Court's indulgence for—"

He cut me off. "The Court's indulgence is exhausted, Mr. Jordan. This is intolerable, a blatant disregard of the State's time and money. A warrant will be issued forthwith for immediate execution by the marshal. If the accused has left the jurisdiction of this Court, bail will be forfeit. Your deadline is tomorrow morning, sir. Ten o'clock." He rapped his gavel and called the next case.

Papa's agitation was understandable. With a worldwide liquidity crisis, ten grand was important money. I disengaged his fingers from my sleeve and went back to the telephone. Still a busy signal. I tried twice more—no change. So I said the hell with it and went out and flagged a cab and rode up to East Seventy-ninth Street.

Jaffee lived on the second floor of an aging brownstone. He didn't answer the bell. The door was open and I walked into utter chaos. The place had been ransacked and pillaged. I headed for the bedroom, expecting the worst.

He was on the floor, propped up against the bed. This time he had been hopelessly overmatched. Somebody, more likely several somebodies, had worked him over good. His face was hamburger. He tried to talk, but it was an incoherent guttural croak. The doctor needed a doctor, but soon.

I looked for the telephone and saw the handset hanging off the hook, which explained the busy signal. I hung up, jiggled, finally got a dial tone, and put a call through to Manhattan General. I told them that one of their interns had been injured, that he was in critical condition, and I gave them his name and address, adding, "This is an emergency. Better step on it if you don't want to lose him."

I turned back and found him out cold, unconscious—probably a blessing.

When the ambulance arrived, I was allowed to ride along, and sat beside the driver while first-aid was being administered in the back. We careened through traffic with the siren wailing, running a few signals and frightening a lot of pedestrians.

"Who clobbered him?" the driver asked.

"I don't know. I found him like that."

"You a friend of Doc Jaffee's?"

"I'm his lawyer."

"Hey, now! He was supposed to be. in court this morning, wasn't he?"

"You know about that?"

"Sure, He was on ambulance duty this week and he told me about it. Said he owed a bundle to his bookie but couldn't raise a dime. Said he banged up a guy who came to collect, strictly self-defense, but his lawyer told him you never know what a jury might do. So he was pretty jumpy yesterday morning. Man, Jaffee was one sorry character, and that's why I couldn't understand the change."

"What change?"

"The change in his mood. All morning he's got a long jaw, his face at half past six, and then suddenly he's walking on air, laughing and full of jokes."

"When did this happen?"

"Right after we got that stewardess."

"What stewardess?"

"The one from Global Airlines." He made a face. "Poor kid. She had taken one of those airport limousines from Kennedy and it dropped her off at Grand Central. She was crossing Lexington when the taxi clipped her. Boy, he must've been moving. She was a mess. Jaffee didn't think she'd make it. I don't know what he did back there, but he was working on her, oxygen, needles, everything, until we got her to Emergency. It was after he came out and hopped aboard for another call that I noticed the change. It was weird. Nothing chewing at him any more. Smiling from ear to ear."

"Do you remember the girl's name?"

"Korth, Alison Korth. I remember because Doc Jaffee was so busy helping the Emergency team I had to fill out the forms."

He swung the ambulance east one block, cut the siren, turned up a ramp, and ran back to help wheel the patient through a pair of swinging doors, where people were waiting to take over. A formidable-looking nurse blocked my path and ordered me to wait in the reception lounge.

I sat among gloomy-faced people, thinking about young Jaffee. The obvious assumption was that his bookie, a man named Big Sam Tarloff, couldn't sit back idly and do nothing after one of his collectors had been so injudiciously handled by a deadbeat. People would laugh. Under the circumstances, how could he keep potential welshers in line? So he would have to make an example of Jaffee.

I was restless and fidgety. Curiosity precluded inactivity. So I got up and wandered over to the reception desk and asked the girl for Miss Alison Korth. She consulted her chart.

"Room 625."

I took the elevator up and marched past the nurses' station, found the number, and poked my head through a partially open door. The girl on the bed was swathed in bandages, eyes closed, heavily sedated, left arm and right leg in traction, her face pitifully dwindled and grey.

A voice startled me. "Are you one of the doctors?"

I blinked and then saw the speaker, seated primly on a chair against the wall. She looked drawn and woebegone.

"No, ma'am," I said.

"Well, if you're another insurance man from the taxi company, go away. We're going to retain a lawyer and you can talk to him."

"That's the way to handle it," I said. "Are you a friend of Alison's?"

"I'm her sister."

"Stick to your guns. Don't let any of those clowns try to pressure you into a hasty settlement."

She stood up and came close, her eyes dark and intense. "Did you know Alison?"

"No, ma'am."

"Who *are* you?" I gave her one of my cards and she looked at it, frowning. "Scott Jordan. The name sounds vaguely familiar . . . but we haven't asked anyone for a lawyer. Are you an ambulance chaser?"

"Hardly, Miss Korth. I don't handle automobile liability cases."

"Then who do you represent?"

"Dr. Allan Jaffee."

"The intern who treated Alison in the ambulance?"

"Yes."

"He's very nice. He looked in on Alison several times yesterday while I was here." Her frown deepened. "I don't understand. Why does Dr. Jaffee need a lawyer?"

"It's a long story, Miss Korth. I'd like to tell you about it over a cup of coffee. There's a rather decent cafeteria in the building." She looked dubious and I added, "There's nothing you can do for your sister at the moment, and the hall nurse can page you if anything develops."

She thought for a moment, then nodded and accompanied me along the corridor to the elevator, stopping briefly to confer at the nurses' station. The elevator door opened and a man stepped out. He stopped short.

"Hello, Vicky."

"Hello, Ben," she said without warmth.

"How is Alison?"

"About the same," she replied.

"Has she regained consciousness?"

"Just for a moment, but they gave her some shots and she's sleeping now. She shouldn't be disturbed."

He lifted an eyebrow in my direction, a tall, blunt-featured man with dark curly hair, wearing sports clothes. Vicky introduced us.

"This is Captain Ben Cowan, the co-pilot on Alison's last flight. Scott Jordan."

He nodded frantically. "Were you just leaving?"

"We're on our way to the cafeteria," I said.

"May I join you?"

"I think not," Vicky said. "Mr. Jordan and I have some business to discuss."

He registered no reaction to the rebuff. "I see. Well, would you tell Alison I was here and that I'll look in again?"

"Of course."

Going down in the elevator there was no further dialogue between them. Captain Cowan left us on the lobby floor and we descended to the lower level. I brought coffee to a small corner table.

"You don't seem overly fond of the captain," I said.

"I detest him."

"Is he a close friend of Alison's?" I pursued the thought.

She made a face. "Alison's infatuated, crazy about him. And I don't like it one tiny bit. I think Ben Cowan is bad medicine."

"In what way?"

"Call it instinct, feminine intuition. Alison and I have always been very close. She shares my apartment whenever her flight lays over in New York. She started going with Cowan about a year ago and she's been moon-struck ever since, sort of in a daze. She used to confide in me. But now, since Ben, she's become withdrawn, even secretive. Alison's not very practical. She was always naive and trusting and I worry about her. And now this— this—" Her chin began to quiver, but she got it under control and blinked back tears.

I sipped coffee and gave her time to recover. After a while, in a small rusty voice, she asked me about Allan Jaffee. So I told her about the gambling debt, the fight and the assault charge, and his failure to appear in court. I told her about going to his apartment and finding him half dead from a merciless beating. Vicky was shocked, but it took her mind off Alison only briefly. She grew fidgety, so I took her back to the sixth floor and then went down to find someone who could brief me on Jaffee's condition.

I spoke to a resident who looked stumbling tired and furiously angry; tired because he'd been working a ten-hour tour and angry because they kept him repairing damages inflicted by people on people. "I'm sorry, sir," he told me. "Dr. Jaffee can talk to no one."

"Not even his lawyer?"

"Not even his Maker. For one thing, his jaw is wired. For another, we've got him under enough sedation to keep him fuzzy for twenty-four hours."

"Will he be able to write?"

"Yes. After a couple of fractured fingers knit properly. Try again in a couple of days."

A couple of days might be too late and I was in no mood to wait. So I went out and was waving for a cab when a hand fell on my shoulder. It was Captain Ben Cowan of Global Airlines.

"I'm sorry if I seem persistent, Mr. Jordan," he said. "But I'm terribly worried about Alison and I can't seem to get any information at the hospital.

Everything is one big fat secret with those people. I thought, since you're a friend of Vicky's, you might know something."

"Why don't you ask her yourself?"

He looked rueful. "Vicky and I aren't on the same wavelength. I don't think she likes me."

"Well, the fact is, Captain, I don't have any information myself."

"Haven't the doctors told Vicky anything?"

"We didn't discuss it. I don't know either of the girls very well, Captain. I met Vicky only today."

"Oh?" A deep frown scored his forehead. "Vicky gave me an entirely different impression. I thought you'd gone to the hospital to see her."

"Not her. A client of mine."

"A client?" he said, puzzled.

"I'm an attorney. I represent the intern who treated Alison at the accident."

"Jaffee?"

"Right. Dr. Allan Jaffee."

"Well, then, I guess you can't be much help."

"Afraid not," I agreed as a cab pulled up in answer to my signal.

Tarloff's was a secondhand bookstore on lower Fourth Avenue, a large and profitable establishment stocking a few splendid first editions and managed by the owner's brother-in-law. On the second floor Sam Tarloff operated a frenetically busy horse parlor with half a dozen constantly ringing telephones manned by larcenous-eyed employees. Big Sam, a heavy, bear-shaped man with an incongruously seraphic smile, sat on a platform watching everything and everybody.

He recognized me and said cordially, "Well, Counselor, good to see you. Let's use my private office." I followed him into a small room. He beamed at me. "And what is your pleasure, Mr. Jordan?"

"Nubile young cheerleaders," I told him. "Right now, however, I would like to see your hands."

"What for?"

"Come off it, Samuel. You know as well as I do that Dr. Jaffee's in the hospital."

"Where else should he be? He works there."

"Not as an employee at the moment. As a patient."

"What happened to him?"

"Somebody clubbed him half to death. I want to see if you have any bruised knuckles."

"Me? You think I did it?"

"You, or one of your men. It's a logical conclusion."

"Because he hurt one of my employees?"

"That, yes, and because he still owes you money."

"You're wrong, Counselor. He doesn't owe me money. He paid off last night, every cent, in cash, including interest."

"Samuel, I'm an old hand. Where would Jaffee get that kind of money on an intern's salary?"

"Not my business, Counselor. I gave him a receipt. Ask him."

"He can't talk. His jaw is wired."

"So look in his pockets. He's got it somewhere."

After countless hours of grilling people on the witness stand, you develop an instinct for the perjurer. Tarloff was not lying. I believed him. "You have lines out, Sam. Tell me, who do you think worked him over?"

He turned up a palm. "I don't know. But it was in the cards, Counselor, it had to happen sooner or later. Jaffee is a very reckless young man. He gambles without capital. Who knows, maybe he was into the Shylocks for a bundle too. I'll ask around if you want."

"I'd appreciate that."

"How about a little tip, Counselor, a filly in the third at Belmont? Only please take your business to an Off-Track Betting window."

"Not today, Samuel. May I use one of your phones?"

"Be my guest."

I rang Manhattan General and got through to Vicky Korth in her sister's room, still keeping the vigil. I asked her if Alison was close to anyone else at Global. She gave me a name, Ann Leslie, another stewardess, who generally stayed at the Barbizon, a hostelry for single females. Vicky offered to phone and tell her to expect me.

I found Ann Leslie waiting in the lobby, a slender girl, radiating concern, wanting to know when she could visit Alison.

"In a couple of days," I said.

"Darn!" She made a tragic face. "We're flying out again on Wednesday."

"Where to?"

"Same destination. Amsterdam. Same crew too, except for Alison. I'll miss her."

"I imagine Captain Ben Cowan will miss her too."

She squinted appraisingly. "You know about him?"

"Vicky told me. And she's not happy about it."

Ann Leslie tightened her mouth. "Neither am I. That Cowan—he's a chaser, a womanizer. He uses people. He made passes at me too, before Alison joined the crew, but I wouldn't have any part of him. I just don't trust him. Have you met Ben?"

"Yes. He seems genuinely fond of Alison."

"It's an act, believe me."

"Is he openly attentive to her?"

"They're not keeping it a secret, if that's what you mean."

"Would you know why he didn't accompany her into Manhattan yesterday when you put down at Kennedy?"

"Yes. Because he was held up at Customs. They wanted to talk to him in one of those private rooms. I was there and I heard him tell Alison to go ahead without him and that he'd meet her later."

"Are members of the crew usually held up at Customs?"

"Not as a rule. They never bothered me. But it couldn't have been much because I know he's flying out with us again on Wednesday, on our next flight."

We talked for a while longer and I thanked her and promised to tell Alison that Ann would be in to see her as soon as the doctors permitted it. I left and cabbed over to Jaffee's apartment. The super recognized me and let me in.

I stood and surveyed the chaos. Nothing had been left untouched. Even the upholstery had been razored open and kapok strewed over the floor. Desk drawers were pulled out and overturned. I hunkered down, sifting through papers. I didn't find any receipt from Sam Tarloff, but after about an hour I did find something even more interesting: a duplicate deposit slip from the Gotham Trust, bearing yesterday's date, and showing a deposit of $34,000.

I straightened and took it to a chair and stared at it, wondering how Jaffee, presumably broke, without credit, could manage a deposit of that magnitude. I saw that it wasn't a cash deposit. The $34,000 was entered in the column allotted to checks.

But a check from whom? And for what? As I studied it, I felt a sudden surge of excitement, of anticipation, because the Gotham Trust was my own bank, an institution in which I had certain connections. Bank records aren't quite as inviolate as most people believe.

Twenty minutes later I marched through the bank's revolving doors and approached the desk of Mr. Henry Wharton, an assistant vice-president for whom I had performed a ticklish chore only four months before. He rose to shake my hand. Then he sat back and listened to my request. He frowned at Jaffee's deposit slip and rubbed his forehead and looked up at me with a pained expression.

"Well, now, Mr. Jordan, this is highly irregular."

"I know."

"It isn't the policy of this bank to make disclosures about our depositors."

"I know."

"You're making it very difficult for me."

"I know."

He signed and levered himself erect and disappeared into some hidden recess of the bank. I waited patiently. He was perspiring slightly when he returned. He cleared an obstruction from his throat. "You understand this is strictly confidential."

"Absolutely."

He lowered his voice. "Well, then, according to our microfilm records the deposit was made by a check drawn to the order of Dr. Allan Jaffee by the firm of Jacques Sutro, Ltd. I assume you recognize the name."

"I do indeed. And I'm deeply indebted, Harry."

"For what? I haven't told you a thing."

"That's right. Now would it be possible for me to get a blowup of that microfilm?" He turned pale and a convulsive shudder almost lifted him out of the chair. I added quickly, "All right, Harry, forget it. I'm leaving."

He was not sorry to see me go.

Mr. Jacques Sutro is a dealer in precious gems, operating out of the elegant second floor of a Fifth Avenue townhouse. Sutro, a portly specimen with silver hair and a manner as smooth as polished opal, folded his beautifully manicured hands and listened to me with a beautiful smile that displayed some of the finest porcelain dentures in captivity.

"And so," I concluded, "as Dr. Jaffee's attorney, I would appreciate a few details about any transaction you had with him."

"Why not discuss it with your client?"

"I would if I could, Mr. Sutro. Unfortunately, Dr. Jaffee had an accident and he's a patient at Manhattan General under very heavy sedation. It may be days before he can talk. In the meantime, I'm handling his legal affairs and it's imperative for me to fill out the picture."

Sutro pursed his lips thoughtfully. "Would you mind if I called the hospital?"

"Not at all. Please do."

He got the number, spoke into the mouthpiece, listened intently, then nodded and hung up. He spread his fingers. "You must understand that I knew young Jaffee's father before the old man died."

"So did I, Mr. Sutro. As a matter of fact, he took me into his office when I first got out of law school. That's why I'm interested in the son's welfare."

"I see. Well, the old gentleman was a valued customer of mine. He purchased some very fine pieces for his wife when she was alive. And later he even acquired some unset stones as a hedge against inflation. Young Allan liquidated them through my firm after his father died. Then yesterday afternoon he came here and offered to sell some additional stones he had inherited."

"Merchandise you recognized?"

"No. But young Jaffee assured me his father had bought gems from various other dealers too. I examined the pieces and offered him a very fair price."

"How much did you offer?"

"Forty thousand dollars. He said he needed some cash right away, an emergency in fact, and that he couldn't wait for my check to clear the bank. He said if I let him have four thousand in cash he'd knock two thousand off the total price. So I gave him the cash and a check for the balance, thirty-four thousand." Sutro looked mildly anxious. "Nothing wrong in that, is there, Counselor?"

I shrugged noncommittally. Within a very short time, Mr. Sutro, I suspected, was due for a severe shock, but I was going to let someone else give it to him. He was chewing the inside of his cheek when I left.

What I needed now was Vicky Korth's cooperation. I went looking for her at the hospital but she wasn't in Alison's room and neither was Alison. The room had been cleaned out, the bed freshly made; there was no sign of any occupancy. I felt a cold, sinking sensation and headed for the nurses' station.

Two girls in white were on duty. My inquiry seemed to upset them both. Their response was neither typical nor brisk. Alison Korth had suddenly developed serious respiratory problems and despite all efforts they had lost her.

I had no way of knowing whether Vicky wanted to be alone or would welcome company. My own experience led me to believe that most mourners crave the solace of visitors. I checked her address in the telephone directory and rode uptown.

Vicky answered my ring and opened the door. The shock of Alison's death hadn't yet fully registered. She looked dazed and numb and she needed a sympathetic ear.

"Oh, Scott," she said in a small trembly voice, "it didn't really have to happen. They were careless—"

"Who?" I asked.

"The nurses, the doctors, somebody—"

We sat down and I held her hand. "Tell me about it."

"She   she was having trouble breathing and they put her in oxygen. It's my fault. I left her alone. I went down for a sandwich and when I came back I saw something was wrong. Her face was dark. I saw that the equipment had come loose, the tube from the oxygen tank, and Alison was—was—" Her eyes filled and she hid her face against my chest.

I said quietly, "You couldn't have anticipated anything like that, Vicky. You mustn't condemn yourself for lack of omniscience."

After a while she sat back and wanted to reminisce, to talk about their childhood. She was touched by nostalgia and bittersweet memories. It was good therapy. She even smiled once or twice.

When she finally ran out of words I began to talk. I put her completely into the picture. I told her about my interviews, about my deductions and my conclusions. I told her Alison had been used and that I needed her help—and told her what I wanted her to do.

She sat quietly and brooded at me for a long moment, then she got up and went to the telephone. She dialed a number and said in a wooden voice, "This is Vicky. I thought you ought to know, Alison died this afternoon. I'm calling you because she'd want me to. The funeral is Thursday. Services at Lambert's Mortuary—Oh, I see. Well, if you wish you can see her in the reposing room this evening. I made arrangements at the hospital when they gave me a package with Alison's things. I'll be there myself at six. Please let her friends know."

It was almost seven o'clock. I sat alone in Vicky's apartment and waited. My pupils had expanded to the growing darkness. A large brown parcel lay on the coffee table. Behind me a closet door was open and waiting. Traffic sounds were muted. I kept my head cocked, concentrating, an ear bent in the direction of the hall door.

I was not quite sure how I'd play it if he came. I wasn't even sure he'd come, but then, without warning, the doorbell rang. It seemed abnormally loud. I didn't move. There was a pause and it rang again. Standard operating procedure: ring first to make sure no one's at home. I held my breath. Then it came, a metallic fumbling at the lock. I glided quickly into the closet, leaving the door slightly ajar, giving me an adequate angle of vision.

Hinges creaked and a pencil beam probed the darkness. A voice called softly, "Vicky, are you home?" Silence. Overhead lights clicked on. He came into view and I saw his eyes encompass the room in a quick circular sweep. He walked to the coffee table, picked up the parcel, and tore open the wrapping. He spread out the contents, staring at Alison's clothes.

"It's no use, Cowan," I said, showing myself. "You won't find them here."

His head pitched sideways and he stood impaled, jaws rigid.

I said, "You're one miserable, gold-plated, card-carrying, full-time rat. Conning a naive and trusting little cupcake like Alison Korth into doing your dirty work."

"What the hell are you talking about?"

"That's a dry hole, Cowan. Step out of it. You know what I'm talking about. Diamonds. Unset stones from Amsterdam. Your moonlighting sideline as a co-pilot on Global. You suspected you were under surveillance and you got Alison to smuggle a shipment off the plane and into the country for you. Concealed on her person. That's why you were clean when they fanned you at Kennedy yesterday."

His mouth was pinched. "You've got bats loose, Mr. Lawyer."

"Save it, Cowan. The deal was blown when Alison had an accident and was taken to the hospital. You thought the stones were discovered when she was undressed and you sweated that one out. But when nothing happened you began to wonder and reached a conclusion. The ambulance intern would have to loosen her uniform to use his stethoscope, so he must have found the stuff taped to her body. You checked him out and that's why you knew his name when I told you that the intern who'd treated Alison at the accident was a client of mine.

"You asked me what happened to him. Why did anything have to have happened to him? I'd go to the hospital if I wanted to see him because he worked there, wouldn't I? But you already knew what happened because you made it happen. You broke into his apartment to search for the loot and you heard him come back and you ambushed him. You hit him from behind, but Jaffee's not an easy man to cool, and even wounded he fought back. I don't know, maybe you even had help. Maybe you tried to make him talk."

Cowan stood like a statue carved out of stone.

"You got nothing from Jaffee," I said, "and nothing from his apartment. So maybe you were wrong about him. Maybe Alison had concealed the stones somewhere in her clothes and nobody had found them. That's why you came here tonight after Vicky told you she'd brought Alison's belongings back here to the apartment. You had to find out, and you knew Vicky would be at the mortuary."

He took a step toward me.

"Careful," I said. "You don't think I'd tackle a murderer by myself."

"Murderer?"

"Yes, Cowan. I'd make book on it. You're a shrewd specimen. You had to cover all contingencies. Suppose the hospital *had* found the diamonds and *had* notified the cops and they were keeping a lid on it until they could question Alison. A girl like her, she'd melt under heat. They could turn her inside out. She'd make a clean breast of it, and you'd be blown. So she had to go. She had to be eliminated. So you loitered and waited until you saw Vicky leave, and then you managed to slip into Alison's room and tamper with the equipment. You cut off her oxygen and watched her die. The cops know what to look for now and they're checking the hospital equipment thoroughly for your prints."

That tore it. He thought he could cut his losses by splitting, so he whirled and slammed through the door. But I hadn't been kidding. The cops were all set for him outside in the corridor.

It seldom comes up roses for all.

Vicky lost her sister, but gained a suitor—me. U.S. Customs descended on Jacques Sutro and seized the smuggled diamonds. Sutro's lawyers attached Jaffee's bank account and recovered the $34,000 check he had deposited. Mr. Sutro still wanted his four-grand cash and I referred him to Big Sam Tarloff. Fat chance.

Allan Jaffee healed nicely. The episode may even have cured his gambling addiction. He copped a plea on the gem charge and turned State's evidence against Ben Cowan. Cowan was going to be out of circulation until he was a rickety old man. For me, representing Jaffee was an act of chairty. I never got paid.

Only Nick Papadopolous emerged unscathed. The judge canceled forfeiture of Jaffee's bail bond and Papa got his money back. He was delirious. He invited Vicky and me out to dinner. That was two weeks ago. We're still trying to digest the stuff.

CLARK HOWARD

Money To Burn

It had been snowing for two hours when Phil Madigan woke up at eight o'clock and looked out his hotel-room window. The sight of the grey overcast morning filled with calmly falling snow petrified him for a moment so that he could only stare at it dumbly, hardly believing it to be real. But it was real, all right; great big white snowflakes drifting down so serenely, already covering the sidewalks and street and parked cars below. Yes, it's real, all right, Madigan thought, a wide smile breaking across his face.

He turned from the window and hurried through the connecting bath into Sam's room. He had to tell Sam right away.

Sam Hooper was sound asleep when Madigan rushed in and shook him roughly by the shoulder. "Sam!" Madigan said urgently, "get up! It's snowing, Sam! It's here; the snow's here!"

Hooper, the older of the two by twenty years, did not have Madigan's capacity for coming fully awake the first thing in the morning. He had to prepare himself to face the world, and he did so now, twisting and grunting and yawning while his sleepy senses returned.

"What? What's here?" he said sourly.

"The snow, Sam!" Madigan repeated excitedly. "It's here! It's here!"

What Madigan was saying got through to Sam Hooper then and he forced himself awake, jumping out of bed and stumbling along with Madigan to the nearest window. Together they stared down at the main street of the little town, freshly whitened by the snow. They stared with eyes wide and mouths slightly agape, as if they had never before seen such a phenomenon. Then they looked at each other and smiled happily. It was here, they were thinking. The snow was here at last.

They had been waiting for this, the first snowfall, for more than three weeks. It usually came not later than the middle of October but this year it was way overdue, for today was the twenty-third. Hooper had been complaining for the last seven days, since the fifteenth came and went and no snow appeared, that he would wait only one more day and then ditch the job; but each day he decided to wait another, until now, finally, his patience had been rewarded. His eyes shone with an eagerness to get on with the work at hand.

"What time is it?" he asked.

"Ten past eight," said Madigan.

"O.K., let's get things moving. You check with the weather bureau while I get dressed; then I'll get everything together while you get ready."

"Right." Madigan hurried back into his own room.

Hooper went into the bathroom, washed, and began a fast shave. He could hear Madigan on the phone getting the weather report. Their plans depended on the forecast. Madigan had assured him a hundred times that it would be favorable, that the first snowfall of the season was always a heavy one. It had better be, thought Hooper now, or we'll get caught just as sure as hell is hot.

He finished up and went back into his room and started dressing. Madigan came in a minute later, grinning like a cat with a mouse under its paw.

"We're set, Sam! Weather bureau says the snow is expected to continue for at least six more hours. I told you, didn't I, Sam? Didn't I tell you?"

"Yeah, you told me, kid."

"Hot dog! We're gonna pull it off, Sam. In a couple more hours we're gonna have money to burn!"

"Well, we ain't got it yet," said Hooper calmly, "and we won't have it if you don't get cleaned up so we can hightail it out of here."

"Sure, Sam, sure." Madigan hurried into the bathroom, humming to himself.

Crazy kid, thought Hooper. Acting like some college punk that just made the team. He'd better settle down or he's liable to get a bullet in his gut. Sticking up a bank is serious business.

Sam Hooper was the man to know, if anyone did, just how serious the robbing of a bank could be. This would be his seventh bank. He had made it away clean on four of them, had been caught on the other two. For the two on which he had been caught he had spent a total of fourteen years in Federal penitentiaries; five on the first, nine on the second. He was now forty-four years old and had thought he was finished with this strongarm stuff.

For the past year, since getting out of Leavenworth, Hooper had led a quiet, law-abiding existence; he had a rented room, ate in cafés, and worked nine hours a day as a leather tanner, a trade he had picked up by courtesy of the U.S. Bureau of Prisons. It wasn't much of a life for a guy like Sam, a guy who had lived it up in Miami and Mexico City, been used to fancy cars, fancy clothes, and fancy dames; but at least he was able to look a cop in the eye and not always have to be thinking about some job he could get busted for; at least he could lay down a twenty for change without worrying about the bill being marked; at least he could sleep nights. He hadn't been setting the world on fire, not by a long shot, but he had been doing all right.

And then the kid came along. Phil Madigan, his name was. A small-timer, a candy-store burglar. Madigan was a real sports enthusiast—skin diving, ice skating, skiing, the works. That was how he happened to run up on this job they were getting ready to pull. He had been up in the mountains for some winter sports the previous season and had come across a cabin high up toward the peaks. It was a little place, just one average-sized room, Madigan had told him, and it was so far up that it was isolated from the time the first snow fell until the spring thaw about four or five months later. It was owned by a real-estate company down in the town of Preston where Hooper and Madigan were now, and was rented out to fishermen during the trout season. A perfect place to hide out, Madigan had said the first time he and Hooper met.

The kid had been referred to Hooper by one of the few contacts Sam still retained in the underworld. Hooper had passed the word around that he was out of business, that he intended to make it as a square after his last bit in prison; but apparently he wasn't taken too seriously because Phil Madigan turned up at his room one night saying he had a hot bank job on the line and had been told to look up Sam Hooper.

Sam listened to the plan out of a mixture of professional curiosity and sheer boredom, after first making it plain that he had "retired." But the more he listened, the more interested he became. It began to sound as if the kid really did have a sweet one waiting to be picked. So he took down all the particulars of the job and told Madigan he would look it over and let him know in a few days.

For the next two nights he worked the plan over and over in his mind and on paper, trying to find some weakness in it, some flaw that would give him an excuse to dump it; but each time he went over it, he came to the same conclusion: it was a good, sound bank job that looked like it could be pulled off very nicely if handled properly. And even though it was a small-town bank, the take would probably be well worth the effort and risk involved.

Sam tried to think over the deal rationally. He knew if he got caught on another bank job he'd be in prison until he was an old, old man. But the temptation was just too much for him. He kept thinking how nice it would be to have a briefcase full of money in his hand and step on a plane for Acapulco again. In his mind danced pictures of new clothes, a shiny convertible, and blondes—great big blondes.

The great big blondes did it. Sam Hooper decided to go the route one more time.

He and Madigan began polishing up the plan. The most important detail—the getaway and hideout—had already been taken care of with the little cabin high up the mountain. The one big obstacle in hitting a bank in that area was getting down the winding mountain highway before a roadblock could be set up at the bottom. This was virtually impossible to do; that was why there had never been a stickup in any of the resort towns that circled the mountain. But Hooper and Madigan would eliminate that problem by going up instead of down. It's a perfect setup, Madigan had said. We pull the job on the day of the first snowfall, then beat it up to this cabin. Nobody'll ever think we'd do that. The place is snowed in for at least four months. All we have to do is sit it out until spring and then just kind of drift down through town one day like we were early fishermen. Before anybody can notice us, we'll be gone. Sure, it'll be dull and monotonous up there all alone for four months, but we can hold out. And in the spring, we'll have money to burn!

Hooper finished dressing and threw his extra clothes in a suitcase. Then he sat down on the bed and gave their guns a final check. They had a .410-guage shotgun with a sawed-off barrel and two .38 revolvers. Each would carry a revolver; in addition Madigan would handle the shotgun while Hooper collected the money in the bank. Hooper also had a little .25 automatic he carried in his hip pocket as an extra precaution. That was his hole card, his kicker, in case somebody got the drop on them; not even Madigan knew he had it.

"Hey, snap it up!" he yelled to Madigan in the bathroom.

The younger man came in, drying his face with a hotel towel. "All set and ready to get going," he said.

"There's your artillery," Hooper told him, strapping his own shoulder holster in place. "Are you sure everything's set in the cabin?"

"I told you, Sam, it's all ready. I made a final check last week. There's five hundred bucks' worth of food laid in; a six-hundred gallon tank of fuel oil; a radio, four decks of cards, about a thousand magazines I got secondhand in the city; and we got checkers, dominoes, Parcheesi—everything but a broad, an' I could have arranged that, too, if you'd let me."

"Sure, sure," said Hooper, "that's all we'd need. We'll be at each other's throats soon enough without having a dame to fight over. You don't know how it is being cooped up with the same guy day after day."

Madigan smiled. "We'll make it, Sam, I know we will. And when it's all over we'll have—"

"I know, I know," Hooper interrupted, "we'll have money to burn. Come on, let's get going or spring'll be here before we even get started."

Madigan got into his holster and rolled the shotgun up in newspaper. They both put on heavy mackinaws, fur caps, and rubber overshoes. Then they got their luggage and went downstairs to check out.

The bank opened at ten. Five minutes later Hooper and Madigan pulled up outside and parked. They were driving a four-year-old coupe with heavy-duty snow chains on the rear tires. Getting out, they ducked their heads against the windblown snow and crossed the sidewalk to the bank entrance.

There were six people inside: three tellers, the manager, his secretary, and one customer. Madigan remained just inside the door, folding the paper back from the barrel of the shotgun so they could all see what it was.

"Don't anybody move!" Hooper ordered, leveling his .38. "This is a holdup!" His gaze swept across the three men in the teller cages. "If an alarm goes off, so does that shotgun, understand? Everybody just stand or sit right where you are and look down at the floor!"

When they were all very still, with Madigan moving the shotgun slowly back and forth in an arc that covered the whole room, Hooper slipped the .38 into his pocket and from under his coat drew out a large canvas bag which he quickly unfolded. He hurried behind the railing and methodically emptied the tellers' cages of all currency. Then he stepped over to the bank manager's desk and pulled the man to his feet roughly. "Get the vault open!" he ordered coldly.

The thick outer door of the vault was already standing open. The manager fumbled with a ring of keys to open the barred inner door. When he finally got it unlocked, Hooper pushed him inside and made him sit in a corner while he systematically looted the bank's reserve safe. Looks pretty good, he thought, as he stuffed the sack with bundles of tens and twenties and a few stacks of fifties and hundreds.

Finished, he stepped back out and snapped, "All right, everybody into the vault! Come on, move!" He glanced at the big clock on the wall as the other five people filed into the vault. They had been in the bank about seven or eight minutes. Pretty good time, he thought.

Hooper slammed the barred door and locked everyone in the vault. "Take a look," he said to Madigan, hurrying toward the front door. Madigan peered out at the street; he saw nothing but swirling snow. "Looks O.K.," he told Hooper.

"All right, let's go!"

Madigan folded the newspaper back over the shotgun barrel, tucked it under his arm, and opened the front door. Hooper stepped past him out of the bank and went directly to the car. Madigan followed him, closing the door gently behind him.

In the car, Madigan tossed the shotgun on the rear seat and started the motor. Hooper kept the sack of money between his knees, his revolver ready on top of it. The windshield wipers threw the loose snow away, giving them each a picture of the street up ahead. It was nearly deserted. Madigan guided the car slowly away from the curb and down the street.

Five minutes later they were out of town and approaching the curve where the highway began its winding descent to the lowlands.

"How's it look?" Madigan asked excitedly, nodding toward the sack of money.

"Pretty good, I think," said Hooper. "Looked like maybe fifty or sixty grand."

Madigan grinned and went back to concentrating on the road. Where the highway curved downward, they turned off into a gravel road almost hidden by the snow. Their chains crunched noisily and caught and the car lumbered up a slight incline. As they gradually moved upward from the highway, Hooper looked back and saw fresh snow already beginning to fill their tracks.

Fifteen minutes later they reached a ridge where the road leveled off momentarily. Madigan shifted to neutral and pulled on the brake. Hooper took a pair of binoculars from the glove compartment and they got out. Taking turns with the glasses, they looked back down the mountain. The first section of their tracks leading off the highway were now completely covered and there was a fresh layer of unmarked snow on the highway itself.

"Perfect," said Madigan. "Just like I told you, huh, Sam? First snowfall is always heavy."

"Just like you told me, kid," Hooper admitted. He turned his gaze upward. "How long will it take us to get to the cabin?"

"About three hours, from the looks of the snow."

Hooper turned back to the car. "Well, let's get going."

It was nearly two in the afternoon when the car pulled up the last steep grade and made the top ridge. They were high up now, in a primitive part of the great mountain range, where the sky looked strangely close to them, where there was nothing visible except snow-covered pine trees, where the air was exhaustingly thin, the cold sharp and painful.

Hooper looked back down the road. "Are you sure nobody can follow us up here?"

Madigan shook his head emphatically. "By the time the snow stops, this road and everything around it will be in drifts up to eight feet deep. And it'll stay like that until the spring thaw. It would be impossible for a car to even go down, much less come up."

Hooper looked around at the white wasteland on all sides of them. "Where's the cabin?" he asked.

"Just up ahead."

The car moved through snow already deep across the rutted, narrow little road, and crawled slowly around a thick group of trees into a small clearing. There, with three feet of snow drifted up against it, sat the little cabin.

"Home sweet home," said Madigan as he drove up as close as he could and cut the motor. They got out of the car.

"We'll have to dig our way in, looks like," said Hooper.

"Yeah." Madigan opened the trunk and took out two hand shovels.

"How's that work?" Hooper asked, indicating the large fuel-storage tank mounted on a raised wooden platform next to the cabin.

"There's a line running into the cabin," Madigan explained. "It's got a regular tap like a water faucet. We use the fuel oil for our lanterns, for the stove, and for the heater."

"Sure there's enough to last?"

"Plenty," Madigan assured him. "Probably be a hundred gallons left in the spring."

The two men went to work clearing the snow away. When they got the door open, Madigan took the shovels and put them back in the trunk. "You grab the money," he said easily, "I'll unload the suitcases."

Hooper nodded and got the sack of money from the front seat. He went on inside and looked around. One corner was piled high with magazines. A table in the middle of the room had decks of cards and other games of amusement on it. There was a radio on a shelf on the wall. In a little alcove Hooper saw cases of canned goods and other supplies. There were two folding cots, each with three new blankets stacked on it. Between them was a large kerosene stove.

Not bad, thought Hooper, considering it's only a four-month stretch that we must hibernate.

The door slammed behind him and he turned to see Madigan putting their luggage on the floor. "Get the binoculars out of the glove compartment, will you, Sam?" the younger man said. "If we leave them out there the lenses will freeze."

"Sure, kid. Then let's get a fire going and warm the place up, what say?" Madigan smiled. "Good deal."

Hooper went back outside and waded the snow over to the car. Opening the door, he reached inside and got the glasses. Have to get this car around back and get it up on blocks some way, he thought. Got to be sure and start it every day, too, so it won't freeze up. He closed the car door and made his way back to the cabin. There was a thermometer nailed to the wall just outside the door. Hooper saw it was only fifteen above zero. He shivered and pushed through the door.

Just as he stepped inside, Hooper felt the muzzle of the shotgun jab into his back. He stiffened and held his hands very still.

"That's the ticket, Sam," said Madigan evenly. "Don't even think about moving." He reached around under Hooper's coat and lifted the .38 from Sam's shoulder holster. "O.K., Sam," he said, pushing him away, "go on over there and sit down at the table and keep still so I don't have to blast you."

Hooper sat down, feeling the hardness of the little automatic in his hip pocket, very glad now that he had never mentioned to Madigan that he carried his "kicker," his "hole card." He stared coldly across the room at Madigan. "Double-crossing me, kid?" he asked in a measured tone.

"That's it, Sam," Madigan said, smiling.

"So you lied to me," Hooper accused quietly. "You said there was no way out of here until spring."

"I said there was no way with the car, Sam," Madigan corrected. The younger man picked up the sack of money and emptied it on the floor. Kneeling down, watching Hooper closely, he used one hand to stuff the currency into a knapsack. When it was packed, he slipped his arms through the shoulder straps, switching the shotgun from one hand to the other as he did so.

"What are you gonna do, hike down?" Hooper asked sarcastically.

"Little too cold for that, Sam," said Madigan lightly. He backed over to one of the cots and pushed the blankets off onto the floor. Beneath them lay a pair of shiny skis and matching ski poles.

"So that's it," said Hooper. "You're gonna ski down. A regular all-American boy, aren't you? Don't you think the law will be waiting for you when you get back down there?"

Madigan was kneeling on the other side of the cabin again, lacing on heavy ski boots. He continued to watch Hooper closely, the shotgun lying only inches from his hands.

"I'm not going that way," he told Hooper. "I'm going down the other side. There's a ski lodge down there. By tonight there'll be busloads of skiers up here. Nobody'll notice one more." He stoop up, gathered his skis and poles under one arm, and leveled the shotgun on Hooper. "Outside, Sam," he ordered.

Hooper went back out into the cold, Madigan following him.

"Just stand over there by the door where I can keep an eye on you," said Madigan as he moved a few yards away from the cabin. Hooper watched while the younger man laid his skis in position on the level snow and knelt between them, cradling the shotgun first on one knee, then the other, while he fitted the skis onto his boots. Then he stood up and held the shotgun loosely under one arm.

'You gonna kill me, kid?" Hooper asked, tensing himself for a drop to the ground to try and get the .25 out before Madigan could get him with a load of buckshot.

"What for, Sam?" Madigan said easily. "You never did anything to me."

"Aren't you afraid I'll come after you in the spring when I get out of here?"

Madigan laughed. "Go ahead, Sam," he said simply.

Hooper frowned as suspicion flooded his mind. It doesn't figure, he told himself. The first rule in pulling a double-cross is to make sure the guy you cross won't ever be able to get even. It's a trick, he decided. He's trying to get me off guard for some reason.

"I've got to cut out if I'm gonna make the ski lodge by dark," Madigan said. "You just go on back in the cabin, Sam, and stay put until I get gone. And don't try following me if you've got any sense; you'd never make it on foot. Understand?"

Hooper nodded.

"So long, Sam."

Hooper backed slowly toward the door, still expecting Madigan to raise the shotgun at any second. But the younger man made no attempt to fire; he just stood waiting while Hooper backed all the way into the cabin and quickly shut the door.

Watching through the window, Hooper saw Madigan swing first one, then the other ski around and move off slowly toward the first slope that would take him down the other side of the mountain. Hooper wet his lips and took out the little .25 automatic, snapping the safety off. He looked back out and decided that Madigan was now about a hundred yards away—too far to chance accuracy with the small bore weapon he had. Got to get closer to him, he thought anxiously.

He hurried to the rear of the cabin and climbed out the back window, dropping nearly waist-deep into a drift. Moving through the snow to the corner, he peered around and saw Madigan still moving smartly along on his skis, now about two hundred years away. Hooper thought quickly and bolted from behind the cabin, running in a crouch until he reached the lines of trees edging the clearing. The snow was not so deep under the trees and Hooper was able to move faster.

He began to run through the trees, staying back under their protective covering. He ran until his chest was heaving from the thin air that failed to satisfy his lungs; then he had to rest. He slowed to a walk and moved back toward the clearing. Looking out from behind a tree, he saw Madigan still about fifty yards ahead of him. He leaned up against the tree and counted slowly to thirty, then moved back under cover and started running again.

He ran until he judged himself to be ahead of Madigan, then slowed down and crept quietly back to the edge of the clearing. Madigan was just approaching the place where Hooper stood concealed. They were both almost to the end of the slope now.

Hooper waited until Madigan went by, then stepped out behind him, the gun leveled. "Hold it, kid!" he said sharply.

Madigan tried to whirl around and raise the shotgun but he got his legs tangled in the skis and his arms in the ski poles, and he dropped the weapon and stumbled into a snowdrift helplessly.

Hooper stood over him laughing, the .25 aimed at his chest. "Outsmarted yourself, didn't you, punk?"

"Don't shoot me, Sam!" Madigan begged.

"I'm not," Hooper told him. "I don't want somebody finding you with a bullet in you and wondering how you got it. No, I'm going to take care of you in a different way, punk."

"Give me a break, Sam," Madigan pleaded.

"Sure, I'll give you a break," Hooper said coldly. He reached down and picked up the fallen shotgun by its barrel. Using it as a club, he smashed the stock against Madigan's skull. The younger man fell over unconscious.

"There's your break," Hooper snarled. "A break in the head."

He put the shotgun down and rolled Madigan over, pulling the money-filled knapsack from his back and removing the unconscious man's coat to take off the shoulder holster he wore. When it was off, Hooper took the other .38 from the pocket and worked the heavy mackinaw back onto Madigan's limp form. Then he grabbed the collar of the coat and began to pull Madigan through the drifted snow, the skis and poles dragging behind him.

Stopping near the edge, Hooper surveyed the slope carefully. It fell in a gentle curving grade that angled off to the right and seemed to wind gradually down-mountain as far as he could see. That was the ski trail Madigan had meant to follow down to the lodge, he decided. But off to the left there was no gentle curve, no slope at all; there was only a steep incline that stretched about thirty feet to a sheer drop down into a deep gorge.

That looks O.K., Hooper thought dispassionately. He dragged the unconscious man farther along the edge until he had him right above the incline leading to the drop. There he laid Madigan out on his side, skis straight, poles still attached to his wrists with thongs.

"So long, double-crosser," he said softly, and with the toe of his overshoe he started Madigan down the slope.

Madigan's unconscious form slid downward, the drag of his skis slowing but not stopping him. He moved jerkily, his body weaving and leaving an odd trail in the snow. Seconds later he went over the edge and dropped from sight.

Hooper waited perhaps two minutes but he never did hear Madigan hit bottom. Either it's pretty damned deep, he decided, or else there's a lot of snow at the bottom. Either way it didn't really matter. If the fall didn't finish Madigan, he'd freeze to death before he woke up.

Hooper went back and got the shotgun and Madigan's shoulder holster and the packful of money, and trudged back toward the cabin. It was getting colder now and the light was beginning to fade. The evening air seemed even thinner than it had been earlier and Hooper had to stop twice to rest and catch his breath. When he finally reached the cabin, he saw on the thermometer that the temperature had dropped to two degrees below zero. He hurried on inside.

The cabin was as cold as the outdoors. Hooper was shivering as he put the guns and knapsack on the table and pulled off his gloves. His fingers were numb with cold. He blew into his cupped palms a few times and rubbed his hands briskly. Got to get a fire going, he thought. Got to warm this place up.

He lifted the lid of the stove and saw that it was dry inside. Picking up the kerosene can, he found it empty. He went over to the tap running in from the fuel tank outside and put the lip of the can under it. He turned the tap   and nothing came out.

Hooper stared at the dry nozzle, the empty can, the cold stove. No fuel, he thought dumbly. Then the panic began to rise in him. *No fuel—!*

Outside, the temperature was down another degree and dropping steadily.

The House Guest

The lecture agency called on Tuesday and said they were sending this girl down that weekend. They didn't even ask me; just said they were sending her down. I always take them in though. When you're married to a man who had the fortune or misfortune to discover a new active agent for the medics to mess around with, you get used to people—all kinds of people—all wanting something. There are always a lot of girls.

I hadn't heard about this one before, but that didn't mean anything. The agency always has a few on hand doing busy work. This one probably needed a Florida vacation as much as the next one. We don't have any children and there's a good guest room, and I like to cook and make special drinks, so they don't bother me too much. I do get a little tired of Kramer's constant talk-talk-talk when they're here. The stories and theories may be all new to them, but I've had to hear them all a million times. I just sat on the terrace and cut my mind off and let it drift when he talked. That's what I used to do—cut and let drift, like the ocean out there.

This one was a publicity girl. Kramer went out to the airport and got her and I spent the time thinking up a special drink. It's something to do. I never drink anything but the best rum and soda myself, but I like to mess around with drinks. I tried something with bourbon and a liqueur, but it didn't come out to suit me; it wasn't at all pretty. So I threw it down the sink and started over and came up with a nice pink thing out of gin, grenadine, and white crème de menthe.

Then I heard them in the driveway and put the hors d'oeuvres in the oven. She was a good-looking girl, like they all are: brunette, tall, with good legs and one of those thinned-down bodies from starving herself to death like everybody in New York seems to do. I've never had to starve myself. I'm just naturally skinny. Not slim or slender, just skinny, and little too. It used to worry me, but I've gotten used to it. I wear my hair long and keep the clothes simple and everybody thinks I'm a lot younger than I am, which is definitely closer to forty than thirty. This girl was about twenty. She looked bright and efficient, and she shook hands like a man. I almost liked her.

We went out on the terrace and she took one of the drinks without saying anything cute about it. I was almost sorry for her having to listen to Kramer for the whole weekend, but she was polite enough to him. They always are at first. He's still a good-looking man, though he's started to go pretty bald and all the bounce and energy that used to seem exciting has degenerated into a bunch of annoying habits, like tapping his foot on the floor and snapping his fingers.

"Your ocean is wonderful," this girl said.

"Yes," I said. "I like it. I didn't when we first moved here. It used to drive me crazy. I'd wake up every time the tide changed. But now I can't stand getting away from the sound of the surf. You get attached to it."

"I can see you would," she said. "It must be like listening to rain when you're going off to sleep at night."

Well, when she said that Kramer leered at her, but she acted as though she didn't notice it. I used to wish he'd get enough of girls, just once, so I could have one around to talk to without him playing cavalier at them, but it isn't going to happen, of course. Not now.

I fixed them another drink and had one myself, and then I went to see about the supper. When I came back out Kramer was telling her about the first year after he discovered the mold or whatever, and she was hanging on it. It is a pretty interesting tale the first time you hear it, I guess, but he always brings in that awful place we were living in then, and makes me sound like Marie Curie stirring the pitchblende in the backyard.

"You ought to get more of that into your lectures," she said, earning her vacation.

"Oh, it really isn't very interesting," Kramer said.

"But it is," she said. "It's just like the—well, like the Curies."

She actually said it. Well, I guess it's all right; there was a time when I thought it was sort of like the Curies myself.

That was before all the publicity and the girls and the publicity girls—and the money. The money has been fun. It bought me that ocean out there, but it did things to Kramer. Maybe it did things to me too, only you can't see what's happening to yourself so well. I know what happened to Kramer. He got the idea he was the most important guy in the universe. He'd always had a tendency that way, but if all the publicity and the money hadn't come along he couldn't have convinced himself so thoroughly. He wouldn't have gotten so pontifical about it.

I brought the supper out and they ate. The girl, she was named Linda, ate everything. Kramer ate too. Sometimes he doesn't any more, but I am a good cook. It's about the only thing I am good at.

"Aren't you eating?" Linda said to me about halfway through her shrimp romelade.

"I never want much supper," I said.

I went up to bed early because I figured they wanted to talk business and I wasn't interested in that. I could still hear them on the terrace when I went to sleep. She had gotten out her briefcase and they were going over the new tour route for the lectures. I hoped Kramer didn't bore her to death.

The next day I took her away with me for lunch and let Kramer work on his lecture notes. We drove up to the next key and had lunch at a nice restaurant there. She bragged on the food, but said it wasn't as good as mine. I asked her all about her job and she told me. She made it interesting, and she was bright and clever. She reminded me of the way I used to be a long time ago in college.

That night I suggested we go to a place where there was an orchestra. That surprised old Kramer, I could see. I don't ever go out any more. I've gotten to where I like to go to bed early and listen to my ocean. He jumped on it and said, "Oh, great." I knew he wanted to dance with Linda. That was all right with me. Kramer can't dance. He thinks he's real good at it, but he never has learned how to lead.

We went out to the Beach Club where they have a good combo. Kramer danced with me once and with Linda once and then we just sat and drank and talked. They ordered martinis. I didn't blame them. The bartender wasn't really good at exotic drinks like I am.

I drank my rum and soda and watched all the people in the bar. All of them seemed to have something wrong with them. There was a woman in a sari and she was too fat; there was a tall beautiful girl in a white dress but she had her hair dyed so much it was ruined; there was a good-looking man in a beautiful blue sportcoat but he squinted. I don't know why I've gotten that way lately. I look at people and they seem perfectly plausible. Then I see the really awful little thing that ruins them. I looked at Linda and I decided her wrong thing wasn't apparent. That pleased me. I get tired of all the wrong things. I'm not looking for them. They just seem to be there, like me being too skinny.

We went home about two o'clock and I guess that was the latest I'd been up in over a year. It felt strange to look up and see the moon going down over the water and feel that late-night, early-morning chill.

They didn't want to go to bed so I made them some scrambled eggs with the little green peppers and they ate that. Then I made them a nightcap out of cream and crème de menthe and a secret ingredient and they drank that. Kramer can get real nasty about some of my drinks sometimes, but Linda seemed to like all of them so he went along with it. He'll do anything to impress other people with his reasonableness. He only yells at me when there's nobody else around.

When we went up to bed I said, "Well, I like that girl."

Kramer said, "Finally, the millennium. I didn't know you liked anybody any more."

"I think I'll ask her to stay over another couple of days."

"I guess she'd like that," Kramer said. "New York isn't very pleasant this time of year."

So she stayed. I wonder if she'd gone on back—but then that's a pretty useless thing now, to wonder.

She and Kramer got everything set up about the lecture tour and she and I talked. I hadn't talked to anybody in a long time—just listened to Kramer—so it was fun. We went dancing again, and this time I just left them with the scrambled eggs and drinks. That's how I found out.

Usually when I go up to bed I go right to sleep, but I guess all the talking I'd been doing lately had stimulated me. I couldn't get to sleep. I lay there in my twin bed and listened to my surf, but it didn't have its usual effect. I kept thinking of things I'd like to say I hadn't got around to yet, so finally I got up and put my robe on. I'd been hearing Kramer talking all the time, but as I started downstairs he shut up and there was just the surf sound—and moonlight. I was barefooted—I never wear bedroom slippers—and I walked out the door without making any noise, I guess. She was actually sitting in his lap, just like the cartoons about secretaries, and he was kissing her neck, and she was making little moaning sounds as though he were some great lover instead of Kramer Lytle, the poor woman's lecture idol. I just stood there and stared at them, because right at first I didn't care whether they knew I was there or not.

They were getting pretty sloppy about the whole thing by then so I turned around and went back in the house and upstairs. I knew then what her flaw was. She's got this little picture of herself as some sort of abandoned maiden.

I figured there was no point planning right then what I had to do, so I just turned over and went to sleep. I'd known for a long time it was going to come to this with Kramer anyway. There had been moments when I knew I would have to do it if he snapped his fingers or said "Now in my humble opinion" one more time, but I hadn't counted on having to include one of the girls.

I got up next morning and fixed them a really good breakfast. I figured they needed it. The funny thing was that knowing now exactly what I was going to do made me hungry. I hadn't had any appetite in a long time—not since the money. First I'd gotten to where I just didn't like certain things: eggs and meat. Then it got to be fish too, and lately there just wasn't much of anything I really wanted—a little bread, maybe, with my rum and soda. This morning, though, I ate as much as they did, maybe even a little more.

I saw Kramer watching me and I said, "What's the matter?"

"I just wondered why you were eating like that," he said. "I thought you didn't like eggs and bacon any more."

"Oh," I said, "I guess it's because I've got somebody to talk to these days. Conversation just plain makes me as hungry as a shark."

They both laughed. Ha-ha. Funny. I looked at her, all dewy and virginal. I wondered whether it was really Kramer or the money, but the dewy look probably meant it was Love. She was just a natural-born idiot. If I'd thought it was the money I might have spared her, but there wasn't much point in it if she was really in love with Kramer. That didn't give her much of a future anyway. She had only *seemed* bright and clever after all. It was a veneer, like the New York look. Underneath she was just a dumb broad. I'd been wasting my time talking to her all along, just like the years I'd wasted trying to talk to Kramer when all he wanted was a listening post.

It was so simple I didn't have to do much actual planning. The poison was in the house. We kept various kinds for the various insects. It didn't really matter which one I picked. By the time I got through with one of my extra special stingaroos of a drink they weren't going to taste anything in it anyway, and they'd drink it. Linda thought she was being horribly clever liking anything I whipped up in the kitchen, and Kramer was going along with it to impress her and lull me. That's another thing about him. He never has known that I'm not stupid. He never had the faintest idea he could ever bore *me*.

They sat around all day looking at the ocean with Simple Simon expressions, and once they actually went into the kitchen and started whispering. I guess they figured I was so crazy about her I wasn't going to notice anything. I let them think it. It didn't make any difference. They'd know by tonight.

About five o'clock I said, "Let's go out to dinner."

That took them both aback.

"Why?" Kramer asked. "You know you love to cook and we love to eat it."

"I don't know," I said. "I just want to. I'll whomp us up a good drink first. I've got a real weirdo of an idea for tonight. Then we'll go out."

They looked at each other and both said, "Fine, fine."

I got dressed early so I'd have time in the kitchen while they were getting dressed. I wanted to do it all up really special, so I wore a new dress Kramer had brought me when he came back from one of his lecture trips—a conscience present. Not because he'd actually been up to anything; he'd never really had the nerve for that. It took this girl with the dewy look really to fool him into thinking he was man enough to *try* anything in the first place.

I went outside and put my best straw placemats on the terrace table. I fixed some zingy hors d'oeuvres and even put a big bouquet of flowers in the middle of the table. Appropriate.

In the kitchen I went to work on the specialty. There were some coconuts I'd been saving and I figured they'd do real well. I cut the tops off and left the milk in and added the gin, the mixers, and the poison. Then I got a really good idea. I never used rum in my specialty drinks. I drank only the best, and it was mine. Kramer didn't have enough palate to taste one drink from another anyway. That was one reason I got such a kick out of mixing up all the mess I could and watching him drink it. I started making the drinks really because I couldn't stand watching him drink cola and vodka or cola and bourbon. He never had known that, but he knew I had a thing about my rum. He didn't really like it anyway, so he thought it was funny, me wanting my six-ninety fifth all to myself. I'd heard him telling Linda about it one day and laughing. "Don't touch Miss Iris' rum," he told her. "That is verboten."

So while I was mixing in everything else I thought, Give them a charge, put in some of Miss Iris' six-ninety rum. Why not? It's the last time. I laced it good. Besides, it would cover up anything the least bit odd. I could just hear Kramer saying, "My God, Iris, I taste rum. You really must love us." And I'd say, "Yes, darling. You don't know how much." Even Kramer could taste rum when he hadn't had any in so long.

I stirred it all up and punched holes in the coconut tops and put them back on with a straw through them. Then I hollered, "The sun just went over the yardarm" up the stairs and took the drinks outside. I set the two coconuts square in the middle of two side-by-side placemats. Then I went back and made myself a good stiff rum and soda and brought it out and sat down across the table from where they were going to sit.

They came ambling out, looking like pie, and oohed and aahed over the coconuts.

"You've really outdone yourself tonight, kid," Kramer said. "Sure you won't have one with us?" Then he actually winked at Linda.

"You know I can't quit my good old rum and soda," I said in a good imitation of a submissive voice. "Cheers, dears." I lifted my glass and took a good slug.

They smiled and leaned over and drew through the straws. Then they smiled again, said, "Ummm, good," and took another swig.

I knew they were trying to drink it down fast without having to taste it. I just watched them, drinking my drink, waiting.

Then all of a sudden a simply terrible look came over Linda's face. She went white as a sheet, and she stopped drinking and choked and pushed the coconut back and stared at me. She put a hand out and pushed Kramer's coconut away from him and said, "Oh, my God."

I guessed that mess didn't cover up the taste after all.

Then she said, "Don't, Kramer. Don't drink it. It's got rum in it. It's got rum."

Well, I told you Kramer never thought I had a lot on the ball, but it didn't take me long to figure that one. I knew there wasn't any point in worrying about it either. I'd already drunk half my drink and even Kramer would have had enough sense really to load the bottle, even if Dewey Eyes over there didn't. There wasn't a damned thing I could do about it, so I just laughed. I laughed for what seemed like a long time while both of them looked desperate and scared and started to stand up.

"An emetic," Kramer said. "The doctor, the hospital—"

"Sit down, darling," I said. "You've not only got poisoned rum in your drink, but a good measure of Mother Iris' remedy for you in your coconut milk. I don't really think you'll be able to make it."

I looked at the sun. It was almost ready to touch the horizon. When it does, people here make bets on how long it'll take to go under completely. Two minutes is a pretty good estimate. It goes a lot faster than anyone would think.

"I'll give you odds," I said, smiling at them. "I'll last long enough to watch the sun go under and neither of you will make it."

And that's what I'm doing. Sitting here all by myself looking for the last time at that thin little edge of green that comes up just as the sun goes down.

WILLIAM LINK and RICHARD LEVINSON

The Man in the Lobby

It had been a wasted morning for Wolfson. The captain had sent him over to the Golden Gate Hotel to check out a public nuisance complaint, but after a brief investigation he found that it was groundless—a few conventioneers had blundered into the wrong room after a night of carousing.

He left the elevator and glanced at the people coming in from Powell Street. It was not quite noon, but the hotel bar was already crowded with advertising men from the cluster of office buildings a few blocks away. All riding the expense account, he imagined. What would it take to pull them away from their martinis and black Russians? A stock market crash, probably. Either that or another earthquake.

Well, it was time to report back. As he started across the busy lobby he brushed by a man at the check-in desk. The face hung for an instant in his mind, then he dismissed it. At the street door he hesitated and turned back. The man at the desk was in his early fifties, meek and rumpled, with the slightly dazed expression of someone who had spent his life in front of a blackboard or an adding machine. He wore a cheap summer suit and a frayed blue shirt.

Wolfson strolled back to the counter and tried to get a better look.

"Anything on the twelfth floor?" the man was saying.

"1205 is available," said the desk clerk. "Nice and spacious." He slipped a registration card into a leather holder and pushed it across the counter. "There's a lovely view of the pagodas on Grant Street."

The man mumbled something, then signed the card and started for the elevators. Wolfson, no more than a casual foot away, instantly made the connection. He took his wallet from his back pocket and crossed to the man, tapping him on the shoulder. "San Francisco police," he said, showing his badge. "Sorry to bother you, sir, but would you mind telling me your name?"

The little man blinked at him from watery eyes.

"Miller," he said in a fuzzy, classroom voice. "Charles Miller."

"Mind waiting here just a minute, Mr. Miller?"

Wolfson went to the desk and opened his wallet again. "I'd like to see this gentleman's registration card, please."

The clerk produced the information. "Charles Miller, 10337 Lombard Street, San Francisco."

Wolfson copied down the address and returned the card. When he swung back to Miller, the little man was staring vaguely up at the hotel clock, idly juggling the room key.

"You live here in San Francisco, don't you, Mr. Miller?"

"Yes." The voice seemed on the verge of disappearing.

"Then why are you checking into a hotel?"

Miller shrugged. "Business."

"What kind of business?"

Miller looked up again at the clock, as if he were a small boy waiting impatiently for a recess.

"What kind of business, Mr. Miller?"

"I have to meet a few people. Salesmen, mostly."

Wolfson glanced at the carpet. "And no luggage?"

"Just overnight."

Wolfson studied his face closely. Could he be mistaken? Was there a chance that this was a look-alike, a near-perfect double? There was a tiny white scar just below Miller's left eye that seemed to underscore the man's essential blankness. That scar and the rest of the description could be checked by teletype this afternoon.

"I'm afraid I'm going to have to ask you for some identification."

After a slight pause the man patted most of his pockets and finally fished an old wallet from somewhere inside his jacket. He held it out.

"No, you go through it. Social security card, driver's license. Anything."

The man thumbed through a small packet of cards and handed him a license. It was State of California issue and the name was Charles Miller.

As Wolfson studied it a group of bystanders had begun to gather, trying to edge closer.

"Sorry to trouble you like this, Mr. Miller, but I'd like you to come with me. It shouldn't take more than a half-hour or so."

The little man looked wistfully at the elevators. "But I thought I could . . ." His voice threatened to disappear again. "Is it important?" he asked.

"I've got a car outside. It'll be as quick as I can make it."

"Well . . . I suppose so." He looked down at the key in his white, plump hand. "What should I do?"

Wolfson began to feel a little sorry for him. "You've already registered. They'll hold the room for you." He guided the man toward the door. "You'll be back in plenty of time to keep your appointments."

Outside in the bright, almost holiday air, Miller seemed dazed and lost. A cable car jangled, and he stiffened upright with the sound. Wolfson took his arm and led him up the hill, watching him carefully. The man was blinking hard in the glittering sunlight, but he looked more bewildered than trapped.

When they reached the automobile Wolfson held open the door, then got in and started the engine, throwing his companion a quick, assessing glance. The man was staring down at his hands, still toying with the key.

"Mr. Miller," Wolfson said, driving toward Market, "there's something that bothers me. You haven't once asked why I'm taking you in."

Miller shrugged listlessly. They were passing Union Square and a pigeon sprang gray and frightened across the windshield.

"Why aren't you interested?"

"I imagine I'll find out."

"I imagine you will." It would take only a short time to verify. And he was pretty sure that Miller wouldn't be returning to his hotel.

He parked the car a block off Market and walked the little man up the steps of the station house. There was no one in the squad room, just a few stale newspapers and the smell of new paint. He left Miller alone in the interrogation room and went down the corridor of Sy Pagano's office.

Pagano was leaning on the windowsill, looking up at the sky. "I haven't seen a gull in weeks," he said. "You think it's the fallout of something?"

Wolfson didn't bother closing the door. "Got something, Sy."

"Yeah?"

"Brought in a man by the name of Charles Miller. I think it's an alias."

Pagano was looking up at the sky again. "Who do you think he is?"

"Frederick Lerner. The school teacher from Santa Barbara who killed those two women last week."

Pagano turned abruptly from the window. "Are you sure it's him?"

"The description fits. L.A. sent a wire-photo up yesterday. They mentioned he might have headed for San Francisco."

"Where'd you spot him?"

"The Golden Gate Hotel. He was checking in without luggage."

Pagano picked up the phone and punched a button. "I'll call L.A., get more information. Where've you got him?"

"Interrogation." Wolfson went out and walked back to the other office. Miller was sitting in a chair, looking at the wall. His eyes squinted slightly in the bright rush of light from the window. Wolfson drew the shade and sat down with him. He took his time lighting a cigarette. "Sorry. You want one?"

"I don't smoke."

"How long have you lived in San Francisco, Mr. Miller?"

The little man rubbed his eyes. "Only a few weeks."

"Where did you live before that?"

"New York. My company sent me out here."

Wolfson got up, went back to the window. There was no one in the street beneath the half-lowered shade. A church clock chimed the hour and he checked it with his watch. "What line of work are you in, Mr. Miller?"

"Heavy goods jobbing."

"Married?"

There was a pause while the chimes succeeded each other like ripples in water. "Yes, I'm married."

"Happen to have a picture of your wife?"

"Is it important?"

Wolfson came back to him. The man's face was in half-shadow, but blinked up at the detective.

"It's important, Mr. Miller. Do you have one?"

The old wallet came out again. The man fumbled through the celluloid card folder, then held up a photograph. Wolfson took it over to the light. It was a crisp new picture of an attractive blonde, considerably younger than her husband. There was an interesting pout to the mouth. "Married long?" he asked.

"Few weeks."

The door opened and Pagano came in, carrying a file folder. "This is my partner, Mr. Miller, Lieutenant Pagano. You make that call, Sy?"

"Tried. The lines are tied up."

Wolfson took the photograph over to him. "This is Mr. Miller's wife."

Pagano studied it expressionlessly. He opened the file folder and removed two photos, tilting them so that only his partner could see.

"The victims," he said.

Wolfson touched the photos, moving them to catch the light. They both showed middle-aged women with vacant, trusting faces. Neither resembled the blonde.

"Your wife at home, Mr. Miller?" Pagano asked suddenly. It was his first acknowledgment of the man's presence.

"Yes."

Wolfson picked up the phone. "What's the number?"

Miller swung around quickly in the chair. "No—she's not at home. I made a mistake."

Wolfson met Pagano's eyes. "Oh? Where is she then?"

"She—left for Nevada this norming. Visiting some friends."

"I see. Has she got a phone number there?"

"No."

Pagano came around the side of the desk. "Stand up, Miller."

Miller got awkwardly to his feet.

"See that blackboard on the far wall? Why don't you go over there and pick up that piece of chalk."

Miller did as he was told.

"Fine," said Pagano, glancing at Wolfson again. "Now write something on the blackboard."

The little man seemed ready to cry. "What should I write?"

"Anything. I don't care."

Miller was motionless for a moment, then his hand glided up and he wrote "Charles Miller" in a graceful, sweeping line. He started to turn around but Pagano called, "No, stay there. Write your name again."

While Miller wrote, Pagano took the wallet from the desk and dug out the driver's license. *Nice*, Wolfson thought. *Very nice*. Over Pagano's shoulder, he compared the signature on the card with the writing on the board. They matched.

"You're pretty good at that blackboard," Pagano observed. "Some guys would have that chalk squeaking like a mouse. But not you. You sure you're not a school teacher or something?"

"Well . . . I've had some experience with blackboards," the little man said. He still faced away from them.

"Really?" Pagano said.

"Yes. Before my company sent me out here I was teaching some of the younger men, the sales trainees."

"But you never did any teaching at a school?"

"No."

Wolfson walked to the blackboard. "Here's another name. I want you to write 'Frederick Lerner.' Would you do that for me?"

The hand swung up without hesitation. It wrote the name in the same sure, graceful way.

"Uh-huh," Wolfson said. He went back to Pagano and gestured at the folder. Pagano opened it, and Wolfson removed another photo. He set it face up on the desk under the unlit lamp. "You can come back now, Mr. Miller. Have a seat."

The little man returned to the desk, blinking in confusion at them. He sat down wearily.

Wolfson pointed at the lamp. "Mind turning on the light? I want to show you something."

Miller snapped on the switch and then started, his hands gripping the arms of the chair. He was staring down at the photograph, a slow flush staining his face. "Where did you get that?" he asked.

"From our files," said Wolfson. He and Pagano edged closer to the desk. "It's a picture of a man named Frederick Lerner. He killed two women in Santa Barbara last week."

"But—but that's a picture of me," Miller protested. He picked it up and stared. "That's *me*."

Pagano took the photo out of his hands. "The Los Angeles police got it from the yearbook of that private school where you used to teach."

Miller shook his head. "That's impossible. I was never in Santa Barbara in my life. Anybody can tell you that, anybody!"

"Can they?" Pagano said. "How about your new wife? Can she tell us that?"

Miller turned pale, almost the color of the photograph. He lowered his eyes and brought a cupped hand to his forehead. "There's been a mistake," he mumbled. "You've got me mixed up with someone else."

Pagano dropped down in the chair beside him. "Where'd you get that wallet, Lerner? Who is Charles Miller?"

"*I'm* Charles Miller!" The little man seemed close to tears. "You can ask my friends, my business associates. They can tell you."

Pagano leaned closer. "I think you're a liar. You killed those two women, and you came up here to hide. Look at me!"

"It's all a mistake! Can't you see that?"

Pagano's voice grew louder, more insistent. "I think you should make a statement. I think you should tell us about those two women."

"I don't know what you're talking about!"

Wolfson interceded. "Take it easy, Sy. We still don't have a positive identification."

"This guy is Frederick Lerner. The photo matches, he lied about having a wife, and he used that blackboard like a pro. I say book him."

Wolfson thought it over. For a moment he wished he had never recognized the man, had walked right by him.

"What do we do?" Pagano pressed. "Lock him up or let him run? Come on, buddy, make up your mind."

Wolfson looked down at the little man. He was holding the photograph of Lerner again, studying it with dull incomprehension.

"Okay, we book him. I'm still not as sure as you are, but we can't take a chance."

"Take my word," Pagano said. "Everything checks."

"Let's go, Mr. Miller," Wolfson touched him gently on the shoulder. "First stop is Fingerprints."

Miller nodded. He stood up and groped his way toward the door.

Pagano leaned against the windowsill, slapping the file angrily against his hip. "When you're finished," he said, "bring him back. I'm going to try L.A. again."

He was beginning to dial the phone when Wolfson closed the door.

In the fingerprint office Miller was disinterested as they rolled his fingers on the inked glass. Wolfson sat in a corner, smoking a cigarette and thinking. Something was wrong; Charles Miller—or whatever his name was—was too mild, too apathetic for a murderer.

A minute later there was a soft knocking at the door and Pagano looked in. "Wolfson? Could I see you?"

Wolfson followed him out, stamping his cigarette into the scarred floor. "You reach L.A.?"

"Yeah." Pagano didn't look at him directly. "They picked up Frederick Lerner last night."

"What!"

"Caught him hiding out in a friend's place near the U.C.L.A. campus. It's him, no chance of error."

Wolfson tried not to show his relief. "How do you like that!" he said. "The guy looks just like him. The two could be twins."

Pagano sighed and held up his hands. "We goofed. We've done it before, we'll do it again. Look, you want to explain things to our friend in there? I'm not good on apologies. Tell him we're sorry, we made a mistake, the works." He grinned sourly. "You were always the diplomat. And give him a lift back to the hotel. He looks like he's gonna collapse any minute."

It was a silent drive to the Golden Gate. Miller sat brooding in the front seat, completely withdrawn. He had taken Wolfson's apology blankly, once or twice looking at the smudge marks on his fingers.

"Tell you what," Wolfson said, trying to brighten the atmosphere. "We'll have a drink at the hotel. On me."

Miller shook his head.

"No thanks. You don't have to do that."

"All right, but don't worry about anything. Nobody will ever know it happened. We didn't put you on the blotter so there's no record."

In the lobby of the Golden Gate Wolfson managed an awkward goodbye and sent the little man toward the bank of elevators. When the doors slid closed he breathed a sigh of relief. The next time he would think twice before taking someone in for questioning.

He was about to leave when he heard his name being paged. There was a telephone call for him at the main desk.

Pagano was on the line.

"Thought I could catch you there. On a hunch, I called Miller's place on Lombard. His wife answered."

Wolfson frowned.

"I thought he said she was in Nevada."

"He lied. She's going to Nevada all right, but not to visit any friends. Reno, Nevada."

"She's divorcing him?"

"That's right. You should have heard her on the phone. Sounds like a real swinger. She says it broke him up pretty bad but she doesn't care. Guess it was one of those May and December things."

"The poor guy," Wolfson said. "And we didn't make matters any easier for him."

"Yeah. Well, I thought you'd be interested. That'll be the last you'll ever hear of Mr. Charles Miller."

"Okay, Sy. Thanks."

He hung up and walked across the lobby to the doors on Powell Street. Well, it all figured. That's why Miller had seemed so indifferent and apathetic, even before he was asked to go downtown.

Outside, all along the curb, a crowd was beginning to gather. Cars had stopped and people were running up from the shops on Geary. Curious, Wolfson pushed through the door and looked up the steep stone slope of the hotel building. Miller stood on a ledge high up near the top, looking down at the crowd.

Now he knew why the little man had wanted a room on the twelfth floor.

LAWRENCE TREAT

Family Code

When the wheels touched ground at Tokyo airport early that morning, I breathed a sigh of relief. I was in Japan. I was safe. He hadn't tried to stop me.

I don't know what I had expected. In my fitful sleep on the plane, I'd dreamed that he came down the aisle, knife in hand, looking for me. Awake, I'd worried about a possible bomb planted in the hold and I'd gazed around at the sleeping passengers and wanted to warn them and tell them not to blame me. I was as anxious to live as they were. I, Richard Corwin, had a wife I loved and I wanted desperately to get back to her.

And now we'd landed. No bomb. He hadn't followed me. He'd given up.

I'd hidden the painting between a couple of blueprints, pasted them together, and rolled them up. I had it with me, in my flight bag. The Customs men weren't looking for fifteenth-century Zen paintings. The examination would be cursory. I'd see Iwasa Yazawa, and hand him the treasure.

I felt almost confident of it. Takahito had tried to kill me, and he'd failed. He wouldn't try again.

I thought of that afternoon three days ago when he'd come to my apartment in San Francisco. I import Oriental art goods, and I'd done business with his father and been entertained in his house. I'd known Takahito as a boy, in his student's uniform, and years ago I'd talked to him about America and our different customs while his father smiled gently and approved. Travel was good, a youth should see the world and learn foreign ways. There were other ideas besides the Japanese, and it was useful to study them. And so Takahito had come to America.

Nevertheless, as he walked into my apartment carrying the black portfolio tucked under one arm, I had misgivings. Why hadn't his father written me? why the surprise visit, without even a phone call? And why come here, to my home, instead of to my office?

Takahito's smile was pleasant, courteous—his manners were impeccable. I greeted him, offered him a chair, and asked how his father was and what he, Takahito, was doing here.

"I come for education," he said. "American college."

"Oh," I said. To question him further would have been indelicate and, besides, I could guess the answers. Takahito, the son of a distinguished family, had been brought up in luxury and was destined to enroll at the University of Tokyo. But he disliked work, he was spoiled and lazy, and he must have failed his examinations. His father, rather than see him lose caste and attend a university of lesser standing, had sent him to study in the United States.

"College very expensive," Takahito said. "I wish to sell this." And he untied the ribbons of the portfolio and opened it.

I gasped. Yazawa Senior had shown me that painting two years ago. It was a landscape of the Ashikaga period, with delicate reeds in the foreground and the suggestion of a lake at the foot of high mountains. And even if I hadn't seen the painting before I would have recognized the subtle style and the beautiful brushwork of Saga Shubun, a master of the Chinese school.

"It's your father's," I said in a low, troubled voice. "It's registered as a national treasure, it's illegal to take it out of Japan. Takahito, you must return it."

"National treasure very valuable," he said, still smiling. "I not bring back."

"Then I will," I said.

"Please," he said quietly. "You make mistake."

"Hardly," I said. "Takahito, I think I know your mind. You're in revolt against the old traditions you were brought up in, you feel that the world has changed. You have some wild idea that by breaking with your father and trying to be independent you'll somehow be in step with the new Japan. But you're making a bad mistake. Unless you do what I tell you to, I'll call the police and you'll end up in jail."

"Mistake," he said, "is coming to you." And he grabbed at the portfolio.

I pushed him and he staggered back, wheeled, and charged at me. "I kill you!" he yelled. "You not tell police—I kill you!"

He picked up the heavy standing ashtray, swung it with all his strength, and sent it crashing at me. I grabbed up the coffee table for a shield and ducked. It shattered with the force of his blow, but he still had the ashtray and raised it again and lashed out, switching it like a golf club and driving me back into a corner of the room.

That was when Janet came back with the groceries. At the sight of Takahito she screamed, dropped her bundles, and threw a milk carton at him. She followed it up with a couple of grapefruit.

She missed, but the barrage was too much for him. He scooped up the portfolio, yelled one final phrase at me, and dashed out. He shoved Janet out of his way and raced past her, slamming the door behind him.

Janet rushed over to me. "Are you hurt?" she asked. "Are you hurt? Tell me—what happened?"

I took her in my arms. "I'm O.K.," I said, "and you certainly saved my life." I hugged her tight and glanced past her. "Look!" I exclaimed. "The painting—he left it here—he must have thought it was in the portfolio!"

"What are you talking about?" she asked. "I don't understand."

I explained as well as I could. "Maybe I shouldn't have mentioned the police," I finished. "That would mean disgrace to the whole family, which is unthinkable. I couldn't actually do that, but I thought the threat would bring Takahito to his senses."

"That's why he tried to kill you."

I nodded. "Yes. Because, compared to betraying his father and stealing from him, murder is almost a minor, negligible crime."

"And what about the painting?" Janet said, pointing to it.

"I'll take it back to Yazawa, with the least possible fuss. I'm due to go to Japan next month, so maybe I'll make it a little earlier."

"You'll go as soon as you can," she said. "Richard, I'm scared. We'll move to a hotel and stay there until you leave, because Takahito is bound to come back here. He'll feel he has to kill you now." I agreed, and she knelt down and examined the painting. "It's beautiful," she said softly. "So beautiful."

I left three days later. I thought I saw Takahito at the airport, but I wasn't sure. Naturally I was nervous.

I had no trouble with the Customs or the immigration officials. I took the airport limousine to the hotel where I always stayed. The route was straight down a long avenue flanked by ugly little houses, but to me at least the signs with their lovely Japanese characters gave the street a picturesqueness and graciousness that was far from ugly.

I kept glancing behind to see if we were followed. I saw only taxis and bicycles and trucks, many of which were the small, three-wheeled variety. Shopkeepers were wetting down the streets. When we stopped for a traffic light, I heard the familiar sound of wooden clogs slapping on the pavement. A fair proportion of women still wore kimonos, but the majority were in western clothes. Japan in transition, I thought, and taking it hard. Takahito's problem of adjustment was no exception.

My hotel was a new modern building, and I walked into a broad cool lobby that buzzed with activity. I headed for the desk, where the clerk remembered me and greeted me with the warm courtesy that comes so naturally to the Japanese.

I put down my bag with the precious painting. I straddled it, glanced at the people nearest me. A man with a moustache changing money, a woman arranging a trip to Hakone. He looked English, she was plainly American. I had nothing to worry about. Nevertheless I pressed my ankles tightly against the bag while I unclipped my pen and filled out the registration card. Name, address, date of arrival, passport number. I reached into my pocket for my passport. It wasn't there.

I put the pen down and searched my side pockets. Nothing. I emptied my inside pocket, pulled out papers, letters, my address book. Still no passport.

The clerk smiled. "You find it later," he said, to reassure me. "There is no need now."

"I had it an hour ago," I said anxiously. "I had it when I went through Immigration. I couldn't have lost it. Impossible."

"I will make search," the clerk said, as if he located lost passports every day, knew exactly where to look, never failed.

"I have to find it," I said obstinately. I felt that Takahito was at the bottom of this. Somehow he'd managed to—

Then my eye caught my raincoat lying on top of my big bag at the other end of the lobby. And I remembered. I'd stuck the passport into the pocket of my raincoat.

I laughed in relief. "Over there," I said, and I crossed the lobby. The clerk followed, watched me pick up the coat and shove my hand in a pocket. My fingers touched the all-important passport and I pulled it out. The crisis was over.

"Here it is!" I said happily.

An American tourist, lounging in a chair and obviously bored, asked me what had happened. I explained. He started to tell me how he'd once lost a passport. The anecdote was long and pointless. I listened impatiently and cut him off as quickly as I could. Then I returned to the desk, completed the registration form, and bent down to get my flight bag. It was gone.

"Who?" I exclaimed, and stopped. First I misplaced my passport, now my bag. I felt like an idiot.

"Something is wrong?" the clerk said.

"My bag—I left it here, I had it next to my feet."

The clerk nodded. "You did not carry it across the lobby."

I whirled, saw the Englishman who'd been changing the money, and walked over to him. "My bag," I said. "Did you notice it? Who took it? Did you—"

"Beg pardon?" he said coldly and gave me a blank look.

I wanted to yell out, to tell the fool clerk that a valuable painting had been stolen under his nose while he'd watched me get my raincoat. His job was at the desk, he shouldn't ever have left it.

But I couldn't make a fuss. I had no right to have the painting in my possession. It belonged in Yazawa's collection, he kept it in his stone earthquake-proof vault, and I could be arrested for having it. It was a national treasure, registered with the government, held by Yazawa in sacred trust for the people of Japan. I was helpless.

"It contained something of value?" the clerk asked.

"No," I said quickly. "Nothing much. My overnight things. Somebody must have taken it by mistake. Let me know when it's turned in."

The clerk, cleared of responsibility, smiled gratefully. He handed a key to the boy, who took my big bag and brought it to my room.

I sat there for a while, thinking. If Takahito had the painting, he'd take it back to America as soon as he could. And I had to stop him.

I went out at once, took a taxi to the office of Japan Airlines, and requested space on the first available flight to the States. There was nothing for a full week. I asked them to check with other carriers, and they phoned. Absolutely impossible, they reported. Nothing for at least two days.

Good, I thought. If I can't leave today, neither can Takahito.

I returned to my hotel, called Yazawa, and made an appointment for the morning. I said nothing about Takahito, nor did he.

The ringing of my phone startled me and I picked it up.

"Hello?" I said.

"Mr. Corwin?" The voice, speaking with a Japanese accent, was unfamiliar to me. "You lose something important?"

"Where is it?" I asked excitedly. "Who are you and—"

The phone went dead, and I put the receiver down slowly. Takahito, and no one else, knew about the picture. The voice had not been Takahito's, nor would he need to ask whether I'd lost anything.

Who, then? And why the strange question?

I sat in my room and tried to figure things out. If Takahito had come to Tokyo, his purpose was to get the picture and prevent me from seeing his father. In that case, I knew the danger point—Yazawa's art shop. It was located in the middle of a narrow street, barely wide enough for two small cars to squeeze past each other. It was the bottleneck, and I was certain to go there.

I had, then, no worries until I took that last step, no obstacles until I reached the final one. And there—a hand would grab me, a knife would thrust out, and it would be all over.

And if Takahito was not in Tokyo? Then someone else had stolen the painting and would be caught when he tried to dispose of it. The police would trace it to me, and as a result I'd have to close up my business and look for some other means of livelihood, because the illegal possession of a national treasure would ruin my reputation. I'd be through, and the Yazawa family would suffer a deep disgrace.

At six o'clock my phone rang again.

"Mr. Corwin?" a voice said. It was soft, and the accent was not Japanese. Oriental, I thought, but definitely not Japanese. "Mr. Corwin, I perhaps have something which you lost. I think you desire to have it again."

"What?" I asked. "Where did you find it, and who are you?"

"It is my pleasure to return it, but I think you will wish to offer reward. Please to come to Osacone Restaurant, in Shinbashi section, and bring much money."

"How will I get there?"

"I will be pleased to send taxi, and taxi-man will bring you."

"How much do you want?" I asked.

"It is so very complicated," he purred. "We will talk of that, the two of us. Such a pleasure." And he hung up.

I went downstairs. The hotel was set back from the street, and the driveway and parking area were in front of the entrance. I paced nervously up and down, reentered the hotel, stepped outside again, lit a cigarette, took a few puffs, and stamped it out. I was jittery, but at least I didn't have to deal with Takahito.

The sending of a taxi didn't bother me. Very few of the streets in Tokyo have names, so addresses are complicated. The simplest way to find me would be to hire a cab near the restaurant, send the driver to my hotel, and tell him to bring me back to the restaurant.

I watched a couple of taxis pull up to the hotel, discharge their passengers, and drive off. But the third cab was empty and the driver put on his brakes, took a piece of paper from the seat next to him, and examined the writing. I figured this was my man, and I approached him.

"You came for me?" I said. "Mr. Corwin?"

The driver understood no English, but he climbed out and peered at me uncertainly. After a moment, he handed me the slip of paper. The message on it was in Japanese.

I shook my head to indicate that I didn't understand. He motioned towards the lobby of the hotel, and I nodded. The clerk would interpret. When I turned around, Takahito was standing a few feet away.

"You!" I exclaimed and tensed up, waiting for the attack.

Takahito merely smiled. "I wish to help," he said quietly.

"I don't need your help, or want it," I said stiffly.

Takahito shrugged and spoke to the driver in Japanese. The driver answered him, opened the door of the cab, and got in.

"He say he take you to a Korean gentleman," Takahito said. "What for?"

"None of your business."

"What for?" Takahito asked again. "You lose something?"

I stepped back. "Oh—*you* called this afternoon. Or rather a friend of yours called, and then hung up."

Takahito nodded, admitting that I'd guessed right. "Koreans dangerous, and very tricky," he said. "I accompany you."

"The hell you will!" I said.

"Please—show me paper."

"Get out of my way," I said.

Takahito grabbed and got his fingers on the note. I hit him with my elbow and he bounced sideways, tearing the paper in two. He clawed at the piece I was still holding. In a rage, I have him a vicious shove that sent him reeling back. He fought to keep his balance, couldn't make it, and fell heavily. I jumped into the cab and slammed the door.

"Go!" I yelled. "Fast—quick—get going!"

The cab driver understood what I meant and started with a jerk that slapped me against the back of the seat. Through the rear window I saw Takahito pick himself up, start to run after the car, and then stop. It swung into the street and picked up speed.

I stared at the bit of paper I still held. It probably told the clerk that the cab was the one I was waiting for. I crumpled the scrap and stuck it in my pocket.

During the drive across Tokyo, I kept my eyes closed. Nobody drives in a straight line or relinquishes the right of way. Other cars are enemies and you fight them in a war of nerves, with the horn one of your chief weapons. Passengers should never look, and I didn't.

I had plenty of other things to worry about, and what scared me most was Takahito's relentless determination. He'd followed me five thousand miles across the Pacific, and he'd been watching me all day. Somehow he'd found out about the loss of the bag with its precious contents and he realized I was his only means of recovering it. Temporarily I was safe from him, but as soon as I had the picture again, he'd return to the business of killing me.

I shuddered.

Eventually the cab turned into a narrow street and halted in front of a small house. It had no sign. The door opened almost at once, and a maid bowed and motioned me inside. I paid the driver and stepped into a vestibule with a damp concrete floor. There was a small bar to the right. In front of me, on the raised wooden platform, were a half dozen pairs of slippers. I took off my shoes and exchanged them for slippers.

The maid bowed again and spoke to me. I had no idea what she was saying, but she gestured to me to go upstairs, and I went. I was in a Japanese-style restaurant, and a good one, where you had to make reservations ahead of time and where you ate in the privacy of an individual room. There would be no chairs and no furniture in it except the low table.

At the head of the stairs I saw a doorway. The paper-and-lattice shoji had been slid back. I kicked off my slippers and stepped inside.

A small chubby man was kneeling in front of the table. On it stood a bottle of *sake* and a pair of cups. My flight bag lay on the floor beside him.

He bowed low. "Mr. Corwin," he said.

I nodded curtly and sat down crosslegged on the cushion opposite him. He smiled, indicated the *sake* cups, and lifted the bottle. I held my cup for him to pour. We drank in silence.

"So pleased that you come," he said politely. "I think you have questic s to ask me."

"No," I said. "Just give me my bag or else I'll take it. Obviously you picked it up in the hotel lobby while I went over to my other baggage. You think it's valuable and you want a reward." I opened my wallet and took out a ten-thousand-yen note. "Here," I said.

He didn't touch it. "I think you joke," he said.

"Take it or leave it," I said, and started to get up.

He raised his hand. "If police find contents of bag," he said, "then you have great trouble. They ask how you possess so valuable painting. Then the newspaper tell about the dealer and the stolen painting, and the result—most unfortunate."

He was right about that. He had me boxed. "You have a proposition?" I said.

"I am business man," he said, "and my business is to make money. So I spend day finding out about you. It is so peculiar, I think, that you bring registered national treasure *to* Japan, and that you hide it so carefully. The Customs men much interested."

"You stole my bag," I said. "So where do you come off?"

"Please to use polite words," he said solemnly. "I think the bag is lost, so I try to restore to rightful owner, which I now do. But this—" He indicated the note. "This is not adequate thanks."

"What is?"

"Ten thousand dollars," he said.

"You're crazy!" I said angrily. "I don't have that much. And if I did, I wouldn't give it to you." I stood up and my intention to sock him and take my bag must have been pretty clear.

He smiled, and pulled a gun. "I advise not," he said. "You see, I come prepared."

I took his advice. Then, to my surprise, I saw him gasp and lean back. I heard a light footstep behind me and I whirled. Takahito was there, moving forward slowly. The knife that he held had an eight-inch blade of silvery, gleaming steel.

He kept his eyes on the Korean, but he spoke to me. "The taxi-man paper have restaurant map," he said. "I come, and I listen outside."

I backed up. A man with a knife and a man with a gun. When the man with the knife got close enough, the man with the gun would fire.

Apparently Takahito read my thoughts. "Perhaps loaded," he said. "Perhaps not. Soon I find out."

"Is loaded," the Korean said grimly. I backed off another step.

"I see him take bag this morning," Takahito said. "You cross lobby and leave it, and he take. I wish to follow, but he go out back way and I lose him. Then I wonder, does he have painting, or do you have?"

"And your friend called to find out," I added.

"Take bag," Takahito ordered crisply.

The gun shifted to cover me. "Gentlemen," the Korean said. "Everything so easily arranged." His free hand reached out and touched my bill. "Ten thousand yen is ten thousand yen, and each of us happy."

"No," said Takahito. "You try blackmail once, you try again. I do not trust you with honor of my family."

The gun swung back and pointed at Takahito. Takahito blinked and made a sudden lunge. I leapt back and sought the protection of the wall. I heard a grunt, then an agonized, gutteral moan, but there was no shot. I turned and saw the knife buried deep in the Korean's chest. Takahito was kneeling above him.

"Take bag," he said hoarsely, "and go. You never here, never see him, painting never leave the house of my father."

I picked up the bag and left.

In the morning I read the item in the paper concerning the murder of a Korean named Choi Soo. He was known to the police as a petty thief who hung around hotels and preyed on tourists, and he had been stabbed by an unidentified man who had committed suicide after the act. When found, Choi Soo had an imitation gun in his hand. It was believed that the assailant had killed without realizing that the gun was harmless. His motive for suicide was not clear.

I went to see Yazawa around ten o'clock. He was waiting for me in the Japanese-style room behind his office. The flower arrangement in the recessed *tokonoma* was a work of art, the painting on the scroll above it was a rare and ancient Buddha.

Yazawa bowed low when I entered and I bowed equally low. He motioned me to the seat of honor, with my back to the *tokonoma*, and I sat down. We spoke quietly, as old friends do, while a servant brought in the tea.

As soon as we were alone I handed him the painting. He glanced at it only long enough to identify it.

"It is a burden," he said. "It is not right for one man to hide a thing of such beauty. I think I give it to a museum."

"That's a good idea," I said. "Takahito—"

He raised his hand to his lips, in token of silence. "My son is dead," he said slowly. "There is no Takahito."

I wondered how I could tell him that before Takahito had died he had returned to the truth and the honor of the old ways. But Takahito had discovered them too late, and the real lesson, combining the best of the new with the best of the old, had escaped him.

I lifted my cup and slowly sipped my tea, but I did not speak. Nor did my friend.

WILLIAM BANKIER

To Kill an Angel

I remember the day the letter arrived and things started happening. I rode up on the escalator from the Peel Street Metro station and walked a block to the club on Stanley Street. The place was almost empty at eleven-thirty in the morning. Jonathan Fitzwilliam, the owner, known to most of us as Johnny Fist, was holding a crumpled sheet of note paper, squinting at whatever was written on it.

The Ninety-Seven Club is lit by small lamps on oak tables beside upholstered chairs. Floor-to-ceiling bookshelves cover every wall. There are books stacked on the carpet, books piled on the mahogany bar and a few standing between the liquor bottles on the mirrored shelves. Many of them lay open. You can walk into The Ninety-Seven and find yourself first intrigued, then trapped, by a different book every day. Johnny Fist thinks this is a good thing.

Correction: you can't just walk into The Ninety-Seven. The club has a private membership which Johnny keeps to 100. His accountant, Mervin Stein, says this is bad business but Johnny says he wants room to breathe.

My name is Dennis Masterson. I am a professional singer with a half-hour radio show three days a week on the CBC, and I like to think of myself as Jonathan Fitzwilliam's best friend.

When I walked into the club, Johnny looked up from reading a paper in his hands, peering at me through lamplight. "Milligan is dead. Did you hear?"

"Yes. Killed by some dumb cop in New Orleans."

"Don't blame the cop. Milligan was running with a nasty pair." Johnny lowered this note that seemed to have him puzzled, forgetting it while he considered how our old friend had been conned. "They left a dead body in his bedroom."

"Well," I said, "there goes the ball team."

Milligan was a former pro baseball player who ran a restaurant on Ste. Catherine Street. The restaurant sponsored a team in the Snowdown Fastball League and a few of us used to have some fun on summer evenings, behaving gloriously on the diamond and then going and hoisting a lot of draft beer at the Texas Tavern.

But not any more.

I sniffed the air. "What's on for lunch?"

"Beef curry. Spinach pie."

Dallas came in from the supply room and struggled behind the bar with three cases of beer stacked in front of him. I moved onto one of the upholstered stools where I could relax and watch him work. "Hey," I said, "if you get a minute, you might open me a cold Guinness."

Dallas did, and as he poured the black beer, frowning below the headband that held back his thick blond hair, he said, "How about settling up your tab?"

"I'll clear it on Monday," I said, sipping my beer and wiping my upper lip. "I have a check coming for a couple of commercials."

Singing commercial music tracks was how I happened to meet Johnny Fist in the first place. A few years back, Johnny was the most popular English radio voice in Montreal. He got called on frequently by the ad agencies to do announcer tracks. So we showed up in the same studio quite often and we soon discovered we laughed at the same things.

So we ended up more than once around the same tavern table. One of these times Milligan joined us and graciously, or perhaps drunkenly, invited me to join the fastball team. I went along and booted a few easy chances at second base, absorbing the razzing, accepting the demotion to right field where I could do less harm. And all the time, Jonathan and I drifted closer together.

This was before the catastrophe that turned him upside down and almost buried him. In those days, Johnny had a wife and son, so part of our time together was spent in his apartment watching the golden girl spoon cereal into the golden baby while we sat at the kitchen table and played cribbage.

But I had better keep my mind on this story. It is too easy to slip back into what used to be with me and Johnny, which is not what is today.

I took my beer over to where he was tapping the sheet of note paper against his teeth and blowing across it with a rhythmic buzz like a Walt Disney bee.

"What *is* that thing you're playing with?"

"Something very sad," he said, handing it to me. "And maybe dangerous."

It was a message scrawled in red pencil in the largest hand I have ever seen. I read the note twice.

"Dear Jonathan, For the sake of past friendship be my guide and help me perform the Lord's work. Let not the guilty go unpunished. The man's name is Sieberling, or maybe Emery Disco, and he lives somewhere in Montreal. With God's help, I will bring this evil-doer to justice. First we find him. Then we do what must be done. Don Cleary."

I handed the note back to Johnny. "Sounds like a religious nut. Where do you find your friends?"

Johnny did not smile. He held up a torn envelope.

"According to the postmark, this was mailed in Baytown over a week ago. The address isn't accurate so delivery was held up. Cleary may be in Montreal right now."

"Then he'll contact you."

"He may have tried while I was away. Dallas said there were a couple of phone calls but the guy wouldn't leave his name."

I thought about the name in the note—Emery Disco. It rang a bell. "Isn't Disco a member of the club?"

"That's right."

"How does your friend know that?"

"He doesn't. He just wants me to help locate the man. He assumes Disco is in hiding and he figures I know my way around Montreal."

"Sounds like a spy story."

"It's no joke. Disco did something to Cleary years ago." A key turned in the front door lock and a wedge of noonday sun clanged in. The luncheon crowd was beginning to arrive.

"We should have food, landlord, and fine wine." It was that manic, six-foot redhead, Noble Kingbright, come over from the agency with Linda Lennox. And he was in full cry, green eyes glittering, both rows of teeth unsheathed, heels pounding the floor, little Linda propelled along like a marionette at the end of one of his rangy arms.

"I'll tell you later about Cleary," Johnny said. "And remind me to telephone Disco and warn him."

Johnny confronted the newcomers and took Linda away from Kingbright, lifting her like a doll. Big as Kingbright is, he had to look up to my friend Jonathan.

Linda and Johnny had been seeing each other for several months. She had come from Alabama a year before, following her boy friend who was evading military service. Linda is an advertising writer, one of the good ones, and she soon found a job at Parenti Agency where she makes a lot of bread. Her American friend, whose name I could never remember, was a dour stud hiding his light under a bushel of hair but he must have had something because Linda is no fool. Anyway, he decided to split and fly to Denmark but Linda liked the way Montreal was falling into line for her, so they parted his beard and kissed goodbye.

Enter Johnny Fist who saw something fine in the Lennox girl, sitting by herself nights at his bar, drinking sour mash bourbon and taking down the right books from the musty shelves. Maybe he always wanted a girl one quarter his size. Anyway, soon she was climbing the winding stairs to Johnny's apartment after The Ninety-Seven closed for the night. And our cribbage games became less frequent.

Now Johnny said, without looking at Kingbright, "Keep your hands off my woman, you red-headed, alien sonofabitch, or I'll punch large holes in your body."

He steered both of them to a table and said, "Sit here, have a drink on me, then have lunch on you. I recommend the spinach pie." And he was off towards the kitchen, glancing once again at Cleary's erratic note, folding it, tucking it into his back pocket.

Linda said to me, "Sit down, Denny. Have a bit of lunch with us."

I was not anxious to eat with these two. I liked Linda Lennox but her companion put me on edge so I said, "Save me a place, Linda. I have to settle up with Dallas." I went to where the bar angles out of sight of the main room behind an island bookshelf and called Dallas over.

"Got another Guinness back there?"

He fished one out of the cooler. "What's the matter with Johnny this morning?"

"Is something the matter?"

"The mail came and he opened this letter and got all edgy. Last time I saw a guy that nervous, it was alimony payments."

"It's a note from some old buddy back in Baytown. The way it's written he seems to be around the bend. I suppose Johnny is worried the guy is going to show up."

"That's all we need in this place, another screwball." Dallas looked out into the clubroom. From where he was standing he could see Linda's table and just then we heard Kingbright let go with one of his maniacal laughs.

"Beautiful," he boomed, using all ten cubic feet of chest capacity, "the gun becomes the hero! We build the whole film around the gun."

I could hear Linda trying to hush the man, to bring him back down to the tone of the room.

At this point, perhaps I should explain how Jonathan Fitzwilliam became financially independent. It was three years ago. Johnny's wife and baby were off to Winnipeg to spend a few days with her mother. I drove the car that took all four of us out to Dorval and I stood with Johnny at the gate as we waved them aboard the plane. I can still see those golden heads moving up the stairs in the jostling crowd, and I can feel the empty silence we took back with us to the car.

"Hey," I remember saying, "we're a couple of reckless young bachelors for the next few days."

Johnny did a high kick with one leg in the direction we were heading, hunching his shoulders and flapping his hands. "Which way to the vaudeville show?" he cried.

We heard the news bulletin on the car radio as we neared Montreal. The airplane had gone into a hillside five minutes after takeoff. I wanted to turn around and head back to Dorval but Johnny kept me heading straight. He was like a closed door.

"She's dead," he said. "They're both dead."

We went to the radio station and watched the Telex and he was right, they were all dead, everybody aboard the airplane. Johnny's fellow workers whispered around, some of them coming to him in tears, and through it all he was like the crown of an iceberg floating in a dead calm sea.

That's how he remained when he learned she had taken out two life insurance policies, each one worth a hundred thousand dollars. The company paid and the money went into the bank and Jonathan did not refer to it.

Then one day he came into the studio at six o'clock to do his morning show. He had a Church of England hymn book and began reading it on the air, starting with page one. When the engineer joined him at 7:00 and answered the screaming telephone, Johnny was attending to nothing else—no music, no commercials, no time checks, no sports scores or weather.

The engineer did what the station manager told him to do over the telephone. He put on a musical feed from the control room. Then he went into the studio to tell Johnny he could stop now, but Johnny paid no attention. I was not there, but the way they tell it he was still reading when the manager showed up at nine and when the boss tried to close the hymn book, Johnny bloodied his nose with a backhand.

That brought in the cops and it ended with the studio turned into a room full of kindling and broken glass and with Jonathan Fitzwilliam being taken away in restraints.

He spent a month in the Allen Memorial talking to the doctors and responding to medication. Then he came out, calm and apologetic, and threw away the pills they had given him, switching to booze. Then he disappeared and we thought our old friend had switched cities. But Mervin Stein, who was doing Johnny's personal income tax in those days, checked the bank and found the $200,000 was still there.

For a while we speculated foul play, or even suicide, but a body that size has to show up. And it did, six months later in New York City. They shipped him home under sedation with a big-armed male nurse, all at the radio station's expense. This time my friend was released from the Allen a very healthy man. He was wide open now, absolutely in touch with reality, and ready to resume his life.

"Lenore would think I was pretty stupid," he told me, using his wife's name as if she were in the next room, "leaving all that money in the bank. I'm going to talk to Koshe about a thing I have in mind."

Koshe was Johnny's nickname for Mervin Stein. They did talk, about buying a failed second-hand bookshop on Stanley Street and putting it on a sound business footing as a private club, reading room, drinking and eating place, chess parlour and occasional dance hall. In surprisingly short order it all happened, and they called it The Ninety-Seven. Johnny explained the name to me. "You know, Den, it wasn't just my wife and son who died in that air crash. Ninety-seven souls all went together. I'm not the only one who lost people that day." Later, he harked back to the point. "Don't ever worry about dying, old sod. You won't be alone. It's you and me and everybody who ever lived."

Johnny's smile when he told me this was like afternoon sunshine at the ball park.

So much for my friend leaving the radio business and becoming an independent club owner. You should also know how he got his nickname.

There used to be a late-evening radio show from the lounge of a jazz club called The Riverboat, and it was chaired by Jonathan Fitzwilliam. He would play records from his private collection of Basies and Luncefords, and even an occasional Bing Crosby from the early years when the man was really singing. One night Johnny was talking on the air to Arnie Pender, the club owner. I remember it well; I was schlepping a free drink at the celebrity table. Suddenly we all became aware of an obnoxious patron with a sweating face and a tight blue suit who was leaning into the interview. I remember what he said. He said, "Hey faggot. Did you hear about the two queer radio announcers? Jonathan Fitzwilliam and William Fitzjonathan."

Johnny didn't even stand up. He just drew back and drove a ten-inch right-hand jab into the dimple in the protruding jaw. The heckler went down into an empty chair, head lolling, then slid out of the chair onto his knees, a slow, heavy decline onto the floor face down, like a rolled-up carpet collapsing.

After the applause, Arnie Pender produced a label that would last forever. "Never mind Jonathan Fitzwilliam," he said. "You should be called Johnny Fist."

Anyway, enough with ancient history. Back to what was happening at The Ninety-Seven at lunch hour on this hectic afternoon. Dallas was pushing plates of beef curry across the counter and I wanted mine. I took a plate, went looking for a place to sit and found myself back where I did not want to be, across the table from Noble Kingbright with Linda on my left.

"That curry is hot stuff," Kingbright said. He went to get us another round of drinks which I, for one, did not want. But go argue with Hyperhost.

I looked at Linda. She has a funny way of drinking; she takes a swig, makes a face of mild disgust and then sets the glass down with an abrupt thrust away from her, turning her head at the same time as if that is definitely the last taste of booze she will ever tolerate. But a minute later, she is doing the same thing. I wanted to get her talking because Linda Lennox's speech is in the beguiling cadence of the Deep South. I'd pay to listen to her.

"Well then," I said, "how goes the battle?"

She looked at me; sparkling black eyes in a sweet, round face. "I just wish you would ask Jonathan to keep his hands off Noble."

She pronounced the word "hayunds." I relished it. "You felt the tension too?" I said.

"I declare, it's like the overture to World War Three when those two confront each other. And there's no use my speaking to Jonathan about it. He will not listen to me on the subject in any way, shape or form."

"You have to admit your friend comes on strong."

"Well he does, yes. But that's because he's a creative individual and at the moment he happens to have a very important project on his mind."

On his maaahnd . . . a sweet, hypnotic syllable. Then Kingbright came back with the drinks and broke the spell.

"That's right. I am into an original suspense film in which the pistol, the murder weapon, is the star," he said. "And I know just the pistol to use. A most photogenic weapon, all long and sexy and heavy in the hand."

"I didn't know you were a feature-filmmaker," I said. "I thought you produced TV commercials."

"For wages. Unfortunately, the family income to which I am entitled through blood is denied me on the grounds of a technicality. My baronial, Teutonic father chose not to honor my mother with a wedding ceremony."

I said, "You'll need tons of money to make a film."

"Ve haf vays of gettink ze necessary funds," Kingbright said, leaning back in his chair, eyelids lowered, letterslot lips spread in a slashing smile.

"I wish you luck." I glanced at Linda, who was watching Kingbright's performance with cold eyes. If the man was going to approach a backer for support, it was to be hoped he would sober up first.

The lunch crowd dispersed and it was after two o'clock when I got back to Johnny about the troublesome note. We were upstairs in his apartment above the club, Johnny with the telephone on his lap and a roster of club members in his hand. I was holding his guitar against my chest, plucking a few chords.

"I was hoping Disco might come in for lunch," he said, dialing. "I'd better call him."

"What is this Cleary thing?"

"It happened years ago, before I left Baytown and came down here. Cleary was a cop, the best man on the force. He could have gone on and become Chief if he'd wanted to stick at it. Hell, he could have run for Mayor—he was one of those guys you have to admire. Then this hassle happened with Disco."

"What hassle?"

"It's a long story. I'll tell you when . . ." I heard a natter of response on the phone. "Hello, Emery? It's Johnny. Where are you keeping yourself these days?"

They small-talked for a minute or so and then Johnny filled the man in on the note he had received. Disco seemed to treat it as a joke. I could hear him laughing. By the time the call ended, Johnny had agreed to come up to the house later in the afternoon and talk about how they should handle the situation.

Johnny emphasized his warning. "You may think you know Don Cleary from that one exposure to him, Emery. But believe me, I know him better. He's a stubborn guy."

We got out the cards and killed an hour with the cribbage board. Then my friend got up, a tailored mountain rising into the air. "Come on, let's go have a splash in Emery Disco's swimming pool. We've been invited."

"You've been invited."

"Wherever I go," he said, "you go. Damon and Runyon."

So I went with Johnny Fist on that hot, hazy afternoon and we flagged a taxi. Then we headed up Cote des Neiges onto the shaded plateau of Upper Westmount. Disco's house on Cherry Hill Crescent was concealed by leafy maples, but what we could see of it was grey stone and leaded glass and rich, grainy oak. We walked along the winding flagstone path, listening to the wealthy hush of summertime. There were no growling trucks in this neighborhood, no pedestrians, no kids screaming in the street. Even the grasshoppers kept their activity down to a respectful strum, and the birds whispered.

"How the other half lives," I murmured.

"You mean the other two percent," Johnny said.

He pulled the iron handle jutting from the stone wall beside the doorframe. Inside, at a distance, a well-tuned chime said, "Clong." A minute later it was my turn; a double clong.

"Let's look around at the back," Johnny said.

I followed him over a carpet of grass along the front of the house and between a high hedge and the side wall which was edged with petunias and marigolds.

"I wish you'd tell me what Disco did to your friend Cleary," I said. "I want to know how to act."

"It's a long story. He'll probably tell you himself better than I could."

We walked into the backyard and I closed the iron gate behind me. The area was enclosed on three sides by stone walls eight feet high, which were themselves masked by four poplar trees and one weeping willow which was in a position to cry a few leafy tears into the swimming pool. On the fourth side, the house stared down at us with what seemed like a hundred windows.

At first we thought the yard was empty and, in a sense, I suppose it was. There were a couple of deck chairs drawn up on the concrete patio beside the pool. There was a wicker-and-glass table with a paperback book on it and a pair of sunglasses.

"Emery?" Johnny said in what would pass around these parts for a loud voice. No answer, except a shiver passed along from one poplar tree to the others. Then we saw them in the pool.

I recognized Disco, even face down in the blue water surrounded by the red slick of his blood. He was wearing bathing trunks. The two women were fully dressed except for shoes. One had gray hair. The other was a younger person with long black hair fanning out on the surface of the water. All were floating with arms outstretched as though they were looking for something on the bottom of the pool.

The fourth corpse floated on its side, eyes open and tongue extended—a huge Alsatian dog.

"Good Jesus," Johnny said, "would you look at what he's done?"

"So you think Cleary got there ahead of us," I said. We were walking along Cedar Avenue with the city and the St. Lawrence River spread out below us, on our way back to the club on foot. After our session with the police and all the lifting of wet bodies from the pool, we needed the fresh air.

"I don't want to believe it, but what else is there?"

"Is that why you didn't show the Inspector the note you got?"

"I want to find Don first. I want to talk to him." Johnny was in full stride and I was hard pressed to keep even. "There has to be another explanation. If you knew Don Cleary the way I do, you'd understand why I say that. I can imagine a situation where he might kill Disco in a struggle. But not the wife and daughter. Not the dog."

"When are you going to tell me what Disco did to Cleary?"

"Right now," he said. "When Cleary was a Baytown cop, he happened to arrest Disco for a minor traffic violation. Emery was just driving through. Then he remembered the name and tied Disco in with a con job in Toronto. So he locked him up and called the Toronto cops to come for him."

"Emery a con man?"

"He had his little ways. The point is, he offered Cleary twenty thousand bucks to let him go. That was a mistake. Nobody bribes Don Cleary. But then Disco managed to slip a note and some money to a kid who brought in food from a restaurant. The result was, two friends of Disco's showed up pretending to be the cops who were coming from Toronto. Cleary fell for it and let Disco go with them."

"Okay, so Disco conned his way out of Baytown jail. Why didn't Cleary just put a routine tracer on him and forget about it?"

"Because it ate away at him. It was what everybody in town talked about for a long time. Cleary fell apart the winter after it happened. He disappeared for a while and we heard he was in Kingston sanitarium. He showed up next spring but they never took him back on the force."

"Poor bastard."

"Last I heard he was hustling beer at the Coronet Hotel."

It was rush hour on Sherbrooke Street when we got back down off the mountain. We had made a half-mile descent from heaven on earth into hell on wheels. The office crowd was heading for home in anything that would move. The roads were plugged with cars and the cars were packed with citizens, all windows open, all faces red and wet.

"Anyway," Johnny said, "the rap in Toronto—Disco squared that years ago. Everybody got paid most of what they invested and the book is closed."

"Does Cleary know that?"

"Don wouldn't want to know. There was a crime, there must be punishment. He could never bend an inch."

We were on Drummond Street. I followed Johnny into the Central YMCA lobby, heading for the long corridor that would lead us through to the exit on Stanley Street, a few doors above The Ninety-Seven. We were passing a bank of elevators when Johnny stopped dead. I piled into his massive back. He straightened me out and pushed me into one of the elevators just as the door was closing.

"Are we checking in?" I said. "I never knew you cared."

Johnny was not listening to me. In addition to the old guy handling the doors, there was one other man in the elevator. He was pale grey in color; that was what struck me first. In Montreal, in July, almost everybody carries some degree of sunburn but this long hollow face was made of parchment. His clothes hung on his bones. As he smiled at Johnny, pale green eyes flickered like lamps back inside his head.

"Dennis Masterson," Johnny said, "meet an old friend of mine from Baytown, Don Cleary."

The inside of Cleary's room on the tenth floor was untidy and the air was stale. There was no sign of a suitcase but a paper shopping bag lay on the floor, spilling a crumpled shirt. One rolled blue sock peeked out from under the bed.

Johnny sat on the window ledge, blocking most of the light. "I got your note, Don. Sorry I wasn't in when you telephoned."

Cleary said, "No problem. I was surprised how easy it was to find Disco."

So there it was. The man was so crazy he was about to take credit for the slaughter. Nobody said anything for half a minute. Cleary lowered himself onto the bed as though he had learned a way to keep his bones from separating. This left the leatherette armchair vacant so I sat down in it.

"Why did you kill them?" Johnny said.

"I didn't."

"Come on, Don. We just came from there. We found them all dead."

"That's how I found them. They were all dead."

Johnny Fist looked at me across the room. He wanted to believe this maniac.

"Then I wonder who did kill them," I said.

"The Avenging Angel."

"The Avenging Angel," I repeated, just so it would be clear on the record.

Johnny said, "Nobody is going to believe you if you say that, Don."

"It's the truth. Anyway, Disco has paid the price. That's all I wanted." Cleary put the edge of a thumb to his mouth and gnawed the tattered flesh, his eyes glazed.

We let some moments pile up around us. Then Johnny looked hard at me and said, "You wanted to go to the can, didn't you, Denny? Don, why don't you be a gentleman and show my friend where the can is."

I almost said something but then I realized he wanted to search the room. We went down the hall, Cleary and I, wasted a few minutes in the lavatory, then headed back to the room. He went in first and when I followed him and closed the door, I saw Johnny was holding a pistol with a silencer on the muzzle. It was a long nasty-looking weapon.

"This was in your top drawer," Johnny said. When Cleary remained silent, he added, "The police said the shooting had to have been done with a silencer."

Now Cleary said, "Not my gun."

"It doesn't have to be your gun. Is it the gun that killed Disco?"

"It must be."

"How did you get it?"

"I took it from the Avenging Angel. We struggled, but I had the strength to prevail."

"I wish I could believe that."

"Believe it, Jonathan. God brought me to this city so that I could see the wicked brought to justice."

The scene was starting to spook me. Cleary was standing there, flickering like a candle in the wind and Johnny was hesitating, trying to swallow something that was stuck in his throat.

"I'm sorry, Johnny," I said, "but I think your friend is a sick man. And you are now holding the murder weapon. If you take my advice, you'll deliver Cleary and that gun to Number Ten Station."

"I guess you're right."

"Of course I'm right. And you'd better turn in that note he sent you. That's evidence. It's against the law to conceal it."

Cleary looked right at me then for the first time. He seemed to be admiring me. "Let's get the hell out of here," I said.

We were on Maisonneuve, about a block from the police station, when Cleary made a run for it. He was walking between us and nobody was holding onto anybody. Suddenly he was off into the stream, heading back the way we had come. For a man who looked like he was on his last legs, he sure had pace. Johnny made a token move to go after him but then gave it up.

"You let him get away," I said.

"What could I do? I can't move in all these people."

"Like hell. You should have had a grip on him in the first place."

Johnny Fist looked at me, his eyes full of amusement. "What are you so excited about?"

"The man killed those people. And you let him get away."

"Maybe he killed them, maybe he didn't."

"Oh, come on, don't give me the Avenging Angel. It's him. He's a classic schizophrenic."

"So what if he is? What's it got to do with you?"

I had to think about that. After all, he was Johnny's friend, not mine. I'd never heard of Cleary before this morning. As for the dead Disco family, just read the papers. It's happening every day. Why was I so excited?

"He's a criminal," I said. "He broke the law."

Johnny smiled warmly. "I declare," he said, "you're starting to sound just like him." He headed back towards Stanley Street, his jacket pocket bulging. "Come on, let's get this gun put away in a safe place."

It's a funny thing how waves settle. I told myself when I came away from Emery Disco's backyard that I would never be able to get that scene out of my mind. Now here it was, two days later, with Cleary vanished from his YMCA room, and already I was getting on with the vital business of my life. Specifically, I was hovering around the piano in my apartment, hitting chords and performing my breathing exercises, hoping to extend my modest range by half a tone.

My telephone rang and it was Johnny. "Saturday morning without snooker pool is like a day without sunshine," he said.

"That's a good slogan," I said. "Why don't you sell it to the orange-juice people?"

"We'll shoot a game," he said. "Then if you want, you can stay with me while I go over and see Koshe. He has a quarterly statement for me to sign."

"Mervin Stein works on Saturdays?"

"It gets him out from under Mitzi and the kids."

Johnny and I met on the broad cement steps leading up to the third-floor level at Leader Billiards where all the snooker tables stand on a Saturday morning, shadowy and quiet under their dark green canopies. We selected cues while the attendant snapped on the light over table 19 and stamped our card in the time clock. I took it from him, paying at the same time for a couple of large Pepsis and four small bags of peanuts.

Jonathan led the way to the table, doffing his jacket, chalking his cue. "Who breaks?"

"Be my guest."

He slammed the cue ball into the triangle of reds with a powerful thrust of his cue. I waited until two red balls had dropped into pockets before I said, "No flukes off the break."

Johnny had been lining up his next shot but now he stepped back. "Go ahead," he said. "You'll need all the help you can get."

He was right. He made every shot on the table and I had to concede the first game by the time we got to the blue ball. In the second game, Johnny's attention began to wander. He missed a few shots and I made a good run that included three blacks, so when only the colored balls were left I was twenty points up. Then he was sitting staring at the table not seeing it.

"Your shot," I said.

He stayed where he was.

"The cops are saying it may be a gangland execution," he said. "Did you see the story in the *Gazette*?"

"Yes. But we know better, don't we? We met the Avenging Angel. We have his gun."

"Cleary could be telling the truth. He went there to arrest Disco—that would be his style. But he surprised the killer and took the gun away from him."

I looked at the oily floor and shook my head. "An experienced underworld hit-man gives up his gun to that walking wreck. Some scenario."

"Don't be fooled. Don is stronger than he looks."

"If it was a contract, the killer wouldn't make that mistake."

"They aren't that professional around here," Johnny said. "This isn't New York. Some of the local hoods are real meatballs."

I leaned my cue against the table and put my hands in my pockets. "Are we going to finish this game?"

"My mind isn't on it."

"Then who pays?"

"You pay. I haven't any money."

Johnny's business with his accountant took no time at all but we spent an hour in Stein's office anyway. It was a pleasant visit. Merv keeps a huge samovar on a table in his waiting room. The machine came from Russia with his grandparents who were smart enough to emigrate with dignity and their possessions before later generations had to leave on the run.

His girl made us tea and brought it into the office where we were sitting in deep black leather chairs on a white carpet around a low brass and glass table. The young lady had ebony skin and wore a wine velvet suit. She had gone to the trouble of cutting her hair very short and changing its color to ash blonde. She looked almost as splendid as Mervin himself, who was dressed in a powder blue suit with a white shirt open at the neck. He sparkled at the extremities with gold cufflinks and patent-leather shoes. His face was dominated by eyes as large and dark as ripe olives separated by a nose as bold as a monolith. His hair was a thundercloud.

"I understand why *you* work Saturdays," Johnny said, "but how do you get *her* to work Saturdays?"

"I removed a thorn from her paw," Stein said. "She'll do anything for me."

"Let's talk more about that," I said.

"No, let's talk about the murders," Johnny said. "Disco was a client of yours, wasn't he, Koshe?"

"For a long time."

"What do you think of the story in the paper today? Gangland execution."

Stein got up and went to the window and stood with his back to us, an elegant pose with one hand against the frame, his forehead balanced against his wrist. "It could be," he said. "Disco had enemies."

Johnny sat up in his chair and threw a quick glance at me. I got the message; not a word about Cleary.

"What enemies?"

Stein turned around. He cracked his long fingers at each of their many joints. "That's a matter of professional confidence, Johnny."

"Oh come on, Koshe, you aren't a priest. You don't hear confessions."

"Yeah, but if word gets around that I spill secrets, I could get hurt."

"Spill just this one. I won't say a word."

Stein looked at me. I said, "I'm Johnny's puppet. I only speak when he moves my mouth."

"Okay. I also do the books for The Riverboat lounge."

"Arnie Pender," Johnny said.

"I happen to know Disco was into Arnie for a lot of money and they were having trouble collecting."

"Money problems?" I said. "With that castle he lives in?"

"Don't be fooled. By the time the creditors are paid, the Disco estate will be a negative asset." Stein turned to Johnny. "It's possible they decided to make an example of him. Pender sent a gun around to hit Disco and the family showed up unexpectedly so he wasted them too."

His telephone rang then and it was his wife reminding him that he was going to take the kids to Westmount Park. His voice changed on us; it became a high-pitched, impatient harangue.

"Mitzi, I can't! I have people in the office right now. *You* take them. No, don't put Rodney on the phone. I can't talk to him now. Rod, tell your mother to come back on the line. Daddy is very busy today, Rod, you and Len will have to amuse yourselves. Well of course you can amuse yourselves . . ."

We left poor Mervin and took the scenic walk along Sherbrooke Street past the park, past Atwater Avenue with the Forum below us waiting for September so it could start packing in the hockey crowds again, past the red brick apartment buildings leading to Guy Street, and then past the rows of tiny shops with one dress or one painting in each window.

We arrived at The Ninety-Seven and I hated to go inside. Johnny held the massive oak door open for me, spilling out onto the sidewalk the metallic aroma of air-conditioning mixed with stale beer and a million exhaled cigarettes.

"Can't we go and sit in Dominion Square?" I asked him.

"Are you coming in?" He stood in the doorway, looking at me balefully out of the shadows. "I work here, remember?"

I followed him inside and soon wished I had not. Dallas met us at the foot of the winding staircase with an empty glass in his hand. He said to Johnny, "Linda is on her third one of these. She started at noon."

"Shit a brick," Johnny said and began tramping up the stairs, his shoes clanging on the metal treads. I went to sit at the bar.

"Anything for you?" Dallas asked me.

"It's early for me."

"It's early for most people." Right from the start, Dallas had been immune to the charms of Linda Lennox.

For a few minutes, the dialogue between Johnny and Linda was muted. Then they began to play it like performers on a stage. Their voices came ringing down the stairway.

"I don't want you getting bagged in the morning. It makes you a pain in the ass by four o'clock."

"How would you know? You're always out with your boy friend. When are you and Dennis getting married?"

Johnny talked low and fast for a few seconds. I suppose he was telling her I was downstairs. She sounded only a little restrained as she said,

"I don't care. It's true."

"What's wrong with you? You used to be somebody I could talk to. Now all you want to do is lush it up with that idiot Kingbright."

"He's a great relief after you. He doesn't just use me and walk away. Let go of me. I have to go to another man if I want any kind of consideration."

She came rattling down the stairway, her long skirt hitched up in one hand, her purse under her arm. There were tears on her cheeks and the dark eyes were a little out of kilter, as though she had been hit hard on the side of the head. Something was eating her up these days.

The place seemed awfully quiet after the front door banged behind her. For a few moments, the only sound was the squeak of Dallas's bar cloth on the rim of a glass. I got up and went to the foot of the stairs.

"Big John?"

"Yazzah!"

"How's about Dominion Square?"

"You go, old sod. I think I'll rest here for a while."

I stood listening to the silence, waiting for some further message from above. It came. The sound of one of Johnny's old .78 records on the machine. It was Duke Ellington, the poignant cry of "Lady of the Lavender Mist." If that was where Johnny Fist was going to be on this Saturday afternoon, it was no place for me.

I did go to Dominion Square for a while, sitting on a bench, half in sun, half in shade, watching the people come and go through the main door of the Windsor Hotel. There was a rich, wet, green smell in the air. A lady in a print dress with a newspaper folded on her head threw a handful of breadcrumbs on the pavement and was mobbed by pigeons.

I spent the afternoon in Loew's, watching a science-fiction film. When I came out onto Ste. Catherine Street, it was the time of day I like best in summer. There was a mood of subdued tension among the tanned faces watching themselves as they passed the department store windows. I was torn between roaming for an hour or so, enjoying this idyllic mood, or heading back to The Ninety-Seven to see if Johnny had surfaced out of his indigo, lavender, turquoise pool of Ellington and introspection.

In the end I went home and practiced my scales. Then I lay down and slept for an hour. When I got up and showered and put on a fresh suit, the sky was almost dark and from my high-rise balcony I could see nothing but lights in buildings, on streets and bridges and on chains of automobiles.

I taxied to the club, enjoying the delays in traffic so I could look out my window at the girls. I thought of Françoise, the script girl at CBC who three months ago had tired of waiting for me to get serious and had gone and married her college sweetheart. Maybe it was time for me to get involved again, to whatever extent I could manage.

The Ninety-Seven was as busy as it ever gets. All the tables were occupied, three chess games were in progress, and from the lower room I could hear the throb of electric guitars seeping through the double doors. I drank for a while and exchanged a brief greeting with Johnny, who was busy playing host.

Then, about eleven, there was a savage hammering on the front door, the sort of assault I associate with the arrival of Cossacks in the night. In the shocked silence somebody said, "It's a raid," and a few people laughed. When the locked door was opened by the nearest member, in walked Noble Kingbright clad in a floor-length cloak of black velvet and holding before him a sword, the pommel and guard raised high like a cross, his glittering eyes fixed on it so that he came on like Joan of Arc. The applause was enthusiastic and, I must admit, deserved. Full marks for artistic impression.

Having made his entrance, Kingbright confronted Johnny and said, "If you would grant me a membership in your tacky club, I would have a key and would not find it necessary to bash down your door."

Johnny unfolded his arms and let them hang at his sides but otherwise he did not move. "That is a dangerous weapon you're holding," he said. "It's against the law for you to have it with you."

Kingbright lifted the blade and looked at it, the way a man admires a well-developed muscle in his own arm. He ran his tongue along his teeth and I could hear how dry his mouth was inside. For the first time I sensed how very drunk he was. When he slipped the sword back into its sheath, the room let out its breath.

"To business," Kingbright said. "I am here because Miss Linda Lennox informs me she has left a certain notebook in the upper room. And since she has no desire to present herself in this location ever again, she has sent me to pick it up."

Johnny glanced at me. "Dennis, get the notebook."

I hurried up the winding stairs and found the book on the bedside table. It opened in my hand and I saw pages of scrawled handwriting—some sort of story Linda was working on, I assumed. When I got back downstairs, Kingbright was saying, "The portrait I am posing for will be magnificent. Boulanger is a depraved man but a great artist. You must all come to the studio and see it."

I handed the notebook to Jonathan who passed it to Noble Kingbright. "There you are," he said. "What you came for."

Kingbright swept the notebook under one arm and strode to the bar, upon which he laid down his sword with a clatter. He reached into a pocket and drew out a fistful of money. Some of it fell to the floor, a careless litter of twenty-dollar bills. He tossed several to Dallas.

"Drinks," he roared, "for everybody within sound of my voice!"

Then he made a fast departure, with his sword sloped across one shoulder and his cloak billowing behind him. I followed Johnny to the bar and saw him give to Dallas the money Kingbright had dropped on the floor.

"Put that aside," he said. "I'll see he gets it back."

I said, "Where do you suppose he came into all that loot? He used to complain about being flat all the time."

"Who knows? Maybe the baronial Teutonic father sent his bastard son a birthday present." Then he said, "Let's drop in on Arnie Pender. I want to find out whether Koshe was onto something this afternoon."

The Riverboat lounge was halfway down Stanley Street towards Dorchester Boulevard. The doorman needed a shave, a clean shirt and a few lessons in brushing his teeth.

"Johnny Fist," he said, flinging wide the door and welcoming us into the pungent atmosphere of cheap perfume and beer-soaked carpet. "Why don't you come back and do your old radio show?"

"Them days is gone forever," Johnny said.

We stood for a moment in the doorway to the Bayou Room, looking for Pender. It was quiet in there; the prostitutes were buying each other drinks. All the action was in the main room where we could hear a rhythm-and-blues band scorching the paint off the walls and ceiling. Johnny led the way next door.

The band was a swinging mass of screaming reeds and throbbing strings, playing so far above melting point that they had fused some time ago into one inseparable slab of sequined tuxedos and black skin. When the set finally came to an end, it would be necessary to cut the act up with an acetylene torch and haul it off the stage in sections.

Arnie Pender was nowhere in the main room so we threaded our way along the side wall towards the doorway leading to his upstairs office. We went through, closing the door behind us, which reduced the level of music to muffled hysteria.

Ahead of us stretched a long narrow flight of wooden stairs. A young man in a double-breasted suit left his post at the top and doubled down to meet us.

"You can't come in here," he said. He was a new man; Johnny and I were strangers to him. He had a massive torso and his arms hung loose and slightly in front of him as though he was suspended from a hook in the middle of his back. This was no meatball. His skin was bronzed and his hair was oiled and he had sauna written all over him.

"It's all right," Jonathan said. "We're friends of Arnie." He made as if to go ahead.

"Nobody gets in," the bodyguard said. And here he made his mistake. He walked right into my friend and stepped on the toe of one of Johnny's shoes. Johnny grabbed him with both hands, one of them seizing the material of his suit at the belly, the other his shirt and tie at the collar. His feet were off the floor now and he was being run back up the stairs, carried over Johnny's head like a shield. Nor did the charge end on the top landing. Johnny kept right on going, using the body in his hands like a ram to burst open the door.

By the time I got into the office, Arnie Pender was standing up behind his desk with wide eyes and Johnny had set the bodyguard back on his feet. I could see broken fingernails on Johnny's left hand. Adrenalin is a wonderful thing.

"Tell your new man I'm a friend of yours," Johnny said.

We were introduced to the bodyguard. His name was Ernie and he came from out West where he had been Mr. Prairie Provinces. He gave us a prairie smile—bleak and flat—and left the room.

Arnie Pender sat us down and got us a drink from his cabinet. Pender is in his late fifties and he must carry close to 300 pounds on a frame not much taller than mine. When he moves, you'd think he had large sacks of water suspended inside the legs of his trousers. We were on our second drink when our host said, "Why are you here, Johnny? You didn't come storming through that door just because you miss me."

Johnny opened up then about Emery Disco and, while Pender listened with his big face growing dark, my friend told him how he suspected it was a gangland hit.

"Not in my book," Pender said. "Even if somebody wanted to waste Disco, why go that far? It doesn't make sense." He considered. Then he said, "Why all the interest in Disco? I didn't know he was a special friend of yours."

"I'm interested because of something I heard today," Johnny said. "I was told Disco was into you and your backers for a lot of money."

"Where did you hear that?"

"It doesn't matter where I heard it. Is it true?"

Pender's easy smile had faded. "It's true. Disco owed the organization for a long time. We wanted him to find the money. Now we'll have to write it off." His smile returned. He said, "You don't have to tell me where you heard about the money Disco owed. I can tell you. Merv Stein."

"Koshe never said a word to me," Johnny lied to keep the peace. "I haven't seen him in a week."

Pender's smile became a grin. "Tell you something, John. If you're tracing murder suspects, take a look at Stein. He's a busy guy."

"You're kidding."

"Don't laugh. I happen to know Stein invests money for his clients. Only the way he does it, not all of it goes into secure stuff. Some of it he puts in high-risk ventures with better interest and when it works, he keeps a percentage."

Johnny shook his head but it sounded right to me. I always thought Merv had a swift, elusive look about him.

"Believe it, my friend," Pender went on. "Now suppose Stein had done this with some of Disco's money, only the risk turned sour. We were pushing Disco, I've admitted that. He'd be pushing Stein and Stein might have panicked."

Johnny put his hand on the telephone on Pender's desk. "Do you mind if I tell him you said so?"

"Hey, yeah," he said. "That's beautiful. Call him and tell him I put the finger on him. I know he told you it was me."

Johnny dialed and waited. Then his face brightened and he said, "Hello, Mitzi, this is Jonathan. Can I speak to Merv for a minute? Did he? No, he didn't say a word about it to me. No, there isn't any message. I'll talk to him when he gets back."

Johnny put down the phone and looked at Pender. "Koshe got on a plane tonight for London. I guess he got called away on business."

Pender put a fingertip beneath his left eye and drew the rim down, making the eye wide and innocent. "Yeah, sure," he said.

We were on our way down the narrow stairs when we heard the telephone ring in Arnie's office. On a hunch, Johnny paused and waited. We heard Pender's voice, muffled. In a moment the door opened.

"That was your bartender," Pender called down to us. "He just got a call from somebody named Linda Lennox. You know her?"

"Yes."

"Well, she says you better get right over to the Boulanger studio on St. Denis Street. Somebody went out a window."

They had taken Noble Kingbright's broken body away by the time we got to Boulanger's place. The artist works in a garret up four flights of crusty stairs. There was a uniformed officer on the top landing but we had no trouble with him. It was Lucien Lacombe. We first met Lacombe when he was playing shortstop for a Police Association fastball team. Since then he was playing for us.

"Hey, Johnny," he said, "did you know this guy?"

"He was a mutual friend of mine and Linda's."

"She's in there now." Lucien casually put a fist into my stomach and I responded with an appropriate flinch. "How's our good right fielder?"

"Getting run ragged these days. Too many people dying."

"It's a bad summer. First Milligan, then all those people in the swimming pool. Now this one."

Johnny asked what had happened. Lucien said it was all over when they got there. The jumper had been drunk and was swinging, of all things, an unsheathed sword. Like Willie Stargell at home plate, was how Lucien put it. Boulanger apparently tried to settle the man down and received a cut on the arm. He went away to borrow a bandage from a girl he knew downstairs. Then he heard more yelling and running in the loft and when he got back up, there was only the girl left in the room, standing by the open window with blood on her skirt.

"Thanks, Lucie," Johnny said. "I think I better go in and talk to her."

We encountered the Inspector on his way out of the studio. It was the same man who had seen us in Disco's backyard. We explained our connection with Linda and the deceased. We confirmed that Kingbright had been drunk and a little manic when he left The Ninety-Seven earlier in the evening. We also mentioned his conspicuous affluence with twenties all over the floor. This drew a satisfied smile from the police officer.

"That may wrap up the Disco killings. The girl tells us that Kingbright went to see Disco on the afternoon it happened. He was making a film and he wanted Disco to put up some money."

Johnny was keeping his mouth shut tight but his eyes were alive. The Inspector said, "She tells us there was a pistol to be used in the film and that Kingbright had it with him when he went to see Disco. He didn't have it with him tonight but I've sent somebody to search his room. When it turns up, I think ballistics will show it was the gun that killed the Disco family."

I waited for Johnny to say he could assist the police in their search for the murder weapon, but he said nothing.

"So you believe the guilty man took his own life tonight," I said.

The Inspector nodded. "It seems logical, according to what the girl inside tells us."

He went away, taking Lucien Lacombe with him. Johnny and I went inside. He hurried to Linda while I stopped with Boulanger. The artist was standing in front of the unfinished portrait, frowning at it through half-closed eyes while he reamed a nostril with the tip of his little finger.

"This kind of work is really not my thing," Boulanger said. As support for this statement, a crowd of brilliant abstracts shouted at me from every side of the studio. "But he was a persuasive man. He made me believe I wanted to do it."

"Did he pay you for it?"

Boulanger turned pained eyes upon me. "That is an irrelevant factor now, wouldn't you agree?" he said.

Feeling I had said the wrong thing, I was glad to move away and approach Jonathan and Linda, who were standing now and talking. "He was raving," Linda said. "After he cut Paul's arm, he wouldn't stop laughing."

"When I came earlier, it was like the man was in church. A priest," Boulanger said.

"We were here early," Linda said. "I kept telling Noble to calm down."

"He was on his knees in front of the painting," Boulanger went on, "like at a prie-dieu. The sword was stuck in the floor in front of him and he was chanting about being guilty of something."

"He wouldn't stop yelling," Linda said. "He kept on about guilt and punishment. I asked him if he was talking about the murders at the swimming pool. I knew he went there with the gun to talk to Mr. Disco. When I said this, he got worse and he began pointing the sword at himself."

Johnny took Linda by the shoulders and held her, shaking her to bring her out of it.

"He stabbed himself," she said, her breath bubbling in her throat. "He held the sword in both hands and he ran it into his stomach. He was standing right here." She pointed at the spattered boards below the window ledge. "Then he stumbled backwards and was gone."

I watched Jonathan bury the tiny girl in his arms and I said to Boulanger, more for my own benefit than anybody else's, "Have you got anything to drink around here?"

He had half a gallon of red wine, imported at no great expense. We drank a good quantity of this out of the artist's rare collection of jam jars while sitting with our backs to Kingbright's half-finished portrait and listening to Linda as she calmed herself down.

"It all adds up," Johnny said finally, his gaze directed at the studio window, closed and bolted now that it no longer mattered. "Kingbright must have threatened Disco when he refused to back his film. I imagine the dog went for him and he shot it first. Then Disco himself. And then the wife and kid when they came out into the yard."

"Where did all the money come from?" I said.

Johnny hardly paused. "He took it out of Disco's pocket. Emery always had a lot of cash on him."

We said goodbye to Paul Boulanger and went outside to where Linda's car was parked. Johnny said to me, "This fits in with what Cleary said. He came along just after the shooting and took the gun from Kingbright."

"You see it that way?"

"I wish I could find Don and tell him he can stop running."

We climbed into the car and Linda took us on a swift erratic drive back to The Ninety-Seven. I declined Johnny's invitation to come in for a nightcap and left them to their reconciliation.

My taxi ride home was troubled. I wondered when I would suck up my nerve and tell Johnny his case against Kingbright had at least one obvious hole in it. I could not picture the hysterical killer searching the house for cash with four dead bodies in the backyard. And how could he have gotten the money from Disco's pocket? The dead Disco was wearing nothing but a pair of bathing trunks.

Linda Lennox took a couple of days off work to recover from her ordeal. For this reason, she didn't hear the news at the ad agency. I had to pick it up from Dallas, who got it off the street. It was my justification for going back to Johnny and telling him he was all wet about Kingbright being Disco's killer.

"How do you know?"

"The word is out that Kingbright misappropriated a pile of money from the office. Funds intended to be talent repayments for TV commercial performers. That, my friend, was the cash he was throwing around the club. It also explains all his talk about guilt."

Jonathan had brought a tray from the kitchen to Linda's bedside. He was doing everything now but feed her. It was a subservient side of the man I had not seen before and it made me uncomfortable. He said, "Okay. But we know Kingbright went by himself to see Disco, and he had the gun with him. Right, Linda?"

"That he did."

"But Cleary claims he took the gun from whoever did the killing," I said. "There's no way he could have got it from a big man like Kingbright."

"Cleary. Who's he?" Linda asked.

I told her about the note, Cleary's motive for getting Disco, his presence at the scene, his possession of the weapon, his flight from our custody. An airtight case.

Linda said, "I buy what Dennis is saying. I wouldn't look any further."

But Johnny kept looking, refusing to accept the obvious evidence against his old hometown buddy. That's why he was ready to listen the next day when Mitzi Stein telephoned, full of worry about the missing Mervin. Johnny put down the phone and said to me, "Listen to this about Koshe. He hasn't gone to England on business. He's gone for good. I think that means he was doing what Arnie Pender said. Losing Disco's money in risky investments."

"Tell it all," I said. "Mitzi was going on a lot more than that."

"Koshe has been getting letters from London for a year or so. Since the last time he was there."

"And?"

"Okay, he and Mitzi have been sleeping apart for quite a while. So what?"

"So Mervin has a girl friend in London and he's gone to live with her. He had nothing to do with Disco."

"Could be. But it also could be what I said, with or without the girl friend."

I stood by helplessly while Johnny put through a call to Air Canada. As he made the booking, he raised his eyebrows at me. If something was going to happen, I ought to be with him so I nodded my head. "Two seats."

Seeing England was nice, but the search for Mervin Stein turned out to be a depressing episode I would have been happy to miss. All we had to go on was a name and a return address from the outside of one of the letters Stein had been receiving. A suspicious Mitzi had copied it down in case a divorce lawyer might one day need it.

The address was on Gros enor Street. The name turned out to be a subdued, smooth gentleman with polished nails and manners. No, he had not seen Mervin Stein lately, but last year he had thrown a large party which the Canadian had attended. He was able to supply the name and telephone number of a mutual friend, a television writer, who had spent more time with Stein.

A call to the writer's answering service revealed that he was on the set at Thames Television in Teddington Lock. No, he could not be reached by telephone. But it was only half an hour by train from Waterloo Station.

"At least we're seeing London," I said later as we crossed the station concourse, avoiding squadrons of pigeons milling around a sign that said if we fed them we would be fined £100. Our train eased away from platform 9 and raced through slums, suburbs and green country, stopping at towns with good names like Wimbledon and Hampton Wick.

At Teddington, we rode a taxi to the Thames studios which were located in acres of green fields beside the river, in which hundreds of pleasure boats were moored. We found the writer, not on the set but in the cafeteria. He was a reedy young man with a shaven head and weary gestures.

"Oh, Mervin is here all right, but he hasn't been to see me. When you see him, tell him an old friend hopes he catches fire."

Besides a lot of bitchy sarcasm, we got from the writer the phone number of a hotel in West Kensington where Stein was said to be registered. Johnny asked me to call and to tell Merv I just happened to be in town. He was afraid his voice would panic our man if he was guilty.

From a call box in the studio lobby, I got through to the hotel. Yes, Mr. Stein was staying there. They rang his room and a lush feminine voice with a cultured English accent came on the line. She passed me on to Mervin.

"Dennis! How nice to hear your voice. When did you get in?"

The words were right but he sounded tense. I made arrangements to come and see him that evening. Then, on the train back to Waterloo, I justified Mervin's anxiety. "Sure he was nervous. He's left his wife and he's booked in there with this English broad. He'd be wondering how I'd take it."

"Or he's on the run and doesn't want to be found." Johnny's face was thoughtful. "Never mind this evening. We're going there as soon as this train gets in."

In a way, Johnny turned out to be right. Mervin Stein was on the run from us, but not because he killed anybody. When our taxi let us out across the street from the hotel, we saw a willowy girl pulling a comb through long golden hair as she stood beside a couple of bags on the sidewalk. As we watched, Merv came out of the front door, putting away his wallet. He spoke to her, then he began looking for a taxi. That was when he saw us. He looked around, but there was no place for him to go.

Johnny confronted him. "I think you killed Emery Disco, Koshe. You were gambling with his money in the stock market. You lost and you took the heavy way out."

"Not true, Johnny. I invested Emery's money, but it all came good."

"Then why the sudden departure?"

"It wasn't sudden. It's been on my mind for a long time. You wouldn't understand." Merv threw a reproachful glance at me.

"Try me," Johnny said.

"I've been buried in that life back home—the accountant and family man. It isn't me, Johnny. Never has been. It was all a big lie. Mitzi and I have been nothing for years."

"She said something about that."

"So it was stay there and die, or make a move. That's all. The real Mervin Stein has decided to let himself out of the closet."

I was watching Stein's companion. There was something about the shape of the jaw, the narrow hips in tailored jeans, the vaguely masculine posture. A slight shift of my point of view and there it was; despite the touch of lipstick, the haze of eyeshadow and the glistening hair, this was no woman. Mervin Stein was traveling with a very beautiful boy.

I nudged Jonathan. He looked where I was looking and made the connection a lot faster than I did.

Merv caught our glances and with a defensive tone in his voice, he said, "This is Simon."

So Johnny and I got back on a plane for Montreal, lighter by a few hundred dollars, having learned the secret of Mervin Stein's new existence, which would be considered sordid or liberating, depending on your attitude.

When we arrived back at The Ninety-Seven, descending from the airport limousine in the wee small hours of the morning, we discovered that the next event in the mystery had been programmed to meet us.

Dallas was sitting in a chair holding an icebag to the back of his head. Around him lay the shambles of the club interior; books had been cascaded from shelves, cupboard doors ripped open and contents strewn about. We knew the upstairs would look the same.

"I don't know how long I was out," Dallas said. "But whoever it was didn't touch the cash. I checked it."

Johnny examined the bartender's scalp. "Have you called the cops?"

"I was about to."

"Don't. I know what this is." He went behind the bar and twiddled the dial on the safe. He came back with the murder gun, long and evil. He looked at me.

"It must have been Don Cleary. He was after this. You were right all along."

"You admit that now?"

"It wasn't Kingbright. It wasn't Arnie Pender. It wasn't Mervin Stein." I never saw my old friend look so unhappy. "So I guess I'll have to face the obvious. Let's go find Don Cleary . . ."

We used my car to drive to Baytown, a pleasant 200 miles, much of it beside the St. Lawrence River and the green mounds of the Thousand Islands, with their half-concealed roofs of millionaires' cottages. Baytown is a small place. It should have been easy to locate a well-known citizen like Don Cleary.

Our first call was at the police station.

"We've been looking ourselves," the man behind the desk told us. "We read about the Disco killings in the paper and when there was no sign of Cleary around here we put two and two together. Sent a wire to the Montreal police with a description. So far, no news."

I thought of that incriminating note Johnny had received and how much grief could have been saved had he gone immediately to the police. Again, I said nothing.

We tried the Coronet Hotel, a useless move. The beverage room where Cleary served beer was half full. We stopped for a couple of drafts and quizzed one of the waiters, a crimson-faced man with black leather hair that had a part down the middle half an inch wide. Red thread on his jacket pocket told us his name was Dave. Dave had not seen Cleary in over a week.

We even drove past Cleary's house, a berry-box cottage in a new development where, Johnny told me, the golf course used to be. He had spent childhood days in this area searching pools for lost golf balls and for tadpoles. Now we found Cleary's wife on her knees on the lawn, grubbing weeds out of a petunia bed. She had no idea where her husband was. If we found him, would we tell him there was no money in the house for groceries?

Johnny offered her twenty, but she refused it. As we walked away, a haunted-looking ten-year-old boy came out of the kitchen door unwrapping a popsicle. In the car on the way to his brother's place, Jonathan said, "I'm sorry, but I don't believe Mrs. Cleary."

"Why not?"

"She's an old friend of mine from high school. No reason for her not to take money from me if she was really broke. And the kid with the popsicle—I think that was bought at the supermarket today."

"Pretty thin evidence."

"Call it a feeling then. Cleary is around and she's covering up."

We carried our bags into the old Fitzwilliam residence, half of a frame duplex with hollyhocks standing along the side wall and a noisy fox terrier on his hind legs behind the screen door. I met Johnny's brother Merlin, who is the lone occupant these days. The dark rooms reminded me of a theater after the performance with the cast all gone away; here, amid the unsprung furniture, watched by broad Irish faces in old wooden frames, Jonathan Fitzwilliam had played out the early years of his life, becoming what he is.

Merlin fed us, then invited us to accompany him to the Armoury to witness a practice of the regimental pipe band in which he is a snare drummer. We were inclined to accept when the telephone rang. It was for Johnny.

"Hello? I knew you were. How did you know I was looking for you? I figured she would. Where are you now? Okay. Can we get in? Then we'll see you."

Don Cleary was at Pine Street Public School, hiding out in the basement. He used to do summer maintenance work there, painting floors and such, and had kept a key. His wife told him we were in town and for some reason he was ready to see Jonathan.

There was a smell of oiled floors and running shoes in the old school. Looking through open doorways into deserted classrooms, I expected to hear the bell signaling class changeover and then be trampled by hundreds of stampeding kids.

We found Cleary where he said he'd be, in the caretaker's cubbyhole beside the silent furnace room. He met us in the doorway, an embarrassed smile on his hollow face.

"I'm sorry I busted up your place, Johnny. I wanted to get hold of the gun."

Johnny produced it from his pocket, without the silencer on it now. It was the first time I knew he'd brought the weapon with him. "I should never have let you run away, Don. But the chase is over. Now I'm taking you to the police."

"Why?"

"To tell them what I know. The note you sent me. The fact that you were at Disco's that afternoon, and you were carrying this gun."

"But I didn't do the killing. I took the gun from the murderer."

My voice sounded loud in the concrete hovel. "If it wasn't you, Cleary, who was it?"

He smiled at me. "I promised myself not to tell. The killer should be rewarded for doing God's work."

Johnny stepped aside and motioned with the gun towards the door. "Come on, Don. Let's go."

As we walked by, Cleary turned and was on the gun hand like a cobra. I was blocked out of the action in the narrow space. Johnny seemed hard pressed. He was using both hands to try to wrestle the gun away from Cleary. The man must have been possessed with superhuman strength.

"Grab his head!" Johnny yelled and I tried to squeeze past but it was too late. I saw the muzzle of the gun turning slowly, a dark eye looking for someone. I heard the ear-splitting roar that reverberated in the concrete box, was blinded by the flash, smelled the acrid, burnt powder.

It was over. Don Cleary lay on the floor with Johnny kneeling beside him. My ears cleared in time to hear the dying man's last words.

"That's why I wanted the gun, Jonathan. All I wanted was out."

A couple of weeks later in Montreal, things seemed to be looking up. Johnny Fist had somehow squared the police by telling what he knew about Don Cleary without revealing that he had been concealing the murder weapon. As far as they knew, Cleary had had it all along.

Then, to ice the cake, Linda Lennox came into the club late one afternoon to announce she was on her way to California. She was done with advertising in general and Montreal in particular. Film writing was her future, and the Coast was the place to be.

Johnny seemed ready to let her go and I was delighted. Visions of uninterrupted cribbage and snooker danced in my head. The good old life was coming back.

Linda went upstairs to pack some of her things. Johnny was totalling bar receipts and I was reading an ancient book of Victorian recipes with brown pages that crumbled like dried bay leaves. Then the door opened and in walked Mervin Stein. He looked a little shy, but clearer of eye than I had seen him in some time.

"I'm back," he announced.

We waited for him to say why.

"That scene over there wasn't working. I missed my kids," he said. "And in a crazy way, I missed Mitzi."

"That's nothing to be ashamed of," Johnny said.

"I was hoping you wouldn't say anything about what I was into in England. She doesn't know I go that way."

"Not a word from us," Johnny said and I nodded.

Before he went away, Merv said, "How goes it with you, Johnny?"

"Changes, like everybody. I'm losing Linda Lennox. She's off to Hollywood to write movies."

Merv stuck out his lower lip. "Too bad Disco got killed. Otherwise, he might have backed the film she was writing here."

Our heads lifted as we listened to that new thought. Johnny said, "What film? Wasn't that Kingbright's film?"

"Yeah, he was directing but it was Linda's screenplay. In fact, it was a lot more hers than his."

"How do you know this?"

"Because Disco asked my advice about investing in it. Linda had put one proposition to him. I said films are risky but it was up to him. He told me he'd make up his mind when he talked to the girl. Apparently Linda and Kingbright were coming to see Disco that afternoon."

Merv went home and I followed Johnny upstairs. I didn't like the look in his eyes. We found Linda putting clothes in a bag. Johnny closed the lid, turned her around, held her in both hands.

"I just heard for the first time that you were with Kingbright when he went to see Disco. You never told me you were there."

"Why should I?" She pulled away from him, went to the wall.

"Because Don Cleary said he took the gun from the Avenging Angel. Most people think of angels as women. That never occurred to me before now."

"If you think I killed those people, you're crazy," Linda said. But her liquid southern accent would not cover the lie.

Johnny said in a very quiet voice, "You've nothing to worry about. The case is closed. Cleary is dead and the cops have hung it on him. I just want to know what really happened. For my own satisfaction."

Linda looked at me. "I'll talk to you. But not with Dennis here."

Johnny nodded at me. I made my way down the iron steps. It can't have been more than a few minutes before I heard a muffled scream and a thud. Then I heard heavy footsteps, a slamming door and silence.

I ran upstairs. The apartment was empty. They had to be on the roof. I opened the service door and ran up the final flight and out onto the flat asphalt roof. Johnny was standing by the edge. Alone.

I walked to his side and looked down. Linda Lennox was lying in the stone-paved courtyard five floors below. I waited and then he started to tell me about it.

"She sent Kingbright away that afternoon because he was drunk and hyper. The gun was in her handbag. She laid the story of the film on Disco, poured her heart out to him. He not only refused to back the idea, he laughed at it. Said it sounded like kid stuff. Then he let her know he would be interested in her, but not as a writer. She took out the gun and threatened him. That was when the dog came at her and she shot it first. Disco tried to grab the gun and she shot him. Then when his wife and daughter came running, she had to kill them to protect herself."

I thought about this. "What about Cleary?"

"It was like he said. He came along just then and found Linda with the gun. She was dazed. He took it from her. Told her to go and sin no more. Then he put the bodies in the pool. Just to confuse the situation, I suppose." Somebody had parked a car in the courtyard below us. He saw Linda's body, looked up at us on the roof, and went away running.

"Another thing," Johnny said. "She killed Kingbright, it wasn't suicide. He was getting set to talk about her being with him that afternoon. She used the sword to topple him out the window."

In the distance we heard a siren. "But why this ending?" I said.

"It was the only way. She said she'd never admit to the police what she'd told me. And she laughed in my face. I thought of poor Don with all that crazy guilt on his mind. I saw her skating out of here, clean." He stared at his right hand. "So I hit her and brought her up here."

What bothers me most about all of this is that Johnny Fist now seems at peace with himself. And I am the one with the load of heavy information I have to live with. I'm sitting now in the club nursing a beer and the busy night life is going on as usual. Mervin Stein and Mitzi came in and are two stools down the bar from me, pretending to be okay. But I see the expression on Merv's face when he glances at me. He's heard about what has been logged as Linda's suicide leap and he recalls Johnny's harsh reaction when he talked about her that afternoon.

So what do I do? Do I go to the police? Do I swallow the whole thing, no matter how it poisons me? I just looked up and saw Johnny Fist watching me from the far end of the room. There is a little smile on his face, as if he knows me better than I know myself.

PAULINE C. SMITH

That Monday Night

That Monday night at nine o'clock, as soon as "Laugh-In" was over, Jim Copeland remembered to get up and turn on the porch light. His daughter, Michele, should be home from the store by nine thirty. She always was.

He yawned, stretched, and looked at the TV news. Discarding the movie on Channel Four that would take too long, he switched to Channel Two. Then he went into the kitchen, opened a can of beer, returned, settled down to the television set, and was sound asleep by nine fifteen.

The screen finished its Mayberry problems and began a Doris Day entanglement, continuing then with Carol Burnett's comedic exaggerations. . . .

Jim Copeland slept on.

Mrs. Carrie Mason, the middle-aged widow next door, was also watching television, from her bed. Her bedroom window looked out upon the Copeland porch so that she saw the light when it went on at nine o'clock. For Michele, she thought, knowing that the girl worked on Monday nights at Harper's department store in the Plaza shopping center. She would be home at nine thirty right on the dot, because she always was, then the light would go off.

Carrie became absorbed in the movie, not noticing that the porch light remained on, not until after the movie was over at eleven. Her first thought, then, was that Jim Copeland had forgotten to turn it off after Michele's arrival home. "Just like a man," she muttered, knowing that Mrs. Copeland, Sue, was in Tremont, babysitting for that married daughter of hers, the one with three children. With Sue gone, wouldn't Jim Copeland keep the porch light on until all hours!

Carrie switched off her TV set, went to the kitchen, swallowed a jigger of bourbon to help her sleep, returned to the bedroom, turned off her light, and opened the window a scant three inches. Just before she slanted the blind slats enough so that the morning sun would not awaken her with the terrible start of remembering that she was alone and a widow, she looked out upon the Copeland driveway where Michele always parked her car and found it empty.

Her heart squeezed and her mind formulated four thoughts in rapid succession. The first: *That eighteen-year-old child who had seemed so dependable, so studious and conscientious was, perhaps, like the rest of this young college generation, out whooping it up heaven-knows-where.* The second: *That father, who seemed so nice for a man, was letting her whoop it up while he sat goggle-eyed in front of his television set, which she could see grayly flickering in the Copeland living room.* Her third thought was that there was some kind of trouble: *Michele never stayed out after her evening at the store and her father never stayed up on a week night.* Fourth: *She should go over and find out, being a woman and with Sue gone.* Then she remembered that she was a forty-year-old widow . . . well, all right, forty-five . . . and her act of Samaritanism might be misinterpreted, especially with a jigger of liquor on her breath.

She lay down, but uneasily, and slept restlessly, the empty space in the Copeland driveway on her mind.

It was one o'clock when she was awakened by the rumble of Jim Copeland's car as it backed with noisy abandon from the garage.

She peeked out between the slats of the blind. The Copeland driveway was empty and fog-washed. The Copeland garage was open and dark. The porch light still shone, as did a lamp dimly from the living room.

Something was wrong.

The town lay between the ocean and the mountains, quietly serene. With a sprawling megalopolis to the south and a tightly aloof city to the north, it was left out by the AP and the UPI news reports and ignored during the television weather forecast; a forgotten town.

At nine thirty that Monday night, a co-worker, Linda Fischer—("I'm in jewelry, but Michele moved around from department to department because she went to college, you see, and only worked two nights a week plus Saturday . . .")—saw Michele in the brightly lighted parking lot. "Of course I know it was Michele Copeland. She was standing there by her car, that little green bug she drives, and she waved when my husband and I drove by. My husband picks me up about nine twenty. He parks in the A section, and when I'm through we drive down to the D section which is near the coffee shop, and we go in there for coffee and a snack."

The coffee shop, Linda Fischer explained to the police on Tuesday when they questioned her, stayed open until ten. She and her husband left just before it closed. There was only one car in the D section when they left, probably the coffee shop owner's car, and the owner explained to the police when questioned that, yes, he took off five minutes after the last customers, but he drove out the other side. Out through D, he meticulously explained, to the turnoff on Sargent and, as far as he could remember, there wasn't a car in the parking lot. As far as he could *see* there wasn't a car; but then, of course, he hadn't looked back toward A, the Harper parking lot. Why should he? He was going the other way.

Linda Fischer and her husband drove from D section, after coffee and a sandwich, about nine fifty-five, she thought, out through A again and they saw Michele's car still there, jacked up. They supposed she had gone off with the friend who had been helping her because his car was gone.

"A friend?" asked the police.

How could Linda know that? She and her husband had seen this man there at nine thirty or thereabouts. No, they couldn't see him very well, he'd been tall and thin and had dark hair, she thought. He seemed to be fooling around with the jack, and his car—at least they assumed it was his car—had been parked next to Michele's so they supposed she had come out from the store, found a flat, and called him, a friend.

What kind of car? Linda was asked. She didn't know; light, probably white—at least a pale color.

Anyway, Michele waved to Linda, and she wouldn't wave if anything were wrong would she?

Linda did not add that her husband had wanted to stop. "Maybe I can help," he had said in his involved way. "Don't be silly," Linda had answered. "She's got help." Anyway, Michele was pretty, and it was Linda's mission in life to keep her husband away from pretty girls.

Just the same, ever since that Tuesday morning when the police had questioned her, Linda was nagged by the guilty suspicion that maybe it wasn't a happy hand greeting Michele had waved at nine thirty Monday night, but a frantic wig-wag of terror.

Well, she couldn't tell the police that, could she? And what woud be the use now?

On Tuesday morning Sue Copeland, Michele's mother, prepared to leave her daughter Dorrie's home in Tremont immediately after breakfast.

"But Mom, why so early? It's only a couple of hours' drive and, anyway, by the time you get there, Dad'll be at work and Michele at school. Why not wait and leave this afternoon?"

Sue did not know why unless, being unaccustomed to the demands of three small children during a long weekend, she felt the abrupt need of the quiet of her home. "Oh, I don't know, Dorrie," she said. "I guess I just want to get the house straightened up. . . ."

A limp excuse since Michele was neat as a pin and Jim never got anything out of place.

Dorrie firmed her lips and spoke precisely. "Well," she said, "if you don't want to hear about the trip and the speech Hal gave at the convention," a snappish attempt to cover up and superimpose the selfish guilt of a married daughter who would call a mother out on the freeway two hours away to go through a three-day brat-race just because it was cheaper and more convenient than hiring a babysitter who would babysit only, and not clean and wash and cook and rock. "If you don't want to have a *visit* and just *enjoy*. I thought you'd stay a little while, at least, after we got home and Hal had gone off to work. So we could talk *alone*. I thought you wouldn't leave until afternoon. At least noon."

"I know, honey," said Sue vaguely, gathering her bags together and picking up her car keys. "I know," she said, feeling a compulsion to get home without knowing why.

She kissed the three grandchildren and Dorrie walked with her out to the car.

"I wanted to talk about the trip, Mom," said Dorrie, leaning inside the car, the guilt, now that her mother did not allow her to assuage it with hospitality, melting into tears. "I wanted to have a little while with you. I mean, after you'd taken care of the kids and all, it seems kind of awful that you should pick up and run without a visit with me."

Sue, starting the motor, said, "I know, honey, but another time," unable to explain her obsession that she must hit the freeway and hurry home.

She worked her way through the early morning traffic, away from the city, into the fast lane north through the coastside fog and the overhanging clouds of winter. She made the trip in less than two hours, leaving the freeway and turning onto Sargent, where she drove past the Plaza shopping center's morning-filled parking lot without noticing the little green car jacked up in the A section directly behind Harper's department store.

She crossed the back residential streets toward the old suburban area and turned onto Rio Mesa. From the end of the block, the moment she turned, Sue routinely observed that Michele's car was gone from the driveway, which was as it should be at ten o'clock on a Tuesday morning. She drove up the quiet street, made the sharp turn required to enter the open garage and braked with startled surprise.

What was Jim's car doing home at this hour of the day?

She eased her car in beside it, then hurried from the garage up the steps of the porch. She noticed the forgotten porch light glowing faintly in the gloom of a cloudy day.

Now alarmed, Sue turned the key and flung open the door.

There sat Jim, sunk in the big chair, his head in his hands.

Before she could speak, he lifted his head and said, "Michele is gone."

"Gone?" Sue's voice rose on the word and reached a shrill note. "What do you mean, gone?"

He told her then about dropping off to sleep, and awakening to discover that it was one o'clock in the morning, with Michele not in her bed and her car not in the driveway.

Sue backed against the door so that it closed with her weight. *Is this what she had been hurrying home to?*

Jim told her, in a dead voice Sue had never before heard, how he got out his car and raced through sleeping streets to the Plaza shopping center and found Michele's little green car there, the only car in the entire parking lot, jacked up, with the spare lying on the pavement; not Michele—only Michele's car.

He went on to explain, in this freshly dead voice, his hurried search for a phone booth in among the fog-wet planters and the darkened shops of the mall and how he finally found one and called the police.

The police had it all wrong from the beginning. At first, over the phone, they thought Jim Copeland had wanted them to fix a flat or get someone to fix a flat. Then they thought he was reporting a daughter's stolen car. Finally they got it straight. Well, not really straight because, even after meeting him out there at the lighted parking lot and seeing the jacked-up car and hearing his garbled account, the two patrol officers still confused Michele with the usual teenager encountered during the course of their varied, colorful night duty.

"You know who she might have run away with?" asked one.

The other mentioned drugs and possible pregnancy.

However, they did not press charges when Jim Copeland took a poke at one of the officers, even though they did tell him that was no way to find his daughter.

At headquarters, the man at the desk recorded the necessary descriptive information. Name, Michele Copeland. Age, 18. Height, 5'1". Weight, 98 pounds. Brown eyes. Blonde hair. Occupation, full-time college student, part-time department store employee. It was not a complete description since Michele's dependable character and her reserved personality had been left out, but the man at the desk said that information was unnecessary.

Because Michele was eighteen and legally an adult, the police could not get out an all-points bulletin on her disappearance for seventy-two hours, and by that time, through interviews with students and faculty members of the college as well as co-workers at the store, it had been well established that she was indeed a good, dependable, conscientious, and reserved girl; therefore not the type to take off willingly with some strange man.

This left the police with two theories. Either the tall, thin, darkhaired stranger, described by Mrs. Linda Fischer, had used physical violence to force Michele into his car, necessitating a search of the hillside arroyos and deserted rocky points of the beach for a body, or the tall, thin, darkhaired stranger was a friend with whom Michele had gone willingly and the highway patrol was alerted to cover the brushlands and cliffsides for a wrecked, probably white, car and possibly two bodies.

"Can't you describe the guy's car any better than that?" the police asked the Fischers. "You just say a light-colored car, probably white. How about make? Was it a late model? Sedan, convertible, station wagon, compact maybe?"

Linda said she didn't know one car from another, and anyway she hadn't looked at the car. She had just waved back at Michele as they drove on.

At that, her husband glared at her. He would never forgive her for talking him out of stopping on Monday night. He had wanted to stop. He had slowed down even, but know-it-all Linda, who acted like she owned even the breaths he took, hurried him on as she turned and waved and smiled as if butter wouldn't melt in her mouth at that poor girl who was God-knows-where now.

"I'm sorry, officer," said Linda Fischer's husband, "I didn't notice much about the car either, except that it was light—white, probably—and stuck out farther than her little green job in the diagonal parking space right in front of it. What I was noticing was that her trunk was open and it looked as if the guy was getting out the jack, so everything seemed to be under control, with him there and all . . ." He ended his excuse for noninvolvement with a sigh, feeling only partial absolution and none at all for his wife.

Again he glared at her. "Is it true the tire was slashed?" he asked.

Jim Copeland was sure the tire had been slashed. "The sidewall was punctured with a sharp instrument," he declared for the press. The crime-lab report offered the more conservative view that the tire could have been damaged accidentally and routinely by a sharp rock or a piece of glass.

Carrie Mason didn't know what to do.

She had seen Jim Copeland arrive home on Tuesday morning at seven o'clock, just about the time it was beginning to winter-light. Watching from her bedroom window with the blind slats carefully slanted, she had seen the car pull into the garage and Jim Copeland walk heavily up the porch steps.

The porch light remained on and the driveway remained empty, and she didn't know what to do. She should go over there, shouldn't she? After all, they were neighbors and she was a good friend of Sue's. But then, being a widow and with Sue gone, it might look . . . Well, it might look *funny*, like she was trying to . . . well, trying to promote something.

At eight thirty she saw the patrol car pull up to the curb, and two officers walk up to the Copeland front porch. They went inside the house.

What in the world?

At nine o'clock they left the house and drove the patrol car away, and Carrie Mason was again faced with the question of what to do? Offer her services, her condolence, her sympathy, whatever it was that she should offer? She felt a nagging anxiety that the offer might be coming too late, but she couldn't just stay here in her house with a neighbor in trouble. My goodness, daughter gone, up till all hours, out all night, and then the police. It was time, certainly, to throw caution to the winds. Even if she was an attractive forty-five-year-old-widow—well, almost fifty—still, this was a duty; but first she must do something about her jumping nerves after seeing the patrol car and the policemen, so she tottered to the kitchen and swallowed a jigger of bourbon which calmed her, but also caused her to realize that she could not possibly, being a nice widow and all, visit a man alone with liquor on her breath.

An hour later she saw Sue Copeland's car turn into the garage.

With Jim's shocking announcement, Sue's reaction was immediate. She went into his comforting arms to comfort him. From that moment on, until he drove Michele's little green car home on Thursday, or perhaps it was with Dorrie's arrival which also occurred on Thursday, Sue leaned upon Jim and encouraged him. She was his hope as he was hers, with never a thought of recrimination for this accidental tragedy.

They were interviewed together by a young reporter that Tuesday noon, and together they described their daughter—a good, responsible girl, not the type to go off with a stranger, so it had to be foul play. They described the dress she wore, a brown wool with matching coat, and her quiet, orderly habits which would never allow her to act heedlessly. Her grades were excellent. She had no problems. Yes, she dated on occasion, but seldom, what with her studies and part-time clerking job, and no one steadily.

At the reporter's request, Sue offered him Michele's latest pictures—the year-old graduation photograph, careful to point out that her hair had been long then, but now was cut short, as shown in the more recent snapshots. She broke down and wept, feeling bereft and frightened as if, by relinquishing the pictures of Michele, she were giving up her daughter for lost.

Sue got through the first day by drinking coffee and keeping the pot ready for Jim when he arrived home from either an anxiety-filled trip to the police station or a fearful cruise along lonely roads. She paced the floor and phoned those of Michele's friends who were available and might know something. No one knew anything, or so they said.

She looked with aversion at the plate of cookies Carrie Mason brought apologetically over about two o'clock in the afternoon, smelled Mrs. Mason's mouthwash-spiked breath, and listened with an edge of surprise as Mrs. Mason groped through a perplexing maze of nonintervention excuses for not arriving earlier. Then Sue roused to realize that Mrs. Mason, widowed and somewhat humiliated by it, had probably been on target behind her venetian blind since last night when the pattern of the Copelands had been smashed, wanting to know, to be a part of it, wanting to help but unable to because she was a widow and envious of the non-widowed.

Sue told her all that she knew and they wept together.

The paper, with the front-page item and picture of Michele, was delivered at five, when the winter day began to be night. Sue read about her daughter and looked at the darkening sky, knowing that she was out there someplace.

Through the night, Sue made frequent trips to the front porch to test the black, cold dampness, ashamed of being warm and safe. She stood on the porch in terror of the night and what it might be doing to her child, until Jim urged her back into shamed warmth and safety.

It was during those times that Sue and Jim were close, with the compassion of mother for father and father for mother, not thinking of blame or self-blame, or guilt or self-guilt—not until Thursday, after the seventy-two hour lapse, when flyers would be distributed to 250 law-enforcement agencies within the state and extending into adjoining states, when the case would reach the television newscast and be released to the press through the AP and the UPI services, when the little green car would be returned to the driveway, and Dorrie would arrive.

Wednesday morning, Carrie Mason divided her time between the venetian blinds of her bedroom and the kitchen stove, cooking up food the Copelands could not possibly eat.

She anguished as she watched the television people haul out their equipment from the truck in front and drag it up the porch steps and into the Copeland house. She castigated herself for her Monday-night-eleven-o'clock-bourbon-breath when she identified the reporter returning to the Copeland house for a second interview. She cooked and watched, flagellating herself for her anxious-widow sins of omission, for had she awakened Jim Copeland from his sleep, his daughter might be home now.

The Wednesday evening article in the local newspaper covered the lower section of the front page, displaying another picture of Michele—one of the snapshots showing her hair cut short and with a smile on her face—that broke Sue's heart. The picture looked back at Sue now under the heading: HAVE YOU SEEN THIS GIRL?

It was then that Sue phoned her married daughter, knowing that she could put it off no longer in the hope it would not be necessary at all, because now, if she were not warned, Dorrie would have the shock of finding out from her own newspaper or through her television.

Dorrie became immediately emotional. "When did it happen?" she cried. "On Monday night? When you were *here?*" She was silent for a time, interrupting her mother at last with, "But if you had been home, it might not have happened," and quickly adding, "What was Daddy *doing* all that time? *Sleeping?*" and she had the hook upon which to hang her guilt. "You mean he didn't *do* anything? Mom, I'll be there," making the immediate decision to transfer her fault of needlessly needing her mother, to her father, so that he could be the sinner and not she. "Mom, I'll drive up tomorrow as soon as I can arrange about Hal and the kids."

"No, honey," protested Sue, knowing Dorrie's tendency to dominate, to push like a bulldozer and whack away like a pile driver. Sue did not want to be pushed or whacked at this point, but wanted only to wait and worry and hope so that she didn't go to pieces, with all the pieces flying out into limbo.

"Absolutely, Mom," said Dorrie. "This is awful! Why, it's awful! I'll be there. You don't have to do a thing. I'll take care of everything."

Just as Michele could not legally be presumed a missing person until seventy-two hours had passed, so could her car not be legally presumed to be abandoned for the same length of time, and it stood there in the parking lot just as she had left it. No fingerprints had been found and none had been expected, due to the heavy fog of Monday night and early Tuesday.

Thursday afternoon the sun came out with brief and pale promise as Jim Copeland changed the tire on his daughter's car.

The shoppers who had parked in A section, most of whom had read the front page of the local paper, and many having heard a number of the news spots from the local radio station, walked an arc of sympathetic self-consciousness around Jim Copeland and his daughter's car. All were hurried and embarrassed except for one, the man who drove into A section in a light gray compact and stepped out of it with an offer to help Jim Copeland change the tire.

The man, youngish, about thirty-five, Jim decided, squinting up at him, really wanted to help. He was slim, personable, conservatively dressed, of medium height and with medium brown hair—unless, of course, he might have been seen at night in the deceptive light of the floods with their elongated shadows, making any man tall, especially if standing next to a girl of five feet one inch, just as night light colors all brown hair dark, particularly when contrasted with blonde.

With the spare in place, the damaged tire, jack, and lug wrench back in the trunk, the young man leaned against his car to talk about Monday night.

Grateful for his interest, Jim Copeland listened to ideas that were neither as objective as those of the police nor as emotional as Jim's own, but a combination of emotional objectivity that could be trusted.

"I read about it in last night's paper," said the man, "and I've been hearing radio reports all day. I'm a salesman and in my car a lot and have the radio on. I wonder if the police are going about it in the right way."

"I wonder, too," said Jim Copeland. "They say they aren't even sure if the man with whom those people saw Michele had anything to do with it. They say it's possible he might have driven away and Michele walked off to find a phone, and whatever happened, happened then."

The man shook his head. "He had everything to do with it," he said with certainty. "I'd bet on it. The one with the white car."

"I think so, too," said Jim. "I think he slashed the tire and waited for her."

The man gave the damaged tire a token glance. "No. In the first place, how would he know the driver was a girl? Even if he looked in and saw the registration on the steering wheel post, how would he know the girl would be alone? Whoever it was didn't plan the thing. It just happened."

Jim closed the trunk and leaned against it. "You think the tire was flat and he saw it and just waited and when it turned out to be a girl, especially a pretty girl, he went through all the motions, and then as soon as there wasn't anyone around, he forced her into his car? She sure as hell wouldn't go with him willingly."

"What if he seemed like a nice sort of fellow? Clean-cut, pleasant, helpful, not a long-haired hoodlum kid or old enough to be a dirty old man, but somewhere in between, and he says he'd be glad to help and he gets out the jack and gets to work. What can happen under the lights? Then he hauls out the spare and bounces it up and down on the pavement and says it needs air—"

"But it had plenty of air," interrupted Jim, kicking the tire.

"Okay," said the man, "but would your girl have known any different if somebody'd told her it hadn't?"

No, thought Jim Copeland. All Michele had known about a car was how to drive it. It could have happened the way the man had said.

"So he says he guesses she'd better ride with him down to the filling station to get some air in the tire. The filling station's down on the corner. You can see it from here."

Obediently, Jim Copeland, who was a regular customer of that filling station, shaded his eyes toward the corner of Sargent and Oak where he could see the top of the station sign.

"What's she going to do? Even a girl like yours, who wouldn't willingly get into a car with a stranger, this time she's going to think nothing of it. After all, the guy's knocking himself out for her, and he's honest enough not to want to take off with her tire, leaving her to stand there all alone, scared he might steal it and not come back." The man smiled, curving the smile into a combination of arrogant pity for the father and pompous regret for the daughter.

"You mean you think she might have been tricked into this weirdo's car?" asked Jim Copeland.

"Not tricked, exactly," said the man, "and the guy wasn't necessarily a weirdo. He might have been sick."

"*Sick?*"

"Look, I'm basing this hypothesis on the psychology I have learned. You see, I set out to be a consulting psychologist and then my wife got sick and I had to drop out of school and make money to take care of her. That was years ago. Haven't had any married life since and no career either. Just work at a sales job to give an invalid wife the things she needs and wants . . ." He shook his head with self-pity. "That's what I was doing here Monday night, getting her one of the things she's always after me to get—a prescription, ice cream, a heating pad or an ice bag, anything, something—"

"You mean you were here at the shopping center that night?" Jim Copeland leaned forth from the trunk of the little green car to grab the jacket lapels of the man. "You were here that night? Did you see something? Did you see any of that stuff you've been talking about?"

The man shook loose. "I told you," he said, "everything I told you is theoretical. I think about it. The police in a case like this want fingerprints or a hair or something before they're satisfied, and the relatives keep saying 'My daughter wouldn't,' and all I'm doing *is* showing how your daughter *might*, because I have studied those things and understand them. And I think he's sick, but a kind of a nice guy so your girl got into his car . . ."

Jim Copeland smothered the man's lapels with apologetic pats. He was only trying to help and, God knows, this theory he'd come up with was a lot more believable than those of the police—talking about drugs and pregnancy and running away—none of which could apply to *Michele!*

"So we assume the guy was sick," explained the man. "Oh, not ordinarily, but just when the pressures build up. Let's say he's a nice guy. Your girl wouldn't go with anybody but a nice guy . . ."

Jim Copeland nodded.

"He doesn't plan anything. It gets planned for him."

"Gets planned?" asked Jim.

"That's the psychology of an impulse crime and I think it was a crime of impulse; nothing premeditated, but an extemporaneous impulse triggered by a series of circumstances. The guy's under a lot of pressure, he's at the exploding point. He drives into the parking lot late, just before closing time. He's in a hurry, probably doesn't even notice the little green car with its flat, at first. When he gets ready to leave, he notices but he doesn't think too much about it. The parking lot's thinned out, customers have taken off for their homes filled with loving, healthy, undemanding wives. He starts his motor. Then the girl comes, your girl, and she sees the flat and the guy turns off his motor and gets out."

Jim Copeland swallowed.

It could have been exactly like that.

"He's a nice guy," repeated the man. "He really wants to help, so he helps. He get the jack out. Then the people drive by, those people who saw your girl and the guy. They slow down. They wave. And the guy wonders if your girl might be signaling, might be rejecting him and his help, signaling to her friends.

"But they go on and he jacks up the car and starts to reach for the lug wrench, still helping. Then the explosion comes, the pressures blow skyhigh and he reaches for the spare, instead, and bounces it on the pavement. The whole thing's set up for him. He's sick and can't help what happens."

Jim Copeland looked away, feeling ill.

The pale sun hid behind the clouds that were rising on the horizon. It would rain again; sure enough, it would rain again tonight.

"He gives her the filling station pitch. She goes for it because there's not much else she can do. He helps her around his car and opens the door, then goes around to his side, leaving the spare on the pavement. He jumps in and they're off before she can even yell."

Jim Copeland felt as if he were swimming in the filtered light of the winter day. "You think," he said faintly, "that's the way it happened? That anyone could just—"

"That's the way it could have happened," said the man. "There were no signs of struggle. The police pointed that out. You said your girl wouldn't go off with a stranger willingly, so what other way could there be? It's a psychologically sound theory that a sick man, but a nice guy, found a setup just made for him to act on at a time that his pressures exploded . . ."

Jim Copeland looked away.

Then the man gave him hope. "A sick mind like that, though," he said, "knows he's sick and wants to be stopped."

Jim Copeland jerked his head back, and listened with intent.

"He'll cover—self-preservation, you know, being the first law—but at the same time, he'll drop clues, just hoping someone will find them and stop him from doing again what he has already done."

The man opened his car door and stepped inside. "I'm sorry, Mr. Copeland," he said, genuinely sorry.

He turned on his motor and the radio sounds came on immediately, faintly at first, to grow stronger into the on-the-hour news broadcast. ". . . Nothing yet on the Michele Copeland disappearance," came the voice of the announcer. "If you know of anything, or think you might know, or suspect . . ." The man turned down the volume to a whisper and started to back his car from its parking slot.

Jim Copeland straightened from the trunk of the little green car. "What do you think he did with her?" he asked the man.

"What do *you* think?"

Jim Copeland swallowed again.

The man turned the wheel, straightened out, and started down the A section of the parking lot.

"Hey," called Jim Copeland, "I didn't get your name."

The man shouted it out the window, but the sound was lost in the rising wind of the early evening and the growl of the motor as he turned to make the off-ramp onto Sargent.

The police didn't think much of Jim Copeland's theoretical story as told to him by the stranger in the parking lot when he immediately drove the little green car to headquarters and related it.

"A crackpot," they stated. "We get them all the time. A mother who's had it up to here with this rotten kid of hers thinks he did it and wants us to lock him up and throw away the key. Some dame says it's the kind of trick her ex-boyfriend would pull. You been in this work as long as we have, you expect all kinds of trumped-up stories."

"But this was a theory," argued Jim. "This man seemed to know a lot about psychology, and he was basing this theory on his psychological knowledge."

"Every crackpot is a psychologist," said the officer. "They know everything about nothing and are eager to talk about it."

"But it sounded," said Jim with hesitation, "as if it could have really happened. It sounded right, somehow. If you could talk to him . . ."

"Sure," and the officer poised a pencil over a scratchpad. "Sure, we'll talk to him. We talk to all of 'em. Just give us his name and address."

Jim didn't know his name or where he lived. That bit of information had been snatched away in the wind, and maybe he *was* a crackpot, like the officer said. What had the man offered, after all? Just a theory.

Dorrie arrived late that Thursday afternoon, at the beginning of the storm that had been brewing and slacking off, allowing the sun to peek through, then closing in again. The storm broke, dark and vicious and Dorrie walked in about the same time her father drove the little green car home and parked it, once again, in the driveway.

From then on, every time Sue looked out the window she saw that little green car and shuddered, and every time she turned from the window Dorrie told her it was Jim's fault that Michele was gone, until she believed it.

"Your own daughter," she denounced him, "and you slept through it all."

"What could I have done?" he asked. "She was gone by ten. That's what those people at the parking lot said."

"With you home here, asleep," accused Sue, appalled at her own vindictiveness, but relieved to have a victim at last.

Jim was confused. "If I'd been awake, I wouldn't have gone after her by ten. Why would I? I'd have thought she'd stopped to have coffee with somebody."

"But not Mom," Dorrie broke in. "If Mom had been here, she'd have known Michele is never late. She'd have been out of here like a flash."

"But she wasn't here," said Jim, seeing his opportunity to fix blame, knowing that if the blame were to be circumvented it must be fixed upon someone else. "She was at your house, babysitting. That's why she wasn't here."

Ready for him, Dorrie answered in triumph, "Because she trusted you, that's why she wasn't here. She trusted you to take care of things and protect Michele so this awful thing wouldn't happen."

Thursday evening the story in the paper was more compact and without a photograph, headlined simply, HUNT CONTINUES, with a quick synopsis and the usual vague promise of an expected break.

The taped television interview had been cut to the bone to allow newscast pictures and commentary on the storm in progress, with accounts of sliding hillsides in the city to the north and stories of boiling rivers within the sprawling megalopolis to the south. The town in between lay ignored, as usual, except for the tape-cut interview with the parents of Michele Copeland.

However, it, too, was having its storm troubles with minor erosion of the hills and overflowing river banks, its greatest problem being the flooded streets and, more particularly, that corner at the intersection of Sexton and Sargent where the new tract of houses was under construction. There the water rose and flowed down the grade, bringing with it mud and debris, clogging the curbing outlets and flooding the Plaza shopping center parking area so that the water swirled into the mall and threatened the shops.

The storm lasted three days.

During that time, Sue could not sleep, her fearful nights being filled with terror-thoughts of her baby, out there someplace, out there alone or with a monster in the cold and the rain, out there dead or dying. Sue could not eat, her frightful days being consumed by horror-pictures of ravishment and death. She lived on coffee and the wakefulness it engendered. She lashed out at Jim as an object for her emotion. She worked him over, discovering after all their peaceful years together that she had a talent for it.

Dorrie, having shifted the weight of her own guilt, now carried a new burden. Her parents, always friends, were now enemies, and was that her fault?

"Mom," she cried, "I never heard you talk to Dad like that before."

"He never killed my daughter before," said Sue.

Periodically, Jim drove through the storm to the police station to find the officers engaged with traffic problems and slick-street accidents.

"About my daughter . . ." Jim Copeland asked anxiously, apologetic with this new deep guilt his wife had thrust upon him.

"We're working on it, Mr. Coepland," said the officer. "We've got those flyers out, you know. We wish we had more information, like a better description of the man and what kind of car he drove. We did the best we could with what we have. A picture of your daughter is on the flyer, and anythii suspicious—well, we'll hear about it. I know how you feel, Mr. Copeland."

Jim Copeland looked at him blankly. This officer, too young yet for guilt, too young for teenage daughters, could not possibly know how he felt. Jim turned and left the police station, knowing that he would return shortly, to learn nothing again; but he had to come, a telephone call would not suffice. He had to come through storm-filled streets, and climb the stairs and open the heavy doors, and ask whichever officer was on the desk at the time, "Have you heard anything about my daughter?" He had to. There was nothing else he could do now.

The storm hampered the search, but it did not hamper Mrs. Carrie Mason. Daily, she made a tent of her late husband's raincoat and crouched under it, a platter of baked, fried, grilled, or broiled food covered and clutched, and scampered from her house to the Copelands'.

There she made her offering, always hoping it would be only Sue she might encounter in the kitchen. Even Sue, who had changed so drastically during the last of these few days from a soft and warm anxiety to being anxiously hard and cold, was better than her daughter Dorrie; Dorrie, who looked down her nose from the enviable heights of her youthful, husband-filled life, and caused within Carrie Mason great pangs of guilt for her own manless old age of almost fifty—no, actually fifty-two, almost fifty-three—and sometimes looked it.

So, guiltily, when it was Dorrie in the kitchen, she handed out the covered plate of whatever she had prepared and asked softly if there had been any news, any news at all.

Dorrie, taking the covered plate without even glancing under the cover, looked down from her pinnacle of security and said there was no news but, "We thank you for your kindness."

"No kindness!" protested Carrie. "It was Monday night when I should have been kind, the night I was sure something was wrong. At eleven o'clock I saw the porch light on and the driveway empty. I should have come then, and I didn't."

"Then it would have been too late," said Dorrie.

It might *not* have been too late, worried Carrie. On a Monday night this town was in bed by eleven and so, with the few cars on the streets at that time of night, they might have found Michele.

Carrie could not easily shift her burden of guilt, being neither young enough nor egotistical enough. Her guilt caused her to make a firm resolve: from now on she would be warmly friendly—instantly. She would not hesitate or vacillate, distrustful of her breath, apprehensive as to appearances, but she would, so help her, aid, assist, succor, and befriend anyone who might need her, and she would be watchful for the need.

By Sunday, the storm was over.

On Monday, a week after Michele's disappearance, the street maintenance crews were out in full force and got to work to find out what was wrong in the area extending from the hills into the Plaza shopping center, which was a mess. The trouble was found to be at the intersection where the new tract of houses was under construction and now a sea of mud. The storm drain there seemed to be clogged, allowing an overflow of water and muck down Sargent, where it spread into the side streets and filled up the parking lot.

A work crew was called, and when they opened up the storm drain they found Michele's body doubled up and stuffed into it, plugging up the opening.

Linda Fischer heard it on the radio.

This was her late day at Harper's department store, starting at one and extending to nine o'clock closing time, so she was, that Monday morning, cleaning her apartment with the radio on when the newscast broke in to announce the discovery of Michele Copeland's body. She cringed, thinking what if, oh my goodness, what if she had allowed her husband to stop that night? He, too, might have been killed. Thus she absolved herself of any guilt, and turned her act of remission into one of nobility.

Her husband heard it during his lunch hour. "That girl," said the man on the stool next to him, "they found her. You know, the girl who disappeared a week ago."

Linda's husband swallowed the bite he had already taken from his sandwich and carefully laid the sandwich back on the plate.

"They found her in the storm drain up on Sargent and Sexton. Awful!"

Mrs. Fischer's husband pushed back his plate, got off his stool, and walked woodenly from the drugstore. He walked down the street to the parking lot next to the business-machine office where he worked, got into his car, drove carefully down Main Street, past all the Caution signs to protect the street workers, entered the on-ramp to the freeway at the edge of town, and sped north.

He never wanted to see his wife, Linda, again. He would lose himself somewhere, in some city far away, and try to forget that if Linda had not stopped him a week ago, Michele would be alive now.

On that second Monday morning, Carrie Mason was busy preparing a hearty vegetable soup for the Copeland family. The radio in the kitchen, as always, was turned to the local station but she knew, even before the newscast told her so, that Michele had been found. She knew it when the police car drove up and the two police officers, their faces blankly reluctant, slowly climbed the steps to the Copeland front porch. So Carrie Mason knew, and as soon as the news was announced, remembering her always-be-friendly, help-in-time-of-need resolution, she knew that she would take the bowl of soup over even though, by the time the soup was ready, her breath would be redolent of bourbon, that she would look every minute of her almost fifty-three years, and that she wouldn't know what to say.

Jim Copeland took the news like a doomed man, dully aware of the fact that he was, indeed, doomed.

Sue turned on him with a final, "This is your fault," knowing that she would never speak to him again.

Dorrie, in the depths of her new guilt, wished that she could have the old one back, realizing at last that the guilt she had bequeathed herself would be lasting and difficult to endure.

By Monday night the body, having been properly identified, was properly resting in the funeral home.

Monday night, at nine ten, Linda Fischer emerged from Harper's department store into the parking lot of the Plaza shopping center. She walked out with a part-time co-worker, a college girl from the notions department in which Michele had worked the week before. The girl hadn't known Michele, but claimed acquaintanceship because they went to the same college and worked in the same store and it was all terribly exciting.

"We actually saw him that night," Linda said, and the girl hung on her words. "It was just a good thing my husband didn't stop. He might have been killed, too."

There were few cars left in Section A. The two walked carefully on the dry, caked mud. "Well, here's my car," said the girl. "Isn't your husband here? Do you want a lift?"

"No, thank you. You go ahead." Linda consulted her watch. "He'll be along," she said. "I'm out a little early. He'll be here by nine twenty for sure. He always is."

She didn't begin to worry until nine forty, and the last car was gone from Section A. Then she became frightened and ran past the now darkened shops to the coffee shop, still light, but empty of customers. The proprietor was just closing up.

"Would you drive me home?" Linda asked him breathlessly. "Would you please drive me home? I'm scared to wait for my husband out there all alone because of what happened . . ."

He would be glad to. He closed up the doughnut case, covered the cakes, turned off the lights, and locked the door. He was very kind and solicitous. He helped her into his car and headed toward the apartment section of town where Mrs. Linda Fischer said she lived.

It was not until they reached the turn-off into Sargent that Linda realized she was in exactly the same situation Michele Copeland had been at this very same time last Monday night.

She froze on her side of the seat and her voice, as she gave directions, emerged as a thin thread of sound, stitching together the man's earnest talk of the dangers that lurked for a woman alone in the night. She lived only a few blocks from the Plaza shopping center, and she was sure she would never arrive there, but the man drove her directly to her destination and she was startled when he stopped and she looked out at her very own apartment building. She leaned on the door and staggered from the car, too voiceless from her moments of terror to thank the man. Her strength returned with her relief as she ran toward the apartment door, banged it open, and stumbled up the stairs.

The moment she opened her own door upon darkness, she realized what an awful thing she had done when she prevented her husband from stopping to help Michele Copeland a week ago. It was the next moment that Mrs. Linda Fischer realized that her husband had left her and would not be back, because the awful thing she did to Michele she had also done to him.

Wednesday was the morning of the funeral. In the curtained-off mourners' section of the chapel, Dorrie sat between Michele's father and Michele's mother so that each parent wept alone through the ceremony.

Wednesday afternoon, Carrie Mason took over a pumpkin pie, and Dorrie had to push aside a mountain of dishes and a stack of pans to find room for it.

The kitchen looked as if a tornado had torn through, and there was Sue, dragging out linens and piling them up, making lists, dashing from one task to another. Carrie Mason wondered what in the world was going on and thought perhaps now that Jim and Sue Copeland were to be alone and with diminished needs, they had decided to reward Dorrie for all her self-sacrificing help by sending her home with extra household goods.

"You will probably be leaving now," Carrie said to Dorrie.

"Tomorrow," said Dorrie.

"I am going with her," said Sue without interrupting the even rhythm of her activity.

"Well," said Carrie, doubtfully supposing that maybe it was all right for a bereaved mother to go off and grieve with her daughter and grandchildren instead of staying home to grieve with the bereaved father, but she wasn't sure. "Well," she said, "that's nice. Now you go right ahead and have a wonderful vacation . . ." and halted mid-sentence, appalled at her poor choice of words, and unaware of the conversation going on around her until she heard the last part of Sue's amazing announcement, ". . . and I am not coming back. Not ever. I am going to live with Dorrie and her family."

Yes," said Dorrie. "Mom will live with us."

The minute she said it, Sue knew that she didn't want to go. The minute she said she was never coming back she turned sick at the thought of leaving Jim. The minute she declared, "I am going to live with Dorrie and her family," she wondered how she would be able to bear her daughter's domination and the tyranny of three spoiled grandchildren.

When Dorrie added, to make it stick, "Yes, Mom will live with us," she knew she had saddled herself with a live-in mother, Hal with an unwanted mother-in-law, and the children with a grandmother who would not be good for them and to whom they would not be good. She had done this to herself and hers, and now she would have to live with it.

The two loaded cars, Dorrie's and Sue's, departed on Thursday, leaving Jim Copeland alone. Carrie Mason certainly wanted to take him some food, wanted to be warm and friendly as she had so firmly resolved, but she could not find him. He had gone back to work, of course, but he came home quietly and late. The porch light never went on any more, nor the light in the living room. Carrie Mason could not see even the flicker of the TV screen.

He was home only twice during the weekends; once when a long-haul moving van carted away certain pieces of furniture, and another time when a local van carted away the rest of it.

Three weeks after the funeral, Michele's little green car had been driven away and the house had been dismantled and a For Sale sign went up in the front yard.

Then Jim Copeland came over to see Mrs. Carrie Mason.

She offered him coffee, which he refused, explaining that he was busy and in a hurry. She noticed how thin he had become and she fluttered over him, not caring that she had bourbon on her breath, only wishing to be warm and friendly.

He told her he was living in a small apartment in town and was in the process of selling the house, which was why he was here; he wanted to leave one of the house keys with her, "Just in case," he said, and she wasn't sure whether he meant just in case Sue returned or just in case a prospective buyer wanted to take a look at the house.

The rest of the keys, he explained, were in the hands of the real estate agent who would be showing the house, but he wanted her to have one of them, "just in case."

Then he left and Mrs. Mason had nothing more to look at through the venetian blinds of her bedroom; nothing except the closed drapes of the living room next door, and a corner of the For Sale sign out in front.

Money being tight and interest rates up, not many people came to look at the house, but enough so that Carrie learned to recognize the real estate agent's car and to know it wasn't his when the light gray compact drew up to the curb in front of the Copeland house. It drove on again, but returned a few days later.

The third time she saw it, she was out in her front yard planting the last of her spring bulbs and hopeful that she could finish before the twilight turned to darkness. She rose from her knees when the car pulled up out in front, dropped her trowel, and walked from her yard to the next and down to the curbing.

"If you are interested in the house," she said to the young man in the car, "I have a key and I can take you through. But we'll have to hurry because the electricity has been turned off and it's getting dark. There won't be much time."

"Oh. Oh, yes," he said, momentarily startled, as if he were so fascinated by the house that he had been totally unaware of her approach. "Didn't the Copelands used to live here?"

"Yes. Such a tragedy." Mrs. Carrie Mason could not see the young man very well in the shadows of the car. He seemed nice, though, and personable. "Did you know them?" she asked.

"I met the girl just once," said the man.

"Michele? The one who was killed?"

"Yes. That one. And I talked to her father once." Abruptly, as if suddenly conscious of her existence, the man leaned across the car seat and looked directly at Carrie Mason in the now-purple twilight. "I have a wife, you see," he said, "who is an invalid . . ."

Carrie clucked with sympathy.

"We live in an apartment now, and I thought if we had a house, she could be outdoors more."

"Oh, she could, and that would be wonderful," said Carrie.

"I'm a salesman and out a lot and I would insist upon a good neighborhood, one I wouldn't have to worry about leaving her alone in. Nice and quiet. Decent."

Carrie started to describe the utter niceness, the restful quiet and the pure decency of the neighborhood when he broke in with, "I would like to see the house very much, but as you warned me, it is getting a little dark for that, but if I could look around the neighborhood, Mrs. . . . ?"

"Mrs. Carrie Mason," she said.

"Mrs. Mason, I think this might be just the house I have been wanting. I can come back tomorrow, of course, to go through it, but I do want to get a look at the neighborhood first. It's still light enough for that. I wonder if you would show me . . ."

Carrie moved back a step.

"Just a short drive around the block. Only to point out the market and the nearest drugstore." He chuckled in a half-sorrowful, half-rueful fashion. "My wife needs and wants so many things at all hours—a prescription, ice cream, a heating pad or an ice bag, anything, something—"

Carrie remembered her firm resolve to aid and abet in a warm and friendly fashion.

"And if I had someone to show me around so I could describe the neighborhood to my wife tonight, perhaps rouse her interest, then tomorrow . . ."

Carrie gave one backward glance at her lawn, almost dark now, where the trowel and the remaining bulbs lay on the ground, and at her dark and unlocked house. "It will be only a few minutes?" she asked.

"Only a few minutes," he assured her.

She stepped inside the car, and the gray compact moved down the street.

CHARLES W. RUNYON

The Waiting Room

Pawley watched the rain streak the dirty glass. He liked the way the droplets started out small at the top, hung there for a moment, raced downward until they met a companion, hung for a shorter time, and then began the long swift plunge to the bottom of the pane, taking everything with them. Life is like that. Nobody likes to go down alone.

The air inside the station was warm, diffused with dampness and the smell of road dust and old rubber. New rubber was better, rich and pungent. When he was a kid, he always liked to smell new rubber. He always liked to watch rain on a window, too. Funny, he'd had to run like hell for thirty-two years just to get back where he started. Not in a geographic sense, of course. The southern California plain was a lot different from the piney slopes of Arkansas. Flat as a table, like you weren't on the earth at all, but on some kind of mirror.

Pawley was a tall man, rather gaunt. His prominent nose hooked slightly, and his blue eyes sat steady inside deep sockets. He wore a gabardine jacket and gray trousers, a white shirt and a maroon tie. He dressed as people do who are not aware of clothes; they didn't exactly fit, and he made no attempt to adapt his bony frame to them. There were wrinkles at the collar, and though the tie was pulled up tight below the thrusting larynx, the top button of his shirt was undone. The hat was a chocolate brown felt, crushed on one side, somehow failing to adapt its shape to Pawley's narrow skull. The coarse hair above his ears was threaded with gray.

Pawley placed his palm flat against his face and with his fingers tipped the hat onto the back of his head. He put his forehead to the glass, not surprised that it was the same temperature as the room. Glancing out to the right, he saw rows of cabbages stretching to infinity, pale green, with sheets of water in between. He saw a movement of pale blue. Finding a broken pane, he lifted the heavy .45 from his pocket and thrust it through the window, bending his elbow at a right angle. The gun bucked in his hand. A geyser of muddy water shot up and the patch of blue dropped out of sight.

Pawley withdrew his hand. At least he was dry. The cops were all wet. He laughed.

John looked up, his broad face drawn in a puzzled frown. He was stocky, stooped in the shoulders where his brown suit jacket pinched. He always looked as though he didn't quite understand what he was seeing.

"How many you got left?" he asked.

Pawley flicked on the safety and withdrew the magazine, counting the coppery eyes which glinted through the slot. "Four."

"I'm all out." John spun the chamber of his .38 and let it drop from his fingers. Thunk! on the concrete. Pawley heard the sound echoing inside his head. Thunk. Sound of clean-shot squirrel falling out of high pine tree. Thunk. Sound of bat against ball, grandslam homer in the last of the ninth. Thunk. Fist against jaw. Thunk, thunk, thunk. Well, I've had all those things.

He watched John tie his shoelaces. "Think you'll walk out?"

John stretched his legs in front of him, heels on the floor, toes pointed outward. He cupped his broad, blackhaired hands over his groin and shook his head.

"Wouldn't get far. They dragged back two dead ones. There's another one out in that car. 'Spect they're pretty mad at us."

Pawley looked out the window. The asphalt ribbon dwindled almost to a point before it climbed into the mountains. Fifty yards away sat the patrol car with two sunbursts in the windshield. The front wheels were cramped hard and part way in the grader ditch, the rear wheels were in the road, back end lifted high. Something funny about those wounded cars; Pawley could never see them all shiny and neat in a showroom without imagining how they'd look this way, too. He always thought of dead grasshoppers.

He saw his own car pulled up beside the dry pumps. They'd done all right until they met the patrol car. Must have had a description from the bank guard, because the car did a switch-itch and took after them. One hundred miles an hour, and a lucky shot holed their gas tank. Just made it to here and found the station closed, empty. Pawley had realized, with a certain relief, that it was the end of the road.

He could see the roadblock a quarter mile away, cars beginning to pile up behind it. Word must have gotten out. Spectators, reporters coming in for the kill. Make him famous for a day. Hell, he didn't care about being famous. Just tried to get in a few licks, it was only a game. He always shot to kill, that was part of the game. Always ate till he was full. Always got a woman when he felt like a woman.

A clot of blue reared up among the green. He aimed the gun and felt it buck in his hand. The man fell. He aimed the gun and felt it buck in his hand. The man fell. He aimed the gun and felt it . . .

Take him down behind the shed and shoot him. Acting nonchalant, you snapped your fingers and old Brindle, shaggy old brown mongrel, worth nothing to anybody, followed you down behind the shed and you stood him up there among the round black pellets of sheep droppings. He cocked his head while you raised the old single-shot, octagon barrel .22 with the magic sight. He looked at you, wondering what the game was, and you tried to force the hatred you were supposed to feel. Dirty sheepkiller. He ran and licked your hand and you slapped him and cursed him, you dirty sheepkiller, but only sickness came and Brindle stretched out his long jaw on the two paws, looked up, and you let him have it right between the quizzical brown eyes. Though you didn't know it then, there were two deaths that afternoon, the boy and the dog. You remember the weather, too, hot July day, acrid smell of sheep droppings, the sun had set, but heat still radiated from the old pine building. There are moments like these slicing right through the layers of your life, Pawley, cutting right through and connected, back to back, like a pair of aces and everything in between is just so much filler, like insulation, because if you lived your whole life at that level, man, you'd *burn*. . . .

Dirty sheepkiller. The man in the blue uniform humped along the watery ditch, raising his rear in the air like an inchworm. He wants to be a hero. Pawley raised the gun and it was a clear shot, but the mist in his eyes clouded his aim, and he decided to save the bullet for the creation of another hero. He pulled out his handkerchief and wiped the sweat from his face, wiping his eyes at the same time. "Three left," he said.

"How long do you figure?"

"Half hour, just as a guess. They'll get rifles and stay out of our range. Keep us pinned down while the others make a rush."

The building was built of cinder block, waist high. From there to the tile roof were ten-inch panes of glass set in a steel frame, painted red. It shared the same level as the highway, about five feet above the surrounding fields. The only interruption of view came from the washroom, which was cinder block to the ceiling, and occupied a six-foot square in the northwest corner. Pawley gazed a long time at the closed door. Shirley had been inside a long time. He called out, asked what she was doing.

"Changing my underwear."

He looked at John, who raised his shoulders in a shrug. Then Pawley understood. She knew this was the end and she wanted to die with clean underwear. It struck him as funny, and he started laughing.

She came out a moment later, her eyes naked and defenseless. Strange, the way her high cheekbones pushed up her eyes into narrow slits. They were knife-points that stuck into him and made him tingle. She always did it to him; stripped him clean of pretense. Her red-brown hair was brushed into a soft wave, which curled out beyond her ears, then curled back to lie against her collarbone. The bony structure of her chest showed above the low line of her jersey. Some kind of sleazy material, shot full of gold. He didn't like that kind of material, he wondered why she wore things he didn't like, particularly at this time. No makeup, her mouth wide, upper lip long. Nose a straight shiny line, high forehead. A scent about her that no perfume had ever hidden, like hay molding, like butterscotch and cracked walnuts, a sense of richness which made his nerve-ends stretch until they touched emptiness.

He watched her sit down in the swivel chair behind the desk and light a cigarette. A piece of paper clung to her lower lip, she caught it between long, unpolished nails and peeled it off. Every movement did something for him. The bend in her elbow was more important to him than the articulation of his own muscles. He'd met her when she was sixteen and now she was twenty-four. He didn't know if he liked her or not; just that when she wasn't around, everything was flat and dead and lifeless, and the wine and the other women had nothing for him. Twenty-four. That was too young.

"You could go out," he said. "I don't think they'd shoot you, you could live."

"What for?"

Casual and final. You made your own choice, he thought.

Then he wondered if she'd had any choice. From the time they'd met, they'd fit together like dovetails. He'd never talked about his feelings, never even felt the emotions that raced inside him. She found them and brought them out. She didn't dig. She just knew they were there, and she didn't give a damn for his feelings or his pride, or anything like that—just him.

He watched her open a magazine and start thumbing through it. One of the pages caught his eye and he read a paragraph. The words were like gruel, like food chewed up and swallowed by some Eskimo woman, then regurgitated, absent of all spice, flavor, and sauce. She had her legs crossed, the short skirt off her knees. She had bony knees. He loved her bones. She could have been waiting for a dentist.

He thought of her flesh and the death of her flesh—her teeth shattered, organs ripped and skull blown apart in the smash of lead. He felt a longing for her that was not sexual, a desire to enclose her in his arms and take all the bullets into his own flesh.

He went to a wall calendar. It was eight years old and had obviously hung in the station long after its primary purpose had been exhausted. It was adorned by a picture of a girl whose body was impossibly perfect and unblemished, whose breasts were so impossibly round that they were a—what was the word? Cliché. When he said something that Shirley didn't like, she said he was using clichés. Well, baby, how do you like this for a cliché? We're going to die. Everybody does *that*.

Notes on the side of the calendar. *Call Mrs. Cardoza about grease job.* Probably the car was junk by now, and the woman could be dead. Somebody had written *Thelma* and drawn an arrow to the calendar girl. He wondered where Thelma was in the outside world. Here she was lovely, young as ever, desired and desirable. And Mrs. Cardoza was still waiting for her grease job. Here had nothing to do with anywhere else.

"I wonder if they had kids? Wives and kids?"

Shirley was looking out the window, talking about the cops, and thinking about herself. Eight years of love and violence, now ended.

"It doesn't matter," Pawley said.

"How can you say it doesn't matter?"

"With my lips and tongue and throat. Like this." He leaned over her and spoke with exaggerated lip movements. "It doesn't matter."

She raised her face and gave him a flat, blank stare. The light fell on the planes of her face and revealed the fine white hairs on her cheekbones. For a moment he saw violence lying in her eyes like a coiled viper. Then it melted away and she asked in a tone of sincere curiosity, "Are you crazy?"

He thought about it. "That doesn't matter either."

John scraped his feet on the concrete. "We're all crazy, I think."

Pawley turned to look at him. John sat indolently with his back against the wall, the valise between his knees. With a lopsided smile, he opened the bag, took out a deck of currency, pulled out a bill and wadded it up, then snapped off the rubber band and gave the sheaf a backhanded flip toward him. The neat pile disintegrated and fluttered down like feathers. "There. That's what it was about. Now, what the hell good is it?"

Pawley saw the desolation in his eyes. He leaned over, picked up a fifty-dollar bill, struck a match and lit it. Then he shook a cigarette out of his pack and held it to the flame. He held the cigarette out to John and looked into his eyes.

"Everything is good for something."

For a minute, they looked into each other's eyes. Slowly the fear disappeared, and was replaced by puzzlement.

"Pawley, why is it always . . . ?"

Pawley waited, but the puzzlement deepened.

"What?"

John shook his head. "I don't know. For a minute it seemed like I was somebody else . . . waiting for Indians."

"We used to play Indians, back in Arkansas. You ever play Indians, Shirley?"

"I used to get tied up a lot—and tortured."

He looked at her. They had clawed each other's flesh until the blood had mingled. Life was a melting process. A milking process. Life was . . .

He shook his head. Life was.

John was retying his shoes. "I never liked to play Indians. That was you. I never got to be myself. You wanted to make the team. Okay, I made the team. Quit school and go to the coast, ship out and see the world. I went along. When I met a girl I wanted to marry, you said she was a slob, so I dropped her."

Pawley looked out the window. Quiet too long. *Soon* . . . "She was a slob."

"Okay. I could have discovered that myself."

"Why didn't you?"

"I don't think she was. You turned her into one. You'd look at her and make her feel stupid. You turned her into one."

"Well, no matter how she got that way, she was—that way." Pawley turned. "John, you left her and came with us. Maybe you ought to find out why you came with us."

"*Why*? Why anything? Why are we here? I mean . . ." He slapped his palm on the concrete floor, then waved at the wide expanse of the world. "Here. You know."

"We're here to find out why we're here," said Shirley. She was looking out the window. There was no expression on her face. Pawley wished he were she, having thoughts, nice thoughts. When he considered what was about to happen, his brain turned into an ivory doorknob, all white and shiny and nothing on it at all.

"Why are we *here* then?" asked John. "Sitting in a lousy station. Dad raised us, why did he do that?"

"Because we were there," said Pawley.

"But why were we—"

"Shirley told you. To find out why we're here."

John rose and walked stiff-legged to the center of the room. His shoes crumpled the bright green currency. His eyes were wide. "You mean, there's no reason? None of it makes any difference?"

"None of it."

John looked at Shirley. "You agree with that?"

"I agree."

For a moment longer he looked at her, then his face seemed to settle. "I've wanted to do something for eight years."

She looked at him. "Do it."

He stepped forward and caught the shoulders of her jersey, jerking it downward. Her small breasts thrust into the light.

"Does that make a difference?"

She moved her shoulders slightly. "Does it?"

"Hell!" He jerked himself away fast, strode across the room and turned. "Okay, it doesn't make any difference. So why don't we just walk out that door now?"

"Because I want a cigarette," said Pawley. He lit two, and held one out to John. John took it and slumped down with his back against the wall, looking at the floor between his feet. His wrist hung limply from his knees, his cigarette smoked between his fingers.

After a minute, Shirley pulled up her blouse, walked over to John and sat down beside him. She took the cigarette from his fingers and drew slowly, looking at Pawley. Something glittered in her eyes. Pawley knelt down, facing her. John looked up, and for a moment they were all enclosed in a single sweaty hand, breathing with one breath, seeing with a single eye . . .

A bullet came through one of the upper glasses. Ping! Then another. They had rifles now, but they were shooting high. It wouldn't be long. Pawley reached out and squeezed Shirley's shoulder, and felt the bones give beneath his hand. Then he squeezed John's knee, and stood up, not for any reason, but because he wanted to make one last gesture of free will.

Shirley rose and stood beside him. John rose on the other side. Pawley thought of telling him, *You could have had her any time, boy, but I couldn't stand for that because then I'd have lost both of you,* but there was no need to say anything.

"This is the way it is, John."

"Yeah, but I don't have to like it."

"No, you don't have to like it."

Then the bullets came in.

CLARK HOWARD

The Keeper

Charles Lawson, the new warden, took over the prison at noon on a gray, rainy Monday. He held his first staff meeting one hour later.

"Gentlemen," he said from behind a desk vacated by his predecessor just that morning, "you all know who I am and why I'm here. I've been appointed by the governor to succeed the former head of this institution, and I've been given full authority to act in whatever manner I feel will be in the best interests of the state."

Lawson rose and turned to the window behind his chair. He looked out at the big yard, still scorched and blackened from the riot that had been contained barely forty-eight hours earlier.

"Two inmates dead," Lawson said quietly. "Sixteen men injured; five of them guards. And," he turned back to his chair, "many thousands of dollars in damage done to the prison itself."

He sat back down and fingered a worn pipe from his coat pocket. The men seated in front of him—a deputy warden, the guard captain, and three guard lieutenants—watched as he carefully filled the pipe from a leather tobacco pouch. When the bowl was packed to suit him, he clamped the stem between his teeth and dug one thumbnail into the head of a stick match, snapping it to flame. He put the match to the bowl and lighted the tobacco, puffing pungent, gray whirls of smoke into the room.

"My instructions from the governor are threefold," he said, shaking the match out and tossing it into the former warden's ashtray. "First, and most important, I am to restore complete order throughout the prison. Second, I am to tighten and maintain strict internal security. And third, I am to conduct an in-depth investigation to determine the factual causes of the riot, to place formal blame on any guilty parties, and to rectify, if possible, the conditions that sparked the trouble in the first place. Now then," he leaned back in the unfamiliar chair, "I would like to hear recommendations for a procedure to accomplish the first objective: restoring complete order throughout the prison."

"I can answer that for you," said Fred Hull, the prison's guard captain. "In fact, I can tell you how to accomplish *all* of your objectives. Lock Ralph Starzak in the hole and throw away the key."

"Ralph Starzak," Lawson reflected. He drummed his fingers silently on the arm of the chair. "That's Ralph Starzak, the big-time fence from the early 1950's? Been up here fourteen or fifteen years?"

"Sixteen," said Hull. "Doing twenty, and he'll be with us the max, too. The parole board turned him down for the last time three months ago; they gave him a four-year set, so he'll have to do the full twenty."

"Are you saying that Starzak is the *entire* problem, captain? That he's the cause of *all* the prison's problems?"

"I am," said Hull flatly. "I'm saying exactly that."

"Well," Lawson said.

He puffed at his pipe and nodded slowly. "What about you other men? Do all of you agree with Captain Hull?"

For a moment there was silence in the room. The three guard lieutenants glanced at one another but said nothing. Finally Roger Stiles, the young deputy warden, spoke up.

"Sir," he said to Lawson, "with all due respect to Captain Hull's position and experience, I'm afraid I'll have to disagree with him. I'm sure I'll be a minority of one, but I think the captain is exaggerating Starzak's importance among the prisoners. I don't think he has anywhere near the influence that Captain Hull credits him with—"

"Influence!" Hull roared. "He's behind every racket in the whole joint! He controls every con in every responsible position in the place."

"That's not entirely true," Stiles said mildly. "He doesn't control the inmate teachers in the school—"

"The inmate teachers!" Hull spat the words out scornfully. "Who'd *want* to control them? They're nobodies to the rest of the cons! I'm talking about control over cons who *matter*—the ones in the inmate commissary, the dining room, the laundry. I'm talking about the ones a con has to pay off if he wants clean denims twice a week and a thicker slice of meat on his tray at supper, and a full tobacco allowance instead of a three-quarter measure."

"Are you insinuating that Starzak controls all of that?" Lawson asked.

"That and more," Hull said, "and I'm not insinuating; I'm stating a *fact*. There is no doubt about it."

"An unsubstantiated opinion isn't a fact," Stiles said quietly.

"I'm afraid he has a valid point there," the new warden said to Hull. "Do you have any proof, captain? Any definite infraction of an inmate regulation that you could charge him with?"

Hull glared briefly at the young deputy warden sitting beside him. "No," he said in a near sullen tone.

"Are there any inmates who might be willing to cooperate with us in an investigation of Starzak?" Lawson asked.

Hull shook his head.

"You must have an informant or two on the yard," Lawson said. "I've never seen a prison that didn't."

"Sure," Hull admitted, "we've got stoolies. They'll stool on any con in the joint—except Starzak."

"Then we really have no basis for disciplinary action, do we?"

"Not unless you want to accept my personal recommendation and put him in solitary," Hull said rather stiffly.

Lawson drummed his fingers on the desk again.

"Let me give the matter some thought," he said neutrally. "Let me get a better feel of the place. I'll discuss it with you in greater detail before I make a final decision. In the meantime, I think we'd all better get busy with the primary objective of restoring order in all areas. What is our situation at the present?"

"We're in good shape securitywise," Hull answered. "A and B Blocks are completely under control, and Tiers One through Five in C Block have been secured. Tier Six in C Block is locked in; they're on a hunger strike, haven't eaten since breakfast Saturday."

"How long do you think they'll hold out?"

Hull rubbed his chin reflectively. "Tuesday noon at the latest."

"All right. What else?"

"Eight of the rioters are still holed up in the shoe shop. They're unarmed—" he looked pointedly at the deputy warden, Stiles, "but we've been instructed not to take them out by force."

Lawson turned to Stiles and raised his eyebrows inquiringly.

"We have more than twenty thousand dollars' worth of shoe manufacturing machinery in that shop," the deputy warden explained. "The men will destroy it if we try to force them out. I'm negotiating with them through Father Cahill, the prison chaplain; I think they'll come out voluntarily—" now he looked pointedly at Hull, "*without* costing the state a new shoe shop."

"All right," Lawson said. He directed his attention back to Hull. "What else?"

The guard captain shrugged. "That's about the extent of it. Isolation is more than half full; so is the dispensary, nearly. All three blocks are on early lockup; privileges have been suspended."

"Very well," Lawson said. "Now here's what I want you to do: continue the early lockup, but restore radio and reading privileges in all cells except the tier on hunger strike. At supper tonight have a couple of steam carts sent over and offer a tray of hot food to each man participating in the strike; whoever eats can be restored to dining-hall status. As far as the men in the shoe shop are concerned, let the chaplain continue to try talking them out." He glanced fleetingly at Hull's three guard lieutenants. "By tomorrow noon I want a written appraisal from each of these officers of the situation in each cellblock, along with summary recommendations from you on further general steps to be taken. You can exclude any suggestions regarding Starzak; we'll talk that over between ourselves later." He paused, then said, "Any questions?"

"No questions," Hull answered. He rose from the chair, his three lieutenants doing likewise. The four of them, with Hull in the lead, filed out of the room.

When Stiles and Lawson were alone, the young deputy warden cleared his throat and said, "I'm sorry for the dissension, sir. I'd hoped your first staff meeting would go a little more smoothly."

"Don't give it a thought," Lawson said, smiling. "Frankly, in light of the present situation, I didn't expect it to go nearly as well as it did." He stood up and stuck his pipe in the corner of his mouth. "Let's walk down to the dining hall and get better acquainted over a cup of coffee."

In the huge inmate dining hall, deserted now except for the convicts who worked there, Lawson and Stiles took metal cups and helped themselves to coffee from a large urn behind the steam table. They walked to a nearby aluminum table with self-attached seats, their footsteps resounding hollowly in the great expanse of room. Lawson sipped his coffee in silence for a moment, then looked squarely at the young deputy.

"I hate to put you on the proverbial spot this early in our association," he said flatly, "but as you well know, I myself am also on one. Needless to say, I want to get off of it as quickly as possible. So—what's your evaluation of Captain Hull as a correctional officer?"

Stiles grinned uncomfortably. "You certainly don't beat around the bush about matters, do you?"

"Normally I'd be subtle about it, but in this case I don't have the time. For the present, we'll keep it off the record if you like."

Stiles shrugged. "It's immaterial to me; I'd say the same thing off the record as I would on the record."

"Good," said Charles Lawson. "I like that. Let's have it."

"All right." Stiles swallowed dryly and took a quick sip of coffee. "Fred Hull is probably one of the ablest, most efficient security officers any prison could ask for. He put down a riot in two days that would have lasted a week anywhere else. When it comes to keeping inmates behind walls, there's not a better man in the business than Hull. A perfect example of his ability is the fact that he's been here sixteen years and in that time there hasn't been a single escape."

"But—" Stiles lowered his voice considerably, knowing how it would carry in the big room, "in the areas of rehabilitation, inmate education, vocational training—all the modern aspects of penology—Captain Hull is a total failure. He's completely out of his element; a throwback to sweatbox days. His thinking, as far as motivating inmates toward self-improvement, is as archaic as a chain gang. In short, he feels that the function of a penitentiary is simply and solely to punish, which I think is all wrong."

Lawson pursed his lips briefly. "Do you like Captain Hull personally?" he asked bluntly, quickly.

"No," said Stiles, "I'm afraid I don't. I don't *dis*like him, mind you. It's just that we have nothing in common; there's no basis for a friendship."

"I see," Lawson nodded. "Well, I appreciate your honesty." He drummed his fingers, as he seemed to have a habit of doing, on the gleaming metal tabletop. Stiles noticed that where they touched, faint fingerprints were left on the shiny surface. "What about Starzak?" Lawson said. "Is he top con in here or isn't he?"

Stiles shrugged. "Hull thinks so. I don't."

"Hull doesn't just *think* so," Lawson corrected him. "Hull is flatly and firmly convinced of it. Why?"

"Warden, I don't know," the younger man said. "I'll be the first to admit that Starzak has probably been mixed up in a shady deal or two; I mean, he's been here like a decade and a half, and any old con in any prison is going to cut a touch now and then to make life a little easier. But I don't believe that he controls the entire inmate population."

"Do you think that Captain Hull might have a personal grudge against Starzak for some reason or other?"

Stiles rubbed his chin thoughtfully. "It's possible, I suppose. They've both been here a long time; they could have had some kind of run-in a long time ago."

Lawson thought about it for a moment and then said, "Well, I'll have an opportunity to explore that possibility; tomorrow, as a matter of fact, when I ask Starzak his views on how the prison can be improved."

Stiles frowned deeply. "You're going to ask *Starzak* how to improve the prison?"

"Yes. Starzak and every other old-timer in the place. I tried that tack once before, when I went in as warden of Danville. You'd be surprised at the insight that can be gained from interviews of that sort; not to mention the constructive criticism that comes out of them." He noticed that Stiles had quickly replaced his frown with a smile. "I take it you approve," he said.

"Very much," the young deputy replied at once. "It's just the sort of enlightened thinking that the institution needs."

"Well, I just hope some successful results come of it," Lawson said. "I'd like you to schedule the interviews for me, begining at nine tomorrow morning. Let's make it every inmate with fifteen or more years' time. Give me a quarter hour with each of them. I'd like all their files on my desk by six this evening, too, so I can look them over tonight."

"Yes, sir. I'll take care of it."

"Good." Lawson finished his coffee. "Well, shall we get back?"

The two men rose and walked toward the nearest door, their footsteps again echoing sharply in the vast expanse of the room.

At nine the next morning, Warden Charles Lawson began interviewing privately his new prison's long-time inmates. He went through the routine efficiently, professionally, probing the minds and thoughts of the men much as a skilled surgeon would probe their bodies for a tumor; except that Lawson used not his fingers but rather an alert mind and quick, leading words to encourage the men as individuals to express themselves candidly to him. Having read their records the previous night, he was familiar with them as criminals of society and as prisoners of the institution. Now, in seeking to tap their prison-developed wisdom, he took care to approach them on the basis of one mature man to another.

Lawson was pleased to find that his plan worked in the new prison even better than it had at Danville. Most of the old cons were not only willing, but eager, to help. From the surviving member of a notorious pair of young thrill-killers, for instance, who was now well past middle age after thirty-one years behind the walls, Lawson learned of some serious shortcomings in the operation of the Diagnostic Depot, the separate section of the prison where new arrivals were isolated until let into the general prison population. Then, from a former surgeon serving life for the murder of his wife, came information on laxity in the prison dispensary. From an infamous midwestern gangster, now working as a prison butcher, Lawson found out about a low grade of meat being sold to the prison by a local supplier. From the oldest of the oldtimers, the leader of a kidnap gang which had snatched a wealthy bootlegger in the late twenties, and who had been a convict there for forty-two years, the new warden learned that the general consensus of inmates was that the riot had been the result of a lot of little discontentments built up over an extended period of time, rather than any one incident which could be directly linked to its cause.

After Lawson had spoken with half a dozen long-termers, it came Ralph Starzak's turn. Lawson was surprised at the appearance of the convict as he entered and sat down. Contrary to the flamboyant multi-million-dollar fence who in the early 1950's had been sent to prison for twenty years, the man before Lawson now was a slightly stoop-shouldered, balding, watery-eyed individual who, with his gray, unhealthy complexion, hardly looked capable of influencing even a single inmate, much less inspiring an entire prison population to violence.

"Starzak," the warden said, after he got over his initial surprise at how the man looked, "I am calling in all of the long-termers in the institution in an effort to determine what, if anything, in the minds of the inmates, needs to be done to improve conditions in the prison. Do you have any suggestions which might be helpful along those lines?"

Starzak, sitting on the very edge of the chair, holding his prison cap in both hands almost apprehensively, shrugged noncommittally. "I . . . I don't know anything about . . . conditions, warden."

"Starzak, you don't have to be afraid to say anything that's on your mind," Lawson pointed out. "Before the day is out, I will interview every inmate who has served fifteen or more years. There is absolutely no way for anyone in here to know who told me what. Now, please be frank with me. Surely you have some ideas on improving prison conditions."

Again the shrug. "Well, sure, warden—I mean, you know, there are lots of ways to make things better. The food could stand improvement, too much boiled stuff on the menu; and the movies we've been getting on Sundays are so old some of them still have Dean Martin with his old nose—"

"Those are general complaints," Lawson told him. "Some of the inmates are always going to be displeased with the food; just as some of them will always be unhappy with the movies shown every Sunday. What I'm looking for are *specifics*, Starzak; particularly causes of discontent that might spark trouble. For instance," he casually opened Starzak's thick prison record, "it isn't unusual for guards—or even guard *officers*, for that matter—to favor certain inmates, while at the same time perhaps being too harsh with others. Would you say situations like that exist in this institution?"

Starzak twisted his cap in his hands and avoided Lawson's eyes. "Maybe, maybe not," he said. "I don't know anything about any situations."

Lawson quietly drummed his fingers. "Would you report such an officer if you felt he were being unduly harsh with *you*, Starzak?"

"Sure," Starzak's shoulders raised and dropped. "Why not? I mean, I've been here a long time, warden. I've done my time clean," he bobbed his head at the desk, "you can see for yourself right there in the record. I've hardly gotten a discipline ticket in sixteen years. I'd have been paroled a long time ago if I'd had a job to go to and family to take me in—"

"So you *would* report a guard—even an officer—who was carrying a grudge against you and was out to get you?"

"Yes, sir, I would," Starzak said unequivocally, "and because of my clean record in here, I'd expect to get fair treatment in the matter, too."

"I see," Lawson nodded. "Well, that's a very realistic attitude, Starzak." He pretended to study very thoughtfully a page in the convict's record. Forcing a frown, he then said, "Do you get along all right with Captain Hull?"

Starzak shook his head. "The captain doesn't like me very much," he admitted.

"Why? Did you have some kind of run-in with him?"

"Well, yes, sir, once—but it wasn't anything really serious."

"Let me be the judge of that. What was it about and when did it happen?"

Starzak pulled on one ear. "Let's see, it was about five years ago, maybe a little longer. I was working as a checker in the laundry—same job I've got now.

"What I do is make sure that the sheets are collected from certain tiers in certain blocks on certain days. The cons strip them off their bunks, fold them up, and leave them on the gunwalk outside the cells. Then laundry runners go along and pick them up and bring them to the laundry. They get scalded and bleached, blower-dried, then run through a folding machine, and returned to the cells before lockup the same day—"

"I am familiar with prison laundry routine," Lawson said patiently. "Just tell me what happened between you and Captain Hull."

"Yes, sir. Captain Hull came to me on the second Tuesday of a particular month and said my runners hadn't picked up the sheets on B-Five and B-Six. I told him we didn't do those two tiers until the next Tuesday. The captain said I was crazy, there were sheets outside of every cell door on B-Five and B-Six. I said maybe so, but that second Tuesday wasn't their laundry day. Then he said I obviously didn't know what I was doing and that I shouldn't be in a position of any responsibility; so he relieved me of the job."

Lawson nodded. "And?"

"Well, I didn't think it was fair so I went to the deputy warden—that was Mr. Grimes, before Mr. Stiles came. Well, Mr. Grimes looked into the matter and found out I was right and Captain Hull was wrong. Laundry day for B-Five and B-Six *was* the next Tuesday. What happened was, some con on B-Five got mixed up on the days and put his sheet out by mistake. Another con saw him and without thinking did the same thing. Pretty soon it set off a kind of chain reaction and every guy on both tiers had his sheet out on the gunwalk. When Captain Hull saw it, he naturally figured there was some foul-up at the laundry—"

"Do you blame him for thinking that?" Lawson interjected.

"Not a bit," Starzak said emphatically. "I'd have thought the same way myself if I'd been in his place. I mean, you wouldn't expect two tiers of guys to all make the same mistake at the same time."

"What was the outcome of your complaint to the deputy warden?"

"Mr. Grimes restored me to my job," Starzak answered with a hint of self-righteousness. "It was the only fair thing to do."

"And you don't think it was a serious enough matter to cause Captain Hull to build up a grudge against you?"

"No, sir. It was just a minor thing, and it was all straightened out that same day. I don't think anybody even knew about it except Mr. Grimes, Captain Hull, and me."

Lawson smiled. "You mean you didn't brag to the other inmates about getting the best of the guard captain?"

"No, sir!" Starzak said quickly. "Not me, warden. I've got more sense than to *look* for trouble."

Lawson sat thoughtfully for a moment, staring intently at the slight, balding, altogether insignificant convict who sat before him. So, he thought, it was no more than a petty incident; a case of Hull's being in the wrong and an inmate's being in the right. A thing which in itself was nothing at all, but which to Hull was probably of paramount importance. Hull knew that he had been wrong, and he knew that *Starzak* knew. That, Lawson concluded, was probably the whole rub. Hull was as much an old-timer as Starzak; he had been carrying a club as long as Starzak had been wearing a number. He was, as young Stiles pointed out, a throwback to the sweatbox days; the days when a guard was *always* right, a convict *always* wrong—the old days, when convict riots were put down by shotguns and blackjacks.

Lawson sighed quietly and closed the manila folder on his desk. "Well, Starzak, I think that will be all. I appreciate your frankness and I'm certain what you've told me will be of value in getting our institution back in proper order. Thank you."

Lawson pressed a button on his desk to let the reception guard know that Starzak was leaving.

The warden had his second staff meeting at the end of the day on Wednesday. Once again Captain Hull, the three guard lieutenants, and Deputy Warden Roger Stiles sat in an arc of chairs facing his desk.

"I won't keep you gentlemen long," Lawson said for the benefit of the two lieutenants who were off shift. He laid his pipe aside and shuffled through the reports which had been submitted to him the previous day. "I've gone over the situation summaries on the cellblocks," he said, "and I think they are very well done. The suggestions they contain for general security improvement and protection against future riot incidents are particularly good. After some additional study I'm certain we'll want to implement most if not all of the recommendations." He laid the reports aside and referred to a note pad. "What's the status of the eight men barricaded in the shoe shop?"

"They're out, warden," said Stiles. He could not resist a glance at Hull. "They came out voluntarily, and there was no damage to the shop machinery."

"Where are the eight men?"

"Isolation."

"All right."

He made a checkmark on the note pad and turned to Hull. "I understand that the hunger strike in C-Six has been resolved."

"Yes, sir," said Hull. "Your idea of using steam carts worked just fine. At the morning meal today there were only three men on the tier still refusing to eat. We've removed them to Isolation, so we now have all of C Block on the same routine as the other two cellblocks."

"How's the atmosphere in the blocks?" Lawson asked. "How does it *feel* to you?"

"Quiet," Hull said with the confidence of his years. "I'd say the spark is gone."

"You don't think it could flare up again?"

"I think it would take something big to do it."

"What kind of something big?"

Hull shrugged. "Guard killing a con; something on that order."

"I'm sure nothing *that* serious is likely to happen," Roger Stiles said dryly.

"I wouldn't be *too* sure," Hull replied, looking at him coldly. "It's happened four times in four different prisons in the past year. A con is sent for by an officer, or maybe asks permission to see the officer; he's alone with the officer in a block room or guard office; out of the blue he comes unglued and jumps the officer; the officer guns him." He leaned slightly toward Stiles. "It could happen any time, deputy warden. Any time at all."

"Well," Lawson cut in, "let's assume that nothing of that magnitude will occur. Barring any such serious incident, you are of the opinion that our riot *is* over."

"Yes, sir," Hull admitted quietly.

"Very well." Lawson made another checkmark on the pad and turned to the guard lieutenants. "If all goes well tonight and tomorrow, suspend the early lockup tomorrow night and restore full recreational privileges, including the gymnasium and the tier television sets. Restrict all cellblock movement to the tiers, however, and instruct all tier guards to stay inside the tier control rooms; I want no guards on the gunwalk until after lockup. Understood?"

"Yes, sir," the three lieutenants said in broken unison.

"Good." Lawson's fingers commenced drumming. "As for the men in Isolation, keep them there until we can review their offenses individually. We'll begin that tomorrow." He glanced at his watch. "That's all for now, I think. Captain Hull, would you mind staying a moment longer?"

Roger Stiles and the lieutenants rose and left the office. Hull, his jaw tightening defensively, remained behind.

"Hull," Lawson began when they were alone, "I've done some checking into your theory regarding Ralph Starzak's connection with the riot, and very frankly I can't find any basis for it—"

"You aren't likely to, either," Hull said. "Starzak's a smart cookie."

"He could be the smartest cookie in the whole jar and still not get away with *everything*," Lawson said pointedly. "Isn't there anyone in the entire institution who can support your claim?"

"My lieutenants—" Hull began, but Lawson shook his head firmly.

"You know better than that, Hull. Your lieutenants would simply be giving lip service to your position. Surely there must be someone else, in some other department of the prison. How about the hospital personnel, the civilian shop foremen, the volunteer teachers—?"

"They don't know anything," Hull grumbled. "All they do is work here; they don't have to *run* the place."

"What you're saying then is that you can't produce an independent opinion to corroborate your own. You can't *prove* that Ralph Starzak is anything worse than a long-term con who occasionally stretches a regulation like any other long-term con."

"Are you saying I need proof? Proof to throw a con like Starzak in the hole?"

"That's exactly what I'm saying—not only regarding Starzak but every other inmate in here. We can't teach honesty unless we practice it."

Hull sat back and pursed his lips thoughtfully. "I thought you were here to *tighten* security," he said. "You talk like you're planning to pamper these hoodlums."

"I don't intend to pamper anyone," Lawson said coolly, "inmates or guards." He stood up behind the desk and began to pack his briefcase. "I think we've discussed this particular matter as much as we need to, captain. If you can develop any evidence to support your opinion of Starzak, I'll be happy to review it; if not, please see to it that he is accorded the same treatment as any other inmate. And while we're on the subject of treatment, you may as well advise your lieutenants, and pass it on down through the guard ranks, that I will not tolerate harassment or maltreatment in any form as long as I am in charge of this institution. Any breach of that rule will result in immediate suspension and charges before the civil service board. Is that understood?"

"Yes, sir." Hull had risen now also. He watched quietly as Lawson closed and snapped the catch on his briefcase.

"You know, Hull," the warden said, coming around the desk, "you only have four more years before you're eligible for an early pension. In light of the continuing changes in prison policies and administration, you might do well to consider taking it and finding another line of work." He paused and put a not unfriendly hand on Hull's shoulder. "I don't mean to sound harsh, Hull, it's just that some men don't adjust to change as well as others. You're a . . . well, a *keeper* of men; Stiles and I, on the other hand, look upon ourselves as rehabilitators, remakers of men. You were valuable in your day, Hull, but I'm afraid your day is nearly over." He gripped Hull's shoulder once and removed his hand. "I hope you won't take any of this personally."

"No," Hull said quietly. "No, I won't." He followed Lawson out of the office, through the reception room, and into the hall. They passed out of the administration building and down half a dozen concrete steps to the warden's private parking space. Lawson put his briefcase in the car and got behind the wheel.

"You play it smart, Hull," he advised. "Stop trying to break guys like Starzak. If they become problems, leave them to Stiles and me. You just ride out those four years and collect that early pension."

Lawson backed the car out and swung it in a slow arc toward the personnel gate. Hull stood next to the empty parking space and watched him go. After a moment, one of his lieutenants, Finer, who was on night duty, came out of the building and stood beside him.

"Captain?" he said. His voice carried a hint of nervousness.

"Yeah?" Hull answered without looking at him.

"Do you think the new warden's right? Do you think the riot *is* all over?"

"Probably," Hull replied. "Unless something happens like I said inside. Unless a con gets killed or something like that."

Finer nodded. He was visibly relieved. "Well, like the deputy warden said, that's not likely to happen."

"No," Hull said tonelessly. "No, that's not likely to happen." He looked at Finer. "Made your rounds yet?"

"Just on my way now."

"What order are they in tonight?"

Finer took a card from his shirt pocket. "B Block, then A, and C last."

Hull glanced at his watch. "I'll meet you over in the dining hall when you're finished. We'll have a cup."

"Sure thing, captain," Finer said.

Hull turned back to the concrete steps as Finer started across the yard. He climbed the steps slowly and reentered the administration building. Walking along the hall, he glanced to his right and to his left to see if any of the clerical offices were still occupied; he found they were not. He ignored the warden's office, knowing no one was left there, and came to the closed door of the deputy warden's office. He paused and knocked briefly, then opened the door. Sticking his head in, he saw that Stiles too had gone for the day. The administration building—except for himself—was deserted.

Hull walked farther down the hall to his own office. Entering, he sat at his desk. He waited exactly fifteen minutes, until he was sure Lieutenant Finer had completed his inspection of B Block; then he called the B Block guard sergeant.

"This is Captain Hull," he said. "Have Ralph Starzak, Number 1172307, brought to my office."

The guard who escorted Ralph Starzak to Hull's office was one of the new probationary men whom the captain barely knew. He and Starzak entered and stood before Hull's desk. Presently Hull looked up. He gave Starzak a cursory glance, then reached for the inmate receival slip the young guard was holding.

"No need to wait," he said as he signed the slip. "I'm going over that way in a few minutes; I'll take him back myself."

"Yes, sir," the young guard said. He took the slip back and touched the brim of his cap in an informal salute.

"Close the door as you leave, please."

"Yes, sir." The young guard left and closed the door behind him.

In the quiet that remained in the office, Ralph Starzak and Hull locked eyes for a brief moment across the desk. Then, very casually, Hull opened the bottom drawer and took out a bottle of whiskey and a glass tumbler. He poured a double shot into the tumbler and pushed it across the desk. Starzak grabbed it eagerly and bolted it down. Then he sighed heavily and slumped into a chair.

"I *needed* that," he said.

"I figured." Hull grunted, then capped the bottle and put it back into the drawer.

Starzak leaned forward and put the glass on the desk. "Okay," he said tensely, "let's have it."

"You can relax," Hull said. "Our new warden is a reformer. He's going to be too busy rehabilitating people to pay any attention to prison rackets."

"You're sure?" Starzak asked. "I mean, we've got a nice thing going for us in here—"

"Of course I'm sure," Hull said easily. He rose and walked to the window, from which he could see the lighted cellblocks, the guard towers, the yard, the wall. He looked out on it, knowing that it was his domain. "You don't have to tell me we've got a good thing going for us, Ralph; I *know* we've got a good thing going for us." He put an expensive cigar between his lips and lighted it. He took a deep, expansive drag. "We've got two thousand cons in here," he said reflectively, "and every day of every week at least half of them kick in fifteen cents to a quarter for one thing or another. The little luxuries of life— pressed dungarees; a commissary pass; a book reserved in the library; an extra outgoing letter; a second scoop of ice cream at Sunday dinner; a full tobacco ration instead of sweepings from the floor. Just the little things that make life in here at least bearable."

Hull turned his back to the window and faced Starzak. He smiled around the cigar. "Fifteen cents to a quarter a day, Ralph. Sounds like chicken feed, doesn't it. But how much does it come to? From all sources, how much?"

Starzak shrugged. "We make a hundred and eighty, two hundred a day, on the average."

"Right. And you and I split a hundred a day, and use what's left to pay off the inmate librarian and the inmate dining hall workers and the inmate commissary clerks and whoever else needs paying off. But first," he reached over and hit the desk solidly with his open palm, "first, my friend, you and I, we take our hundred, right?"

"Sure. Right," said Starzak. He shrugged again. "I mean, why shouldn't we? After all, we engineered this scheme, we set it up—"

"Exactly," said Hull. "It's our baby and we get the cream. Fourteen years we've been working this joint; fourteen long years." He smiled again. "Do you know how much money we've got in our Swiss bank account now, Ralph? Better than *three hundred thousand dollars*! Why, we make a thousand dollars a month in interest alone." He removed the cigar from his mouth. "In four years, Ralph, when you finish your time and I apply for my stinking early pension, we'll have close to half a million dollars."

"If this new warden doesn't start getting wise," Starzak said, "like the old one did."

"If he does," Hull's smile faded, "we'll get rid of him just like we did the last one. We'll pull another riot; and anyone who's cooperated with him, given him information, will get what's coming to him during the rioting—just like the two big-mouths we got rid of during the riot we just had." Viciously Hull crushed out the cigar in his ashtray. "*We* are running this joint, Ralph; you and me! And nobody is going to interfere. I haven't devoted fourteen years of my life to this setup for nothing." He snatched up Starzak's glass and put it in the drawer with the whiskey. "No do-good warden or anybody else is going to undo what I've spent fourteen years building," he said self-righteously. He closed the drawer and reached for his hat. "Come on, I'll take you back to the block."

The two men left the office and walked side by side down the long corridor. They went outside and down the concrete steps and started across the yard. Hull took a deep breath and looked up at the sky.

"Pleasant night," he said casually.

"Yeah," Starzak agreed, also looking up. "Lots of stars. When you're a con, it's nice to have nights with lots of stars. Gives you something to look at after the cell lights go out."

"I never thought of that," Hull said. "That's interesting, Ralph."

They continued walking together across the broad prison yard until finally they were just two darkly shadowed figures and it was impossible to tell them apart.

BILL PRONZINI

The Jade Figurine

La Croix had not changed much in the two years since I had last seen him. He still wore the same ingratiating smile. We sat together in a booth in the rear section of the Seaman's Bar, near the Singapore River. It was eleven thirty in the morning.

La Croix brushed at an imaginary speck on the sleeve of his white tropical suit. "You will do it, *mon ami?*"

"No," I said.

His smile went away. "But I have offered you a great deal of money."

"That has nothing to do with it."

"I do not understand."

"I'm not in the business any more."

The smile came back. "You are joking, of course."

"Do you see me laughing?"

Again, the smile vanished. "But you *must* help me," he said. "Perhaps if I were to tell you of—"

"I don't want to hear about it. There are others in Singapore. Why don't you try one of them?"

"You and I, we have done much business together," La Croix said. "You are the only one whom I can trust. I will double my offer. I will triple it."

"I told you, the money has nothing to do with it."

"*Mon ami,* I beg of you!" His gray-green eyes were pleading with me now; sweat had broken out on his forehead.

We had done business before, that was true enough, but I did not owe him anything. I would not have helped him, even if I had.

I stood abruptly. "I just can't do it, La Croix," I said quietly. "I'm sorry, but that's the way it is. I hope you find somebody else."

I turned away from him, walked through the beaded curtains into the bar proper, and ordered beer, on ice.

La Croix hurried through the curtain and pushed in beside me. "I beg of you to reconsider, *M'sieu* Connell," he whispered. "I will be in most grave danger if I remain in Singapore."

"La Croix, how many times do I have to say it? There's nothing I can do for you."

"But I have already—" He broke off, his eyes staring into mine, reading them accurately, and then he turned and was gone.

I finished my beer and went out into what the Malays call the *roote hond*, the oppressive, prickly heat that was Singapore at midday. There were a few European tourists about—talking animatedly, taking pictures the way they do—but the natives had sense enough to stay in where it was cool.

I walked down to the river. The water was a dark, oily bluish-green. Its narrow expanse, as always, was crowded with sampans, *prahus*, small bamboo-awninged Chinese junks, and the heavily-laden, almost flat-decked *tongkangs*, or lighters. There was the perennial smell of rotting garbage, intermingled with that of salt water, spices, rubber, gasoline, and the sweet, cloying odor of frangipani. The rust-colored tile roofs that cap most of Singapore's buildings shone dully through the thick heat haze on both sides of the river.

I followed the line of the waterfront for a short way until I came upon one of the smaller *godowns*—storage warehouses. I found Harry Rutledge, a large, florid-faced Englishman, without any trouble; he was supervising the unloading of a shipment of copra from one of the lighters.

"Can you use me today, Harry?" I asked him.

"Sorry, ducks. Plenty of coolies on this one."

"Tomorrow?"

He rubbed his peeling red nose. "Got a cargo of palm oil coming in," he said musingly. "Holdover, awaiting transshipment. Could use you, at that."

"What time is it due?"

"Eleven, likely."

"I'll be here."

"Right-o, ducks."

I retraced my steps along the river. I had never really been able to get used to the heat, even after fifteen years in the South China Seas. I wanted another iced beer, but I thought it would be a better idea if I had something to eat first. I had not eaten all day.

Here and there along the waterfront are small eating stalls. I stopped at the first one I saw and sat on one of the foot-high wooden stools, under a white canvas awning. I ordered shashlick and rice and a fresh mangosteen. I had gotten down to the mangosteen—a thick, pulpy fruit—when the three men walked up.

The two on either side were copper-skinned, stoic-featured and flat-eyed. They were both dressed in white linen jackets and matching slacks.

The man in the middle was about fifty, short and very plump, and his skin had the odd look of kneaded pink dough. He was probably Dutch or Belgian. He wore white also, but there any similarity between his dress and that of the other two ended. The suit was impeccably tailored, the shirt was silk; the leather shoes were handmade and polished to a fine gloss. On the little finger of his left hand he wore a huge gold ring with a jade stone in the shape of a lion's head—symbolic, I supposed, of the Lion City.

He sat down carefully on the stool next to me. The other two remained standing.

The plump man smiled as if he had just found a missing relative. "You are Mr. Connell, are you not?" he asked. His English was flawless.

"That's right."

"I am Jorge Van Rijk."

I went on eating the mangosteen. "Good for you."

He thought that was amusing. Gold fillings sparkled. His laugh had a burr in it that made my neck cold. "You were observed at the Seaman's Bar a short while ago," he said. "You were conversing with an acquaintance of mine."

"Is that right?"

"Yes. *M'sieu* La Croix."

"Interesting."

"Isn't it?" Van Rijk said. "May I inquire as to the nature of your conversation?"

I met his eyes. "I don't suppose that's any of your business."

"Ah, but it is, Mr. Connell. It is, indeed, my business."

"Then why don't you ask La Croix?"

"An excellent suggestion, of course," Van Rijk said. "However, it seems that *M'sieu* La Croix is, ah, nowhere to be found at the present time."

"That's too bad."

"Necessarily, then," Van Rijk said, "I must ask you."

"Sorry. It was a private discussion."

"I see." Van Rijk smiled, studying me with his mild blue eyes. "I am given to understand, Mr. Connell, that you are an aeroplane pilot."

"You've been misinformed, then."

"I think not," he said. "This is, of course, the reason La Croix spoke with you."

"Is it?"

"He wished you to transport him from Singapore."

"Did he, now?"

"And did you agree to this proposal?"

"What proposal?"

"I desire to know his destination, Mr. Connell."

I shrugged. "I couldn't tell you."

"His destination, Mr. Connell."

"Well, he did mention something about Antarctica," I said. "They say it's very nice there this time of year."

He stiffened slightly, and said in a cold voice, "I have become rather bored with this game of verbal chess, Mr. Connell. You would be most wise to tell me what I wish to know. Most wise."

"I don't have to tell you a damned thing," I said, keeping my own voice equable. "I don't know who you are, and I really don't much care. I do know that I don't like you or your manner or your implications. Do I make myself clear?"

I watched his eyes change. They were no longer mild. "I am not a patient man, sir," he said. "When I have lost what little forbearance I possess, I am also not a very pleasant man. Ordinarily, I abhor violence in any form, but there are instances when I find it to be the only alternative."

"I see." I put my hands flat on the table, leaning toward him slightly. "All right, Van Rijk," I said. "You've made your point. Now I'll make mine. I'm not going anywhere with you, if that's what you had in mind. I'm sure your two bodyguards, or whatever they are, are armed to the teeth, but I doubt if you'd have them shoot anybody in a crowded bazaar like this. In fact, I doubt if you'd want to make any trouble at all. Your boys would get into it, too, and I think you know what that would mean. Would you care to spend some time in a city *penjara* for street brawling, Van Rijk?"

Anger blotched his pink cheeks. The other two were poised on the balls of their feet, watching me. They were waiting for Van Rijk to let them know which way it was going to be.

Abruptly, he stood. "There will be another time, Mr. Connell," he said softly, acidly. "When the streets are not so crowded, and when the sunlight is not so bright." Then he pivoted and stalked off, threading his way between the closely-set tables, the other two at his heels. The three of them disappeared into the waterfront confusion.

I sat there for a time, thinking. I was a little bothered by Van Rijk's threats, but they could have been a bluff; I decided I had handled the situation well enough. I was also a little curious about his relationship with La Croix, but not enough to get myself involved in it. It had an odor about it with which I was all too familiar.

I got to my feet and put it out of my mind, decided it was time for that iced beer now.

On Jalan Barat, there is a bar which is called The Malaysian Gardens. The appellation is a gross misnomer. If any flower, shrub, or plant has ever been cultivated within a radius of one hundred yards of the place, I am not aware of it. With a facade reminiscent of nothing so much as a Chinatown tenement, its barn-like interior does little to dispel this image, both in decor—or rather, lack of decor—and in the distinctive smells of human close-quarter living and the perfumed incense called joss.

In short, The Malaysian Gardens is a dive which I first discovered many years ago, and I cannot explain why I continue to frequent it on the somewhat regular basis that I do. Perhaps it is because their price for beer is unparalleled in moderation anywhere on the island, or perhaps it is because they cater to those individuals like myself who desire a minimum of conversation and a maximum of solitude in which to do their varying degrees of drinking.

I had my iced beer there that afternoon, and then, after a nap in my flat and supper at a small, inexpensive restaurant, I had decided to return to the Gardens for a generous portion of both their solitude and their beer; there was not much else to do.

I had been there for perhaps three hours, sitting alone at a rear table and thinking a lot of old and useless thoughts, when I noticed the girl for the first time.

She stood just inside the arched entranceway, and she seemed to be staring at me, or at least in my direction. Her bearing appeared uncertain, as if she were prepared to bolt at the slightest disturbance.

I watched her over the rim of my glass, and after a moment our eyes met. Her mouth made a small, round circle and she half-turned toward the street; then her body stiffened, perhaps with a resolution of sorts, and she walked toward me quickly.

As she approached, I saw that she was very tall, finely-proportioned; her face was heart-shaped and perfectly symmetrical, suggesting European—or at least Western—ancestry. She wore her dark hair long and sweeping. In the smoky dimness of the Gardens it was difficult to determine her age, though I thought she could not have been much more than twenty-one.

She stopped in front of my table, appearing very nervous or very embarrassed, or perhaps it was a combination of both, and said, "You're . . . Daniel Connell, aren't you?" Her voice reflected the uncertainty in her manner.

I nodded. "Yes."

"I wonder if I could speak with you. It's . . . it's very important."

I indicated an empty chair and invited her to sit down.

"I don't know quite how to say this," she said. "I'm . . . not very well versed in this sort of thing."

"What sort of thing is that?"

She hesitated. "Well, *intrigue*, I guess you would call it."

I smiled. "That's a very melodramatic word."

Her voice dropped to a furtive whisper. "Mr. Connell, I've been told you sometimes . . . do favors for people."

"Favors? I don't think I understand."

She chewed at her lower lip. Then, in a rush, as if she needed to relieve herself of the pressure of the words: "I've been told you're a pilot, a pilot-for-hire, and that you would fly persons anywhere they wanted to go no matter why they wanted to go there, just as long as they could get enough money to pay you."

I was silent for a moment, then asked, "Who told you this?"

"Some . . . some people I talked with."

"What people?"

"I don't know their names. There were several. I tried to be very discreet about it, but I'm just not very good at such things. I asked along the waterfront and in Raffles Square if there was anybody in Singapore who would be able to fly me home without asking a lot of questions and some of the people said that Daniel Connell was the man I wanted to see and they said I could find him here most likely at night, and so I . . ." Her voice trailed off, and she looked down at her hands.

I drank from my glass, and then I said, "Just where is it that you want to go?"

"The Philippine Islands," she answered. "Luzon."

"Those people of yours were wrong about my not asking any questions," I told her. "Why do you have to get to Luzon in such a hurry? And why so secretively?"

She paused, as if debating confiding in me. Then, in a hushed voice, she said, "It's . . . my father."

"Your father?"

"There was a telegram this afternoon, when I returned to my hotel. It was from the . . . the police in Luzon. It said my father had been arrested. There have been a rash of terrorist attacks there lately, and they think he's involved with some kind of Communist guerrilla organization responsible for them." She took a deep, shuddering breath; she had, I decided, desperately needed someone to confide in. "It's not true! It can't be true! I know my father. He's a very patriotic and individualistic man, and he would never get mixed up with such people."

I did not say anything for a time. Then, slowly, I said, "I think it would be better if you began at the beginning. Suppose you start with your name."

Again, she gnawed at her lower lip. "Tina Kellogg."

"You're on a holiday in Singapore?"

"Yes, sort of. I just graduated from the University of Manila, and I thought I would take a tour of the Orient before I settled down to a position I've been offered at home."

"Your home is Luzon?"

"Yes."

"And your father—who is he?"

"He's an import-export dealer, just a small businessman, really, with a few American and European clients. That's why it's so ridiculous for anyone to believe that he would be involved with Communist guerrillas. What would he have to gain?"

Her question was rhetorical. I said slowly, "I can understand your wanting to get home so quickly. But why can't you simply take one of the scheduled flights to the Philippines?"

"I haven't any money, and no means of obtaining credit with any of the airlines. My father was supposed to send me a check to cover my expenses for the next month, but he . . . he didn't, he just didn't."

I said, "Can't you wire home for the money? To your mother, someone in your family?"

"My mother died when I was eleven," Tina answered. "My father is the only family I have."

"His business associates then? Personal friends?"

She shook her head convulsively. "There's no one. I suppose I could arrange something with his bank, but that might take days, weeks. And we have no close friends in Luzon; we were sort of self-sustaining, do you know? But even if we had, they wouldn't agree to send me money for fear of being implicated with the Communists."

I asked, "Have you tried the Philippine Consulate?"

"Yes," Tina said. "I went there immediately after I received the telegram, but they refused to help me. They said that if my father was involved with guerrillas there was nothing they could do. I tried to tell them it was all a mistake, but they just wouldn't listen."

"I see." I rotated my glass slowly on the scarred surface of the table. Even in the half-light, I could see the pleading in Tina's eyes. I ignored it; there was no other way. I said, "Tina, I'm sorry. I wish I could help you, but there's nothing I can do. I don't fly any more; what those pepole told you is false rumor. I haven't flown a plane in two years now."

"But I can pay you, really I can," Tina said with a note of desperation in her voice. "After we arrive, I can arrange with my father's bank—"

"I don't mean to be harsh, but don't make it any harder than it is to say no. I can't help you. That's all there is to it."

"Then . . . then what am I going to do?" She seemed on the verge of tears.

I felt like a heel at that moment, but I had enough burdens of my own. "Come on," I said gently. "I'll get you a taxi back to your hotel. Maybe something will turn up tomorrow."

"No, no . . ."

"Tina, this way is no good for you. If I agreed to do what you want, or if you found somebody else to do it, you would be breaking the law. You don't need that kind of grief, too. Listen to what I'm saying; it's good advice." I paused. "Now if I were you, I'd go back to the Philippine Consulate in the morning and camp in front of the ambassador's door. He'll see to it that you get back home, I'm sure of it."

I thought for a moment that she was going to protest, to beg, but she gave a resigned little sigh and then stood. I took her arm and led her out to the street.

It was very dark—street lamps on Jalan Barat are few and far between—and the night air held the same overt mugginess of the afternoon. There were few automobiles on the street. On the next block, I knew, was a taxi stand and I steered Tina in that direction. She looked up at me once as if to say something, but she apparently thought better of it and remained silent.

We had taken a few steps into the next block when I heard the car coming down Jalan Barat behind us, traveling very fast. Curious, I turned to look, and the car, a small English car, was just coming through the intersection. There was the pig squeal of hurriedly applied brakes then, and the driver pulled the wheel hard, skidding the car in at an angle to the curb ten yards in front of where Tina and I stood.

Both front doors opened simultaneously, and two men came out in a hurry. In the pale yellowish glare of the tropical moon, I could see their faces clearly. They were the two flat-eyed men who had been with Van Rijk that afternoon.

I had time for the quick thought that he was carrying out his threat after all. I pushed Tina out of the way just as the driver reached me. His right arm was raised across his body, and he brought it down in a backhand, chopping motion, karate-style. I got my left arm up and blocked his descending forearm with my own. The force of his rush threw him off balance, and he was vulnerable; I jabbed the stiffened fingers of my right hand into his stomach, just below the breastbone. All the air went out of him. He stumbled backward, retching, and sat down hard on the sidewalk.

The other one had got there by then but when he saw the driver fall, he came up short, and I saw him fumble beneath his white linen jacket. I took three rapid steps and laid the hard edge of my hand across his wrist. He made a pained noise deep in his throat, and there was a metallic clatter as the gun or knife dropped to the pavement. I hit him twice in the face with quick jabs, turning him, and then drove the point of my elbow into his kidneys. The blow sent him staggering blindly forward, and he collided with the side of the car, slid down along it, and lay still.

I looked at the driver again, but he was still sitting on the sidewalk, holding his stomach with both hands. I let my body relax, breathing jaggedly. There was no sign of Tina. The whole thing must have scared the hell out of her, and I was sorry for that. She seemed to have enough troubles.

I heard shouts from the direction of The Malaysian Gardens, and when I looked up there, several people began to run down toward us. I thought briefly about waiting for the *polis* and telling them about it, but I decided against that. The less I had to do with them, the better it would be for me. Even though it had been two years since the trouble, memories are long in the South China Seas.

I could decide later what to do, if anything, about Van Rijk, so I began to walk toward the running group from the Gardens.

A tall, grayhaired man was in the lead, and when he reached me he asked breathlessly, "What happened here?"

"An accident," I said. "Happened right in front of me."

He looked past me. "Are they all right?"

"I think so."

I started to push past him. "Where are you going?" he asked.

"To call the constabulary."

He seemed satisfied with that, and the group left me to see about the two men from the English car. I angled across the street and walked west. I did not look back.

Somebody was at the door.

I rolled over on the perspiration-slick sheets and opened my eyes. It was morning; the sun lay outside the bedroom window of my Chinatown flat like a red-orange ball, suspended on glowing wires. I closed my eyes again and lay there, listening to the now impatient knocking. I listened for several minutes, not moving, but whoever it was did not go away.

"All right," I called finally. "All right."

I drew back the mosquito netting covering the bed and swung my feet down. Then I stood and crossed to the rattan chair near the bed. The fan on the bureau had quit operating sometime during the night, which accounted for the stagnant air. I put on my khaki trousers and went to the door and opened it.

Standing there was a little, wiry, dark-skinned man beneath a white, pith-type helmet, dressed in white shorts, knee-high white socks, black shoes, and a short-sleeved bush jacket. He wore his uniform proudly, the way only a native Malayan in an official capacity can.

He said, "You are Mr. Daniel Connell?"

"Yes?"

"I am Inspector Kok Chin Tiong of the Singapore *polis*. I would like to speak with you, please."

"What about?"

"May I come in?"

"If you don't make any comments about my housekeeping," I said, and stood aside.

He came in past me and stood in the middle of the room, looking about him. He turned to face me as I shut the door, his eyes expressionless. "Do you know a man by the name of La Croix, Mr. Connell, a French national?"

I went to the bureau and shook a cigarette from the pack there. "Why?"

"Do you?"

"Maybe."

"We have reliable information that you spoke at length with him yesterday."

I decided I would be wise in leveling with him. "All right, then," I said, shrugging. "I know him."

"So? And how well, please?"

"We've met a few times."

"You have been acquainted how long?"

"Two or three years."

"How did this meeting yesterday occur?"

"He looked me up."

"For what purpose?"

"He wanted to hire me."

"To do what?"

"Fly him out of Singapore."

"To what destination?"

"He didn't tell me."

"Singapore has excellent airline service to all major cities," Tiong said pointedly.

"Maybe he couldn't get immediate passage."

"This was his reason?"

"He didn't give me one."

"Did you agree to his wishes?"

"No."

"Why not?"

"I don't fly any more," I said.

"Ah, yes," Tiong said. "There was an accident two years ago, was there not? Involving an aircraft belonging to you."

"Yeah," I said shortly. "There was an accident."

"You were co-owner of an air cargo company at that time, Connel and Falco Transport. The aircraft, piloted by you, I believe, crashed under rather strange circumstances one night in a remote jungle sector on Penang. You escaped without serious injury, but your partner, Lawrence Falco, was killed in the crash."

I pressed my lips tightly together, not speaking.

"What were you and Mr. Falco doing in that particular area on Penang, Mr. Connell? And at that hour? No flight plan had been filed for such a journey."

"There was a full investigation at the time," I told him. "I gave a statement. Look up the records."

He smiled slightly. "I have already done so. There was strong speculation that you and Mr. Falco were involved in the smuggling of contraband. Among other things."

"Nothing was proved," I said slowly.

"Yes, the plane's cargo was burned beyond recognition," Tiong said. "But your commercial license was nonetheless revoked."

I'd had enough of this. "Listen," I said, "I don't know why you're here, inspector, but what I was or wasn't doing two years ago is a dead issue, just like Larry Falco. I haven't been up in a plane since then, and I don't intend to go up in one. Now, if you don't mind, I'd like to wash up and get dressed."

His black eyes searched my face for a moment, and then he put his hands behind his back and walked to the window. He looked down at Punyang Street, and the palpitating ebb and flow of Chinese there. After a time he said, "I would like to know your whereabouts last evening, Mr. Connell."

I told him. He asked what time I had arrived at the Malaysian Gardens and what time I had left, and I told him that, too. He rubbed at his upper lip with the tip of one forefinger. "Are you familiar, Mr. Connell, with the East Coast Road, near Bedok?"

"A little."

"The French national was found there shortly past midnight," Tiong said. "He had been dead for some three hours at that time. He was quite badly used, and then shot through the temple with a .25 caliber weapon."

Very carefully I stubbed out my cigarette in the glass ashtray on the bureau. "How do you mean, badly used?"

"Tortured," Tiong said. "Quite methodically, it would seem, and quite without compunction."

The back of my neck felt very cold. I said, "And you think I had something to do with it, is that it?"

He turned away from the window and looked at me squarely again. "Did you, Mr. Connell?"

"I told you where I was."

"Yes," he said. "Do you own a gun, please?"

"No."

"Would you object to a search of your quarters?"

"Be my guest," I said. "But I'll tell you something. You're wasting your time coming around to me. I didn't kill La Croix, I didn't have any reason to kill him. But I've got a very good idea who did. Look up a guy named Van Rijk, Jorge Van Rijk, and ask him the questions you've asked me."

Tiong's eyes narrowed. "What do you know of Van Rijk?"

I still did not want to get involved in this thing, but La Croix's death, and the way Tiong had said he died, seemed to make it necessary. "We had a little chat yesterday," I told him. "He wanted to know what La Croix and I discussed, too. I wouldn't give him the time of day, and he made a few very plain threats. Last night, when I left The Malaysian Gardens, the two men he'd had with him earlier jumped me. They didn't have any better luck."

"I see," Tiong said slowly.

"I take it you're familiar with Van Rijk?"

"Most familiar."

"Who is he?"

Tiong hesitated for a moment. Then he shrugged lightly and said, "Ostensibly, Jorge Van Rijk is a tobacco merchant in Johore Bahru. But we have reason to believe he has some other, more profitable—and more illegal—interests. He is also quite an avid collector of rare jade."

Tiong had made that last statement as if I should have attached some significance to it. I said, "Rare jade?"

"Quite so. You are aware, of course, of the recent theft from the Museum of Oriental Art?"

"No," I said.

"It has been prominent in the newspapers."

"I make it a point never to read the newspapers."

"Early last week," Tiong explained, "a priceless white jade figurine, the Burong Chabak, was taken from an exhibit at the museum. The robbery was quite cleverly accomplished, suggesting most careful premeditation."

"You think Van Rijk was involved in it?"

"We are quite certain he was. And we are also quite certain the Frenchman was involved as well."

I was beginning to get an idea what it was all about. La Croix, I knew, had once put in time in a French prison for burglary; he was accomplished at that sort of thing. And he had never heard, from what I knew of him, of that old saw about honor among thieves. It looked like a nice little doublecross on La Croix's part, a doublecross that had backfired. I said so to Tiong, but it didn't stun him.

He made a noncommittal gesture. "Possibly."

"Have you picked up Van Rijk?"

"We have been unable to locate him as yet."

I had a sudden thought. "Listen, Tiong," I said, "if you've got all this information, then why did you come around to me at all? Unless you've got some foolish idea that I was in on the doublecross with La Croix."

"The possibility entered our minds," Tiong said mildly. "You are, after all, known to us as a dealer in contraband. And you were seen with the French national the very day of his murder. We are naturally most curious about this."

I felt a slow anger begin to burn at my neck. Once you acquire a reputation in the South China Seas, it clings to you like a satellite; any time there is any trouble, and the *polis* can put you within fifty miles of it, they come around badgering the way this Tiong had done. I said coldly, "Are you satisfied now?"

"Possibly yes, and possibly no," he said. "Have you anything else you would care to tell me?"

"No."

He stood there for a moment, trying to read something in my eyes, and when he couldn't, he said. "Very well. I will take up no more of your time. But may I suggest that you do not attempt to leave Singapore until this matter is disposed of?"

"I hadn't planned on it."

He went to the door and opened it, nodding curtly as he turned to me again. "Then, *selamat jalan*, Mr. Connell."

"Yeah," I said, and shut the door in his face.

The sun bore down with a merciless fire on the bared upper half of my body. My khakis were soaked through with a viscid sweat, and the back of my neck was blotched and raw from the *roote hond.*

I rolled another barrel of palm oil from the deck of the *tongkang* across the wide plank and onto the dock. One of the Chinese coolies took it there and put it onto a wooden skid. An ancient forklift waited nearby.

I rubbed the back of my forearm across my eyes and thought about what an iced beer would taste like when we were through for the day. It was a fine thought, and I was dwelling on it when Harry Rutledge came walking over to me.

"How's it going?"

"Another hour or so should do it."

"Well, you've got a visitor, ducks. An impatient one, at that."

"Visitor?"

"Bit of a pip, too," Harry said. "You bloody Americans have all the luck."

"A woman?"

He nodded. "Fetch Mr. Dan Connell, she tells me. Urgent. Now I don't like the birds coming round here bothering my lads when they're on the job. But like I said, she's quite a looker. Young, too. Never could say no to them."

"Did she give you a name, Harry?"

"Tina, she says: Tina Kellogg."

I frowned. I had thought I had seen the last of her after my gentle but firm refusal of last night—and after the incident on Jalan Barat. "Okay," I said to Harry. "Where is she?"

"My office," he told me. "You know where it is."

"Thanks, Harry."

He gave me a grin. "My pleasure, ducks."

I picked up my shirt and put it on, then went inside the huge, high-raftered *godown* and threaded my way through the stacked barrels and crates and skids to Harry's small office.

Tina was sitting in the bamboo armchair near the window. She wore a tailored white suit today; the skirt was very short, revealing fine legs. In the light of day, she looked somewhat older than I had first thought.

She stood as I entered, smiling hesitantly; I saw that her eyes were green, and that they had a kind of frantic pleading in them. She said, "Mr. Connell, I . . . I'm sorry to bother you like this, but I was, well, worried about you. Those men last night . . ."

I tried a reassuring smile. "Street muggers," I lied. "They're a native hazard in Singapore."

"Yes," she said. "Well, I guess I shouldn't have run away like I did. But I was very frightened."

"You did the right thing."

"Yes." She sat down in the armchair again, and began twisting her hands nervously in her lap.

I sighed softly. "Your concern over my well-being is very flattering, Tina," I said, "but I don't think it's the only reason you looked me up again today. Am I right?"

Her cheeks flushed. "I . . . I went back to the Philippine Consulate this morning, as you advised, but the ambassador is in Manila attending some sort of conference and won't be back for a week, and the man there told me the same thing he had yesterday. They just won't help me. I . . ."

Abruptly, she began to cry. Her shoulders trembled, and large, glistening silver tears spilled down over her cheeks. I stood there uncomfortably, not speaking. What was there for me to say?

Silence began to build, a strained silence, for we both knew what was coming next; I became aware of how damnably hot it was in there. Finally, Tina said in a tiny voice, "Mr. Connell, please, please help me. I know what you said last night, but I don't know anyone else in Singapore. I don't know where to turn, and if I can't get home to help my father . . ."

"Tina," I said as quietly, as gently, as I could, "there are reasons I can't help you, several reasons. For one thing, it's strictly illegal. I'm treading on very thin ice with the government here; they've made it plain that if there's one more mark against me, I'll be declared *persona non grata*. For another, when I said last night that I don't fly any more, I meant it. I don't have access to a plane any longer. I couldn't fly you to Luzon for just that reason alone."

"But . . . one of those people I talked with said that you used to keep a DC-3 in a hangar at an abandoned airstrip on the island." She brushed at the wetness beneath her eyes. "Isn't it still there?"

I studied her for a long moment, and then I went over to Harry's paper-littered desk. I sat on one corner and took a cigarette from my pocket. "Yes, it's still there."

"Then . . . ?"

I did some thinking, some very careful, methodical thinking. I weighed things in my mind. It's not up to me, I thought. It's none of my concern. I don't have to get into it.

Then I said, "All right, Tina."

"You'll help me?"

"I'll help you."

"Oh, Mr. Connell, thank you, thank you!" She came up out of the bamboo chair and threw her arms around my neck. "I'll never forget you for this!"

I pushed her away gently. "I'm probably a damned fool, but if your father is falsely accused, as you think he is, then I guess it's worth the risk."

Her eyes held a mixture of eagerness and relief now. "When can we leave?"

"It will have to be tonight," I said. "Late, around eleven. It would be idiocy to try it in the daylight."

"Where shall I meet you?"

I thought about that. "Are you familiar with the Esplanade on Cecil Street?"

"I think so, yes."

"There, then, at ten thirty."

"Whatever you say." She stood looking at me, and then quickly, lightly, daughter to father, she kissed me. "Thank you, Mr. Connell," she said again, and seconds later she had stepped into the storage area and was gone through one of the side entrances into the bright, sunlit afternoon.

It rained the early part of that evening, a torrential tropical downpour that lasted for perhaps two hours and left the air, as the daily rains always did, smelling clean and sharp and sweet; but by ten, when I left my flat, it had grown oppressively hot again.

Tina was waiting in the shadows near the Esplanade when I arrived at Cecil Street. She had shed the white suit of the afternoon for men's khakis and a gray bush jacket.

After exchanging soft hellos, I said, "No luggage, Tina?"

"No," she answered. "I didn't want to bother with it. I can send for it later."

I nodded. "All right. Then we'd best get started."

I hailed one of the yellow taxis that roam the streets of Singapore in droves. The driver, a bearded Sikh, did not ask any questions when I told him where we wanted to go. I did not imagine he got many fares to the remote Jurong sector of the Island that I named—there was nothing much there but mangrove swamps and a few native fishing *kampongs*—but like all competent drivers in the South China Seas he kept his thoughts to himself. We rode in silence.

It was ten fifty when he turned onto Kelang Bahru Road, leading toward the abandoned airstrip, Mikko Field. The moon was orange brilliantine in the black sky; the road was illuminated enough so that you could have driven it without headlights.

When we neared the access road that led to the strip, the Sikh began to slow down. "Do you wish me to drive you directly to the Mikko Field, sahib? The road is very bad."

"Go as far as you can," I told him. "We'll walk the rest of it."

"As you wish, sahib."

He made the turn onto the access road. It was badly scarred with chuckholes and heavily grown over with tall grass and tangled vegetation. We crawled along for about a quarter mile. Finally, in the bright moonlight, I could see the long, pitted concrete runway, raised some ten feet on steep earth mounds from the mangrove jungle on both sides. At its upper end, to our left, were the rotting wooden outbuildings, and farther behind them the huge domed hangar. The airstrip had been deserted since the Japanese were driven from Singapore at the tag end of the Second World War. Few people remembered, or cared, that it was still there.

The Sikh braked the taxi to a stop. The road was impassable here; the marsh grass was very tall and thick, and parasitic vines and creepers and thornbushes braided together to form a barrier that was more effective than any man-made obstruction. The Sikh turned to look at me. "We can go no farther, sahib."

"This is fine."

Tina and I stepped out into the night. The air was alive with the buzzing hum of mosquitoes and midges, and with the throaty music of Malayan cicadas. There was the smell of decaying vegetation, and of dampness from the rain.

I paid the Sikh and thanked him and stood there watching while he made a U-turn, and started back along the access road. I watched his taillights fade, disappear, and then I turned to look again at the airstrip.

Tina had not spoken during the ride out. Now she said, in a voice that was almost breathless, "Where do we go?"

I wet my lips. "Suppose—"

I broke off, listening. There was the high, unmistakable whine of a four-cylinder automobile engine being held in low gear, and it was approaching, not retreating. I pivoted to look along the access road. I could see nothing, even in the moonshine, and it was very close now. They were coming without headlights.

A coldness crept over me. "Somebody's coming," I said.

"But who—?"

"I don't know yet. But I've got a good idea."

I caught her arm and we ran for the protective cover of the mangroves, but they must have seen us outlined against the moonlit sky. Headlights stabbed on, and I heard a familiar pig squeal of brakes. Without halting stride, I veered to the left, into the tall marsh grass at the edge of the road. There was a hoarse shout behind us. I pulled Tina deeper into the swamp jungle, parallel to the airstrip. Thorns ripped at my bare arms; unseen creepers tugged at my clothing; something brushed my face, whispering, cold.

We had traveled perhaps fifty or sixty yards when the grass began to thin out, leaving us without protection. I could hear two men, possibly three, moving through the morass behind us. I looked about wildly. To the left was the access road, relatively free of growth here and bathed in moonlight, where it curved around to the outbuildings. I discarded that direction immediately.

The only other way was up onto the airstrip. The outbuildings were only a distance of a hundred yards down the runway, and I knew that if we could make them, find a hiding place, we would have a chance.

I pushed Tina to the right, through a clump of wild shrubs, and up to the base of the embankment. The mounded earth was a quagmire from the evening rain, but we managed to fight our way up onto the strip. "Run!" I hissed to Tina.

We ran. Our muddied boots slapped wetly on the concrete. There was another shout from behind us, and I heard the roar of a large-caliber pistol. I glanced back over my shoulder. There were two of them at the base of the embankment; I could not see their faces. A third stood in the twin headlamp beams of an English car where we had been on the access road. He was doing the shouting, and even though I could not see his face, I knew, of course, who he was—Van Rijk.

I turned my head. We were almost to the outbuildings now. I heard another roar from the pistol behind us, but they were not going to hit much at the range from which they were firing.

The closest building was a long, rectangular, low-roofed affair that had been used to quarter duty personnel. All the glass had been broken out of its windows, a long time ago, and some of the wooden side boarding had rotted or pulled away, leaving shadowed gaps like missing teeth. Off to one side was a much smaller, ramshackle substructure, a shed of some kind.

I steered Tina toward it, and we went around the corner of the rectangular building and along the side of the shed. At the rear, a semicircular, jagged-edged hole in the wood yawned black, like a small cave opening.

I came to a stop, fighting breath into my lungs. "Through there!"

She obeyed instantly. She dropped to her knees and scrambled through the hole, inside the shed. I followed close behind her.

Thin shafts of moonlight made a pale, irregular pattern on the debris-ridden floor inside. The shed was empty, and it was close, humid in there—a pervasive heat like that in an orchid hothouse.

Tina's breath came in thick gasps. She crouched on her knees with her head bowed. I left her and crawled across the damp wooden floor to the front of the shed. I peered through one of the smaller gaps there. I had a full view of the airstrip.

I saw the headlights then—two sets of them—coming down the access road, coming very fast. I felt some of the tension in my body ease. I could not see the portion of the road where the English car and Van Rijk were, but the other two, up on the runway now, fifty yards away, could see it clearly. They pulled up, looking back, uncertain.

The sound of jamming brakes, of doors slamming, of men shouting, carried faintly to me on the night air. They had not used their sirens. Part of the strip was illuminated from the automobile headlamps.

"What is it?" Tina asked, coming beside me to look out. She had got her breath now. "What's happening?"

"The *polis* are here, Tina," I said.

"The *polis*?"

I watched the two men on the airstrip. One of them extended his arm, crouching, and I saw the gun in his hand, but before he could use it, there was a short, sharp burst from an automatic weapon. The man fell, sprawling headlong. The other one veered off to the right, running in a low zigzag. The automatic weapon sounded again. He went off the side of the embankment, feet first, like an Olympic broadjumper. Pistol shots rang out, three of them, and then another burst from the automatic weapon. After that, there was only silence.

I turned away from the opening. "It's all over now," I said.

Tina's fingers dug into my arm. "The plane!" she breathed. "Maybe there's still time to reach the plane, Mr. Connell . . ."

I straightened, placing my hands flat on my knees, looking at her. "There isn't any plane, Tina."

Her face was shadowed, and I could not see her eyes. "I . . . I don't understand."

"There's no plane here," I repeated slowly. "There hasn't been one here for two years now."

She stared at me for a full minute, and then, suddenly, her hand flashed to the belt of her khakis, under the bush jacket. She was very quick, and I did not have time to react before she had the gun pointed levelly at my stomach. It was plainly visible in one of the shafts of pale moonlight, and I saw that it was of Belgian manufacture, a .25 caliber automatic. I said quietly, "Is that the gun you shot La Croix with? After you tortured him?"

She leaned forward slightly, and I could see her face then. The frightened little girl no longer existed; in her place was a cold, hard, and very deadly woman. "All right," she said. "So you know."

"I've known since this afternoon, Tina," I said. "Oh, it was a very nice act you put on, a clever little farce. I'll admit you had me fooled last night at The Malaysian Gardens, and that you had me fooled for a while this afternoon. But you made a mistake, then, and it didn't take long before I saw the whole thing for exactly what it was."

I watched the automatic; it did not waver. I went on.

"You said that one of those fictitious people you talked with mentioned an abandoned airstrip where I used to keep a DC-3. But you didn't know, couldn't have known, that there were only three people besides myself—and eventually the *polis*—who ever knew I once kept a plane in a hangar here. One of those men was my partner in an air cargo business, and he's been dead for two years. Another is a German named Heinrich; he's serving ten years in a Djakarta prison for hijacking. And the third man, the only man you could have gotten the information from, was a French national named La Croix. But La Croix was on the run, trying to get out of Singapore. He sure as hell wouldn't have been wandering around Raffles Square; he couldn't possibly have been one of the people you claimed you'd talked to.

"That started me thinking, Tina, about a lot of things, and the way they added up. But just to make certain, I went down to the Philippine Consulate after you left the *godown* this afternoon, and asked a few pertinent questions. They had never heard of any Tina Kellogg, much less a Luzon import-export dealer being arrested for Communist conspiracy. So I went to see an Inspector Tiong at the government precinct building and told him about it, and he did some very efficient checking. He uncovered a bit of interesting information. Like the fact that your real name is Tina Jeunet, and that you're a Canadian by birth. The fact that, although nothing was ever proved, you were implicated in the theft of several valuable uncut diamonds in England two years ago. And the fact that you were in Brussels last July when an original Gauguin was stolen from a private collector there. Again, nothing proved. But there was no doubt in police minds.

"When we had all this, the inspector and I devoted a long and careful discussion to the theft of the Burong Chabak, the jade figurine, from the Museum of Oriental Art. I suggested this little trap tonight and paved the way by agreeing to fly you to Luzon. We didn't expect Van Rijk to fall into it, too, but I guess it worked out all right that way. I would have had you picked up right away at the Esplanade tonight, if I'd thought you were carrying the figurine—the inspector was waiting there for my signal. It had me a little puzzled when I saw you didn't have it, and later when you didn't make some excuse so we would stop and you could pick it up. But then I remembered something La Croix had started to tell me, that I hadn't let him finish, when he talked to me two days ago. I'm sure what he had started to say was that the figurine was here at Mikko Field. You never had it at all. And that's the reason you came to me: to find out the name of this strip, and because I would know where the Burong Chabak was hidden."

She smiled, an ugly curving of her mouth. "You're going to take me to it," she said. "Right now."

"Don't be a fool, Tina. This whole area is alive with *polis*. You can't get past them."

"*We'll* get past them," she said pointedly.

I smiled in the darkness. "If you're thinking about using me as some kind of hostage, you can forget it. They don't give a damn about me."

"We'll see about that."

"No," I said, "we won't see about it at all."

She moved the automatic again, and that was exactly what I had been waiting for. I brought my left hand off my knee, swinging it out and up, palm open. My closed fingers hit the barrel of the automatic, driving it upward. There was a roar as she squeezed the trigger reflexively, and I felt a searing heat along my forearm, but the bullet thudded somewhere into the shed's roof. I caught Tina's wrist with my right hand and pressured it heavily. She cried out in pain; the automatic fell to the floor.

I picked it up, sliding back away from her. Then I got to my feet and put the gun in my belt. My arm was blistered from the discharged bullet, and stung badly, but I thought that it would be all right. I looked out through one of the gaps in the boarding. Four men were on the airstrip now, running. One of them had a machine gun and the others drawn pistols. Inspector Kok Chin Tiong was in the lead. I turned, looking down at Tina Jeunet; she was crouched there on the floor, hating me with her eyes. "Let's go," I said.

She did not move. I shrugged. I felt very tired, and it did not make any difference now anyway. I went to the rear of the shed and crawled through the hole and came around onto the strip. The running men slowed when they saw me. Tiong approached. He was out of breath. "You are all right, Mr. Connell?"

"Yeah," I said. "I'm just fine."

"The woman?"

"In the shed there. She's not hurt, but I don't think she's going anywhere."

Tiong said something in Malay to one of his men. The officer nodded and hurried off toward the shed.

I asked, "What about Van Rijk?"

"We have him in custody."

"And the other two?"

"They are both dead."

"You could have been saying the same thing about me," I told him. "You took your sweet time getting here."

He smiled. "When your taxicab drove away from the Esplanade, we saw an automobile following closely behind it. An automobile with its headlamps dark and containing three men."

"And you figured it was Van Rijk," I said.

"Yes."

"Why didn't you just pick him up instead of letting him come out here?"

"We wished to—how is it you Americans say—give him further rope with which to hang himself?"

"Yeah," I said. I lifted the automatic from my belt and handed it to him, butt first. He accepted it with a polite gesture, then turned it over to one of his men.

There was a sound from the direction of the shed. The officer Tiong had dispatched was bringing Tina Jeunet out, her hands shackled in front of her. The officer led her toward the access road and the waiting *polis* cars.

I watched them for a moment and then I told Tiong what I had said to Tina Jeunet about the Burong Chabak. He nodded silently. I said, "I think we'll find the figurine at a drop point La Croix and I used when we did business together. He would leave payment there for whatever I was carrying if everything went all right."

I led Tiong to the rear of the huge domed hangar, near two large and heavily corroded tanks that had once been used for the storage of airplane fuel. There, set into the ground beneath a layer of foliage, was a wooden box housing regulating valves for the airstrip's water supply.

The Burong Chabak was there.

I learned the full story the following morning, in Tiong's neat little office at the government precinct building; it was just about as we had speculated when I saw him the previous afternoon, after Tina Jeunet's visit to the *godown*.

La Croix and Tina had done the actual stealing of the figurine from the museum, but it had been Van Rijk's idea originally. But instead of delivering the Burong Chabak to Van Rijk afterward, the two of them had decided to pull a doublecross. It would have worked out all right for them, too, if La Croix had not attempted to make a triplecross out of it by taking the figurine for himself, and leaving Tina in virtually the same position as Van Rijk.

Then La Croix came to me. Someone who knew that Van Rijk was looking for both Tina and La Croix had seen La Croix talking to me, and called Van Rijk. He knew, of course, that he had been doublecrossed, but he still thought both La Croix *and* Tina were in it together. His idea was that I would lead him to La Croix, and Tina, and eventually to the figurine.

Tiong had told me La Croix was killed somewhere around nine; assuming it was Van Rijk who had done it, then he would have had no reason for having me followed at eleven. He would have got the information he wanted from La Croix.

Tiong and I had reasoned earlier that this meant Van Rijk had not killed La Croix; that left only one person who could have—Tina Jeunet. She found out where he was hiding, and she tortured him. He told her then that he had hidden the figurine at an abandoned airstrip, at a place known only to him—and to me—but he had died before he could name the strip, and the cache point. Tina Jeunet had shot him in the head in blind anger, and then she had come looking for me.

That was all of it.

I saw the jade figurine for the first time there in Tiong's office. Intricately, painstakingly carved, it depicted a nightbird—a *burong chabak*—in full flight, wings spread, head extended as if into a great wind. The bird itself was of white jade, the purest, most valuable of all jade; the squarish pedestal upon which it rested was of a dark green jade.

"Is it not beautiful?" Tiong asked when I had examined it.

I said nothing; it had felt cold, a faintly repulsive coldness, in my hands. "How much is it worth on the black market?" I asked him. "To an underground collector, say?"

"Perhaps four hundred thousand Straits dollars," he said. "I would not know the exact figure, of course."

"A hundred and fifty thousand or so, American," I said. "That's why Tina Jeunet wanted to get to Luzon. She had a buyer there."

"Yes," Tiong said. He gave me a thoughtful look across his desk, as if something was puzzling him. "That is a great deal of money. Enough to tempt any man."

I said that it was.

"And yet you chose to notify the *polis* when you suspected the woman of possessing the figurine. Your past record indicates no hint of such civic-mindedness. Why, Mr. Connell?"

"All right," I said. "The main reason is Larry Falco."

"Your former partner?"

"My *dead* former partner," I said. "A nice guy, with a lot of fine ideas about how to make a comfortable living from an air cargo transport company, who is dead because I had other ideas—running contraband, for instance, to a small airport in disrepair. Larry tried to talk me out of it, but I wouldn't listen. I could take the plane in, I said. Well, I was wrong, and Larry died because of it. It should have been me."

Tiong was silent for the longest time. Then, finally, he said quietly, "I see."

I do not think he really saw at all.

REYNOLD JUNKER

The Volunteers

Somewhere he could hear a bell ringing. It was a faraway sound, lost in a dark attic under a heap of broken old toys or hidden in the bottom of a barrel that smelled of dark, sour wine. There was a child, a boy, in a white First Communion suit searching frantically. He could feel the warm sting of the starched collar against his freshly scrubbed neck. It had been his brother's suit. And before his brother? And since?

Then the ringing was right there inside his head, pushing against the warm numbness of sleep. The child was crying.

Santro Ristelli shifted his bulk into a half-sitting position and ran a hand over his black, day-old beard. The bed creaked someplace in its joints. He leaned back against his elbows and listened. The only sound was the hoarse, strained breathing of the child sleeping on the couch in the front room.

The phone rang. Santro didn't move. He wondered sleepily how many times it had already rung. He had been awake only seconds. Maria, his wife, jerked awake at the sound. She, like her husband, was a dark, heavy person but had learned to move quickly. With five children, she had to. "What's wrong? What is it?" Her voice was thick with sleep.

In a few seconds, Santro thought, she will be wide awake, but now her voice is like that, as though she was afraid to say all of the things that are bottled up inside her. In the old days she sang and cried and laughed, but now there is nothing to laugh and sing about, and what's the use of crying? There is only the slow, heavy voice always asking, "Is anything wrong?"

Without answering, Santro slipped from the bed onto the bare wooden floor. He picked his way through the darkness past the front room and out onto the landing. Outlined against the dirty grey light from the open roof, his squat hairy body looked like a circus bear. He lifted the phone from the wall before it stopped ringing. "Hallo?"

"Santro?"

Even in his sleep he would have known the voice. It was like a loud hissing in his ears, someone telling another a great secret, but very anxious that everyone should overhear. "Johnny—What the hell do you want?"

"Santro, my old friend, is that any way to talk to a buddy?"

"*Buddy*. It's the middle of the night. I need sleep, not smart talk. I'm the one who works for a living, remember?"

"Sure, Santro, sure. How could I possibly forget? Work all day, sleep all night. Someday you'll be the patron saint of the working class."

"Don't make fun, Johnny. Don't make fun." Santro could feel all of the sleep seeping out of him.

"Then listen, friend, and listen good. This is no smart talk. There's been a train wreck just outside of Fairfield. One of the specials coming up from Miami jumped the track or missed a stop. I didn't get it all exactly."

"So?" Santro heard the child groaning awake in the front room.

Johnny breathed sharply into the phone. "Is that all you can say? Think, Santro. Use something besides your belly for once. The special is loaded with a bunch of rich so-and-sos who have nothing to do but ride back and forth between New York and Miami looking for someplace to throw their money around."

Johnny paused, then continued slowly. He was saying each word carefully as though he were driving nails. "Fairfield is a small town. They're calling for volunteers to help with the bodies. The police can't handle it. They need help—with the bodies."

"I don't know," Santro said, more to himself than into the phone.

Johnny's voice became an angry hiss. Santro remembered the time the younger man had spoken at a local union rally. He remembered the voice and eyes and the arms rising and falling wildly.

"Santro, listen, do I have to go down there myself and bring back the stuff to show it to you? All you have to do is pick it up off the ground—at most empty a few pockets or fingers. They're dead! It's no good to them any more. They're dead! What do you say?"

"Shut up. Shut up for a second, will you? I've got to think about it. There are other things—" He shut his eyes and tried to ask himself what they were, these other things. The old words and answers he had learned as a child floated back across the years, but he could never be the child in the white communion suit again. How easy the answers had been then. He had learned all of the answers, but nobody had ever really explained the questions. They had never told him that he'd have to choose and that no matter what the choice, someone had to get hurt. He had had to learn that for himself. Someone is always getting hurt. Every door you open leads to another door.

Johnny's voice was a whisper. "What about your old lady? And the kids? Is young Santro still having that trouble? It's a terrible .cough. Sometimes, it's almost as though his chest were breaking in—"

"Liar," he whispered, but there wasn't any anger in his voice. Santro ran a hand across his face. He was wet with perspiration. Johnny was whistling softly under his breath. Santro tried to swallow. His mouth tasted of something stale and brown. "How soon will you be here?"

"Just as soon as I can."

"I've got to get dressed."

"Better get something to eat."

"I'm not hungry. I'll only need time to dress."

"Just as well. Tonight we'll be eating steak. Your old lady—"

"Don't come to the house. I'll meet you at the corner."

"Okay. I'll be driving my cousin Guido's truck. We'll need a couple of picks and a shovel and maybe some—"

"Bring them. Whatever you think." Santro hung up the phone without waiting for an answer and stood listening to the silence around him. He felt a little sick. He tried to think, but he could only remember.

Maria was sitting up on the edge of the bed. "Is anything wrong?" she asked dully. "Who was that?"

Santro picked up his clothes from the chair on which he had laid them the night before and began pulling them on.

"Where are you going? What's wrong?"

"That was Carlo," he lied quickly. "There's been a train wreck over near Fairfield and he wants us to go over and help with the—hurt. The police can't handle it. I guess it's pretty bad."

"Why you? What about the others? The younger ones?" The sound of her voice made him want to scream, to strike out at her.

"A bunch of us are going. It's pretty bad." He could feel the words catching at the bottom of his throat. It was hard to keep from shouting.

"Will you lose any time on the job? Will they pay you?"

He turned to face her. She looked far away, like a ghost or part of a dream. "Money!" he answered angrily. The words were coming loose now. "Always money. Isn't there ever anything else? Why can't there ever be something besides money?" He looked at her and found himself hoping that she'd be able to tell him something he hadn't been able to find for himself. There was still a chance. Somewhere, someplace maybe he had missed something.

"How can there ever be anything else for us?" Her voice neither fell nor rose. The words tumbled across her lips simply because the muscles expanded and contracted.

"I'm sorry," he said softly. "The company wants us to go. It will look good for them. We'll be paid. Maybe even a bonus."

He finished dressing in silence. When he looked back at the bed, Maria had rolled over on her side and lay facing the wall. He couldn't tell whether or not she had fallen back to sleep. He picked up his jacket, turned off the light, and started out through the front room.

Santro walked slowly through the soft grey morning. The streets smelled sweet and damp and a kind of freshness ran through them like something lost. His mind was flooded through with thoughts of Maria and of the children. They came into his mind, not separately and distinctly, but fused together, a jumble of names and faces without any real name or face: Maria's voice, the boy's eyes, a cough, a cry. They tumbled together crazily. It was like looking into a toy kaleidoscope or even more like being inside one. Everything was lost in the shifting patterns of colored glass. Everything he once thought was sure seemed to become tangled and changed each time he moved. He couldn't be certain of anything except that he seemed to be moving all the time; not going anywhere, just moving.

He turned quickly at the sound of the truck pulling up at the curb beside him. It rattled to a stop and the door swung open. Santro climbed up into the pickup and pulled the door closed behind him. He leaned back against the worn seat and tugged the collar of his jacket up around his chin. Johnny laughed lightly, shrugged his shoulders, and gunned the engine. The truck groaned around the corner and jerked heavily toward the highway.

"Don't be so gloomy, Santro. It's not the end of the world."

"Maybe it is. For some." He avoided looking at Johnny.

"The weak must die so that the strong may live, eh, Santro?"

"And vultures. What about the vultures?"

Johnny laughed softly. He reached across the seat and slapped Santro sharply across the thigh. "You and me, vulture and friend. The vultures going to loot the vultures. They loot from us when they are alive and we, like any self-respecting vultures, return the favor. Ha-ha."

They drove in silence to the highway where they turned north toward Fairfield. Johnny whistled the same tune over and over until it became like a faucet dripping someplace in the middle of the night. Santro shut his eyes against it and tried to relax.

"You know what's wrong with you, Santro? You're an Italian—" He said "Eyetalian" as though it were a word he'd never heard before except in street jokes. Santro opened his eyes and stared out along the narrow white ribbon of highway. It had already begun to grow quite light. "And, you know what's wrong with *Eye*talians? They're a whole race of nothing but stomachs. Stomachs. The women are always pregnant and the men are always eating. I don't think there's been an *Eye*talian with an idea since—since Da Vinci."

"And you, Giovanni *mio*, of course we mustn't forget you," Santro said wearily.

"Not me. Not the kid." Johnny grinned at him and tapped his head just in front of his ear. "Up here, plenty of ideas, American ideas."

"Johnny, Johnny the American. Excuse me."

They approached Fairfield from the south along the highway that paralleled the railroad and then turned onto a dirt road that ran along the tracks on either side. The wreck wasn't visible until they had made a jogging turn to the right and drove up over the top of a softly sloping hill. The pickup jerked down the incline slowly. Santro had never seen a train wreck before. The only trains he could remember seeing were the shining blue and silver limiteds that screamed past the gangs working near the tracks and the faded red-brown locals that labored up and down the coast between the small resort towns. What he saw before him now looked like something he might have seen in a newsreel somewhere, something quick and alive and violent that had broken and snapped into silent deathlike pieces. Beams and splinters of wood and metal stuck out at crazy angles from the tangle of the wreckage. At places up and down the line he could see small puffs of smoke rising and settling. The narrow shoulder beside the tracks was dotted at places with dark blankets. He felt the same stale brown taste come up into his mouth. A couple of bodies hadn't been covered over yet. Maybe they had run out of dark blankets.

Johnny drove down the sloping road to a small canvas tent that had been set up about halfway down the line. A dark, squat man came out and motioned for them to stop. Johnny waved back at him and pulled up beside the tent.

"Just in time." He grinned at Santro.

"There's hardly anyone here."

"That's what I mean. Just in time."

Santro reached over to open the door at his side. Johnny grabbed at his sleeve. "In case they ask us for our names, I'm Johnny Williams and you're Santro Candoli. Get it?"

"Got it, Johnny Williams." Santro nodded.

They dropped down from the truck and Johnny came around quickly, past Santro, to where the fat man was standing. "I'm Johnny Williams and this here's my friend, Santro Candoli. We came over to help. They said over the radio that the police couldn't handle it and you were sending out a call for volunteers."

The fat man spat into the dust at his feet and shrugged at Johnny. "Leave it to the radio."

"What do you mean?"

"I mean leave it to the radio to figure out a way to exaggerate the thing— anything."

"You mean this—" Johnny motioned with his arm at the wrecked train "— isn't the special from Miami?" He had stopped grinning.

"Kid, this ain't even the special from Hoboken." He spat again.

Santro looked closely at the faded red cars. He smiled weakly.

"But I guess since you're here, we can use you to help finish cleaning up this mess. We're short of tools. Did you bring any?"

"A pick and a couple of shovels," Santro answered. He felt sort of giddy, as though he were listening to someone telling a very funny joke. He could still get breakfast and make it to work on time, but there was something he wanted to watch: the American; the idea man. After all, they had come to help, he and Johnny Williams.

"You may as well grab them and start on down the line. We figure we already got all or mostly all of the bodies. There couldn't have been too many passengers. If you find one, call for one of the guys and he'll tag it and cover it up. Maybe you'd better check and see if they want you to start any place in particular." He spat again and went back into the tent.

Johnny stared down the line at the small group of men bending over their shovels. Santro walked back to the truck and pulled out the two shovels and the pick. He shouldered the shovels and tossed Johnny the pick.

"Let's go, volunteer."

"Of all the luck! Of all the rotten luck! It makes my blood boil!"

Santro laughed softly. He wanted to laugh out loud and clap Johnny across the back. Here they were, volunteers, clearing the track so that the Miami Special wouldn't be delayed. All of the rich devils who have nothing to do but ride back and forth between New York and Miami looking for someplace to throw their money around would be back in New York for dinner—thanks to the volunteers.

They started down the line toward the small cluster of men. Johnny walked behind Santro, kicking up the dirt with his feet. He didn't look at the older man. Santro didn't figure that he would, not for a while anyway.

"Son of a—of all the rotten, stinking luck!"

"Oh, well, it was an idea." Santro spoke evenly. He wasn't about to give Johnny the chance to explode. That would get it out of his system too soon, and Santro wanted him to live with it for a little while longer.

They made their way to a man who was standing over a shovel watching a couple of others. A small pack of yellow tags showed from inside his jacket pocket. "Volunteers," Santro said when the man looked up at them.

His eyes were like those of the man in the tent, and Santro half expected him to spit. Instead he straightened up and looked down the line to the rear of the train. "We already finished up most of it on this side. I don't know why he sent you down here. How about going around to the other side and checking with the boys around there? They started after we did."

Santro nodded and motioned to Johnny. They started slowly down the line toward the last car. Santro glanced at his watch. He should have been leaving for work. Neither of them spoke. Johnny picked up a rock and heaved it ahead of them at one of the beams that lay across the track. It hit something soft and kicked up a small puff of dust. Something yellow caught the light and flickered through the dirt. Something groaned.

Santro caught at Johnny's shoulder. "Listen!"

The groan came again. Santro caught his breath. He looked quickly back toward the others. One of the cars jutted out between them. They wouldn't be able to see him and Johnny. Something yellow flickered again in the dust.

Johnny dropped to his knees and began pawing at the dirt with his hands. He dropped back against his haunches and held a woman's gold bracelet in the sun for Santro to see. Santro dropped the shovels and shoved him aside, away from the woman. The younger man fell back heavily into the dust and glared up at Santro. He grabbed for the pick.

"You fool, she's alive! Didn't you hear it?"

"You're nuts. You're hearing things." Johnny pulled his hands away from the pick. It had been only a gesture. Santro knew that he wouldn't use it.

"Help me get her out of here."

Each of them grabbed at one end of the beam and lifted it from the woman's body. They cleared away the dirt and dragged her out from under the wreckage. She had been pinned there on her stomach.

"Turn her over gently."

They laid her out on her back. Santro dropped to his knees beside her and pressed his ear against her chest. He could hear her heart beating faintly. There were other sounds. Sounds of something breaking or broken inside her. He pulled himself up to his knees. "She's alive."

Johnny had moved off to one side behind him. Santro looked back at him. The younger man's eyes were like those of a frightened child. He tried to say something, but the words caught inside him and all that came out was a small whining sound. He pulled the bracelet out of his pocket and let it fall into the dirt. "Her face—her poor face," he muttered weakly.

Santro looked down at the face for the first time. It was broken and blue with bruises, and the eyes were open.

Santro heard Johnny drop to his knees. He was retching. Santro placed his hand against the woman's chest. He could feel the soft tapping cadence of the heartbeats. He looked down into the woman's face again. The colored glass dropped away. All of the faces in his mind became one final, distinct face—

He placed the flat of his hand against her chest and forced down against it. One final spurt of blood ran purple from the twisted mouth before the eyes rolled up into the lifeless head.

Santro reached down and removed a pin from the dead woman's dress. He took two rings, one a diamond engagement ring, from her fingers. "She was all but dead," he said to the stillness around him. "The children deserve a chance to live. I'm sorry, but that's the way it is—for us, anyway."

He stood up beside the body. Johnny was gone. The pick was still where he had dropped it. Santro reached down and picked up the bracelet. He turned and started back to the truck. The jewelry was heavy in his jacket pocket.

EDWARD D. HOCH

Arbiter of Uncertainties

Arthur Urah was a tall, slender man with thick white hair and the bearing of a dignitary. He wore silk shirts with the monogram *AU* over the left breast pocket, and this was what had led some in the business to dub him the Arbiter of Uncertainties. It was a good name. It fit him perfectly.

He had never been to the Brenten Hotel before. It was in an old section of town, and in truth it was an old hotel, dating back some fifty-five years in the city's history. No one of importance stayed at the Brenten any longer, and thus it was perhaps a bit odd to see a man of Arthur Urah's obvious character entering the lobby on a Sunday afternoon.

"I'm to meet some people here," he told the desk clerk, a seedy little man chewing on a toothpick. "My name is Arthur Urah."

"Oh, sure. Room 735. They're waiting for you."

"Thank you," he said, and entered the ancient elevator for the ascent to the seventh floor.

The corridors of the old hotel were flaky with dead paint, and a dusty fire hose hung limply in a metal wall rack. Arthur Urah eyed it all with some distaste as he searched out room 735 and knocked lightly on the door.

It was opened almost at once by a slim young man with black hair and pouting lips. Arthur Urah had known the type for most of his life. The room itself was as shabby as the rest of the hotel, and its big double bed had been pushed against one drab wall to give more floor space, revealing in the process a long accumulation of dust and grime.

"Arthur! Good to see you again!" The man who came forward to greet him first was Tommy Same, a familiar figure around town.

Arthur Urah had always liked Tommy, though personal feelings never entered into his decisions. "How are you, Tommy? How's the family?"

"Fine. Just fine! Glad to have you deciding things, Arthur."

Urah smiled. "I don't play favorites, Tommy. I listen to both sides."

The other side was there, too. Fritz Rimer was a little man with a bald head and large, frightened eyes. It was obvious at once that he was out of his league. "Pleased to meet you, Mr. Urah," he mumbled. "Hate to get you down here like this on a Sunday."

"That's his job," Tommy Same pointed out. "You and me've got a disagreement, and Arthur here is going to settle it. He's an arbiter, just like business and the unions use."

Arthur Urah motioned toward the door. "I'm not used to settling cases with a gun at my back. Get rid of the kid."

Tommy Same spread his hands in a gesture of innocence. "You know Benny. His father used to drive for me. Benny's no kid gunman."

Urah eyed the slim young man with obvious distaste. "Get rid of him," he repeated. "Let him wait in the hall."

Tommy made a motion and Benny disappeared out the door. "Satisfied?"

Urah gave a slight nod, running his fingers through the thick white hair over one ear. "Now, who else is here?"

"Only Sal. She won't bother us."

Urah walked to the connecting door and opened it. Sally Vogt was lounging in a chair with a tabloid newspaper. "Hello, Arthur," she said. "Just catching up on the news."

He closed the door. "All right," he decided. "She can stay. Nobody else, though. Tell the room clerk noboby comes up till we're finished."

"I told him that already."

Arthur Urah opened the slim briefcase he carried and extracted a notepad. "We'll sit at this table," he said. "Since Fritz is the offended party, he gets to talk first."

It was only an outsize card table, with rickety legs, supplied by the hotel. Sitting around it on their three chairs, they looked a bit like reluctant poker players defeated by the odds.

Fritz Rimer cleared his throat and nervously fingered a pencil. "Well, everybody knows what the trouble is." He paused, as if suddenly aware of his smallness at the table.

"Suppose you tell us anyway," Urah prodded gently.

"There are thirty-six horse rooms in this city where a man can lay a bet on the races or the pro games. Twenty years ago, when I started in business, there were thirty-six individual owners of these places. We all knew each other, and helped each other out. When the cops closed down one place occasionally, the rest of us came to the owner's aid. We were one big family, see?"

Tommy Same moved restlessly in his chair. "I'm crying for you, Fritz. Get to the point."

"Well, about a year ago, Tommy Same and some of his syndicate friends moved in and started taking over the city's entire bookmaking operation. Some places they forced out of business and then bought up cheap. Others, they demanded a big cut of the take and sent somebody around to babysit and make sure they got it. Right now the syndicate is a partner in thirty-five of the thirty-six places in this city—all but mine."

Arthur Urah nodded. "And now he wants yours, too?"

"Right. He sent that guy Benny down last week to scare me, but I told him this wasn't like the old days. I don't scare. If he wants to kill me, he can, but that just might be the end of Tommy Same." As he talked, a certain courage seemed to flow into the little bald man. Now his cheeks were flushed and there was an unmistakable power in his words. The others had not stood up to Tommy, but little Fritz Rimer had, even though it might cost him his life.

Tommy Same cleared his throat. "When do I get a chance to talk? You going to listen to this guy all afternoon?"

Urah smiled slightly. "You can talk now, Tommy. Is Fritz telling the truth? Are you trying to take over his operation?"

Tommy Same leaned back in his chair, frowning. "It's like labor unions, Arthur. We all have to stick together, to protect ourselves from the law, and deadbeats, and occasional swindlers. With all thirty-six horse rooms in town linked together in a sort of syndicate, it's better for everyone."

"And that's your defense for this?"

"Sure. I'm not trying to force anyone out of business. I'm giving valuable services, and I just want a share of their profits in return."

"Did you threaten Fritz here?"

"Look, this isn't the old days. If I'd threatened him, do you think I would have allowed him to call you in? Do you think Capone or some of the other old timers would have sat still for arbitration?"

"You're not Capone," Arthur Urah reminded him quietly.

"No, but I can realize the importance of us all sticking together. If Rimer goes his own way, pretty soon the others will start to, and then where'll we be? Back to the old days when the cops could knock off the places one at a time."

It went on like that for another hour, with each man arguing for his side. Arthur Urah had heard it all before, in a dozen different contexts, and at these times the dialogue took on a soporific quality that dumbfounded him. Petty criminals, the dregs of society, taking up his time in a shabby hotel room while he listened to their sordid tales. He had sat, a year earlier, as mediator in a boundary dispute involving some big underworld names in Brooklyn, and it was the peaceful settlement of that potentially dangerous situation which had made his reputation as a gangland mediator. It was a reputation he had never sought and never fully accepted, and yet it stuck and grew through a half dozen other disputes. He was Arthur Urah, the Arbiter of Uncertainties, the one to call when there was bloodshed to be prevented.

"That's enough for now," he told them finally, pushing back from the card table. "I think I have enough information to reach a decision."

"When?" Rimer asked him.

"Leave me alone for a bit to ponder it all."

They went out of the room, Rimer to the hallway, and Tommy Same to the girl who waited next door. Urah stood and stretched, feeling at that moment every one of his fifty-three years. He walked to the window and looked down at the Sunday afternoon street seven stories below, ominously deserted.

Presently, as he stood there, he heard a footstep on the rug behind him. It was Tommy Same, returned for a few private words. He slipped his arm around Urah's shoulder and spoke in tones of brotherhood. "You and I know how to handle these things, don't we, Arthur? These punks like Rimer have to be coddled just so far. Imagine—sitting down at a table with the guy when I should be kicking his teeth in!"

"Times are changing, Tommy."

"Sure they are. That's why I'm taking over the horse rooms in this town. The day of the independent operator is gone forever."

"Fritz Rimer doesn't think so."

Tommy took his arm away. He was nearly a head shorter than Arthur Urah, and standing there close to him he reminded Urah somehow of the wayward son he'd never had. "Look, Arthur, be good to Rimer. Tell him he's all through and save the poor guy's life."

"You're telling me something, Tommy, and it's not something I want to hear."

"I'm telling you the facts of life in this town. I like to keep everybody happy and look respectable, so I go along with this arbitration bit. But I can't afford to lose the decision. The other thirty-five guys would all bolt if Rimer got away. They wouldn't be still a week."

"So?"

"So you rule against me, Arthur, and I gotta score on Rimer. I'm up against a wall. There's no other way."

"You'd be crazy to try it."

"Arthur . . . I already told Benny. He's waiting out in the hall. If you rule that Rimer stays in business, he never leaves this hotel alive."

Urah stared out the window at the occasional passing cars below. The afternoon shadows were already long, offering a hint of approaching night. "Get out," he said to Tommy. "I'll pretend I never heard that."

"Whatever you say, Arthur."

Then he was gone, and the room was quiet once more. Urah sat down at the card table and began to make a few notes. He'd been at it for ten minutes when another visitor entered through the connecting door.

He glanced up and smiled. "Hello, Sal."

Sally Vogt was a cute blonde trying hard to stay under thirty. Most of the time she succeeded, thanks to her hairdresser. "What have you been doing with yourself lately, Arthur?"

"Bringing people together. Making peace."

"I mean besides that. We used to see you often down at the club."

"That was a long time ago. We travel in different circles now."

"Arthur . . ."

"Yes?"

"He sent me in to talk to you. He thinks he handled it badly."

"He did."

She shifted her feet and gazed at the worn carpet. "He's uptight, Arthur. If he loses control of these horse rooms, he's all finished in the organization. They don't give anybody a second chance."

Arthur Urah shrugged. "Maybe they fire him and hire Fritz Rimer in his place."

"Don't joke, Arthur."

"I'm not. Is he really going to kill Rimer?"

"Of course not."

"Then what's Benny for? Just to scare people?"

She lit a cigarette and inhaled slowly. "Benny's left over from the old days. Tommy inherited him, along with everything else in town."

"Not quite everything."

"Arthur, Arthur! This isn't your big moment in Brooklyn with the syndicate chiefs. Nobody cares what happens here. Give Tommy Rimer's place and everybody lives in peace."

"You just said Tommy's bosses cared what happened here. That makes it important to him, at least."

"How much would you take to give Tommy the decision, Arthur?"

Urah rubbed a hand across his eyes. "First Tommy, and now you. Do I get Benny in here next, with his gun?"

She didn't answer that. Instead she said, "I suppose you'll make a decision this afternoon."

"There's no reason to delay it. In fact, I think you can tell them to come in now."

As he waited for Rimer and Tommy Same to appear, the room clerk from downstairs stuck his head in the door. "Some of the big boys are waiting in the lobby. They want to know how long you'll be."

"Not long," Urah said, resenting the intrusion. Their presence in the lobby meant that someone didn't trust him to handle the situation.

Fritz Rimer came in alone, shuffling his feet over the faded carpet, hardly able to look at Urah. "It's going bad for me, isn't it?"

"Not so bad."

"Even if I win, I lose. He'll kill me—I know it."

"Then why did you fight him? Why didn't you just pull out?"

"That place is my life. I don't just see my whole life crumble without trying to hang on."

Tommy Same and Sal came in, and she stood behind his chair while they waited for Arthur Urah to deliver his verdict. He cleared his throat and snapped on one of the table lamps because the room was growing dim in the afternoon twilight.

"I've studied the issues," he began, "and tried to arrive at a fair decision." He cleared his throat once more. Sally Vogt caught his eye and seemed to be telling him something, but he paid no attention. "My ruling is that Fritz Rimer has the right to remain in business as long as he desires. If he should sell his establishment, or pass away, the business should be made part of Tommy's syndicate. But until that time, Rimer is to continue as sole owner and manager."

Tommy leaned back in his chair, saying nothing.

Rimer got to his feet, shaking. "Thanks, Mr. Urah. Thanks for nothing. That decision just sealed my death warrant."

"You can sell out to Tommy," Arthur pointed out.

"Never! He'll have to kill me if he wants my place."

"That's something I can arrange," Tommy said quietly.

"There'll be no violence," Urah told them, but even to his own ears the words carried a hollow ring.

Fritz Rimer turned and headed for the door. Tommy Same got up and started after him but then Fritz turned and showed them the little silver pistol in his hand. It looked like a .22, like something he might have borrowed from his wife. "I'm leaving here," he said. "Alive."

Then he was in the hall. Tommy bolted and ran after him, and Arthur was at Tommy's side. Fritz was halfway down the dingy hallway, heading for the elevator, when Benny appeared at the opposite end of the corridor. He saw the gun, and immediately drew his own weapon.

"No!" Sally screamed. "Don't shoot!" but it was too late for anyone to listen now.

Benny fired one quick shot without aiming, and Rimer's little gun coughed in echo. Tommy Same was shouting above the roar, and then he seemed to stumble back into Arthur Urah's arms. He tore free, lurched into the dusty fire hose on the wall, and then fell forward on his face.

"Tommy!" Sally Vogt was on the floor at his side, trying to turn him over, but her left hand came away all bloody from his back and she screamed once more.

Down the hall, Benny had dropped his gun and was running forward. Fritz Rimer simply stared, more terrified than ever, and then he suddenly darted into the elevator. Within moments the room clerk had arrived, summoned by some hotel guest lurking terrified behind his locked door. There were others on the scene, too; the big boys whom Arthur Urah knew so well—Stefenzo and Carlotta and Venice, big men in the syndicate—bigger men than Tommy Same had ever hoped to be.

"What happened?" one of them asked, staring down at the body on the floor. This was Venice, a slim, almost handsome man.

"There was a shooting," Urah explained carefully. "Benny here took a shot at Rimer and missed."

"I didn't mean to," Benny mumbled, too frightened to say more.

The room clerk looked up from the body. "He's dead."

Somebody had taken Sally aside, but her sobbing could still be heard. One of them picked up Benny's fallen gun and brought it down the hall.

"This looks too big for the hole in him," somebody observed.

"Search everyone," Stefenzo ordered. "The girl, too."

"Rimer's gone with his gun," Benny said. "He did it, not me."

A quick search of Arthur and Benny and Sal and the dead Tommy revealed no other weapon. There was only Benny's big .38 and the missing gun with which Rimer had fled.

"We don't want the police in on this," Venice told Arthur Urah. "Not yet, anyway. We'll never convince them it was an accident."

"No," Arthur agreed.

They wrapped Tommy Same's body in a sheet and carried it into one of the rooms.

"Check everybody on this floor," Stefenzo ordered the clerk. "Make sure there's no one who'll talk."

"Most of the rooms are empty."

"Check anyway."

Arthur Urah walked past the still-stunned Benny and into Sally's room. She was over by the window, staring out at the lights coming on all over the city. "He's dead," she said without emotion to Arthur.

"Yes."

"So what good was all your arbitration? In the end, it came back down to a couple of people shooting it out in a hallway."

"I tried to avoid that."

"Tommy wanted too much. That was always his trouble. Too much. Not thirty-five horse rooms, but thirty-six. He wanted to be too big."

"Yes," Arthur agreed quietly.

She turned suddenly to face him. "What did you do before?" she asked. "Before you started to arbitrate their disputes?"

"Various things. I studied law once."

"But they trust you. Both sides trust you."

"I hope so."

After a time she left him and went in to look at Tommy's body in the next room.

Venice came in to sit with him. "We've taken Benny away," he told Arthur. "He was always a little nuts."

"I suppose so."

"Dangerous."

"Yes."

The telephone rang and Arthur answered it, then passed it to the syndicate man who listened intently. After a moment he held the receiver down against his chest. "They've run Rimer to earth. He's home, packing, apparently getting ready to skip. They want to know if we want him alive or dead."

"Alive," Arthur Urah said without hesitation. "There's been enough killing."

"I suppose so." Then, into the telephone, "Bring him down here."

Arthur Urah sighed and sat down to wait.

An hour later, they had gathered in the room again, around the rickety card table. Rimer was there, under protest, and Benny had been brought back, too. The room clerk from downstairs, and Sally, and the three big men from the syndicate were all seated, their eyes on Urah as he spoke.

"What we have here," he said, "is an interesting problem. We cannot, like the police, dig into Tommy Same's body and compare bullets under a microscope. We cannot do anything except take testimony and examine the facts. I was there in the hall myself, and I saw what there was to see. The hall, for our purposes, is about fifty feet in length from the door of Tommy's room to the spot where Benny stood. Fritz here was about halfway between the door and Benny, at the elevator, when the shooting started."

"Benny fired toward us," Sally interrupted to explain. "Fritz fired away from us."

"And there was no third shot?" Venice asked in a puzzled tone.

"No."

"Tommy just staggered and fell," Urah said. "And therein would seem to lie the impossibility of the thing. The wound indicates to us a small caliber weapon—as nearly as we can tell without being able to dig for the bullet—yet Rimer's small caliber gun was fired in the opposite direction from where Tommy was standing. Benny's larger gun, fired toward Tommy, would have left a bigger entry hole."

Stefenzo grunted, lifting his bulk from the chair. "Yet there was no other shot, no other gun."

"Why waste time, anyway?" Carlotta asked. "Tommy's death was an accident, no matter how you look at it. The bullet bounced off the wall or something. Let's get on to splitting up his holdings."

"Well, I don't think it was an accident," Sally told them all. "I think he was murdered by Fritz Rimer."

"I didn't . . . " Rimer began, and then fell silent.

Arthur Urah cleared his throat. "I was called in to decide the matter of Rimer's horse room and Tommy Same's claim to it. In that affair, my original judgment of this afternoon still stands. The horse room remains in Rimer's control and, since Tommy is now dead, there's no question of his taking over after Rimer's possible death."

"You can talk about this all you want," Sally told them, "but I'm more interested in how Tommy died." She stormed out into the hall, seeking perhaps some sign, some scrawled revelation on the wall.

"You don't need me for anything," Fritz Rimer said. "Let me get out of here."

"Wait a bit," Carlotta told him.

"I have a business to attend to!"

"On Sunday night? Wait a bit."

Arthur Urah interrupted. "Let him go. The killing of Tommy was accidental."

Rimer left, a little man and fearful. Then they settled down to the business at hand.

In the hour that followed, Tommy Same's empire was divided. Arthur Urah listened to it all, taking little part in the discussions. This was not his job, and he would only be needed if a dispute arose. He wandered over to the window at one point, and then into the next room. It was there that Sally Vogt found him.

"I was in the hall," she said.

"Yes?"

"If you look, you can see the marks where both bullets hit the wall."

"I didn't look." He was starting to zip his briefcase. It was time to be going home.

"Arthur . . ." Sally hesitated.

"What is it, Sally?"

"Are they still in the next room?"

"Yes. The territory has to be reassigned."

"Reassigned. Tommy dies, and the territory is reassigned."

"Life must go on, Sal. You know that."

"And what about his body, wrapped in a sheet like some mummy?"

"The body will be given a decent burial."

"In the Jersey dumps?"

"Sal . . ."

"The wound was in his back, Arthur. In his *back*! He was facing the other two, but you were right behind him. He stumbled into you, just before he fell."

"I had no gun," Arthur Urah said quietly.

"No, but you had this!" She brought her hand into view and dropped the ice pick on the low table between them. "Tommy wasn't shot by a small caliber bullet at all. He was stabbed with this ice pick just as the other two fired at each other. Then, while we bent over the body, you simply pushed the ice pick up the nozzle of the fire hose in the hall—where I just found it."

"You try too hard, Sally. You look too closely. This world isn't made for people who look too closely, who find ice picks in fire hoses."

"You killed him because he wouldn't go along with your settlement, because he was going to get Rimer."

"Perhaps I killed him to save Rimer's life, Sally."

"I'm going in there and tell them, Arthur," she said. "It won't bring Tommy back, but at least it'll avenge him just a little."

She had moved toward the door when he reached out to stop her. "Not that way, Sally. Listen a bit."

"To what? To the Arbiter of Uncertainties, while he foxes out another decision? What will it be this time, Arthur? What will they give you when I walk in there and tell them? Life or death?"

"You don't understand, Sal."

"I understand. I'm going to tell them."

"You don't have to. They know."

She paused again, backing against the coffee table, staring at him with widening eyes. "They know?"

"You asked once what I did before I became the Arbiter. I did many things, Sally. Some of them with an ice pick," he admitted.

"No!"

"Tommy was getting too big. They wanted his territory. They thought Fritz might do the job for them, but Fritz was a coward. When I saw my opportunity, there in the hall, I had to take it."

"And all this talk, this investigation?"

"For your benefit, Sally. And Benny's."

"If they won't do it, Arthur, I will." She bent down for the ice pick again, but he merely brushed it away, onto the floor.

"Get out, Sally. You don't want to get hurt."

"Damn you! You're not human, Arthur! You're some sort of monster!"

He smiled sadly. He'd been called worse things in his life. He picked up the ice pick and dropped it into the briefcase, and finished zipping it shut.

After a time, when Sally had gone, he went down in the elevator. He nodded to the room clerk as he passed, and then went out into the night.

FLETCHER FLORA

Variations on an Episode

"This one," said Marcus, "is fancy." Bobo Fuller, deliberately spaced the maximum distance away on the seat of the police car, stared gloomily out the window at the passing buildings. They were moving through sparse traffic at an almost leisurely pace, and the siren was silent. This, to Fuller, was a violation of proper procedure, almost an offense against propriety. Two cops going to a murder, in his opinion, should be going at high speed with siren howling. But Marcus, unfortunately, believed that should be left to the ambulances and the fire trucks. After all, there was no great rush. The scene of the murder was secured in status quo by uniformed patrolmen, sent early to the scene, and it was certain the corpse wasn't going anywhere. High speeds made him nervous, Marcus said, and sirens made his head ache.

"Fancy how?" Fuller asked.

"As I get it," Marcus said, "this guy named Draper was asleep in his bed this morning, and someone walked in and stabbed him."

"That doesn't sound fancy to me. It sounds simple."

"I didn't mean fancy that way. It happened to a fancy guy who lived in a fancy place. That's what I meant."

"Thanks." Fuller's voice was tainted just enough by bitterness to register his animus while sustaining diplomacy. "It's nice to be informed. Was this Draper married?"

"He was."

"Where was his wife when he was getting stabbed?"

"A good question, Fuller. At the first opportunity, let's ask her."

They had turned, meanwhile, onto a broad boulevard split down the middle by a raised median strip that was planted with bluegrass and evergreens, in an area devoted largely to apartment buildings and hotels. They stopped in front of a hotel, the Southworth, and got out. In spite of a bronze name plaque and a canopy from curb to entrance, the place was not really so fancy. What Marcus had meant was that the Southworth was undoubtedly expensive. This conviction was in no degree weakened by the resplendent doorman who held the door open for them.

"It's on the fifth floor," Marcus said over his shoulder as he crossed the lobby to the elevator, with Fuller trailing. "We'll go right up."

Getting out on the fifth floor, they went down the hall and around a corner to 519. Marcus opened the door, already slightly ajar, and entered a short hallway created by the protrusion of a bathroom, which was immediately on his right. A few feet farther on, he came into the bedroom of a two-room suite. Again to his right, headboard flush against the interior wall of the bathroom, was a double bed. Beside the bed, staring down as if bemused by death and the prospects of heaven, was a gray, dehydrated little man with a stethoscope hanging out of his side coat pocket. The stethoscope was just dressing, a kind of professional emblem in support of the caduceus. The gray little man had not needed it, for the man on the bed, the object of his bemused stare, was as clearly dead as a knife driven into the soft hollow at the base of his throat could make him. He had bled a lot, and the blood had soaked the front of his white silk pajamas and spread in a great stain over white cotton sheets. The gray little man looked up at Marcus with curiously angry eyes.

"Hello, Marcus," he said. "You're running late."

Marcus walked around the bed and stopped beside it in the narrow clearance between the bed and the wall. Fuller remained on the other side, behind the medical examiner, and surveyed the carnage with a forced air of detachment. It was Fuller's secret shame that the sight and smell of blood made him queasy.

"Sometimes I do." Marcus, returning the stare of blind eyes, resisted a desire to close them. "He certainly bled a lot, didn't he?"

"You generally do when your throat's cut."

"How long has he been dead?"

"Since seconds after he was stabbed."

"When was he stabbed?"

"Not long ago. Say around nine o'clock. Shortly before he was found."

"Who found him?"

"Should I know? I just pronounce them dead, Marcus. You're the cop."

"Right. He was sleeping when it happened, sleeping on his back. How did whoever did it get in here? These hotel doors lock automatically when they're closed. You can't open them from outside without a key. Don't bother to answer, doc. You've already told me that I'm the cop."

Marcus, sacrificing a handkerchief, reached down with a faint fastidious feeling of revulsion and extracted the knife, carefully preserving in the process the fingerprints which he was convinced would not be there.

The knife was a common kitchen paring knife. It was of poor quality, but plenty good enough and sharp enough, for all that, to peel a potato or trim a steak or cut a throat. You could buy it, or one like it, in thousands of hardware stores or department stores or dime stores. In brief, it was impossible to trace or to identify as the property of any person. Were knives like this available in the hotel kitchen? If so, it would be at least a beginning, but Marcus, the perennial pessimist, bet bitterly that they weren't.

He had been aware all the while of voices and movement in the room behind him, the second room of the suite. Now, abruptly, carrying the knife in the handkerchief, he went through the communicating door. A couple of technicians were working expertly at their scientific hocuspocus. One of the pair of patrolmen who had arrived first on the scene was standing by the hall door. Marcus, with a wave of a hand to the technicians, approached the patrolman. The latter identified himself and, at Marcus' request, gave a report so brief and orderly that it had apparently been arranged and edited in his mind beforehand for the purpose of making a high efficiency rating. It did, in fact, do so and Marcus mentally noted it.

The patrolman and his partner had received at nine twenty the radio message which had sent them to the Southworth. They were cruising nearby and had arrived at nine twenty-seven. They had found the hotel manager, a Mr. Clinton Garland, fresh from the chamber of horrors, maintaining a resolute guard in the hall outside the bedroom door. The body had been discovered by a hotel maid who had come in on her regular routine to put fresh towels in the bathroom. The maid had set up a howl that had reached in relays to the manager's office, and he had come at once in the company of the captain of the bellboys, who had been dispatched to summon the police. The patrolmen, arriving, had relieved the manager of guard duty. Nothing, subsequently, had been touched until the invasion of investigators.

"Where," asked Marcus, "is his wife?"

The patrolman looked stricken, realizing at once that he had, in his orderly report, been guilty of an egregious omission. "Wife, sir?"

"Right. Wife. He had one, you know."

"As a matter of fact, sir, I didn't know."

"I take it, then, that she hasn't been in evidence since you got here?"

"No, sir. No wife."

"No matter. We'll turn her up in good time. Where's the manager now?"

"Waiting in his office on the ground floor. He was pretty badly shaken up. I thought it would be all right to let him go."

"You did everything fine. Now you and your partner better get back on patrol."

Marcus turned back into the room and put the paring knife in its cotton nest on a table near a technician who was methodically dusting for prints.

"You can check the handle of this," he said, "but you won't find anything."

He walked back through the communicating door into the bedroom. The medical examiner had gone, but Fuller lingered.

"Have a look around, Fuller, and see what you can come up with. Odds are you won't find anything that means anything, but I guess we ought to try." Marcus, speaking, reached the hall door. "I'm going down to see the manager. I'll be back up pretty soon."

He went out, and Fuller began looking for something that meant something.

Marcus, however, did not go directly down to the manager. He was delayed, almost before he started. In the hall, he was arrested by a sudden sharp hissing sound, rather like the warning of a startled snake, and he saw that the door across the hall had opened far enough to allow the passage of what appeared to be the decapitated head of somebody's grandmother. It had white hair parted in the middle and drawn back on both sides of the part into a bun; an avid little face, full of wrinkles, with a tight little mouth that looked very much like another wrinkle with teeth; rimless glasses slipped down the bridge of a pointed nose, and behind them, peeping over the rimless glass with an effect of slyness, a pair of alert, inquisitive eyes.

Marcus thought wildly of a wicked wren.

"Did you hiss?" he asked politely.

She nodded briskly and darted a glance both directions in the hall, seeming thereby to invite Marcus into a conspiracy. "Is it true?" she whispered.

"It may be," Marcus said. "Is what true, precisely?"

"Is Mark Draper dead?"

"He is."

"Murdered?"

"Unfortunately, yes."

The white head nodded again. The bright eyes glittered over glass. "Small wonder."

"Oh? You think so? Why?"

"Some people are born to be murdered." The whisper was now barely audible. "And some people are born to be murderers."

"That's an interesting theory. I'd be pleased to hear you develop it."

"I know a thing or two. I do indeed."

"I shouldn't wonder."

"I have an instinct. I feel things."

"Madam, instinct is not allowed in a court of law. However, when supported by adequate evidence, it may prove useful in an investigation. May I come in?"

"Please do."

She widened the crack in the door just enough for him to slip through, then quickly and quietly closed it behind him. The conspiratorial atmosphere, Marcus thought, was really becoming a bit absurd.

"Permit me to introduce myself," he said. "Lieutenant Joseph Marcus."

"I'm Lucretia Bridges. Won't you sit down?"

They looked at each other across five feet of green carpet in a room which betrayed itself by the presence of many small additions of whatnot, obviously personal, as a place of permanent residence. Lucretia, clearly, was no transient. She was one of a swelling company of hotel dwellers.

"You have a theory," Marcus said. "Also an instinct. I'm interested in both."

Her white head bobbed, and again Marcus was wildly reminded of a wicked wren.

"Mark Draper," she said, "was no better than he should have been."

"Most of us aren't."

"He drank and he gambled and he kept late hours."

Marcus, who was guilty of the first and the last, although not the second, clucked disapprovingly. "Is that so?"

"It is. Moreover, he was a wastrel, and he didn't work."

Marcus' cluck was somewhat more genuine now. He himself was not guilty on either of these counts, being far too poor to afford them. "If he didn't work, how could he afford to maintain residence in a place like this? It must be very expensive."

"It is. He had money. He inherited it, more than he could spend in a lifetime, wastrel though he was. Why else do you imagine that sly little baggage married him?"

"Baggage?" Marcus made a rapid mental adjustment. "Oh, yes. His wife, of course."

"She's much younger than he was, years and years. Disparity in ages makes for a bad situation. It invites trouble."

"How so?"

"I was never unfaithful to Mr. Bridges. Never!"

"That's commendable, I'm sure. Mrs. Draper, you think, was unfaithful to Mr. Draper?"

"I know what I know."

"Instinct?"

"I have eyes. I see what's going on."

Marcus didn't doubt it. Witnesses, however, to be of value, must be somewhat more specific.

"What did you see? When did you see it?"

"Comings and goings. Mr. Draper was gone much of the time, you see. He didn't work, but he was forever off somewhere, and she was always having callers. In the daytime, mind you. I always think it's so much more shameful in the daytime, don't you?"

Marcus had no preference, day or night, but he repeated his useful cluck. "So flagrant," he said.

"Exactly. I could drop a few names that would surprise certain folk." She waited for Marcus' cue.

"Surprise me."

"That young Mr. Tiber who lives on the floor above, Jerome Tiber. He was most brazen of all. As you said, so flagrant. I'm certain that she had given him a key."

"To her room?"

"She must have. I've seen him enter, bold as brass, without knocking."

"That's interesting. That's very interesting, indeed."

"He wasn't the only one, however. There are those, so to speak, who have keys by right of position."

"Such as?"

"Well, I'm sure that Mr. Clinton Garland visited her far more often than was necessary."

"The hotel manager?"

"There is simply no occasion, I mean, for a hotel manager to go to a guest's room so frequently. And that bell captain, Lewis Varna. One would think Dolly Draper spent half her time thinking up one pretext or another to get him to her room."

"Her tastes, if I understand your implications, were remarkably catholic."

"It's more to the point to conclude that she had no taste at all."

"She seems to be missing this morning, incidentally. Do you happen to know where she is now?"

"I'm sure I don't," Lucretia Bridges said, then added with a monstrous improbability that took Marcus' wind away, "I am one who strictly minds her own affairs."

The shock of it brought him to his feet. He had acquired enough food for thought, in any event, to tax his mental molars. He looked around and tried to think of a graceful exit line. "You have a pleasant room," he said. "Do you live here as a permanent guest?"

"Yes. I find residing in a hotel so convenient. I've been here nearly ten years, since shortly after Mr. Bridges died."

"He must have left you well off."

"Indeed he did. Winston was a wonderful man, poor dear. He died so suddenly. No warning whatever. We were just beginning dinner, and he fell right over into his soup. There was not time even to fetch a doctor."

"Well, thank you for your help, Mrs. Bridges. It's possible that I may want to talk with you again."

"I am at your service," said Lucretia, and followed Marcus to the door, where he said goodbye. As he passed through, she had, woman-wise, the last word.

"When you find Dolly Draper," she said, "you must be on your guard. She is quite deceptive, and appears to be what she is not. I tell you she's a bad woman. She's *evil*."

The ancient and ominous adjective seemed to hang in the air and repeat itself in whispers. The hall, as Marcus walked down it toward the elevators, seemed suddenly colder and darker than it was.

Mr. Clinton Garland, surrounded by walnut paneling, was waiting behind his walnut desk. He was impeccably dressed, his hair was all present and sleekly brushed, and his face, properly composed for a tragic occasion, was handsome enough to qualify him as the moderator of a TV quiz show, although a bit long in the nose. As he rose and extended manicured fingers, Marcus could detect that Mr. Garland had taken a very large drop for his nerves.

After introductions Marcus said, "This is bad business."

"Indeed it is," Garland said, retrieving his hand after token contact. "It will do the Southworth no good, lieutenant. No good at all."

"It didn't do Mark Draper any good, either."

"It's dreadful. Simply dreadful. Whoever could have done such a monstrous thing?"

"We'll try to find out. I'm hoping you can help."

"I'll do what I can, of course, but I'm afraid it will be very little."

"Perhaps," said Marcus, "you will just tell me about your own part in the affair."

"Certainly. I was right here in my office, discussing several routine matters with Lewis Varna, the bell captain. When the news reached the lobby, one of the bellboys reported it to the desk clerk, and the desk clerk brought it immediately to me."

"What time was that?"

"I'm not sure. I was naturally so distraught by the news that I failed to make proper note of things. It was after nine. Before the half hour, I think. Sometime between."

"Never mind. Go on, please."

"Well, Lewis and I rushed up, of course, and I went into the room and verified the report." Garland repressed a shudder. "So much blood! It was dreadful. Simply dreadful."

"Which room did you enter?"

"Which room? Why, the room in which Mr. Draper had been stabbed, of course."

"I thought you might have entered the adjoining one."

"No, no, I went directly from the hall into the bedroom."

"Was the door closed and locked?"

"If it were closed, it would automatically be locked. It wasn't. Poor Mrs. Grimm, the maid, had rushed into the hall screaming and had left the door standing open behind her. What a dreadful experience for the poor soul!"

"Draper was apparently sleeping when he was stabbed. Do your maids enter the bedrooms of your guests when they are sleeping?"

"Certainly not. However, Mrs. Grimm had encountered Mrs. Draper on the floor below about half an hour earlier, and Mrs. Draper had told Mrs. Grimm that Mr. Draper was sleeping late, but that it would be quite all right to slip in quietly and change the towels. As a matter of fact, Mr. Draper was chronically a late sleeper, and it was understood that the maid could slip into the bathroom when necessary. After all, our maids must perform their services."

"Where was Mrs. Draper going when she encountered the maid on the lower floor? Do you know?"

"She was in the company of Mrs. Bryan Lancaster, who occupies a two-room suite on that floor with her husband. Mrs. Draper and Mrs. Lancaster met the maid just as they were descending the stairs. They had been up in Mrs. Draper's suite and were walking down to Mrs. Lancaster's. The maid saw them enter."

"You seem to have a fair number of permanent guests in this hotel."

"That's true. We rather cater to them. Our rates are not excessive for the comforts and services offered."

"Naturally. Anyhow, I'm delighted finally to have crossed the trail of Mrs. Draper. I've found her rather elusive."

"Elusive? Not at all. She has been in Mrs. Lancaster's suite all this while. After she heard the news about her husband she was prostrate, of course.

Simply prostrate. What a dreadful thing to happen to the poor little thing! Mrs. Lancaster has been taking care of her."

"What's the number of Mrs. Lancaster's suite?"

"421. I trust, if you must talk with Mrs. Draper, that you will be considerate."

"I am always," said Marcus, "considerate of everyone." He fished for a cigarette, found one, and lit it. "What did you do after seeing the body?" he continued.

"I sent Lewis Varna to summon the police, and I remained in the hall outside the door until the police came. Then, with their permission, I came back here. I was limp. Simply limp!"

"I know. It was a dreadful experience. Where is the maid now? I'll need to talk with her."

"I have her standing by. Lewis Varna, too. I was certain that you'd want to see them sometime."

"Good. I'll see them together. Two birds, you know, with one stone."

Clinton Garland left the room, and was back in less than two minutes with Lewis Varna and Mrs. Grimm. The former was a slender, swarthy, young man with black curly hair, courteous but not deferential, who undoubtedly would be attractive to the ladies. The latter was a small woman, almost dainty, neatly uniformed in crisp white. Her hair was going gray, but her face still retained a smooth, youthful quality, and her throat, in the vulnerable area beneath the chin, its taut elasticity. Marcus was surprised. He had expected, somehow, someone canted sidewise from carrying a mop bucket.

Lewis Varna, at Marcus' request, reported first. His report was concise, and it supported in all significant details the prior report of Clinton Garland. Which might mean, Marcus realized with the detached skepticism of his race, that the pair had told separately the simple truth, or that they had, on the other hand, plotted their stories in the ample time that had been allowed them. Marcus was invariably skeptical of any pair who alibied each other so neatly, especially, in this case, a pair who carried passkeys. Still, the alibi was not airtight. There was, after all, the crucial time *before* Garland and Varna met in the office for their discussion of hotel matters.

"Let's see," Marcus said casually. "You and Mr. Garland were right here together when you first heard the report of the murder. How long would you say you had been here?"

Varna got the point. So did Garland. Their eyes met, struck sparks, and passed, but Varna's expression did not otherwise alter. He remained a perfect picture of candor, as one who was willing to accept the digressions of a police investigation, but recognized, nevertheless, the basic absurdity of them.

"It's hard to say. We were not, of course, particularly conscious of time. What would you say, Mr. Garland? Half an hour?"

"There was quite a number of things on the agenda," Garland said. "Half an hour would be a conservative estimate. Nearer forty-five minutes, I'd say."

"I see." Marcus turned to Mrs. Grimm. "Madam, you had a trying experience."

"It was a shock. A terrible shock."

"Have you sufficiently recovered to talk about it?"

"I'm all right now, thank you."

And she did, indeed, seem quite composed. She stood erect with her feet together and her hands folded in front of her. Her eyes, with the proper deference of a servant before masters, were fixed on an imaginary spot somewhere over Marcus' head.

"You entered the bedroom shortly after nine, I understand. Is that correct?"

"It must have been. I'm not positive."

"The medical examiner estimates that Mr. Draper was murdered around nine. You must have just missed a scene more shocking than the one you saw."

"I try not to think of that, sir."

"Right. Nothing to be gained from magnifying horrors. Did you see anyone near the door before you entered?"

"No, sir."

"Anyone in the hall at all?"

"No one."

"You went in to change the towels in the bathroom, I believe. Were you also going to change the sheets on the bed?"

"No, sir. Mr. Draper was sleeping late. I had seen Mrs. Draper on the floor below, and she told me it would be all right to slip into the bathroom quietly."

"Did you, indeed, change the towels?"

Mrs. Grimm thought for a moment, then slowly shook her head.

"Now that you put the question, sir, I don't believe I did. It was the shock, you see. I'm rather confused in my mind about things."

"Understandably so. Just tell me briefly what you did after seeing the body of Mr. Draper."

"I screamed and ran from the room and down the hall. I must have screamed several times, and my head was spinning. At the elevator, I ran into a bellboy who had just come up from the lobby. He helped me to a vacant room and put me on the bed there. The guest had checked out early, you see, and the door was standing open. A few minutes later, when I was not so faint, I thought that I had better see Mr. Garland at once, but when I went into the hall again, I saw Mr. Garland standing guard outside Mr. Draper's door. I didn't wish to go near that room again, so I came down here and waited. That's all, sir. That's all I can remember."

"Very good. Thank you, Mrs. Grimm."

"Are you finished, lieutenant?" Garland asked.

"For the present, yes."

Garland nodded at the bell captain and the maid. "You're free to go."

They left, and so, after a polite word of parting with the manager, did Marcus.

He rapped lightly beneath the neat chrome numbers: 421. A mnemonic gem, second number half the first, third number half the second. Remember the first, you got them all.

The mnemonic gem retreated as the door swung inward, revealing a young man wearing a gray cardigan. He had thick brown rebellious hair, a slightly crooked nose, and an expression that was, all in all, inordinately cheerful for the circumstances.

"Mr. Lancaster?" Marcus queried.

The young man grinned and shook his head.

"No such luck. Old Bryan's off doing his daily stint. Tiber's the name. Jerome Tiber."

"Oh? I'm Lieutenant Marcus. Police. I'm looking for Mrs. Mark Draper."

"This is as far as you go, lieutenant. Dolly's here, safe and sound, although, as you will understand, a bit upset. I must say that you've been an unconscionable time getting to us. We've been waiting for you."

"Well, here I am at last. Now where is Mrs. Draper?"

"Come in. I'll get her for you."

Marcus entered. On a low table before a sofa stood a silver pot that emitted the aromatic odor of hot coffee. Beside the pot, a cup, half full, sat in its saucer. Marcus sat on the sofa, smelled the coffee, and coveted a cup.

Jerome Tiber, at the communicating door, spoke cheerfully into the adjoining room. "Dolly, my darling, your sins have found you out. You had better emerge and face the consequences."

In response to this airy summons, two young women came into the room. One of them was rather tall, with bright red hair, and had about her the firmly benevolent attitude of one who is determinedly giving aid and comfort to someone else. This one, Marcus guessed rightly, was Mrs. Bryan Lancaster.

The other, then, was Dolly Draper. Marcus, rising to meet her, was aware instantly of a feeling to which he should have, at his age, developed immunity long ago. Tenderness? Affinity? The faint siren singing of "September Song"? Say, for decency's sake, fatherliness. For Dolly Draper, who was surely at least in her middle twenties, looked to be in her late teens. And she was small; small and slim with an innocently seductive body now poured into a white cashmere sweater and a pair of red slacks. Her hair, the soft yellow color of ripe field corn, was little longer than a contemporary male folk songster's. Her eyes were grave and gray. She sat down on the edge of a straight chair and folded her hands on her knees. She did not seem grieved. She seemed only infinitely sad.

"Damn it, Jerry," said the redheaded Mrs. Lancaster, "please don't be quite so cheerful. It's absolutely obscene."

Tiber, undaunted, waved a hand and made a little bow. "Gloom accomplishes nothing. 'The Moving Finger writes; and, having writ . . .' You know the bit, darling. One must have a philosophical attitude, I say. Besides, I must add, someone, however reprehensible his method, has done me a service. He has, in brief, removed my competition."

During this remarkable speech, Dolly Draper sat quietly with her grave gray eyes turned on the speaker, and the faintest shadow of a sad and tender smile touched her pink lips. "Darling," she said, "I know you mean well, but you mustn't say such things. It isn't proper."

"It's obscene, that's what it is," said the redhead. "Jerry, mind your manners."

"What? Oh, yes. Introductions are in order. Mrs. Draper, Mrs. Lancaster, Lieutenant Marcus. Lieutenant Marcus, as we have anticipated, is of the police. Since we are clearly to be on familiar terms in this business, I suggest that we abandon formality at once. If you choose, lieutenant, you may call these alliterative ladies Dolly and Lucy."

Marcus did not choose.

"Mrs. Draper," he said, "this is a grim affair, and I understand that it must be very difficult for you. I'm sorry."

"I feel much better now." She smiled sadly at her folded hands. "I suppose, now that the shock has worn off, that I'm not even particularly surprised."

"Oh? What do you mean by that?"

"Well, to be truthful, poor Mark was really a rather disagreeable man, and he was always running around to all sorts of places and associating with all sorts of undesirable persons."

"What places? What persons?"

Dolly Draper lifted her hands in a helpless little gesture, and immediately folded them again. "I don't know, actually. Just places and persons."

"Didn't he ever take you with him?"

"Oh, no. I don't care for such places and persons."

"Mrs. Draper, men are seldom murdered simply for being disagreeable."

"On that score," said Jerry Tiber, "you can make an exception of old Mark."

"Shut up, Jerry," Lucy Lancaster said. "Lieutenant, why do you keep looking at the coffee pot? Would you like a cup?"

"No, thank you," Marcus lied.

"Nonsense. Of course you would. I can tell by the way your nostrils twitch. Jerry, get a cup for the lieutenant."

"There isn't a clean one. Room service only sent up three, and we've used them all."

"Well, I'm sure there's no insurmountable difficulty. Go and rinse a cup in the lavatory."

Jerry went obediently, with reasonably good grace, and Marcus, feeling uneasily that he was somehow not controlling the situation, turned his attention again to Dolly Draper to revive the case at hand.

"Are you suggesting," he said, "that an outsider slipped into the hotel and murdered your husband?"

"Perhaps a guest. A transient. I suspect he's checked out and gone by this time."

"That's possible, of course. But how did he get into the room?"

"I suppose he came through the door. Isn't that how one usually gets into a room?"

"Usually. In this instance, I don't see how. Mrs. Draper, the door of the bedroom was locked. So was the hall door of the adjoining room. How would a transient guest, not possessing a key, get into either room of the suite?"

"Is that a problem? I would say, offhand, that Mark let him in."

"Your husband was sleeping when he was stabbed."

"Was he? How do you know?"

Marcus started to respond and stopped suddenly before making a sound, his mouth open in the middle of a rather foolish expression. Which was, for Marcus, extraordinary.

"He looked as if he'd been sleeping," he said finally, and the words limped in his own ears.

"If you care for my opinion," Dolly Draper said, "you have started off with a very large assumption that may be wrong. Anyone could arrange a body on a bed so as to make it appear to have died sleeping."

"Have you heard that he was stabbed at the base of the throat from the front?"

"I've heard that, yes. It was a cruel thing to do to poor old Mark."

"How in the devil could someone have approached your husband with a knife and stabbed him neatly in such a spot when he was awake and erect and aware of what was going on?"

"Did I say he was erect? I don't believe I did. When Lucy and I left my suite this morning, Mark had a terrible headache. He was so beastly about it, grumpy and all, that he was simply intolerable. That's why Lucy and I decided to move down here to her place. Before we came, however, I gave a Mark a sedative and sent him back to bed. If someone came to the door soon after we left, before the sedative had taken effect, Mark would have let him in, and then, if it was someone he knew well, he would have lain back down and closed his eyes. It's quite possible, you know, to carry on a conversation while lying on your back with your eyes closed. As a matter of fact, he has often done it with me. He was always having severe headaches in the morning, often from hangovers, and he frequently lay in bed while I was up and about, and we would talk, and all the while his eyes would be closed. It's better for a headache, of course, if you keep the light out of your eyes."

Marcus, who was not without experience himself, was forced to concede the point. He looked at Dolly Draper with a kind of growing wonder.

"It's a reasonable explanation," he said. "Do you have any idea who may have called on your husband this morning after you left?"

"Oh, no. It was quite impossible to know who might call on Mark, or when, or why."

"We must at least conclude that the purpose this time was murder."

"Must we? Maybe not. Maybe it was something that was incited and done on the spur of the moment."

"I doubt it. I doubt if anyone, unless he plans to use it, goes calling with an ordinary kitchen paring knife in his pocket."

"Was that what poor Mark was stabbed with? Imagine it, Lucy, an ordinary kitchen paring knife!"

Thus summarily challenged, it remained unknown if Lucy Lancaster's imagination was equal to the occasion. At that moment, carrying a rinsed cup on a saucer, Jerome Tiber came back into the room. He poured coffee into the cup and handed it to Marcus.

"There you are, lieutenant. Compliments of the house."

"Thanks," Marcus acknowledged, then turned to Lucy. "Why did you go upstairs to Mrs. Draper's suite so early this morning?" he asked.

"It wasn't particularly early. It was just after eight o'clock. Do you imagine that we are all the indolent rich or something?"

"Excuse me. Why did you go?"

"Because Dolly called me on the telephone and asked me, that's why. She wanted to show me a silver cigarette box she bought yesterday afternoon. It plays 'Smoke Gets in Your Eyes' when you open the lid."

"I thought it was rather clever," Dolly said. "Cigarettes and smoke in your eyes and all that, I mean."

Marcus was not diverted. "And shortly afterward you decided to come down here?"

"We were practically forced to," Dolly said. "We were going to have our coffee there, but Mark behaved so abominably and kept shouting at us to keep quiet and everything, that we left."

"On the way here, I understand, you met the maid in the hall."

"Yes. The maid who always does our rooms."

"And you told her that it would be all right if she slipped in and changed the towels in the bathroom?"

"I didn't think it would disturb Mark. He'd had the sedative, as I said, and I was sure he'd be asleep again by the time the maid got around."

"I've talked with the maid. She says she saw no one near the bedroom. If your husband admitted someone to the room, he was gone before the maid got there."

"Well, murderers seldom stick around after committing murder, do they?"

Marcus was compelled to admit that they seldom did. He decided also that he had stuck around as long as it was profitable. He drained his cup, set it aside, and rose to his feet. "Thank you very much," he said. "It's time I was getting on to other things. I'm sorry to have intruded."

"Are you going back upstairs?" Jerome Tiber wanted to know.

"That's right."

"I'm going that way. I'll just drop you off if you don't mind."

Marcus didn't mind. In fact, he welcomed the chance to get the remarkable Jerome Tiber a few minutes alone. Having said goodbye to Dolly and Lucy, they departed together.

"I understand," said Marcus, "that you and Mrs. Draper are what some may call good friends."

"I'm working at it," Tiber said cheerfully.

"It has even been suggested that you have a key to her door."

"A key? Nonsense. Why should I need a key? If the coast was clear, as they say in the cheaper thrillers, Dolly could always give me a ring and extend an invitation. I had no wish, believe me, to wander in on old Mark with a hot key in my hand." He stopped and shot Marcus a startled glance. "Are you by any chance implying, lieutenant, that I could have admitted myself this morning and done old Mark in?"

"One has to explore the possibilities."

"Well, you may have guessed that I wasn't exactly one of old Mark's fans, but on the other hand I wasn't his mortal enemy either. Dear as little Dolly is, she isn't worth the risk. Suggested by whom?"

"What?"

"Who suggested that I might have a key?"

"Someone who claims to have seen you enter without knocking."

"Never mind. It must have been the old witch across the hall. When Dolly invited me down, she sometimes left the door slightly ajar. It expedited matters."

"I see."

They had climbed the stairs to the upper floor, and now they paused for a breather before Jerome Tiber continued his ascent.

"Well," he said, "I suppose we must part here. Friends, I hope. I don't suppose you'd be willing to let me come along and poke about the murder scene a bit?"

"No."

"I thought you wouldn't. Well, no matter. It's just that I have such a morbid curiosity. Good sleuthing, lieutenant."

Jerome Tiber went on up the stairs, and Marcus, lingering, heard him begin to whistle softly as he went.

Fuller was at a window with his head out. He pulled it in and turned as Marcus entered. Marcus, however, veered off into the bathroom.

Mrs. Grimm's memory, he saw, had served her well. The towels in the bathroom had been used, and there were no fresh ones in evidence.

On the wide surface into which the lavatory was sunk, among a variety of jars and bottles, was a clear plastic container of capsules. Marcus, examining it, satisfied himself that the capsules contained the sedative which Mark Draper was reported to have taken, then went into the bedroom. Fuller was still standing by the window. The police ambulance had come and gone, and the body of Mark Draper was no longer on the bed. Marcus, who was not fond of bodies, was relieved.

"There's a narrow ledge," Fuller said. "Outside, a narrow ledge below the windows. It would be a risky trick, but a man could conceivably inch his way along it. The window was unlocked."

"Oh." Marcus seemed abstracted. "I don't think so."

"Why not?"

"As you said, too risky. Not only of falling, but of being seen from the street. Besides, how could anyone coming in that way be sure that Draper was in bed and asleep at nine o'clock in the morning? For that matter, how could he be sure that Mrs. Draper wasn't here?"

"I didn't say I had all the answers." Fuller's voice was abrupt, almost harsh. "It's just something to think about."

"Oh, right, Fuller. Any signs of a search in the room?"

"Nothing apparent."

"Anything seem to be missing?"

"Nothing obvious. We'd have to ask Mrs. Draper to be sure."

"I don't think it will be necessary. Draper wasn't killed by any burglar. That's plain."

"It is? I admit it doesn't look likely, but how can you be so sure? The ledge isn't *that* narrow."

Marcus' air of abstraction still pertained. He stood by the bed and pinched his lower lip and stared at the floor. He seemed for a moment not to have heard.

"I'm sure," he said after the moment had passed, "because *I know who did kill him.*"

Fuller, trained by experience in stoicism, said quietly, "That's very interesting. Maybe you wouldn't mind telling *me.*"

"Not yet, Fuller, not yet." Marcus perked up, as if he were brushing the whole vexing business from his mind. "Because I don't know *why.* I can't for the life of me see *why.*"

He turned toward the door abruptly. "Come on, Fuller. We might as well get out of here. There's nothing more at the moment to be done."

In Fuller's opinion, there was, on the contrary, a lot to be done. There was, for example, a murderer to be arrested. If, that is, Marcus actually knew the murderer's identity. Personally, Fuller doubted it. To put it kindly, Marcus was merely trying to measure up to some exaggerated image he had of himself. Behold the great detective! To put it less kindly and more honestly, Marcus was a liar.

Fuller didn't venture the accusation, but his conviction was supported by what happened in the next six days. Indeed, so far as Fuller himself was involved, nothing happened at all. Marcus, for two days, was around headquarters. He had a session with the chief and another session with the chief and the district attorney together. He spent quite a lot of time on the telephone discussing with someone something that Fuller wasn't privileged to know and couldn't get into position to overhear. Then Marcus disappeared. He simply dropped out of sight. To all appearances, Mark Draper had been judged expendable. His murder, apparently, incited no concern.

Then, after four days, Marcus reappeared. He simply turned up again. Fuller, invading his office in the afternoon of the fourth day, found him sitting slumped behind his desk looking across it silently at Mrs. Grimm, who was sitting erect in a straight chair with a purse gripped in her lap. The knuckles of her hands were white. Her face was like a stone.

"Oh, Fuller, there you are," Marcus said. "I've been asking for you."

"That's considerate of you," Fuller said. "Where have you been?"

"Why, I've been all over, Fuller. Both coasts and back. On the Draper case, you know. Incidentally, you remember Mrs. Grimm, I'm sure. Or did you ever meet her?"

"I didn't."

"You know who she is, don't you? Well, meet her now. Mrs. Grimm, Sergeant Fuller."

Fuller nodded at Mrs. Grimm. Mrs. Grimm did not nod or speak. She did not move.

"Mrs. Grimm," said Marcus, "is the murderer of Mark Draper."

Fuller sucked in his breath, held it until his chest hurt, and then released it in a long sigh, barely audible. Taking a step forward, he leaned heavily against Marcus' desk. "Is that so?" he said.

"Unfortunately, it is. Isn't it, Mrs. Grimm?"

Mrs. Grimm didn't answer. She did not move.

"I would be interested in knowing," Fuller said slowly, "how you reached this conclusion."

"Oh, it was plain enough, Fuller, from the beginning. You were right, you know, when you said this case didn't sound so fancy. It wasn't. Mrs. Grimm had a passkey. Mr. Draper was sedated and presumably asleep. Mrs. Grimm simply admitted herself to the bedroom, stabbed Mr. Draper in the throat, and then, after a brief delay which permitted Mr. Draper to get good and dead, rushed out into the hall screaming murder." He smiled benevolently.

Fuller looked with wonder at Mrs. Grimm. Mrs. Grimm did not move or speak.

"How," asked Fuller, "did you know?"

Marcus sighed and built a little tent of fingers on his stomach. "Mrs. Grimm came, presumably, to change the towels. But the towels had not been changed. Mrs. Grimm explained it by saying that she was naturally too distraught by what she found on the bed. Good enough. But what would most women do if, carrying an armload of towels, they came suddenly upon the body of a murdered man? I submit that they would throw the towels all over the place. Anyhow, as they screamed and ran, they would at least drop them. Did you see any towels on the floor, Fuller?"

"No," said Fuller, "I didn't."

"Let it go. That wasn't the big point, at any rate."

"What," asked Fuller, "was the big point?"

"You saw the room, Fuller. You saw how it was shaped. The bathroom is constructed in the corner, next to the outside hall, leaving between the bathroom and the opposite wall a short, narrow hallway. In the bedroom, the bed was placed against the interior wall of the bathroom. Around the corner, that is. *Mrs. Grimm could not possibly have seen the body of Mark Draper unless she walked on into the bedroom.*"

"So," said Fuller, "she couldn't."

"And there was absolutely no reason why Mrs. Grimm should have done so. She was merely going to change the towels. She had been instructed, moreover, to slip in and out quietly so as not to disturb Draper. Instead, she went right on into the bedroom. Does that sound sensible to you, Fuller?"

"No," said Fuller, "it doesn't."

"Neither did it to me. I decided that Mrs. Grimm could bear investigation."

Again Fuller looked with wonder at Mrs. Grimm. Still Mrs. Grimm did not move or speak.

"Why?" said Fuller. "Why?"

"Why indeed? As usual, Fuller, you come directly to the heart of things. Unless Mrs. Grimm was a homicidal maniac, which she wasn't, there had to be some kind of reasonable motive. Had Draper fleeced her at one time or another? Had he, perchance, ruined her daughter or destroyed her husband? I was led, you see, to all sorts of melodramatic speculations. Anyhow, that's where I've been the last few days, Fuller. I've been on the backtrail of Mrs. Grimm, and I dug up, I must say, a couple of rather, ah, enlightening episodes."

"What episodes?"

"Out on the west coast three years ago, Mrs. Grimm, then calling herself Mrs. Foster, worked as a maid in the private home of a well-to-do young couple. One afternoon, while the wife was away, the husband was shot and killed at close range with his own rifle. Mrs. Grimm, who was present, reported that he had been preparing to clean it and had shot himself accidentally. Circumstances aroused some suspicion, but the case, for lack of evidence to the contrary, was eventually closed as accidental death.

"But as you know, Fuller, I have a littered mind. There was one element in the case that reminded me vaguely of another case I'd read about, and after a while I remembered just what it was. On the east coast some six years ago, a wealthy young husband was knifed to death in his home, presumably by a surprised prowler. The wife was spending the night with a friend, but the maid was in the house and testified to what had happened, prowler and all. Again suspicion was aroused, but the bulk of the evidence seemed to support the story. Case closed, and you are right as rain, Fuller. The maid, I discovered, although she called herself Mrs. Breen, and later called herself Mrs. Foster, was no one but the woman who now calls herself Mrs. Grimm."

Whatever her name, she was made of stone. If she heard, she gave no sign. Whatever she felt, she felt in secret.

"And still," said Fuller, "I don't see why."

"Don't you, Fuller? Neither did anyone connected with those two cases. But I do. I see and I understand because all three cases, those and ours, have a common denominator. In each case, *the young wife was away and securely alibied.*"

Abruptly, almost angrily, as if he wanted suddenly to be done with the matter as quickly as possible, Marcus stood up and walked to the door that opened into the next office. He pushed the door open and stepped back. "Come in, Mrs. Draper," he said. "Your mother needs you."

"A mother and daughter team of professional murderers!" Fuller explained.

"That's what they were. Daughter, damnably attractive, marries a reasonably rich man. Mother, in good time, is hired as a maid. Later, exit husband. Still later, much money inherited, including insurance. Later still, reunion of mother and daughter in another place far removed. Plush living, bright prospects of many husbands to come, routine repeated. In our case, there was a slight complication. Draper insisted on living in a hotel, so Mother had to get a job on the staff and work herself onto the right floor. She managed. Mother was clever."

"They were making a career of it!"

"Well, don't let it shake you too much, Fuller. It's been done before by others. Most of them have been poisoners. One of them, you may recall, was a chronic husband who kept drowning his wives in bathtubs. This time, at least, we had some refreshing variations."

Fuller looked at Marcus with surprising, if somewhat grudging, respect. You must, he conceded, give the devil his due.

"Tell me something," Fuller said. "The simple truth?"

"Nothing else. It is my code."

"You suspected Mrs. Grimm from the beginning. That's clear. Did you also suspect Dolly Draper?"

"I did."

"Why?"

"Because she's evil."

"Oh, come off. How could you possibly have known that?"

"I knew because a woman named Lucretia Bridges told me so. To everyone else she was poor little thing, sweet little thing, dear little Dolly. Not to Mrs. Bridges. You know why? Because like reacts to like, and one dog always smells another."

"If you want to know what I think, I think that's crazy."

"Nevertheless," Marcus said, "I'd give a pretty penny to know what was in old Winston's soup."

ED LACY

Finders-Killers

I admit it sounds childish but I was pretty excited about the Frankie Sun murder. It wasn't because it happened on my post and I knew—by sight anyway—about everybody connected with the case. Nor was it taking me out of uniform and placing me on fly assignment with Homicide. It was just . . . well, frankly, being a cop gets dull and boring. There were big things doing like the armored car robbery in Brooklyn, the chorus girl murder downtown, the drug raids over in Queens. And me, I was still trying locked store doors up on Washington Heights, running in a drunk now and then.

Understand, I don't go looking for trouble, but in the ten months I'd been on the force there *had* to be more to law enforcement than a pair of tired feet.

So now I sat in the precinct detective squad room and politely listened with the others as the Homicide inspector from downtown outlined the case. I was up with the big wheels; I thought I was living.

"Here's what we know," the inspector said, his voice soft for a guy his size. "A thug named Frankie Sun is found stabbed in front of a private house. Frankie has a long yellow sheet: rapped for assault, armed robbery, stolen cars, forced entry, carrying a gun, did time for pimping—the works.

"I don't have to tell you that when a hardened criminal like Frankie is knocked off, it isn't a simple murder. Not to mention that he was first sapped, then deliberately knifed while he was out cold. I want this case solved fast because it isn't only a killing, it will give us a lead on other crimes. So far all we've been able to learn from stoolies is that Frankie was in on something 'big,' but nobody knows exactly what." The inspector paused, looking at me, seemed satisfied when I didn't ask any jack questions but waited for him to finish.

"Frankie," the inspector went on, "seems to have been working with an out-of-town hood named Marty. We haven't a thing on this Marty, except his first name. Get the picture: Frankie was killed in a low-income block on Washington Heights. Only two people live in the private house—the landlady, a Mrs. Austin, and her only roomer, a nineteen-year-old girl named Ruth Thomas. Both deny knowing or ever having seen Frankie Sun." The old inspector jerked a thumb at me. "This is Patrolman Stewart, the block is part of his post. He'll be on assignment with us for a while. Stewart, what sort of neighborhood is this?"

"Well, sir," I said, standing up, feeling like a schoolboy among all these vets, "as you said, sir, it's an average low-income area. And crimewise it's . . ."

"What?" the inspector asked.

"I said crimewise it's also an average block."

"Come on," he barked, "talk English, we haven't time to waste!"

Some of the others chuckled and I couldn't stop my face from turning red.

"Yes, sir. I meant as far as crime goes it's a respectable area. Some minor numbers playing, a few penny-ante crap games, maybe a small bookie; but no big or organized crime, certainly nothing that would interest a crook like Frankie Sun.

"About the two women. I think we can forget about Mrs. Austin. She's an elderly lady who only leaves her house to buy groceries. Most of the time she's puttering around her back yard garden. I don't know much about the younger woman except that she's been rooming there for the past three months, works as a sales girl in a five-and-dime store over on Amsterdam Avenue. In my opinion she hardly looks the type that would associate with a punk, a—"

"If she's nineteen," a snappily dressed detective cut in, "sounds like the kind of quail who would interest Frankie. He went for young stuff."

The Homicide inspector said, "This Miss Thomas—she isn't exactly a glamor gal. Plain, scrawny kid, fresh from a hick town. Tell them what else you found out, Stewart."

"Yes, sir. Naturally a murder is big talk in the neighborhood. There's a shoemaker named Jake Cook who has a small shop across the street from Mrs. Austin's house. He's never gotten over the fact he was an M.P. sergeant during World War II. He likes to talk about police methods with me. He claims he's seen Frankie Sun watching the house, tailing Miss Thomas for the last few days. He positively identified a picture of Frankie as the man he thought was a jealous boyfriend."

"This Cook sounds like a crime-happy jerko to me," another detective said.

"It's a fact that Jake is a frustrated cop," I said, "but I would hardly call him a jerk. He's . . ."

The inspector held up a heavy hand for silence. "Now you know everything we have. I've talked to this Cook, he's positive about seeing Frankie hanging around. We've wired Miss Thomas's hometown for any info on her. Stewart and I will talk to her this morning. I want you," he nodded at two of the detective squad dicks, "to shake down Mrs. Austin, dig into her past. Rest of you are to work the bars, keep after your stoolies. I want to know where Frankie Sun lived, what he was doing that far uptown. Keep in touch with me. That's all."

We didn't get much from Miss Thomas. She was a shy kid, obviously afraid of the police, despite the inspector's fatherly voice; a little angry at being called from her job, losing a few hours' pay. She'd come to New York from a tiny upstate village three months ago to find a job, moved into Mrs. Austin's, and found work in the five-and-dime the first day she was in the city. No, she didn't know a soul here except Mrs. Austin and the girls in the store. Oh no, she certainly didn't have any boy friends. She looked pathetically thin and young in her worn, plain dress. I always thought farm kids were sure of plenty of food, if nothing else, but Ruth Thomas sure looked as if she'd missed a lot of meals.

The inspector kept asking if anything unusual had happened recently, but she insisted nothing unusual ever happened to her. All she did was work, cook on the one burner stove in her room, spend her evenings reading books on stenography and office work. No, she never went out, not even to a movie; she couldn't afford to and besides, wasting money was almost sinful. She hoped to attend a business school when she had saved enough money. She proudly showed us her bank book. She'd been putting away five dollars a week since her first pay day. She also sent five home to her folks every other week.

When she left I was told to tail her. The five-and-dime was eleven blocks from the precinct house and she saved bus fare by walking, doing a little window shopping. It struck me as odd, though, that for a kid so desperately poor she only looked into the windows of the expensive stores.

I left her at the five-and-dime, spent the rest of the afternoon talking to storekeepers. They all examined Frankie Sun's picture and said they'd never seen him before. At four I returned to the squad room. Seemed like we were running in circles. A team of detectives had traced Frankie to a cheap room near Penn Station. There wasn't much of anything in his room—he'd only moved in there the last week. They also found a waitress Frankie had been running with; she said he'd talked about making a "big score soon," but she had dismissed that as big talk. Frankie acted like he didn't have money, was tight with a buck. She had never heard of any Marty, nor did she know where Frankie lived, or anything about him.

Stoolies hadn't come up with anything new, and there wasn't anything interesting about old lady Austin, as I had known there wouldn't be.

I shadowed Ruth Thomas the following day. I took her to the store and back home at night. I asked routine questions of the other salesgirls, found only that they considered her a "real square," and she was not very popular because she nursed her pennies, never talked about dates. When I returned to the station house and made out my report, it seemed to me downtown had lost interest. The inspector was off the case and I was told to report back in uniform the following day, on the four o'clock tour. I was sore about the sudden change in tours because I had a movie date with my girl for the following night.

The next day I walked my beat and after phoning into the platoon sergeant, stopped to talk with Jake Cook. I asked him if he was still positive about seeing Frankie Sun following Miss Thomas about. That seemed to me to be the odd point in the case. Jake went into a lecture about how he could spot a tail and while we were talking in the doorway of his shop there were screams and shouts from around the corner. It was a few minutes after six, growing dark, as Jake and I sprinted around the corner into an hysterical group of women standing about Ruth Thomas. She was on the sidewalk, unconscious, her dress torn at the shoulder, her mouth and right eye bleeding.

Two women said they'd heard Ruth shouting, "No! No!" and saw a heavy-set man slugging her. He had run when the women shouted at him. I told Jake to call an ambulance as I tried to get the women to calm down, give me a description of the guy. But it was too dark for them to tell me anything except he'd been beefy, wore a hat and grey top coat, and ran fast. A squad car came about the same time the ambulance arrived. The doc said Ruth Thomas was okay, was suffering from shock more than anything else. He gave her a sedative and the squad car drove her home.

When I phoned in, the sergeant told me to keep a post in front of her house. Jake lived above his shop and after supper he came out to ask what was new. I told him about Ruth being given a sedative and taken away before I had a chance to question her.

Jake puffed on his pipe and said, "It's clear what the guy had in mind." His tone told me what he meant.

"At this time of night, on a street full of people returning from work?"

"Look, I had a case something like this when I was in the army," Jake said patiently. "A joker tried to attack a girl on a busy street in broad daylight. After all, a guy like that must be a moron to start with. Everybody heard her shouting, 'No! No!' What else could it be?"

I said, "There has to be a tie-up with the Frankie Sun killing, that's what else."

Jake didn't agree. He bent my ear for about an hour, then Mrs. Austin came out to give me a cup of coffee and talked for another half hour on how she didn't know "what the neighborhood was coming to. When I first moved here thirty-two years ago it was an elegant . . ." and so on. When I could get a word in, I asked her to let me know the second Miss Thomas came out of the sedative.

About midnight a prowl car drove me back to the station house. Seemed they were taking away the guard but would have the night beat man keep an eye on where she lived. When I said I was surprised at their removing me from the front of her house, the midnight tour sergeant made a few sarcastic remarks about eager-beavers.

I got into my old roadster and drove back to Mrs. Austin's. I let the beat cop believe I had been sent back. Mrs. Austin opened the door in a nightgown and a comical lace cap. When I asked if I could speak to Ruth Thomas, the old biddy snapped, "At this time of night? That's what you got me out of my bed for? Let me tell you, young man, the neighborhood may have changed but I still run a respectable house and—"

"Mrs. Austin, this is a police matter."

"She's awake, go up if you wish. But remember, keep the door wide open."

Ruth Thomas was sitting up in this plain metal bed, her face various shadings of blue and purple. I asked, "Miss Thomas, can you tell me exactly what happened?"

"A man stepped up and suddenly punched me in the face. That's all I remember."

Her voice was frightened, and sullen.

"Didn't he say anything?"

"No. And I never saw him before, either. Hardly had a good look at him when—"

"Miss Thomas, I don't know what you're mixed up in, but I'd advise you to tell me all about it. You're playing with a killer. What were you yelling, 'No! No!' about?"

She seemed to shrink against the pillow for a moment, become even more childlike. Then she let it go. "All right," she said, "I'll tell you. I'm afraid. He asked for the money and I told him no. He just came up and asked, 'Where's the money? Give it to me!'"

"What money?"

"I . . . I found a wallet with two one hundred dollar bills in it a few days ago, as I was coming home from the store."

"Where's the wallet now?"

She hesitated a second, her puffed eye glaring at me; then she pulled this battered wallet from under her pillow. It was an old, beat-up brown leather wallet, not a thing in it but a couple of one hundred buck bills.

She said, "It's mine, I found it," and tried to grab the wallet. She was wearing a thin nightgown and her arm and shoulder were so skinny I wondered how Frankie or any man ever could get interested.

I pushed her hand aside. "Have you told anybody about finding this?"

"No. Give it back to me!"

"You should have told us about this yesterday," I said, a lot of bells ringing in my head. I started to put the wallet in my pocket. Her thin, sharp face grew hysterical. "That's *mine*!" she said, her voice almost a scream. I started to tell her a citizen was supposed to turn over found money to the police, but she wasn't in any shape for a lecture. I took down the serial numbers and gave her back the bills and wallet.

"Miss Thomas, I don't want you to tell anybody else about this money. No one. Not even Mrs. Austin."

"I won't. It's mine, nobody's business but mine." Her hand was clenching the wallet.

"Now you try to relax, get some sleep. I'll be back to see you early in the morning. Don't you leave the house, for any reason, until I return. Do you understand?"

She said she did, shoved the wallet under her pillow, closed her eyes. I went downstairs. Mrs. Austin was standing there. I was pretty sure she'd been listening. How much she could have heard I didn't know.

I drove back to the precinct house. The detective in charge of the night tour of the detective squad was a fat fellow with a big grin and full of laughs. When I started to tell him about Ruth finding the dough, he laughed, told me, "It'll hold until morning, son. I know how it is. Your first big case and you see clues all around. I'm busy. In the morning take it up with the lieutenant. It'll keep." He leaned back in his swivel chair. I thought his weight would take it over.

"You're new on the force, Stewart, so here's some advice—when you're off duty, stay that way. Just patrol your beat, don't play like a movie dick; we got detectives for detective work."

Sure, I thought, getting their pants shiny on the mahogany.

At the desk I phoned downtown to Homicide. When I asked for the inspector's home phone I was told, "Sonny, are you sure this is important?"

"Well, I have a theory about—"

"A theory? Bust up his sleep for a crackpot idea and he'll beat your brains out. For your own sake, wait until morning . . . after he's had his second cup of coffee."

I phoned Central Bureau and at least they had somebody who didn't object to giving me a couple of facts on the armored car robbery. I scouted around the locker room, got two empty shoe boxes and wrapped them in a newspaper. Then I got in my car and parked in front of Mrs. Austin's house for the balance of the night. I didn't make out anyone else watching the house, but then there were too many parked cars and other rooming houses where a guy could safely take a plant on the place. At seven I took my shoe boxes-package through the back of an apartment house, and over a couple of fences until I landed in Mrs. Austin's fancy garden.

I gave the old lady a start, coming in the back way, and she bawled me out for stepping on her flowers. Ruth Thomas was dressed, having a cup of coffee in the kitchen. Her face wasn't puffed but her lips were still bruised and her eye purple. I told her, "I want you to do me a favor, Miss Thomas."

"I was thinking about going to work. Otherwise I'll lose a day's pay."

I hesitated, decided to gamble.

"I'll take care of it."

She looked at me, as if wondering how a cop could cover the day's pay even of a five-and-dime girl. If I was right, I knew that the department would pay.

She said, "I suppose my eye looks pretty bad. What's the favor?"

"Take this package and walk to the library, then walk back here. Walk slowly."

She gave me what she must have thought was a shrewd glance, asked, "Why?"

"Let me worry about the why. Just do it. There'll be an extra five added to the day's pay," I threw in expansively, telling myself that I was right as I talked.

"Sounds like foolishness to me," Mrs. Austin said. "You want some coffee, young man?"

"No, thank you. Will you do it, Miss Thomas?"

"What will happen?"

"Nothing—maybe. But if the guy comes up and grabs for the box, let him take it. Don't put up a fight or say a word." I started to tell her to drop to the ground if Marty showed, get out of the way, but I needed a pigeon and it had to be Ruth.

She asked, "If I do it, can I keep the . . . what I showed you last night?"

I said, "Yes," as Mrs. Austin's ears perked up like they were wired for sound.

Ruth Thomas left the house at eight, the package under her arm. I followed her in my car, my gun out on the seat beside me. She walked the three blocks to the library, which was closed, and not a damn thing happened. Then she started back.

As she turned into her street, this beefy guy in a baggy brown suit jumped out of a doorway, grabbed the package, and took off. Happily he ran in the direction my car was pointed. I overtook him and shouted, "I'm a police officer! Stop or I'll fire, Marty!"

It was like shooting deer from an automobile, which I've read about. Still running, he tucked the package under his left arm and went for his shoulder holster with his right. I dropped him with a slug in his shoulder, anchored him with another shot—a lucky one—in the right leg.

We were all in the detective squad room again, and by all I mean everybody: all kinds of brass from downtown, and even little Ruth Thomas looking very pale and scared. I was feeling swell. I was a cinch to be made Detective, 3rd Grade. Also I was enjoying telling them, all these police vets, how I did it.

"When Miss Thomas told me about finding the two one hundred bills, Frankie Sun's following her made sense to me. Last week when the armored car guard was slugged and two men made off with a bag of hundred dollar bills . . . well, my idea was that the two men had to be Frankie and Marty. As we know now from Marty's confession, Frankie crossed him, took off with sixty grand in hundred dollar bills. Okay, now two things were worrying Frankie Sun—his partner finding him, and whether the money was 'good.' By that I mean Frankie had to know if he was carrying bait money, a few bills whose numbers are known, or since these are large bills, whether *all* the serial numbers were known, hence . . ."

"All the numbers were known, written down before the money was shipped," the detective squad lieutenant cut in. "The money wasn't any good to Frankie. Nor was checking the package at Penn Station smart; he should have known that a routine check, once we knew he was the bank robber, would have . . ."

The Homicide inspector said sharply, "Let's hear the rest of this before going into details. Continue, Patrolman Stewart."

"Yes, sir," I said proudly. "Well, there was only one way for Frankie to learn if the money was good—spend some. Better yet, let somebody else spend it and see what happened. So he put two bills in a wallet and dropped it on the street. Miss Thomas 'found' it and Frankie tailed her to see what broke when she spent the money. As it turned out, she didn't spend it and Marty caught up with Frankie while he was watching Miss Thomas's house. Obviously Marty thought Miss Thomas was Frankie's girl, must have the sixty grand, so with her help I set a trap . . . and collared him."

"Fine work, Stewart," the inspector said, "although you were lucky, too." He turned and smiled at Ruth Thomas. "Why didn't you spend the money?"

"*Spend* two hundred dollars?" Ruth asked, awe in her thin voice. "Why that would be downright silly. I never saw so much money before in my life. I was going to put it in the bank, toward my schooling, but I kept putting it off. Those two bills looked so terribly pretty I just couldn't stand letting them out of my sight."

"That reminds me," the lieutenant said, holding out his long hand, "let me have them. They belong to the bank."

Ruth looked at me, her eyes big with alarm. "But you promised I could keep . . . ?"

"Give him the money, Miss Thomas," I told her. "And don't worry; there's either all or a good part of a five-thousand-dollar reward coming your way, depending on how the inspector sees it."

"Half and half," the inspector said.

That was all right with me, even minus the five bucks. I couldn't have done it without her.

The Pearls of Li Pong

Mei Wong carefully shut the door that led to the outer office and showroom of his Bombay Art & Curio Co. and snapped its lock against any unwanted visitors. His huge frame padded across to the wide window overlooking the street. He listened for a moment to the monotonous chant of a snake charmer's reed and gourd far below; then with a deft movement he closed the venetian blind. Satisfied, he lowered his great body into an oversized chair behind a littered mahogany desk. He fitted a cigarette into a long holder, lighted it, drew several casual puffs, and studied the once famous artist, Gilbert Rendell, who, dirty and dejected, sat opposite him.

The artist shifted uneasily in his chair, rubbed his beard-stubbled chin with a trembling hand. "You weren't expecting me, I suppose," he mumbled and regarded the floor with red-rimmed eyes.

"I remember I advised you," the old Chinaman said tonelessly, "that you were not to come to this establishment again."

Rendell lifted his blotched face and leaned forward. "I'm here only because I'm desperate. I've got to get away. It means my life. Let me have a thousand dollars to get back home."

Mei Wong shook his head. "It wouldn't do any good, my dear Mr. Rendell. Surely you remember the other sums I have let you have—each time to pay for your trip home. You've destroyed a great talent. Once I had hoped to save it, but I hope no longer."

The young man sneered. "I see. Now that there are no more canvasses in prospect, you're not interested. Surely you made enough on my work in the old days to—"

"I paid you well," Mei Wong interrupted calmly, "and since you have ceased painting I have continued to give you large amounts of money. But I am finished."

At this pronouncement, Rendell's bravado disappeared. "I must have a thousand dollars," he pleaded.

"You will not receive it from me, my friend," the old Chinaman smiled. "It seems you have lost your last shred of pride. I believe that now you would do almost anything for a price."

"I want to quit drinking—get right with myself again."

"Idle words, Mr. Rendell, idle words. You are past saving. Drink means everything to you. You'd even kill to get money for it."

There was a moment of silence. Then Rendell said: "Possibly I would."

Mei Wong watched him with expressionless eyes. "Yes—yes, you would. So perhaps we may come to an understanding, after all, you and I. You may be able to undertake a delicate mission for me. One that does involve killing a man."

The old Chinaman puffed easily on his cigarette and studied Rendell, who had slumped back in his chair.

Finally the young man spoke in a tired voice. "What will it pay?"

"Three thousand dollars."

"A neat price for murder."

Mei Wong spoke coldly. "This is not a joke. I am willing to pay for a man's death."

For the first time Rendell looked him in the eye. "And I am willing to accept your money," he said. "Who is the man?"

"A stranger to you. It will be like eliminating a symbol. His name is Han Lee. He lives in the mountains on the mainland of Hong Kong. He has in his possession the Pearls of Li Pong. I have tried to bargain with him. His last word was that he would not part with them while he lived. So, he must cease to live, Mr. Rendell." Mei Wong put aside the cigarette holder. "You shall have help in your task. I have a good friend in Hong Kong, an Englishman, John MacDonald. He lives close to Han Lee and will give you my final instructions. He is trustworthy and will be of great assistance to you."

Gilbert Rendell stood up, nearly sober now. "I want to make sure of the details," he said. "I take a boat to Hong Kong. Go to the mountains on the mainland and look up this MacDonald."

"John MacDonald. And he will have your orders in a sealed box." Mei Wong pulled out a drawer and extracted a small key and passed it to him, "This key will open it."

"Following your orders, and MacDonald's, I locate this Han Lee. And when I find him, I kill him. It shouldn't be too difficult."

Mei Wong shrugged. "Han Lee is wily, he is strong. But you were once a fine, talented man, Mr. Rendell."

"I have an added advantage. Han Lee will not be suspicious of me. A shot in the back—sounds easy." The young man chuckled without mirth and went over to the window.

"There are other means," Mei Wong lifted a small enamelled case from his desk and with a quick pressure released a blade that converted it into a dagger which he sent hurtling across the room to a vibrating stop in the wall a few inches about Rendell's head. "I suggest you take my little weapon with you," he said. "Become familiar with it. It is a weapon of surprise and silence and more suited to your task than the vulgarity of firearms."

"Murder should not be vulgar!" Rendell replied mockingly and removed the beautiful yet sinister instrument from its resting place. He snapped back the blade and put it in his coat pocket. "And what about the three thousand?"

"I will have the money for you when you bring back the Pearls of Li Pong. And I must have them within nine weeks."

"Nine weeks. Should give me time enough. But suppose I decide to keep them for myself?"

"It would be too risky, Mr. Rendell. You wouldn't be able to dispose of them to your advantage." Mei Wong's smile was bland. "You will do best to place yourself entirely in my hands."

Rendell remembered this scene four days later as he roused himself from a drunken stupor and sat, head reeling, on his dirty, sagging bed. The room was small and hot. The only other furniture in it was a washstand and an *elmirah*, the Eastern substitute for a clothes closet. He reached in his pocket for a cigarette and instead brought out the evil little enamelled dagger case. It reminded him of his bargain. It was a killer's weapon.

He released its blade and raised himself to a standing position by steadying his body against the foot of the iron bedstead. The washstand was at the other end of the room, perhaps eight feet from him. He raised the dagger and aimed it. But the washstand wavered in a blurred mist. His hand trembled. He tried to control it, and failed. If he threw the thing he knew he would miss his target. He was in no shape to look after himself. Han Lee could easily kill him before he could kill Han Lee.

Disturbed by this truth he put the dagger back in his pocket. He made his way out of the room and into the street. The blazing sun temporarily blinded him and his lips burned. It was time to begin the day's serious drinking. The bar around the corner would be crowded. There were always some American tourists who could be cadged for drinks.

He stumbled down the narrow street, elbowing through the crowds. An ancient and watery-eyed beggar blocked his path with a whining, "*Baksheesh, master, baksheesh!*" He pushed him aside without hesitating but then as he neared the entrance to the bar he stopped. The ornate gilded clock over the doorway gripped his attention. Time was passing for him—he had only a little better than eight weeks left. He remembered the enamelled case and his shaking hand. He couldn't chance drinking now. It was time to ready himself for his meeting with Han Lee.

Back in his room he paced restlessly till darkness came. Now came the struggle against gnawing thirst. He spent a tormented, sleepless night. He dreaded the dawn when he knew his thirst for a drink would be unbearable. But he knew he would have to suffer in soberness until his hand was steady and his brain alert. He must be fit, fit to murder without risking his own life.

He suffered on for another week, his throat burning and his body aching. But he stayed sober. And all the time, his hatred of the art dealer Mei Wong grew. He pictured him as a satanic schemer, an ugly monster who had cheated him of the last shred of his decency. When the day arrived to board the vessel for Hong Kong his face was lined with pain. Since the morning he had turned back from the bar he had drunk nothing stronger than coffee.

He had gained enough strength to bargain a place for himself on the ship's crew to pay his passage. He pitched into the heavy new work with a strange eagerness. It exhausted him and gave him the pleasure of sleep once again. Sleep that would build his strength further for the murder of Han Lee.

He spent his free time reading quietly in his bunk. He wanted no friends among the crew. Several times a convivial bottle was passed to him. Just once there had been a long second's lapse between the offered drink and his refusal.

After a while the days became a stimulating and pleasant experience. But the nights were suddenly filled with troubled dreams. Dreams of death as the dagger became an expert and precise weapon in his steady hand. He practiced with it until his control was perfect.

He tried to picture what Han Lee might be like. Always he conjured up a vision of an ancient, white-bearded Oriental. Perhaps a gentle man, a man of great culture. And each day brought him nearer to Hong Kong, nearer the day when he would become a paid assassin. With his cleared brain and returned health, Rendell's whole being was revolted by the idea. How had he sunk low enough to be willing to kill a man?

He stepped ashore at Hong Kong sick with fear. There were only three weeks left to complete his mission. And now he had no wish to murder this stranger. There must, he felt, be some way out.

He soon located the whereabouts of Mei Wong's confederate, John Mac-Donald, and began the journey up to the mountains. After a day he arrived at a luxurious bungalow and John MacDonald, hearty and gray-haired, gave him a boisterous greeting. "Deuced glad to see a new face," he exclaimed, pumping his hand vigorously. "Mei Wong sent word you were coming last mail. I have a box for you."

Rendell studied him as they went into the house. It was hard to imagine this pleasant man as a criminal. But the plan was taking shape. The box had arrived.

As soon as they were inside MacDonald went to his desk and brought the box to him. Rendell took it carefully. It was of medium size and not too heavy. "You know what is in this?" he asked.

MacDonald shook his head. He said: "Haven't an idea. Came just a few days ago."

Rendell put the box under his arm. "But you have heard of Han Lee?"

"Han Lee? Yes, everyone here has heard of Han Lee."

"And you know that Mei Wong has sent me here to settle things with Han Lee, and bring back the Pearls of Li Pong?"

MacDonald stared at him. "Han Lee is a term the village people here use when they refer to the evil spirit."

"Yes, I suppose we can admit, you and I, that Han Lee is evil."

"A local superstition, goes back centuries. That's why . . . The Pearls of Li Pong? Come out to my back verandah."

Rendell followed the man outside. There stretched before them a breathtaking view of three tiny lakes at the base of a range of stately gray mountains. A scene of such perfect balance and splendor as to excite any artist—and in Rendell grew an excitement he had forgotten, almost entirely lost.

MacDonald chuckled. "*Those* are the famous Pearls of Li Pong. You might be able to settle your differences with the evil spirit, Han Lee. But as for taking back the Pearls of Li Pong, you will admit that would be quite some task. I'm afraid Mei Wong has been having one of his little jokes. He's been making a fool of you, my good man."

Rendell's eyes remained on the magnificence before him. "Just the opposite," he said quietly. "He's been making a man out of a fool." He remembered the box underneath his arm. He laid it on the bamboo table at his side, found the key, and opened it. He saw tubes of paint, a palette, brushes, and canvas. He looked up at MacDonald, his eyes bright and eager. "And you're wrong about the Pearls of Li Pong. I will take them back with me."

MICHAEL COLLINS

Who?

Mrs. Patrick Connors was a tall woman with soft brown eyes and a thin face battered by thirty years of the wrong men.

"My son Boyd died yesterday, Mr. Fortune," she said in my office. "I want to know who killed him. I have money."

She held her handbag in both hands as if she expected I might grab it. She worked in the ticket booth of an all-night movie on 42nd Street, and a lost dollar bill was a very real tragedy for her. Boyd had been her only child.

"He was a pretty good boy," I said, which was a lie, but she was his mother. "How did it happen?"

"He was a wild boy with bad friends," Mrs. Connors said. "But he was my son, and he was still very young. What happened, I don't know. That's why I'm here."

"I mean, how was he killed?"

"I don't know, but he was. It was murder, Mr. Fortune."

That was when my missing arm began to tingle. It does that when I sense something wrong.

"What do the police say, Mrs. Connors?"

"The medical examiner says that Boyd died of a heart attack. The police won't even investigate. But I know it was murder."

My arm had been right, it usually is. There was a lot wrong. Medical examiners in New York don't make many mistakes, but how do you tell that to a distraught mother?

"Mrs. Connors," I said, "we've got the best medical examiners in the country here. They had to do an autopsy. They didn't guess."

"Boyd was twenty years old, Mr. Fortune. He lifted weights, had never been sick a day in his life. A healthy young boy."

It wasn't going to be easy. "There was a fourteen-year-old girl in San Francisco who died last year of hardening of the arteries, Mrs. Connors. The autopsy proved it. It happens, I'm sorry."

"A week ago," Mrs. Connors said, "Boyd enlisted in the air force. He asked to be flight crew. They examined him for two days. He was in perfect shape, they accepted him for flight training. He was to leave in a month."

Could I tell her that doctors make mistakes? Which doctors? The air force doctors, or the medical examiner's doctors? Could I refuse even to look?

"I'll see what I can find," I said. "But the M.E. and the police know their work, Mrs. Connors."

"This time, they're wrong," she said, opening her purse.

It took most of the afternoon before I cornered Sergeant Hamm in the precinct squad room. He swore at crazy old ladies, at his work load, and at me, but he took me over to see the M.E. who had worked on Boyd Connors.

"Boyd Connors died of a natural heart attack," the M.E. said. "I'm sorry for the mother, but the autopsy proved it."

"At twenty? Any signs of previous heart attacks? Any congenital weakness, hidden disease?"

"No. There sometimes isn't any, and more people die young of heart attacks than most know. It was his first, and his last, coronary."

"He passed an air force physical for flight training a week ago," I said.

"A week ago?" The M.E. frowned. "Well, that makes it even more unusual, yes. But unusual or not, he died of a natural coronary attack, period. And in case you're wondering, I've certified more heart attack deaths than most doctors do common colds. All right?"

As we walked to Sergeant Hamm's car outside the East Side Morgue, Hamm said, "If you still have any crazy ideas about it being murder, like the mother says, I'll tell you that Boyd Connors was alone in his own room when he died. No way into that room except through the living room, no fire escape, and only Mrs. Connors herself in the living room. Okay?"

"Yeah," I said. "Swell."

Hamm said, "Don't take the old woman for too much cash, Danny. Just humor her a little."

After leaving Hamm, I went to the Connors' apartment, a fifth-floor walkup. It was cheap and worn, but it was neat—a home. A pot of tea stood on the table as Mrs. Connors let me in. She poured me a cup. There was no one else there, Mr. Patrick Connors having gone to distant parts long ago.

I sat, drank my tea. "Tell me, just what happened?"

"Last night Boyd came home about eight o'clock," the mother said. "He looked angry, went into his room. Perhaps five minutes later I heard him cry out, a choked kind of cry. I heard him fall. I ran in, found him on the floor near his bureau. I called the police."

"He was alone in his room?"

"Yes, but they killed him somehow. His friends!"

"What friends?"

"A street gang—the Night Angels. Thieves and bums!"

"Where did he work, Mrs. Connors?"

"He didn't have a job. Just the air force, soon."

"All right." I finished my tea. "Where's his room?"

It was a small room at the rear, with a narrow bed, a closet full of gaudy clothes, a set of barbells, and the usual litter of brushes, cologne, hair tonic, and after-shave on the bureau. There was no outside way into the room, and no way to reach it without passing through the living room; no signs of violence, nothing that looked to me like a possible weapon.

All that my searching and crawling got me was an empty box and wrapping paper from some drugstore, in the wastebasket, and an empty men's cologne bottle under the bureau. That and three matchbooks were under the same bureau, a tube of toothpaste under the bed, and some dirty underwear. Boyd Connors hadn't been neat.

I went back out to Mrs. Connors. "Where had Boyd been last night?" I asked.

"How do I know?" she said bitterly. "With that gang, probably. In some bars. Perhaps with his girlfriend, Anna Kazco. Maybe they had a fight, that's why he was angry."

"When did Boyd decide to join the air force?"

"About two weeks ago. I was surprised."

"All right," I said. "Where does this Anna Kazco live?"

She told me.

I left and went to the address Mrs. Connors had given me. An older woman opened the door. A bleached blonde, she eyed me until I told her what I wanted. Then she looked unhappy, but she let me in.

"I'm Grace Kazco," the blonde said, "Anna's mother. I'm sorry about Boyd Connors. I wanted better than him for my daughter, but I didn't know he was sick. Poor Anna feels terrible about it."

"How do you feel about it?" I asked.

Her eyes flashed at me. "Sorry, like I said, but I'm not all busted up. Boyd Connors wasn't going to amount to a hill of beans. Now maybe Anna can—"

The girl came from an inner room. "What can Anna do?"

She was small and dark, a delicate girl whose eyes were puffed with crying.

"You can pay attention to Roger, that's what!" the mother snapped. "He'll make something of himself."

"There wasn't anything wrong with Boyd!"

"Except he was all talk and dream and do-nothing. A street-corner big shot! Roger works instead of dreaming."

"Who's this Roger?" I asked.

"Roger Tatum," the mother said. "A solid, hard-working boy who likes Anna. He won't run off to any air force."

"After last night," Anna said, "maybe he won't be running here again, either."

"What happened last night?" I queried.

Anna sat down. "Boyd had a date with me, but Roger had dropped around first. He was here when Boyd came. They got mad at each other, Mother told Boyd to leave. She always sides with Roger. I was Boyd's date, Roger had no right to break in, but Mother got me so mad I told them both to get out. I was wrong. It made Boyd angry. Maybe that made the heart attack happen. Maybe I—"

"Stop that!" the mother said. "It wasn't your fault."

Under the bleached hair and the dictatorial manner, she was just a slum mother trying to do the best for her daughter.

"Did they get out when you told them?" I asked.

Anna nodded. "They left together. That was the last time I ever saw poor Boyd."

"What time was that?"

"About seven o'clock, I think."

"Where do I find this Roger Tatum? What does he do for a living?"

"He lives over on Greenwich Avenue, Number 110," Anna told me. "He works for Johnson's Pharmacy on Fifth Avenue. Cleans up, delivers, like that."

"It's only a temporary job," the mother said. "Roger has good offers he's considering."

The name of Johnson's Pharmacy struck a chord in my mind. Where had I heard the name? Or seen it?

Roger Tatum let me into his room. He was a small, thin youth who wore rimless glasses and had nice manners; the kind of boy mothers like—polite, nose to the grindstone. His single room was bare, except for books everywhere.

"I heard about Boyd," Tatum said. "Awful thing."

"You didn't like him too much, though, did you?"

"I had nothing against him. We just liked the same girl."

"Which one of you did Anna like?"

"Ask her," Tatum snapped.

"Not that it matters now, does it?" I said. "Boyd Connors is dead, the mother likes you, an inside track all the way."

"I suppose so," he said, watching me.

"What happened after you left the Kazco apartment with Boyd? You left together? Did you fight, maybe?"

"Nothing happened. We argued some on the sidewalk. He went off, I finished my deliveries. I'm not supposed to stop anywhere when I deliver, and I was late, so I had to hurry. When I finished delivering, I went back to the shop, then I came home. I was here all night after that."

"No fight on the street? Maybe knock Boyd Connors down? He could have been hurt more than you knew."

"Me knock down Boyd? He was twice my size."

"You were here alone the rest of the night?"

"Yes. You think I did something to Boyd?"

"I don't know what you did."

I left him standing there in his bare room with his plans for the future. Did he have a motive for murder? Not really; people don't murder over an eighteen-year-old girl that often. Besides, Boyd Connors had died of a heart attack.

I gave out the word in a few proper places that I'd like to talk to the Night Angels—five dollars in it, and no trouble. Maybe I'd reach them, maybe I wouldn't. There was nothing else to do that I could think of, so I stopped for a few Irish whiskies, then went home to bed.

About noon the next day, a small, thin, acne-scarred boy with cold eyes and a hungry face came into my office. He wore the leather jacket and shabby jeans uniform, and the hunger in his face was the perpetual hunger of the lost street kid for a lot more than food. He looked seventeen, had the cool manner of twenty-seven with experience. His name was Carlo.

"Five bucks, you offered," Carlo said first.

I gave him five dollars. He didn't sit down.

"Boyd Connors' mother says Boyd was murdered," I said. "What do you say?"

"What's it to you?"

"I'm working for Mrs. Connors. The police say heart attack."

"We heard," Carlo said. He relaxed just a hair. "Boyd was sound as a dollar. It don't figure. On'y what angle the fuzz got? We don' make it."

"Was Boyd with you that night?"

"Early 'n late. He goes to see his girl. They had a battle, Boyd come around the candy store a while."

"What time?"

"Maybe seven thirty. He don' stay long. Went home."

"Because he didn't feel good?"

"No. He feel okay," Carlo said.

I saw the struggle on his face. His whole life, the experience learned over years when every day taught more than a month taught most kids, had conditioned him never to volunteer an answer without a direct question. But he had something to say, and as hard as he searched his mind for a trap, he couldn't find one. He decided to talk to me.

"Boyd, he had a package," Carlo finally said, tore it out of his thin mouth. "He took it on home."

"Stolen?"

"He said no. He said he found it. He had a big laugh on it. Said he found it on the sidewalk, 'n the guy lost it could rot in trouble."

That was when I remembered where I had seen the name of Johnson's Pharmacy.

"A package when he came home?" Mrs. Connors said. "Well, I'm not sure, Mr. Fortune. He could have had."

I went through the living room into Boyd Connors' bedroom. The wrapping paper was still in the wastebasket. Mrs. Connors was neglecting her housework, with the grief over Boyd. A Johnson's Pharmacy label was on the wrapping paper, and a handwritten address: 3 East 11th Street. The small, empty box told me nothing.

I checked all the cologne, after-shave and hair-tonic bottles—the box was about the size for them. They were all at least half full and old. I thought of the empty bottle under the bed, and got it; a good men's cologne—and empty. It had no top. I searched harder, found the top all the way across the room in a corner, as if it had been thrown. It was a quick-twist top, one sharp turn and it came off. I saw a faint stain on the rug as if something had been spilled, but a cologne is mostly alcohol, dries fast.

I touched the bottle gingerly, studied it. There was something odd about it; not to look at, no, more an impression, the *feel* of it. It felt different, heavier, than the other bottles, and the cap seemed more solid. Only a shade of difference, something I'd never have thought about if I hadn't been looking for answers.

I could even be wrong. When you're ready to find something suspicious, your mind can play tricks, find what it wants to find.

I decided to see Roger Tatum again. He was working over a book, writing notes when I arrived.

"Not working? Fired, maybe?"

"I don't go to work until one P.M.," he said. "Why would I be fired?"

"You lost a package you were supposed to deliver last night, didn't you?"

He stared at me. "Yes, but how did you know? And you think Mr. Johnson would fire me for that? It wasn't worth five dollars; Mr. Johnson didn't even make me pay. Just sent me back this morning with another bottle."

"Bottle of what?"

"Some men's cologne."

"When did you miss the package, notice that it was gone?"

"When I got to the address. It was gone. I guess I just dropped it."

"You dropped it," I said. "Did anything happen between the drugstore and Anna Kazco's place? Did you stop anywhere? Have an accident and drop the packages?"

"No. I went straight to Anna's place. I had all the packages when I left, I counted them."

"So you know you dropped the package after you left Anna Kazco's apartment."

"Yes, I'm sure."

My next stop was the Johnson Pharmacy on Fifth Avenue. Mr. Yvor Johnson was a tall, pale man. He blinked at me from behind his counter.

"The package Roger lost? I don't understand what your interest in it is, Mr. Fortune. A simple bottle of cologne."

"Who was it going to?"

"Mr. Chalmers Padgett, a regular customer. He always buys his sundries here."

"Who is he? What does he do?"

"Mr. Padgett? Well, I believe he's the president of a large chemical company."

"Who ordered the cologne?"

"Mr. Padgett himself. He called earlier that day."

"Who packed the cologne? Wrapped it?"

"I did myself. Just before Roger took it out," he said slowly.

I showed him the empty bottle and the cap. He took them, looked at them. He looked at me.

"It looks like the bottle. A standard item. We sell hundreds of bottles."

"Is it the same bottle? You're sure? Feel it."

Johnson frowned, studied the bottle and the cap. He bent close over them, hefted the bottle, inspected the cap, hit the bottle lightly on his counter. He looked puzzled.

"That's strange. I'd almost say this bottle is a special glass, very strong. The cap, too. They seem the same; I'd not have noticed if you hadn't insisted, but they do seem stronger."

"After you packed the cologne for Mr. Padgett, how long before Roger Tatum took out his deliveries?"

"Perhaps fifteen minutes."

"Was anyone else in the store?"

"I think there were a few customers."

"Did you and Roger ever leave the packages he was to deliver unwatched?"

"No, they are on the shelf back here until Roger takes them, and—" He stopped, blinked. "Yes, wait. Roger took some trash out in back, and the man asked me if he could look at a vaporizer. I keep the bulky stock, like vaporizers, in the back. I went to get it. I was gone perhaps three minutes."

"The man? What man?"

"A big man, florid-faced. In a gray overcoat and gray hat. He didn't buy the vaporizer, I had to put it back. I was quite annoyed, I recall."

"Roger took the packages out right after that?"

"Yes, he did."

That conversation prompted me to visit Mr. Chalmers Padgett, president of P-S Chemical Corp. Not as large a company as Johnson had thought, and Dun & Bradstreet didn't list exactly what the company produced.

Padgett met me in his rich office down near Wall Street. He was a calm, pale man in a custom-made suit.

"Yes, Mr. Fortune, I ordered my usual cologne from Johnson a few days ago. Why?"

"Could anyone have known you ordered it?"

"I don't know, perhaps. I believe I called from the office here."

"Are you married?"

"I'm a widower. I live alone, if that's what you mean."

"What would you do when you got a bottle of cologne?"

"Do? Well, I'd use it, I suppose. I—" Padgett smiled at me. "That's very odd. I mean, that you would ask that. As a matter of fact I have something of a reflex habit—I smell things. Wines, cheeses, tobacco. I expect I'd have smelled the cologne almost at once. But you couldn't have known that."

"Who could have known it? About that habit?"

"Almost anyone who knows me. It's rather a joke."

"What does your company make, Mr. Padgett?"

His pale face closed up. "I'm sorry, much of our work is secret, for the government."

"Maybe Rauwolfia serpentina? Something like it?"

I had stopped at the library to do research. Chalmers Padgett looked at me with alarm and a lot of suspicion.

"I can't talk about our secret work. You—"

I said. "Do you have a heart condition, Mr. Padgett? A serious condition? Could you die of a heart attack—easily?"

He watched me. "Have you been investigating me, Mr. Fortune?"

"In a way," I said. "You *do* have a heart condition?"

"Yes. No danger if I'm careful, calm. But—"

"But if you died of a heart attack, no one would be surprised? No one would question it?"

"There would be no question," Chalmers Padgett said. He studied me. "One of our subsidiaries, very secret, does make some Rauwolfia serpentina, Mr. Fortune. For government use."

"Who would want you dead, Mr. Padgett?"

A half hour later, Mr. Padgett and I stopped for the drugstore owner, Mr. Johnson. Padgett rode in the back seat of the car with Sergeant Hamm and me.

"Rauwolfia serpentina," I said. "Did you ask the M.E.?"

"I asked," Sergeant Hamm said. "Related to common tranquilizers. Developed as a nerve gas for warfare before we supposedly gave up that line of study. Spray it on the skin, breathe it, a man's dead in seconds. Depresses the central nervous system, stops the heart cold. Yeah, the M.E. told me about it. Says he never saw a case of its use, but he'd heard of cases. Seems it works almost instantly, and the autopsy will show nothing but a plain heart attack. A spy weapon, government assassins. No cop in New York ever heard of a case. Who can get any of it?"

"P-S Chemical has a subsidiary that makes some; very secret," I said. "Under pressure in a bottle, it spurts in the face of anyone who opens it to sniff. Dead of a heart attack. The bottle drops from the victim's hand, the pressure empties the bottle. No trace—unless you test the bottle very carefully, expertly."

"In my case," Chalmers Padgett said, "who would have tested the bottle? I die of a heart attack, there would be no thought of murder. Expected. I ordered the cologne, the bottle belonged in my apartment. No one would even have noticed the bottle."

We stopped at a Park Avenue apartment house and all went up to the tenth floor. The man who stood up in the elegant, sunken living room when the houseman led us into the apartment was big and florid-faced. Something happened to his arrogant eyes when he saw Chalmers Padgett.

"Yes," Mr. Johnson said, "that's the man who asked me to show him the vaporizer, who was alone in the store with the packages."

Chalmers Padgett said, "For some years we've disagreed on how to run our company. He won't sell his share to me, and he hasn't the cash to buy my share. He lives high. If I died, he would have the company, and a large survivor's insurance. He's the only one who would gain by my death. My partner, Samuel Seaver. He's the one."

I said, "Executive vice-president of P-S Chemical. One of the few people who could get Rauwolfia serpentina."

The big man, Samuel Seaver, seemed to sway where he stood and stared only at Chalmers Padgett. His eyes showed fear, yes, but confusion, too, and incredulity. He had planned a perfect murder. Chalmers Padgett's death would have been undetectable, no question of murder. No one would have noticed Seaver's lethal bottle, it *belonged* in Padgett's room.

However, Roger Tatum had dropped the package, Boyd Connors had taken it home and opened the bottle. Boyd Connors had no heart condition. Boyd Connors' mother did not believe the heart attack. The bottle had *not* belonged in Boyd's room.

Sergeant Hamm began to recite, "Samuel Seaver, you're under arrest for the murder of Boyd Connors. It's my duty to advise you that—"

"Who?" the big man, Samuel Seaver, said unwittingly. "Murder of who?"

STANLEY ABBOTT

A Quiet Backwater

I had been wandering about Malaya for many months, picking up material for a book I had in mind, when suddenly I felt sick of it all. I couldn't wait to get away from the steam-sodden heat and hot-spiced native food. Even the brilliant eye-shattering colors and lush greenery which at first had seemed so exciting and attractive had become unbearable.

I needed a change. I longed for the crispness of northern California in the fall.

To catch the small coastal steamer that sails twice a month for Singapore I took a native prahu down river to Tenah Solor. It was little more than a village with several hundred Malays, Dyaks, and the inevitable Chinese quarter, clustered together close by the river; higher up, the bungalows of the white population were scattered around an immense padang. It looked like a well-kept English village green, except for the tall cassias which surrounded it and shaded the bungalows.

I had nearly a week to wait and the thought of spending it in this sleepy backwater, which looked as if it hadn't changed in a century, appalled me. I settled in for a boring stay in a bungalow belonging to the district officer, Jeff Hawkins.

Hawkins was a bachelor and he had offered to put me up. He was very British and military looking in khaki shirt and shorts, and we got on well together. During the day he had his job to look after. In the evenings we met on the verandah where the houseboy set out the drinks. After a couple of gin slings, if we felt like it, we'd walk over to the club to find a game of bridge.

The club was a converted bungalow and there were usually a few planters there who had driven in with their wives to have a drink. It was here one evening that Jeff Hawkins introduced me to the Thorntons and asked them if they'd like to make up a game. Harry Thornton said he would but his wife didn't play. She was just about to leave, but while Jeff went off to hunt up a fourth she stayed and talked with me. I was glad she did, for her husband had very little to say, and it had been a long time since I'd set eyes on such a lovely girl.

Harry Thornton had an intelligent-looking face, but a couple of deeply etched furrows at the corners of his mouth gave him a bitter look. Though what he had to be bitter about, with such a charming wife, I could hardly imagine.

Most of the women I'd met made the climate and the distance from civilization an excuse to let themselves go. But Julia was an exception. Her makeup was immaculate, and the coloring of her dark blue eyes and soft dark hair was set off to perfection by a pink linen dress.

She told me they'd been there about ten years. They owned their own rubber plantation and, now that there was no longer trouble from Communist guerillas, all was going well. The price of rubber was good, and there was little to complain about. Except, as she told me with a laugh, she simply could not get used to keeping her lipstick in the refrigerator.

I found myself wishing Harry Thornton weren't there. When I told her I lived in San Francisco she was delighted, for she had been born there and wanted to hear all about it. I noticed, while we talked, that she kept glancing at her husband. It might have been just a nervous habit, but I got an impression that maybe she was frightened of him.

Jeff Hawkins returned, accompanied by a tall man, and after Julia had left I was introduced. His name was Peter Endrik; he was half Dutch, I learned later. He was goodlooking in a flashy sort of way, and was only in his early thirties, but he showed all the signs of being a heavy drinker. I try not to be prejudiced, but I didn't like him. We were partners, and every time he went wrong, he tried to bluff his way out of it. We were no match for Jeff and Harry Thornton, who made full use of their opportunities. After about an hour of this we'd had enough and there was nothing to do but pay up and look pleasant.

Jeff Hawkins had something to do, so I went into the billiard room with Harry Thornton and had my revenge playing snooker. From time to time shouts of laughter came from the bar and later, as we were leaving, Peter Endrik came up to us. He had a drink in his hand and was swaying about.

"How about a game, Harry?" he asked in a thick, slurred voice.

"Make it another time, Peter—I've got to get home," Harry Thornton replied as we tried to get by.

"Gotta go home to the little woman, eh?" Endrik put a hand on Harry's shoulder to steady himself. "Well, give her my love; she'll like that." And he roared with laughter.

I saw Harry Thornton stiffen. Then he pushed by Endrik and turned to me. "Let's get out of here."

I dislike a brawl, but I was surprised he'd let Endrik say that about Julia and get away with it. With Endrik's mocking laughter to accompany us, we left quietly.

"I must say I admire your self-control," I said.

Harry Thornton dismissed it with a shrug of the shoulders. "He's just a drunken bum."

But there was a brooding look in his deep-set eyes, and he had very little to say as we walked across the padang.

Later that evening, Jeff Hawkins and I stretched out on long chairs on the verandah. It was very pleasant and peaceful. A breath of cool air was moving in from the sea and the moon had just risen, revealing the long line of jungle stretching to the mouth of the river on the far bank.

Jeff turned to me with a grin on his big red face. "Well, I suppose you're boning up on the Romance and Mystery of the Malayan jungle." There was a mocking note in his voice but I didn't mind. As a writer I've got used to it, and I can't say I blame him when I think of some of the stuff that's been written about Malaya.

"No," I replied, "far from it. That's been done to death." Then I went on, "We had a little excitement at the club earlier this evening," and I told him about the scene with Endrik.

"I wish somebody'd give him a good hiding," Jeff said. "Peter's big but he's flabby, and I don't doubt Harry could do it if he wanted to."

"There's something strange about him," I said. "I get a feeling he's like a tightly coiled spring—something kept suppressed."

"I know what you mean," Jeff replied. "Ever since they've been out here, Harry's been jealous of any man who dances with Julia or even talks to her. And she's the best looking girl for miles. What does he expect in a place like this? Of course, Peter plays on that. Knowing Harry hasn't any sense of humor, he gets even by making him the butt of his crude jokes."

A houseboy padded out onto the verandah with a note for Jeff. He read it, wrote something on it, and gave it back to the boy.

"You must have made an impression. We're invited to the Thorntons' tomorrow night—dinner and bridge."

Suddenly the lights dimmed, came up, and then went out completely.

"Pay no attention to it," said Jeff, "this is always happening. We've a lousy old generator and not enough money to replace it."

The houseboy appeared with an oil lamp and put it on the table between us.

"I'm afraid Peter's the one rotten apple in the barrel," Jeff went on. "The strange thing is, he's not such a bad fellow when he's sober, but he won't last long the way he's going. This climate has finished off better men than he. Also, he plays around with the Malay girls. I've warned him he'll find a kris at his throat one dark night."

Jeff knocked out his pipe and yawned. "Time I turned in. I've got to be up early tomorrow."

At the Thorntons' the following evening an Englishman and his wife, whom I'd met at the club, were there. Their name was Barwell. I hoped they both played bridge so I'd get a chance to talk to Julia.

We had an excellent rijstafel served by a couple of Malayan houseboys in white jackets. But the conversation didn't match the dinner. As usual, Harry Thornton had very little to say. Then, somehow, Peter Endrik's name came up and Mrs. Barwell turned to Julia.

"Oh, darling, I forgot to tell you; did you hear what happened at the club last night?"

Barwell said it was of no importance, but she wouldn't be stopped. I couldn't help feeling that Mrs. Barwell was getting a certain satisfaction in the telling.

"And what do you think Harry did to Peter Endrik?" she asked. "He simply ignored him. I thought he was quite magnificent, didn't you, Mr. Manson?" She looked across at me, the smile of the Borgias on her pudgy face.

Thornton shrugged as he said, "He was drunk."

Julia put down her knife and fork and stared at him angrily. There was an awkward silence. I was glad when we finished and returned to the living room.

The Barwells both played bridge, so it was arranged that Mrs. Barwell should play the first rubber and then that I should take her place. Julia suggested that we sit on the verandah. It extended around the house on all four sides, and she led the way to the far end where there was a view over the mouth of the river. I guessed she wasn't interested in small talk, so I gave her a cigarette and we sat in silence watching the fireflies flickering through the bushes.

Suddenly she surprised me by asking, "Do you think I could get a job back home?"

I didn't answer immediately, for I guessed there was more behind the question than appeared on the surface.

"Is it as bad as that?" I asked her gently.

She looked at me and nodded, as though not trusting herself to speak. I waited while she slowly twisted a handkerchief to shreds between her fingers.

Presently it all came pouring out. "He hasn't spoken a word to me for over six months. You've no idea what it's like. He gives messages to the boys or leaves notes, but not a word. I don't know what to do. I'm nearly out of my mind."

Though I'd figured there was something strange about Thornton, I was shocked. It was such a cowardly form of mental bullying that I could hardly believe it.

"Has he always been like this?" I asked.

"Not in the beginning. He's always been jealous, but now, if I dance with anyone or say more than a dozen words to a man, he imagines the worst. He used to break things and hit me. Now he doesn't say a word. Once it went on for nearly a year. But I can't take it any more."

She bent her head so that I shouldn't see, but in the dim light I caught the gleam of tears. I put a hand on hers; it must have been the first gesture of sympathy she'd had in years.

The sound of footsteps echoed on the verandah. Julia got up quickly and left as Harry Thornton came down the verandah towards us. She obviously didn't want him to see that she'd been crying.

"Do you want a drink?" he asked me, but his eyes followed Julia. He couldn't have cared less what I wanted.

"Not for me, thanks—I've had enough," I said.

Thornton stood looking down at me and it seemed a very long time that we stared at each other. I wondered what he was thinking. Then I felt I didn't care what he was thinking. I was ready to get up and knock him off his own verandah. Fortunately he turned on his heel and left me, without a word.

Julia didn't appear again, and when we left, Thornton made it clear he didn't care if he ever saw me again. Jeff must have guessed something had happened but he didn't question me and we walked across the padang to his bungalow in silence.

We both turned in but it was a long time before I slept. It was obvious Julia needed help, otherwise she wouldn't have told me what she had. And it was equally obvious she wasn't in love with Thornton. Then why didn't she leave him? It could only be a question of money. If I were right, that could easily be remedied. I could lend her the money for her passage, and I had several friends in San Francisco who would have her to stay and help her find a job. I tried to keep any emotional feelings about Julia out of it. But I found myself wondering what was going on over at their bungalow, and my imagination ran riot. It was dawn before I fell into an uneasy sleep.

I had decided to tell Jeff what had happened, as I wanted his advice. While we were having a drink that evening I told him what Julia had said.

He said quietly, "I didn't know he was as mean as that."

"What I can't understand is why she hasn't left him, or got a divorce."

"Oh, she'd be worse off than ever," Jeff said. "In this country she'd get a mere pittance, barely enough to live on."

I told him how I thought I could help with a passage and my friends in San Francisco. He looked at me steadily for some moments. "I hope you know what you're getting into."

I was about to say something when a sound like a firecracker came clearly on the still night air. It might have been a shot fired some distance away. For a moment we were alert, listening.

Jeff said, "That's probably Peter Endrik. He goes after crocodiles on the mud flats with a flashlight fixed to a rifle."

"That must be exciting."

"Too exciting for me. One false step and you've had it."

For a time we sat looking out over the river. Jeff had just finished pouring drinks when we heard someone running fast across the padang. Almost immediately a Malay houseboy in white jacket appeared below the verandah, carrying a lantern.

"Tuan, come quick," he gasped, "come quick!"

In an instant we were off the verandah, and running hard across the padang toward the lights of a bungalow. The boy led the way across a wide verandah and into the living room. On the floor beside a couch lay Peter Endrik. He had been shot in the chest. Jeff ripped his shirt away and examined him.

"He's dead," he said quietly.

Peter was lying on his back, and a few feet away was a six-chambered revolver. Jeff knelt down and looked at it without touching it.

"A .38," he said. "We'll leave that where it is for the moment."

He spoke to the houseboy in a dialect I couldn't understand, and when they went outside through a garden at the back and on to a lane that ran around the padang, I followed. It was dark and Jeff was examining the ground with a flashlight.

"The boy says the front door was locked. He only got back a few minutes ago himself, so whoever shot Endrik must have come in this way, the only other door."

But there was nothing to be found. We went back inside. The first thing I noticed as we entered the living room was a faint musky smell—strange, and yet familiar; and then that the revolver which had been on the floor had vanished.

We both made a rush for the door and the verandah. Though we searched all around and stood listening, there wasn't a sound. We could only have been out at the back about ten minutes, but it had been enough for someone to slip in and take the revolver.

"I could kick myself for a fool," Jeff cried.

He stood staring down at the body of Peter Endrik for some time, lost in thought. Suddenly he turned to me. "I'm going over to the Thorntons'. Would you mind coming along?"

Their bungalow was on the far side of the padang. When we got there the lights were on. Jeff said in a low voice, "If you don't mind, I think I'd better talk to them alone, but I'd like you to hear what's said."

I nodded and Jeff went ahead.

When he'd gone in I waited, and then crept closer to the verandah, from where I could see Harry Thornton and Julia. Jeff had told them what had happened.

"But, Jeff," Harry Thornton was saying, "you don't think we had anything to do with it, do you?"

"Of course not, Harry. I just wanted to know if you saw or heard anything, but if you haven't been out all evening, how could you?"

Julia said, "I got in about half an hour ago, Jeff. I heard the shot after I left the Barwells. I thought it was Peter Endrik out on the mud flats."

"Which way did you come home?" Jeff asked her.

"Across the padang. I always do; it's shorter than the lane and not so dark."

"So at the nearest point you'd be about a hundred yards from Endrik's bungalow. Did you see any lights on?"

"Not that I remember. There were lights in several bungalows, but I can't say I noticed Endrik's."

Jeff turned to Harry Thornton.

"You say you hadn't been out all evening?"

Thornton nodded. "That's right."

Jeff said quietly, "Yet you were seen by a houseboy. I won't say whose, near Endrik's bungalow."

Thornton straightened up in his chair instantly. He opened his mouth to say something, but before he could do so Jeff stopped him.

"Don't be hasty, Harry. You would be well advised to think carefully before you say anything."

For some moments he stared hard at Jeff. Then his eyes dropped. "It slipped my mind," he said in a low voice. "I did go out, but only for a few moments. I was worried about Julia. I went to see if she was on her way back."

Julia stared at him wide-eyed. For some time not a word was said.

Suddenly the lights dimmed, came up, and then went out completely. I heard Thornton say, "Wait—I'll get a lamp."

Then I heard a crash. The silence that followed seemed endless, and I was beginning to wonder what had happened when I heard Jeff say, "Are you all right?"

A match was struck and I could see Thornton lighting a lamp. "I walked into that darned door," he said, as he brought the lamp over and set it down on the table. He was rubbing his right hand.

"Isn't your houseboy here?" Jeff asked him.

Julia answered quickly. "I let Hassan go to his kampong for the night."

Thornton shot a look at her. "Why did you do that?" he asked.

"He said his father was sick."

Jeff turned to Thornton. "So when you went out to look for Julia, Hassan wasn't here?"

"That's right."

"Was Julia here when you got back?" Jeff inquired quietly.

Thornton looked at Julia. "No, she wasn't."

To my surprise, Jeff got to his feet and said he was sorry he'd had to trouble them. He came out, and we'd only taken a few steps when Jeff stopped and put a finger to his lips. From the bungalow we could hear voices but not what was being said. Suddenly Thornton started shouting. Jeff said, "I wondered if this would develop."

He hurried back and crept up onto the verandah. I followed him. Julia and Thornton were standing, facing each other across the table, the lamp between them. Thornton's face looked awful in the greenish-white light.

"You lied! You were in Endrik's bungalow; I saw you go in!" he was shouting.

"What if I was?" Julia flung at him. "I went to do what you should have done if you were any sort of a husband—to tell him to stop insulting me. But he wasn't there."

"You're a liar! He was your lover, wasn't he? Answer me," Thornton shouted. "Wasn't he?"

"That's not true, and if you weren't so crazy with jealousy you'd know it."

"Then why did you kill him? You were jealous of his Malayan girl, weren't you?"

Julia gave a gasp and the color left her face. Before she could say anything Thornton leaned across the table towards her and asked, " Do you realize what Jeff Hawkins could do if he knew?"

For a minute Julia was silent; then quite quietly she said, "If that was a threat, perhaps you'll tell him at the same time what you were doing out there in the dark."

Thornton's lips worked but no sound came. She'd called his bluff. He was incoherent with rage and glaring at her like a tiger ready to spring. I could see a vein standing out on his head, pulsing. I don't like to think he intended to throw the lamp at her, but he must have lost control of himself, for he grabbed it up suddenly from the table, and as he did so it slipped from his hand. He tried to recover it, but it hit a corner of the table and fell at his feet. Instantly he was enveloped in flames. A terrifying scream broke from him.

For a moment neither of us moved. We were frozen with horror. Julia had fallen trying to get away. We grabbed her, and dragged her out onto the verandah just as the oil covering the floor went up with a roar. We tried to get back in but there wasn't a hope. The flames were utterly beyond control. We had to watch from a distance as the bungalow went up like a torch.

It was much later, after Julia had been taken in and cared for by the Barwells, that Jeff said something that I realized I didn't want to face. We'd returned to his bungalow, and he was mixing a drink.

"If I'd known it would finish like this," he said, "I wouldn't have done what I did. But I wanted to spring it on Thornton, in front of Julia, that I knew he was lying, that I knew he'd been out. Now it's difficult to say which of them killed Endrik."

"Do you really think Julia could have done it?" I asked.

"Who knows?" he said, handing me a drink. "After twenty-five years out here you get so you believe that anybody's capable of anything. But somehow I can't see Harry Thornton taking such a risk. Anyway, it's all over. Endrik got what was coming to him, and Julia's got her own life to make now."

He looked at me as though expecting some comment, but I said nothing.

The coastal steamer was due the next afternoon. I couldn't make up my mind if I should see Julia before I left. I put it off until it was too late, then wrote her a note, and sailed for Singapore where I caught a plane for Manila. I had intended staying two or three weeks, but after a few days I couldn't stand it. I cabled Jeff that I was leaving for Hong Kong to catch a boat back to the States, and to forward my mail to the Palace hotel.

I thought a lot about Julia. I couldn't make up my mind if it made any difference to my feelings about her, if she *had* killed Endrik.

Then one morning, when I was sitting in the lounge of the Palace reading my mail, Julia walked in. "George Manson," she cried. "I can hardly believe it." She had just arrived, and hadn't even been up to her room. "Can we meet in about an hour?" she asked.

She looked radiant and happy. It was hard to believe what she had put behind her so quickly. I wanted to ask her a question to which I had to have an answer, so I suggested the roof garden, which was always deserted in the morning.

When Julia joined me she looked cool and attractive. We talked of Tenah Solor. She had sold the plantation to an Anglo-American outfit and had done very well. As I leaned towards her to light her cigarette, I caught a whiff of her perfume and I had to ask the question. For a moment I didn't know how to put it; then I decided that the only thing to do was to be blunt about it.

"Why did you come back for the revolver that night after Endrik was shot?" I asked her.

The color left her cheeks. She stared at me wide-eyed. "How did you know?" Her voice was barely above a whisper.

"Your perfume."

"Ah! Now I understand why you left without seeing me. You thought I'd killed Endrik."

I nodded.

She continued, "It was Harry's gun—that's why I went to get it. No, he didn't shoot Endrik, he didn't know anything about it, but I had to get it to protect him. It was Hassan, our houseboy."

"Hassan?" I exclaimed. "How did you know?"

"I lied to Jeff," she said. "I got home earlier than I said, and I caught Hassan coming out of Harry's room. He hurried out the back in such a suspicious way that I knew he was up to something. I looked in Harry's dresser and found the gun was gone.

"It was common knowledge that Peter Endrik had been playing around with Hassan's sister. Hassan had told me he was going to marry her. Of course Endrik had no intention of doing so. The Malays don't take that lightly; for them there's only one answer to that. But what could I do? If I were right, I couldn't stop him, even if I went after him. I was all alone, and there was no time to get a message to anybody."

"So when you heard the shot you were at home."

She nodded. "And then I remembered the gun. If Hassan had left it there, it would point right at Harry. However much I hated him, I couldn't let him be accused of murder. That's why I took the chance I did."

I felt a tremendous relief, and shame that I had doubted her.

"I'm sure Jeff Hawkins thinks you did it," I said.

She laughed. "I won't lose any sleep over that."

I moved closer and put an arm around her. "Am I forgiven?" I asked.

She nodded and put her head on my shoulder.

"I can't get over the way our paths crossed," I said. "Another day, and I'd have left."

"It was fate, darling," she murmured.

I smiled to myself, for in a letter from Jeff he'd mentioned that Julia had been in to say goodbye, and had asked him where I was.

But I didn't say a word. And to this day Julia doesn't know. After all, there are some things it's better not to tell a woman, particularly if she's your wife.

PHIL DAVIS

Murder, Anyone?

If it weren't for my wife I might never have hunched out the murders. There were four of them and a fifth was on the fire. Homicide didn't see anything that resembled homicide. They liked accident, mainly, except for the one that went into the books as suicide.

Though cops and robbers weren't my thing any more, I liked to keep my brain in. When I was with the department I was no great shakes—just a digger who liked to play hunches. Now that I'm retired (not because of age, but due to a rich, departed uncle), I could play without being reprimanded.

The first so-called accident made no impression on me. It happened to a veterinarian who died because of a faulty gas heater. So what. You read about it all the time, right?

Then a carpenter gets his hand mixed up with an electric saw, in his own shop, yet. That doesn't happen too often to a professional carpenter. To an amateur, yes. Anyway, they found the poor guy two days later near the telephone, with his arm outstretched, apparently trying to reach the phone with the hand that was still attached.

I said to my friend at the precinct, "Something smells, Marty. A pro wouldn't go near one of those power saws without the safety guard in position. How come this one did?"

Marty was a shrugger. "Careless," he said.

I nodded, my brain acting like it still belonged in a detective's skull. It's possible that a carpenter could be careless, but before a person can get his hand sawed off, first the machine's got to be trying to saw something else besides hands, right? *There wasn't a hunk of wood anywhere near that sawing table.* "How come?" I asked Marty.

Marty gave me one of those tolerant, sighing looks. "He wasn't sawing any wood, Hank. He accidentally flipped the switch while his hand was on the table."

All right, that's an answer. I filed it away.

Then there was this druggist who was found cold in the back room of his store with a bellyful of cyanide. It was obviously suicide. If a druggist wants to go, he knows how—fast and easy.

I didn't argue too much on that one. It was a fairly open-and-shut suicide, but one thing bothered me that didn't seem to bother the department. *All three of these cash-ins happened on a Monday afternoon at around four thirty.*

Marty threw up his hands in disgust. "Why don't you go home," he said, "and watch the crime shows on television? Better yet, write some."

I ignored both suggestions. "Imagine that," I said, pressing the point. "Everything happens on a Monday afternoon at around four thirty, a week or two apart. Funny, right?"

Marty didn't think it was funny. He admitted it was strange and gave me a lecture on the theory of coincidence. I'm a patient man. I didn't belabor it.

During one of my usual visits to the precinct, a report came in that a Mr. Adams, owner of the East Side Exterminating Company, choked on the fumes of some bug killer he'd been mixing. I said to myself, *Murder Number Four?* I also thought, *Why not? It was a Monday, and it was around four thirty in the afternoon.*

Nora was on her side of the bed trying to solve her weekly acrostic puzzle while I stared at the ceiling hoping maybe I'd find some answers up there. Mr. Adams, the exterminator, had been mixing formulas for twenty years, and all he ever killed were bugs. Now he mixes some stuff which any high school chemistry student knows is lethal, and bye-bye, Mr. Adams. How come? Marty had told me, after the usual investigation, there was a mix-up of labels on the bottles. Another pro is careless? Come on . . .

Nora squealed: "I got it! I got it!"

Big deal—another acrostic puzzle solved.

"Listen to this, darling," she said. "This one is real profound."

I gave her my "big-deal" attitude and said, "Do tell."

"Don't belittle me, darling. It was the hardest acrostic I ever worked."

I leered at her well-formed breasts pressing against her sheer nightgown. "Me, belittle you?"

She pulled the covers up to her chin. "Nervy," she said.

That's Nora, a regular square. I slid over to her side and asked her to read me the profound solution to the acrostic. She gave me a smug look and read: "'To liquidate the liquidator, the insects must rise and devour the devourer the day next when the moon is full.'"

She waited for my reaction. I let her wait because I didn't understand it.

"Well?" she said, finally.

"What's so profound about that?"

"Don't you know what it means?"

"It's supposed to mean something?"

"It means that nature will some day rise up and destroy us all because we've been fiddling around with her entirely too much."

"Not bad," I said, grudgingly. "Like that little exterminator guy I was telling you about. All his life he mixes stuff to kill bugs—now the stuff kills *him*." I frowned. "That's a funny coincidence."

"What is?"

"Read that again."

She did, and this time I listened carefully. "'To liquidate the liquidator, the insects must rise and devour the devourer the day next when the moon is full.'"

I nodded and wrinkled my forehead. "That bug killer—his place is next to the Moon Cafe."

"So?"

"So he dies at four thirty, *when the Moon is full—of beer drinkers*. The acrostic tells when it's gonna happen, where and to who."

"Whom," she corrected. Then she mimicked me with an icky face: "'When the Moon is full of beer drinkers.' That isn't worthy of you, Hank."

I grinned. "My wisdom can't all be pearls. But I still think it's a funny coincidence."

"Well, you're going to Teresa Trimble's tomorrow night. You can ask her about it."

"Who's she?" I said, scowling.

"That's the little old lady who makes up the acrostics for the magazine."

My wife was giving me one of her teasing-type smiles, obviously enjoying the scowl I kept on my face. So I teased her back by removing the scowl and replacing it with a shruggy look.

She couldn't stand it for long.

"Don't you want to know," she said, "how come we're going there tomorrow night?" Her tone revealed she had lost the tease contest.

"You're about to tell me, right?"

"Right. I sent her a fan letter and she invited us for dinner."

I rolled my eyes to the ceiling. "Great. A dinner date with an ancient female who makes up weirdo puzzles."

"She's a very remarkable woman. Do you know what she said in last week's acrostic? I memorized it. 'The walrus speaks of cabbages and the carpenter speaks not at all since he cannot be heard above the din.' You know what that means?"

I didn't wait for her to tell me. My hunchy brain was clicking like an overheated computer. I scrambled out of bed and made for Nora's desk. I heard her call out: "Hey!"

"I want to see all the other acrostics you worked out," I said, riffling through her papers.

"Welcome to the intelligentsia," she said smugly.

I sent her a wry look and went back to the puzzles. I found nothing that said anything about a druggist or a vet—not in those exact words—but there was enough to make me wonder about Miss Trimble. I looked forward to tomorrow's date.

We waited in the living room while Teresa Trimble flitted out for some goodies. Her place could have inspired a Charles Addams drawing: the mohair furniture, the beaded portieres, the antimacassars, and the faint aroma of rose sachet. I was about to tell Nora the room gave me the creeps, when she said: "Isn't it charming, Hank?"

What can you say to a question like that? So I nodded and let her believe it was charming.

Miss Trimble minced in through the beaded portieres carrying a tray of watercress sandwiches and three small glasses of wine. She was a tiny, birdlike woman, about seventy. "This is such a joyous occasion for me," she said in a voice that rustled as if it were filtered through some willows.

"We were so happy to be able to come," Nora said with a stickiness that might have attracted a swarm of bees. "Monday is usually Hank's poker night."

I nodded with a suffering, oh-what-I-gave-up! look.

Miss Trimble rushed on. "Well, when I got your gracious letter compliment- ing my acrostics I just knew I had to meet you. And when you accepted my humble invitation—" She broke off, staring at Nora with a semiglazed look. Then slowly she reached out and touched her cheek. "You're so young," she said softly. "So fresh—" She halted abruptly as a thought developed. "Oh, I have a wonderful idea! I'll just be a minute!" She turned and floated out. I started to browse.

"Stop fidgeting," Nora whispered. "It won't destroy you to miss your poker game one night."

By this time I was at the secretary-desk in a corner going through an assortment of papers. Nora reprimanded me sharply. "Hank, you just can't come into this woman's home and start going through—"

"Listen to this . . . " It was a galley proof of next week's acrostic. "'Green is his trade though many shades of yellow are his wares. Black is the nature of his soul, and death finds repose in pale pink.'"

Nora's eyes flashed. "Hank, you can't—"

"How do I look?" Miss Trimble's voice caused us to whirl. She'd changed into a gown of a vintage of fifty years ago, pausing in the portiere and striking a pose as if asking for admiration.

I managed, "Exquisite. Like a Dresden doll, Miss Trimble."

"What a nice thing to say, Mr. Barnes. It's been fifty years since I wore this dress. It has wonderful memories." She gave Nora a warm, tender look. "And seeing you reminded me of all those young yesterdays." Her glance fell on the tray she'd brought in. "Oh, you haven't tasted my sandwiches. They won't interfere with your dinner—they're very light." A note of sadness crept into her voice. "Although I'm afraid the watercress is a bit of a disappointment. It isn't as crisp as it should have been." Now her face turned a shade cunning. "My greengrocer's been neglecting me. I'm going to have to change him."

There went my brain clicking again. "Your greengrocer?"

She gave me a pleasant nod, then picked up a glass of wine and raised it to Nora. "I want to drink a toast to you, Mrs. Barnes. To beauty—who has found faith in a lost art." She had lifted her glass to her lips when her attention was attracted to an empty bird cage hanging on a tall stand nearby. Her eyes clouded and she stood silently gazing at it for a couple of seconds. She caught our puzzled reaction. "I lost Jonathan three weeks ago today," she explained. "The veterinarian was so careless." She extended the tray. "Now, won't you try one of these? You'll find them refreshing."

I reached for a sandwich and accidentally knocked over a glass of wine which spilled on the rug.

"Oh, Hank—" Nora began, chidingly.

"I'm sorry, Miss Trimble." I stooped down to mop it up with a paper napkin, but Miss Trimble stopped me.

"Don't worry, Mr. Barnes," she said. "Moths got to my rug long before that little glass of wine. The exterminator was preparing a special solution, but apparently the moths were smarter than he."

From my stooped position, I looked up at her and said cautiously, "Would that happen to be an exterminator who had his place on East 47th Street?"

She reacted with a surprised smile. "Why, yes, Mr. Barnes. Do you use Mr. Adams, too?"

I rose slowly. "No," I said. "And I don't think Mr. Adams is in a position to take on any more business."

Nora swiveled her stare from me to Miss Trimble in dismay.

In my sleep I heard myself repeating: "'Green is his trade though many shades of yellow are his wares. Green is his trade—'"

Then I heard Miss Trimble's voice saying: "My greengrocer's been neglecting me. I'm going to have to change him."

"'*Green is his trade—*'"

"*I'm going to have to change him—*"

I awoke sharply and cried out: "Oh, no!" I turned and started to shake Nora. "Honey . . . sweetheart . . . baby!"

She offered me her glaze-filled eyes.

"I've got it!" I yelled. Then added in a lower voice: "I'm afraid."

Nora yawned in my face and said, "You've got what? You're afraid?"

"I think that weirdo Trimble dame is going to change her greengrocer, all right. She's going to change him from a live one to a dead one." I reached for the telephone on the night stand.

"It's not a coincidence, Marty," I said. "All your accidental deaths are tied in with these acrostics." Nora refilled our coffee cups.

"Three thirty," Marty muttered dazedly. "In the morning yet."

Nora nodded in agreement. "Imagine—popovers, at three thirty A.M."

"And very good, too," Marty said with a mouthful. "I'll have another."

I waved a handful of solved acrostics under his nose. "Remember the veterinarian who died because of a faulty gas heater? I'll bet you'll find he took care of Miss Trimble's bird with the broken wing. And the exterminator who fought a losing battle with the moths in her rug." I riffled through the stuff. "It's all here—the carpenter, the druggist. And I'm warning you, Marty, next Monday at four thirty a greengrocer's going to die."

Marty sighed. "Do me a favor, Hank? What the hell is a greengrocer?"

Nora leaped in with her super-intellect. "A man who sells fruits and vegetables." Then she attacked me with her super-logic. "We had dinner with her last night, Hank. Did she act like a woman who committed four murders in as many weeks? And if she did, why lay it out in an acrostic puzzle?"

"Who is this dame?" Marty wanted to know. "A Lucrezia de Bergerac? A master criminal? I don't get it, but I've played your hunches before and you've been right, so I'll go along with you now. Just don't tell my boss."

"Right." I turned to my wife. "Nora . . ." She was asleep on her feet, so I did what any red-blooded ex-detective husband would do under the circumstances. I yelled in her ear. "*Nora!*"

Her head snapped back, and she spouted: "A greengrocer is a man who sells fruits and—"

She broke off at the sight of my grin. "You told us that before, dear," I said patronizingly. "What we need to know now is *which* greengrocer is going to be the next victim."

I gave her the assignment.

Nora was a good operative. Teresa Trimble's greengrocer was a frail little man by the name of Pincus. His store was on Lexington Avenue not far from Miss Trimble's apartment. The customers called him Pink, as in the last sentence of the acrostic: *Death finds repose in pale pink.*

The following Monday Marty and I staked out Pink's place. At about four fifteen, Miss Trimble materialized on the sidewalk and glided into the store. We got out of the car and paused at the entrance. We heard Mr. Pincus greet Miss Trimble warmly. She wanted to know if her mushrooms were ready. "You promised me, Pink," she said in that wispy voice. "Today . . . Monday . . . four thirty. Remember?"

"Of course," Pincus said. "I haven't had a light on in the cellar all week. They should be beautiful. I'll just be a minute."

Mr. Pincus went through a back door and we went in through the front. Miss Trimble was surprised. "Why, Mr. Barnes," she said, "how nice to see you. Are you going to buy some of Mr. Pincus's mushrooms?"

"Not exactly." I introduced Marty.

"So nice to meet you, Mr. Gordon."

Marty said, "Thanks."

Miss Trimble turned to a display of persimmons. "Mr. Pincus says it bruises his persimmons to squeeze them. But how else can you tell if they're ripe?" She gave one a delicate pinch and tossed me a conspiratorial smile. "He'll never know."

Miss Trimble went back to examining the persimmons, giving them a pinch here, a pinch there. A clock on the wall ticked ominously. It was obviously fast. Then, after what seemed to be a short forever, I checked my watch and glanced at Marty. "What time've *you* got?"

Before Marty could answer, Miss Trimble turned from the persimmons and told us: "It's four thirty."

It was the way she said it that caused Marty and me to exchange a couple of alarmed looks. Enough for Marty to scoot out the back door.

"It was so sweet of Mrs. Barnes," Miss Trimble was saying, "to drop by last Wednesday. I gave her some of my special jasmine tea. I have such a wonderful tea man—"

I glanced nervously toward the rear door. "She told me," I said.

"She's so young and pretty," Miss Trimble went on. "You're a very lucky man, Mr. Barnes. If I had my way she'd never grow old."

I caught sight of a magazine on a counter beside her. It was the same one Nora subscribed to—the one with the acrostic puzzles. Before I could question her about it, Marty came in from the rear room, his features frozen in shock.

"He's dead," Marty said with complete disbelief.

Miss Trimble looked concerned. "But what about my mushrooms?" she said.

Inspector Crowley, a fat, florid, perspiring cop with a nervous habit of cracking his knuckles, was questioning Miss Trimble in her apartment. I had to hand it to her, the way she sat so calm and controlled.

Crowley cracked a knuckle and said: "Tell me again, Miss Trimble, what was the meaning of the acrostic—" He started to read from a copy: "'Green is his trade,' et cetera, et cetera, et cetera—?"

"I wish you wouldn't do that," Miss Trimble said.

"It's my job to ask questions."

"I didn't mean that. I meant crack your knuckles."

Crowley flashed Marty and me an irky look. With Crowley's permission, I took over the questioning. "Didn't your acrostic contain a warning to Mr. Pincus?"

"A warning?" she said innocently. "About what?"

I repeated the acrostic: "'Green is his trade though many shades of yellow are his wares.'" I gave her my interpretation. "That means he was a green-grocer, but sold yellow stuff like bananas, squash, pears, and so on. Right?"

"That's a very interesting interpretation, Mr. Barnes," she said impressed.

I went on. "'Black is the nature of his soul.' Was that your way of saying you disliked him?"

"Oh, no, Mr. Barnes. I was just sorry he disappointed me in the watercress, that's all. Actually, I was very fond of Pink."

I nodded. "Pink. Death finds repose in pale pink." I put on one of my friendliest faces. "Now, Miss Trimble, didn't you intend that to be a threat?"

"The text," she said simply, "of each of my acrostics is always controversial. That's why they're so successful. Everyone finds his own meaning in them."

"What's yours?"

"I just like the way they sound."

Marty put his two cents in. "Did you like the way it sounded when Pincus slipped on those cellar steps and cracked his head open on the cement floor?"

"I didn't hear anything," she said sweetly.

It was Crowley's turn. "You got into that cellar, waxed those steps, and unscrewed the light bulb—didn't you?"

Marty pounced in with: "And what about the exterminator? Did you slip into his back room and prepare the solution that killed him?"

"And the vet," Crowley barked. "The one you took your bird to. Did you open the jet on his gas heater while he took his afternoon nap?"

"And the carpenter—"

"The druggist—"

They suddenly stopped the interrogation to stare at Miss Trimble as she took out a little pillbox from a table drawer, and poured some water from a carafe.

"I can't remember," she said, "when I've had such a stimulating evening." She opened the pillbox and extended it to us. "Peppermint?"

Nora let out three "oh's," one after another. The first one came when I handed her a special delivery letter. It was an "oh" filled with wonder. Like if it were for me I'd say: "Oh? Who the hell would send me a special delivery?" But my wife's a lady. The second "oh" was one of surprise when I told her that the letter was from the little old acrostic banana. The third "oh" came when she opened the note. "An advance copy," it said, "of my next acrostic. I sincerely hope you can solve it." She frowned at me. "Why do you suppose she did that?"

I wasn't in the mood for supposing. I grabbed the acrostic and hightailed it to Center Street where they have computers that decipher cryptograms, coded messages, and all kinds of stuff like that.

The computer solved the puzzle in three minutes flat, but as smart as that machine was, it couldn't give me an interpretation. When it comes to interpretations my wife and I are smarter than machines.

I showed it to Nora and she drew a blank.

I read it over and over: *X plus too much Y equals death, since neither a found hope nor a lost faith can halt the hour of doom where the sun declines.* I gave Nora a worried look. "I'm batting zero."

"You're in a slump, darling," she said. "Maybe you ought to bench yourself."

I repeated the beginning: *"X plus too much Y equals death.* Read the next line, honey." I closed my eyes and listened.

". . . *since neither a found hope nor a lost faith*—Got that, love?"

I repeated it slowly. "—since neither a found hope, nor a lost faith—" I opened my eyes. "What do you suppose she means, 'a found hope'?"

"What about 'a lost faith'?"

"Yeah. A lost faith. A found hope."

"You can't accuse her of using bad grammar," Nora said.

"What's that got to do with it?"

She shrugged her shoulders. "Nothing. Just that she was very grammatical. She didn't say 'neither or,' she said 'neither *nor.*'"

I felt the hairs on the back of my neck getting bristly. I repeated the line. "'—neither a found hope nor a lost faith.'" I droned on: "'Neither a found hope—neither a found hope—neither a found hope—'" I switched to: "'—nor a lost faith—nor a lost faith—nor a—'" I screamed it. "*Nora!*"

Nora almost jumped out of her chair. "What?"

"'*Nora* lost faith!'"

Nora gulped and said very faintly, "Me?"

The cops were in our living room Monday afternoon. Nora sat on the edge of the couch looking very unhappy. "What am I supposed to do," she complained, "just sit here and wait for the hour of doom?" She pointed to her watch. "That's a scanty five minutes from now."

I said, "Relax, baby."

Crowley said, "There's nothing to worry about, Mrs. Barnes. We've got men stationed all over this building and a stake-out at Miss Trimble's."

Marty said, "Of all the cases I've been on, this is the wackiest. X plus too much Y equals a pain in the neck."

"For your information, Marty," I said, "the X refers to me as an ex-detective. And too much Y means I've asked too many questions. Which adds up to—"

Marty signed me off with: "I know, I know. But what about that 'hour of doom where the sun declines'?"

I wasn't too sure about that part of the acrostic. I figured it was Miss Trimble's way of telling us the action would take place around four thirty. At this time of the year that's about when the sun declines.

The phone rang and Crowley went to answer it. Nora was hoping it was a reprieve from the governor. One of the men who'd been staked out around Miss Trimble's building told us that she had left thirty seconds ago. Nora reacted with a sick gulp and made with a sick joke. "Murder, anyone?"

We checked the time. My watch said four thirty; Marty's, four twenty-nine; Crowley had four thirty-one.

We waited . . . and waited . . . and waited. Zero.

At five thirty the phone rang again. The report was that Miss Trimble just got back to the house. It seems she'd only gone on a little shopping tour.

Marty and Crowley told me off. They'd had enough of my shadow-chasing. Nora told me off, too. She'd had enough of cops, threats, and my profound acrostic interpretations and brain-damaged hunches. I told myself off, then sat in a corner nursing my wounds.

My wife, being the kind of wife she is, soothed my ego with a "can't-win-'em-all" type of remark, kissed the back of my neck, and sent me off to my Monday night poker game. I was glad to go.

It was seven twenty when I left the building. *Had I waited until seven thirty I might have met Teresa Trimble coming in.*

The poker game was at George Bogin's place, a couple of blocks away. His wife was in L.A. so he started the game early. I got there in five minutes.

George looked at me in surprise. "Hey, I thought you weren't coming. I called Nate to take your place."

Nate said, "I'd give you my seat, Hank, but I'm out a hundred and fifty big ones."

"Forget it," I said. "I'll kibitz a while."

George looked at his watch. "I promised to call my wife at four thirty, Hank," he said. "You can take my seat. She'll keep me on the phone for an hour."

I laughed. "You're a little late. It's seven thirty now."

He got up from the table and I sat down.

"Four thirty L.A. time," George explained. "You know Vera. Everything belongs to her. 'Call me at four thirty my time.' You think she'd say, 'Call me at seven thirty your time'? No. *Her* time. I gotta add the three hour difference to her time and subtract it from my time. To make a telephone call I gotta be a mathematician." He slapped my shoulder. "It's a lucky seat."

I picked up a pat straight to the king and my head was buzzing with a jumble of acrostics. The boys were asking me if I could open. I heard myself say, "'—The hour of doom where the sun declines—*where the sun declines!*'" The stark realization hit me like a ten-ton truck. *That dame laid it out! It was four thirty in the West!* I jumped with a convulsive motion that sent the chips flying and leaped for the door, leaving a bunch of surprised poker players.

I don't know how long it took me to cover the distance from George's to my apartment, but when I skidded into the lobby I had very little breath left; just enough to breathe a prayer of thanks that the elevator was there waiting.

I punched the button for the twelfth floor and nothing happened. "Dammit, move!" I punched it again and again. Zero. I lunged for the stairs.

I used to be a fairly good runner in my day, but a mountain climber I never was. Twelve floors to me was a mountain. I ran up that mountain like I'd been doing it for years. I'm still not a mountain climber—a mountain runner, yes.

I made the twelfth floor corridor in time to see Miss Trimble holding a small pistol on Nora in front of the elevator door. Only there was no elevator there—just a deep, empty shaft.

Nora's face was frozen in terror. She didn't see me. Her wide eyes were leveled at the barrel of the gun. Miss Trimble didn't see me either—she was too wrapped up in her game of murder. Needless to say I had to be careful. If I made too much of a thing, the gun might go off or Nora might be shoved down the shaft. Or both.

Miss Trimble was saying: "One so young, so fresh, so pretty should never grow old. But I'm glad I can prevent that." Her face turned to a pout. "Though you did disappoint me. You shouldn't have permitted your charming husband to ask so many questions. You lost faith, Nora. Don't you see that now?"

I moved along the corridor very slowly, thanking the landlord for the thick carpeting. I hoped Miss Trimble didn't hear the wheeze of my breath.

"This is so exciting," she went on. "Composing acrostics used to be dull and uninteresting until I thought of this game. You know, my dear, I wasn't sure I could outwit your husband—but I did." She raised the gun a little higher. Nora's terror-stricken eyes followed it. "Step in, dear," she said. "Just another accident. It wasn't difficult for me to fix that door and still have the elevator go down. A metal contact, that's all. And now the elevator won't even go up. I'm very good at arranging things." She urged her gently. "Take one small step back, dear. Go on—"

Nora was now at the edge of the shaft. So how do you handle it? No time to figure a plan.

"Well, hello, Miss Trimble," I said very quietly.

Nora gasped, and Miss Trimble turned and gave me a surprised, welcome look. "Why, Mr. Barnes," she said. "How nice that we meet again."

I advanced slowly, walking on eggs. The gun was on me. "You look exquisite in that dress," I said. "Like a Dresden doll." I repeated with a little more emphasis: "—a *Dresden doll*."

She was no longer with it. "What a nice thing to say," she said mechanically. "It's been fifty years since I wore this dress . . . It has such—"

Very gently I took the gun from her. She didn't even notice.

"It has such wonderful . . . memories."

Nora swayed. I moved quickly past Miss Trimble and extended my arm to keep her from falling backward into the empty shaft.

"Easy, baby," I said under my breath. Then, in my most suave tone, I said, "We're having Miss Trimble in for tea."

"That reminds me," Miss Trimble said. "My tea man mixed some orange pekoe in my jasmine. He shouldn't have done that."

I agreed with her as we led her to our apartment door.

WILLIAM JEFFREY

The Island

When Flagg was within two hundred yards of the island's leeward shore, he cut off the muted throb of the skiff's ten-horsepower outboard and used the oars to take him the rest of the way in. He grounded the skiff at the corner of a slender strip of gravel beach that gleamed whitely in the darkness—the only spot other than the manmade inlet on the north shore where a boat could be landed safely. He tilted the outboard out of the water, then dragged the small craft into a shelter of pines and thickly-grown ferns. There was no moon, and the stars winked coldly, distantly, in the night sky. It was a few minutes past eleven.

Flagg knew that the island was a quarter mile wide and a half mile long, and he knew all of its contours and contents; Churlak had given him an air reconnaissance map just before Flagg had left San Francisco for Seattle the previous afternoon. He set out to the north, skirting a wooded knoll. Dressed in black clothing and black woolen cap, he was just another shadow etched against the motionless, ebony waters of Rosario Strait.

Several minutes later, using an alternating route through trees and along the rocky shore, he had come around to the inlet where Parish kept his rented, twenty foot inboard-outboard cruiser.

He paused in the pines which ringed the small cove, listening for the dogs. He heard nothing, but that didn't have to mean much. The dogs were Dobermans, a breed that, if properly trained, would strike as silently and as swiftly as a sniper under the cloak of darkness—and Parish's dogs were reputed to be well-trained.

There were two boats tied at the end of the long wooden pier which jutted out like a pointing finger into the cove: the cruiser, and a fourteen foot skiff that was reminiscent of the one in which Flagg had arrived. The skiff undoubtedly belonged to the man named Denman, who was the island's permanent caretaker.

Flagg moved to where he could look upward along the sloping path leading from the pier to the brick-and-pillared main house. It sat high on the bluff which comprised the eastern section of the island, screened by trees. There were no lights that he could see. Silhouetted against the night sky, the house had a Gothic look about it that might have amused Flagg in another situation;

the owner, a Seattle businessman, had built it for his wife in the mid-fifties, the wife had tired of it, and now it was rented to anyone who had enough money and enough desire to want to live on his own private island. Parish had plenty of both, but his reasons went deeper than that—which was why Flagg was here.

He slipped out of the trees, running silently on canvas shoes, keeping to shadow as much as he could. At the base of the pier, he crouched behind a small structure which might have been used as a boathouse. Silence held, except for the soft and serene lapping of water against the wooden pilings, for the cry of a nightbird in the surrounding forest. There was no movement anywhere.

Where were the dogs? Flagg wondered. He had been expecting trouble with them all along, which was the reason he had brought along the hunting knife and the silent, compressed-air gun which were tucked into the utility belt at his waist. He hadn't been worried about Denman; the caretaker went to bed early and let the dogs do his patrolling for him. So where were the dogs?

Flagg pondered the question for a time, and then decided that they were probably after something—ground squirrels, rodents—on the other side of the island. He didn't have time to worry about it. Moving carefully, he edged away from the boathouse and started out along the pier, running bent over to lower his silhouette against the horizon.

When he reached the end of the pier he went to his knees beside the skiff, dropped down into it, and unbolted the engine from the transom. He allowed it to sink into the black water, paused to listen, and then took out the oars and pushed them away. He crawled along to the cruiser and swung into the stern, found the engine compartment, and lifted the housing. It took him ten seconds to remove the rotor and sink it into the water. He lowered the housing, climbed onto the pier again, and ran back to the boathouse. Still there was no sound, no movement.

Flagg stepped out and began to sprint upward along the slope, moving parallel to the crushed oyster-shell path. He had to reach the side gardens now, and the only other way would have been to go through the thick undergrowth between them and the boathouse. He was more vulnerable and exposed this way, but it was quieter and there was less chance of attracting the dogs.

The gardens had been built in tiers, half rock and half shrubbery with strips of grass. They arced around to the northern face of the bluff, ending with a cliff that dropped away to the strait on one side, and small flagstone steps cut into the bluff on the other. Flagg ducked through a hedge and began to scale the narrow, slick steps; from the aerial map, he remembered that they connected with a patio which extended the rear width of the house.

He was halfway up when a muffled and yet explosive report shattered the nocturnal quiet.

Flagg stopped, his right hand on the air gun at his waist. It had been the unmistakably gutty eruption of a shotgun, and the blast had come from above and to his right, a short distance away. He waited another second or two, ears straining, but quiet had settled on the night again. Taking the remaining steps two at a time, he gained the patio and crouched behind a low concrete wall. The air gun was in his hand now, his finger hard against the trigger, and he listened intently.

One ground floor room on his right was lighted, a dim yellow glow spilling through a series of narrow-paned french windows and drawn curtains. The back of the house was otherwise as dark as the front had been. Softly, Flagg trod between the maze of wrought iron garden furniture spread across the patio, coming up to one side of the windows. He peered through the glass and the semi-opaqueness of the curtains.

The room was obviously a study. There was a small, ornately decorated fireplace surrounded by glass-doored bookcases. Niches between the cases were filled with ponderous oil portraits, age having dulled them to the point of obscurity. At the far end of the study was a massive hardwood desk of the Empire period; its surface was taken up with a brass ashtray, a gooseneck lamp with its crown tilted over an electric typewriter. Behind the desk was a padded leather swivel chair, canted to one side, and sitting in the chair was a white-haired, heavy-jawed man Flagg knew to be Eric Parish.

Parish appeared extremely relaxed sitting there, his hands draped loosely in his lap, his head resting gently against the high, open collar of his white shirt. His eyes were open and half-lidded as though filled with sleepiness. The dark, round hole between them leaked blood over the bridge of his nose in a congealing stream.

Flagg put on a pair of thin leather gloves to twist the handle on one of the french doors; it was locked. With the butt of the air gun he broke one of the panes, reached in, and unlatched the door. The sound of the glass breaking hadn't been particularly loud, and the patio remained empty, the night silent. He slipped into the room, stepping around the shards of broken glass now cushioned on the thick carpeting, and crossed hurriedly to the dead man.

In addition to the neat little hole in Parish's forehead, there was a gaping, jagged-edged exit wound the size of a silver dollar that had stained his white hair a dull crimson. Following an imaginary line of trajectory, Flagg found another hole in the wood paneling behind and to one side of Parish. Turning then, he saw the inner door, and it was obvious to him that somebody Parish had known had stood there, perhaps just entering or leaving—and Parish, swiveled in that direction, had been shot before he'd been aware of the threat.

Flagg set about searching both the study and Parish's body. The dead man's wallet, diamond ring, and expensive watch hadn't been touched. The desk drawers were filled with odds and ends, typing paper, a checkbook drawn on a Bellingham bank and showing a large balance in five figures. The electric typewriter still hummed softly, but there were no written or typed papers either on the desk, in the typewriter, or anywhere else in the room. Flagg stood staring down at Parish with a tight feeling of frustration and impotent anger in his throat.

The assignment had somehow gotten screwed up before he'd even been able to start it. Parish's death in itself wasn't regrettable; it was the fact that the papers were missing which made it as bad as it was.

Parish had been one of the Organization's top men in the Washington, D.C., area for a number of years, living the fat-cat life in Alexandria, Virginia. Then there had been a death in one of the Families, and a subsequent struggle for control; new leaders with new brooms had come on the scene, and Parish had suddenly found himself in danger of being swept out by young blood with stronger organizational ties. Embittered and vengeful, Parish had denounced the Circle and had then dropped out of sight.

Shortly afterward, the Organization had learned through informants that he was planning to write a book. *The* book, the biggest and the most volatile yet, naming names and including documentation not only of past history but of current operations as well. Considering his position in the nation's capital, his revelations would have caused a scandal of unprecedented proportions, and nobody on either side of the legal fence wanted that to happen.

But Parish had been hard to find. He'd planned well, coming cross-country and renting a cruiser and this island hideaway by proxy. The island was one of the smallest in a series between the coast of Washington and the southern tip of Vancouver Island. Volcanic in origin, some of the islands were quite large— such as Orcas Island, which had seven small communities on it. Others were unnamed vacation spots only big enough for one or two houses, and were the exclusive retreats for the well-to-do of nearby Seattle and Bellingham.

The waters surrounding the islands were frigid and treacherous, a mixture of currents from the Strait of Juan de Fuca and the Strait of Georgia. The mainland could be reached only by boat, either private or the twice-daily ferry which plied between Sidney, British Columbia, and Anacortes, Washington. Eric Parish had found the perfect location at which to write his book without interference—or so he'd thought.

With the word out, and thousands of informants looking for him, his hiding place had finally been pinpointed in spite of all his precautions. The Washington, D.C., branch of the Organization had immediately contacted the head of the West Coast Security Division, a man named Churlak; and Churlak had assigned Flagg, his primary troubleshooter.

Flagg had rented a car in Seattle and driven to Anacortes, then had taken the morning ferry to Orcas Island and driven around to the opposite side to the hamlet of Doebay, the nearest port to Parish's island. Arrangements had already been made with a Northwest contact, and Flagg had found a boat waiting for him there, all the gear he would need, and an assurance that Parish was home. He had waited until ten o'clock and then he had begun the cold, silent crossing.

The idea hadn't been to kill Parish; his sudden death might have caused more trouble in the long run than the book itself, especially if Parish had managed to cover himself with some sort of insurance. The Organization hadn't even been overly concerned with the publication of a book—books were always being written about the Organization—just as long as that one dealt only with past matters and with nothing happening now in areas like the nation's capital. Flagg's mission was merely to talk to Parish, to convince him that he was vulnerable no matter where he hid, to persuade him to hand over his notes and papers. Failing that, Flagg had been instructed to take all documentation one way or another.

Only now somebody else had gotten to Parish and to the papers first. Why? And who? And what had been the significance of the shot Flagg had heard as he was climbing the outside steps? It had been a shotgun blast, all right—*not* a small-caliber weapon of the type which had killed Parish. . . .

Flagg moved across the study to the door, and went down a short hallway. Darkness and silence filled the massive house. He glided through the down-stairs rooms—parlor, kitchen, pantry, servants' quarters—and found no sign of anyone. A curving staircase led up to the second floor bedrooms, and a quick search there yielded him nothing either.

Downstairs again, Flagg went to the front entrance, slipped through onto a wide verandah cluttered with wicker chairs and settees, with ferns and plants in narrow boxes. To one side of the house, set into the trees, was a smaller dwelling, obviously the caretaker's cottage. A dim light burned in a room on the facing side, casting pale illumination at the edges of the night; it hadn't been on when he'd looked up at the house from the inlet earlier.

With the air gun clenched tightly in his fist, Flagg moved down off the porch and made his way across to a large alder which grew a few feet from the front door. He paused there, watching, listening. After a time he moved forward, put his back to the wall next to the door. The cottage was quiet—too quiet. Flagg reached out with his left hand and rotated the knob on the door, felt it turn. He set himself, shoved open the door, and went into the cottage in a low crouch, the gun leveled and ready.

A tall, thin man lay in the middle of the circular living room rug, sprawled on his back; his head had been nearly severed from his body. The wall behind him was peppered with buckshot, spattered with blood and bone and brain. Flagg kicked the door shut and went through the cottage quickly. It was empty save for the dead man, and there was no sign of the missing papers.

He went out through the rear door. Just beyond the cottage, on a bed of pine needles and leaf mold, he discovered the reason why he hadn't been bothered by the dogs; the two sleek, black Dobermans lay twenty feet from one another, stiff and dead. They had each been shot once in the head with the same type of gun that had killed Parish.

Flagg worked his tongue over dry lips, and moved away in the shadows, to the side of the brick-and-pillared mansion. He stood in darkness there, letting thoughts run free in his mind, trying to put it all together. Parish dead; Denman dead; the dogs dead. Parish and the Dobermans shot with a handgun, the caretaker with a shotgun? Who? And why?

Well, all right. There were no answers to those questions just yet. He had to look at it from the standpoint of what he *did* know, of what seemed logical. To begin with, whoever had been responsible for the carnage tonight had been after the papers and notes for Parish's book, for some as yet unknown reason. Flagg would have found them if it had been otherwise; Parish would have had them by the typewriter, where he'd obviously been working when he was shot. Flagg knew, too, that Parish had apparently been killed by someone he knew—a house guest, maybe—and that it was unlikely, owing to the contours of the island, that another boat of requisite size could be secreted along the shoreline.

That meant the killer had very likely been planning to use either Parish's cruiser or the caretaker's skiff to make his escape—and since Flagg had disabled both craft, the killer, and the papers, were still somewhere on the island.

Flagg had to believe that was the way it was; if it were any other way, there was nothing he could do. His first thought was to check the cove. He moved away from the house again and ran silently to the path and down it, letting darkness camouflage him. Crouched at the bole of an oak, he looked out at the pier, at the near-motionless boats tied there. Nothing stirred.

Flagg swore mentally. Now what? The killer could be anywhere, hiding, waiting, searching. He had no idea how well the guy—assuming it was a man—knew the island. One thing was certain, though: if the killer had intended to use one of the craft out there, and had come down here to find them disabled, he had to know that there was someone else on the island besides himself; someone alive and with a purpose.

What would *he* do, then?

He wouldn't know who Flagg was, or why he was on the island, but he would have to know that the intruder had come by boat—the only boat that was operable now. There was only one thing he *could* do: search out and appropriate Flagg's craft.

The search could take a matter of minutes, if the guy knew the island, or an hour or more if he didn't; but eventually he was bound to find the gravel beach and the hidden skiff. If he were able to do that before Flagg found him—if he were able to make good his escape with Parish's papers—Flagg would be trapped on an island with two dead men, and a mission in ruin.

He crossed the path running, and plunged into the dense woods, moving as fast as he could in darkness and unfamiliar surroundings. The forest was oddly silent, save for an occasional rustling of an animal or a bird, and somehow it gave the impression of vastness far out of proportion to its size. Flagg knew that misdirection was an immediate danger, and he tried to keep the murmuring of the ocean strong in his right ear, an infrequent glimpse of the mansion visible over his left shoulder—due south in as straight a line as possible. The house remained jagged and dark against the paler night sky, but the forest seemed to continue endlessly through a series of small slopes and valleys, thick with brush and trees. The evergreens took on strange shapes as urgency grew inside him and the slender strip of beach failed to appear.

Flagg topped a knoll, thinking that it could be the one he had skirted earlier after beaching the skiff, but beyond it was a higher elevation, rocky and densely grown. He came down off the hill, crossed the brief valley below, and scrambled upward again through several gnarled oaks growing bent from the wind. When he had reached the crest, breathing heavily, he saw the beach below him, clear and empty and still gleaming a faint white.

He worked moisture through his mouth, peering into the darkness. He saw nothing. As rapidly and as silently as he was able, he went down the hill to the beach, clawing at the earth with his hands, grasping plants and saplings to maintain his balance. In spite of his efforts at stealth, a shower of loose stones and dirt cascaded with him. He reached the bottom, then eased around an outcropping of rock until he saw where he had dragged the skiff into shelter. The craft was still there—untouched.

Ten feet beyond the end of the beach was a marshy hollow, filled with thorn bushes and young firs—a place to hide, a place to wait. Flagg started there, the compressed-air gun held in close to his body. He was two steps away when a massive explosion, a brilliant flash of fragmented light, erupted on his right.

Bits of earth and splintered tree branches and shrubbery peppered his lower body along with the buckshot, a stinging rain of it like shrapnel from a burst hand grenade. The shock straightened him up for an instant; then, reflexively, he threw himself into the hollow, rolling, scrambling along wet earth into the bramble thicket.

The killer had been there all along, waiting at some vantage point in the bush; he hadn't wanted to leave a witness of any kind, and he had likely wanted to know who Flagg was, and those were the things that had kept him on the island. Flagg's heart thudded painfully against his ribs as he turned his body on the moist ground. His gun was gone, lost in the first shock of impact or in his wild dive for cover. The killer had the shotgun and the handgun he'd used on Parish and the dogs; Flagg had nothing now except the hunting knife sheathed at his belt.

He lifted his right hand and eased it downward. His torso was bloody, the knife was bloody, but he knew that the full force of the shotgun blast had missed him. He drew the knife, wiped the haft on his trouser leg, and gripped it tightly in his right hand, waiting.

He could hear the killer stalking him, coming to end it.

Covered with mud, leaves, twigs, Flagg lay motionless so as not to betray his position. His only chance was that the guy would not be familiar with jungle-type fighting, that he would be overconfident after that first almost point-blank shot. It was difficult to see anyone lying motionless in a pocket of darkness, and Flagg was counting on that, on the element of surprise.

The killer came out of the thick brush on the hillside, a few feet below where Flagg had stood at the moment the shotgun erupted. He was less than ten yards from where Flagg now lay. In his left hand he carried a leather briefcase, with a single-barrel shotgun crooked down in the elbow; in his right was a small automatic, held up and ready. His eyes ranged the brush. Flagg waited until the man's body was half turned away from him, and then he raised up fluidly and threw the hunting knife.

The overhand pitch was hard and it was true, and the blade flashed through the darkness and disappeared into the killer's exposed right side just below the ribs. His body stiffened in a rigid pose. Flagg was already on his feet and rushing forward. He caught the haft of the knife just as the killer began to sag at the middle. The blade came free cleanly. The man turned, facing Flagg fully, their eyes only inches apart. There was a look of astonishment in the pain-washed glance, then dull emptiness. He fell into a small heap, staring sightlessly upward.

For the first time since the sprayed buckshot had struck his body, Flagg felt pain across his own right side, his stomach. The front of his black sweater was stained darkly with blood, and there was enough of it so that tiny streams flowed downward over his trousers, but he knew he wasn't badly hurt, that none of the wounds was deep. He would be able to patch himself up with strips of cloth until he could get to a safe doctor.

He knelt, hurting, pulled the dropped briefcase to him and opened the catches. There was a pencil flash in his utility belt, and he used that to examine the contents: Parish's notes, all right, and several pages of typescript for the projected book.

He put the flash on the dead man's face and body. He was tall and thin, like the other dead man in the caretaker's cottage. Flagg turned him slightly and went through his pockets. There was a wallet there and inside it a California driver's license issued to a Thomas Sanders; but the face that looked back at Flagg from the photograph was *not* the face of the killer.

Flagg returned the wallet to the dead man's pocket, stood up with the briefcase held in his right hand. He was thinking about the dogs, the two dead Dobermans lying twenty feet apart behind the caretaker's cottage; and he was thinking about how those dogs—and Eric Parish—had died of handgun wounds, while the man in the cottage had had his face blown away with a shotgun. It began to make sense for him then. A pair of trained Dobermans, like Parish, would not have allowed anyone near enough to them to fire a single bullet into each brain unless they knew that someone and trusted him— and the only other man on the island whom they would have known and trusted was Denman, the caretaker.

It was Denman, then, who lay dead at his feet.

The man in the cottage was a ringer, maybe an acquaintance of Denman's, maybe a drifter Denman had lured out to the island on some pretext or other; someone with the same general build as the island's caretaker, someone to be found without a face and carrying Denman's wallet. It had been a clumsy effort at best, but then men like Denman, taking one big gamble for the brass ring, weren't always rational.

Flagg figured Denman had discovered what Parish was doing on this island, who he really was, and had learned also of the incriminating papers and notes which Parish had brought with him. Maybe he had believed he could sell them back to the Organization—or to the government, if they were willing to make a cash offer. In any case, he had evolved his plan and had put it into operation on this night.

He had killed the dogs first, sometime earlier in the evening, maybe telling Parish that he was target-shooting to cover the sounds of the shots. Then he had lured the ringer out to the island and installed him in his cottage. Later, he had entered the mansion, and the study, killed Parish, and then returned to the cottage and used the shotgun on the ringer. All nice and neat, he must have thought; an unexplainable, and therefore unsolvable, double murder on a lonely Northwest island; a case to baffle the police for years if they accepted the prima facie evidence that the second dead man was in fact the caretaker. Denman could have gone anywhere afterward, using the ringer's identification, to put the papers on the market to the highest bidder.

Flagg turned away from Denman, found the compressed-air gun where he'd first been struck by the buckshot, and tucked it away in his belt. Then he limped slowly to where he had secreted the skiff, and put the briefcase in the stern. He managed to drag the craft into the waters of the strait, to lower the outboard and get it started.

The police were going to be baffled, he knew. When the bodies were discovered, as they would be one of these days by some curious local, the police would *really* have a mystery on their hands, one that would very probably receive national attention and be written up in one of those true-crime magazines. But that wasn't Flagg's problem; he had done the job he came to do, and that was all that mattered.

He pointed the skiff's bow at Doebay and slipped away into the night.

HAL ELLSON

Room to Let

Rain spattered the sill of the window where she stood, her gray eyes angry and her chin out-thrust. Forlorn drops sounded a dirge beyond the curtain and glass; she didn't hear it, didn't notice the dreary street dropping swiftly toward the river. They were carrying the stretcher down the high stoop without trouble, for the dead man weighed no more than a stick.

The bloody bugger cheated me, thought Mrs. Flynn, her gaze on the gray blanket. Not a cent to his name and owing me for his room. She shook her head and watched the stretcher slide into the morgue wagon, the door slam, attendant and driver in black gleaming raincoats wave to the policeman standing by and climb into the wagon. As the wagon drove off, the policeman glanced up at the house and walked away, head thrust against the wind of the wild March day.

"Well, that's that," said Mrs. Flynn aloud, turning from the window and hustling on her short fat legs for the hall door. Only one flight to the empty room above, but she was wheezing through her pinched nostrils when she reached it. The door was still ajar, the room brackish with shadow, silent and hollow as a shell. Another woman would have hesitated before entering, but not Mrs. Flynn. She went in like the March wind blowing across the world outside and quickly did what had to be done, sweeping the room, stripping the bed and making it anew, with no thought at all for her late departed roomer.

The wind rattled the window as she finished, rain flailed the glass. Even the bloody elements are against me, she thought, for she was a greedy one and her greed couldn't wait.

Now out of the room she swept and down the stairs. There was the sign in the vestibule which had to be hung no matter the weather. Stooping, she snatched it up and opened the outer door to be met with a rush of wind and icy rain that took her breath but didn't stop her. Out she stepped onto the proud high stoop of the decaying brownstone, hung the sign on its appointed hook, and popped back into the vestibule shaking herself like a wet hen. It was done now, the bait set for the proper fish. The trouble was the terrible March weather.

From a front window, peering through a gray curtain, she watched the desolate street which was now half obscured by a blinding fall of icy sleet. Finally out of the dim veil a man appeared. Once at the house, he stopped and looked up, caught by the creaking music of the sign swinging wildly in the wind. Moments later up the steps he came and rang the bell. The door swung open in his face and there stood Mrs. Flynn, chin thrust out, sharp eye probing him.

"I saw your sign," he began.

"I've a room to let," she answered quickly, noting his clothes which were neat enough, but not quality. "Will you look at it?"

"I will, but first . . ."

"It'll be ten a week if you like it, payment in advance."

He grinned at this and said, "I'll take a quick look if you don't mind."

She led him up the stairs, showed him the room, bed, bureau, lamp, and closet, making no excuses for the cracked ceiling and ancient wallpaper.

"A good old fashioned room. Very comfortable," he observed.

"You'll have it?"

"I've already taken it," he said and out came his wallet, well worn but of good leather and well accommodated with bills, one of which he deftly plucked from among the others and handed to her.

"That should keep me for ten weeks," he said, smiling when he saw her eyes light up. "Unless you raise the ante."

"Ten it is and ten it'll be," she answered quickly, not wanting to lose one like this. "I'm Mrs. Flynn, and what did you say your name was? I'll need it for the receipts."

"John Walker, and you can forget the receipts."

"Ah, you're too trusting. I'll slip them under your door, or I wouldn't rest."

"If it'll make you feel better," he said, moving to the door. "I'm going for my bag."

She followed him down the stairs and shivered at the front door. "A terrible day," she observed. "Maybe you'll have a spot of tea before you go out in that?"

"Thanks. Maybe when I get back," he answered and left.

Back to her place at the window she flew to watch him vanish in the swirling veil of snow that was falling now. The mad March day no longer mattered, for this time she had the right one, a roomer with money actually in his possession.

John Walker returned in half an hour, looking like a snowman, and she was waiting, pot, cups, saucers, best silver and linen there in the high-ceilinged parlor. "Put your bag down and come in," she said, taking his arm.

He laughed and allowed himself to be led through the folding door. "Very nice," he remarked of the room as she poured. "Very pleasant."

"A bit old fashioned, but I like it," she answered, handing him his cup and saucer.

It was good dark tea, steaming and almost black, demanding sugar and cream, which he added and stirred. Then he raised his eyes to see her smiling at him.

"Nothing like a good cup of proper tea on a day like this," she said. "I was afraid it wouldn't fetch you."

"Oh, but it does, especially the way you make it."

"Without no dirty little teabag floating in a bit of tinted water," she laughed, slapping her thigh. "Now mind you, drink that while it's hot."

It was a good beginning, exactly the way she'd wanted it, and now she gave thanks to the madness of the day outside; the snow had stopped and freezing rain slashed at the windows again.

Tea's the grand beverage, thought Mrs. Flynn, recalling Mr. Walker's sudden shyness when she offered to bring a cup to his room now and then. The pleasure was all hers, for the man in him had conceded to comfort. That was part of the plan, to keep him happy as a bird while she went about the business of discovering what she wanted to know.

But Mr. Walker, pleasant and outgoing as he was, didn't reveal himself so easily for all his willingness to talk at length and sit to two and three cups of fine Irish tea. Nor did his room give up any secret about himself, though she fine-combed it daily for the evidence she wanted before acting.

It was his money she was after, and he had it. She was as sure of that as of the sun coming up each day, but where was he keeping it? Not in the bank. He wasn't the type. She was convinced of that.

For four weeks she pursued her routine, waiting till he left the house in the morning, then running up the stairs with broom and duster to clean and search, but to no avail. He kept no money in his room.

On the fifth week she gave up searching. At the end of the sixth week she had decided to send him packing when she found the money she was sure he had, neatly tucked in his extra shoes and covered by a pair of dirty socks. Out it came, ten crisp hundred dollar bills which she counted twice with trembling hands.

"Ah! I knew it," she moaned and counted the money again for the pleasure of counting. Then went below for a cup of tea and to make preparations. It was April now, a fine day with the warm fresh fever of spring in the air, which was not to her liking. But at times April is as daft as March and by afternoon the air grew raw and the balmy air freshened till by dark it was battering the city in wild gusts.

Mrs. Flynn waited at the window, but Mr. Walker didn't show at his regular time. It was ten when he finally plodded up the high stoop and opened the door.

"Ah, it's Mr. Walker, and late and chilly you are," she greeted him in the hall. "Your tea's waiting and steaming."

But for once he refused. He was tired, he said, a bad day, and went up the stairs to his room.

The first time he refused her tea. It was a bad sign. Later, she heard him descend the stairs and out he went. The door closed with a dismal sound and opened again ten seconds later.

She flew to the folding door and pushed it aside. "Something wrong, Mr. Walker?"

"Nothing at all," he said, starting to mount the stairs and halting with a frown on his face.

"What is it, Mr. Walker?"

"I'm leaving tomorrow," he said. "For Chicago."

"You're joking," she said, turning pale.

"I wish I were, but I'm not. Well, it was a pleasant stay."

"Ah, then, a last cup of tea," she said desperately.

"Thanks, but it'll keep me awake. I've got to be up for an early start," he replied, starting up the stairs again.

"For old times sake," she called after him. "And it won't keep you awake. You'll sleep like a baby."

He paused again, smiled, and said, "Well, then," and came down the stairs.

She poured for him in the high-ceilinged parlor and they chatted a while. Then he went above, with the tea she'd poisoned already doing its work.

By morning he was dead. "A fine man," she said as they carried him down the high stoops under a gray blanket. Then she handed the policeman his coat, bag, and a pack of cigarettes. "Not much," she said. "But, then, he doesn't need much where he's going."

"That's right," the policeman answered and out of the hall he went. The stretcher was already in the wagon. The policeman descended the stoop, handed over coat and bag and watched the morgue wagon move off, then walked away.

Mrs. Flynn closed the door and flew up the stairs to her late tenant's room. Panting, she entered it and went to the closet. There were the shoes she hadn't given up, with the dirty socks still stuffed in them. Greedily, she snatched them up and pulled out the socks, but the money was gone.

Took it with him, he did. Why didn't I look through his pockets before I called the police? She groaned and went below, sick with her terrible mistake, but not too sick for a cup of tea.

She poured for herself, sat for a while in the high-ceilinged parlor, then got up and went out on the stoop to hang her deadly sign once more—ROOM TO LET.

AL NUSSBAUM

The One Who Got Away

It was Saturday evening and I was standing beside the line of traffic coming from Tijuana. As each car stopped beside me, I asked the occupants the usual questions: "Where were you born?" and "Are you bringing anything back with you?"

Once in a while I'd check a truck or tell a driver to pull over for a closer examination, but I didn't do it often. I only did it when we'd had a tip from an informer, or the people seemed exceptionally gay and friendly, or I had one of my hunches. I didn't have many hunches, but they'd proved correct in almost every case, so I always paid attention to them.

When I saw Jack Wilner I had a hunch he was up to something. He was in one of the opposite lanes, heading into Mexico behind the wheel of a shiny yellow convertible. The top was down and the blaring radio was tuned to a San Diego rock station. The whole thing seemed too showy—like a magician's antics when misdirecting his audience.

It was the beginning of my shift—I was working the eight P.M. to four A.M. tour—so I made a note of his license number with the intention of giving him a good going-over when he came back.

I watched carefully for the car, but it didn't return before I went off duty. I gave the other customs officers copies of the license number and a description of the car, and went home.

By the next night I had almost forgotten about the yellow convertible, but the following Saturday evening I saw it again. The top was down, the radio was blasting, and it was on its way to Tijuana as before. I had the same feeling as I'd had the first time. I ran to the telephone and called the *aduana*, the Mexican customhouse, and asked them to check out the convertible.

When I got back to the traffic lane, I saw in the distance that the convertible had already been pulled over. Khaki-uniformed men swarmed around it, and a couple of them were busy removing door panels, while others checked the trunk and beneath the hood. Jack Wilner—of course, I didn't know his name then—stood to one side, nonchalantly smoking a cigarette. He was tall and thin, and even from far away I could see that he dressed with a youthful disregard for color.

I got busy with the cars coming into the country and didn't look over that way again for almost an hour. When I did, I was just in time to see the convertible as it pulled away from the *aduana*. Wilner turned to wave goodbye to the Mexican officers lined up watching him, then picked up speed.

So, they had found nothing. In that case, I reasoned, he must be smuggling something *into* the United States, so I watched for him to return. I stayed around a little after my shift was over and gave out the car's description and license number again. I asked everyone to be sure to pass the description and number to the next shift, if one of them didn't stop him.

Monday and Tuesday were my days off, but I called the customhouse both nights to see if the convertible had been checked out yet. It hadn't—and that's the way it went the rest of the week. The convertible didn't pass our border station.

But on Saturday evening I looked across the far lanes, and there it was, heading into Mexico again.

I watched it with my mouth hanging open and then mentally kicked myself for being so stupid. Just because he'd left the country at this point didn't mean he had to return at this point. Mexico and California shared over a hundred miles of border, and there were many places where he could cross back into the United States.

Up until now, my inquiry into the activities of the driver of the yellow convertible had been just that—*my* inquiry. That wasn't good enough any more. I went to my supervisor and told him about my hunch, and he sent out notices to all the other checkpoints along the California-Mexico border. A customs officer has to rely on informers and instinct. Informers account for ninety percent of his arrests, but hunches like mine provide the other ten percent.

I went back to my post and waited. We were supposed to be notified once the convertible had been searched, but we received no word. None.

Then on Saturday evening, at the height of the traffic rush, I saw the yellow convertible heading into Mexico again.

At first we thought it had checked out all right, and the people at its crossing point hadn't bothered to let us know. My supervisor decided to be sure, though, and sent out a call to find out where the car had crossed back into the States.

In half an hour he had the answer—nowhere. None of the official crossing points had seen the car.

Somewhere along the hundred-mile border, Wilner had found a way to slip across without stopping for a customs check. He was able to drive into Mexico, load the car with whatever contraband he cared to, and return to the United States without worrying about paying duty or fearing arrest. We had to find out where the hole was and plug it up.

A telephone call to the motor vehicles bureau gave us Jack Wilner's name and San Diego address. A twenty-four hour watch was set up on his apartment, and we went back to waiting. Wilner was away until Wednesday, then he parked his yellow convertible in his carport and went inside.

Except for shopping and normal housekeeping trips, he remained at home until Saturday evening. Then he drove across the border into Mexico while a car filled with customs agents followed fifty yards behind him. I watched the little parade from my post and felt pleased. I was confident we had him hooked and would soon reel him in.

But I was wrong. An hour later the agents returned. They had been trapped in the traffic on Avenida Revolucion when he had made a sudden turn near the Jai Alai Fronton.

They had lost him.

I was disappointed, and they were angry. They were certain his maneuver had been deliberate, so they applied for a warrant to search his car when he returned. If they found so much as a marijuana seed, Wilner was in trouble.

I was given a special permission to accompany the agents and was on the scene when Wilner returned to his apartment on Wednesday. It was obvious, from the way his jaw fell when they presented the warrant, that he hadn't lost his followers intentionally on Saturday. Until the warrant was thrust in front of him, he hadn't known he was suspected of anything.

We went over his car and found it spotless—literally spotless. It must have been cleaned recently, both inside and out, because even the ashtrays were empty. Wilner watched us take the car apart and put it together again, but he wasn't as much at ease as he had been that day at the border. He kept licking his lips and shifting his weight from foot to foot. As far as he knew, the search at the border had been routine, but this certainly wasn't. We were on the scent of something, and he must have known we'd keep after him until we found it.

That's why I was amazed to see him drive into Mexico on Saturday evening. I was even more surprised to see him stop voluntarily at the *aduana* and go inside. We learned later from the agents following him that he'd applied for a residence permit and took care of all the other paperwork necessary for an extended stay in Mexico. He wouldn't be coming back for a while; he was even more frightened than I'd figured.

I thought about Wilner a lot during the following months. In my mind he was the one who got away. In all the time I had been in the customs service, he was the first man who had eluded arrest when I was sure he was a smuggler.

I didn't see Jack Wilner again for over a year, and then I had to go to Mexico to do it. Every spring there's a yacht race from Newport Beach to Ensenada. There are always between three and four hundred boats in the race and they draw a huge crowd to witness the finish. I drove down to see it and found Jack Wilner standing alone not ten feet from me.

I walked over to him and touched him on the arm. "Hi!" I said. "Remember me?"

He gave me a hesitant smile, then it slipped away as he remembered. His eyeballs jerked as he searched the crowd for more so-called familiar faces.

"I just came down to see the race," I said. "Running into you wasn't planned."

That eased his nervousness and he relaxed visibly. We stood side by side and watched the boats. As the day wore on, he become more friendly and told me a little about himself. He was the owner of a small hotel and marina about twenty miles south of Tijuana, and he was in Ensenada to look at a few boats he was thinking of buying. He invited me to stop at his place sometime.

"Did you buy it with your profits from smuggling?" I asked boldly. I wanted to get him to talk about it, and I was sure he never would if I tried to be clever and circuitous.

He smiled with surprise at my directness. "I don't want to sign a statement," he said, imitating a TV villain. Then, after a few moments, he nodded. "Yes, that's how I got the money to buy it."

"You're not smuggling any more?"

"No."

"That's hard to believe," I said. "You must've been pretty successful to afford a business, and few professional smugglers quit before being caught."

"I'd made up my mind to quit if anyone became curious about me. You people were too curious, so I quit."

We bought tacos from a street vendor and stood eating them.

"In that case, you won't mind telling me how you managed to return to California without being noticed when all the border stations were watching for you," I said.

"No, I don't mind. It was easy. I simply stuck my license plates under my jacket and walked back across the border," he said with a grin. "I was smuggling yellow convertibles, a new one every week."

BRYCE WALTON

Unidentified and Dead

Suddenly Fred Nebel was cold sober and heading through a Saturday morning blur to the telephone. Only the name of Rudy Weldon had been released in the special news bulletin that had touched off Nebel's grieving drunk. The bulletin had said that all the passengers had been killed, but it hadn't mentioned any other names, nor the number of passengers.

Good God, why had he assumed so quickly and unquestioningly that his wife was one of them? You don't just assume a thing like that, he thought guiltily as he dialed. You ought to make very sure first.

Patiently, the woman at the Los Angeles *Daily News* said, "Sorry, we can't release a list of casualties until completed identification, and notification of next of kin."

"But my wife could have been on that plane. Luella Nebel."

"Only four passengers have been tentatively identified. Your wife's name isn't among the four."

"There were more than four?"

"Yes."

"What information *can* you give me?"

"The crash occurred three hours ago," she seemed to read from a teletype. "The two-engined Beechcraft exploded and burned. The remains of the victims are being removed to the chapel of A. Ribesto and Sons in Ten Palms where identification will be completed. The sole witness of the disaster, a sheepherder named Steve Myerson, reported that the plane seemed to lose altitude approaching the San Padres Hills, and crashed and burst into flames a few hundred yards from Myerson's house. It is believed that the plane may have been overloaded. So far, only four of the seven passengers have been identified, and—"

"Thank you," Nebel cut in, "thank you very much." He almost laughed as he hung up. Ironic that the one among all of Luella's eccentricities he had found the least tolerable should now furnish the joyful assurance that she was alive. He had been surprised to find out that Luella was very superstitious about black cats, ladders, broken mirrors, unlucky numbers. Her psychiatrist had said she needed a belief in magic because people had failed her. But Nebel wouldn't fail her. Maybe her fear of the unlucky number, seven, hadn't failed her.

She wouldn't have been the seventh passenger. After being married to Luella for a year, he knew *that* much at least about his wife.

He put through a long distance call to Rudy Weldon's number near Ten Palms, and sat listening to the distant nervous buzzing. He sat still, eyes closed. But the lids couldn't shut out the image of Luella projected by his brain. He stared guiltily at the torn bits of paper on the rug, the note Luella had written him saying she was going to Rudy Weldon's for the weekend, that he wasn't to get jealous, that she was just too bored, that they might fly up to Big Bear in Rudy's new sportsplane, and cheers. He'd gotten mad, very mad, before he could help it. And then he'd gotten drunk.

The buzzing continued. His eyes strained, searched as if his life depended on some absolutely necessary answer. He poured a pony glass of bourbon. He'd never drunk much until the last few months—

"Sorry. You want us to keep trying and call you back?"

His mouth sagged. His eyes pleaded with the phone, a tense and frightened look. "Yes, of course, keep trying."

He stood up. He refused to believe that Luella was—dead. She wouldn't have gone on that flight. Her behavior was too erratic and irresponsible for him to have expected her to call him. No one had answered at the Weldon house, but that didn't necessarily mean that everyone guesting there had gone on that flight. Not at all. Those who hadn't gone had undoubtedly left the premises by now and who would blame them? Luella might be in Ten Palms. She might be comforting bereaved friends and relatives. She might be very upset and needing him.

He tried to call the chapel of A. Ribesto and Sons in Ten Palms but the phone was busy, and when he did get through no one would talk with him.

He demanded to know why they just didn't check the guest list at the Weldon house against the number of passengers. If there had been only seven guests, then that would mean that all of them had gone on the flight. They would have a list of the casualties. But it wasn't quite so simple, it seemed.

"Friends and relatives might assume wrongly," the woman said. "Identification must be positive before we can release such a casualty list." She said something else about moral responsibility.

Nebel sat like a forlorn passenger in a station waiting room. He was a big man turning gray, and his mild meaty face was drawn tight with puzzled anxiety. Because he could not stand the strain of waiting, he decided he would drive out to Ten Palms. Rudy Weldon's hacienda was on the way. As he started for the door, the phone rang. "Hello!" Nebel shouted. "Hello!"

"Go ahead, please," the operator said.

A woman's faint voice said, "Go ahead, dear? Please name it. I'm sure I've been there."

A frantic sort of syllogism scurried speciously through Nebel's brain. The voice was that of a drunken woman. Luella got drunk at places like the Weldons'. Luella was a woman. This woman could be Luella.

"Luella?" he said.

He heard the throb of a dead line. He called again. There was no answer. Fighting a draining weariness, he went out the back door, across the yard past the barbecue pit to the garage. The housing tract's supermarket dome was dirtied by glinting April sunlight.

The solid heavy slam of his big conventional car door was comforting. He tried to ignore the oily emptiness left by the absence of Luella's MG. He hadn't approved of that MG. He didn't approve of sportscars. They suggested reckless abandon, made him uneasy. Luella drove hers as if she didn't give a damn about her life or anyone else's. Once she had said she cared about as much for life as for the long white beard of God, which turned out to be a quotation from Baudelaire. She did care, of course. Luella's psychiatrist said she did. He said Luella's self-destructive drive stemmed from self contempt, a feeling of unworthiness. She tested everybody and everything. "Will he love me in spite of what I do? Does fate love me enough to spare me no matter how much I push my luck?"

Without that psychiatrist, Nebel would know from nothing about his own wife. He respected her psychiatrist. Everything turned into simple, easy to understand, incontrovertible logic. It was comforting to know that an authority seemed optimistic about Luella's chances for improvement, and an early escape from her deep emotional disturbances.

He had met her at that rather wild party—the sort of party he almost never attended—and married her three days later. She had seemed so lovely, young, charming, and witty. No one could have guessed how much emotional disturbance lay behind such a beautiful mask. The complexity . . .

Nebel was a cautious driver who took his own skill for granted, and regarded every other vehicle and pedestrian in sight as a potential menace. But only halfway along the straight, sunglazed desert stretch to Ten Palms, between arid sandstone buttes and cactus-studded gullies, he noticed with a numbing sort of shock that the speedometer registered ninety-seven miles per hour. And the needle was still climbing.

Something entirely new and terribly alien happened to Nebel. His familiar, controlled self seemed to recede and there was a sense of thrill, of doom, of awful necessity. He wanted to laugh out his defiance of caution and reason. There was a wild sense of surrender to something, and his face suddenly shone with sweat.

He had been driving in a sort of daze, a suspension of feeling. A dreamlike distortion settled over things. The desert with its monotonous landscape gave no impression of movement. Air whooshed. Metal faintly throbbed. Cars that he passed effortlessly seemed to stand still. Detachment, distortion, the nightmare feeling of watching himself heading into disaster, helpless, a sort of onlooker who knew he was a great deal more . . .

The ribbon of desert road seemed to expand, extend into infinity, dipped down through glittering mirages. The needle passed the hundred mark . . .

Nebel remained parked in the shade of yucca trees beside the road for some time. He could still hear the warning echoes of his own yells in his ears. He rubbed at his eyes, then jerked his hand away as if he had been caught in an act of weakness.

It wasn't just the whisky, tension, fatigue. Something else waited, a madness inside of him—kin to Luella's, perhaps—which he had never suspected before.

Again he drove with slow caution—all the way to Rudy Weldon's adobe hacienda. But his caution wasn't the same. Now it was self-conscious. And with every mile a tautness stretched in him to squeaking tension. As if he were one of those trick cyclists he had once, as a kid, seen pedaling along a high tightwire.

Luella's blue MG wasn't among the other sportscars parked in the court-yard. He exhaled a long sigh of affirmed relief. He even felt good when it occurred to him that perhaps Luella hadn't come out to Weldon's at all. She could merely have said she was coming out here for the weekend. She knew how he despised that wild, existential bunch who sat around candlelit tables reading Baudelaire and smoking tea. Her psychiatrist had explained how, because she felt unworthy of it, she would go to extremes to test Nebel's love.

But her car's not being here meant one thing definitely—that if she had been here she hadn't left in Rudy's sportsplane.

Nebel considered driving on into Ten Palms. No, he had better at least check, see if Luella had been here at all, and if she had been here, to find out where she had gone.

As he walked through flowered cactus and up onto the wide, columned porch a quick breath of hot air seemed to dry out his face, stretch the skin tight over his cheekbones. Above the red tiled roof, the crests of arid hills were spread with a dirty yellowish light.

The heavy oaken doors were slightly open. He knocked several times, then went into a long, raftered, and coolly shaded room. There was the dead fireplace at one end. At the other, a suit of armor watched him from the bottom of a staircase. His eyes moved quickly over the room, only half seeing the tragic remains of a lavish smorgasbord turned stale, bright cushions ringing a huge redwood coffee table, ceramic mugs stained with lipstick smudges, candles as big as his arms still glowing deep in tallow pits. He shivered a little, then walked through an atmosphere of heavy, brooding melancholy to the sideboard and poured a double shot of bourbon. There was a hint of silent, ghostly laughter. He stood, listening. He called out several times. No answer. But someone had been here when he had phoned from Van Nuys.

"Boooo!"

Nebel spilled half his bourbon as he turned. A tall, model-thin brunette, walnut tanned, wearing a thin blouse and a pair of toreadors, rose up from the couch near the fireplace. She extended a long leg upward and flexed green-lacquered toes like a monkey.

"Would you pour me something, too, please, honey?" She waved an empty glass and studied him. "It's scary. I feel like a ghost myself because I'm supposed to be dead. I ought to be. But I didn't go on the flight, you see. I got sozzled and passed out and when I came to—they were gone."

"What are you drinking?"

"Anything straight and very Lethean."

He handed her a glass of bourbon straight. Up close, her face appeared slack, her eyes glazed. But they were lovely eyes, and behind them he sensed things buried and transformed.

"You look weird, too, sort of wrecked. Sit down." He sat on a hassock.

"You looking for ghosts, honey? If I believed in them I'd be hearing a gibbering chorus of them now, but I don't. But ghouls I believe in and hate in any form. Such as reporters. People who ask morbid questions."

"My name's Fred Nebel."

"You were the frantic caller! You? God, how Luella misrepresented you. I pictured a thing with watery eyes, bifocals, like a pekinese."

The phone started ringing. Nebel jumped. "Ignore it, honey. And here you are, big, shaggy, Charles Bickford type. Saint Bernard, naive strength, etc. That Luella!"

The persisting ring of the telephone scraped Nebel's raw nerves. He started to get up.

"No, honey. I've already told them who was here for the weekend. The hell with ghouls regardless of race, creed, or color."

"I noticed that Luella's car isn't outside. I'm wondering where she went, or even if she was here at all."

"Luella said that she left you a note, honey, like with the milkman or something."

"Yes, but—"

"Luella was here all right," the woman said. "Incidentally, my name's Barbara."

"Do you know where she went then?" Nebel asked. His voice came out with a small squeezed sound. He repressed an urge to scream back at the phone that had started ringing again.

"Luella's favorite weapon, Fred. Keep them guessing. The favorite weapon of the Freudian age—the official excuse of sick, sick, sick. Wife takes off for the weekend; it's because she's psychoneurotic."

The phone stopped ringing, but left a painfully ringing silence. Barbara sipped bourbon as if it were coke. "You suffer, I know. But it's hard to sympathize with marital hell. As Sartre said, hell is a restaurant where you serve yourself. But suffering looks good and masculine on you, Fred. I mean, sweat, the beard. Do you smoke Marlboros? Show me your tattoo."

"All I want to know, Barbara, is where did Luella go? Her car's gone. She went somewhere. Try to remember."

Barbara's eyes grew small. Her full lips stretched to a thin hard line. "I remember all right. Luella was here, unforgettably. She was wherever a male was momentarily unattached."

Anger rose with heavy reluctance in Nebel. With it came a kind of guilty fear. "That's none of your business. Just tell me where she went, if you know. If you don't know, tell me that."

"Pardon my Fredness, Frank, but Luella was my problem. Problem people like Luella become problems for everyone in reach. I loathed little Luella. You see I had a very passionate thing for Rudy. And little wide-eyed, helpless little Luella got her hooks deep into him. Little Luella couldn't get enough of anything, especially if it was supposed to belong to someone else. Like the so-called irresponsible child of nature, she had no respect for private property."

Nebel wiped his mouth with his flat hand. "Barbara—just tell me where Luella went. That's all I, ask."

"When I'm sozzled I don't much care what I say or do or anything, Fred. And I'm really sozzled. I'll never sober up again. Then I might think it all mattered, and I couldn't live with that. I loved old Rudy."

Barbara stared at Nebel's jaw, at the nerve twitching in it. "Luella's an obsession of yours by now. Listen—start now, get rid of your obsession."

"By God, she left in the car and went somewhere, and you—"

"Oh—you mean you're sure she drove away in the car because the car isn't here? I see, Fred. Sorry, sorry. But the car never was here . . . never."

"You said Luella was here."

"Yes, but not the car. And therein lies a sordid tale. Her car broke down somewhere down the line. She called in—poor helpless little Luella, you know. Rudy went out and brought her in. They took a mighty long time getting back . . . mighty long."

Nebel rubbed his hand across his eyes. There was a peculiar constriction in his throat. So Luella had been here. And she hadn't left in the car. Then—

The phone started ringing. But now it had a dull, distant, meaningless sound. A voice within Nebel whispered, "What are you doing in this accursed place? Go, get out, go home, go somewhere, anywhere, before it's too late."

He started to ask, "Was Luella on that plane?" He couldn't ask it. He couldn't ask anything.

But Barbara could. Barbara not only could, but would. Nebel knew with a horrible certainty. Barbara would never run down.

"I really was attached to Rudy. Though crazy and wild, he was genuine. Luella was pure phony. All phony, no real Luella anywhere. No core. A chameleon. Pretend to be or believe one thing, but all the time several other people or things. Nothing real. Her psychoneurosis, her love life, all phony, too. An act, a diversion, little charade. She may have been nuts, but she didn't want to be cured. There never was a real Luella to cure. Luella was just a figment of her greedy little imagination."

The phone must have stopped, for now it began ringing again. Nebel sat dazed, listening to this deadly, coherent, drunken woman speaking of Luella in the past tense. He gripped her wrist. "Where's Luella?"

"I told the reporters who the guests were here," she said, her voice getting higher. "Answered telephones all morning. Don't you know how I feel? I mean, weekend guests were all here having a ball, laughing it up, you know, trying to make the tired old merry-go-round go a little faster. Then all at once—they—they were dead and gone."

He shook her. She laughed shrilly. She gripped his wrists with both hands. The glass shattered on the floor. Sensing the pitiable terror under her mask as her hands turned to clawing panic, he quickly released her.

"And then there were none," she said tonelessly. "None but Barbara all alone in limbo. I might even feel self-pity if I sobered up. I loved Rudy."

Nebel stood up. He started for the door.

"Where are you going, Fred?"

"To find Luella."

She screamed at him. He turned. "You're alive, Fred. Don't look for Luella. Don't you want to stay alive? You ought to feel lucky you're free. All right, I'm sozzled. I'll tell you honey. She's dead. Luella's dead. Real dead. Completely dead. Dead, dead, dead!"

"You're lying!" Nebel shouted, swinging the palm of his hand at her. She stumbled back and fell sprawling. He stood staring at his opened palm, then down at her welted face. She laughed up at him. "Don't be nice, Fred. Hit me again. You're beginning to look human. How does it feel? Ever hit a woman before? Ever hit anybody before? You're built for it. You hit real good. Only it's better when you hit the right guy."

His voice hadn't sounded like his own. His actions were the incredible shocking actions of someone else. He'd driven his car over a hundred miles an hour; he'd struck this woman.

He sat down and put his hands over his face.

He heard her voice as though through a wall. "What are you trying to prove, Fred? That she really is dead? Can't you believe how lucky you are?"

"Shut up!" he snarled through his hands. "Why take your hatred out on me?"

"I like you, Fred. You're big and nice. Why did you do it, Fred? Because you're over forty, and Luella looked so wide-eyed and young and innocent? Was it flattering to have the old libido pumped by a sweet thing only twenty-two? Be glad that sort of childishness isn't contagious. I see it all over you, the old values, responsibility, loyalty. Luella never heard of them. She laughed at, ridiculed you. She laughed about how you were putting out a hundred a week to that Beverly Hills quack. I'm not against psychiatry. But her guy happens to be one of the greediest quacks since Cagliostró."

He took his hands slowly from his face and looked at her.

"How many guests were here?"

"Eight."

"That's all? How about servants?"

"No servants. Servants have big eyes. They talk."

"And you didn't go on the flight. Seven went which means that you're telling me that my wife—that she was—"

"That's what I've told you. But I won't repeat it. There were seven passengers. There were only seven others besides me. Little Luella had to have gone, and that's it, my good man."

"You said you were too drunk to go. Did you actually see Luella go aboard that plane?"

She stared at him, neither condemning, nor reproachful, nor with pity, but highly speculative. "All right, Fred. I was passed out, cold as a Christmas turkey. I didn't see her go aboard."

He stood up and took a deep breath. "Thanks, Barbara. Then they must have picked up someone else. You see my wife was very superstitious. She wouldn't accept a license plate from the Department of Motor Vehicles because of the number seven in it. She wouldn't make appointments on the thirteenth. She was scared to death of unlucky numbers. By some people seven's considered lucky; to her it was poison. So I know she couldn't have been the seventh passenger."

Barbara shrugged. "So, they could have picked up someone else. That's possible. Anything's possible." Her eyes were wet. "I'm sorry, Fred," she whispered. "I'm really sorry that you have to suffer for nothing. We all of us ought to stay young forever."

"Goodbye, Barbara," he said, and went out onto the porch. He walked to the car, got in, and slammed the door.

"Fred!"

As he looked toward Barbara running across the courtyard, the sun was a stinging glaze, low and reflecting at a sharp angle into his eyes.

"Where are you going, Fred?"

"To find Luella."

Her face was close to his. Her eyes were soft and dark. "I'm sorry I hurt you, but I'm not sorry for what I said. People like her hurt people like you because you're decent. You won't give up, will you? Your kind never gives up."

"She was my wife—she didn't have any real friends."

"I understand. But—I'm sober now, you sobered me up. I can't stay out here alone any longer, not sobered up."

"Why don't you go home?" he asked gently.

"I will. I'm practically on my way home right now, Fred. Listen—give me a ring sometime. In North Hollywood directory. Name's Barbara Allerson. A, as in Aphrodite."

Nebel got out of the car. "Fill it up," he said to the Shell attendant, a kid in a buckskin shirt and tight levis. He looked down the length of the main drag of Ten Palms, baking in the late afternoon sunlight, down between blurred glares of gambling casinos, bars, pizza and hotdog and beer signs, drugstores. His eyes were bloodshot and there was a stubborn set to his jaw. "Check the oil. May need a quart of special X. Check the brakes. I'll be back after a while."

The kid unlocked the gas cap. "Hear about the plane crash this morning?"
"Yes, I did."

"Movie actress supposed to have got it, too. Private plane, guy named
Weldon. He lives a little way from here. Plane went down just over on the hill
there. Brought seven in here all at once."

Nebel didn't say anything. He didn't feel much of anything now either,
except a curious sense of injustice. If he didn't know Luella well enough to
know she wouldn't have been the seventh passenger on that plane, then he
didn't know Luella at all. Didn't know *any*thing about Luella. If you could
marry someone, be married to them a year, and not know anything at all about
them, not one thing, then you couldn't trust yourself either, not in the least.

"Who were the seven passengers?" Nebel asked.

"They don't know yet," the kid said. "They're over at the mortuary putting
them together. Who would want to work in a mortuary? I wouldn't."

"Where is it—the mortuary?"

The kid told him. It was two blocks away, a block off the main street. Nebel
walked over there where the chapel nestled next to the church. A crowd
loitered. Someone had brought up hotdog and ice cream wagons.

Someone said to someone else, "Steve Myerson saw the crash all right, in
fact, he was almost number eight. The plane darned near landed on his roof.
He reported it, and now he's a TV star. Been on TV and everything. Like a
celebration for Steve. Ain't seen him so loaded since last Fourth of July. He's
really livin'."

"Well, that's logical," someone answered. "He ain't been in town without the
old lady since last Fourth."

But Nebel was walking up to the khaki-clad officer standing before the
chapel door.

"Name's Fred Nebel," he said. The officer shuffled his boots, and looked
over the top of Nebel's head. "Are all of them identified yet, officer?"

The officer shook his head. "All of them but one, Mr. Nebel."

"There's a possibility that my wife may have—"

"I know. I've got a list of the seven guests who probably made that flight,
Mr. Nebel. Got it right here."

"I know my wife's name is on that list. But I'm equally sure she didn't make
that flight," Nebel said.

The officer shifted his boots and then wiped his fat, sweating face with a soggy
bandanna. He looked over the top of Nebel's head and didn't say anything.

"You've identified six of them, but not my wife," Nebel said. "Isn't that
right?"

The officer dug a wet, folded paper from his shirt pocket and looked at it.
"Your wife isn't on the list."

"What about the seventh one then?" Nebel asked. "Is it a man or a woman?"

"It's—a woman," the officer said. "And you could be right, Mr. Nebel,"
he added quickly, "it may not be your wife at all. We don't know who it
is yet."

"I know it isn't my wife," Nebel said. The setting sun burned like pins in his eyeballs.

The officer shook his head, embarrassed and hardly able to speak. "Well, we got a guest list from a Miss Barbara Allerson over at the Weldon place. There were eight guests there, and Miss Allerson didn't go. Your wife was one of the seven. Of course, I guess someone else could have been number seven, but on the other hand it doesn't seem—"

"I happen to know my wife couldn't have been on that plane," Nebel said.

"I sure hope you're right, Mr. Nebel. They can't find anything at all to identify this number seven. Completely unrecognizable, and no rings, or any identification found, nothing, just nothing at all. They'll have to check with dentists and doctors, check for dental X-rays and broken bones. That's the only way."

"We were married a year," Nebel said. "My wife had no dental work or anything like that done, no broken bones."

"Well, Mr. Nebel, we'd like a little information. Just in case, you understand. So we can check. Where did she come from? Was she born here? If we could check in other towns, where she may have had dental work done, bones set, well—we can make absolutely sure it isn't your wife that way, you see, Mr. Nebel? Could you give us information of that kind?"

Nebel hesitated.

"I don't guess you've heard from her since the crash," the officer asked uneasily. "Or you don't know where else she might be, or something?"

"I soon will know," Nebel said. "But I'll give you what information I can." The officer brought out a black notebook, and a pencil. "Her maiden name is Luella Sawyer. She came from Lakeville, Arkansas. She had a stepfather until she was five, then spent the rest of her life until she was eighteen in an orphanage in Lakeville. Then I believe she went to work in a bank there. Three years later she came to Los Angeles."

Nebel felt a bit dizzy. He started down the steps, hearing the officer mumbling something. But he paid no attention and went on.

He sat in the bar drinking beer and listening to the rhythm of slot machine handles for a long time. He called home several times, but there was no answer. He should, he told himself, have stayed home. He would have been there when she called in, or drove in.

He sat at a corner table and looked into his memory.

He had been lonely and afraid and then he met her at that party and married her three days later . . . and that morning after the first night of their honeymoon in Miami, there she was on the balcony, stark naked, calmly feeding the pigeons. Someone called the cops. Nebel managed to convince them that Luella was a sleepwalker. That was the beginning. The beginning of pranks, irresponsible behavior of a complex and unbelievable variety. Finding her gone, never knowing where, or when she would be back. Calling hospitals, police stations. A child in a lovely woman's body. And how would anyone have guessed? But afterward you love, feel responsible. It's like having the responsibility for something lovely and precious and helpless. None of the anxiety and pain and irritations mattered to him now.

She was here behind his closed eyes the way she had been the first time he saw her, radiant and always young and reckless and lighting up lonely dark rooms. She was with him now, her breath on his face, her hands and lips caressing him, the distinct lavender scent of her perfume all around, her warmth entering into him. Am I my brother's, my sister's keeper?

"How about another, sir?"

He looked up at the waitress. "Sure," he said.

And for the first time in a long time he thought about his first marriage, his first wife. He remembered everything and he remembered with sharp clarity her warm gentle strength, the color of her eyes, and how she had waved and blown him a kiss that evening before walking through the falling snow to catch a streetcar to her mother's house because her mother had the flu. He even remembered hearing the scream, and without a shirt running through the snow and seeing her there, a dark sooty wet blob under the wheels of a truck. "Oh come on, Fred," she had said. "I can't, I've got to study," he had said. And all he had remembered for years after that was that if he had gone with her it would never have happened.

It would never happen again, he had said. He remembered saying that, too, over and over as he walked all night in the snow. And for years and years it had not happened.

It hadn't happened this time either.

But wishing didn't make it so. The idea that it did was an old myth to which Nebel had never subscribed. Everyone else assumed that the seventh body in the chapel of A. Ribesto was that of Luella Nebel. There was every reason for this assumption. And the sole fact for his assuming that it was not Luella would hardly convince anyone else. Barbara knew that Luella was dead. Luella had been at Weldon's. There were only seven guests other than Barbara. By all logic, the seventh unidentified body at the chapel was Luella.

But Nebel insisted that it couldn't be. Or was he insisting that it shouldn't be? Was he afraid to face the truth? He would feel responsible, just as he had for his first wife, and he knew that he couldn't bear it again.

Luella wore several rings. She wore a necklace and earrings. She always carried a wallet. The searchers could easily have overlooked something. But he wouldn't. If anything of Luella's was up there in the wreckage, he would see it, and he would know it.

He left the bar. The sun had set as he got his car and the directions on how to reach the crash site and drove up into the foothills. As he drove over the winding road through the clear moonlight, he knew something else. That he wanted to be up there alone where those people had died. There was a strange, unexplainable feeling that, up there, alone, he would come nearer to knowing the truth. He had to know.

And in any case, when he found out the truth, whatever it was, he preferred to be alone when he found it.

The moon seemed balanced on the crest of the arid hills. Nebel looked a while through the wreckage with his flashlight, then sat on a rock and felt the slow steady push of the desert wind. It whispered around him through charred grass, blackened rocks, bits of molten wreckage, tatters that were sooty and formless.

He had searched through the wreckage and found nothing. And he kept telling himself that he wouldn't find anything, so why go on looking? It was ridiculous. Why doubt his own powerful hunch? Go on back to Ten Palms. They've probably already identified that seventh victim as someone else. Go back and call home, go home, Luella's probably there waiting and afraid.

And if it isn't that way, if it's the other way, you'll find that out soon enough, too. You can't be absolutely sure of everything all the time.

Something moved, a sound, behind the blackened boulders. His heart pounded as he stood up and he seemed to catch a whiff of Luella's perfume mixed with burned earth, seared grass, dead waste.

He walked quietly toward the sound, leaned over the top of the rock, and flicked on his flashlight. Like an animal fixed and hypnotized by such a sudden glare in the night, the man rose and faced into the light, blinking. His face a dirty grayish pallor. And he was breathing heavily, showing a toothy grin at something nameless and unseen.

Nebel switched off the flashlight. However, he could still see, vividly, the face, the long creases in the cheeks like scar furrows, the thick shoulders, ragged sleeves. The torn shirt, the missing buttons. The hands and wrists of both arms badly and recently burned. The raw redness of the burns still shone in the moonlight like the claws of crabs.

And out of his hand those buttons falling on the rock as the man straightened up, startled.

"Just poking around here, you know," the man said. "You scared me."

"Sorry," Nebel said. "You found some buttons?"

"Few little old buttons, that's all. Just sort of looking things over. It's practically in my back yard anyway now. Name's Steve Myerson. I saw it happen, whole thing. Live down the hill a piece. Thought it was coming right down on my head. It was hot, hotter than hell. I could feel it like a furnace blast all the way down the hill. You looking for something?"

"Yes I am. They've identified six of the seven down at Ribesto's Chapel. The seventh one hasn't been identified yet."

"Hasn't?"

"No. No identification of any kind. So I was looking, seeing if maybe something had been overlooked."

"Well, they know who it is all right," Myerson said. "It's just a question of verifying it, I guess. They know who the seven was that went up in that plane, but I guess they got to be sure."

Nebel shivered then. The long howling wail of a dog came from a little way down the hill. He was big and crouching a little, making a gnarled shadow under the moon. "That damned dog. Been howling and howling. I'll kill the mutt, so help me. My old lady pulled stakes, you know, up and left me, and that dog's been howling for her."

Nebel saw the shine of Myerson's eyes in which there was no warmth, no trust, but a naked fear that had gone off and on like a light bulb. The dog gave another long wail.

"Well, I got to get back down to my shack," Myerson said. When he started walking away, Nebel walked behind him. Myerson stopped.

"Maybe you got something to drink down there," Nebel said. "I sure could use one."

Myerson looked at him. Finally he said in a kind of mumble, "You a detective, a reporter maybe?"

"No. I just have a very special interest in that seventh unidentified woman whose body they found up here this afternoon. You see, I happen to know it isn't who they think it is."

"I see," Myerson said. "Sure, you come on down for a snort or two. I got some brandy down there, some whisky, too. Brought it up from town today."

"Thanks," Nebel said. He followed Myerson's big but noiseless padding movement down the hill, along a narrow winding path through stunted sage.

Myerson was saying, "I keep goats. They said over the radio I was a sheepherder. I ain't no sheepherder. Goats, and they're a headache. Sometimes I don't know if I'll make it go. But they's money in goats' milk."

"Didn't your wife like goats, Myerson?"

Myerson began swearing and hurling rocks down the hill at a grove of cottonwoods where the dog kept howling. "Shut up, Queeny, or I'll put a bullet in you! You hear!"

They had moved past peeled railings to where a small two-roomed shack threw a pale, sickly, coal oil light through an open door. Myerson opened the door wider. "Go on in, and make yourself comfortable. Ain't much, but it's home." Myerson chuckled.

"I've heard dogs howl like that before," Nebel said. "Always for somebody dead."

Myerson grabbed at the wall and leaped crouching across the path of lamplight. A double-bitted ax swung up above Myerson's mad, flushed face.

Nebel moved out of the light. His stomach felt as if a rope were squeezing around it. "Killing me won't help you any," he said. Running would hardly help Nebel much either. He didn't know where the paths went, and it was steep, rocky terrain. "They'll find out who that seventh body is, or was. That it's your wife's."

"They won't find out from you though. Not now, you—you—snooping—"

The ax whistled around and Nebel fell back and the wall of the shack held him as if he were pinioned. The ax came back like a snake's head poised. Nebel slid down the side of the boards, then swung under the ax, rolled and felt his feet slipping in gravel as he tried to regain his feet. Myerson's bulk bent over him, the double-blade ax silhouetted against the moon.

In that moment lying there, fear boiled something latent out of Nebel. And hate was like a fire coiling in him. It was all the more violent because it had been so long delayed, like a charge of dynamite going up, a roaring flood breaking down a drywash, a lightning stroke out of an empty sky. It broke suddenly and completely. And he came up with a hoarse cry under the down-swinging ax. He caught the handle of it on his shoulder and grabbed Myerson's wrist with both hands, felt the burned skin slipping under his fingers like the skin of a rotten peach.

He dropped his right hand and smashed Myerson in the stomach. Myerson stumbled and gasped, sobbed slightly, and tried to get the ax up again. Nebel smashed him twice in the mouth. Myerson stumbled back, flopped against the side of the shack, slipped down to his hands and knees. Nebel stomped on his wrist and the ax slid down the hill. When Myerson came up, Nebel pounded away at him and, finally, laced his hands together, brought them down across the back of Myerson's neck.

Then he picked up the ax.

An hour later, Myerson confessed everything to the sheriff in Ten Palms. He had seen the crash and the flames and had beaten his wife unconscious, then pushed her up there in a wheelbarrow and dumped her into the fire. Everyone knew that Mrs. Myerson had been threatening to leave her husband for some time and her disappearance would have aroused no suspicion. Myerson had figured the bodies would be completely burned, or at least that it would be assumed that seven passengers had been on the plane. She had regained her senses long enough to put up a terrible struggle, had torn Myerson's shirt, ripped the buttons off. His hands and wrists had been badly burned.

"I had a strong hunch my wife couldn't have been that seventh passenger," Nebel said. "Yet there were seven passengers. Then I saw Myerson up there picking up those buttons, and noticed that buttons were missing from his shirt. I got another hunch then when he talked about his wife leaving him. And seeing those burned hands. What really did it was that dog howling not for someone gone away, but for someone dead."

As Nebel drove into the driveway of his house in Van Nuys, he noticed that the light in the front room was on. He didn't drive into the garage. He parked in the driveway, then walked across the front yard to the door and opened it.

"Freddy, darling!"

He saw Luella standing there in a wispy negligee, and he knew she appeared very appealing in it, but Nebel didn't take a very close look. He heard her giggling and swinging her arms in a little dance, and he felt the same hot coiling in his stomach and his hands clenched, but then the tension went away. It might be some time yet before any such rage as he had known this afternoon would come back. Maybe it never would.

He went into the bedroom without saying anything, threw a few items into an overnight bag, and walked back across the living room to the door. She ran toward him, then stopped. She was still laughing, but it sounded grotesque and unreal. He saw a kind of savagery beneath the giggling prankster face, something venomous and unforgiving in her eyes even as she laughed more shrilly and yelled.

"But, darling, it's April Fool's Day!"

"I know," Nebel said. "I just remembered it as I drove up to the house."

He shut the door.

He drove through the still darkness of the housing tract toward the bright lights of Ventura Boulevard. Familiarity might blunt perception. But a sick need could blind you to reality.

He parked by the Owl Drugstore and went inside to the phone booth. Kids make life bearable for themselves, he thought, by pretense and fantasy, by this facility for self-deception. And it was possible to go on being a kid for years. But it was also deadly. Deadly to stay young too long.

He looked up the number in the North Hollywood directory. Then he dialed HOllywood 7-1313. "Hello," he said after a sleepy voice answered. "Is this Aphrodite?"

EDWIN P. HICKS

The Lure and the Clue

Turning my boat around to head out of the cove, I saw the other boat bearing down and headed straight for me. It came with a rush, under the full power of a forty-horse outboard motor, and never slackened speed until at the last second the big guy in the stern cut the motor completely. The waves raced in in great rolls, and *Lucy*, that's the name of my boat, rocked wildly. If it had happened in the streets in the old days I'd have given the fellow a ticket for reckless driving.

It was my fishing cabin neighbor, Bill White, whom I'd met the day before, and two companions. White, who was around sixty and who claimed to be an Oklahoma City oil man, was dressed like a dandy—red coat, red cap, and khakis. The man in the bow, medium sized and roughly dressed, was about forty-five. He held a pair of field glasses and grinned insolently at me, getting a kick out of the way my boat was rocking. My ex-police sense told me this gentleman was a cop-hater and dangerous.

"Hi there, Joe Chaviski," White greeted. "Meet my fishing partners, Frank Caprino and Jim Brown. Frank was watching you through the glasses and saw you pull out that big bass, and we thought we'd join you over here and see what you were using. Where is that bass? Let's see how big he is."

"Didn't know you fellows wanted him," I said. "I didn't need him to eat, so I turned him loose."

Brown swore. Caprino spat into the water.

"I don't understand you damn fellows who drive miles to fish, then when you luck into a big one turn him loose again," Caprino said with a sneer.

A policeman's blood doesn't boil easily. He's used to men spouting off. I ignored Caprino and looked Brown over. Here was a youngster who would be tough handling. He was young—in his early twenties—and he was big, at least two hundred and thirty pounds, and probably would stand six feet three or four inches tall. His shoulders were the shoulders of a heavyweight boxer, and his weight was sinewy bone and muscle. There was no fat on his entire frame. The boy was a perfect physical specimen.

Caprino was ready to kill at the drop of a hat, and you knew what to expect; but Brown was the one who could do the most damage, because you wouldn't be sure what he would do. Brown's face was suntanned, but his eyes were blue. He looked like a big, friendly, innocent kid—a bit too innocent. Through bitter experience I had a great deal of respect for baby-faced youngsters. You never knew what a friendly-faced juvenile delinquent like Brown would do.

I spoke to White. "I was just getting ready to pull out of here. You can have the cove if you want it."

Caprino chuckled as I started the motor. He dropped his field glasses to the end of the leather thong about his neck and thrust his right hand beneath his coat, towards a bulge below his left shoulder. At that instant, White dropped a restraining hand on Caprino's arm, just like a man steadying a vicious dog that was about to leap on a stranger.

I was glad to get away from there and scooted clear across the lake to a forest of dead treetops sticking out of the water. Here I searched for a small buoy-marker bobbing on the surface, among the tree tops. This marker, a slab of wood, anchored by wire to the bottom, marked a crappie bed.

Finding the marker, I tied up, unlimbered a couple of cane poles, lines, and bobbers, baited with minnow, and began fishing for crappie. This was a lazy man's way of fishing. I stayed over the crappie bed for hours, mainly dozing, enjoying the warm October sun. The crappie began hitting about one thirty in the afternoon. I pulled out crappie until I got tired, keeping only a few of the big slabs. Then in an hour or so the flurry was over, and the crappie went back to sleep and so did I.

As I dozed there, half awake, I dreamed about the past. I was thinking of my wife Lucy, for whom my boat was named. Lucy had been dead more than five years now. And I thought of Johnson and Sauer, wild young buckaroos, whom I had made into plainclothesmen, although the effort nearly killed me. And, with something akin to physical force, I pushed back into their graves the eleven men I had killed during my thirty years on the police force. Then I thought of Billy Hearston. Billy was my good friend.

He had broken in with me as a rookie patrolman—in those dim, dead days of long ago. I had the First to the Main Hotel Alley beat, and Hearston had the Alley to Thirteenth Street. We worked seven nights a week, in twelve-hour shifts. If a policeman made any arrests, he had to appear in Municipal Court next day to testify. A court appearance made one or two more hours in uniform, during the twenty-four-hour day. Our pay was eighty dollars a month, but eighty dollars was good money in those days.

Day after day drunks had been wandering up on my beat. Day after day I walked them dutifully down the Main Hotel Alley and to the city jail—and appeared sleepy-eyed and red-faced next day in court.

One night it appeared there were going to be no drunks, and I was looking forward to grabbing a bite to eat and then just dying in my bed. I was that tired. Five minutes before off-duty time, a wobbly soul met me at the Alley. I grabbed the poor fellow by the shoulders and shook him. "Tell me," I bellowed, "why do you drunks always have to come on my beat?"

"Why—" said the intoxicated one, between hiccoughs, "that other cop down the street told me to come up here and report to you."

A great light dawned on me then. Next afternoon, right after five o'clock, just after I had started on duty for the night, I met Billy Hearston at the Main Hotel Alley. Billy was every bit as big a man as I was—about two forty-five, and six feet tall. I walked straight up to him. "You so-and-so!" I yelled in his face.

"Whatta you mean, Joe?" Billy asked, grinning from ear to ear.

"Why the hell are you always sending your drunks over on my beat and making me lose two hours' sleep every day?" I slapped Billy with my open hand across the cheek so hard it sounded like a whip cracking.

Holding his ground, Billy returned the slap. For five minutes we engaged in a face-slapping exercise—both of us as stubborn as two young bull-calves butting heads in the pasture. We were still at it when Chief Ingersoll appeared and grabbed each of us by the coat collar.

"What are you two pups doing? Trying to kill each other?"

The chief took us both over to his office, gave us a sizzling lecture on the dignity of our uniforms, threatened to fine us a month's salary, then sent us both back on the beat, grinning sheepishly.

It was a week later we learned that the major, who lived in an apartment across the street, had seen the slapping incident and had called the police station: "Hurry over here, chief, before two of your policemen beat each other to death!"

Poor Billy had died of Japanese bullets on a South Pacific island in 1944.

But all the time as I lazed away there in the autumn sunlight—drinking in its warmness and haunted with a loneliness for Lucy—the Oklahoma dandy Bill White, killer-type Hank Caprino, and the baby-faced young giant, Jim Brown, were in the back of my mind.

There was something wrong with that trio. I felt it—I knew it—and yet I knew also that criminals, gangsters, hoodlums, do not fish and hunt, and they do not enjoy the outdoors. And then I said to myself—oh hell, Joe Chaviski, you're no longer a cop. But my mind was still a cop's mind.

The sunset was a scarlet band above the pines as I nosed my boat back into the cove where I had taken the lunker at sunrise.

Hank Caprino had reached for a rod that morning, fisherman or no fisherman. I hadn't seen the gun, but I had seen the movement, and I was just as sure as anything that he would have blasted me out of the boat if White hadn't restrained him. And here I was, clear away from base, without a sign of a firearm. I had left everything that would remind me of police work back at home.

I cast a big redhead surface plug about the shallows of the point without success and then headed back for the landing, my cabin, a quick meal, and a soft bed. A patch of light showing beneath the drawn window shade in the cabin next to mine as I drove up, and the blare of a radio told me that White,

Caprino, and Brown were at home. I hoped they would quickly knock it off and let me get some sleep.

But before I got inside, the baby-faced giant, Jim Brown, was there. "Mr. Chaviski, come over and have a drink with us. A shot will do you good."

"No thanks, Brown, I'm all worn out. Think I'll eat a bite and turn in."

"Aw come on, Chaviski, we caught some fish. Want to show them to you."

I followed the boy into the cabin. The place was thick with tobacco smoke, and the radio was loud enough to burst your ear drums. "Turn off that damn noise," shouted White, who appeared to be the only man in the room not drinking. When nobody stirred, White turned it off himself.

"Look, Mr. Chaviski, we followed your system and caught some good ones today," Brown said.

Caprino said something that was between a snarl and a laugh.

A fourth man came into the room from the kitchen. He was about forty-five, blond, six feet in height, even though caved in in the chest, and his long jaw ended in an underthrust chin. His eyes were glazed and green, and through the thick tobacco smoke the newcomer looked like a walking cadaver. He had a heavy black skillet in his hand, and the skillet was filled with smoking crappie. He piled the hot fish onto a platter on the table, and Caprino and Brown pounced on the fish with forks. The emaciated cook cackled: "Take yore time. There's another skilletful just like that one."

"Sit down," said White. "Sit down, Chaviski, and have supper with us."

I sat down, and a plate of fish, surprisingly well cooked, was placed before me.

All five of us pitched in and ate the fish greedily. I was as hungry as a bear myself, and the others appeared just as hungry.

"I didn't introduce you to our cook," said White, when the thin fellow had cleared the table and returned to the kitchen. "He's a sort of oddball—not all here." White tapped his forehead. "But he's the best cook in seven states. Name's Lenny Hamm. Got a machine gun bullet through his chest at Omaha Beach."

"I didn't see him this morning," I said.

"Oh, we picked him up later after he had cleaned up the cabin. He's not much of a fisherman, but he likes to go out on the lake now and then when he's on a fishing trip."

"Well, thanks for the supper. It sure saved me a lot of work. Where did you get those crappie?"

"Right off the point where we saw you this morning. We went back to the dock and bought some surface plugs like you were using."

"You mean Luckies?"

"Yep. Same color, same size, and everything."

"Well, sometimes they hit over there. You never can tell. I'd have thought you'd have got them on minnows, though.

"No, just what you were using this morning."

Back in my own cabin I got up a real head of steam. You don't catch crappie on big surface lures like a casting size Lucky and very seldom on the surface at all. When crappie hit an artificial lure it is something that looks like a small minnow flashing through the water, and usually a few feet down. But then I started to get drowsy. I'd get the news and turn in.

I turned on the radio and got rock and roll music on three stations. It wasn't time for the newscasts. I switched to the police calls—and instantly came alive. The Blakely City police and the Garland County sheriff's office were keeping the airwaves hot. The First National Bank at Blakely had been robbed at noon that day by four bandits who wore stocking cap masks. The four had gotten away cleanly with forty-five thousand dollars in cash, in a red convertible bearing a Texas license plate. The convertible had been found an hour later in the woods near the intersection of U.S. Highway 270 and a national forest road about twenty-five miles northwest of Blakely City, and at the bottom of a ridge a quarter of a mile south of the southern edge of Pine Valley Lake.

A four-state hunt for the bank robbers was underway, but so far the officers were following a cold trail. I listened to the physical descriptions of the four. There was one tall, big man, two of medium height, while the description of the fourth varied. Some said he was tall, others said he was stooped. But black stocking cap masks had hidden the features of the bandits completely.

I turned off the radio after a while, switched off the lights in the cabin, and walked back to the lodge dining room. A couple of fishermen and their wives were watching a fight on TV. Sam Willoughby, operator of the lodge, was tidying up behind the fountain. Jim Taylor, who was in charge of the dock, was at the end of the counter, eating a late dinner.

I moved over to the counter and chose a stool next to Taylor. I ordered a dish of vanilla ice cream. I love vanilla ice cream.

"The four fellows in the cabin next to mine, I was just wondering if they drove off anywhere in their car during the day?" I asked Sam, as I dug into the ice cream.

Sam wiped at the spot of water on the counter. "You too?" he said, low and under his breath.

"What do you mean?"

"Half a dozen lawmen have been over here off and on since that bank robbery in Blakely City. They searched every cabin this afternoon, inside and underneath—yours included—and every car, and they found nothing."

"No guns?"

"Nothing but a .22 rifle for shooting snakes and plinking around, like a lot of fishermen take with them. Your friends had a .22."

"What about their car, has it been anywhere today?"

"Not that I know of. Taylor says all four of them been out on the lake all day fishing, the same as everyone else. Isn't that right, Jim?"

Taylor nodded. "They went out in two boats. First time they ever took two boats since they been here."

"What I can't understand," I said, grinning, "is the way they catch crappie. They had me over to eat tonight, and they said they caught all their crappie on big top water lures—large size Luckies. Never heard of such a thing before."

Taylor laughed. "Those poor devils. They have been here since the first of the week and haven't caught fish one. So a fellow with more crappie than he could use give them a mess today, when they come in about the same time to the dock, about four P.M. It was that guy on the left over there watching the fights. He'll tell you about it."

"Now that's more like it," I said. "I knew good and well they hadn't taken them the way they said. You mean they were out there all day today and didn't catch a thing?"

"Never saw any harder fishermen in my life. Went out right after you did— the three of them in one boat. Come back in about three hours and rented another boat, like I said. Said they were going to take their cook out. In a few minutes he came down to the boat—a tall guy, bent over and sickly looking. They kidded a lot about what a fisherman he was, but he took it all right. He and the dark, mean looking guy got in one boat, and the big young fellow and the old duffer from Oklahoma City got in the other. Both boats headed back up the lake the way you went. Didn't come off the lake until around four or a little after, like I said, and they were really riding the cook. They said they were transferring their icebox from one boat to the other, and the cook let it slip, and it sank fifty feet down in the water, beer and all."

Taylor paid his bill, picked up a toothpick, and ambled out of the restaurant. "Something about those four neighbors of yours you don't like, Joe?" Willoughby asked, low enough that Taylor couldn't hear.

"Yes," I said. "Maybe it's because I can't get out of the habit of thinking I'm still a policeman. You know you can't shake off thirty years wearing a badge and gun in two months' time."

"I guess that's right."

"Ever see these four fellows here before?"

"No," Sam said, "never did."

"When the law searched their cabin and car, you sure they didn't find anything—anything at all?"

"They were clean," said Willoughby, "except for that little .22 rifle, like I told you. Usually they took that with them in the boat, but they hadn't today. There wasn't a thing out of the way—nothing."

I sidled over towards the crappie fisherman, who was watching the last round of a fight on television. The man looked up and nodded, but I waited for the round to end and the decision.

"What time did the crappie start hitting for you today?"

"About eleven o'clock—clear up until one thirty or two, I would judge. Couple of fellows came by about noon. I asked them what time it was—always leave my watch in the cabin to keep from dunking it. They said it was twelve o'clock. The poor duffers hadn't had a nibble all day—though the Lord knows why. Later I ran into them at the dock as they were coming in and gave them eight or ten nice crappie."

It took me some time to go to sleep. The guys in the next cabin were hotter than a firecracker, it seemed to me, and yet they had established alibis all over the lake. They couldn't have robbed the Blakely bank. When you are on the lake fishing, you aren't robbing banks, and that definitely was where these four were.

Oh well, maybe I was getting old—brain softening up or something. Everything in me was screaming that I was sitting right on top of a bank robbery that I ought to blow wide open—and yet nothing in the whole business fit together. The four had been on the lake, same as I. They had been seen all over the lake, and their car hadn't left the fishing camp all day. So I turned off my feeble mind and went to sleep.

The sun was already up when I hit the lake next morning. I had overslept an hour, and the old navy wound in the left hip was paining me, and that was a sign that a spell of weather was on its way. The eastern sky was red, too. "Red at morn, sailor's warn—red at night, sailor's delight." The bass had read the signs, too, long before I had. They were still sulking, as they had been at sunset. Oh well, if the whitecaps started rising on the lake I would pull off and go to the cabin and get some sleep, or I'd go over to Blakely City and nose around the police station and see if they had any sign—any line on the bank robbers.

I used the paddle to edge silently into the cove, and then threw everything I had in the tackle box at the bass, but they wouldn't hit. Then, throttle at a crawl, I started pulling out of the cove, changing to an eel and jig combination as I did so, intending to fish the deep water off the points. Something hit me right between the eyes—figuratively.

I yanked the boat around and sent it back towards the center of the cove. Yes, I hadn't been seeing things. One hundred feet out from the short line was a floating wooden marker—a fresh pine slab, about three feet long, with a bright copper wire attached and leading down into the depths!

Such a marker is frequently used by fishermen or lake men for various reasons—to mark a good fishing spot, or to serve as a direction guide, or as a depth marker. *Yesterday morning this marker hadn't been there.* It could have been there yesterday evening because it was late when I passed that way and I could have gone within a few feet of it without seeing it.

I edged the boat towards the marker and caught hold of the copper wire and began heaving on it. Something tremendously heavy was attached to it on the bottom. I put my back into the work, and the thing began to move. I began bringing it up slowly, while the boat careened over almost to the gunwale.

Hand over hand I brought up the length of bright copper wire, some twenty-five feet of it. Then, several feet down, I saw it—shining metal. It was a large fishing icebox, with the lid padlocked, and attached to the icebox by wire was a rubberized bag!

Puffing and grunting I got the whole into the boat, wire and all, and sat there panting like a porpoise. The whine of a speeding outboard came to me, from the center of the lake. I turned to see a boat headed directly towards me and cutting a great swath through the surface. It was time to get moving.

By the time I had the motor started and underway, the other boat was within two hundred yards. I headed up the shore line, throttle open, picking up speed and going hell for leather. The other boat came right after me, wide open, spray flying wide. Three of my cabin neighbors were in that boat, and they were after me and no question about it. By the time I was full speed, the other boat had cut the distance to one hundred yards.

We went up the north shore line, with my twenty-five-horse outboard now holding its own. White and Caprino were waving their hands and yelling. The roar of the motors made it impossible to hear what they said, but I knew damn well what they meant. If they caught me I'd wind up at the bottom of the lake, wire and icebox attached but no buoy to mark the spot where the body lay.

Something that wasn't a bumblebee hit the top of the icebox and ricocheted in a screaming whine out over the lake. They were using that .22 rifle! I bent my two hundred and fifty pound anatomy down as far as I could behind the motor and kept pouring on the coal, running towards a small island ahead. Passing the island, I made a ninety degree turn sharply to port, then reversed my course completely, ducking around the island, and headed back towards the center of the lake.

The maneuver, which caught White and company by surprise, gained a little distance, but not too much. The wind was freshening, and out in the middle of the lake tiny whitecaps were showing. I aimed at a rocky point on the opposite shore, a mile and a half away, watching the surface ahead closely and thanking the good Lord that I had filled the gasoline tank before starting out that morning.

A minute passed, and I sighted what I was looking for, another marker, a block of wood bobbing on the surface and attached to a wire. I made a turn to starboard around this marker, doubling as if I intended to reverse my course again.

The pursuing boat turned instantly and cut across the arc of my course, thus gaining a full fifty yards on me. Two bullets whistled by my ear. Caprino was coming close!

And then it happened—what I had been praying for! The boat that was chasing me smashed into a low-water rock bar with a resounding crash, and the three occupants went flying through the air. They came up one by one, sputtering and cursing, Caprino, Hamm, then White—to find themselves up to their waists in water, a good half mile from shore. Their boat with shattered bow had capsized, and the .22 rifle had been lost in the smash-up.

I cut my motor and circled back, to idle about fifty yards from the bedraggled trio. "Now, you're marooned on a low-water bar, and I'd advise you to stay right where you are and not try moving around unless you're darn good

Channel swimmers. The water is fifty feet deep in every direction from where you are, and the whitecaps are rising. Stay right there and be good boys and maybe you can keep your noses above water."

"But I can't even swim!" bawled White. He looked really terrified.

"Now ain't that just too bad!"

At the dock I got Jim Taylor to help lift the heavy icebox and the rubberized bag out of the boat and told him to keep watch over it.

At the lodge I put in a call to the Blakely City police department. "Yep, all of it!" I said. "They used boats instead of a getaway car, and they put the money in a rubberized sack inside a fishing icebox. They put their tommy guns and their other heavy artillery in another rubber sack, attached everything to a floating surface marker by wire, and sank the whole business into the lake—to stay there until things cooled off. They probably dumped their masks and the clothes they used in the holdup into the water, too, weighted down with rocks—and had their fishing clothes on under what they took off.

"Yeah, captain, they're stranded out on a reef helpless as flies on flypaper— three of them. Yeah, I'll have the fourth one hogtied and ready for special delivery when you get here. Take all the time you want."

Sam Willoughby was goggle-eyed. "The big guy is down at the cabin. I saw him just a few minutes ago." Sam took a shotgun from under the counter and handed me a .45 automatic.

"Put those guns down," I said. "Guns get people killed. You stay out of this, Sam. Not a gun on the place in that cabin. You said so yourself. I think I'm still man enough to take him."

"But you're not as young as he is, and he's as big as you are, Joe!"

"This will separate the men from the boys, Sam."

I limped down to the cabin, trying to fit all the pieces together on the way. I'm not too fast with the think tank. Anything obvious takes me about thirty minutes to comprehend when my brain is working real good. But it came to me on the way. The cook, Lenny Hamm, who didn't go out with the three of them the first time on the lake the day of the robbery, already was in Blakely City. It was he who stole the getaway car and he parked it in the woods over the ridge from the lake. Then, at the appointed time, he had met them on the lake shore, and they had taken him back to a point near their cabin. He had left the boat then, gone to the cabin, while the three others returned to the dock and rented another boat and motor. They waited at the dock, and Hamm came down to them after apparently just having finished his cabin chores.

The four then sped out across the lake in the two boats, heading for known fishing points, but once out of sight of the landing they had turned and headed for the south shore. There they beached the boats, picked up their artillery from some shore-line cache, made their way the quarter of a mile over the ridge to the hidden car—and had gone into Blakely right on schedule to rob the bank at twelve noon. They had then raced back with the bank loot, abandoned the car, climbed back over the hill, and soon were back in their boats. They then made it a point to be seen all over the lake, lying to the crappie fisherman that it was noon—the time of the bank robbery—when it was around two o'clock. The rest everybody knew.

I didn't knock on my neighbor's fishing cabin door—just turned the knob and walked right in. Maybe I couldn't handle the youngster, but I wanted to try. Brown read my intentions and didn't waste a word. He came off the cot like a charging bull, throwing a punch from right field that tickled my left ear as it just missed. I sank a right hook up to my wrist in his middle, judo-chopped him across the back of the neck with my left hand, and came up under his sagging chin with a knee. It was real pretty for an old man. Jim Brown wouldn't think I was old at all. That is, he wouldn't think so when he woke up and met all those Blakely cops.

BORDEN DEAL

The Big Bajoor

Vanya hurried down the side of the highway to the place where the trailer was parked. The trailer was pulled off the side of the road into a small clearing. When she stepped across the ditch, she saw Sandor lying on his back under the nearest tree. He had his fiddle in his hand, but he was not playing.

Vanya stopped to look at Sandor from a distance, before he should be aware of her presence. He was a Rom any gypsy girl could be proud of loving. He was tall, handsome, his black hair curled about his ears, and he played the fiddle as the old ones had played it. Vanya herself was small, dark, pretty; but she had never expected to capture such a Rom as this one. Watching him, she felt the old familiar stab of love and pride inside her.

She came on, then, and Sandor looked up to watch her approach. He scowled, slightly, and she knew that he had planned the scowl for her appearance.

"Well, Vanya," he said. "Are you through dukkering? It was yesterday that I wanted to coor the drom and get started traveling."

"We can travel tomorrow," Vanya said breathlessly. "Today is the day for telling fortunes."

"So how much money did you make?" Sandor said indifferently.

"None," she said. She saw the frown again between his black eyes and she hastened with the news. "But I've got a big bajoor."

Sandor sat up. Vanya watched him with pride and joy. For a year, now, they had been married and she had not had a big bajoor. Every good wife makes the big bajoor for her Romany husband. Without the big bajoor she was not a good wife; and for a year now Vanya had not found it.

"Boro Dad!" Sandor said, his voice tense with the excitement. "You don't mean to say. Who are we going to swindle?"

Vanya sat on the ground beside Sandor. She took off her kerchief and loosened her hair to cool the heat from her head. "There's an old gajo woman who lives up the road," she said. "Yesterday I stopped for a drink of water. She lives in a big house just on the edge of the town, a house that was painted twenty years ago. It has seventeen rooms and it sits on a very large lot. The old woman lives there alone."

"So?" Sandor said impatiently.

"So today I stopped again. Today I told her fortune. She believed the fortune, for more than an hour I had to tell her all the bad she has seen and all the good that she will see. She is a very lonely old lady."

"She's probably got next week's grocery money," Sandor said. "This is a big bajoor?" But his eyes were sparkling with the excitement and the smile was in them that was not on his lips.

"I told her that I was a queen of the gypsies," Vanya said. "I told her I had the power to bless money in such a way that would keep it safe and increase it by as much again. The old gajo woman believed. I could tell that she believed."

Vanya turned to Sandor, put her hand on his arm. She squeezed the arm tightly. "She showed me the money, Sandor. She opened the trunk to show me this great bundle, wrapped in newspapers and tied with string. I told her I would prepare the magic and this afternoon I would bless the money for her because she was a kind lady who gives a gypsy a drink of water."

Sandor grinned. He loved Vanya. But it is good for a man to be proud of his wife, too. He could hear himself now, telling the story of the big bajoor and how his lovely young wife had worked it.

"The old gypsy switch," he said.

Vanya nodded her head. "Yes," she said.

He frowned uncertainly. "Can you work it?" he said. "Have you ever tried?"

Vanya drew herself straight. "My mother worked a great bajoor," she said. "Ten thousand dollars for my father. In one day."

He grinned ruefully. "Don't I know it? That's all I heard about when I set out to buy you from your father. It raised your price nearly out of my range."

She touched him again. "I will work the big bajoor," she said. "Or I will not come back."

She went then to prepare the meal. While she worked she sang, because she was so full of the happiness she had found today. She knew that her price had been high and she knew that Sandor loved her for he had paid a great deal of money for her. And until now she had made them only a living, nothing more.

They sat on the ground and ate companionably of the noon meal. They did not speak of the swindle again. After the meal would be soon enough. When the meal was finished, they went silently to work to prepare. Sandor helped her with the preparations. He drove into town and bought two reams of white paper and an ample supply of newspapers. They cut the white paper into dollar-sized pieces, stacking them carefully, Vanya measuring the stack from time to time with her hands.

"That's about the size of the bundle she had," she said at last.

"Then your daughters will be old maids," he said, laughing. "For no Romany will be able to afford them."

She laughed with him, tasting the sheer happiness in the sound of his voice, and together they wrapped the bundle in newspaper and tied it with the red string. She went into the trailer and changed into the dress with ampler folds, and put on the cloak over it. She wrapped up some of the leftover newspaper with a supply of the red string, and put the incense into a pocket of the dress.

She came outside again and picked up the bundle of blank paper wrapped in the newspaper and tied with the red string.

"Can you handle it all right?" Sandor said anxiously. "It's a pretty big bundle."

"I can handle it," she said confidently. She smiled at him and her hands moved quickly, concealing the bundle inside the voluminous dress. "See?"

"But the switch . . ."

She laughed, "Don't worry, Sandor," she said. "I can make the switch. I am the daughter of my mother, and I am Sandor's wife."

"I will be ready," he called after her as she started toward the road. "We will leave as soon as you return."

She tried not to hurry. But she was anxious for the deed to be accomplished, to have it a fact of her life that she had made a bajoor bigger than her mother had ever done. There was the love of Sandor and the thirst for fame strong in her throat and both were urging her on in spite of the flutter of fear deep down in her stomach. Vanya was young, only twenty, and her mother had been already old when she had accomplished her great feat.

There was nothing to arouse her suspicions. Everything looked as it had this morning. She entered between the old broken concrete gateposts and went up the walk. She stopped on the porch and the door opened immediately without her knock.

She looked at the woman standing in the doorway. She was tall, spare, with a large nose. Her hair was white and once, you could tell, she had stood erectly. But now her shoulders were stooped.

"I have come," Vanya said in an impressive voice.

"I followed your instructions," the old lady said, her voice whispering. "You must bless my money. You must keep it safe."

"And double it," Vanya said.

"I don't care about doubling it," the old woman said. "But I must keep it, for if I don't I could never face my father again."

Vanya had started for the room where she had told the fortune this morning. Now she stopped, turned.

"Your father?" she said. "Is he . . . ?"

"He is dead," the old lady said. "If I lost the money I would even be afraid to die."

Vanya went on, followed by the old lady. She went into the room and looked about her. It was the same as this morning, cool, high-ceilinged, dusky with darkness from the thick drawn drapes in spite of the great sunlight outside. No preparation of the room would be necessary.

There was a chair before a table and the old lady had placed the bundle of money, wrapped in tattered newspaper, on the table.

"Sit in the chair," Vanya said.

The old lady sat down. Vanya lit the incense and placed it on the table. The fragrant, sweet smoke billowed up into the room, making the old lady blink her eyes. Vanya spoke some words in Calo, the gypsy tongue, reverberating them with her diaphragm so that they echoed in the room.

"Now," she said. "Take this newspaper and this red string and wrap your money carefully. Tie it with many knots."

The old lady took the newspaper and string uncertainly, with trembling hands. "I have arthritis," she said. "You will have to wrap it and tie it."

Vanya drew back in horror. "No" she said. "I cannot touch the money. If I touched the money while I was blessing it, I would die."

She began chanting in Calo while the old lady began to prepare the bundle with the newspaper and the red string. She was slow and uncertain but Vanya pushed down the impatience that rose within her.

"You are so kind," the old lady said. "No one has been kind to me for so long. Nobody comes here any more, you know. People used to come here. Before the War Between the States they held great dances here. People still came in my father's time. But they don't come any more."

"When you are kind to a gypsy, great blessings come into your life," Vanya said. "For this reason I bless your money."

"I want to pay you, though," the old lady said. "I have five dollars right here to pay you with."

"I cannot take pay for the blessing of money," Vanya said. "This is a thing that gypsies do only for friends, and from a friend a gypsy cannot take money."

Vanya did not let herself think about the old woman and her loneliness and her money. She kept herself thinking about Sandor instead, and how much more he would love her now, and be proud of her. The woman was a gajo, wasn't she?

At last she was finished. The bundle sat on the table in the gloominess of the room. The room was filled with incense now, making it hard to see, the incense overwhelming the mind as well as the senses.

"Now," Vanya said. "you must close your eyes, for no one may look upon the blessing. To look upon the blessing would strike your mind, for it is a terrible and a hurting thing."

She watched closely to see if the old lady obeyed her. The eyes were tightly closed, the hands held stiffly in the lap, clenched into fists.

Vanya began chanting in Calo. She started low and far away, began coming nearer and louder, her body beginning to thump and beat against the sound of the voice. Her legs jerked out from under her and she thumped to the floor, where she thrashed, uttering terrible cries. She inched her way toward the table, making the sounds and watching the old lady. Not once did she look toward the table as her hand took out the fake bundle and held it ready. The eyes were closed. Swiftly, soundlessly, she switched the bundle, keeping up the thump and bang of her body against the floor while she edged away from the table. When she had reached her place, she began to let the terrible sounds subside, going gradually away into the distance until she lay silent.

At last she sat up and said, "You may open your eyes."

The old lady looked at her and Vanya stood up, wearily, making her face vacant and drawn.

"I have blessed the money," she said in a dull voice. "I have made it safe and it will double within three months. You must put it away into your keeping place and speak of it to no one. At the end of three months you may open it and see the increase my magic has brought you."

"Are you all right?" the old lady said, peering at her. "You look . . ."

"I must sleep for twenty-four hours," Vanya said in the weary voice. "Then I shall recover my strength. Gypsy magic is very strong. Remember. You must not look at the money. You must not speak of the money. Or the magic will be destroyed."

The old lady followed her as Vanya edged toward the door, anxious to be gone. "It worked all right?" she said anxiously. "It will be safe? My father gave the money to me, just like his father gave it to him."

"The magic worked," Vanya said. "I must go. I must sleep. I will be very ill, perhaps even die, if I do not sleep soon."

She got to the doorway, but the old lady was right behind her. The old lady put her hand on her arm. "You're sure it's all right?" she said.

"Of course it's all right," Vanya said, her voice cracking with the strain.

"Maybe we'd better look," the old lady said, her voice getting frenzied. She started toward the table where the package lay.

Vanya froze, watching her. Then her voice snaked out at her. "No," she said. "Not for three months."

The old lady turned to look at her and Vanya knew that she was suspicious now. It had risen up in her suddenly at the thought of the three months without seeing the money.

"I've got to be sure," the old lady said. "I don't care whether it doubles or not. That part doesn't matter. But it must be safe. I'll look. Then it'll be safe, even if it won't double . . ."

Already she was fumbling with the string. Vanya felt an impulse to flee. But she knew it would be wrong. That would certainly arouse the old lady. She stood with her hand on the doorknob, not knowing what to do, thinking, I tried it too soon. I am too young for the big bajoor.

The old lady's impatient hands ripped the newspaper and the white paper showed beneath. She looked toward Vanya, clutching a dollar-sized sheet of paper.

"What have you done with the money?" she screamed.

She came toward Vanya, almost running, clutching at her with both hands. Vanya, panicked, wheeled toward her, pushing her away, thinking now only of escape. She still had the money. If she could escape . . .

The old lady fell backward, clawing at the air. She made a strange cry when she landed on the floor, and there was in her an immediate limpness that frightened Vanya. She stood holding the door, looking down at the old woman, who lay twisted in a strangely familiar way.

At last Vanya left the door. She stood over the old lady, then she knelt down and put her hand on her face. "Mullah," she whispered. "Dead. Dead."

She squatted beside the old woman's body. It had been such a little push. But the old gajo woman had been so old. She knelt there, feeling the disaster that had come upon her in her youthful pride. She was no good for Sandor, no good for herself. She scarcely deserved to be called by the name Romany.

After a time, how long she did not know, she began to think more calmly. She still had the money, didn't she? She could hide the other bundle, clear away the incense and the other signs of a gypsy presence, and go away. The old lady lived alone. When she was found everyone would assume that she had fallen. She *had* fallen. Vanya had given her only a little push.

Vanya cleared the table of the incense holder, looked about the room. She didn't know what to do with the fake bundle. She picked it up, then, and took it to the chest where the old lady had kept her money. She put the bundle inside the chest, under a quilt, and locked the chest door. Let her relatives figure out why the old lady kept a bundle of paper tied up in newspaper and red string.

She went to the door and looked out carefully. Nothing stirred. She walked out on the porch, turned once and waved back toward the house as though speaking farewell to the old lady, and then went casually toward the highway. She made herself go slowly down the highway until she had covered more than a mile. Then she began to hurry.

She would not tell Sandor. She would tell him only that the big bajoor had worked, that she had the money. He need not know how she had failed. No one would ever know that the old lady had fallen.

When she arrived, Sandor was ready. She got into the car beside him and immediately Sandor pulled into the highway.

"Did you get it?" he said briefly.

"Yes," she said, taking the bundle out of the voluminous dress and putting it on the seat between them.

They drove for a long time. At first Vanya slept, for she was weary, but when she awoke they were very gay. They laughed and sang and Vanya was warm with his love and with the coming fame of the big bajoor when their people should be told the story.

They did not stop until daylight.

"Time for breakfast, little one," Sandor said tenderly. He put his hand on her head and tousled her gently. "But first . . . let's look at our fortune."

His lean strong fingers began to undo the red string. Vanya watched him, not looking down at the money but watching his face as he saw it for the first time. She saw the change in him and her mind could not understand it. At last he looked up at her and his voice was strange when he spoke.

"Well, little Vanya," he said. "We're rich now. We're rich—just as soon as the Confederate States of America come back into power."

Vanya looked, then. She saw the bundle of carefully preserved Confederate bills, large and strange-looking, and she felt her soul curl inside her.

Sandor had never punished her as gypsy men punish their wives. But she knew that he was going to do it now. Her mind revolted. She had killed the old woman and then the big bajoor had been a swindle on her instead. But her body did not move as she waited for Sandor to begin.

There was a silence. Then he opened the door of the car on his side. "Get out," he said. "Build a fire."

She got out of the car and went around to his side. She kept her eyes to the ground. He did not touch her.

"Build a fire," he repeated. "I want my breakfast, woman."

"Sandor," she said.

There was no pleading, no tears, in the voice.

"You are going to cook breakfast with the heat of your great bajoor," Sandor said above her.

She went away from him, began gathering the dry pine limbs. She moved numbly, as though she were an old woman. Sandor stood still, watching her as she knelt before the pile of sticks. He threw a match at her feet. Dazed, she struck it.

"A bigger fire," Sandor said.

She piled on the limbs she had brought. With one foot he kicked the package of Confederate money near her. Her hands tore the bills out of the stacks. She stopped, then.

"I can't burn money," she said. "Not even . . ."

"Burn it," he said.

She began putting the bills into the resin-hot fire. The flames licked at them, curling the edges, wisping them into ashes that preserved still the engraved pictures. She fed the fire steadily with the bills, her hands moving with a slow hurt that came from deep within her. It was a greater punishment than a beating from his broad leather belt.

Sandor went away, came back with the utensils for cooking. He dropped them by her side. "You have swindled me a great breakfast fire," he said. "See now if you remember how to cook my breakfast."

She put in the last handful of bills, scrabbled in the old newspaper to see if there were more. She picked up the thin booklet that had lain under the bills, hidden by them, and looked at it stupidly. It fell open in her hands. She kept on looking at it, laughing, a laughing that sounded like crying.

Sandor came back to her side, his face angrier still. "What's the matter with you, stupid woman?" he said.

She looked up at him, for the first time. She thrust the booklet toward him. "Look," she said. "Look. Where she has made the mark with the pencil."

He looked. His face turned white. He stalked away from her toward the car. She looked at the booklet again, seeing where the old woman had marked the page.

"This money catalogue is old, too," she called after him. "Yet here they are worth seventeen dollars apiece. Bodo Dad alone knows how much they are worth now."

He was gone into the trailer. She stood up shouting after him. "The father of the gajo woman was wise," she shouted after him. "He told the truth when he told her never to let it go. And you burned it. You burned my big bajoor. Seventeen dollars apiece!"

There was only silence. The anger and the weeping laughter left her. She squatted again beside the fire and looked into its red heart. She could still see the ashy outline of the last bill. She touched it with a stick and the ash crumbled so that it could not be distinguished from the rest.

She added the rare-money catalogue to the flames. Then she began cooking breakfast for her Romany man.

JACK RITCHIE

The Operator

Inside the police station, I found the Motor Vehicle Section and approached the sergeant.

He took his time about going through some papers on his desk, but finally he looked up. "Well?"

I cleared my throat. "I'd like to report the theft of an automobile."

He yawned, opened a desk drawer, and reached for some forms.

"It was a 1963 Buick," I said. "Four door. The body is dark green and the top cream."

He looked up. "Buick?"

"Yes. I parked it on the bluff above the lake, on Lincoln Drive. I just got out for a minute or two and walked around. When I came back, it was gone."

"The license number?"

I rubbed the back of my neck for a moment. "Oh, yes. E 20-256."

He looked at the civilian clerk at the next desk. They both grinned.

"As soon as I found that my car was gone," I said, "I flagged down a taxi and came here. This is the right place to report this, isn't it?"

"Yeah. It's the right place." He turned to the clerk. "Fred."

Fred left his desk and came over. He had a slip of paper in his hand.

The sergeant glanced at it and then looked up again. "Let's see your ignition keys."

"Ignition keys?" I reached into my right trouser pocket. Then I tried my left. I began patting my other pockets. Finally I smiled sheepishly. "I guess I must have lost them."

"No, mister. You didn't *lose* them." His face lost the grin. "Don't you know that it's against the law to leave your ignition keys in an unlocked car?"

I shifted uneasily. "But I was gone for just a minute."

"You were gone a lot longer than that, mister. The boys in the squad even took the trouble to look for you. They couldn't find you any place around there."

I frowned. "The boys in the squad?"

"That's right. They waited fifteen minutes and then one of them had to drive the car away."

"A *policeman* took my car?"

"He didn't steal it. If that's what you mean. He just took it to the police garage for your own protection." His eyes became cold. "Mister, did you know that in eighty percent of automobile thefts, the owner left his keys in the ignition?"

"Well . . . I guess I read something about that, but . . ."

"No buts," he snapped. "It's people like you who make it possible for the punks to steal cars."

I bristled. "Wouldn't it have been simpler just to lock the car and take the ignition keys? And maybe leave a note under the windshield wiper?"

"Sure it would be simpler, but it wouldn't teach people like you anything. But *this* you'll remember." He seemed to relent a little. "It's just your tough luck, mister. We've got orders to crack down this week and haul away any car if we can't find the owner. You should have read about it in the papers." He reached into another drawer this time and came out with a smaller form. "Like I said, it's against the law to leave your keys in the ignition. The fine is twenty-five dollars."

"*Twenty-five* dollars?"

"You can pay right here or take it to court. So far that's never done anybody any good. Just adds twelve dollars and ten cents to the tariff. That's costs."

I exhaled slowly. "I'll pay here." I took out my wallet and put two tens and a five on his desk.

"Let's see your driver's license."

I put the wallet on the desk in front of him.

He filled out the form, shoved it toward me, and pointed. "Sign there."

I signed. "Where can I pick up the car?"

He tore off the stub along the perforated line and handed it to me. "Your receipt. Show that to the sergeant in the basement garage. He'll let you have your car and keys."

Seven minutes later I drove out of the garage.

It was a clean car and handled nicely.

I wondered who it belonged to.

Earlier that morning, I had parked my car where the Lincoln Driveway arched down to the lake front.

It had been cool and only a scattering of cars were parked along the drive. I lit a cigarette and walked easy, taking in the automobiles I passed. Some of them were occupied and the empty ones appeared to be locked.

And then I came to the 1963 Buick. It was parked two hundred yards from the nearest other car and the keys were in the ignition.

I investigated the paths near the car and saw no one. At the bluff's edge, I looked down.

A man and a woman strolled along the beach far below and it seemed like a good bet that they belonged to the Buick. Even if they started back up right now, it would take them fifteen minutes to get up the twisting path to the top.

I walked back toward the Buick and was almost there when I saw the squad car parked behind it.

Both cops were out of their car. The taller one glanced my way. "Your car, mister?"

"No. But I wish it was." I kept walking and got back to my car ten minutes later.

I looked back down the long drive. One of the cops was still at the Buick, but the other had disappeared.

I watched. Five minutes later the tall cop reappeared. I guessed that he'd been looking for the owner of the Buick and hadn't found him down there on the beach.

He got into the Buick and pulled away. The squad car followed.

I turned on my ignition and kept about two blocks behind them. They took the Buick to the downtown police headquarters and it disappeared into the basement garage.

I parked my car and slowly smoked a cigarette. The tall cop finally came out of the basement drive and got back into the squad car. It drove away.

I thought it over and then grinned. I opened my glove compartment and took out the wallet that had once belonged to somebody named Charles Janik.

I drove the Buick the half mile to Joe's Garage and he opened the doors when I blew the horn. I eased the car to the pair of doors at the rear of the shop and into the room no legitimate customer of Joe's ever saw.

In twenty-four hours the Buick would have a different paint job, the motor block number would be changed, and it would leave here with a new set of license plates. By tomorrow afternoon it would be across the state line and on a used car lot.

Joe closed the doors behind us and looked the car over. "Nice buggy."

I nodded. "Cost me twenty-five dollars."

He didn't get that. "Where did you pick it up?"

I grinned. "You'll probably read about it in the papers this afternoon."

We went into his office.

"I'll phone in," Joe said. "You should get your money in the mail tomorrow."

"Have it sent to the Hotel Meredith in St. Louis."

"Taking a vacation?"

"You might say that."

But it was more than a vacation. After what I'd just done, every cop in the city would have a complete description of me down to the last button.

I phoned for a taxi and took it back to where I'd parked my own car.

At my apartment I packed a suitcase and then drove to St. Louis. The trip took three hours and I checked in at the Meredith at two thirty in the afternoon.

The clerk swiveled the register back so he could read my name. "How long are you staying, Mr. Hagen?"

"I don't know. It all depends."

Maybe I would stay three or four weeks before I thought it was cool enough to go back. Or maybe I wouldn't have to go back at all—if I got the telephone call I was hoping for.

The story got into the St. Louis evening papers, all about the man who walked into a police station and stole a car. The newspapers seemed to think it was hilarious, but the police didn't, especially not the sergeant I'd talked to. He had been suspended.

I stuck to my room and the phone call came the next afternoon. It was a voice I'd never heard before.

"Hagen?"

"That's right."

He wanted to be a little more sure he had the right party. "Joe says we owe you some money for the last errand."

"Send it here."

He seemed to relax. "I see you got into the papers."

"Not my picture."

He laughed slightly. "Some people would give a lot to have it."

I waited, because I didn't think he had called just to congratulate me.

"The man in Trevor Park wants to talk to you," he said. "You know who I mean?"

"I know."

"Eight tonight." He hung up.

I got to the main gates of Trevor Park at about seven thirty.

You couldn't call Trevor Park a town. It had no stores or gas stations and the big houses were far apart and not even numbered. But it was a place of trees and acres and money. It had its walking guards to keep the ordinary people out and a private police force to help them.

The cop at the gate came to my window.

"Hagen," I said.

He checked the clipboard he carried and nodded. "Mr. Magnus is expecting you."

"Which is his place?"

"The fourth one on your right."

The fourth one on my right didn't come up until half a mile later. There was another gate at the entrance, but it was open. Another two hundred yards brought me to a circle driveway in front of a three story Norman.

Eventually I found myself in a large study facing two men.

Mac Magnus was big and graying at the temples. Looking at him you would have thought he was born to the clothes he wore. He was that far away from where he had started.

The other man was tall and thin, with shrewd gray eyes, and when he spoke I recognized his voice as that I'd heard on the phone. His name was Tyler.

We got drinks served on a tray and Magnus looked me over. "Did you read about yourself?"

"In St. Louis. Page three."

He indicated some newspapers on the desk. "You did better than that locally."

I walked over and glanced down. The front page, bottom. There was a picture of the unhappy sergeant, too, but I didn't think he would save it for his scrapbook.

When I looked up, Magnus was still studying me.

"I suppose you know you cut your own throat," he said.

I shrugged.

"You'll never be able to go back. At least, not for a long time. Right now if you passed even a rookie patrolman, he'd look you over sharp and wonder if he should have a talk with you."

I sipped my drink. "There are other cities."

Tyler spoke now. "Hagen, just why did you take a chance like that in the first place?"

"I just wondered if it could be done. And so I tried."

But that hadn't been the real reason. I stole the Buick in the way I did because I wanted somcone up high to notice me. I didn't want to be doing nothing but stealing cars the rest of my life.

Magnus glanced at Tyler. "I still think it was a fool thing to do."

"Maybe," I said.

My eyes went around the room, taking in the expensive furnishings. "The car racket must be good, if you can afford all this."

Magnus laughed softly. "Not that good, Hagen. But I'm like a supermarket. I got all departments. The canned goods, the fresh vegetables, the meat counters, the frozen foods. Hot cars is just a little counter somewhere in the back of the store."

But I had known that, too. Magnus had his finger in everything that paid. He *was* everything. He was on top, and safe.

Magnus looked at Tyler. "He's got your okay?"

Tyler nodded.

Magnus went to the map on the wall and pointed. "Ever been there?"

I looked at the dot. "No."

"It's a medium-type city of about two hundred thousand. I don't have a big operation there, but I want you to report to Sam Binardi."

"I go to work for him?"

"No. You replace him."

"You don't like him any more?"

Magnus selected a cigar from a humidor. "Don't get any movie ideas, Hagen. Sam's sixty-five and worried about his ulcers. He wants to retire to one of those colonies in Florida and play golf all day." He lit the cigar. "Like I said, Hagen, it's not a big operation, so don't get excited. And you can thank Tyler for the promotion. He seems to think you got something—nerve, maybe—but as far as I'm concerned you're still only a second lieutenant, and that's way down on the ladder."

I decided to find out just where Tyler stood in the organization. "Tyler's second in command?"

Magnus laughed. "There *is* no second in command. You might say that Tyler's my personnel and recruitment officer. And that's only for the operating personnel. Not the bookkeepers. He's got his job and I don't want him to know any more than that."

I reported to Sam Binardi the next day.

Sam was a small, florid man with nervous gestures, and his office was on the second floor of a toy factory.

He shook hands. "Tyler phoned. Said you were taking over." He indicated a cabinet. "If you want a drink, help yourself. I don't drink myself. Bad for the stomach."

"Later, maybe."

He looked me over. "They're sending them up young these days. I been in this business forty years—thirty before I got to sit behind this desk." He sighed and looked at some papers. "Well, let's get at it. We've got ninety-six people on the payroll, and they're all good men."

"Counting the toy factory?"

"No. That's legitimate. Thirty-two employees. Mr. Swenson is the supervisor." He looked down at the papers again. "The real business is organized into four divisions. D-1. That's all the gambling, including the bookies. D-2. Junk. Riordan in charge. He's not hooked himself, so you can depend on him. D-3. Mable Turley. The girls like her. And D-4. Cars."

"What do I do? Just sit here?"

"Most of the time. There's the toy factory to consider, too. That'll keep you busy a couple of hours a day." He beamed. "We cleared twenty-eight thousand last year. Mostly because of the Dottie Dee dolls. Ever see one?"

"No."

"I'll show you around the factory later." He got up and went to the city map on the wall. "This is our territory. Everything north of the river, including the suburbs."

I looked at the map. The river divided the city into two almost equal sections. "What about the south side of the city?"

Binardi shook his head. "We leave that alone. That's Ed Willkie's territory. We mind our business and he minds his. That way we got no trouble." He came back to the desk. "We got a treaty like. There's no sense in fighting. I play golf with Ed twice a week."

He sat down. "I'll be in every day for about a month to break you in."

I phoned Captain Parker and we arranged a meeting at the Lyson Motel just outside of Reedville.

Walt Parker listened to what I had to say and then grinned. "So it was you who stole the car?"

"I had to get attention from the right people some way. This fell into my lap."

Parker agreed. "You could be stealing cars for twenty years and maybe never get noticed by Magnus. You got away with five cars so far?"

"Including the Buick."

He nodded. "They ship them to a place called Karl's Used Cars in Hainsford. Just across the state line. We could clamp down, but there's no point to that now. We're after bigger things. So we dip into the fund, buy up the cars for real, and store them in the garage for now. After this is all over, we'll make the adjustment with the owners or their insurance companies."

"Pretty rough on the fund."

"If this all works out everyone will forgive us."

"What about the sergeant?"

"In a way he's got it coming, considering how he let you get away with what you did. But we'll pass the word to the chief and it won't be too hard on him."

Parker sat down on one of the beds. "So now you're a second lieutenant in the operation."

"It's still a long way from the top. Magnus won't be handing me any secrets for some time yet."

"At least it's a toehold. Magnus has got himself a great big organization. I wouldn't be surprised if it covered every one of the fifty states and Puerto Rico for frosting. And this isn't the type of operation where you can carry the bookkeeping under your hat or in a little black notebook. There's *got* to be a central bookkeeping headquarters and we're out to find it. It's the only way we can really nail Magnus."

Parker lit a cigar. "We know how Magnus runs the operation. Take Binardi's, for instance—it's just like any of the hundreds of others Magnus controls. Once every month Magnus has a crew come in to microfilm Binardi's books. The film is mailed to a box number. Somebody picks it up and mails it somewhere else. Maybe it goes through five or six hands before it reaches that bookkeeping headquarters. But Magnus has so many safeguards on the way that we've never been able to follow the mail all the way through.

"And when the film gets to headquarters, half a dozen or more trusted accountants get to work on it—and the hundreds of others like it—and Magnus gets to know how much he made and where and when and by whom.

"Magnus's empire is like a head of hair. We can snip off a little here and there—maybe even give him a crewcut—but the roots are still there. We've got to get at those roots, and our best bet is to find out where in these whole blessed United States he's hidden that bookkeeping headquarters."

After a month, Sam Binardi left for Florida, and I was left to play golf with Ed Willkie on Tuesday and Thursday afternoons.

Willkie was in his fifties, tanned, and played in the eighties. His wife was dead, but he had a twelve-year-old son named Ted.

I learned that Willkie's organization was long established and conservative. Everybody waited patiently for his promotion. There was no idea of mutiny. Everyone took his orders from Boss Willkie and didn't feel frustrated about it.

On a Tuesday afternoon, two months later, when I pulled up in front of Willkie's house, I noticed Ted duck back behind the garage.

I was about to ring Willkie's doorbell, but then I changed my mind. I went to the garage and found Ted hiding behind it. "Aren't you supposed to be in school?"

He glanced uneasily toward the house. "There's no school today."

"On a Tuesday?"

He didn't meet my eyes. "Well . . . I didn't feel so good. So I stayed home."

"But your father doesn't know that?"

Ted didn't say anything.

"Do you play hooky a lot?"

"You're not going to tell my father?"

"No. I never cared much for school myself. How do you get away with skipping school?"

He grinned. "I write the excuses and sign Dad's name."

"What do you do when you skip school? You go somewhere special?"

His eyes brightened. "Mostly I go down to the lake and watch the boats. They have races almost every day now. There's a big one Thursday afternoon."

"And I suppose you'll be there?"

He grinned. "I guess so."

I went back to the front door and pressed the button. Willkie and I drove to the Wildwood course. He shot an eighty-two and I came in with a seventy-six.

The next morning I left the office for an inspection trip of my territory. I found the two big men I thought I could use and had them report to my office in the afternoon.

I came right to the point. "I've got a little job for you."

They looked at each other a little uneasily. "Job?"

"It's about the simplest thing you've ever done in your lives. I just want you to sit on the back seat of my car. I'm going to pick up Ed Willkie tomorrow afternoon. I'll drive the three of you a couple of blocks, and then I want you to get out. Go back to work and forget everything."

They looked at each other again and then the bigger one spoke. "Just that? Nothing else?"

"Nothing else."

"I don't get it."

"You're not supposed to. Just do as you're told."

He had one more question. "You don't expect us to do any rough stuff? I mean . . . well . . . those days are gone. I got a wife and . . ."

"No rough stuff. Nothing but what I told you. I'll pick both of you up at noon on the corner of Sixth and Wells."

At noon Thursday I packed my golf bag in the trunk of the car and stopped at Sixth and Wells. We drove on to Ed Willkie's big house and I honked the horn.

Willkie came down the walk carrying his golf clubs. He opened the car door. "A foursome today?"

"No," I said. "Just giving them a lift."

I drove two blocks and then pulled to the curb. The two men got out of the back seat.

When I pulled back into traffic, Willkie said, "Who were they?"

"Just a couple of friends from Chicago."

After the eighteenth hole, Willkie and I went to the clubhouse. We got some cokes and sandwiches at the counter and took a table near the window overlooking the first tee.

I glanced at my watch. "As soon as you're through eating, Ed, you'd better call a meeting of your division heads."

Willkie took a bite of his sandwich. "Why?"

"I want you to make the announcement that you're retiring because of your health. And you're appointing me to take your place."

His eyes narrowed. "You're crazy."

"No. You'll make that announcement if you ever want to see your son alive again."

He stared at me unbelievingly.

I smiled. "Remember those two nice men who were in the car when I picked you up? They've got your son by now." I tried my sandwich. "He's perfectly safe, Willkie. And he will be. As long as you do what I say."

He glared at me for thirty seconds and then rose abruptly. He strode to the telephone booth. I followed and kept him from closing the door. "I'll listen. I wouldn't want you to say anything rash."

I watched him dial his home number. He got his housekeeper, Mrs. Porter.

"Amy," he said. "Is Ted there?"

"Why, no, Mr. Willkie. He came home for lunch and then went back to school."

Willkie hung up and began paging through the phone book. I watched his finger run down the list of public schools. He dialed the number of Stevenson Grade and got the principal. "This is Edward Willkie. Is my son, Ted, in his class?"

It took about ten minutes for the principal to get the information. "No, he isn't, Mr. Willkie. And I've been meaning to speak to you about the number of times . . ."

I touched the hook on the side of the telephone and disconnected us. "Are you satisfied, Willkie?"

His face was gray. "I want to speak to Ted. I want to be sure he's all right."

"I can't accommodate you, Ed. I don't know where they took him."

He didn't understand that.

"Self-preservation," I said. "If I knew, you might be able to beat it out of me. But this way it wouldn't do you any good."

I gave him another minute to think things over and then cracked down. "All right. Start phoning your division heads. Have them meet at your office."

By the time we got to his office on the third floor of a furniture factory, his chief lieutenants were waiting.

Willkie took a deep breath and made the announcement, and the reason for it. They seemed to believe him. He didn't look too healthy.

I watched their faces for signs of resentment over the fact that an outsider had been promoted over their heads. I didn't see any. If there were some, they kept it off their faces. And possibly they were just specialists in their line. None of them ever really expected to get the number one position.

When they were gone, Willkie turned to me. "Now do I get my boy back?"

"Not for a week. You'll be gone at least that long yourself."

I drove him to the airport and explained things on the way. "You'll take the first plane out of here to Los Angeles. You'll stay there one week. At the end of that time you can come back and you'll get your son safe and sound. One week will give me enough time to consolidate everything here. By the time you come back you won't be able to do anything about anything." The smile left my face. "But if I were you, I wouldn't bother to come back at all. It might not be too healthy for either you or your son. Why not just send for him? I think he'll like California."

At the air terminal I bought him a nonstop ticket to L.A. and we walked to Ramp 202. I glanced at the waiting passengers. They were all strangers to me, but I nodded to a heavy man whose luggage seemed to indicate that he collected hotel stickers. He nodded back, probably wondering who the hell I was.

I turned my back on him and spoke to Willkie. "See that big man all wrapped up in the light tan coat?"

His eyes flicked that way. "The one you nodded to?"

"That's right. When you get to Los Angeles, I want you to follow him."

"Follow him?"

I nodded. "Check in at the same hotel he does. Stay there one whole week. He'll always be somewhere around to see that you do."

"He's one of your . . . ?"

"Don't talk to him. And don't try to buy him. He doesn't know any more than his part of the job. And remember, no phone calls to anyone. I don't want you arranging things behind my back. Remember, we've got your son. Don't even try phoning your home. If you do, I'll know about it. Mrs. Porter has orders to . . ." I stopped and shrugged irritably as though I'd revealed something.

Willkie must have felt surrounded. He certainly looked that way.

Ten minutes later, I watched him walk up the ramp and disappear into the plane. He was still wearing his billed golf cap and sports shirt. He looked small.

When the plane took off, I phoned Mrs. Porter and told her that Willkie would be gone for a week and not to worry. It was a business trip.

I expected a telephone call that night, but it didn't come until eight days later. Tyler told me to report to Magnus right away.

When I pulled into the circle drive in front of Magnus's house I noticed a darkhaired girl on the lawn near the lake. She had set up an easel and was painting. She gave me only a momentary glance and returned to her work.

Her picture was in the Mac Magnus file. Valerie Magnus. Twenty-three. His only child.

Tyler and Magnus were waiting for me in the study.

Magnus let me stand for a while and then he said, "I hear you took over the south side."

I nodded.

"That was eight days ago," Magnus said. "Why didn't you let me know?"

"I wanted to be sure the merger would take."

"Did it?"

"Willkie could come back today and I don't think anybody would listen to him."

Magnus went to the humidor. He took out a cigar, looked it over, and finally lit it. He walked to the TV set and tapped it with a knuckle. "If I turn this thing on I'll probably find somebody giving a spiel about soap. The talk will be that there's only one thing you're supposed to use when you do your washing. Soap. Don't use harsh detergents."

He tapped the set again. "And if I turn to another channel, I'll probably find somebody else pushing detergents. Detergents are the new, the modern thing. Don't use old fashioned inefficient soaps."

I noticed that Tyler was smiling.

Magnus went on. "What most people don't know is that the *same* company . . . the same *syndicate* . . . manufactures the soap *and* the detergent. They really don't give a damn *which* you buy . . . as long as you buy one. The money all goes into the same pocket."

He waited for that to sink in and then he said, "Willkie works for me, too."

I blinked. "Binardi didn't say anything to me about that."

"Binardi didn't *know* that. And Willkie doesn't know that Binardi worked for me either. I wanted it that way."

Tyler spoke. "Divide and rule. Empires are built that way."

Magnus held up a hand. "I don't want one finger to know what the other's doing, but I want to control the hand." He took a deep puff of his cigar. "Tyler, I'm beginning to think that you made a mistake about Hagen."

Tyler rubbed his jaw. "Hagen, how many people helped you pull this off?"

"None." And I told them all about it.

Magnus was impressed in spite of himself. "Damn. You scared Willkie silly. He didn't do a thing but stay in that L.A. hotel for a week. When he got up enough nerve, finally, to phone his home, he found that his son hadn't been kidnapped at all. The next thing he did was to phone me." Magnus glared at me. "I told Willkie to come right back. And as for you, Hagen, I want you to get back to the north side and *stay* on the north side."

Tyler stepped forward. "I've been thinking Mac. If Willkie scared that easy, maybe he's not the right man for the job."

"He was scared because of his kid," Magnus said.

"Sure. But he still shouldn't have waited eight days before he told us what happened to his organization. Do you want somebody like that working for you?"

Magnus worked on the idea for half a minute. "Tell Willkie he's through. He should have reported."

Tyler nodded. "And as long as the district's consolidated, why not leave it that way?"

Magnus showed teeth. "And I suppose you mean leave Hagen in charge?"

"Why not? I'd say he can handle the job. He has been, as a matter of fact. And it would cut down on overhead."

Magnus looked as though his arm had been twisted, but he said, "All right, Hagen, you got it." Then he glowered. "But if you get any other fancy ideas, you'd better clear them with me *before* you do anything."

Outside the house, I stopped for a moment to watch Magnus's daughter. Her back was toward me and she was still at the easel. She was slim, but from the picture in the files, you could hardly call her pretty. I had the suspicion that she did a lot of painting mostly because there was nothing else to do with her time.

I wondered what kind of a part she played as Magnus's daughter. Did he try to keep her ignorant of what he was? It seemed almost impossible that she could fail to know about him. Maybe she knew a lot more than he thought.

It was tempting to walk over there, admire her painting, and introduce myself. But on the other hand, I thought that if I were that direct, and Magnus heard about it, I'd be broken down to private.

And yet, it might pay to know her.

I went to the left rear wheel of my car and let the air out of the tire. The wind came off the lake and I didn't think she could hear the hiss.

I got the jack and handle from my trunk, and I made some noise while I was doing it.

As I jacked up the car, I covertly glanced her way. She had turned and was watching.

When I pried off the hubcap, I allowed the iron to slip and strike my knuckles. I jerked to my feet, holding the fingers of my left hand. I walked stiffly in a circle, cursing softly. It hurt more than I had anticipated.

That brought her over. "Are you hurt?"

"No. I always dance this way."

She looked down at the jacked-up wheel. "I can get somebody to change that for you."

"Thanks. But I think I can manage as soon as my wound heals." I flexed the hand. "Nothing seems to be broken." I knelt down and began removing the bolts from the wheel. "Do you work here?"

"Would I be sitting on the lawn painting second-rate pictures if I did?"

"Why not? I imagine you'd get time off and all the free scenery you can eat. No reason why a maid can't paint."

"I'm Magnus's daughter."

"Oh," I said. I removed one bolt from the wheel. Then the next. And the next.

"You're still allowed to talk to me," she said acidly.

I shrugged, but still said nothing. I removed the fourth bolt.

She took an exasperated breath. "I suppose you work for my father?"

I nodded. The fifth bolt came off and I removed the wheel. I went to the trunk for the spare. She followed me. "You just don't talk to anybody at all? Is that it?"

I took the spare out of the trunk and when I straightened, we were eye to eye. I kept it that way for about ten seconds, then I smiled faintly. "Let me put it this way. You're country club and I'm corner tavern. Kismet."

"I am *not* country club. As a matter of fact, we've never even been invited to join the one in Trevor Park."

I grinned. "Why not just buy the place? Your father ought to be able to do that."

"Of course he could. But you just don't *do* things like that. You've got to be *asked*. It makes all the difference in the world."

"To you?" I was mildly curious.

"No. I really don't care much one way or the other. But it does bother Dad."

I rolled the wheel to the side of the car. "Why doesn't he just send the club a five thousand dollar gift. But make it anonymous."

"Anonymous? What good would that do?"

"The members of the board, or whoever runs the place, won't be able to send the money back, because they won't know who gave it to them. So they'll think, 'Well, now, that's nice, and we do need a new bar.' And they'll spend it."

I began tightening the bolts. "That's the first hook. A month later, your father ought to send another five thousand. Again anonymous. Keep that up for four or five months."

She was interested. "And then?"

"And then *stop* sending money. But by now they'll be accustomed to getting the money regularly. They'll be wondering how they ever got along without it. They've begun to depend on it. As a matter of fact, they wouldn't have started building that new swimming pool if they hadn't expected the dollar rain to continue."

I tapped the hubcap into place. "And then let it leak out that your Dad is the one who's been sending all that beautiful cash—out of the goodness of his heart, and in the spirit of general neighborliness."

I looked up at her. "And so there'll be a meeting of the board, and nobody will say anything direct about money, but someone will clear his throat and say, 'Everybody in Trevor Park belongs to the country club, except Mr. Magnus. Now I was thinking, isn't that just a little inhospitable?'

"And somebody else will say, 'After all, he's never been convicted of anything. There are just rumors. And this *is* America, isn't it? We shouldn't convict a man just on hearsay.'

"And they'll all feel good, and American, and virtuous, and besides they still need another five thousand to finish that swimming pool. And the next thing you know a delegation will call on your father, and within another six months he'll be the chairman of the Memorial Day Dance Committee."

She grinned when I finished. "I'll be sure to tell Dad."

And don't forget to mention who gave you the idea, I thought. I put the spare in the trunk and wiped my hands on a rag. This time I looked at her longer, bolder. I grinned faintly. "I still wish you only worked here."

Then I got into my car and drove away, not pausing to look back.

I thought I had played things just about right. I didn't press the situation, yet I thought that she would spend some time thinking about me.

After I told Captain Parker how I'd taken over Willkie's territory, he frowned. "But we know that both Binardi and Willkie worked for Magnus. It's in the files we gave you to study. You should have remembered that."

I grinned. "I did."

"Then why. . . ?"

"Because it was time for me to get noticed again. To move up another notch. And I did just that."

Parker rubbed his ear. "What did Magnus think about it?"

"He wasn't too happy at first, and maybe he's not enthusiastic now. But the point is that he was impressed."

Parker sighed. "You have a lot of luck."

"Maybe some. Tyler seems to think I've got possibilities. As a matter of fact, I might not have been able to make it if Tyler hadn't been on my side."

Parker still looked unhappy. "Why don't you let us know before you do any of these crazy things?"

"I never really *know* what I'm going to do next. I make plans and wait for the situation. If it doesn't show up, I forget them. But if it does come up, I have to act fast."

Something else bothered Parker. "We can have you stealing cars, because we're working on a bigger thing. But this kidnapping . . ."

"There wasn't any kidnapping."

"Not actually, I suppose, but still if Willkie had some other trade and could be in a position to complain, you'd get yourself into trouble we couldn't get you out of."

He took an envelope out of his pocket. "Your check. If you'll endorse it, I'll bank it for you."

I looked at it. One month's pay. Twenty years from now the figures probably wouldn't be much different.

I turned it over and signed my real name.

When I got back to the city, I had Willkie's chief clerk bring in the books. I went over them, hoping to find something wrong, something I could run to tell Magnus about and get another gold star in my record, but the books were clean.

I did notice something else, though. Even if there was nothing wrong with the books, the handwriting had changed abruptly eighteen months ago.

I called the clerk back into the office and wanted to know why.

"That was when Fielding retired, sir," he said. "And I took over the job. Is there anything wrong with the books?"

"No."

"Fielding was a very sick man, sir. His kidneys. You might say that he didn't exactly retire; he just wanted to spend his declining days in a warmer climate. California, sir."

"How is he getting along?"

The clerk sighed. "I received a letter from his wife last week. Fielding passed away."

When the clerk was gone, I lit a cigarette and mulled things over. What the hell, I thought finally, you can't hurt a dead man.

I studied Fielding's handwriting and for a while considered trying to imitate it. But I gave that up. I didn't think anybody was going to be comparing handwriting anyway.

I got some blank paper and copied two of the pages from the account books Fielding had filled out. I kept the items the same, but I changed the figures.

I folded the paper and rubbed it on the floor a few times. I wanted to make it look at least eighteen months old, but it wouldn't have to pass a laboratory test.

At one o'clock I made a call to Magnus's place in Trevor Park.

I got a formal voice. "This is the Magnus residence."

"Could I speak to Mr. Magnus?"

"He isn't here, sir. He won't be home until five. Do you wish to leave a message?"

"No." I hung up. Perhaps it was just as well Magnus wasn't in. While I was working on this, I might as well keep something else going, too. And make it seem accidental.

I phoned the Magnus place again.

"The Magnus residence," the butler said again.

I hung up without saying a word. Five minutes later I called again and did the same thing.

Eventually the butler would get tired of picking up the phone and having no one to talk to. I thought he'd go to somebody and complain. And since Magnus wasn't there, it would be Valerie.

He must have been a patient man. It wasn't until twelve calls later that I finally heard Valerie's voice.

"Who *is* this?" she demanded.

"I'd like to speak to Mr. Magnus."

"Have you been phoning every five minutes and then hanging up?"

"Why, no. I just got to my office and . . ." I stopped. "The voice is familiar. Is this the girl who paints?"

"Hagen? Pete Hagen?"

"I didn't think I left the name."

"You didn't. I asked Dad." She laughed lightly. "He sent the first five thousand to the country club. He liked the idea."

"Good. Can I talk to him?"

"He's not here right now."

"Tell him I'll be there around five."

"Now look, Pete . . . Hagen. Nobody just *says* that he's coming here. That much I know. You wait until . . ."

I hung up.

At a little after five, the patient butler showed me into the study once again. Tyler was with Magnus and they had evidently just returned from a golf course.

Magnus glowered, but held himself in until the butler closed the door. "Damn it, Hagen, nobody, *ncbody* calls up and tells me he's coming here. If I want to see anybody here, *I'm* the one who does the inviting."

"I thought I ought to see you personally. I don't know how clear your phone line is."

He seemed to go along with that precaution, but he still wasn't happy. "All right. What is it?"

I took the sheets out of my pocket. "While I was going over Willkie's books, I found this. It must have slipped behind one of the shelves."

Magnus glanced at them. "So?"

"I checked these with the ledgers and found the right pages. The items are identical, but the figures are different. It looks like you were being taken, Magnus. For about five hundred a week."

He wouldn't believe that. "I have those books checked every month."

"There's nothing wrong with the books. The juggling takes place *before* the entries themselves are made."

He frowned. "Willkie?"

"No. A clerk Willkie used to have. Fielding. I compared the handwriting and it checks."

The name Fielding meant nothing to Magnus or Tyler. He was just another one of hundreds of clerks.

"I thought I'd let you know before I did anything about it," I said. "You told me you wanted things that way."

He studied me. "*You* want to do something about it?"

I nodded. "Fielding retired eighteen months ago. To California. But that isn't good enough for us. I think I'll take a trip out there."

Magnus waited.

"At least we'd have his hide," I said. "If not the money. We can't let anybody in the organization get away with something like this."

"And you'd take care of that little thing yourself?"

"Sure. But I wanted to clear it with you first."

Tyler looked worried and I thought he'd say something.

But Magnus laughed softly. "Thanks for volunteering. But all I need is Fielding's address. I've got a division that specializes in people like him."

And Magnus would arrange for Fielding to have visitors. But the visitors would discover that he fortunately died before they could see him.

But I had scored two points. For one, I could be trusted to keep the books honest. For another, so far as Magnus knew, I was willing to commit murder for the organization.

The phone on Magnus's desk rang and he picked it up. He listened for a minute and then hung up.

His eyes were thoughtful. "Benson's dead."

Tyler and I looked at each other. The name didn't mean a thing to either one of us.

"Heart attack," Magnus said. "Went just like that." He puffed his cigar and finally looked at Tyler. "You once mentioned that you had some kind of degree in accounting?"

Tyler nodded.

Magnus let things ride for a quiet half minute. Then he said, "Tyler, you got the job."

"The job?"

"Benson's job," Magnus said. "It's a promotion, Tyler. You'll be the only one besides me who knows where central bookkeeping . . ." He stopped and looked my way. Evidently he had forgotten I was still there. "You can go now, Hagen."

Outside the room, I walked past doors to the front of the house. None of them opened.

I began to wonder about Valerie. I'd made the phone call specifically so that she'd know I'd be here, and when.

At my car, I waited. Still nothing.

I'd been wrong before in my life and this looked like another time.

I got into my car and drove down the winding drive.

Valerie waited at the gate. She gave the hitchhiker's sign and I slowed the car to a stop.

She smiled. "Hello."

"Hello."

"How about a lift?"

I rubbed my hand along the steering wheel and tried to look uneasy. "Car break down?"

"No." She smiled. "Are you afraid of something?"

I took a breath. "No. Get in."

I waited until we were out of Trevor Park before I said anything. "How will you get back?"

"I'll take a taxi."

"Wouldn't it have been much simpler if you'd just taken your car?"

"I walked down to get the mail. There wasn't any, so I decided to go to town. Flash of the moment type of thing."

"Does the mail come this late in the day?"

She looked at me. "Did you think that I deliberately waited for you to come along?"

I didn't say anything.

She stiffened. "You might as well stop right here. I'll *walk* the rest of the way."

I slowed the car down to about twenty and then stepped on the accelerator again. I sighed. "Care for a cigarette?" I took the pack and lighter out of my pocket and handed it to her.

She lit two cigarettes and passed one on to me. "Suppose I weren't Magnus's daughter?"

"Maybe I'd ask you for a date. Maybe."

"Why?"

"What do you mean, 'why'?"

Her eyes were level. "I have a mirror. People don't ask me for dates."

I stared at her as though I didn't have the faintest idea of what she was talking about.

"Watch the road," she said. But she had blushed, and she was pleased.

I got the car back into my lane. "You wouldn't happen to know if there's a good restaurant in town? I haven't had anything to eat since breakfast."

"There's Henrich's."

After a while I asked, "Have you had dinner?"

"No."

This time when I looked at her, I smiled. And so did she.

In the restaurant we kept the talk small, but at coffee she said, "I wish you didn't work for my father."

"He gives out nice money."

"No, he doesn't." She looked away. "As my father, I love him. And he loves me. But I know what he does. What he is. I'm not a little girl who thinks her father's in the investment business."

After I paid the check, I drove her back. At the entrance to Magnus's estate, she touched my arm. "I'll get out here and walk the rest of the way."

I had intended to stop here anyway. I didn't want Magnus to see me with his daughter. But I made the motions of protest. "I'll take you up to the house."

"No. I think it would be better if we just . . ."

"Sure," I said. "I guess you're right. We're both right. It's better to say goodbye."

"I didn't mean that," she said desperately. "I mean—just for *now*."

I stopped the car, got out, and opened her door. She stepped out, looking small and lonely.

It was evening and a full pale moon hung in the sky. I looked down at her. "I like that restaurant. Henrich's. I don't suppose you'd like another lift to town? Say tomorrow night at eight?"

Her smile was sudden. "I'll be here. I will."

When I drove away, I glanced back. She still stood beside the road, watching me.

I got to my apartment at about nine. I made myself a stiff drink and walked to the mirror. I looked about the way I felt. A little dirty.

I went to the window and stared out over the lights of the city. How long would it take before I found out where Magnus kept that damn bookkeeper's nest? One year? Two?

And then what? Another assignment and a three-figure monthly check?

I took out my wallet and counted the money. Nineteen hundred dollars. And that was just spending money. Something you carried around to keep from feeling insecure. Just for odds and ends.

But I'd never had that much in my wallet before. I'd never expected to.

I had a good deal going here. Suppose I kept it that way?

Suppose I told Captain Parker to go to hell.

I swallowed half the drink.

There was a lot of money to be made with Magnus. A lot. But there was something else, too. Just working for him was one thing, but suppose . . . suppose . . .

It could be done, I thought. Get Magnus to see me more often. Get *him* to invite me to his house. Like Tyler. Get Magnus to trust me completely. Depend on me.

Make it so that when he saw what was happening between Valerie and me, it wouldn't bother him at all. Maybe I could even get him to think that it was his own idea.

Yes. It would take time. But I could sell it.

And what about Parker?

There wasn't much he could really do except to let Magnus know why I had gotten into the organization in the first place.

How could I get Magnus really to believe that I'd switched sides? How could I convince him? How?

My phone rang.

It was Tyler. "Hagen? I'm at the Carson hotel in Bellington. That's about an hour's drive north of where you are. I'd like to see you right away. Room 408."

When I got there and knocked, Tyler opened the door. I noticed a bottle and two glasses on the table.

Tyler patted me on the shoulder. "Come on in and help me celebrate."

I closed the door behind me. "Sure. Your promotion."

He grinned. "I just finished inspecting Magnus's central bookkeeping headquarters. It's right here in Bellington. The front is the Spencer Insurance Agency. The complete books are there, Hagen. Everything."

I frowned. "I thought that kind of information was something you were supposed to keep under your hat."

Tyler laughed again. "There's no reason why I can't tell you, Hagen. We're both working for the same organization."

"I know. But . . ."

Tyler's face became serious. "Hagen, did you think that in something this big, Captain Parker would have only *one* man working on the job?"

I stared at him.

"There are at least a half dozen besides you and me, Hagen. I don't know who the others are, but I was told about you."

It took a little while for what he had said to sink in. I shook my head. "Why didn't Parker tell me about you? Or the others?"

"Because if something went wrong, he didn't want any single man to pull down all the rest."

"But still he told *you* about me."

"Because I was in a position to help you along. Did you think that you alone made all your luck? You might still be stealing cars if I hadn't been there to keep calling you to Magnus's attention."

He poured whisky into two glasses. "I've been on this assignment for five years, Hagen. And that's a long, long time. But it looked like I'd gotten into a dead end. So my instructions were to help you along whenever I could—try to get you to the top, and maybe you could do what I hadn't been able to. And then this good thing came along. Benson died. Luck? Sure. But it wasn't luck that I was up there for Magnus to tap on the shoulder."

I took one of the glasses and almost emptied it. "Have you told Captain Parker about the books?"

"Not yet. I phoned his office and got referred to his home. But his daughter told me that Parker and his wife went out for the evening. She didn't know where they went. I left a message for him to call me here just as soon as he gets home." Tyler lifted his glass in a toast. "Parker will get his squads busy and we ought to have this thing wrapped up before morning."

I stared at the liquor in my glass. No one knew about the books yet, but Tyler.

He frowned slightly. "About this clerk, Fielding. We've got to stop that. We don't want anything to happen to him."

"Fielding died about two weeks ago."

Tyler grinned slowly. "You're a smart operator, Hagen. For a while there you had me worried. Murder's going too far."

Is it? I smiled faintly to myself.

I would kill Tyler. I would kill him and tell Magnus who he was. What he had been.

And then I would tell him who *I* was—and that I'd changed sides.

Even then he might not believe me—until I told him I knew where central bookkeeping headquarters was and hadn't gone to the department with the information.

I reached for the bottle and filled my glass.

"Easy on the liquor, Hagen," Tyler said. "You want to be on your feet for the raid, don't you?"

"Sure." But I took another long drink.

The phone on the table rang. When Tyler picked it up, his back was toward me.

I slipped the .38 out of my holster, leveled it at Tyler's back.

Tyler spoke into the mouthpiece. "Parker?"

I found myself perspiring. Just one shot and it would be all over. It could be as simple as that. My finger touched the trigger.

And then I closed my eyes.

No. I couldn't do it.

I cursed myself for being a fool. A sucker. But I slipped the .38 back into the holster.

Someday I would figure out why a badge was more important than a million dollars, but I didn't want to work on it now.

When Tyler was through, he turned. "It's all set. Parker's getting the wheels moving. He's even going to pick up Magnus tonight."

A reflective haze came into Tyler's eyes and he grinned wryly. "There's a lot of money to be made with Magnus. There were times . . . well . . . you know . . . there were times when I was a little tempted to change sides."

I pulled a cigarette slowly from my pack. "Yeah. I know what you mean."

I parked and waited outside the car. The road ahead was white with moonlight.

There wasn't any reason for being here, I thought. Not now.

I glanced at my watch. Eight fifteen.

Then I heard the footsteps and in a moment Valerie stood at the gates.

She was a nobody now, I told myself savagely. She didn't mean millions. She didn't mean information I wanted.

And yet I was here.

She walked slowly to the car. "Why did you come?"

"I don't know." Was it pity?

"Everything was planned, wasn't it? Meeting me? Talking to me?"

"Yes. I planned it."

"You didn't have to come back now," she said. "Everything has been done."

"I know."

"Did you travel all this way just to say goodbye?"

I touched her face lightly and she began to cry.

I held her and I knew why I'd come back.

DONALD OLSON

The Souvenir

It was my custom to stay on for a week or two at The Buckeye after the season ended; it was then that I did my best work and in my spare time I would help Margit, my landlady, prepare the ancient rooming house for winter. Her grandmother and aged aunt, with whom she had passed a dull, migratory existence for many years, opening the place in Glen Avon in May, closing it after Labor Day and journeying to St. Petersburg for the winter months, had both died down there within weeks of each other two years before, but Margit still practiced the same ritual; she was like a bird who finds its cage is open at last but can't decide where to go or even if its wings will work.

I happened to be alone in the house, trying to finish the last chapter of my novel and so deeply absorbed I jumped a bit when the bell rang, and when I went down to open the door I found an attractive but doomed-looking woman with blue eyes and cinnamon-colored hair peering through the screen. A foreign sports car was parked at the curb.

"I'm looking for Miss Fanchon. I'm Helen Maier."

The name didn't register at first. I told her Margit had gone for a walk but should be back at any minute.

"I was told the Fillmore—is that its name?—is the only hotel still open. Maybe I ought to go around there and see about a room for the night. I've been driving for hours."

She gave a sudden cry as she followed me into the parlor and I put out my hand, thinking she might have twisted her ankle on the little step-down. Her face was sickly pale and when I saw the direction of her gaze I knew at once who she was.

"Good heavens, how stupid of me! You must be Paul's wife."

She kept staring at that piece of sculpture on the mantel.

"Who's the artist?" she asked faintly.

"Margit—Miss Fanchon." Then, idiotically trying to dispel the awkwardness of the moment, I added, "The head in the middle—that's mine." I always had to tell people because, in truth, it only vaguely resembled me. Margit always said I had the sort of face to which only Rodin could do justice.

Mrs. Maier's next question was obvious. "And the woman's? Could that be—her?"

"Juliette Bardo. Yes."

She studied the head with the feigned indifference of a gallery visitor. "I might have known she'd be stunning." She asked me if I'd known Paul and I said yes, fairly well, as well as one gets to know fellow lodgers in a rooming house during a short summer season.

"Please sit down," I told her. "Or would you rather wait in another room? I shouldn't have brought you in here."

She was already more composed. "Don't apologize. I'd known for years that my husband had *feet* of clay. He played first violin in that orchestra for fifteen years. I played second fiddle in his life for twelve. This Juliette Bardo person was simply the latest of a long string. It never bothered me that much, really. I'm not a romantic schoolgirl. Paul always came back to me when the season ended. He was always mine for those long winter months." She read my expression and quickly laughed. "Don't get the wrong idea. I'm not tracking him down. I've been spending the summer at Lake Placid and on my way south thought it might be fun to see this place. I never came up when Paul was with the symphony all those summers. He never urged me to. Naturally. But I must say I was shocked when I got his letter. Formal as a letter of resignation— which of course is what it was. And typewritten at that! Saying he'd fallen in love with this Juliette Bardo and was going away with her to start a new life. Oh, it was a masterpiece of cruelty, that letter. Wish now I'd never burned it. So, I just suddenly took it into my noggin to see the place where this great romance flowered."

She surveyed the tacky-looking parlor with the sort of disappointed frown one might see on the face of an avid Shakespearean at his first glimpse of Verona.

She said, in reply to my question, that she hadn't heard a word from Paul since that letter. "I suppose he was too ashamed. He's never even tried to claim any of the money. He can't be playing with any well-known orchestra. I would have heard. But then I suppose they're living in Love Land, where material worries are unimportant. You knew her, too, I assume?"

I nodded but didn't feel it necesary to tell her that I'd thought Juliette Bardo to be a rather sweet young creature. No innocent—she was an actress of sorts and had been around—but not tawdry, either. Exactly the sort of girl who would run off with a handsome dark-eyed violinist.

"Were you here when they left?" she wanted to know, and once again I wondered if she were not secretly in pursuit of the pair. Well, I certainly couldn't give her any clues to their destination. Margit had asked me to take some clothes to the dry cleaners in the city for her that day. When I'd got back she'd broken the news to me that the couple had run off.

I told her this, and she looked at her watch with a frown. "I'm hungry and tired. And frankly, this place gives me the willies. I suppose it's the sort of atmosphere only a writer—or musician—could appreciate." She stood up and wrapped her fur stole around her shoulders. "Tell Miss Fanchon I was here, will you? If she doesn't mind, I think I'll drop back later this evening." Then, glancing back, "Maybe I could get her to sell me those heads. Think what a joy it would be to smash them against a brick wall!"

I laughed. "If she thought you'd do that she'd never let you have them. They're the best things she's ever done."

I supposed I owned the worst—that head of the busboy Adonis she'd been working on the first year I knew her—her maiden effort.

Glen Avon, if you've never been there, is rather like Tanglewood or Chautauqua or that place in Vermont where my old college professor used to dry out while lecturing on the metaphysical poets. It has a miniature panorama of the Holy Land, a shaded plaza, an amphitheater where Glenn Miller *and* Toscanini had performed—it was that sort of place, something for everyone, and picturesque enough for the most demanding: quaintly narrow streets of eccentric-looking hotels and rooming houses huddled together in a vast leafy gloom which would abruptly end as you emerged from the shadow of the rambling hotel onto a greensward stretching between the bathing beach and the bell tower, and bordering one of the prettiest lakes in the Adirondacks.

Its eight-week midsummer season was crammed with a potpourri of operas, concerts, plays, lectures, and art classes, and then after Labor Day, when it all came to an end, its population would dwindle to a relative handful. I liked it best then, when its atmosphere was curiously mellow, as if ghostly strains of music still floated upon the quiet air, and a gentle autumnal haze would settle over the lake, and the Westminster chimes from the bell tower would echo among the narrow empty streets with an unearthly resonance, and I would look up from my work with that pleasant feeling of sheltered, isolated cosiness reminiscent of college days on a deserted summer campus.

This place to which I'd been coming for the past four summers was the typical frame rooming house in the center of the grounds, damp and umbrageous, in thickets of lily of the valley and spidery rhododendrons, with a painted sign, *The Buckeye*, nailed over the front door, and a buckeye tree planted beside the porch, because Margit's Auntie Belle and Nanna had come from Ohio in the antediluvian past.

My landlady herself, the spinster survivor of those two formidable dragons, was "an overgrown, clumsy, young-old woman with a plain, intense, kindly face which looked as radiantly sallow as a cloistered Carmelite's, and as ignorant of the more robust emotions,"—which is how I described her in a story I tried to write about her the first season I was here—a story I never finished, incidentally, because its main character seemed to resist my attempts to involve her in any sort of dramatic situation.

While the two female dragons were still alive I would occasionally come upon Margit sitting alone on one of the benches near the bell tower, watching the sailboats or the sunset, and we would exchange the shyest of hellos. Then one day I'd seen her at the Plaza Art Festival where, with others in the beginners' modeling class, she was trying her best to reconstruct in clay on a wire armature the head of a model, but it was pathetically clear to me as I watched her that she would never succeed, not from any specific lack of talent but because she was trying to get more than was there. The handsome youth the class was using as a model was all blue eyes and jawline, whereas Margit was trying to make something spiritual out of him, and I'd felt like stopping behind her and whispering in her ear: "Forget it, my dear. Apollo *has* no soul."

Instead, I'd waited till the rest of the class and spectators had dispersed, leaving her gazing sadly at the result of her wasted efforts, and I'd felt sorry for her and impulsively declared I wanted to buy it. She blinked at me. "Whatever for? It's hideous." I badgered her until she gave in, although she insisted on making me a present of it. It still sits here on my desk. Hideous, yes, but with a singular kind of honesty about it which makes it rather precious to me. In its way, I think it superior to those heads of Paul and Juliette, which seem to me too cheaply attractive, too spiritless.

Helen Maier drove off toward the Fillmore and I returned to Chapter Fifteen. I heard Margit come in about a half hour later and when I went down she was laying out the tea things. Auntie Belle and Nanna had been staunchly British and this habit of afternoon tea was one of their legacies Margit had not abandoned. Her tenants during the season found it rather endearing, and so did I.

My news surprised her. "Paul's *wife*? How very odd. Whatever brought *her* here?"

"She said she was on her way home from Lake Placid and decided to look the place over. Although, between you and me and the buckeye tree, I think it's more of a sentimental pilgrimage than she lets on."

"What do you mean?"

"Or else she's actually trying to track him down. Maybe that's why she wants to see you."

Margit looked scornful. "Well, land sakes, *I* can't tell her anything. If she thinks I played Friar Lawrence to *that* Juliette and her Romeo I'll soon set her straight. I can't tell her a thing she doesn't already know. Her husband was a charming man, but a philandering cheat. That's all I can tell her."

I sat down at the table and she poured the tea. "Your aunt and grandmother were such strict old ladies, I've often wondered why they allowed him to live here."

"Oh, he was smooth as syrup and sweet as honey, you know that. Could worm his way into any woman's good graces—without half trying."

I detected the faintest shadow of a blush and it occurred to me to wonder if Margit herself hadn't had romantic yearnings toward the passionate fiddler. Now, with Auntie Belle and Nanna dead and Paul no doubt far away, I felt bold enough to tease her about it. "I may be wrong, but I seem to recall his flirting with you, as well."

She responded with such a frank and painful blush I quickly backed off. "But then, that was probably my writer's diseased imagination."

She became unexpectedly thoughtful, sipping her tea with a musing, distant look, and then she put the cup down and looked at me with an expression which was brave almost to defiance.

"If you weren't going to Europe next summer I'd be quite willing to have you think so—that it was just your imagination, I mean."

Her face began to shine with an unaccustomed excitement, and once more she blushed.

I was intrigued. "You mean it wasn't only my imagination?"

"Well," this time she was tremulously coy, "not entirely, maybe."

I thought she was going to lose her nerve and pass it off as a joke, but I was wrong.

"You won't ever come back here, will you? I mean, after your summer in Europe. You'll go to other places. You won't ever come back here."

There was no point in lying. "No, I suppose not, but then, who can tell? I'm very fond of this place."

She continued to shake her head. "You won't ever come back. I can tell. The way you look at everything. You're storing it all up, aren't you?"

I admired her perceptiveness. "You should have taken up writing instead of sculpture."

"You said once you'd write a story about Auntie Belle and Nanna. Remember? My, but weren't they flattered? And you listened so patiently to their tales and reminiscences . . . You will write about them someday, won't you?"

"It's very likely."

The next thing she said caught me off guard. "I wish you'd write a story about me someday."

This may not look in print as touchingly wistful as it sounded. She sat across from me, this awkward-looking, soft-eyed, no longer young woman, and she was so painfully sincere it was embarrassing.

"Oh," I said, "I no doubt shall."

She lowered her eyes and shook her head. "No. I'm not the sort of person stories are written about. My life is too dull."

I couldn't help thinking about that story I'd tried to write about her and couldn't. Presently she looked up and gave me a slow, almost provocative smile. "If I tell you something—something I would never in my life tell another soul—will you promise to write a story about me?"

Still thinking of that one paragraph that had led nowhere, and trying not to look as guilty as I felt, I nodded.

"And you must promise never to tell anyone. I mean, in a story, that's different. No one will know it's me. You can change my name and appearance and all that."

"Of course."

She drew her chair in closer to the table. "Well, to tell the truth, Paul did flirt with me. When I'd bring up his towels and things. It was all in fun, of course. I knew he didn't mean anything by it, but how Auntie Belle and Nanna did tease me about it. Then one evening we ran into each other on the plaza and he took me to the Refectory and bought me an ice cream cone. And walked me home. I went to every one of the concerts that season. And the rehearsals. I'd sit way up there in the amphitheater behind the orchestra where he couldn't see me. But he knew I was there. He always knew . . . Want your tea warmed up?" She said this very crisply and I could tell she needed a moment to discharge the emotion in her voice—or to get her story straight in her head. I was almost sure she was making it all up.

"Then one night just a few days before the season ended, after the last concert, I waited for him and he walked home with me. He held my hand and we took a roundabout way along the shore. He kissed me by the bell tower. That night, after everybody was asleep and the house was quiet, he came to my room."

Curiously, she said this without blushing. "I can't believe Auntie Belle and Nanna really found out. They couldn't have. But there was something in the way they looked at me the next morning . . . but they didn't say anything and the season ended and Paul went home. To his wife, I suppose, although none of us knew he even had a wife then. I honestly didn't expect to see him again, you know."

She sipped her tea with a mildly sour expression, as if she found the beverage—or the memory—bitter. "I think I hoped that he wouldn't come back to The Buckeye. But, miracle of miracles, he did. I guess I thought it was a sign from heaven. I behaved foolishly, though I tried to be discreet, of course, and implored him to be. That's why it surprised me now when you said you thought he'd flirted with me. It was a wonderful summer . . . I was older than any of those sweet young things who used to hang around Paul, mooning over his Haydn and Bach; so cool, so resilient. *I* had no resilience left, and that's why I ought to have known better. But it was now-or-never time for me, and I knew it. Age comes so suddenly when there's been nothing to gauge your progress by. Life is just a landscape without figures. No growing children, no aging husband, no fellow workers, no friends. Auntie Belle and Nanna? Don't be funny. They were always old, far back as I can remember. Walking mummies. Two mummies and a zombie, that was us!"

She emptied her cup and folded her hands in her lap. "But it was all an act. He would have been kinder if he'd broken into the house and—attacked me. Then sneaked off. But the concerts, the after-dark walks along the lake, our special bench behind the bell tower, that funny little tearoom where they were always short of forks, the trip around the lake that night on the *Gadfly*, the mist along the banks and the moonlight on the water. It all meant . . . nothing!

"That winter both Auntie Belle and Nanna died—so unexpectedly. I would have come unraveled if I hadn't had Paul to think about. Paul . . . and the summer to come. I was almost sure he wouldn't return."

The more she said now the uneasier I became, because the conviction kept growing in me that it was all make-believe, wishful thinking.

"But he did come," I was forced to prompt her.

"Oh, he came. Yes, indeed, he came. He was shocked to hear about Auntie Belle and Nanna, and for a while he was nice enough to me. But you remember we had a new roomer that season—dear Juliette. I began to notice how they looked at each other when they thought I wasn't looking. Then as time went on they grew reckless, brazen. Well, I don't have to tell you. You were right here. You remember. Oh, yes, they made no bones about their feelings for each other. You can imagine how *I* felt. People couldn't help remarking how nervous and moody I was—but you all thought it was because of Auntie Belle and Nanna. Well, now you know the truth. Finally, I just couldn't take it any longer. We had it out, Paul and I. And that's when he told me."

She flicked a hanky out of her sleeve and dabbed at her eyes, a gesture that seemed too consciously theatrical. "The reason he'd come back to The Buckeye, you see, after that first season, was that Auntie Belle and Nanna had told him he could stay here *rent free*! As long as he was *nice* to *me*! Yes. God's truth. And that's only part of it. They paid him! Actually gave him *money*. And he'd taken it! That's the kind of man he was. Those two sweet, ridiculous old ninnies had *bribed* him to be nice to me. They were actually going to try to *buy* me a husband."

My astonishment seemed to please her immensely. "There! Isn't that a story for you?"

A story—that is to say, fiction—was what I felt sure it was, but I merely said, "Is that all? That's the end?"

"Ah, well . . . you can supply whatever ending you please. I leave that entirely up to you. They ran away together when the season ended. You can say they lived happily ever after, I don't care."

"Did Juliette know about you and Paul?"

"Of course. I had to tell her. I felt it was my duty. I wanted her to know what sort of wretch she was involved with. But it did no good. She was too moonstruck to care."

I'm not saying that I believed the *entire* story to be a lie. I was sure she was fond of Paul Maier, and I'm sure he did flirt with her in a mild, half-joking manner; and though I supposed it was not inconceivable the two old ladies might have been capable of such a stratagem to get a man for their spinster niece, I couldn't see Paul Maier being a party to it. He hadn't struck me as being that depraved a character. I felt sure that that part, and the part about his going to bed with Margit, was pure fantasy. The story was far more interesting and dramatic the way she told it, of course, but I hadn't a shred of what the courts call "hard evidence" to back it up.

That evening, true to her word, Helen Maier called at The Buckeye again. Margit greeted her warmly. I went to my room and did some more work and when I went back downstairs the visitor was just leaving.

"That head you did of Paul," she was saying to Margit, "May I buy it from you?"

Margit smiled, a very generous smile. "No. But you're welcome to it as a gift."

Helen Maier regarded it dryly, once it was in her hands. "As I told your friend here, I always knew my husband had *feet* of clay. This will be a most appropriate souvenir of our marriage."

"Take the other one, too, if you'd like it."

"No, thanks. I think it's time the lovers were separated."

I believe she half hoped there might be some voodoo-like significance attached to this transaction, that by removing Paul's effigy from the company of his paramour's she was magically effecting some faraway separation of their two bodies.

When she had gone, Margit looked at me with wry satisfaction. "I can see what you're thinking. No, I didn't tell her any of what I told you. That's *our* secret. You can send her a copy of your story—if you ever write it, that is."

The next morning we were standing on the porch of that prim-looking white frame house, the porch that was shaded by morning glories on one side and by the buckeye tree on the other, and we, too, were saying goodbye.

"I ought to have a souvenir, too," I said. "May I have the other head? Juliette's?"

Her eyes twinkled. "Let's trade. Give me back the one I did of you. Don't pretend. You never did like it. And you can have hers."

As we made the exchange she said, "There. Now you own my first and last artistic efforts. As well as my worst and my best."

I never saw her again, and I didn't think I ever would get around to writing that story about her. I suppose I might even have forgotten about Margit altogether if I hadn't had those two heads to remind me of her. The one of the young Adonis, though artistically regrettable, makes a splendid paperweight; Juliette's I used as a bookend, which my friends admired very much, praising the sculptor's superb plastic sense and assuming he must have been someone of renown. I would merely smile and keep the secret to myself.

Then one day as I was reaching for a book I accidentally dislodged the head, which toppled from the shelf and shattered on the hardwood floor. When I knelt to exmaine it more closely I discovered why it was so nearly perfect a replica of Juliette's head, for the clay was not molded around the conventional armature but instead adhered to an actual human skull—a skull which could only have been Juliette's.

Then I understood why Margit had sent me away on some errand the night Paul and Juliette had "run away together," and why she had said she was going to stay on a while longer than usual at the end of that season, telling me she had some "loose ends that must be tidied up."

As a man, I was quite naturally horrified by this discovery, but as an artist I must admit I couldn't have been more pleased, for now at last I could sit down and finish writing that story about Margit.

I had my hard evidence.

NANCY SCHACHTERLE

Speak Well for the Dead

O'Hara was frustrated, and when Daniel Epstein O'Hara was frustrated, the reverberations were felt for miles around. Harried nurses found themselves cherishing the hope that, since he was obviously not going to leave the hospital soon, he might die inexplicably. Or, desperately, they even weighed the possibility of arranging his untimely demise themselves. At times they considered that their subsequent punishment could never outweigh the relief they would obtain.

Not only was O'Hara confined to a hospital bed, but O'Hara was in traction—and O'Hara in traction was not to be taken lightly.

Aside from his actual detention in the hospital, O'Hara was frustrated by the nature of his injury. It was no honorable gunshot wound, taken in the line of duty, but a spiral fracture of the left leg suffered during the last weekend of the skiing season that had him strung up like, he thought privately, a Christmas goose.

The morning bath and its concomitant insults now over, O'Hara, or most of his lean length, lay in a rat's-nest of bed sheets surrounded by sections of the two morning papers. His torso rocked dangerously toward the edge of the bed as he tried to reach for part of the *Clarion-Register* which had slid to the floor, and for a moment it seemed as if he would be suspended from the cast-encased leg strung up to the overhead pulley.

"I'll get it!" Sergeant Giovanni arrived opportunely and dived for the paper before O'Hara could tumble to disaster.

"It's about time," O'Hara growled, over the pronouncements of a newscaster on a television set on the wall opposite him. "The most important murder of the century and I'm left here like a turkey on a spit, trying to scrounge a few facts from the daily papers like any man in the street."

"You're on sick leave," Giovanni reminded him.

"I'll go crazy in this place if I don't have something to keep me busy. My body may be out of action, but my mind isn't."

"I was just supposed to bring some mail that was on your desk," Giovanni said, handing O'Hara several envelopes banded together.

The sufferer barely glanced at them, and shoved them into the drawer of his bedside table. Then he settled back against the pillows, arms firmly folded, his wiry copper-with-gray hair thrust upright by rampaging fingers. "Come on, Giovanni, clue me in."

"Well," Giovanni said, gesturing at the newspapers, "it's pretty much all there."

"Don't give me that, me boyo. There's nothing there. Probyn's dead. That's all that's there. Start at the beginning. How am I to help solve this case if I don't get the facts?"

"Well . . ." Giovanni was hesitant, casting a look at the door. "I guess a few minutes won't make much difference. Deceased was Gerald Probyn," he began, as if reading from a notebook.

"I know that!" O'Hara interjected. "Every schoolchild knows Gerald Probyn. He owns the mines, he owns the mill, and he owns the state senator, if the truth were known. He lives, or used to, at Highgates, an aptly named estate eight miles east of town that is just a little harder to get into than Fort Knox, and somebody bumped him off. Now, are you going to give me the facts, or do I have to hobble down to headquarters and get them myself?"

Giovanni blushed. He was a mild man, short and solid, still a little over-whelmed by O'Hara, but after six months' association becoming almost used to him. He stood at a respectful distance by the window.

"We don't know what time Probyn was shot. It seems he spent most of his spare time in his greenhouse, had been out there since early afternoon. He had a great German shepherd named Vulcan, who prowled the place on his own—more of a pet than a watchdog. A little before five o'clock—she's not quite sure of the exact time—the cook heard Vulcan howling, a real mournful sound, she said, and sent one of the maids off in a hurry to see what was wrong. The maid found Probyn just outside the greenhouse, dead, with the dog howling over him."

O'Hara was leaning forward, listening intently. He threw a murderous glance at the television set, now dripping a fatuous soap opera. "Turn that idiot box off!"

Giovanni studied the set above his head. "You've got the controls," he pointed out reasonably.

O'Hara thrashed among the bed sheets and came up with the remote control. Snowy dead channels flashed intermittently with ancient westerns and cheery game shows as he fumbled the buttons, then finally the set subsided into a black stare. "That's better. And you could come a little closer so I don't have to holler. I'm not infectious, you know."

Giovanni moved to the side of the bed.

"How long had he been dead?" O'Hara asked.

"Well, it was an abdominal wound, and the doc said he could have lasted anywhere from ten minutes to half an hour. He'd dragged himself around—you could follow the trail in the dirt floor—and he'd bled most of the way. I couldn't see much sense in it, the way he went. You see, he was standing at the far end, away from the entrance, when he was shot. My guess is the dog scared off the murderer, or he'd have finished the old man off. Looked like he'd lain there, bleeding, for a little while, then he started off dragging himself. There are three aisles to the place, like this—" Giovanni leaned over the bed, drawing a crude sketch on a corner of the nearest paper with a dull pencil stub. "One aisle leads straight from the door down the center. Probyn was at the back end of that. Now, if he were going for help you'd think he'd head straight to the door, but his tracks are clear as can be, and he swung around the end like this—" A swift jab of the pencil drove through the paper to the bedding. "Then he went halfway down the outside aisle, if that's what they call it. There was a big spread of blood where he'd lain for a minute, then some stains along the upright of the . . . the whatchamacallit—"

"Bench," O'Hara threw in.

"Yeah. Whatever, there was blood on it where he'd reached up, trying to drag himself upright. There was a big bunch of flowers torn out—he still had them in his hand when the maid found him. I guess he fell down, couldn't get up again, so he dragged himself on out the door. But the funny thing—I suppose he must have been pretty much out of his head by then—he didn't go toward the house. He turned the other way, and the maid found him stretched out by a water butt—"

"A what?"

"A water butt. Sort of a cistern affair, but above ground, to catch rainwater. The granddaughter said old Probyn claimed rainwater was best for the plants, more natural nutrients than tap water, or something. Anyway, he was stretched out there, as if he'd been trying to hang onto it. And that's as far as he got." Giovanni's voice dropped with dramatic finality.

"What kind of flowers were they?"

Giovanni shrugged. "The ones in his hand? I dunno. I don't know one from another."

The leg in traction swayed dangerously as O'Hara's torso surged forward. "Well, find out, dammit!"

"Yes, sir!"

The door opened with a muffled swoosh and a heavily built, busty nurse in her middle years bore down on O'Hara.

"Can't you see we're busy?" O'Hara growled.

"Come now, Mr. O'Hara, we mustn't be like that." She slipped a thermometer under his tongue as he opened his mouth to protest, and placed firm fingers along his wrist, her head bent to her watch.

The patient made an urgent *Get on with it!* gesture at Giovanni with his free hand. The latter eyed the pair nervously, cleared his throat, and got on with it.

"The maid found him around five. Probyn'd had a session of intestinal flu most of the day before and all that day, so he wasn't eating regular meals. Hot tea and crackers off and on, whenever he felt up to it, so there was no way of knowing by the stomach contents exactly when he died. The dog, Vulcan, was lying across him, which probably kept him from cooling down normally. Figure how long he lived, and how long till he was found, the doc said he could've been shot anywhere from half an hour to two hours before that."

The nurse drew the thermometer from between O'Hara's lips and held it up to read with a professional turn of the wrist. "Well, Mr. O'Hara," she remarked wryly, "I don't know about poor old Mr. Probyn, but at least *you're* cooling down normally." She made an entry on her records.

O'Hara snapped with a pained air, "Looks like everybody's a comedian around here!"

The nurse bustled out the door, casting a satisfied smile behind as it closed.

"They don't give you any peace in this place," O'Hara said. "But I've got to admit that The Bride of Baal's handy to have around in the wee hours of the morning when the pain's gettin' just a bit too much for a body." He shifted self-consciously among the tangled bedding as if afraid he'd exposed a soft spot, and glowered at Giovanni. "Okay, let's hear the rest. Who've you got for suspects?"

"Nobody firm, yet. First of all there's the household. Besides Probyn himself, there's his sister-in-law, who seems to be some kind of a poor relation, and a granddaughter, Marla . . . Marla . . ."

"Wyman," O'Hara supplied. "I've seen her around town. A darlin' of a colleen, about twenty." O'Hara's one-sixteenth Irish blood was inclined to go to his tongue. "Long black hair, worthy of the sweet Deirdre, and eyes as blue as the River Shannon."

Giovanni wondered privately just how blue the River Shannon might be. "That's her," he went on. "Then there's a butler; a cook, who's his wife; two maids; a chauffeur-handyman type; the old fellow who minds the gate; and his wife. I tell you, O'Hara, nobody gets into that place without old Probyn wants him to."

"Didn't I tell you the place is like Fort Knox? That wall must be eight feet high, solid stone around the whole place, miles of it, and the only gate that isn't locked is guarded day and night."

"Right," Giovanni agreed. "The gatekeeper's wife swears he wasn't gone from his post all day. Unless we can find somebody to swear differently, we can rule him out. And only three people came in after the last time Probyn turned up in the kitchen looking for some tea."

Wrinkles on O'Hara's florid brow tangled as he concentrated his thoughts. "You're sure it was intestinal flu he had, and not a little arsenic or something that somebody slipped into his supper a couple of nights before? The shooting could have been the second try, y'know."

Giovanni perked up like a schoolboy who'd gotten an unexpected A. "That's the first thing I thought of. Doc says he'll be looking out for it when he does the P.M. We'll soon have his report."

"Who's on the case besides us?"

Giovanni hesitated. One of the first things he'd heard on his transfer was: "With O'Hara you never know which way the cat'll jump." Confinement to a hospital bed wouldn't have lessened his sensitive ego.

"Lindstrom and I did the initial investigation."

O'Hara nodded, with a wry twist of his mouth. "He's coming along well. Did a good job on the Masterson case." Giovanni felt a twinge of surprise. O'Hara's previous reference to Lindstrom had labeled him as "a clod in thick boots."

"But remember," O'Hara continued, "I'll be working with you all the way. There's no need to worry. I won't let you down." He wore a gentle smile, as if in contemplation of the comfort this would bring to his colleagues. "Who were the three you said got into Fort Knox?"

Giovanni consulted his notes. "Rupert Kendall clocked in precisely at three o'clock. I've been talking to Probyn's secretary at the plant, and Kendall would be a good man to put your money on. He's been storming around the past couple of weeks claiming the old man stole some milling process he invented."

"Developed."

"Whatever." Giovanni shrugged. "It's supposed to save millions, or thousands anyway, and he's been raising quite a stink. Hawkins, the chauffeur type, was washing one of the cars outside the garage—a four car affair—which is about fifty yards from the greenhouse. He said the two of them were going at it hot and heavy, from what he could hear. Said Kendall called the old man every name he could lay his tongue to."

"Kendall . . ." O'Hara mused. "Seems to me I should know him."

"Early forties, tall and slim, dark, getting a little bald in front. Real intense eyes, look as if they could see right through you."

O'Hara nodded in satisfaction. "I know him. Hawk nose, and a sensitive mouth. Looks like a cross between a poet and a pirate. What does he say for himself?"

"He admitted they'd had words," Giovanni said, "but he swore up and down that Probyn was alive when he left."

"Wouldn't you?"

"I suppose so. Anyway, the gatekeeper clocked him out at three twenty. Ten minutes later a fellow called John Locke turned up."

O'Hara nodded. "Him I know. Medium height, in his early fifties? A sarcastic type, used to be married to Probyn's daughter. Not Marla's mother, the other one. She's dead now, and he works for the old man—or did the last I heard."

"That's the guy. An accountant. He went up to the house, the butler told him Probyn was down at the greenhouse, and he headed that way. But he says he changed his mind and decided not to disturb the old man. He didn't check out till three forty-five, though. I asked him what took so long, and he said he'd noticed Marla's Ferrari in the garage, poked around it for a while, checking out the features and wondering if he might ever be able to afford one."

"Wasn't the chauffeur there?"

Giovanni shook his head. "He finished washing the car about the time Kendall left, then came on into town on an errand for the cook. The gatekeeper says he drove out not long after Kendall, and he was seen at the market."

O'Hara leaned across to his bedside table, pulled out one of his letters, and began to make notes on the back of the envelope.

"Locke left at three forty-five?"

Giovanni nodded. "We've got two witnesses to that. Just as he was leaving, the granddaughter's boyfriend, Loren Renaldi, drove up. There's an unsavory type, if you ask me. About twenty-three, I'd guess. He's tall, with a good build, but he's got one of those homely faces, you can't tell if he's a budding genius or verging on moronic. Long, straight hair, down over his collar, and probably none too clean—and his clothes are something else. Of course, old Probyn himself looked as if he'd ridden the rods, in baggy old pants and a jacket that could have been dragged through a stovepipe."

"Millionaires can afford to look like bums," O'Hara remarked. "Did the boyfriend go out to the greenhouse?"

"He says not. Miss Wyman and her aunt both confirm that he spent about twenty minutes with them, and then he took off to hunt the old man out. Renaldi was supposed to be trying to talk Probyn into letting him marry the granddaughter. But he claims he lost his nerve, wandered around the place trying to get it back again, and finally headed out the gate, figuring he could find a better time to tackle the old man than when he was suffering from what Renaldi called 'the gripes.'"

"If the boy married Marla with the old man dead, he'd be married to a nice piece of money. It might seem smarter to marry her first, though, and then knock off the old man, if he's the one who did it." O'Hara cocked his head to one side; bright, birdlike eyes seeming to assess abstracts in the air before him. "It might be even smarter, though, to knock the old man off first. Marla'd get the money either way, and the old man wouldn't be around to object." He swung his gaze back to Giovanni. "How's the pie going to be sliced, now that Probyn's dead?"

"The biggest chunk goes into a foundation, medical research, new library for the city, things like that, with a board controlling it. Marla gets three million outright, in trust till she's twenty-one, and shares in the mill. The aunt, or great-aunt—she's a brother's widow—gets a pension, twenty thousand dollars a year if she lives at Highgates, or thirty-five thousand dollars if for any reason she wants to move. The staff all come in for a nice chunk, except one maid who's fairly new—anywhere from five thousand to fifteen thousand dollars apiece, depending on how long they've been at Highgates. There are a few minor beneficiaries, but nobody who's involved."

O'Hara whistled. "Three million! Nurses and governesses when she was little, the best schools here and in England, a year at the Sorbonne, and now all that money. The luck of some people. But I don't think my little colleen'd do a thing like that, especially when she had it so good already. Is she covered?"

"Pretty much. Either her aunt or one or other of the staff can testify to her whereabouts except for one period of about twenty minutes just after the boyfriend left the house. She says she was in the library making some notes for a report she's working on—she's a junior at the university—but nobody saw her during that time. Theoretically, she could have slipped out and shot him, but I'm with you, I don't think she's the type. She seems pretty much broken up about the old man's death."

"How about the others?"

"All accounted for. The aunt was in the kitchen with the cook, going over some new gourmet recipes, while Marla was in the library. The maids were both upstairs. The way they were working, they cover each other pretty thoroughly, so they're in the clear, unless they're in it together."

"How about the butler?"

"He was feeling wonky all day, probably the same bug Probyn had. After Renaldi left, Marla made him go to his quarters and lie down. One of the maids saw him go up, and she was working in that area most of the afternoon, said she'd have seen him if he'd come down."

O'Hara scribbled on the envelope. "So much for the people. Now, what do we have by way of physical evidence?"

"Not much. He was shot with a .38. There are several guns around the house, but only one pistol, a .22 in the old man's desk. It hadn't been fired since the last time it'd been cleaned. Wasn't even loaded."

"Any pertinent fingerprints?"

"The team's working on it, but so far nothing of any use."

"Footprints?"

Giovanni nodded. "One. The greenhouse floor is dirt, pretty hard-packed, but the chauffeur—he's nurseryman, too—knocked over a watering can near the doorway a couple of days ago. It had pretty much dried up, but we've got one partial that looks promising. Hawkins, the chauffeur, said the old man wouldn't let Vulcan in the greenhouse any more. He was always knocking something over with his tail. But our partial has one of Vulcan's paw prints on it, pointing toward the door. That suggests it was made after the dog interrupted the murderer. Not one of the outsiders had been on the grounds since the water was spilled, except that afternoon. The print's real smooth, but there's a sort of scar as if the wearer picked up a rock that got ground into the sole, and then dropped out. A good clear impression of the hole."

O'Hara's cheeks creased in a wide smile. "Good! We can use something concrete like that. If it is the murderer's and he doesn't know we've got it, we might match shoes before he gets rid of them."

Giovanni looked at his watch with dismay. "Look, O'Hara, I know you want to hear everything, but I was only supposed to bring your mail and get on with the job. Lindstrom'll be waiting."

"Okay, okay," O'Hara grumbled, "get on your way. But you keep me posted, hear? And don't forget to find out what kind of flowers the old man had in his hand."

Giovanni turned toward the door. "I'll try, and I'll come back tonight, or tomorrow morning at least, and bring you up to date."

"Tonight!" O'Hara called imperiously as the sergeant disappeared. He glowered at the closed door for a moment, then settled back to think.

Out of his frustration, rather than by intention, O'Hara made the second floor staff miserable for the rest of the day. When the shift changed in the afternoon, the most important word passed was not about Mrs. Hurley's violent reaction to the new medication, or Dr. MacCallum's orders to screen Mr. Janeway's visitors for contraband liquor. Rather, the watchword was: "Look out for O'Hara!"

The head nurse at the station drew something like a breath of relief when shortly after supper she saw Sergeant Giovanni ambling down the hall toward 204. Perhaps things would get better soon.

"Well," O'Hara growled when Sergeant Giovanni peered around his door. "You certainly took long enough! Where have you been?"

"I had a lot of work to catch up on, spending so much time here this morning," Giovanni replied, with less of an apologetic air than he would have had a few months earlier. "I found out quite a bit, though."

"Like?"

"For one thing, there was no sign of poison, not even in the small amount that might have made it look like an intestinal upset. No fingerprints in the greenhouse that aren't accounted for in the ordinary way. We've got a nice cast of the one footprint, showing the scar in the sole, and Miss Wyman told me it was gillyflowers the old man had in his hand."

"Gillyflowers?"

"That's what she said. I don't know a thing about flowers."

"Well, what color were they, what did they look like?"

"The old man just caught a handful as he fell. What does it matter?" Giovanni asked with a daring degree of heat.

"Matter! I'll give you *matter*, me boy. You got a look at them, didn't you?"

"The ones in his hand were so wilted by the time we got there you couldn't tell what they were, but the ones on the bench, where he'd grabbed for a hold, were all sorts of colors." He screwed up his eyes and his brow knitted in concentration as he cast his mind's eye back to the greenhouse. "There were some pink ones, and white, and yellow, and some sort of purplish ones—and there were some red ones, too, real pretty. Tall, sort of clustery, real flowery, if you know what I mean."

"I don't know what you mean, if you really want to know," O'Hara complained, "but it's a poor workman that blames his tools."

Giovanni was silent in the face of this apparent *non sequitur*.

"Anything else? Have you found the shoes to fit your cast yet?"

Giovanni shook his head. "Judge Clayton won't issue search warrants for the suspects' houses as things stand. He said if we could come up with something to point to one person, that'd do the trick, but right now there isn't enough evidence to back up a warrant."

"And in the meantime somebody does some figuring and decides it'd be the wise thing to get rid of those shoes. That'd be just our luck. Damn, I wish I were out of this place! I'd find the right shoes, regulations or no."

Giovanni backed a few paces away from the bed. "Well, if you don't need me for anything else I'll . . ."

O'Hara waved him away absently, studying his back-of-the-envelope notes on the case. "Go on. Go on. I'll work with what I've got." The staff at the nurses' station shared apprehensive glances as Giovanni left the floor. The respite had been so brief.

The evening, however, was comparatively quiet. After visiting hours, peace reigned for an unexpected length of time. Charts were brought up to date, shelves were cleaned, nails were polished, and bits of gossip exchanged in hushed voices. Then the sword fell. O'Hara's light went on. "Not me!" several nurses declared in unison.

"I'll go myself," the senior nurse offered, and moved briskly and silently down the hall.

"What is it, Mr. O'Hara? Do you need a sleeping pill?"

The room was suitably dark for the sleeping hours, except for the soft glow from a lamp behind the bed. It showed O'Hara teetering on the edge of the bed, his traction equipment straining, one hand braced on the bedside table. The other hand groped ineffectually for the telephone, just out of reach.

"Sleeping pill! I've got to catch a murderer. I don't need a sleeping pill, I need an outside line!"

"Mr. O'Hara please! You'll wake the other patients. Don't you realize it's after two o'clock?"

"Get me an outside line, or I'll not only wake the other patients, I'll wake the dead," he threatened, but in a slightly subdued voice.

"Mr. O'Hara . . ."

"Please?"

This approach was so unexpected that the nurse found herself with the receiver in her hand before she realized what she was doing. "What number do you want?"

O'Hara told her. After a moment she passed him the handset.

"This is O'Hara. Let me talk to Giovanni."

There was a short wait, then a drowsy voice came through the receiver.

"Giovanni, I've got the pointer you need. Roust up Lindstrom, then see if Judge Clayton'll issue a warrant. Get him out of bed, if you have to. Find those shoes, before it's too late."

A crackle of protests and questions from the receiver sounded through the still room. In a series of succinct sentences O'Hara told his sergeant exactly what he'd come up with, and who it pointed to. The nurse standing by, listening eagerly, gave a startled gasp.

"Now get going, and report to me in the morning." O'Hara handed the phone back to the nurse.

"And now, me pretty, I'd be obliged if you'd take yourself out of here. Don't they teach you nowadays that hospital patients are supposed to have plenty of rest?" O'Hara snuggled against the pillow and wormed himself into as comfortable a position as was possible in the circumstances. He directed one long, outrageous wink at the nurse, then closed both eyes and settled himself to sleep.

Orderlies were trundling cartloads of breakfast trays down the hall when Giovanni next entered Room 204. O'Hara greeted him with a smug grin, an effect slightly marred by a mouthful of scrambled eggs. "Find 'em?"

Giovanni nodded. "Judge Clayton said he'd take a chance on your reasoning, and gave us a search warrant. They were at the bottom of a Goodwill collection sack. The pit mark on the sole is clear, and the shoe fits the cast perfectly. And we found a bonus, too." He waited, glowing with pleasure, for O'Hara's reaction. Raised eyebrows and an expectant silence prompted him to go on. "The gun. It'd been cleaned, but we roused the ballistics men, and it was the one that did the job, all right."

O'Hara beamed with satisfaction. "Good work. I figured I'd got the answer before the evidence was gone. Now I'd guess you want to know how I solved the case."

Giovanni hesitated. Had O'Hara forgotten the telephone conversation at two in the morning? Well, he was entitled to his kicks. "I didn't quite catch it all this morning. Your line of reasoning, I mean," he answered finally. "Sounded like a stroke of luck."

O'Hara slapped a triangle of toast back down on the tray. "Stroke of luck! Hardly. It's knowledge of the ways of the world that gave me the answer. That's where those of us who've seen more of life have it over you young fellows. Oh, don't worry, you're bound to catch up, given time and a little more experience. You see, old Probyn's behavior after he was shot was the clue to the whole thing. You spotted it yourself, but didn't follow it up. Why did he drag himself the long way around to the door, and then away from the house? *Away*, mind you, not toward it, where you'd expect him to go for help."

"I can see it now," Giovanni replied. "Before, I thought he was just irrational from pain."

"I've had more time to think than you did," O'Hara admitted. "Probyn didn't grab those flowers while he was falling. No, he deliberately dragged himself up to that bench to *get* those flowers, 'cause he was afraid there wasn't a snowball's chance of him living with a wound like that. Then, with his very lifeblood marking the trail for us, he forced himself to make it to the door and beyond, to seal his killer's death warrant."

"A gutsy old man," Giovanni murmured respectfully.

"Identifying them as gillyflowers almost cancelled out that dying effort, you know."

Giovanni bridled. "I told you I didn't know one flower from the other. Miss Wyman, she's the one said they were gillyflowers. Weren't they?"

"In a manner of speaking." O'Hara paused for effect, while Giovanni shuffled uncomfortably by the bedside. "But you've got to remember, our little Marla had nurses when she was little—English nannies—nothing being too good for the old man to give her. And she went to boarding school in England. So what is it that the English call a gillyflower? What do we call the flower that fits your rather inadequate description? Tall, clusters of flowers, pink, white, yellow, purple? I finally got it. Stock! That's what it is. Stock."

"Never heard of it. But then, I don't know much about flowers."

"Probyn did. He grabbed a handful of stock, then headed out the door, to the water butt, you said."

"That's right."

"Sort of a cistern, you said.. Why in the name of all that's good and holy didn't you say, 'Sort of a barrel'?" O'Hara asked peremptorily.

"Anybody knows what a water butt is."

"Not everybody," O'Hara admitted. "But once I thought about it, the whole thing fell into place. All I had to do was ask myself what—or, in this case, who—goes with 'stock' and 'barrel'?"

"Even dragged out of my warm bed, I followed you there," Giovanni remarked. "Locke. And now, if you'll excuse the expression, we've got him under lock and key. When we found the shoes, and showed him the cast of the footprint in the greenhouse he claimed he'd never been in, he hemmed and hawed around, finally admitted he'd gone to see the old man, but swore up and down he'd left him alive. Then we hit him with the dying man's accusation, and he broke down completely. It was the old story. He was a darn sharp accountant, and started doctoring the books. He'd salted away a tidy little sum on the side, but the old man was just a little bit smarter. He found out about it, even though a couple of audits had missed it. I suppose Locke thought that being family, even by marriage, old Probyn wouldn't see him go to jail. But he wasn't much of a judge of millionaires. Out in the greenhouse Probyn told Locke he was going to prosecute, and he'd end up in the pen, so Locke shot him. He had the gun with him, so there won't be any question about lack of premeditation. And now that we have the gun, the case is wrapped up neater than a Christmas present."

"Thanks to old man Probyn," O'Hara declared. "A real present it was, too— handed to you on a silver tray, like the head of the sainted John the Baptist by Salome."

"Yeah," Giovanni said.

"So now," said O'Hara, stroking jam onto a toast triangle, "you can get on with your other work."

"Well, thanks for the help," Giovanni told him, sidling toward the door. "And it was 'to' Salome, not 'by,'" he muttered—but not until the door had shut silently behind him.

JONATHAN CRAIG

The Girl in Gold

It was supposed to look like either suicide or accidental death. It was neither. It was murder.

A detective is rarely the first police officer at the scene of a homicide, but this was one of those times. Stan Rayder, my detective partner, and I had been cruising Greenwich Village in an unmarked patrol car, matching faces in the streets against our mental files of wanted criminals, when a small boy had run from the alley behind the hotel, shouting that there was a dead man back there.

The boy had kept on running, and Stan, who was driving, turned into the alley.

Now, at a few minutes past six on as steamy an August evening as I could remember, we stood looking down at the body of a well-dressed, darkhaired young man who had, it would seem, fallen only minutes ago from the open window of the third floor hotel room directly above.

He lay flat on his back, spreadeagled, and in spite of the crushing impact of his body on the concrete there was very little blood. There was a dark swelling across the bridge of his nose and a purplish discoloration of the skin on the left side of his face and on his left hand and wrist.

In New York, detectives aren't supposed to touch a body until the medical examiner has looked at it, but sometimes we cheat a little. I pushed a fingertip against the jaw, and the head moved easily to my touch.

"Any rigor mortis, Pete?" Stan asked.

"No," I said, and slipped the man's wallet from the inside pocket of his jacket. It held eighty-three dollars, some business cards, and an I.D. card that said he was Harry B. Lambert, of 684 East 71st Street. I read the name and address to Stan, put the wallet back, and stood up. We'd make a closer examination, of course, after the M.E. arrived.

"That's quite a bit of postmortem lividity on his left side, there," Stan said. "It'd take about an hour for that much to show up, wouldn't it?"

"About that, yes," I said. Postmortem lividity results from the blood's settling to those parts of the body nearest the floor. In Harry Lambert's case, it meant he had lain on his left side for at least an hour before someone pushed him through that third floor window.

"He'd been boozing a little, it smells like," Stan said, glancing at me with mild surprise.

Stan, who always appears to be mildly surprised about everything, is a tall, wiry young cop with a soft voice, a sprinkling of premature gray in his old fashioned brush cut, and a deceptively mild manner. He also has a black belt, the hardest fists in the department, and an almost complete lack of physical fear.

"You figure that knock he took between the eyes finished him off?" he asked.

"Could be," I said. "Maybe somebody hoped he'd hit the pavement face down. Sort of blot out the evidence, so to speak."

"It just might have worked, too," Stan said. "Well, you're the head man on this one, Pete. What now?"

"Stay here with the body until the M.E. gets here. I'll get on the horn in the hotel and stir things up."

I walked around to the entrance of the Corbin and used one of the phone booths in the lobby to call Lieutenant Barney Fells, Stan's and my superior. Barney would take Stan and me off the duty roster and assign us full time to the homicide. He would also immediately notify the communications bureau. They, in turn, would dispatch an ambulance, and notify the other departments concerned with homicide.

The Corbin was just another small hotel, a little smaller and older and scruffier than most, perhaps, with a minimum of lobby and a bird-cage elevator no larger than a phone booth.

There was no one behind the desk. I tapped the bell a couple of times and waited.

The middle-aged man who finally came out from the room behind the desk was short and slightly built, with a large, almost perfectly round head, thinning strawlike hair, moist gray eyes, and very little chin.

"Yes, sir," he said in a voice much deeper than I would have expected. "May I help you?"

I showed him my badge. "Detective Selby," I said. "You have a Mr. Harry Lambert registered here?"

He nodded. "Yes sir. He checked in this morning."

"Anyone with him?"

"No."

I got out my notebook. "I'll need your name."

"Dobson. Wayne Dobson."

"Did Mr. Lambert have any visitors?"

"Not that I know of. Why? What's happened?"

"He's dead. Out in the alley behind the hotel. He went out the window."

Dobson sucked in his breath. "A suicide?"

"You know him personally?"

"No. But I . . ." He shook his head slowly. "This is the first time anything like this has ever happened here."

"You only come to the desk when someone rings the bell?"

"Usually, yes."

"What room was Lambert in?"

"Just a moment." He turned to check his file of registration cards. "304."

"He put his home address on there, on the registration card?"

"Yes, sir. It's the law. He put down 684 East 71st."

"What time did he check in?"

"Eleven forty-five."

I put my notebook away. "I'll need a key to his room, Mr. Dobson. And please stay close to the desk. There'll be other police along any minute."

He nodded. "Of course," he said as he handed me a master key on a big loop of heavy wire. "I'll do all I can to help."

I crossed to the elevator, but I had second thoughts. I have a thing about elevators of that size and vintage. I took another look at it, and then walked to the other side of the lobby and started up the stairs.

I might have been in a smaller hotel room at one time or another, but I couldn't remember it; I knew I'd never been in a hotter one. The metal bed and metal dresser seemed to have been painted over with green house paint, and the ratty lounge chair looked to be on the verge of giving way to its own weight.

There were no indications of a struggle, but Harry Lambert appeared to have had at least one visitor, and that one a woman. There was a nearly empty fifth of whisky at one end of the dresser and a couple of hotel glasses at the other, and one of the glasses had a smear of lipstick on the rim.

There was nothing under the bed but dust, and nothing in the closet but more dust and two rusty coat hangers. There was nothing in the bathroom, either.

I went over to search the dresser. There was a handsome black attaché case in the top drawer, nothing at all in the others. I put the case on the bed, handling it carefully to avoid obliterating fingerprints, and opened it.

The case held, among other things, another black case, about ten inches long, six inches wide, and half an inch thick, embossed with Harry Lambert's name in gold, and to which was attached about two feet of gold chain with a clip on the end of it. I'd seen a number of such cases; they are used by diamond salesmen to carry gems and are known as jewelers' wallets. It was empty.

The attaché case also held, in various compartments, a jeweler's loupe, a miniature pair of scales and a set of weights in a clear plastic box, and a large number of the squares of white tissue paper in which diamond salesmen wrap their stones.

I put the case back on the dresser, took off my coat, and began stripping down the bed. I found the tube of lipstick in the space between the pillows.

It was no ordinary lipstick. Even the cheapest ones can look expensive, of course, but this one was the genuine article. It was of heavy gold, with a beautifully engraved floral design along its length and the initials "L.C." in a monogram on the cap.

It was the kind of thing women never buy for themselves. It was also the kind of costly, handcrafted item that just might have a secret jeweler's mark.

Headquarters maintains a file of hundreds of such marks, just as it does of laundry marks.

I found the mark with the help of my handkerchief and the loupe from Lambert's attaché case. It was inside the cap, at the top: an anchor surrounded by three concentric circles.

I put the lipstick on the dresser beside the attaché case and finished searching the bed. I was just putting my jacket back on when there was a knock on the door and two techs and a photographer from headquarters came in.

"Hi, Pete," the chief tech said, wiping the sweat from his forehead. "You think it might warm up a little?"

"We can hope," I said. "You finished in the alley?"

"Nothing to do down there. Just the pictures was all. They're done."

"I'd better get a couple of bird's-eye shots from the window," the photographer said, moving off.

"The M.E. show up yet?" I asked.

"He got there just as we left. Doc Chaney."

"Well, it's all yours, Ed," I said, turning to leave. "I want to have a few words with the desk clerk."

Before I went downstairs, I knocked at the doors at either side of Lambert's and at the one directly across the hall. There was no answer at any of them.

When I reached the lobby, I found that Wayne Dobson had abandoned his desk again. The door behind it was slightly ajar. I went back and opened it the rest of the way.

Dobson was lying on the bed in a room that, except for a portable TV set and the iron bars usually found on first floor windows in New York, was the mirror image of the one I'd just left upstairs. He looked even smaller lying down than he had behind the desk, and his eyes seemed drawn with pain.

"What's wrong?" I asked.

He smiled up at me thinly. "Ulcers. That suicide got me pretty upset."

"Can I do anything for you?"

He shook his head and pushed himself up on the side of the bed. "It'll pass. At least it always has."

"Feel up to talking a little?"

He shrugged. "If I have to, I have to. What do you want to know?"

"Well, first, where are the bellhops? I haven't seen any."

"Joe Moody's on. The trick is to find him."

"Moody go up with Lambert when he checked in?"

"No. Joe wasn't around at the time."

"Lambert had some company," I said. "A woman. You see any women pass through the lobby?"

"I saw one, a beauty. She took the elevator."

"You have any idea who she was?"

"No, but she was something to see; silver blonde, a terrific build, and a gold dress like a second skin. Real bright, shiny gold dress. Must have cost a mint."

"When was this?"

"Oh . . . about four, I'd say. Maybe a little later."

"She the only woman you saw?"

"Yes. Mr. Selby, would you do me a favor, please? There's a shoebox out beneath the desk with a lot of odds and ends in it, stuff people have left in their rooms. I just remembered I put a bottle of antacid tablets in it the other day. Maybe they'd help."

I went out to the desk, dug around in the shoebox until I found the tablets, and took them back to Dobson.

"Thanks," he said. "Don't ever get an ulcer."

"Just one more thing, and I'll let you rest. Do you handle the switchboard?"

"Yes. The desk clerk here does everthing but make a living."

"Did Lambert make or receive any calls?"

"Damm!"

"What's wrong?"

"I completely forgot. Yes, he did get a call. And the guy that called him was plenty sore about something. He started right off cussing him. Mr. Lambert kept saying, 'Now, just a minute, Rocky,' and 'Listen, Rocky' and 'Let me explain,' and things like that."

"All right. But aside from the cussing, what did this man *say?*"

"Nothing. He just kept blessing him out. Then all at once Mr. Lambert hung up."

"The man call back?"

"No."

"When did he call?"

"I can tell you exactly. It was ten minutes of four. As it happened, I'd just set my watch." He suddenly grimaced with pain and lay back on the bed. "Like I told you, " he said, "never get yourself an ulcer."

I made a few notes in my book, thanked Dobson for his help, and walked around the hotel to see how Stan Rayder and the M.E. were coming along with their work in the alley.

There were two more police cars and an ambulance there now, and perhaps a hundred or so onlookers.

"Doc Chaney here says he can get a pretty close fix on the time of death, Pete," Stan said, after I'd shouldered my way through the crowd. "He puts it somewhere between four and five P.M."

"That's right," the M.E. said, looking up from where he knelt by the body. "This is the one time in a hundred when I can set fairly tight limits."

"How about that bruise between his eyes, doc?" Stan said. "You figure it could have killed him?"

"*Could* have, yes. It's likely a depressed fracture. But we'll have to wait till I autopsy him, Stan." He stood up and glanced in the direction of the ambulance. "I'm finished, Pete. If you'll release the body, I can take it back with me."

"You get everything out of his pockets, Stan?" I asked.

"Yes," Stan said, tapping the bulge in the side pocket of his jacket. "Nothing helpful, though. There was nothing in his billfold but the cards and money."

I had the M.E. sign a receipt for the body. Then Stan and I pushed through the crowd to the car we'd come in and got inside.

"So Lambert was a diamond salesman, eh?" Stan said, after I'd filled him in on my search of the hotel room and my talks with the desk clerk. "What a way to run a railroad. A hundred people could have gone in and out, but the only one we know about for sure is that girl in the gold dress."

"We may pick up some others from the bellhop." I started the engine and began to back the car out of the alley. "I'm going uptown to check at the address on Lambert's I.D. card, Stan. You—"

"Yes, I know," he said wryly. "I get to stay here and boss the operation in that bake-oven upstairs."

"Somebody always has to do the dirty dishes, Stan."

"Sure, but why does it always have to be me?"

"First of all, get hold of that bellhop. Then see if any of the other guests on Lambert's floor saw or heard anything. Also, there's a newsstand across the street. Maybe the man that runs it noticed something."

I turned the corner and pulled up in front of the hotel entrance. "One more thing," I said. "Send somebody over to headquarters with that lipstick. I want a check made on the jeweler's mark."

Stan sighed. "You sure you can't think of any other little things I can do for you?"

"Not offhand," I said. "Still, if I really worked at it . . ."

He grinned. "Never mind," he said, opening the door. "I'll see you at the squad room."

684 East 71st turned out to be a posh-looking converted brownstone. I found a mailbox with a name card that read LAMBERT/MANNING—2A, and pushed the button beneath it. A moment later the buzzer released the inner door of the foyer and I climbed the stairs to the second floor.

A heavyset man with his arms folded across his chest was standing in the open doorway of 2A, frowning at me as I approached. He was about thirty, I judged, with a lot of thick, sand-colored hair, a deep widow's peak, and unusually heavys brows over very small hazel eyes with yellow flecks in them.

"You the one that buzzed 2A?" he asked, giving it a little edge.

I showed him the tin. "Detective Selby," I said. "Are you a friend of Mr. Lambert's?"

"He lives here. We both do. What's up?"

"We could talk a little better inside."

He hesitated for a moment, then shrugged and motioned me into the apartment.

The living room wasn't very large, but the furnishings had cost someone a lot of money. I sat down in a cream leather easy chair and nodded to the sofa across from it.

"Let's see, now," I said as I got out my book. "Your full name is what?"

He glowered at me, but he came over and sat down. "David D. Manning," he said. "And make yourself right at home, Selby."

"Thanks. You and Mr. Lambert pretty close friends?"

"We're roommates," he said. "We get along. Why?"

"I've a little bad news for you, I'm afraid. He's been killed."

He started to say something, then changed his mind and sat looking at me as if he were trying to decide whether I was telling the truth.

I waited.

"How?" Manning asked.

"We're not just sure. Somebody tried to cover it up by pushing him out a window."

"Somebody? Does that mean you don't know who did it?"

"Not yet."

He got up suddenly and walked over to a bar in the corner. "I could use a drink," he said, pouring a couple of inches into a highball glass. "How about some for you?"

"No, thanks."

He took a pull at his drink, walked slowly back to the sofa, and sat down again. "It's hard to believe," he said.

"He married? Separated?"

"No."

"Divorced?"

"No."

"We'll want to notify his next of kin. You know who that might be?"

"No, I don't. He never mentioned any relatives. His parents are dead, I know."

"He have a good income?"

"We averaged about the same, I guess. Twenty thousand one year, twenty-five the next."

"You're a diamond salesman, too, then?"

"Yes."

"Well, the big question is, of course, do you know anyone who'd want him dead?"

Manning smiled sourly. "I can think of two or three who'd like that just fine."

"Who?"

"Well, there's this girl he used to be engaged to, Barbara Nolan. Harry threw her over for another girl. Barbara swore she'd kill him."

"He take her seriously?"

"Not at first. Then he started to. It was beginning to sweat him plenty. I guess she convinced him."

"You know where she lives?"

"It's in the Village. 542 Waverly Place."

"You said there were others."

He took a sip of his drink. "Well, there's a guy named Mel Pearce, another diamond salesman. He thought Harry stole a big sale from him. He had almost an obsession about it. Once I had to get between them to keep them from climbing all over each other."

"You know where I can find him?"

"He lives on Central Park West, I think. I don't know just where."

I turned over to a new page in my notebook. "That's two," I said. "Anyone else?"

"Not that I know of."

"Harry got a tough phone call from somebody named Rocky. That name mean anything to you?"

Manning frowned thoughtfully, then shook his head. "No."

"Was Harry in trouble of any kind? Any dealings with shylocks? Any civil suits? Gambling debts? Anything at all like that?"

"No. At least not so far as I know."

"You said he threw Barbara Nolan over for another girl. What's her name?"

"Elaine Greer." He nodded toward a large color portrait on the coffee table. "That's her picture."

I went over to examine it. The girl was very young, very blonde, and very beautiful, but it was a cold beauty, and the smile that curved her lips had somehow failed to reach her slightly tilted blue eyes.

"I'll want to talk to her," I said. "You know her address?"

"No. She's in the Manhattan book, though, I know."

"Harry pretty much of a ladies' man, was he?"

"No. He practically had to beat them off with a club, but he always stuck pretty much to one girl at a time." He paused. "She must be a very potent proposition, that girl, Elaine, I mean. Harry was practically out of his skull over her. As I said, he and Barbara were going to get married. But when he met Elaine, he forgot all about Barbara. She had Harry so crazy for her he didn't know which way was up."

"You know Elaine yourself, do you?"

"No, I never met her, and I reached the point where I wished Harry hadn't, either. She was all he talked about. He went around mooning over her like a fifteen-year-old kid with his first big crush. You had to see it to believe it."

I shifted my weight around in the chair and ran out a fresh point on my pencil. "Who'd Harry work for?"

"Nobody. He took stones out on memo."

"On memo?"

"On consignment. He might be peddling stones for half a dozen dealers at the same time. A memo is the dealer's record of the stones he gives you. You just sign the memo, and that's it."

"His reputation must have been pretty good, then."

"Better than good. Perfect."

"When was the last time you saw him, Mr. Manning?"

He glanced at me sharply, then raised his glass and finished his drink, watching me over the rim.

"Don't tell me I'm a suspect," he said.

"Just a routine question, Mr. Manning," I said. "But when?"

He put the glass down on the end table beside the sofa. "This morning," he said. "And it was a very strange thing. I didn't know what to make of it."

"What happened?"

"Well, the phone in Harry's room rang early, about six or so. It woke me up. I went out to the kitchen to make coffee, and a few minutes later Harry came in with his attaché case under his arm, all dressed to go out. He looked like something had just scared the hell out of him."

"What did he say to you then?"

"Nothing. I asked him what was wrong, but he walked right past me and grabbed a fifth of whisky out of the cabinet and took a heavy belt straight out of the bottle. I was amazed. It was the first time I'd seen him take a drink in more than a year. He used to have a drinking problem, you see. No tolerance for the stuff at all. And here he was, suddenly gulping it straight out of the bottle."

"He didn't say anything at all?"

"Not a word. I think he was only half aware I was there. I asked him who had called so early, but I don't think he even heard me. He wasn't in the kitchen more than half a minute."

"And he left the apartment right away?"

"Yes."

"Did you overhear any of what he said on the phone?"

"No," Manning said, and got up to pour himself another drink.

I watched him carefully. There was something about Dave Manning that bothered me. He was just too cool for the circumstances; but when he came back and took his seat again, I noticed something that told me the coolness was all on the surface. He sat leaning back comfortably against the cushion, apparently completely relaxed, perhaps even a little bored, but he was gripping his highball glass so tightly that the knuckles of his hand were bone-white.

I thumbed back through my notes, then got to my feet. "Your phone book handy?" I asked.

"Over there, by the bar."

"This diamond salesman you said was feuding with Harry," I said. "Mel Pearce. His first name Melvin?"

"No. Melford."

I located a Melford Pearce at 216 Central Park West. Elaine Greer, the girl for whom Harry had thrown over Barbara Nolan, was listed at 734 East 58th.

"I think that'll do it for this time, Mr. Manning," I said as I crossed to the door. "Thanks very much."

"No trouble at all," Manning said easily. "I wish you luck."

I went down to the street and walked along to where I'd left the car. It was completely dark now, but the soggy air was just as stifling as it had been at noon, and it would be that way all night. There was a lot of heat lightning flickering around the spire of the Empire State Building to the south, and the blare of the boat horns from the East River had that muffled sound they have when an early evening fog has set in.

I worked the car out into the traffic and headed downtown for a talk with Barbara Nolan, the girl whose threat against Harry Lambert's life had caused him considerable concern.

The one room apartment above the curio shop on Waverly Place was small, even by Greenwich Village standards, and the girl who had let me inside was petite and pretty and very angry. She had shoulder-length hair so black that it had blue highlights in it, a small oval face with skin like fresh cream, and deep brown eyes under sooty lashes so long that at first I'd thought they were false.

"So why come to me about it?" she said, glaring at me from her perch on a hassock. "What am I supposed to do? Throw myself on his funeral pyre or something?"

"Not necessarily," I said. "I'll settle for the answers to a few questions."

She brushed the hair from her forehead with the back of her hand and crossed her legs the other way.

"You're pretty sure I killed him, aren't you?" she said.

"I didn't say that, Miss Nolan."

"You don't have to. It's written all over your big ugly cop's face."

"We also have a big ugly station house. Would you rather talk there?"

"Well, just for the record, I didn't do it. And also, just for the record, I definitely wish I had."

"And yet, at one time, you were going to marry him."

"Dave Manning certainly gave you a full briefing, didn't he?"

"What do you do for a living, Miss Nolan?"

"I'm a designer. Jewelry, mostly. Also money clips, belt buckles, compacts, lipsticks, perfume bottles, eyeglass frames—et cetera."

"You at work this afternoon? Say, between four and five?"

"Oh, so that's it. That's when he was murdered, wasn't it?" she said.

"Just answer the question, please."

"I work at home. I haven't been out of the place all day."

"You threatened Mr. Lambert's life more than once, I believe."

"I meant it, too." She paused to light a cigarette. "Dave Manning told you about that, too, I suppose?"

"Most girls don't threaten to kill a man just because he changes his mind about getting married."

"Just *because!* You make it sound like nothing at all, like he merely changed his mind about going to a movie or something." She took a short, angry drag on the cigarette and exhaled the smoke through her nostrils. "And besides, I'm not 'most girls.' I'm me. And I just don't take a thing like that."

"And is that all he did to you?"

"Is that all!" Her dark eyes seemed to have tiny fires behind them. "Why, yes, you simple man, that's all he did to me. What more would he have to do? Stake me out on an anthill?"

"You know a girl named Elaine Greer?"

"No. Should I?"

"How about someone named Rocky?"

"No. No Rockys, either."

"You ever been in the Corbin hotel?"

"I've never even *heard* of the Corbin hotel."

"You know anyone who'd have liked to see Lambert dead?"

"Yes. Me. I—"

"Let's cooperate a little here, Miss Nolan. All right?"

She stabbed the cigarette out in a tray on the floor beside the hassock and crossed her legs again. "Just for starters," she said, "how about that fink, Dave Manning? He hated Harry, you know. I mean, *really* hated him."

"Why?"

"Because of me. Harry took me away from him. Did he tell you that? No, of course he didn't." She paused meaningfully. "Dave took it very hard. *Very* hard. It tore him up in little pieces." She raised one eyebrow and smiled at me. "Get the picture?"

"They continued to live together, though."

"What does *that* prove, for heaven's sake?"

I asked Miss Nolan a few more questions, none of which bought me anything, and got up to leave.

"Thanks for your help," I said. "It's possible we'll want to talk to you again, Miss Nolan."

"Oh, no doubt about it," she said. "And thank *you*—for bringing me such good news."

When I reached the squad room at the station house the hands on the big electric clock over the wall speaker stood at nine forty-two. Stan Rayder was at his desk, hammering at his ancient typewriter, a look of faint surprise on his lean face, as if the complaint report in his typewriter were the first one he'd ever seen.

I draped my jacket over the back of my chair and sat down. "How'd it go over at the hotel?" I asked.

"All buttoned up," Stan said. "Police seal on the door and all."

"Come up with anything?"

"Not in the room, no. Somebody'd wiped all the prints off the bottle and the glasses, though. I sent them over to the lab anyhow, along with everything else."

"Good. How about the lipstick? You ask for a check on the jeweler's mark?"

He nodded. "We just had a call on it. They had the mark on file, all right. The engraver lives in Brooklyn. I had them send a man over to see if he can round him up."

"You talk to the bellhop?"

"Yes, for all the good it did. Same goes for the maids. And none of the people in the rooms around Lambert's were in. The newsstand operator across the street saw the girl in the gold dress, though, the one the desk clerk told you about. She went in somewhere around four, he thinks. He didn't notice her come out again."

"Did you get anything else?"

"Yes. We've had a couple of panic calls from diamond dealers. It seems Harry Lambert took out about fifty thousand dollars' worth of stones on consignment this morning." He paused. "Maybe he was murdered for them, maybe not. Maybe he was going to run with them. Maybe a lot of things."

I told Stan what I'd learned from Dave Manning and Barbara Nolan, and then phoned the I.D. bureau to ask for checks on Dave Manning, Barbara Nolan, Elaine Greer, Mel Pearce, and Harry Lambert himself.

A few minutes later they called back to say they had nothing on any of them except Elaine Greer. A cross-reference check had shown that she was the wife of an ex-convict named Ralph Greer, who had been released four days ago from the State Hospital for the Criminal Insane at Matteawan.

Ralph Greer's rap sheet showed bits for grand larceny, aggravated assault, and extortion. His only known criminal associate was another ex-con, Floyd Stoner, now thought to be living at 631 West 74th Street. The present whereabouts of Greer himself were unknown.

"So Lambert's new girlfriend had a husband," Stan said when I relayed the information to him. "And the husband hits the street only four days ago. That sounds pretty good, Pete."

I dialed communications, asked that a pickup order be put out for Ralph Greer, then stood up and reached for my jacket.

"I think Mrs. Greer deserves the pleasure of our company, Stan," I said. "Let's not deny her any longer."

As it happened, Mrs. Greer was to be denied that pleasure, after all. She wasn't home.

We had the same luck when we drove uptown to talk to Floyd Stoner, the man who had once been Ralph Greer's criminal associate. Stoner wasn't home, either.

"We're batting a thousand," Stan said as we walked back down the stairs. "At this rate, we'll wrap things up just in time to put in for our pensions."

I used the wall phone in the first floor hall to ask for pickups on both Elaine Greer and Floyd Stoner, and arranged for plainclothes stakeouts to be stationed at their apartment houses. Then we went out to the car.

"I'll drive," Stan said as he got behind the wheel. "Your driving's too hairy for my nerves. Where to?"

"216 Central Park West."

"Who's there?"

"Mel Pearce, the diamond salesman who thought Lambert cheated him out of a sale."

Stan sighed. "Poor Lambert," he said. "There must be at least one person in this town who wasn't gunning for him. I wonder who it could be?"

Mel Pearce was about fifty, I judged, a graying, slightly stooped man with protuberant eyes behind thick, rimless glasses, abnormally long arms, and very fast answers to every question except the one about his whereabouts between four and five P.M.

He had, he said, spent the time "just walking around the midtown area, mulling over some deals I hoped to make."

As for his troubles with Lambert over the disputed diamond sale, that had all been a misunderstanding. He'd found that he had been in error, had apologized to Lambert, and that had been the end of it.

I called the squad room to see whether there had been any developments. There had.

The stakeout I'd had stationed at Floyd Stoner's apartment house had called to say that a man answering the description of Ralph Greer's former criminal associate had been seen entering the building.

It was a five story house with paper tape across the cracks in the first floor windows, trash in the foyer, and garbage on the stairs. There was no problem getting in; someone had propped the door open with the tattered remains of a phone book in a futile effort to encourage ventilation.

I knocked at the door of 301. There was a faint sound of movement from somewhere inside, but no one came to the door. I knocked again. This time, there was no sound at all.

"Police," I said.

"You're too polite," Stan said. "You got to give it more clout." He stepped close to the door. "It's the law!" he called loudly. "Open up here!"

About fifteen seconds passed.

I drew Stan a little way back from the door. "Stay here," I said. "I'll cover the fire escape. If you hear anything interesting, break in."

I went up to the top floor, climbed the metal ladder to the roof, and eased myself down the fire escape until I was outside the rear window of the apartment.

There was a half-inch gap between the bottom of the window shade and the sill. I peered through it into the room beyond. The blonde girl with the slightly tilted eyes who lay trussed and gagged on the bed was the same girl I'd seen in the photograph in Dave Manning's apartment: Elaine Greer. She was struggling against the towels with which she'd been bound, her bright gold dress bunched up around her hips.

I tried the window. It was locked. I stood back and kicked the glass out of the frame. Then I unholstered my gun, jumped inside, and ran toward the bedroom door.

I jerked the door open just as Stan, alerted by the sound of breaking glass, burst through the front door with a crash of splintering wood, gun in hand.

We stood looking at each other across an empty room.

"What the hell?" Stan said. "I heard something in here. So did you."

"There's a girl tied up in the bedroom," I said. "Elaine Greer. What we heard was her trying to get loose."

"Elaine Greer?"

I nodded. "In a shiny gold dress. Just like the girl at the Corbin hotel was wearing."

The noise had brought some of the tenants to investigate, and now they stood gaping at us from the hallway.

"Police business," I said. "Clear the hall, please."

Mrs. Greer was almost hysterical. It was several minutes before she calmed down enough to talk to us. Even then, it took considerable backtracking before we got a coherent story from her.

She had, she said, been an unwilling participant in a phony kidnapping. Her husband, of whom she was terrified, had learned of her affair with Harry Lambert while he was still in the state mental hospital. When he had been released, four days ago, he had looked up his old friend, Floyd Stoner, and together they had worked out a way to make the most of Lambert's feelings for Mrs. Greer.

The two men had taken her to Stoner's apartment, where, under threat of death if she refused, she had been forced to make the early-morning phone call that Lambert's roommate had told us about. She had told Lambert she had been kidnapped, and that she would be killed unless he came up with a ransom of fifty thousand dollars' worth of small, easily sold diamonds. Lambert, whose insurance would cover that amount, was to claim that he had been robbed by two armed men who had forced themselves into his car.

Lambert was to put the gems in a chamois bag, take a room at the Corbin hotel under his own name, and wait for a phone call giving him further instructions. When Ralph Greer had called him there, however, Lambert had not answered the phone. Greer got mad.

"I was half out of my mind," Elaine Greer said. "I knew I had to do something about it. Then I saw a chance to slip out of the apartment, and I did."

"And?" Stan said.

"I'd heard my husband tell Stoner what Harry's room number was at the Corbin. I got a cab and went there. I knocked and knocked, but Harry didn't answer his door. Then I heard someone behind me—and there was my husband, with a gun in his hand. For a minute I thought he was going to kill me right there. I could see it in his eyes. But then he put the gun away and said something about getting the diamonds one way or another. He opened Harry's door with a piece of celluloid. He slipped it between the door and the jamb and—"

"We know the technique," Stan said. "Go on."

"Well, the door opened right up. We went in, and—and Harry was lying there on the bed. He was dead. I must have gasped or something because Ralph slapped me hard and told me to shut up. He looked for the diamonds, but they weren't there. Then he slapped me again and put his jacket over his arm so nobody could see he was holding a gun on me, and brought me back here in a cab."

"Why'd they tie you up?" Stan asked.

"They were going to kill me. I heard Ralph say so. They didn't want me left around to tell what they'd been up to."

"Where are they now?" I asked.

"I don't know. They left about twenty minutes ago." Her eyes suddenly flooded with tears. "They made me do what I did," she said. "They'd have killed me if I hadn't. They were going to kill me anyway."

Stan and I stood looking at her.

"It's true!" she said. "Everything I've told you is the truth!"

We arranged for additional stakeouts in and around the apartment building, beefed up the pickup order on Greer and Stoner to a thirteen-state alarm, and then took Mrs. Greer down to the station house.

On our way through the squad room to one of the interrogation rooms at the rear, I paused at my desk to see whether there was anything on my call spike or in my IN basket that pertained to the homicide.

There was a lab report saying that the lipstick in the tube I'd found in Lambert's bed and the lipstick on the glass were the same. The smear on the glass, however, had not been left there by a woman's lips; it appeared, rather, to have been put there with the ball of someone's thumb or fingertip. A test had revealed that at the time of his death Lambert's blood had a point five concentration of alcohol.

There was a brief, preliminary report from the medical examiner saying, in essence, that Lambert had died as the result of a blow inflicted by some blunt object to the base of his nose.

There was also a messge on my call spike to phone Ed Gault, the detective who had checked out the jeweler's mark in the lipstick I had found in Lambert's room.

"Good news on that lipstick, Pete," Ed said when I got through to him. "I not only found the guy that made it, I even talked to the girl he made it for. It was a gift from a friend of hers, and her name was on the gift certificate."

It had been the wrong thing for Ed to do, since he might have flushed a prime suspect, but I let it go.

"What'd you find out?" I asked.

"Well, the girl's name is Linda Cole. She lives at the Pendleton, and a prettier little liar you won't find, believe me. She finally admitted being at the Corbin hotel, and she even admitted that she might have lost her lipstick there. But she says she was there almost a month ago, and she hasn't been near the place since." He laughed. "Some story."

"Thanks, Ed," I said. "We'll take it from there."

I hung up and sat drumming my fingertips on the desk for a moment. There had been some lying done, all right, but I had a feeling it hadn't been done by Linda Cole.

I motioned Mrs. Greer to a seat on the chair beside my desk, and then drew Stan away a few paces to tell him about the reports and my talk with Ed Gault.

Stan shook his head, and for once some of the surprise on his face was real. "It looks like somebody ought to get his mouth fixed, doesn't it?" he said. "It just doesn't work right."

"Make sure Mrs. Greer knows her rights and gets a lawyer."

"You're going over there?"

"Yes."

"I'll go with you."

"I don't expect that much trouble, Stan," I said. "Besides, one of us ought to be here in case something breaks on Greer and Stoner."

I went downstairs, checked out a car, and drove the few blocks to the Corbin hotel.

Once again there was no one behind the desk, but there was a light beneath the door of Wayne Dobson's room beyond it, and I could hear someone moving around in there. I went back to the door, turned the knob very slowly, and inched it open.

The desk clerk was moving between his bed and the dresser, packing a suitcase. He was completely dressed for the street, even to a hat, and he was moving quickly, as if he had a lot to do and very little time in which to do it.

"Leaving us, Mr. Dobson?" I said as I stepped inside.

He spun to face me. His jaw sagged for an instant, but he recovered fast. "What's this?" he demanded. "Why didn't you knock?"

"We're old friends by now," I said. "I thought I'd be welcome."

There was an airline envelope on the dresser. I took the ticket out and looked at the name on it. It was made out to "J. Jackson" for a flight to Los Angeles.

"And a one-way ticket, too," I said.

"That belongs to a guest. What's the meaning of this, Selby?"

"And is that suticase you're packing also a guest's?"

"It's no concern of yours, either way. Is there any law that says I can't go anywhere I want to, *when* I want to?"

"There just might be," I said. "Impeding a homicide investigation is a serious charge."

"Impede? What's the matter with you? Impede in what way?"

"You told me Harry Lambert got a phone call from someone named Rocky at exactly three fifty P.M. You were certain about it."

"So?"

"There wasn't any Rocky, Mr. Dobson. And Lambert didn't do any talking on the phone. He was an ex-alcoholic with no tolerance for liquor at all, but he drank a lot of it in that room, and he died with a point five concentration of alcohol in his blood. At three fifty he wasn't only drunk, he was too drunk even to mumble." I paused, "Why'd you lie?"

"I didn't. I—"

"And there's that fancy tube of lipstick you planted in Lambert's bed. It was lost here a month ago, and you put it in the shoebox under the desk, the one from which you had me get the antacid tablets. What you took for just another jazzy drugstore lipstick was an expensive, hand-engraved—"

"Now I get it," Dobson broke in. "You think you're going to frame me for—"

"And another thing," I said. "You smeared some of the lipstick on a glass to make us think Lambert had company in his room. That puzzles me a little, Mr. Dobson. Why'd you do it?"

"I—" Dobson began, then suddenly compressed his lips and stood there, glaring at me.

I moved to the bed and lifted the top layer of clothing out of the suitcase. It was there, all right—a chamois leather bag, no bigger than the kind that kids keep their marbles in.

I glimpsed the bag in the same instant I felt the stab of Dobson's gun in my back. We stood that way, neither of us moving or speaking, for what must have been a full ten seconds.

Then, "Get into the bathroom," Dobson said. "Take it real slow."

"Why?" I said. "A gunshot will carry just as well from there as it will here."

"Real slow, now," he said. "Get going, Selby."

I shrugged, took one slow step in the direction of the bathroom—and then dropped, clawing for my gun, starting to roll the instant I hit the floor.

Dobson's first shot missed, but his second burned a path across my left bicep. Then my own gun bucked in my hand and I saw Dobson's body jerk back from the impact of a slug in his stomach.

It was like watching a slow-motion film. Dobson's right arm lowered almost inch by inch until the gun fell from his hand, and he folded first one arm and then the other across his middle, stood there swaying back and forth for several seconds. Then, very slowly, he sank to his knees.

I kicked Dobson's gun under the bed, put my own back in its holster, and took two of the clean undershirts from the suitcase.

Dobson had lost interest in everything except the blood seeping from the bullet hole in his abdomen. He watched with dull eyes as I wadded one undershirt beneath his belt to serve as a compress and wrapped the other one around my arm where his slug had furrowed the skin. Then I went out to the switchboard to call an ambulance. The shots had brought several guests to the lobby, but I ignored them.

The ambulance was there in eight minutes. I helped the intern put Dobson's stretcher in the back and took a seat on the bench across from it. The intern climbed in beside me, and a moment later the ambulance lurched away from the curb.

"I'm going to die," Dobson said, almost completely without emotion. "You've killed me, Selby. I'm dying."

There wasn't a chance in a thousand of his dying, of course, and the intern opened his mouth to say so, but I kicked his ankle and he shut his mouth again. When a person is sure he is dying, even though he is not, anything he says has the full legal weight of a "deathbed confession," technically known as a dying declaration. It was my job to get such a declaration if I could.

"I guess there are some things you'd like to say, Mr. Dobson," I said. "Maybe now would be the time."

He lay looking at me unblinkingly while the ambulance traveled the better part of a block. Then his eyes drifted away from mine and he moved his head slowly and sadly from side to side.

"I should never have learned karate," he said quietly, almost as if to himself. "If I hadn't, Lambert would still be alive and I . . . I wouldn't be here dying." His voice was resigned and weak, but steady, with an undertone of irony in it.

"Is that how he died?" I asked softly. "From a karate blow?"

"Yes. When I saw all those diamonds, I . . ." He took a deep breath, held it for a moment, and let it out with a sigh. "I was passing his room. The door was half-open and I could see him in there on the bed with a bottle in his hand. I thought it was just another case of a drunk leaving his door open, and I started to close it for him, but then I saw the diamonds, where he'd spread them out on the bed beside him."

I waited. When he didn't go on, I said, "Too much temptation?"

He nodded. "I knew it would be the only chance I'd ever have to be rich. I've always had to scrounge for every dime. It's been just one grubby little job after another all my life, and I . . . I don't know, I thought I could just take them, and who would ever know?"

"And then, Mr. Dobson?" I said.

"I put them in a leather bag that was there, and started to leave, but Lambert's head moved a little, and I . . . Like I said, I should never have learned karate. I didn't even think about hitting him; I just did. I was afraid he was coming to and that he'd see me and . . . You have to understand. It was suddenly like they were *my* diamonds, not his, and he was about to take them away from me."

"And you thought that by pushing him out the window you might cover up?"

"Yes. But I didn't think of that till later. Then I went back upstairs and did it."

He paused, breathing a little more slowly now, his voice a bit fainter. "All the rest was like you said, the lipstick and the phone call and all. I was trying to divert suspicion, but I was so nervous and rattled and sick with my ulcer that I just . . ."

"Go on, Mr. Dobson," I said.

He turned his face away from me. "I've always been a fool," he said, almost inaudibly, and closed his eyes.

The ambulance was nearing the hospital. I sat watching the neon streak past through the window beyond Dobson's stretcher, suddenly tired to the bone. I didn't like the idea of leaving a man, Dobson or anyone else, under the impression he was going to die any longer than I had to.

"All right," I said to the intern beside me. "You can tell him the truth now."

The intern leaned forward, studying Dobson's face. Then he reached out and raised one of his eyelids.

"He didn't make it," he said. "He's dead."

DONALD HONIG

Minutes of Terror

Mel Gifford's house was the last one on the dirt road, which ran nearly a mile in from the highway before becoming a dead end. There were only two other houses along the road and then Gifford's, and beyond that nothing but the pine forest, slowly elevating itself along the mountain slope, rising higher and higher, cresting at two thousand feet. There were ski trails on the other side of the mountain and when the Vermont winter drained the sky of color and spilled its snows, the area became a bustling ski resort.

Now it was November, one of the two transitional seasons (the other occurred in April); the fall foliage was gone and the snows had not yet come. Gifford called it the quiet season. There were no tourists on the roads or in the woods, and things were quieter in town too. Certainly there were fewer people coming into the bank. Many of the local businessmen took their vacations this time of year, just before the onset of the ski season.

"I wish my business were seasonal," Gifford said that morning after the alarm had brought him jarringly awake. He sat up in bed and with dull eyes faced the dim gray morning. Helen had barely moved. He looked at her inert bulk under the covers. No one ever looked graceful lying under covers.

"I said—" he began again.

"I heard you," she said, talking into her pillow.

"I wouldn't mind a month's vacation right now. Hadley left for Florida yesterday, for a month."

Hadley owned the next house down the road. The third house, the one nearest the road, had been rented as a ski lodge for the winter; the owners had already vacated and the new people had not arrived yet. So both houses were empty.

"A whole month," Gifford said, yawning. "He was in the bank the other day to say goodbye. Said he was going to turn off the gas, the electricity, the phone and pack up and go. The lucky stiff."

"You'd better get up," Helen said, "and wake the kids."

Gifford got out of bed and stood by the window. He gazed listlessly for a moment and then, as he turned away, he thought he saw something move among the pine trees. He turned back and stood at the window again, squinting.

"I think I saw a deer," he said.

"Must be a crazy one," Helen said drearily. "Doesn't know the hunting season's started, I guess."

He continued to peer out at the woods, hoping to catch sight of whatever it was that had moved, but all he saw was the extraordinary stillness of the pine in the windless gray light. After several minutes, he said, "I *think* I saw a deer."

"Mel," his wife said, still talking into her pillow, "please wake up the kids. You've got to take them to school."

"And open up the bank and sit behind my desk and smile at everybody. Look, I think I saw a deer and if I did, then it's the most exciting thing that's happened to me in six months."

"Don't be bitter, darling."

"Who's bitter?" he muttered leaving the window.

He put on his bathrobe and walked across the hall, first to Jennifer's room. He opened the door and paused, listening to the seven-year-old snoring lightly. Then he walked to the bed, gazed for a moment at the sleeping face, the dark hair sprawled over the pillow. Gently he put his hand on her shoulder and shook her. A querulous look crossed her sleeping face as she began to turn.

"Good morning, Jennifer," he said.

Her eyes opened, searched sleepily for a moment, then found him standing there by her bed.

"Get up, sweetheart," he whispered.

She stretched and yawned.

"Okay?" he asked.

"Okay."

Then he went to Billy's room. The towheaded eight-year-old was already up.

"I was dreaming, Dad," he said when Gifford walked in.

"Tell me about it later. First, get dressed."

Gifford returned to the bedroom window and peered out again, a puzzled frown on his face. Helen was fully awake now, lying in bed watching him.

"I thought I saw a deer," Gifford said, studying the pine forest with gravely thoughtful eyes. The night shadows seemed to be lingering among the poised, graceful trees. Nothing was moving.

"Maybe it was a hunter," Helen said.

"The woods are posted."

"Since when has that stopped them?"

"Well," Gifford said, "they'd better keep away from here."

After he had washed and shaved and dressed, he sat down to breakfast with his family. Billy and Jennifer yawned, and toyed uninterestedly with their food. Gifford noted it but said nothing; there was a general ennui in the house this morning which was catching.

While Helen helped the children into their coats, Gifford stood at the hall mirror, gazing at himself in a rather detached way. He was thirty-eight and he supposed he looked it. His brown hair had begun to thin. Soft, passive lines were appearing around his mouth. His brown eyes were cool, unreadable, good eyes for a banker to have; good eyes for listening. He thought he was getting a bit flabby, though he did not really want to admit it. He'd ski again this winter, maybe do some hiking. Tone up those muscles.

He put on his topcoat, opened the door and went outside. He stood on the porch feeling the cool, fresh morning air on his face, then headed for the garage, hoping he wouldn't have any trouble starting the car this morning.

As he approached the garage—the door was open—he turned and looked over his shoulder one more time at the pine forest. Had he seen a deer or not? So he was not looking at the garage and did not see the man step from inside it and stand in the doorway. When Gifford finally did turn back and found himself being confronted by the stranger, they were about ten feet apart. He stopped dead in his tracks.

The man was much younger than Gifford, perhaps in his mid-twenties, but there was a lot of hard experience etched into his face, into the calculating steadiness of his gaze, and in the almost contemptuous nonchalance with which he stood. He was wearing a plaid jacket which was two-thirds unzipped, and one hand was concealed inside, at once calmly and menacingly.

"Who are you?" Gifford asked. "What are you doing in there?"

"Just relax, Mr. Gifford," the man said, the tone of his voice suggesting he was giving some very good advice. "You just keep your head and do as you're asked and nobody is going to get hurt."

"I want to know what you were doing in my garage."

"We were waiting for you."

"We?" Gifford said.

The second man appeared then, stepping out of the garage. This one was older, perhaps Gifford's age, with that same steady gaze that wasn't necessarily hostile or threatening, that was simply there to be observed, noted. He was wearing a trenchcoat and a small felt fedora and he looked almost European. He was holding a small revolver in his hand, pointed at Gifford.

"Get into the house," he ordered.

"Why?" Gifford asked, making a conscious effort not to look at the gun, as if refusing to acknowledge it, its primacy.

"Because I tell you to," the older man said impatiently.

"My family is in there."

"We know that. And the best way you can help them is to do exactly as we say, with a minimum of fuss and talk."

"There isn't much money in the house," Gifford said. "But whatever there is, you're welcome to."

"Just get in the house," the older one repeated, putting the gun in his coat pocket but keeping his hand on it. Gifford turned and, followed by the two men, walked back to the house. The door was still open. He could hear Helen talking to the children.

When she heard his footsteps on the porch, she said, "Don't tell me the car won't start."

When he walked inside, followed by the two men, Helen took one look and moved the children around behind her. She didn't have to be told that this was trouble. It was written on her husband's face.

"It's all right, Helen," Gifford said. "They haven't explained themselves yet, but it's all right."

Helen turned to the children and said, "These are friends of your Daddy's. Say hello to them."

Shyly, the children nodded to the men.

"Now take off your coats and go upstairs to your rooms," Helen told them. "We'll call you when it's time to go."

Slowly, uncertainly, with backward looks, the children went upstairs. The two men smiled pleasantly at them.

When the children were gone, the older one said, "Well done, Mrs. Gifford. Now, if this kind of cooperation is maintained everything is going to be just fine."

"What do you want?" Helen asked.

"Sit down, both of you," the older one ordered. "It's very simple, really. All cut and dried, from point A to point Z."

The Giffords sat down on the living room sofa. While the younger man lounged in the doorway, his hand still inside his jacket, an expressionless, uncompromising look on his face, the older one stood before the Giffords.

"I'm going to drive into town with you, Mr. Gifford," he said. "My partner is going to remain here, to oversee your wife and children, as a sort of guarantee for your cooperation until our return."

"You mean you're going to hold them hostage," Gifford said angrily.

"Well, yes. I know you don't like it, but it's the best way, all around, believe me. Now, here's what's going to happen. Instead of opening your bank at nine o'clock, as you normally do, you're going to open a bit earlier today, before your staff gets in."

"And you're going to clean it out," Gifford said, "Well, you've overlooked one thing: there's a time lock on the vault. It doesn't open until nine o'clock and there's not a damn thing I can do about it."

The gunman stared sternly at Gifford for a moment, then began to laugh softly. "We know that, Mr. Gifford," he said. "Look, if it makes you feel any better, we're not amateurs. We know about these things. We've been studying you and your bank and the habits and procedures of all concerned. We've been here nearly a week, and the fact that you haven't noticed us tells you something about our expertise."

"You're not perfect," Gifford said. "I saw you in there yesterday at closing time."

The gunman laughed again, a short, mirthless chuckle. "So we're not perfect," he said, "but don't let that reduce your confidence in us. There's nothing like a smalltown bank. You're very trusting people here. You don't lock up all of your cash at night. Your tellers leave their cash drawers full. That's what we want."

Gifford looked at the floor. The man was right. It was not recommended practice, but out of old habits the tellers did leave their cash in their drawers overnight as crime was virtually nonexistent here. Bank robbers or other serious criminals all seemed so remote.

When Gifford looked up at the gunman there was resentment in his eyes, as if his trust had been betrayed.

"Now," the older man said, looking at his watch, "it's exactly seven thirty. The drive into town is forty minutes, which means we arrive at the bank at eight ten. It shouldn't take us more than fifteen minutes to do what we have to do. So it's then eight twenty-five. With the drive back, we should be returning here at a few minutes after nine."

"That's if he doesn't make trouble," the other gunman added.

"Don't worry, Alf," the older one said, smiling at Gifford. "He won't make any trouble. He knows what's at stake, don't you, Mr. Gifford?"

Gifford said nothing.

"Because," the gunman went on, "if we're not back here on time, and let's allow a few minutes for delays, then his family will be in deep trouble. If we're not back by, say, nine twenty, Alf will safely assume that someone tried to upset our plans."

"And then what?" Gifford asked. "What happens then?"

The gunman smiled, shrugged, and said, "Who can tell—with Alf's temper?"

The implied threat infuriated Gifford; the very idea that anyone would think of harming his family almost deranged his thinking for a moment and he had to suppress the impulse to leap at these men.

"All right," the older gunman said curtly, "let's get moving. For you and your family, Mr. Gifford, the clock has begun to tick."

Gifford did not, would not, get up until the revolver had reappeared. Gesturing with it, the gunman brought Gifford to his feet and followed him outside.

"We'll take your car, Mr. Gifford," the man said as they went down the porch steps.

So for the second time that morning, Gifford headed for his garage. This time he went in with his companion, got into his car, and backed out. As he turned to head down the driveway Gifford took a last, longing look back at his house. It suddenly had an aspect of closed, cold inaccessibility. It provoked in Gifford one single, driving resolve: to get this over as quickly as possible and get back to his family. He had no intention of trying to play the hero. They could take the money and be damned.

As he drove toward the highways he passed the two empty houses and for the first time realized how isolated he was back there. He passed the gunmen's car along the side of the road and knew that no one would see it, no one would pass who might be curious enough to question its presence.

When they got to the highway, Gifford pressed down hard on the accelerator and headed for town.

"Please observe the speed limit, Mr. Gifford," the gunman said. "We don't want to break the law," he added with a sardonic chuckle.

They drove in silence after that. Occasionally they exchanged glances and when they did, the gunman nodded politely and showed a faint, whimsical smile.

As they neared town, Gifford broke the silence. "Won't it look strange to people," he said, "you walking into the bank with me?"

"No, the people here don't have suspicious minds. No reason for them to."

"Suppose some of my staff show up early?"

"Have they ever?"

"No," Gifford said glumly. "But what happens when they arrive and the bank is closed?"

"I can tell you what will happen. They'll call your home, where your wife, with Alf standing right next to her, will tell them you overslept and are on your way in."

"But if someone has already seen me there, entering and leaving . . ."

"We'll let them puzzle it out, Mr. Gifford. By the time they begin to become overly-curious, it won't matter any more. Alf and I will be well on our way."

When they reached the bank, Gifford was told to park in the alley adjacent. They got out of the car and, without being seen by anyone, entered the bank. The blinds were drawn, concealing the bank's interior from the street.

"Eight ten on the button," the gunman said with a note of quiet satisfaction in his voice.

Gifford suddenly whirled and confronted him and, in an unnaturally loud voice asked, "What happens to my family if we don't get back there on time?"

As if annoyed or perhaps alarmed by this sudden belligerence, the gunman drew his revolver.

"I'm asking you a question, damn you!" Gifford shouted, taking a step toward the other, and as he did the gunman lifted the revolver to eye level and pointed it coldly and directly at Gifford.

"Get on with it, Mr. Gifford," he said testily. "If you have your family's well-being at heart you won't tempt the fates by wasting time. Now, you have the keys to those cash drawers, so get on with it."

Gifford got his keys and began unlocking the drawers. The gunman went with him to the tellers' stations, holding a canvas bag which he had pulled from his pocket, and watched Gifford go from drawer to drawer filling it. The gunman had figured fifteen minutes in the bank; it took less than ten.

"All right, Mr. Gifford," the gunman said when all the drawers had been emptied, "now comes the delicate part—walking out of here carrying an obviously stuffed bag. I might add that with the money now in my possession my outlook on things becomes a bit obsessed. The idea of a large sum of money is one thing, the possession of it is another. If anyone challenges us I'm prepared to use this gun—on you or them. Do you understand?"

"I understand," Gifford said.

"So give me your car keys. In the event I have to shoot you dead I'll have to leave in your car."

Frightened now, Gifford handed him the keys. The gunman seemed tense, even angry, as if the mere thought of having to relinquish the money was intolerable.

They opened the door and walked outside. The sidewalk was empty, for which Gifford was grateful, for he had taken quite seriously the man's threats. They walked around to the alley and got into the car, Gifford in the driver's seat. The keys were returned to him.

"Now head back."

"What time is it?" Gifford asked, then looked at his watch. It was eight twenty.

"This is no problem, Mr. Gifford. Just get moving."

Gifford backed out of the alley. Several people passing on the sidewalk seemed to take no notice. In this small, insular New England town they were so conditioned to minding their business that they seemed to feel it was an intrusion even to glance at someone. Gifford damned their aloofness now. If any one of them had any brains they would notice that something was amiss here and call the police—except that the police in this town consisted of two middle-aged men who were totally inadequate to cope with a situation like this.

As they drove back along the highway, Gifford began having some disturbing thoughts. What would happen after they returned? Would the two gunmen simply take the money and leave? The more Gifford thought about it the more his doubts began to grow. At best, they would tie up the family, so as to have ample time in which to get away; and the worst—but Gifford didn't want to think about that.

Grimly silent, Gifford sped along the highway, anxious to get back, to be with his family, to face together whatever happened.

They passed few cars on the highway; there was only the constant passing on either side of the road of the endless evergreen. Between the monotony of the drive and the consuming depths of his thoughts, Gifford was paying only mechanical attention to what he was doing, to the extent that it was the gunman who had to point out that they were nearing the side road.

"The turnoff is coming up," he said, noting that there had been no deceleration to allow for the turn.

His voice barely penetrated Gifford's reverie and, with an uncomprehending expression, he turned his head to look at the man.

"The turn is coming," the gunman yelled, pointing ahead with his finger.

Instinctively, without thinking, without braking or even decompressing the accelerator, Gifford suddenly swung the wheel, but the car was going too fast, the angle too sharp. There was a shuddering and a skidding as the car bounded off the highway onto the dirt road; the trees seemed to be flashing through every window, swooping and abrupt, as if doing some wild dance around the car. Unable to make its turn, the car made a screeching sound and plunged off the dirt road. It bolted furiously through the roadside brush, ran over some scrub pine and came suddenly and barbarously to a stop with a sickening thud against an enormous boulder that had been cast from the mountaintop in another age.

Gifford remembered his head hitting against the window. He thought he had been knocked unconscious then, yet he remembered the car flattening the scrub pine and then the boulder looming up like something rising from the undersea. He also remembered the jolting and unceremonious stop to which they had come, but it was all vague and unreal, ill-recorded by memory.

He was lying against the door, aware of a dull aching in his head, his thoughts unable for the moment to emerge coherently from under the pain. He blinked several times before he was able to understand what it was he was seeing. The hood had been thrown into the air by the impact of the crash and hung now like the open jaw of some voracious bird of prey. He could not immediately remember where he was, what had happened. Then he turned and saw his companion, and he remembered.

The gunman looked as though he had been hurled against the door with great fury; he seemed crushed and crumpled. His face, in profile, wore an expression of shocked anger, made the more furious by a copious flow of blood. His hat was gone and his hair looked as though it had been about to leave his head and then stopped.

Gifford gazed at him with simple, uncomplicated curiosity, until the realization had set fully in—the man was dead.

Then Gifford remembered all the rest of it and a shock of terror rushed through him. He looked at his watch: it was ten minutes after nine. He turned around and stared with building panic at the road, then undid his seat belt and opened the door and got out. He walked around behind the smashed and seething car to the other door and opened it. The gunman, who had not been using his seat belt, tumbled softly to the ground. Gifford reached down and took the revolver out of the man's pocket.

He glanced at his watch. There was still time. Alf was expecting them back at nine twenty and there would surely be allowed some margin for delay, but how much? He thought about the possibility of going back to the highway and hailing a car but that would consume time.

Another thought occurred: take the bag of money to the house, tell Alf what had happened, and perhaps he would go. The idea was appealing, except that Alf might suspect a trick, might suspect that Gifford was trying to trap him, and in that situation there was no telling what the man might do.

Then, under the pressure of elapsing time, with the determination to help his family, Gifford disdained all further thought and speculation and began to run toward his house, revolver in hand. He passed his neighbors' empty houses. A fleeting thought to break in and telephone the state police had to be rejected; the telephones in both houses had been disconnected.

What am I going to do? Gifford kept asking himself. He couldn't simply burst in there, gun or no gun. There was no telling what Alf's frame of mind was, nor what it would become. Doubtless an awful tension had been building in that house during the past hour. The young gunman had to be getting more and more concerned and nervous, and consequently unpredictable and dangerous.

Gifford stopped in the middle of the road, panting. He lifted his hand and covered his eyes for a moment. Get out of the road, he told himself. Alf would almost certainly be watching the road.

So he began approaching the house in a roundabout way, through the pine forest, moving slowly, cautiously. When the side of the house came into view he lay down on the pine needles, trying to formulate some plan, some kind of assault that held a reasonable chance of success. *Think*, he told himself. *Think. Think.*

He could enter through a basement window, carefully and quietly, and work his way upstairs and take Alf by surprise—but the least sound, with his wife and children sitting in front of a gun . . . He closed his eyes for a moment. Were the basement windows locked? He hadn't checked them in months; there was never reason to, in this "crime-free" environment. If they were locked, how could he get in without breaking one? There was no telling what the least sound might provoke in Alf's mind.

He should have gone back to the highway and summoned help, he realized now. This was foolhardy. He had no experience at this sort of thing. He was jeopardizing his family.

Then, as he lay there agonizing over his situation, a shot suddenly rang out, shattering the pristine silence of the pine forest. Gifford instinctively pressed himself tensely to the ground, his eyes glaring. He looked at his watch: ten minutes after nine.

Only ten minutes after nine?

With his eyes widening in terror he studied the face of the watch. The sweep hand was still. The watch had stopped, probably during the accident. But when? How long ago? How long had he been unconscious in the car?

Now the echo of the shot began to reverberate through him. What was happening in the house?

Without waiting to shape another thought, suddenly seized and impelled by an uncontrollable terror, he got to his feet and began running at breakneck speed for the house, pointing the gun out ahead of him. He crashed through the underbrush and out onto the road, running faster and faster, driven forward by the single, maniacal thought of getting the man who was inside the house, unmindful of his own safety, unencumbered by any idea of stealth or strategy. That was all gone now, replaced by the primitive urge to protect his family.

He ran across the front lawn, took the porch steps in two bounds and burst through the front door. He ran through the front door. He ran through the hallway—and was suddenly confronted by Alf. The gunman was in the act of running from the living room to the hallway, his gun swung out from his body.

Without stopping, Gifford fired, his finger suddenly frozen on the trigger. The revolver's recoil made him shudder and stagger as a fury of motion was enacted before him. The running Alf was struck several times in mid-flight and now his animation became spastic and grotesque as one after the other the bullets struck him. He slammed into the wall, then arched back, spun in a half circle and dropped to the floor.

Gifford raced into the living room where he found his startled wife standing, her clasped hands covering her mouth.

"Where are the children?" Gifford demanded.

Helen gasped, her fixed eyes upon the smoking revolver in her husband's hand.

"Where are they?" Gifford shouted.

"Upstairs," she said in a small, strained voice that sounded like a gasp.

"Are they all right? Are you all right?"

"Yes-yes-yes," Helen said, trembling.

Then she ran to him as Gifford let the gun fall to the floor and he threw his arms around her.

"I heard a shot . . ." he said, wracked by unspent tension.

"He was getting more and more restless and nervous," Helen said. "It was terrible."

"He didn't harm any of you, did he?"

"No."

"But what was he shooting at?" Gifford asked.

"He said he saw something moving in the trees. He thought it was the police. But I saw it. It was only a deer . . . but he didn't believe me."

She looked once at Alf's inert, bloody, bullet-torn body, then closed her eyes and pressed her forehead against Gifford's chest.

"A deer?" Gifford said softly. "That's what he shot at?"

"What happened?" Helen asked. "Are you all right? Are you all right?"

Gifford sighed and shook his head. "Not yet. Give me a little time," he said, closing his eyes as he heard his children calling from upstairs.

ARTHUR PORGES

Puddle

A great poet promised to show us fear in a handful of dust. If ever I doubted that such a thing were possible, I know better now. In the past few weeks a vague, terrible memory of my childhood suddenly came into sharp focus after staying tantalizingly just beyond the edge of recall for decades. Perhaps the high fever from a recent virus attack opened some blocked pathways in my brain, but whatever the explanation, I have come to understand for the first time why I see fear not in dust, but water.

It must seem quite absurd: fear in a shallow puddle made by rain; but think about it for a moment. Haven't you ever, as a child, gazed down at such a little pool on the street, seen the reflected sky, and experienced the illusion, very strongly, so that it brought a shudder, of endless depth a mere step away—a chasm extending downward somehow to the heavens? A single stride to the center of the glassy puddle, and you would fall right through. Down? Up? The direction was indefinable, a weird blend of both. There were clouds beneath your feet, and nothing but that shining surface between. Did you dare to take that critical step and shatter the illusion? Not I. Now that memory has returned, I recall being far too scared of the consequences. I carefully skirted such wet patches, no matter how casually my playmates splashed through.

Most of my acquaintances tolerated this weakness in me. After all, I was a sturdy, active child, and held my own in the games we played. It was only after Joe Carma appeared in town that my own little hell materialized, and I lost status.

He was three years older than I, and much stronger; thickset, muscular, dark—and perpetually surly. He was never known to smile in any joyous way, but only to laugh with a kind of *schadenfreude*, the German word for mirth provoked by another's misfortunes. Few could stand up to him when he hunched his blocky frame and bored in with big fists flailing, and I wasn't one of the elect; he terrified me as much by his demeanor as his physical power.

Looking back now, I discern something grim and evil about the boy, fatherless, with a weak and querulous mother. What he did was not the thoughtless, basically merry mischief of the other kids, but full of malice and cruelty. Where Shorty Dugan would cheerfully snowball a tomcat, or let the air

395

out of old man Gruber's tires, Carma preferred to torture a kitten—rumor said he'd been seen burning one alive—or take a hammer to a car's headlights.

Somehow Joe Carma learned of my phobia about puddles, and my torment began. On several occasions he meant to go so far as to collar me, hold my writhing body over one of the bigger pools, and pretend to drop me through—into that terribly distant sky beyond the sidewalk.

Each time I was saved at the last moment, nearly hysterical with fright, by Larry Dumont, who was taller than the bully, at least as strong, and thought to be more agile. They were bound to clash eventually, but so far Carma had sheered off, hoping, perhaps, to find and exploit some weakness in his opponent that would give him an edge. Not that he was a coward but just coldly careful; one who always played the odds.

As for Larry, he was good-natured, and not likely to fight at all unless pushed into it. By grabbing Carma with his lean, wiry fingers that could bend thick nails, and half-jokingly arguing with him, Dumont would bring about my release without forcing a showdown. Then they might scuffle a bit, with Larry smiling and Joe darkly sullen as ever, only to separate, newly respectful of each other's strength.

One day, after a heavy rain, Carma caught me near a giant puddle—almost a pond—that had appeared behind the Johnson barn at the north end of town. It was a lonely spot, the hour was rather early, and ordinarily Joe would not have been about, as he liked to sleep late on weekends. If I had suspected he might be around, that was the last place in the world I'd have picked to visit alone.

Fear and fascination often go together. I stood by the huge puddle, but well away from the edge, peering down at the blue sky, quite cloudless and so far beneath the ground where it should not have been at all; and for the thousandth time tried to gather enough nerve to step in. I *knew* there had to be solid land below—jabs with a stick had proved this much before in similar cases— yet I simply could not make my feet move.

At that instant brawny arms seized me, lifted my body into the air, and tilted it so that my contorted face was parallel to the pool and right over the glittering surface.

"Gonna count to ten, and then drop you right through!" a rasping voice taunted me. "You been right all along: it's a long way down. You're gonna fall and fall, with the wind whistling past your ears; turning, tumbling, faster and faster. You'll be gone for good, kid, just sailing down forever. You're gonna scream like crazy all the way, and it'll get fainter and fainter. Here we go: one! two! three!—"

I tried to scream but my throat was sealed. I just made husky noises while squirming desperately, but Carma held me fast. I could feel the heavy muscles in his arms all knotted with the effort.

"—four! five! Won't be long now. Six! seven!—"

A thin, whimpering sound broke from my lips, and he laughed. My vision was blurring; I was going into shock, it seems to me now, years later.

Then help came, swift and effective. Carma was jerked back, away from the water, and I fell free. Larry Dumont stood there, white with fury.

"You're a dirty skunk, Joe!" he gritted angrily. "You need a lesson, your own kind."

Then he did an amazing thing. Although Carma was heavier than he, if shorter, Larry whipped those lean arms around the bully, snatched him clear of the ground and with a single magnificent heave threw him fully six feet into the middle of the water.

Now I wonder about my memory; I have to. Did I actually see what I now recall so clearly? It's quite impossible, but the vision persists. Carma fell full-length, face down, in the puddle, and surely the water could not have been more than a few inches deep. But he went on through! I saw his body twisting, turning, and shrinking in size as it dropped away into that cloudless sky. He screamed, and it was exactly as he had described it to me moments earlier. The terrible, shrill cries grew fainter, as if dying away in the distance; the flailing figure became first a tiny doll, and then a mere dot; an unforgettable thing, surely, yet only a dream-memory for so long.

I looked at Larry; he was gaping, his face drained of all blood. His long fingers were still hooked and tense from that mighty toss.

That's how I remember it. Perhaps we probed the puddle; I'm not sure, but if we did, surely it was inches deep.

On recovering from my illness three weeks ago, I hired a good private detective to make a check. The files of the local paper are unfortunately not complete, but one item for August 20, 1937, when I was eight, begins:

NO CLUES ON DISAPPEARANCE OF CARMA BOY

After ten days of police investigation, no trace has been found of Joe Carma, who vanished completely on the ninth of this month. It is not even known how he left town, if he did, since there is no evidence that he went by either bus or train. Martin's Pond, the only deep water within many miles, was dragged, but without any result.

The detective assures me that Joe Carma never returned to town, and that the name is unlisted in army records, with the FBI, or indeed any national roster from 1937 to date.

These days, I skin dive, sail my own little sloop, and have even shot some of the worst Colorado River rapids in a rubber boat. Yet it still takes almost more courage than I have to slosh through a shallow puddle that mirrors the sky.

LAWRENCE BLOCK

When This Man Dies

The night before the first letter came, he had Speckled Band in the feature at Saratoga. The horse went off at nine-to-two from the number one pole and Edgar Kraft had two hundred dollars on him, half to win and half to place. Speckled Band went to the front and stayed there. The odds-on favorite, a four-year-old named Sheila's Kid, challenged around the clubhouse turn and got hung up on the outside. Kraft was counting his money. In the stretch, Speckled Bank broke stride, galloped home madly, was summarily disqualified, and placed fourth. Kraft tore up his tickets and went home.

So he was in no mood for jokes that morning. He opened five of the six letters that came in the morning mail, and all five were bills, none of which he had any prospect of paying in the immediate future. He put them in a drawer in his desk. There were already several bills in that drawer. He opened the final letter and was at first relieved to discover that it was not a bill, not a notice of payment due, not a threat to repossess car or furniture. It was, instead, a very simple message typed in the center of a large sheet of plain typing paper.

First a name:

> Mr. Jospeh H. Neimann

And, below that:

> When this man dies
> You will receive
> Five hundred dollars.

He was in no mood for jokes. Trotters that lead all the way, and then break in the stretch, do not contribute to a man's sense of humor. He looked at the sheet of paper, turned it over to see if there was anything further on its reverse, turned it over again to read the message once more, picked up the envelope, saw nothing on it but his own name and a local postmark, said something unprintable about some idiots and their idea of a joke, and tore everything up and threw it away, message and envelope and all.

In the course of the next week he thought about the letter once, maybe twice. No more than that. He had problems of his own. He had never heard of anyone named Joseph H. Neimann and entertained no hopes of receiving five hundred dollars in the event of the man's death. He did not mention the cryptic message to his wife. When the man from Superior Finance called to ask him if he had any hopes of meeting his note on time, he did not say anything about the legacy that Mr. Neimann meant to leave him.

He went on doing his work from one day to the next, working with the quiet desperation of a man who knows his income, while better than nothing, will never quite get around to equalling his expenditures. He went to the track twice, won thirty dollars one night, lost twenty-three the next. He came quite close to forgetting entirely about Mr. Joseph H. Neimann and the mysterious correspondent.

Then the second letter came. He opened it mechanically, unfolded a large sheet of plain white paper. Ten fresh fifty dollar bills fluttered down upon the top of his desk. In the center of the sheet of paper someone had typed:

Thank you

Edgar Kraft did not make the connection immediately. He tried to think what he might have done that would merit anyone's thanks, not to mention anyone's five hundred dollars. It took him a moment, and then he recalled that other letter and rushed out of his office and down the street to a drugstore. He bought a morning paper, turned to the obituaries. Joseph Henry Neimann, 67, of 413 Park Place, had died the previous afternoon in County Hospital after an illness of several months' duration. He left a widow, three children, and four grandchildren. Funeral services would be private, flowers were please to be omitted.

He put three hundred dollars in his checking account and two hundred dollars in his wallet. He made his payment on the car, paid his rent, cleared up a handful of small bills. The mess in his desk drawer was substantially less baleful, although by no means completely cleared up. He still owed money, but he owed less now than before the timely death of Joseph Henry Neimann. The man from Superior Finance had been appeased by a partial payment; he would stop making a nuisance of himself, at least for the time being.

That night, Kraft took his wife to the track. He even let her make a couple impossible hunch bets. He lost forty dollars and it hardly bothered him at all.

When the next letter came he did not tear it up. He recognized the typing on the envelope, and he turned it over in his hands for a few moments before opening it, like a child with a wrapped present. He was somewhat more apprehensive than a child with a present, however; he couldn't help feeling that the mysterious benefactor would want something in return for his five hundred dollars.

He opened the letter. No demands, however. Just the usual sheet of plain paper, with another name typed in its center:

Mr. Raymond Andersen

And, below that:

When this man dies
You will receive
Seven hundred fifty dollars.

For the next few days he kept telling himself that he did not wish anything unpleasant for Mr. Raymond Andersen. He didn't know the man, he had never heard of him, and he was not the sort to wish death upon some total stranger. And yet—

Each morning he bought a paper and turned at once to the death notices, searching almost against his will for the name of Mr. Raymond Andersen. *I don't wish him harm*, he would think each time. But seven hundred fifty dollars was a happy sum. If something were going to happen to Mr. Raymond Andersen, he might as well profit by it. It wasn't as though he was doing anything to cause Andersen's death. He was even unwilling to wish for it. But if something happened . . .

Something happened. Five days after the letter came, he found Andersen's obituary in the morning paper. Andersen was an old man, a very old man, and he had died in his bed at a home for the aged after a long illness. His heart jumped when he read the notice with a combination of excitement and guilt. But what was there to feel guilty about? He hadn't done anything. And death, for a sick old man like Raymond Andersen, was more a cause for relief than grief, more a blessing than a tragedy.

But why would anyone want to pay him seven hundred fifty dollars?

Nevertheless, someone did.

The letter came the following morning, after a wretched night during which Kraft tossed and turned and batted two possibilities back and forth—that the letter would come and that it would not. It did come, and it brought the promised seven hundred fifty dollars in fifties and hundreds. And the same message:

Thank You

For what? He had not the slightest idea. But he looked at the two-word message again before putting it carefully away.

You're welcome, he thought. *You're entirely welcome.*

For two weeks no letter came. He kept waiting for the mail, kept hoping for another windfall like the two that had come so far. There were times when he would sit at his desk for twenty or thirty minutes at a time, staring off into space and thinking about the letters and the money. He would have done better keeping his mind on his work, but this was not easy. His job brought him five thousand dollars a year, and for that sum he had to work forty to fifty hours a week. His anonymous pen pal had thus far brought him a quarter as much as he earned in a year, and he had done nothing at all for the money.

The seven fifty had helped, but he was still in hot water. On a sudden female whim his wife had had the living room recarpeted. The rent was due. There was another payment due on the car. He had one very good night at the track, but a few other visits took back his winnings and more.

And then the letter came, along with a circular inviting him to buy a dehumidifier for his basement and an appeal for funds from some dubious charity. He swept circular and appeal into his wastebasket and tore open the plain white envelope. The message was the usual sort:

Mr. Claude Pierce

And, below the name:

When this man dies
You will receive
One thousand dollars.

Kraft's hands were shaking slightly as he put the envelope and letter away in his desk. One thousand dollars—the price had gone up again, this time to a fairly staggering figure. Mr. Claude Pierce. Did he know anyone named Claude Pierce? He did not. Was Claude Pierce sick? Was he a lonely old man, dying somewhere of a terminal illness?

Kraft hoped so. He hated himself for the wish, but he could not smother it. He hoped Claude Pierce was dying.

This time he did a little research. He thumbed through the phone book until he found a listing for a Claude Pierce on Honeydale Drive. He closed the book then and tried to put the whole business out of his mind, an enterprise foredoomed to failure. Finally he gave up, looked up the listing once more, looked at the man's name and thought that this man was going to die. It was inevitable, wasn't it? They sent him some man's name in the mail, and then the man died, and then Edgar Kraft was paid. Obviously, Claude Pierce was a doomed man.

He called Pierce's number. A woman answered, and Kraft asked if Mr. Pierce was in.

"Mr. Pierce is in the hospital," the woman said. "Who's calling, please?"

"Thank you," Kraft said.

Of course, he thought. They, whoever they were, simply found people in hospitals who were about to die, and they paid money to Edgar Kraft when the inevitable occurred, and that was all. The why of it was impenetrable. But so few things made sense in Kraft's life that he did not want to question the whole affair too closely. Perhaps his unknown correspondent was like that lunatic on television who gave away a million dollars every week. If someone wanted to give Kraft money, Kraft wouldn't argue with him.

That afternoon he called the hospital. Claude Pierce had been admitted two days ago for major surgery, a nurse told Kraft. His condition was listed as *good.*

Well, he would have a relapse, Kraft thought. He was doomed—the letter-writer had ordained his death. He felt momentarily sorry for Claude Pierce, and then he turned his attention to the entries at Saratoga. There was a horse named Orange Pips which Kraft had been watching for some time. The horse had a good post now, and if he was ever going to win, this was the time.

Kraft went to the track. Orange Pips ran out of the money. In the morning Kraft failed to find Pierce's obituary. When he called the hospital, the nurse told him that Pierce was recovering very nicely.

Impossible, Kraft thought.

For three weeks Claude Pierce lay in his hospital bed, and for three weeks Edgar Kraft followed his condition with more interest than Pierce's doctor could have displayed. Once Pierce took a turn for the worse and slipped into a coma. The nurse's voice was grave over the phone, and Kraft bowed his head, resigned to the inevitable. A day later Pierce had rallied remarkably. The nurse sounded positively cheerful, and Kraft fought off a sudden wave of rage that threatened to overwhelm him.

From that point on, Pierce improved steadily. He was released, finally, a whole man again, and Kraft could not understand quite what had happened. Something had gone wrong. When Pierce died, he was to receive a thousand dollars. Pierce had been sick, Pierce had been close to death, and then, inexplicably, Pierce had been snatched from the very jaws of death, with a thousand dollars simultaneously snatched from Edgar Kraft.

He waited for another letter. No letter came.

With the rent two weeks overdue, with a payment on the car past due, with the man from Superior Finance calling him far too often, Kraft's mind began to work against him. *When this man dies*, the letter had said. There had been no strings attached, no time limit on Pierce's death. After all, Pierce could not live forever. No one did. And whenever Pierce did happen to draw his last breath, he would get that thousand dollars.

Suppose something happened to Pierce—

He thought it over against his own will. It would not be hard, he kept telling himself. No one knew that he had any interest whatsoever in Claude Pierce. If he picked his time well, if he did the dirty business and got it done with and hurried off into the night, no one would know. The police would never think of him in the same breath with Claude Pierce, if police were in the habit of thinking in breaths. He did not know Pierce, he had no obvious motive for killing Pierce, and—

He couldn't do it, he told himself. He simply could not do it. He was no killer. And something as senseless as this, something so thoroughly absurd, was unthinkable.

He would manage without the thousand dollars. Somehow, he would live without the money. True, he had already spent it a dozen times over in his mind. True, he had been counting and recounting it when Pierce lay in a coma. But he would get along without it. What else could he do?

The next morning headlines shrieked Pierce's name at Edgar Kraft. The previous night someone had broken into the Pierce home on Honeydale Drive and had knifed Claude Pierce in his bed. The murderer had escaped unseen. No possible motive for the slaying of Pierce could be established. The police were baffled.

Kraft got slightly sick to his stomach as he read the story. His first reaction was a pure and simple onrush of unbearable guilt, as though he had been the man with the knife, as though he himself had broken in during the night to stab silently and flee promptly, mission accomplished. He could not shake this guilt away. He knew well enough that he had done nothing, that he had killed no one. But he had conceived of the act, he had willed that it be done, and he could not escape the feeling that he was a murderer, at heart if not in fact.

His blood money came on schedule. One thousand dollars, ten fresh hundreds this time. And the message. *Thank you.*

Don't thank me, he thought, holding the bills in his hand, holding them tenderly. Don't thank me!

> *Mr. Leon Dennison*
> *When this man dies*
> *You will receive*
> *Fifteen hundred dollars.*

Kraft did not keep the letter. He was breathing heavily when he read it, his heart pounding. He read it twice through, and then he took it and the envelope it had come in, and all the other letters and envelopes that he had so carefully saved, and he tore them all into little bits and flushed them down the toilet.

He had a headache. He took aspirin, but it did not help his headache at all. He sat at his desk and did no work until lunchtime. He went to the luncheonette around the corner and ate lunch without tasting his food. During the afternoon he found that, for the first time, he could not make head or tails out of the list of entries at Saratoga. He couldn't concentrate on a thing, and he left the office early and took a long walk.

Mr. Leon Dennison.

Dennison lived in an apartment on Cadbury Avenue. No one answered his phone. Dennison was an attorney, and he had an office listing. When Kraft called it a secretary answered and told him that Mr. Dennison was in conference. Would he care to leave his name?

When this man dies.

But Dennison would not die, he thought. Not in a hospital bed, at any rate. Dennison was perfectly all right, he was at work, and the person who had written all those letters knew very well that Dennison was all right, that he was not sick.

Fifteen hundred dollars.

But how, he wondered. He did not own a gun and had not the slightest idea how to get one. A knife? Someone had used a knife on Claude Pierce, he remembered. And a knife would probably not be hard to get his hands on. But a knife seemed somehow unnatural to him.

How, then? By automobile? He could do it that way, he could lie in wait for Dennison and run him down in his car. It would not be difficult, and it would probably be certain enough. Still, the police were supposed to be able to find hit and run drivers fairly easily. There was something about paint scrapings, or blood on your own bumper, or something. He didn't know the details, but they always did seem to catch hit and run drivers.

Forget it, he told himself. You are not a killer.

He didn't forget it. For two days he tried to think of other things and failed miserably. He thought about Dennison, and he thought about fifteen hundred dollars, and he thought about murder.

When this man dies—

One time he got up early in the morning and drove to Cadbury Avenue. He watched Leon Dennison's apartment, and he saw Dennison emerge, and when

Dennison crossed the street toward his parked car Kraft settled his own foot on the accelerator and ached to put the pedal on the floor and send the car hurtling toward Leon Dennison. But he didn't do it. He waited.

So clever. Suppose he were caught in the act? Nothing linked him with the person who wrote him the letters. He hadn't even kept the letters, but even if he had, they were untraceable.

Fifteen hundred dollars—

On a Thursday afternoon he called his wife and told her he was going directly to Saratoga. She complained mechanically before bowing to the inevitable. He drove to Cadbury Avenue and parked his car. When the door-man slipped down to the corner for a cup of coffee, Kraft ducked into the building and found Leon Dennison's apartment. The door was locked, but he managed to spring the lock with the blade of a pen knife. He was sweating freely as he worked on the lock, expecting every moment someone to come up behind him and lay a hand on his shoulder. The lock gave, and he went inside and closed it after him.

But something happened the moment he entered the apartment. All the fear, all the anxiety, all of this suddenly left Edgar Kraft. He was mysteriously calm now. Everything was prearranged, he told himself. Joseph H. Neimann had been doomed, and Raymond Andersen had been doomed, and Claude Pierce had been doomed, and each of them had died. Now Leon Dennison was similarly doomed, and he too would die.

It seemed very simple. And Edgar Kraft himself was nothing but a part of this grand design, nothing but a cog in a gigantic machine. He would do his part without worrying about it. Everything could only go according to plan.

Everything did. He waited three hours for Leon Dennison to come home, waited in calm silence. When a key turned in the lock, he stepped swiftly and noiselessly to the side of the door, a fireplace andiron held high overhead. The door opened and Leon Dennison entered, quite alone.

The andiron descended.

Leon Dennison fell without a murmur. He collapsed, lay still. The andiron rose and fell twice more, just for insurance, and Leon Dennison never moved and never uttered a sound. Kraft had only to wipe off the andiron and a few other surfaces to eliminate any fingerprints he might have left behind. He left the building by the service entrance. No one saw him.

He waited all that night for the rush of guilt. He was surprised when it failed to come. But he had already been a murderer—by wishing for Andersen's death, by planning Pierce's murder. The simple translation of his impulses from thought to deed was no impetus for further guilt.

There was no letter the next day. The following morning the usual envelope was waiting for him. It was quite bulky; it was filled with fifteen hundred dollar bills.

The note was different. It said *Thank you*, of course. But beneath that there was another line:

How do you like your new job?

ELIJAH ELLIS

Public Office

On any Saturday afternoon, the ancient courthouse in Monroe is a lonely place. All the county offices, except for the sheriff's office down on the ground floor, close at noon. By one o'clock or so, the ugly old pile of stone and marble and worm-eaten wood is about as lively as a mausoleum.

This particular Saturday was raw and rainy, much too wet and dismal for golf. So I'd decided to stay on at my office on the third floor and catch up on my paperwork. By two o'clock I was regretting my decision. I leaned back in my chair, lit a cigarette, and sourly eyed the heap of work yet to do. Then the phone rang. Eagerly I picked it up. "Yes?"

"This the country attorney's office?" The voice was curiously muffled. "County Attorney Gates?"

"Yes, this is Lon Gates speaking. Can I help you?"

"Go look in the dome."

I took the receiver away from my ear, frowned at it, then replaced it. "Go do what?"

"Go look in the courthouse dome. And I hope it makes you happy. You dirty rat."

Click. My caller hung up quickly.

Slowly I cradled my phone. "Now what?" I asked the empty office. I swiveled my chair around to stare out the tall, narrow windows in the far wall. Beyond them, the sky was a smear of cold gray-black. Rain fell steadily, speeded on its way by occasional jabs of lightning, followed by sullen booms of thunder. A lousy day.

Look in the dome?

Well, why not? It'd give me a few minutes away from this mass of paperwork. And besides, I'd never been up there, even though it was a famous place in Pokochobee County folklore. About seventy-five years ago, a disgraced county official had hanged himself from one of the beams that supported the dome.

Lightning streaked across the stormy sky. Thunder crashed.

Yes, this was surely the day to inspect the famous dome. I laughed, but I didn't enjoy it much. I was remembering the cold venom in that voice on the phone. ". . . I hope it makes you happy. You dirty rat."

I got up, left the office, and went along the dim, echoing corridor. Between the county courtroom and the court clerk's office, I found an unmarked door. I pulled it open with a creak of hinges. I stepped inside. It was a small narrow room, crowded with junk. At the far end was the beginning of a spiral iron staircase leading upwards.

Everything—the floor, the walls, the staircase—was furred with inch-thick dust. Squinting through the thick, musty gloom, I saw a trail of scuffed footprints, leading to the iron stairs. I followed them up the corkscrew of the staircase. I was halfway up before I realized that there was no sign of footprints coming down . . .

I hesitated. Sure, all this was probably someone's idea of a joke. He'd be there in the dome, ready to jump out at me, but I couldn't see the fun in it.

Slowly I went on up. The stairs emerge on one side of the large, round, sheet-iron dome that crowns the old courthouse. There are small windows around the dome, caked with the grime of years, and now these admitted just enough light to make out an elongated figure suspended from one of the central beams that supported the roof—the figure of a hanging man!

I could feel sweat popping out on my face, and the hairs bristling on the back of my neck. I told myself firmly that it was a joke. The jokester, remembering the old story of the county official who had hanged himself here, had now hung a lifelike dummy in the same spot. Very funny.

I walked toward the dangling figure. It swayed gently in the vagrant puffs of wind that found their way through the cracks and crevices of the ancient dome. I shivered and told myself it was because of the chill and the damp.

Then lightning glared at the windows.

I jumped back and yelled. In the brief flicker of light, I saw the face of the hanging figure. It was a man's face—swollen, congested, and very dead. I forgot all about jokes. I forced myself to walk to the dead man. I squinted up through the gloom, waiting for the next bolt of lightning so that I could see the face suspended above me. From the corner of my eye I noted a ladder propped against the beam, some feet to my right.

It all made a pretty clear picture. Suicide. But, who . . . ? Another sheet of lightning, and I saw who. It was like a kick in the stomach. "Oh, no," I breathed.

Turning away, I stumbled back to the stairs and down them to my office. I fumbled for the phone, dropped it, picked it up again. I called the sheriff's office. In a moment Ed Carson's familiar drawl came on the line.

"Ed, this is Lon Gates. Come up to my office. Quick!"

The sheriff of Pokochobee County didn't waste words. "Be there in a minute."

He was, in less than a minute. I was glad to see him. He ran a handkerchief over his craggy face and panted, "Now what is it? You sounded like a dead man on the phone."

"Leland Russel," I said. "He's up in the dome. . . . Dead."

The sheriff stared.

I took a long drag at a cigarette. "Yeah. It looks like the old codger went up there and—and hanged himself. Suicide."

Carson tugged fiercely at a corner of his pepper-and-salt mustache. Then his suddenly icy gaze hit me. "Let's hear about it."

I told him about the phone call, the single trail of footsteps leading up the spiral stairs into the dome—and none coming down. I mentioned the ladder propped against the beam, and the old man's body, at the end of a seven-foot length of rope.

The sheriff's big, rawboned frame seemed to shrink into itself. Lines of pain appeared in his face, and then lines of bitter anger. He didn't speak. He didn't have to; I knew what he was thinking.

Now he whirled around, picked up the phone. He called his office and snapped an order to the deputy on duty. He broke the connection, immediately called another number—that of Dr. James Conley who served as county coroner.

When he'd finished, he put down the phone. He kept his back to me. Leland Russel had been one of his oldest and best friends. Now I heard quick footsteps in the corridor outside the office. Carson turned.

"It wasn't enough you took his job away," he said. "You had to take his life, too."

The sheriff was gone before I could reply. I started to follow him, the hot words rising in my throat, but I didn't. I stopped in the doorway and watched Carson and his deputy pound along the corridor toward the door that led to the dome. The deputy, Wally Hooper, was carrying a battery-powered floodlight and other equipment.

I turned back into my office. I went to my desk, sat down in the swivel chair. I'd never felt so sick in my life.

Leland Russel . . . a dry, straight, white-maned old man who had been Pokochobee county attorney for twenty years, even longer than Ed Carson had been sheriff.

Last year, I'd been brash enough to run against Russel, and I'd beaten him. The campaign had been rough, even brutal, in its final stages. Pokochobee County politics is no place for the faint of heart.

I'd thought Russel's ideas of justice, and the administration of the county attorney's office were strictly nineteenth century, and he himself little more than a relic. And I didn't hesitate to say so. Enough of the new generation of voters had agreed with me to put me in office.

But it had destroyed Leland Russel. He was like a man who has seen a beloved father turn on him and kick his teeth out. After the election, the old man had withdrawn almost completely from life. Callers were not welcome at his home, and the few who did get in to see him wished they hadn't. They found a gray-lipped, vacant-eyed shell.

He was seldom seen in downtown Monroe, and never seen at the courthouse, though he had many old friends there. He had crumbled away without even the solace of booze; he was a strict teetotaler. Now, a little over a year later, he'd come to this: the sick gesture of making himself the second "disgraced" county official to hang himself in the ancient dome of the courthouse.

But what about the phone call?

The cobwebs of shock and remorse began to lift from my mind. I sat forward in my chair. Yeah, and what about a couple of other things—like a man Russel's age carrying a heavy, twenty-foot ladder up that steep and winding staircase?

"Like hell," I said, and jumped up and left the office. In the gloomy corridor I bumped into the just-arriving Dr. Conley. We went on up to the dome together. There we found that Carson and Deputy Hooper had set up the floodlight.

The dangling body was bathed in the floodlight's hard white glare. Hooper was up on the beam, examining the rope. ". . . It's just looped around a couple of times and tied in a plain old hard-knot," Hooper was saying when the doctor and I arrived.

Dr. Conley brisked forward. He spoke to the sheriff. He eyed the body from several angles. He whistled tunelessly between his teeth. Then he said, "All right, let him down."

While Carson held the body, Hooper undid the knot that held the rope to the beam. Carson lowered the slack body to the floor and stepped back. Then the sheriff came over to stand beside me near the mouth of the staircase.

"Sorry about what I said a while ago," he muttered. "I was just—well, anyhow, I had no business poppin' off. Even if old Leland had killed himself . . . which he didn't."

I blinked. "That's what I was thinking. The phone call, the ladder—"

"Well, sure, that too," Carson said, "but the main thing is, his neck ain't broken, which it sure as heck would be if he'd got up on that beam, tied the rope around his neck and jumped off. Just look at the poor old fellow. He died of strangulation."

A moment later Dr. Conley rose from his examination. He dusted absently at the knees of his trousers and said, "I don't know what kind of wild theory you men have, but I'll tell you right now, Mr. Russel did not commit suicide."

No one spoke. Outside, the rain still pattered down. A burst of thunder made the iron dome tremble. Wally Hooper asked, "Then what did happen?"

"How should I know?" Dr. Conley complained. "The body has a bruise on the point of the jaw. At a guess, I'd say the blow that made the bruise was struck not long before death. That's all I'm saying. You want detective work out of me, you can ask the county commissioners to raise my salary."

Ed Carson snorted. Then his hawk-nosed face sobered. "How about this, doc? He was slugged, and his unconscious body was hoisted up on the end of the rope so that he died of strangulation."

The pigeon-chested, fussy-mannered little doctor grimaced. "Could be," he nodded. "Whatever, this man certainly didn't hang himself. The fall from that beam to the point where the rope became taut would have snapped his neck like a toothpick," the doctor added, repeating what Carson had said a few moments ago.

There was a sudden clatter of footsteps on the spiral staircase. Then the familiar rotund figure of Jeremiah Walton, editor of the semi-weekly Monroe

Dispatch, panted into view. Walton surveyed the scene. His small, puffy eyes fastened on the corpse. "Ah," he wheezed happily.

Ed Carson exclaimed in annoyance. "How did you get word of this so quick, Walton?"

The editor waddled forward to peer down at the body. Then he whirled and aimed a forefinger at me. "So. How do you feel now, Gates? Now that you've driven this poor old man to take his own life—"

"Oh, shut up, you fat jackass," Ed Carson growled. "Mr. Russel didn't kill himself. He was murdered."

That stopped Walton for a few seconds. His tiny eyes flickered toward Deputy Wally Hooper. "But, I thought . . ."

"The last thought you had was thirty years ago," I said. Needless to say, the *Dispatch* and I are on opposite sides of the political fence. During last year's campaign, Walton had done everything from questioning my ancestry to accusing me of being a card-carrying communist.

He blinked a couple of times, nibbling at his small, pursed lips. Again his eyes flickered toward Hooper. The deputy was bending over the corpse, carefully keeping his broad back turned to the rest of us.

Sheriff Carson said softly, "Wally?"

Hooper turned. His face was a study in innocence.

"Wally, did you call Mr. Walton here? After I called you from Mr. Gates's office?"

The big deputy ran a finger around the open collar of his khaki shirt. He swallowed. Then he blurted, "Well, it wasn't supposed to be a secret, was it?"

Carson squeezed his eyes shut. He opened them again. "All right, Wally." There was something very final in the way he said the two words. Like, "You're through."

Even in the grim circumstances I couldn't help smiling to myself. I'd never liked Wally Hooper, and the feeling was mutual. He was a big, muscular towheaded guy a couple of years younger than me. This past spring he'd gotten his law degree from the state university. During the last two or three summer vacations, and now full time, he'd worked as a deputy to Ed Carson.

Which all sounds very fine and industrious, but not the way Hooper played it. Actually, his one purpose in serving as a deputy sheriff was to make political contacts. He had been a strong worker for Leland Russel last year, no doubt with the agreement that, if Russel were reelected, Wally Hooper would become the assistant county attorney, with every prospect of taking over the office when the old man retired. After the election, Hooper had the nerve to come to me and ask for the assistant's job. I took a good deal of pleasure in laughing in his "boyish" face.

No, Wally Hooper and I didn't care for each other.

But now Jeremiah Walton was thrusting his paunch forward, tilting his head back, and peering down his broad nose at the sheriff. He had recovered his composure. "Are you trying to tell me this was murder?" he sneered.

Carson's Adam's apple bobbed up and down his neck as he swallowed a mouthful of angry words. After a moment he said mildly, "It looks that way to me. Mr. Russel didn't die of a broken neck; he was strangled to death."

"So what?" Walton argued. His eyes darted about the dome, up to the beams that crisscrossed overhead, to the ladder leaning against the beam from which the body had been suspended. "Why, it's obvious what happened. Russel attached the rope to the beam, then he descended the ladder. He had a chair or something placed directly beneath the dangling rope. He then put the noose around his neck and stepped off the chair. Hah! Therefore, he did not drop a sufficient distance to break his neck. He simply strangled."

The editor luxuriously scratched his chins.

I said sardonically, "Where's the chair?" I paused, then added, "Or something?"

The editor again peered about him. There was nothing in the dome but the dust and grime of years. Walton shrugged fat shoulders. "Obvious. Someone carried away the object upon which Russel stood . . ."

"Oh, for God's sake," Dr. Conley barked. The little doctor waved his stubby-fingered hands in disgust. "Politics—politics. You people would debate over the ravished body of your own mother. I'm resigning as county coroner tomorrow."

The doctor stumped toward the stairs. I said, "Doc, could Mr. Russel have packed that ladder up here from the janitor's closet on the third floor?"

Conley paused. "Oh, yes. As far as that goes, Lon, when a man sincerely wants to do something, there's very little he can't do. Long as he don't care what it costs. But in this particular case, I'm here to tell you, Leland Russel didn't. Now I'm going to call the meatwagon."

"Use the phone in my office," I called, as the doctor bustled down the steps.

An outraged cry responded. "I'll use the phone booth in the hall, thank you!"

After that, no one spoke again for a long moment, while the wind and rain howled outside the shuddering dome.

The glaring white circle of light illuminated the sprawled body on the floor. Walton drew Hooper off to the other side of the dome, and the pair were soon deeply engaged in a whispered conversation.

Carson muttered wryly, "Looks like the end of a beautiful friendship there."

I gave him an absent nod. I was staring at the corpse, particularly the dust-coated shoes on the small slim feet. "Those footprints on the stairs," I said, "there really was just one set, leading up."

"Yeah," Carson grimaced. "No good to us now. What with all the trampin' up and down since you first saw them."

The sheriff lit a cigarette. I lit one of my own.

"Not that there's any problem about how they were made," the sheriff went on. "The killer was just careful to place his own feet in the prints old Leland made—you can be sure he had Leland in front of him, comin' up the stairs. And the same thing in reverse, when the killer went down, alone."

Carson sighed, rubbed his eyes. "Course I ought to be doin' a dozen things, but I feel like I've been clubbed. I don't care how long you're in this lousy business, or how hardened you think you've become. When it hits close to home . . ." He broke off, ended with a weary shrug.

By now the newspaper editor and Wally Hooper had finished their talk. They moved over to join us. Hooper looked chastened. Jeremiah Walton, as usual, looked like a pompous bullfrog, but he tried to sound friendly even though it was obviously a strain on him.

"Boys, I want to apologize for my somewhat rude language a while ago. But you understand that Mr. Russel was an old and dear friend, and I'd been given to understand he had killed himself."

"Yeah," I broke in, "and if he had, you would have a field day tearing me to pieces in your paper. 'The young upstart who drove the old and honored public servant to a disgraceful death.' I wouldn't be able to get elected dog catcher by the time you got through spraying your venom all over the county."

As I spoke, I took a few steps toward the editor. He quickly backed away, waving his hands before him. "Now, now. Nothing of the sort. I . . ."

A sudden yelp of pain interrupted us. We turned to find Wally Hooper crouched above the body. He had a finger in his mouth. Carson asked, "What's the matter with you?"

Hooper took his finger from his mouth and frowned at it. "I was just going through the old man's pockets again to see if we missed anything. I caught my finger on the point of a stickpin here, on the lapel of his jacket."

Carson snorted. "Too bad you didn't sit down on it."

By now Jeremiah Walton was at the top of the staircase. He passed and backed out of the way as Dr. Conley appeared. The doctor came on up the last few steps and brushed by Walton.

"The wagon will be here in a few minutes," Conley said. The little pigeon-chested doctor's face looked drawn and tired. I remembered that he too had been a close friend of Leland Russel's.

There wasn't anything to do right now but wait for the arrival of the ambulance. My burst of anger towards Jeremiah Walton was gone; this was hardly the time or the place.

The five of us milled slowly around the dome, not speaking. For something to do, I climbed the ladder that was propped against the beam overhead. At the top, I looked along the length of the massive, worm-holed oaken beam.

I sighed and started down. Then I stopped. I bent my face closer to the point where the ladder rested against the beam. There was a fur of undisturbed dust there. Even a cobweb draped from the beam to the side piece of the ladder.

Quite obviously, this ladder had rested in this position for months—maybe years. It was not, as I had thought, the ladder that was kept in the janitor's closet on the third floor. I backed down slowly to the floor of the dome. As I did, a lot of little things that hadn't seemed important began to come together and form a picture.

Maybe I was crazy. But—

I caught Ed Carson's eye, beckoned him over to the side of the dome, away from the others. "Listen," I asked softly, "when's the last time you talked to Russel?"

Ed blinked at me. "Why, I talked to him a couple of minutes on the phone, this noon. Tried to get him to come downtown and have lunch with me. Course, he wouldn't do it."

I swallowed. "Did you happen to mention to him that I'd be working this afternoon?"

"Why—I might have. Think I did. In connection with what a lousy day it is, something like that. Too bad for even you to get out on the golf course. But what the . . . ?"

"Tell you in a minute," I said. I ran down the twisting staircase to the narrow, long room at the bottom. I fumbled along the wall near the corridor door, found a light switch, flicked it on.

A single dusty bulb shed a dim glow over the room. Stacked along the walls and at the far end were a jumble of old packing crates, broken office equipment, a few discarded desks and chairs.

Almost at once I spotted what I wanted. On top of a pile of wooden chairs was a chair like the rest—only the dust on it was smudged in many places and the seat was clean, as if it had been wiped off recently.

Leaving the dingy light on, I went back upstairs.

I remembered certain ugly rumors I'd heard, but hadn't been able to substantiate. Back in the dome again, I went across to Carson.

He looked at me like he wondered if I'd lost a few more of my marbles, I was wondering myself, but it all made a weird kind of sense—up to a point.

"I was right the first time," I told him.

"What are you talking about?"

I didn't answer just then. I walked over to the edge of the glaring circle of light that centered on the dead man. I said, "Listen, would you all come over here a minute?"

The four men sauntered across the dome to form a little knot around me; Ed Carson, puzzled and worried; Dr. Conley, tired and irritable; Wally Hooper, looking as if he wished he were somewhere else; and the editor, Walton, who was very, very nervous, and stayed several feet distant from me.

"Just take a minute to tell," I said casually, though I was feeling far from casual. "Maybe I'm as crazy as Walton there thinks. It's this. I believe a sick, weary old man came up here this afternoon, sometime shortly before two. He knew the courthouse would be deserted practically—especially on a day like this. He also knew I was in my office. From one of the phone booths somewhere in the building, he called—a friend—and told the friend what he intended to do. He asked the friend to wait a few minutes, then call me. See? He wanted me to find his body."

The sheriff exploded, "Are you trying to say now that Russel really did commit suicide?"

"Exactly."

"But that's nonsense," Dr. Conley cried.

There was a confused babble of talk. Finally I shouted, "Shut up, and let me finish."

When they were quiet again except for an occasional mumble, I went on. "So then Russel came on up here. He brought a length of rope with him, and he stopped in the room at the bottom of the stairs long enough to pick up a straight-back wooden chair. Up here, he climbed the ladder to the beam, attached the rope, then climbed down. He placed the chair under the noose in the free end of the rope. He put the rope around his neck, and kicked the chair out from under him."

In the dead silence, I turned slowly to face Jeremiah Walton. "Just as you said, Mr. Editor, the drop wasn't far enough to break his neck. So he strangled to death."

Walton licked ashen lips. "But . . . I was just guessing."

"Good guessing," I said. I looked around at the pale, strained faces. "But then Russel's 'friend' entered the picture. Soon as he got Russel's call, he rushed over here. He was just too late. He was careful to step in Russel's footprints on his way up and down the stairs. He found Russel . . . dead. Pinned to the lapel of his jacket was a note. Remember, Wally? You stuck your finger on the pin a few minutes ago."

The big deputy mopped his face on his sleeve.

"Not much more," I said. "The friend couldn't afford to have Russel found a suicide. Certainly not with that note on his lapel, and probably a sheaf of very revealing documents in his pocket. So he took the note and the papers, and the chair. He left, again being careful to stay in the footprints made by Russel. Down in the anteroom he put the chair back on a pile of similar chairs. He hurried out of the building, noticing that my lights were on. He went across the square to his office. He called me—"

Suddenly everything happened at once. The floodlight smashed over on its face, breaking the lens and the bulb, plunging the dome into near darkness. Startled yells. Vague figures shifting about, silhouetted against the brief flares of lightning at the windows.

I was nearest the staircase so I blundered toward it. At the top, I turned back, meaning to block the way. But before I could set myself a pair of open palms plowed into my chest. I sprawled back and down, windmilling my arms. My flailing hands smacked into the iron railing at the first turn. I grabbed the rail with all my strength.

I was on my back, my head and shoulders hanging over into empty space. A dark figure loomed above me. I cried out, "Stop! Look out!"

Too late, the man tripped over my body. He went over the railing and emitted a grunt that turned into a brief scream. Then he hit the floor thirty feet below.

He was still alive when the rest of us got down there. He was looking up blankly at the dingy bulb that gave the only light. As we gathered around, his lips formed a wry smile. Blood seeped from a corner of his mouth and from his nose.

Ed Carson knelt down by him. He asked, "Why?"

The dying man coughed. "Couldn't be—suicide. Be too much—searching—into past. Someone sure to find evidence, sooner or later—deals Russel and I made. But if it was murder—then—then—search would be for killer. I'd be safe." He struggled for his breath.

Dr. James Conley rose up on his elbows, his eyes glaring. "Safe," he repeated. He fell back. He was gone.

For a long moment no one spoke. Wally Hooper was bent over an empty box. Jeremiah Walton backed away, toward the door at the other end of the room. Suddenly he turned and ran. Ed Carson and I exchanged glances. Ed shook his head, got to his feet.

I said, "I heard, here and there, rumors that Russel and Conley had pulled some shady deals—payoffs to call murder suicide—that kind of thing. I never believed it."

Carson scrubbed his hands over his face. "I heard that, too, but I never for a minute . . ."

"Yeah, I know." I wanted to get out of there. "Listen. Let's leave Hooper here. You and me, let's go along to my office. I got a bottle there."

I had to take Carson's arm, lead him away.

At the door, he turned. He spat, "Politics!"

Then we left.

MARGARET B. MARON

The Beast Within

Early summer twilight had begun to soften the harsh outlines of the city when Tessa pushed open the sliding glass doors and stepped out onto the terrace. Dusk blurred away the grime and ugliness of surrounding buildings and even brought a kind of eerie beauty to the skeletal girders of the new skyscraper going up next door.

Gray haired, middle-aged and now drained of all emotion, Tessa leaned heavily-fleshed arms on the railing of the penthouse terrace and let the night enfold her.

From the street far below, the muffled sounds of evening traffic floated up to her, and for a moment she considered jumping—to end it all in one brief instant of broken flesh and screaming ambulances while the curious stared. What real difference would it make to her, to anyone, if she lived another day or year, or twenty years?

Still, the habit of life was too deeply in her. With a few cruel and indifferent words, Clarence had destroyed her world; but he had not destroyed her will to live. Not yet.

She glanced across the narrow space to the uncompleted building. The workmen who filled the daylight hours with a cacophony of rivets and protesting winches were gone now, leaving behind, for safety, hundreds of tiny bare light bulbs. In the warm breeze, they swung on their wires like chained fireflies in the dusk.

Tessa smiled at the thought. How long had it been since she had seen real fireflies drift through summer twilight? Surely not more than half a dozen times since marrying Clarence. She no longer hated the city, but she had never forgiven it for not having fireflies—or for blocking out the Milky Way with its star-quenching skyscrapers.

Even thirty years ago, when he had married her and brought her away from the country, Clarence had not understood her unease at living in a place so eternally and brilliantly lit. When his friends complimented them on the penthouse and marveled at the size of their terrace (enormous even by those booming wartime standards of the Forties), he would laugh and say, "I bought it for Tessa. Can't fence in a country girl, you know; they need 'land, lots of land 'neath the starry skies above!'"

It hadn't taken her long to realize that the penthouse was more a gift to his vanity than to still her unspoken needs. After a while, she stopped caring.

If the building weren't high enough above the neon glare of the streets to see her favorite stars, it at least provided as much quiet as one could expect in a city. She could always lie back on one of the cushioned chaises and remember how the Milky Way swirled in and out of the constellations; remember the dainty charm of the Pleiades tucked away in Taurus the Bull.

But not tonight. Instead of star-studded skies, memory forced her to relive the past hour.

She was long since reconciled to the fact that Clarence did not love her; but after years of trying to fit his standards, she had thought that he was comfortable with her and that she was necessary to him in all the other spheres which hold a marriage together after passion is gone.

Tonight, Clarence had made it brutally clear that not only was she unnecessary, but that the woman she had become, to please him, was the antithesis of the woman he'd chosen to replace her.

In a daze, Tessa had followed him through their apartment as he packed his suitcases. Mechanically, she had handed him clean shirts and underwear; and, seeing what a mess he was making of his perfectly tailored suits, she had taken over the actual packing as she always did when he had to go away on business trips. Only this time, he was going to a hotel and would not be back.

"But why?" she asked, smoothing a crease in his gray slacks.

They had met Lynn Herrick at one of Alison's parties. Aggressive and uninhibited, she wore the latest mod clothes and let her straight black hair swing longer than a teenager's although she was probably past thirty. Tessa thought her brittle and obvious, hardly Clarence's type, and she had been amused by the girl's blatantly flirtatious approach.

"Why?" she demanded again and was amazed at the fatuous expression which spread across Clarence's face: a blend of pride, sheepishness and defiance.

"Because she's going to bear my child," he said pompously, striking a pose of chivalrous manhood.

It was the ultimate blow. For years Tessa had pleaded for a child, only to have Clarence take every precaution to prevent one.

"You always loathed children. You said they were encumbrances—whining, slobbering nuisances!"

"It wasn't my fault," Clarence protested. "Accidents happen."

"I'll bet!" Tessa muttered crudely, knowing that nothing accidental ever happens to the Lynn Herricks of this world; but Clarence chose to ignore her remark.

"Now that it has happened, Lynn has made me see how much I owe it to myself and to the company. A 'pledge to posterity' she calls it, since it doesn't look as if Richard and Alison are going to produce an heir, as you know," Clarence said.

Richard Loughlin was Clarence's much younger brother. Together, they had inherited control of a prosperous chain of department stores. Although Tessa had heard Richard remark wistfully that a child might be fun, his wife Alison shared Clarence's previous attitude toward offspring; and her distaste was strengthened by the fear of what a child might do to her size eight figure.

With Clarence reveling in the newfound joys of prospective fatherhood, Tessa had straightened from his packing and snapped shut the final suitcase. Still in a daze, she stared at her reflection in the mirror over his dresser and was appalled.

In her conscious mind, she had known that she would soon be fifty, that her hair was gray, her figure no longer slim; and she had known that Clarence would never let her have children—but deep inside, she felt the young, half-wild girl she had been cry out in protest at this ultimate denial, at this old and barren woman she had become.

The siren of a fire engine on the street below drew Tessa to the edge of the terrace again. Night had fallen completely and traffic was thin now. The sidewalks were nearly deserted.

She still felt outraged at being cast aside so summarily—as if a pat on the shoulder, the promise of lavish alimony, and an "I told Lynn you'd be sensible about everything" were enough to compensate for thirty years of her life—but at least her brief urge toward self-destruction had dissipated.

She stared again at the bobbing safety lights of the uncompleted building and remembered that the last time she had seen fireflies had been four years ago, after Richard and Alison returned from their honeymoon. She and Clarence had gone down to Pennsylvania with them to help warm the old farm Richard had just bought as a wedding surprise for Alison.

The hundred and thirty acres of overgrown fields and virgin woodlands had indeed been a surprise to Alison. Her idea of a suitable weekend retreat was a modern beach house on Martha's Vineyard.

Tessa had loved it and had tramped the woods with Richard, windblown and exhilarated, while Alison and Clarence complained about the bugs and dredged up pressing reasons for cutting short their stay. Although Alison had been charming, and had assured Richard that she was delighted with the farm, she found excellent excuses for not accompanying him on his infrequent trips to the country.

Remembering the farm's isolation, Tessa wondered if Richard would mind if she buried herself there for a while. Perhaps in the country she could sort things out and grope her way back to the wild freedom she had known thirty years ago, before Clarence took her away and "housebroke her"—as he'd expressed it in the early years of their marriage.

A cat's terrified yowl caught her attention. She looked up and saw it running along one of the steel girders which stuck out several feet from a higher level of the new building. The cat raced out on it as if pursued by the three-headed hound of Hell, and its momentum was too great to stop when it realized the danger.

It soared off the end of the girder and landed with a sickening thump on the terrace awning. Awkwardly writhing off the awning, the cat leaped to the terrace floor and cowered under one of the chaises, quivering with panic.

Tessa watched the end of the girder, expecting to see a battle-scarred tomcat spoiling for a fight. Although cats seldom came up this high, it was not unusual to see one taking a shortcut across her terrace from one rooftop to another, up and down fire escapes. But no other cat appeared.

The night air had roused that touch of arthritis which had begun to bother Tessa lately, and it was an effort to bend down beside the lounge chair. She tried to coax the cat out, but it shrank away from her hand. "Here, kitty," she murmured, "it's all right. There's no one chasing you now."

She had always liked cats and, for that reason, refused to own one, knowing how easy it would be to let a small animal become a proxy child. She sensed Richard's antipathy and sympathized with him whenever Alison referred to Liebchen, their dachshund, as "baby."

Patiently, she waited for the cat to stop trembling and sniff her outstretched hand. She kept her tone low and soothing, but it would not abandon its shelter. Careful to make no sudden moves, Tessa stood up and stepped back a few feet.

The cat edged out then, suspiciously poised for flight, and the light from the living room beyond the glass doors fell across it. It was a young female with crisp black and gray markings and white paws; and judging by its leggy thinness, it hadn't eaten in some time.

"Poor thing," Tessa said, moved by its uneasy trust. "Wait right there, kitty— I'll get you something to eat." As if it understood she meant no harm, the cat did not skitter aside when she moved past it into the arpartment.

In a few minutes, Tessa returned, carrying a saucer of warm milk and a generous chunk of rare beef which she'd recklessly cut from the heart of their untouched dinner roast. "You might as well have it, kitty. No one else will be eating it."

Stiff-legged and wary, the young cat approached the food and sniffed; then, clumsily, it tore at the meat, almost choking in its haste.

"Slow down!" Tessa warned, and knelt beside the cat to pull the meat into smaller pieces. "You're an odd one. Didn't you ever eat meat before?" She tried to stroke its thin back, but the cat quivered and slipped away beneath her plump hand. "Sorry, cat. I was just being friendly."

She sat down heavily on one of the chaises and watched the animal finish its meal. When the meat was gone, it turned to the saucer of milk and drank messily with much sneezing and shaking of its small head as it inadvertently got milk in its nose.

Tessa was amused and a bit puzzled. She'd never seen a cat so graceless and awkward. It was almost like a young, untutored kitten; and when it finished eating and sat staring at her, Tessa couldn't help laughing aloud. "Didn't your mother teach you *any*thing, silly? You're supposed to wash your paws and whiskers now."

The cat moved from the patch of light where it had sat silhouetted, its face in darkness. With purposeful caution, it circled the chaise until Tessa was between the cat and the terrace doors. Light from the living room fell full in its eyes there and was caught and reflected with an eerie intensity.

Uneasily, Tessa shivered as the cat's eyes met her own with unwavering steadiness. "Now I understand why cats are always linked with the supernatu—"

The cat's eyes seemed to bore into her brain. There was a spiraling vortex of blinding light. Her mind was assaulted—mauled and dragged down and under and through it, existence without shape. She was held by a roaring numbness which lasted forever and was over instantly, and she was conscious of another's existence, mingling and passing—a being who was terrified, panic-stricken, and yet fiercely exultant.

There was a brief, weird sensation of being unbearably compacted and compressed; the universe seemed to tilt and swirl; then it was over. The light faded to normal city darkness, the roaring ceased and she knew that she was sprawled upon the cool flagstones of the terrace.

She tried to push herself up, but her body would not respond normally. Dazed, she looked around and screamed at the madness of a world suddenly magnified in size—a scream which choked off as she caught sight of someone enormous sitting on the now-huge chaise.

A plump, middle-aged woman held her face between trembling hands and moaned, "Thank God! Thank God!"

With a shock, Tessa realized she was seeing her own face for the first time, without the reversing effect of a mirror. The shock intensified as she looked down through slitted eyes and saw neat white paws instead of her own hands. With alien instinct, she felt the ridge of her spine quiver as fur stood on end. She tried to speak and was horrified to hear a feline yowl emerge.

The woman on the chaise—Tessa could no longer think of that body as herself—stopped moaning then and watched her warily. "You're not mad, if that's what you're wondering. Not yet, anyhow. Though you'll go mad if you don't get out of that skin in time."

Snatching up one of the cushions, she flung it at Tessa. "Shoo! G'wan, scat!" she gibbered. "You can't make me look in your eyes. I'll never get caught again. Scat, damn you!"

Startled, Tessa sprang to the railing of the terrace and teetered there awkwardly. The body responded now, but she didn't know how well she could control it, and twenty-eight stories above street level was too high to allow for much error.

The woman who had stolen her body seemed afraid to come closer. "You might as well go!" she snarled at Tessa. She threw a calculating glance at the luxurious interior beyond the glass doors. In the lamp lights, the rooms looked comfortable and secure. "It's a lousy body—too old and too fat—but it seems to be a rich one and it's human and I'm keeping it, so *scat!*"

Her new reflexes were quicker than those of her old body; and before the slipper left the woman's hand, Tessa had dropped to the narrow ledge circling the outside of her apartment. Residual instinct made her footing firm as she followed the ledge around the corner of the building to the fire escape, where it was an easy climb to the roof. There, in comparative safety from flying shoes and incipient plunges to the street, Tessa drew up to consider the situation.

Cat's body or not, she thought wryly, *it's still my mind.* She explored the sensations of her new body, absentmindedly licking away the dried milk which stuck to her whiskers, and discovered that vestigial traces of former identities clung to the brain. Mere wisps they were, like perfume hanging in a closed room, but enough to piece together a picture of what had happened to her on the terrace below.

The one who had just stolen her body had been young and sly, but not overly bright. Judging from the terror and panic so freshly imprinted, she had fled through the city and had taken the first body she could.

Behind those raw emotions lay a cooler, more calculating undertone and Tessa knew *that* one had been more mature, had chosen the girl's body deliberately and after much thought. Not for her the hasty grabbing of the first opportunity; instead, she had stalked her prey with care, taking a body that was pretty, healthy, and, above all, young.

Beyond those two, Tessa could not sort out the other personalities whose lingering traces she felt. Nor could she know who had been the first, or how it all had started. Probing too deeply, she recoiled from the touch of a totally alien animal essence struggling for consciousness—the underlying basic *catness* of this creature whose body she now inhabited.

Tessa clamped down ruthlessly on these primeval stirrings, forcing them back under. This must be what the girl meant about going mad. How long could a person stay in control?

The answer, of course, was to get back into a human body. Tessa pattered softly to the edge of the roof and peered down at the terrace. Below, the girl in her body still cowered on the chaise longue as if unable to walk into the apartment and assume possession. She sat slumped and looked old and defeated.

She was right, thought Tessa, *it is a lousy body. She's welcome to the joys of being Mrs. Clarence Loughlin.*

Her spirits soaring, Tessa danced across the black-tarred roof on nimble paws. Joyfully, she experimented with her new body and essayed small leaps into the night air. No more arthritis, no excess flab to make her gasp for breath. What bliss to think a motion and have lithe muscles respond!

Drunk with her new physical prowess, she raced to the fire escape, leaped to the railing and recklessly threw herself out into space. There was one sickening moment when she felt she must have misjudged, then she caught herself on a jutting scaffold and scrambled onto it.

Memories it had taken thirty years to bury were uncovered as Tessa prowled through the night and rediscovered things forgotten in the air-conditioned, temperature-controlled, insulated environment which had been her life with Clarence.

Freed of her old woman's body, she felt a oneness again with—what? The world? Nature? God? The name didn't matter, only the feeling. Even here in the city, in the heart of man's farthest retreat into artifice, she felt it.

What it must be like to have a cat's body in the country! Tessa thought, and then shivered as she realized that it would be too much. To be in this body with grass and dirt underneath, surrounded by trees and bushes alive with small rustlings, and uncluttered sky overhead—a human mind would go mad with so much sensory stimulation.

No, better the city with its concrete and cars and crush of people to remind her that she was human, that this body was only temporary.

Still, she thought, descending gracefully from the new building, *there can be no harm in just a taste.*

She ran west along half-deserted streets, heading for the park.

On the cross-town streets, traffic was light; but crossing the avenues terrified her. The rumble and throb of all those engines, the glaring lights and impatient horns kept her fur on end. She had to force herself to step off the curb at Fifth Avenue; and as she darted across its wide expanse, she half-expected to be crushed beneath a taxi.

The park was a haven now. Gratefully, she dived between its fence railing and melted into the dark safety of its jumble of bushes.

In the next few hours, Tessa shed all the discipline of thirty years with Clarence, her years of thinking "What will Clarence say?" when she gave way to an impulsive act; the fear of being called "quaint" by his friends if she spoke her inmost thoughts.

If Pan were a god, she truly worshiped him that night! Abandoning herself to instinctual joys, she raced headlong down grassy hills, rolled paws over tail-tip in the moonlight; chased a sleepy, crotchety squirrel through the treetops, then skimmed down to the duck pond to lap daintily at the water and dabble at goldfish turned silver in the moonbeams.

As the moon slid below the tall buildings west of the park, she ate flesh of her own killing; and later—behind the Mad Hatter's bronze toadstool—she allowed the huge ginger male who had stalked her for an hour to approach her, to circle ever nearer . . .

What followed next had been out of her control as the alien animal consciousness below surged into dominance. Only when it was over and the ginger tom gone, was she able to reassert her will and force that embryonic consciousness back to submission.

Just before dawn, her neat feline head poked through the railing at Fifth and East 64th Street and hesitated as she surveyed the deserted avenue, emptied of all traffic save an occasional green and white bus.

Reassured, Tessa stepped out onto the sidewalk and sat on narrow haunches to smooth and groom her ruffled striped fur. She was shaken by the night's experiences, but complacently unrepentant. No matter what lay ahead, this night was now part of her past and worth any price she might yet have to pay.

Nevertheless, Tessa knew that the strength of this body's true owner was growing and that another night would be a dangerous risk. She had to find another body, and soon.

Whose?

Lynn Herrick flashed to mind. How wickedly poetic it would be to take her rival's body, bear Clarence's child, and stick Lynn with a body which quite probably, after last night, would soon be producing offspring of its own! But she knew too little about Miss Herrick to feel confident in that role.

No, she was limited to someone familiar; someone young and financially comfortable; someone unpleasantly deserving; and, above all, someone *close*. She must be within transferring distance before the city's morning rush hour forced her back into the park until dark—an unthinkable risk.

As Tessa formulated these conditions, the logical candidate came into focus. *Of course!* She grinned. *Keep it in the family.* Angling across Fifth Avenue, she trotted uptown toward the luxurious building which housed the younger Loughlins.

Her tail twitched jauntily as she scampered along the sidewalk and elation grew as she considered the potentials of Alison's body, which was almost twenty-five years younger than her old body had been.

It might be tricky at first, but she had met all of Alison's few near relatives; and as for the surface friends who filled the aimless rounds of her sister-in-law's social life, Tessa knew they could be dropped without causing a ripple of curiosity. Especially if her life became filled with babies. That should please Richard.

Dear Richard! Tessa was surprised at the warmth of her feelings for her brother-in-law. She had always labeled her emotions as frustrated maternalism, for Richard had been a mere child when she and Clarence married.

Since then, somewhere along the line, maternalism seemed to have transmuted into something stronger. Wistful might-have-beens were now exciting possibilities.

Behind the heavy bronze and glass doors of Richard's building, a sleepy doorman nodded on his feet. The sun was not yet high enough to lighten the doorway under its pink and gray striped awning, and the deep shadows camouflaged her gray fur.

Keeping a low silhouette, she crouched beside the brass doors. As the doorman pushed it open for an early-rising tenant, she darted inside and streaked across the lobby to hide behind a large marble ash stand beside the elevator.

The rest would be simple as the elevator was large, dimly lit, and paneled in dark mahogany. She had but to conceal herself under one of the pink velvet benches which lined its sides and wait until it should stop at Alison's floor.

Her tail twitched with impatience. When the elevator finally descended, she poised ready to spring as the door slid back.

Bedlam broke loose in a welter of shrill barks, tangled leash and startled, angry exclamations. The dog was upon her, front and back, yipping and snapping before she knew what was happening.

Automatically, she spat and raked the dog's nose with her sharp claws, which set him into a frenzy of jumping and straining aganst the leash and sent his master sprawling.

Tessa only had time to recognize that it was Richard, taking Liebchen out for a pre-breakfast walk, before she felt herself being whacked by the elevator boy's newspaper.

All avenues of escape were closed to her and she was given no time to think, to gather her wits, before the street doors were flung open and she was harried out onto the sidewalk.

Angry and disgusted with herself and the dog, Tessa checked her headlong flight some yards down the sidewalk and glared back at the entrance of the building where Liebchen smugly waddled down the shallow steps and pulled Richard off in the opposite direction.

So the front is out, thought Tessa. *I wonder if their flank is so well-guarded?*

It pleased her to discover that those years of easy compliance with Clarence's wishes had not blunted her initiative. She could not be thwarted now by a Wiener schnitzel of a dog.

Halfway around the block, she located a driveway leading to the small courtyard which serviced the complex of apartment buildings. From the top of a rubbish barrel, she managed to spring to the first rung of a fire escape and scramble up.

As she climbed, the night's physical exertion began to make itself felt. Paw over paw, up and up, while every muscle begged for rest and her mind became a foggy treadmill able to hold only the single thought: paw in front of paw.

It seemed to take hours. Up thirteen steps to the landing, right turn; up thirteen steps to the landing, left turn, with such regular monotony that her mind became stupid with the endless repetition of black metal steps.

At the top landing, a ten-rung steel ladder rose straight to the roof. Her body responded sluggishly to this final effort and she sank down upon the tarred rooftop in utter exhaustion. The sun was high in the sky now; and with the last dregs of energy, Tessa crept into the shade of an overhanging ledge and was instantly asleep.

When she awoke in the late afternoon, the last rays of sunlight were slanting across the city. Hunger and thirst she could ignore for the time, but what of the quickening excitment which twilight was bringing?

She crept to the roof's edge and peered down at the empty terrace overlooking the park. An ivied trellis offered easy descent and she crouched behind a potted shrub to look through the doors. On such a mild day, the glass doors of the apartment had been left open behind their fine-meshed screens.

Inside, beyond the elegant living room, Alison's housekeeper set the table in the connecting dining room. There was no sign of Alison or Richard—or of Liebchen. Cautiously, Tessa pattered along the terrace to the screened doors of their bedroom, but it too was empty.

As she waited, darkness fell completely. From deep within, she felt the impatient tail-flick of awareness. She felt it respond to a cat's gutteral cry two rooftops away, felt it surfacing against her will, pulled by the promise of another night of dark paths and wild ecstasy.

Desperately, she struggled with that other ego, fought it blindly and knew that soon her strength would not be enough.

Suddenly the terrace was flooded with light as all the lamps inside the apartment were switched on. Startled, the other self retreated; and Tessa heard Alison's light voice tell the housekeeper, "Just leave dinner on the stove, Mitchum. You can clear away in the morning."

"Yes, Mrs. Loughlin, and I want you and Mr. Loughlin to know how sorry I was to hear about—"

"Thank you, Mitchum," came Richard's voice, cutting her off.

Tessa sat motionless in the shadows outside as Liebchen trotted across the room and scrambled onto a low chair, unmindful of a feline.

As Richard mixed drinks, Alison said, "The dreadful thing about all this is Tessa. Those delusions that she's really a young girl—that she'd never met Clarence—or either of us. Do you suppose she's clever enough to fake a mental breakdown?"

"Stop it, Alison! How can you have watched her wretchedness and think that she's pretending?"

"But, Richard—"

"What a shock it must have been to have Clarence ask for a divorce after all these years. Did you know about Clarence and Lynn?" His voice was harsh with emotion. "You introduced them. Did you encourage it?"

"Really, darling! You sound as if Tessa were the injured party." Alison's tone held scornful irony.

"Well, really, she is!" Richard cried. "If you could have seen her, Alison, when Clarence first married her—so fresh and open and full of laughter. I was just a child, but I remember. I'd never met an adult like her. I thought she was like an April breeze blowing through this family; but everyone else was appalled that Clarence had married someone so unsuitable. I remember her face when Clarence lectured her for laughing too loudly."

Richard gazed bleakly into his glass. "After Father died, it was years before I saw her again. I couldn't believe the change; all the laughter gone, her guarded words. Clarence did a thorough job of making her into a suitable wife. He killed her spirit and then complained that she was dull! No wonder she's retreated into her past, to a time before she knew him. You heard the psychiatrist. He said it often happens."

"Nevertheless," Alison said coolly, "you seem to forget that while Clarence may have killed her spirit, he's the one who is actually dead."

In the shadows outside the screen, Tessa quivered. So they had found Clarence's body! That poor thieving child! At the sight of Clarence lying on the bedroom floor with his head crushed in, she must have panicked again.

"I haven't forgotten," Richard said quietly, "and I haven't forgotten Lynn Herrick either. If what Clarence told me yesterday is true, she's in an awkward position. I suppose I should make some sort of arrangement for her out of Clarence's estate."

"Don't be naive, Richard," Alison laughed. "She merely let Clarence believe what he wanted. Lynn is far too clever to get caught without a wedding ring."

"Then Clarence's request for the divorce, his death, Tessa's insanity—all this was predicated on a lie? And you knew it? You *did!* I can see it in your face!"

"You're being unfair," Alison said. "I didn't encourage his affair with Lynn. I introduced them, yes; but if it hadn't been Lynn, it would have been someone else. Clarence wanted a change and he always took what he wanted."

As she spoke, Alison moved between the kitchen and living room, arranging their dinner on a low table in front of the couch. Liebchen put interested paws on the edge of the table, but Richard shoved him aside roughly.

"There's no need to take it out on Liebchen," she said angrily. "Come along, baby, I have something nice for you in the kitchen."

On little short legs, the dachshund trotted after Alison and disappeared into the kitchen. Relieved, Tessa moved closer to the screen.

When Alison returned from the kitchen, her flash of anger had been replaced by a mask of solicitude. "Must you go out tonight, darling? Can't the lawyers wait until morning?"

She sat close to Richard on the couch and tried to interest him in food, but he pushed the plate away wearily.

"You know lawyers," he sighed. "Clarence's will can't be probated as written, so everything's complicated. There are papers to sign, technicalities to clear up."

"That's right," Alison said thoughtfully. "Murderers can't inherit from their victims, can they? Oh, Richard, don't pull away from me like that. I'm not being callous, darling. I feel just as badly about all this as you do, but we have to face the facts. Like it or not, Tessa did kill Clarence."

"Sorry," he said, standing up and reaching for his jacket. "I guess I just can't take it all in yet."

Alison remained on the couch with her back to him. As Richard took papers from his desk and put them in his briefcase, she said with careful casualness, "If they decide poor Tessa killed him in a fit of insanity and she later snaps out of it, would she then be able to inherit?"

"Probably not, legally," he said absently, his mind on sorting the paper. "Wouldn't matter though, since we'd give it back to her, of course."

"Oh, of course," Alison agreed brightly; but her eyes narrowed.

Richard leaned over the couch and kissed her cheek. "I don't know how long this will take. If you're tired, don't bother to wait up."

"Good night, darling. Try not to be too late." She smiled at him as he left the apartment; but when the door had latched behind him, her smile clicked off to be replaced by a grim look of serious calculation.

Lost in thought, she gazed blindly at the dark square of the screened doorway and was unaware when Tessa slowly eased up on narrow haunches to let the lamplight hit her eyes—eyes that glowed with abnormal intensity . . .

It was after midnight before Richard's key turned in the lock. Lying awake on their wide bed, she heard him drop his briefcase on the desk and open the bedroom door to whisper, "Alison?"

"I'm awake, darling," she said throatily and switched on a lamp. "Oh, Richard you look so tired. Come to bed."

When at last he lay beside her in the darkness, she said shyly, "All evening I've been thinking about Tessa and Clarence—about their life together. I've been a rotten wife to you, Richard."

He made a sound of protest, but she placed slim young fingers against his lips. "No, darling, let me say it. I've been thinking how empty their marriage was and how ours would be the same if I didn't change. Richard, let's pretend we just met and that we know nothing about each other! Let's completely forget about everything that's happened before now and start anew. As soon as the funeral is over and we've settled Tessa in the best rest home we can find, let's go away together to the farm for a few weeks."

Incredulous, Richard propped himself on one elbow and peered into her face. "Do you really mean that?"

She nodded solemnly and he gathered her in his arms, but before he could kiss her properly, the night was broken by an angry, hissing cry.

"What the devil is that?" Richard asked, sitting up in bed.

"Just a stray cat. It was on the terrace this evening and seemed hungry, so I gave it your dinner." With one shapely arm, she pulled Richard back down to her and pitched her voice just loud enough to carry through the screen to the terrace. "If it's still there in the morning, I'll call the ASPCA and have them take it away."

C.B. GILFORD

Murder in Mind

It began, Cheryl Royce remembered, as a kind of parlor game—a slightly dangerous game, dealing with the dark unknown, but it was the danger, and the venture into the unknown, which made it interesting.

Hypnosis.

"Sure, I can hypnotize people," Arnold Forbes said.

Nobody at the party except the hosts, the Cunninghams, knew Forbes very well. Naturally, someone challenged him, someone else begged him for a demonstration, then Liz Cunningham very sweetly chimed in, "Arnold used to do a nightclub act. Would you like to show them, Arnold, dear?"

So Arnold Forbes performed. He was a short, chubby fellow, very jolly; very deceiving. His blue eyes could suddenly transfix one with a very penetrating, very commanding stare. Somehow, maybe because he thought she was pretty, or maybe because she looked like a scoffer, an unbeliever, he chose Cheryl Royce.

With Forbes' blue eyes probing into her own, she "went to sleep" in about thirty seconds. Only she didn't exactly go to sleep. Her eyelids closed, but she was far from unconscious. She could hear Forbes' voice quite clearly. "Your eyelids are very heavy . . . your arms are heavy. . . your entire body is very heavy . . . very relaxed . . . you are drifting down . . . down . . . down . . . into a very deep sleep . . ."

No, I'm not, she answered silently. *I'm not going to sleep, because I can hear you. Besides, I know I'm not asleep. I'm sitting in this easy chair, and everybody is gathered around, and . . .*

Nevertheless, she had to admit that the state she was in was strange indeed. Her body did feel heavy, and yet almost weightless. She hadn't wanted to close her eyes, and yet she had closed them. Now she wanted to open her eyes, and she couldn't.

She was entirely at the hypnotist's mercy. He gave her commands—to read a book, type a letter, drink a glass of water—and she obeyed him, pantomiming the actions, even though she knew perfectly well that the objects weren't there, and even though she resented going through the silly motions. Forbes passed his finger around her wrists, "tying" her to the chair arms, and she couldn't move, even though she knew there was no rope binding her. The game went on and on, and all the while she felt foolish, for being tricked, for being helpless.

Yet when Arnold Forbes wakened her finally, with a snap of his fingers, she laughed and joked about it, playing at being a good sport. Forbes found another victim, and Cheryl drifted off to the sidelines, gratefully out of the limelight.

Wint Marron followed her. Wint was darkly handsome, in his middle thirties, with a pretty blonde wife. Cheryl had attended perhaps three or four parties where the Marrons had been present.

"How did it feel being hypnotized?" Wint asked her.

"It was fun," she said.

"No, it wasn't," he contradicted her. "You hated it. You fought that guy every minute."

She stared at Wint Marron for a moment. "How do you know that?" she demanded.

He smiled, showing his perfect white teeth. "I know a little about hypnosis. One of the things that happens sometimes is that under hypnosis, telepathic powers are sharpened. Maybe you and I are on the same wavelength. Anyway, I saw into your mind all the time you were asleep there. You kept telling Forbes, 'No, I won't do it . . . I don't have a glass of water in my hand . . . you don't have a rope to tie me with.' And you were angry."

"You saw that from the expression on my face," she argued.

He shook his head, still smiling at her. "Your expression was completely serene. Ask anybody." He waited for an answer, but she had none. "It's interesting, don't you think?"

"I don't know . . ."

"Don't worry that I'll be able to read your thoughts all the time. I won't. It doesn't work that way." He had leaned closer. They were all alone. Everybody else was watching Arnold Forbes and his act. "Telepathic powers are sharper while under hypnosis, like I said. But I might catch a random thought of yours some other time. For that matter, you might catch a thought of mine. It usually works in both directions. Like I said, we seem to be on the same wavelength."

"What am I thinking now?" she demanded.

He hesitated, looking straight into her eyes. With an effort, she met his gaze. "You don't like what I've been telling you," he said finally. "You think your privacy has been invaded. The whole thing disturbs you. Now tit for tat. What do you think I'm thinking?"

She didn't want to, but she kept staring back at him. Was she trying to read the expression in his dark brown eyes? Or was she going beyond his eyes . . . to his thoughts? Then she found herself saying, involuntarily, "I think you want to kiss me."

He laughed softly and winked at her. "I don't know what you're using now, honey," he said. "I don't know whether it's telepathy or not. But you're close. Mighty close . . ."

She didn't see Wint Marron again for months. Perhaps she was even, subconsciously, trying to avoid him. During that interval she perhaps thought *about* him a time or two, but she certainly didn't receive any telepathic messages from him, for which she was grateful. And she didn't send him any messages. At least she didn't think she did.

Once, however, she saw Paula Marron, Wint's pretty blonde wife, in a dim corner of a dim cocktail lounge. She was shoulder to shoulder with another man, acting in a way no married woman should act with a man not her husband.

The incident shocked Cheryl, for several reasons. Paula's obvious infidelity, for one, and that she should be unfaithful to a man as attractive as Wint Marron, for another. Wint was handsome, charming, and doing very well in advertising. Why should Paula be dissatisfied?

It was a while after that incident, a month perhaps, that Cheryl first began to get the strange sensations. Sensations . . . she looked for a better word to describe the experiences; forebodings . . . feelings of uneasiness . . . that came to her at odd times and for no apparent reason.

They came for no apparent reason because everything seemed to be going so well in her life. She'd met Alan Richmond, and had almost decided that Alan was her long-awaited dream man. He was tall, lean, pleasant-looking, ambitious, very fond of her, very devoted to her. They'd been going out together frequently; she'd been with Alan when she'd seen Paula Marron in the cocktail lounge. Her life was happy, and there was the promise of even greater happiness.

But there were those queer sensations, the feeling now and then that a threat lurked somewhere. More than that. An emotional response to that threat . . . a vague kind of anger . . . or hatred . . . or jealousy . . .

Jealousy. She could almost laugh at the notion. She had no cause for jealousy. Alan had proposed marriage—she could have him any time she wanted him—and she knew that he didn't go out with other girls. Why on earth should she be jealous where Alan was concerned?

Well, she couldn't be, and she wasn't. She wasn't jealous . . . *she* wasn't jealous . . . why then did she feel . . . ?

The answer came suddenly.

She'd had a difficult day at her job, had begged off going to the movie with Alan. She was tired. She was in bed, in her dark bedroom, falling asleep, perhaps already asleep. When it happened, she came awake with a jolt.

For a sudden, searing, painful moment she wasn't in her bedroom. She was in that dim cocktail lounge. There was Paula Marron sitting in that corner with that stranger, leaning her shoulder against the stranger's shoulder, stroking his chin with her fingertips, whispering into his ear, her lips very close to the ear. Then Paula turned, distracted by something. Paula was full-face, her expression blank for a second, then her eyes widening, her lips parting.

Paula said one word, loud, in a tone of complete surprise. "Wint!"

The vision faded. Cheryl Royce was in the darkness of her bedroom again. The cocktail lounge, the strange man, Paula Marron, had all departed.

What was left, and it was inside Cheryl Royce, was a bursting flame of anger . . . hatred . . . jealousy! Her hands clutched the blanket in a death-grip, her mouth contorted, she stared at the empty air. It was a minute or two before the feeling subsided, and she lay there afterward limp, drained, her skin clammy with perspiration.

She knew then exactly what the experience had been. Wint Marron had discovered his wife in the company of that other man. Wint Marron was insanely angry and jealous. She, Cheryl Royce, knew all that, because she had been there in that cocktail lounge with him. She had read his mind, been inside his mind.

She and Wint Marron were on the same wavelength.

She didn't confide in Alan, or in anyone. She considered trying to find Arnold Forbes, the hypnotist, asking him to help her. She wanted to get off Wint Marron's wavelength. She didn't want to share his thoughts. But she didn't seek out Forbes. The whole business was too ridiculous, too embarrassing—too incredible, in fact.

She didn't want to believe it. It was quite possible, wasn't it, that she'd been dreaming there in her bed? She had once seen Paula Marron in that cocktail lounge, and so she was able to dream about it. The dream had put her, as it were, in Wint Marron's place, but there was an explanation for that too: the power of suggestion. Wint Marron had suggested that they were "on the same wavelength."

So she spoke of the matter to no one, and she was sorry for that.

Just three weeks later, on a Thursday, at dusk, her consciousness sat inside Wint Marron's skull again, looked out through his eyes, felt his emotions, and decided upon an action.

She was alone again, sitting at her dressing table, combing her hair in front of the mirror. Alan was due to pick her up in half an hour. Her thoughts were on Alan, not on Wint Marron, but then they were wrenched violently away from Alan. Her own face disappeared from the mirror. She was looking not into the mirror, but through the windshield of an automobile.

Ahead was a road, dim and shadowy in the dusk; not a road that she recognized. Then, however, she lost awareness of herself completely.

The car was going slowly at first. The road curved. The headlights swept a border of trees that lined the road. The lights were very bright. The trees showed up very distinctly, but not the road. The road was blacktop, dark.

Something appeared in the road . . . or at the edge of it . . . or just at the side of it . . . the right side. Something white, very brilliant in the lights, in great contrast to the blacktop. White, fluttering . . . a woman's dress.

A woman was standing there by the side of the road, as if waiting to be picked up. Yes, to be picked up, because in her right hand she carried a small suitcase. Definitely a suitcase, blue, very bright blue against the whiteness of the dress.

But she was not waiting for the driver of this car. No, because when she saw which car it was, she made a funny little gesture of surprise, throwing up her left hand, the fingers spread wide. The face registered surprise also. The car was close enough now for the driver to see her face.

Paula Marron's face, almost as white as the dress. Framed in yellow-blonde hair. Blue eyes very wide, very blue, as blue as the little suitcase. Emotion in the eyes. Fear.

Emotion in the driver too. Relentless hatred, and soaring triumph. Here was Paula, the hated object, caught in the act. Where were you going, Paula? I thought if I took your car keys away from you, you'd have to stay home. But you're waiting for your chauffeur, aren't you? *Him.* Where are you going with him? For how long? You're taking the small suitcase, I see. So maybe it's just overnight. Or maybe not. Maybe you're going for good, and you decided not to bother to take all those "rags" hanging in your closet. Well, you're not going anywhere, baby. Not with *him* you aren't!

The car was going faster now. The engine responded to the accelerator with a rasping roar. Paula seemed to comprehend suddenly. She tried to back away, off the road, into the trees. She'd be safe among the trees. The car couldn't follow her there.

But she wasn't quick enough. She hadn't comprehended soon enough. She dropped the suitcase, tried to turn and run, but in her high spike heels she stumbled on the rough gravel along the road. She wasn't in costume for racing a car, and she seemed to know that she couldn't win. She turned again toward the car. Her arms stretched out in a gesture of pleading.

Don't kill me, Wint!

The gesture of the arms changed. They rose, trying to shield that soft white face from the onrushing metal. The face grew larger, almost filled the windshield. The red mouth opened wide, and a scream competed with the roar of the engine, overcoming it for a moment.

In the same instant there was the impact, so hard that the glass in the windshield shook. The trees, the whole scene pictured through the windshield, shuddered as if in an earthquake. The white face and the white dress sank down out of the picture. The last visible parts of Paula were her white hands with their long tapered fingers . . . reaching upward . . . begging . . .

The car didn't stop. It went relentlessly forward, the tires protesting as they dug into the gravel at the side of the road. Why was the ride so bumpy? Why was the woodsy scene in the windshield jarring up and down? Were the wheels of the car passing over something? Was there an obstacle in the road? Ah . . .

The road smoothed, the jarring ceased. The car swerved back onto the blacktop, negotiated the curve adroitly . . .

And as it did, the windshield scene faded. Cross-faded rather, into a face in the mirror. The face of Cheryl Royce, contorted into an ugly mask of hatred.

Hands went to the face, Cheryl Royce's hands, covering the staring eyes, desperately trying to shut out the vision. *What did I just see?*

After a long time, the hands lowered, and Cheryl looked at her own face again. The ugly lines had softened, but there were beads of perspiration on her forehead, and her hands were shaking.

She staggered from the dressing table to the phone, managed to dial Alan's number. "I can't go out tonight," she told him in a trembling voice. "I have this terrible headache."

Which was true.

There was nothing in the morning newspaper, but the afternoon edition told the story completely.

Paula Marron, aged 28, apparently had been the victim of a hit-and-run driver. The accident had occurred sometime early last evening, on Morton's Mill Road, almost in front of the Marron home. Mrs. Marron was struck, run over, and then dragged along the road for about thirty feet. She had died, the examining physician said, immediately. There had been no witnesses.

The Marrons lived in a wooded, exurban area of rather expensive houses, each set on five or six acres. The Marron home was several hundred feet from the road, and the road was invisible from it. Mr. Marron, who was at home at the time of the accident, stated that he had not heard any unusual sounds, nor could he explain why his wife was walking along the road at that time of the evening. Police were questioning neighbors, hoping to find someone who had seen the hit-and-run car.

Cheryl Royce read the newspaper account with growing horror. She had really seen Paula Marron die. In a fit of jealousy, her husband had run her down with his own car. He had committed murder. Cheryl had seen him do it. She had practically ridden in the driver's seat with him.

So of course she should go to the police.

Then she stopped, right there on that crowded downtown street where she'd bought the newspaper. What was she going to tell the police? All that stuff about telepathy, thought-transference, mental wavelengths? Could she, Cheryl Royce, who had been in her own apartment at the time of the murder, qualify as a witness? She felt she had to try.

At police headquarters she was eventually allowed to see a detective sergeant named Evatt, who listened frozen-faced to her story.

"You realize, Miss Royce," he said at the end, "we'd have to have more evidence than what you just told me." Evatt was lean, tired-looking, but polite.

"Yes, I know," she told him, "but I thought this might alert you to look for evidence in Wint Marron's direction. Doesn't a car usually get a bent fender or broken headlight or something if it hits a pedestrian? You could tell them to look at Wint Marron's car."

Evatt nodded. "I can pass on the tip," he agreed, but not too convincingly. "Now, you mentioned, in one of these scenes you imagined—excuse me, one of these times you saw into Mr. Marron's mind—you said you saw another man with Mrs. Marron. Who was he?"

"It wasn't anybody I recognized—well, I really didn't look at him. I was looking at Mrs. Marron most of the time, you see."

"It would help," the detective pointed out, "If we knew something about this guy. It would establish a possible motive."

"Yes, I realize that," she said, "but I don't think the man was anybody I know."

"Well, I'll pass the word on to the officers investigating the accident," Evatt promised, and he jotted down her name, address, and telephone number. But he had called the case an "accident," she noticed, not a murder or a homicide.

As she left the detective's tiny office, she thanked him, and then she paused in the doorway. "I could be wrong, of course," she said. She felt forced to make the admission. "It could have been my imagination."

Evatt nodded again. "It could have."

"I'm not accusing Wint Marron of . . ."

Evatt seemed to understand. "If the boys ask Marron any questions or look around," he promised, "your name won't be mentioned."

She left feeling better. She had done what she could. It was up to the police now. If Wint Marron had committed murder, it was their job to bring him to justice, not hers.

She had dinner with Alan that evening. The restaurant was a quiet place, the music soft and unobtrusive, the lights dim. She didn't confide in Alan. He apparently hadn't even read the newspaper, didn't know that Paula Marron was dead.

She was uneasy the entire evening, as if she were trying to think of something, to remember something, and the elusive little fact kept dodging away. Finally, however, after a long time, the message came through.

Cheryl told them. The three words beat in her brain over and over again. *Cheryl told them.*

Then she knew that Wint Marron knew. Either his suspicions had been aroused by a visit from the police and fresh questions asked, or else he was seeing directly into her mind, as she'd seen into his.

She sent Alan home early, spent the rest of the night tossing in bed, unable to sleep. In the morning she called Detective Sergeant Evatt.

"Your story interested the officer in charge," Evatt told her. "He went back to the Marron home. He made an excuse to get into the Marron garage. There were two cars there, neither with any signs of front-end damage. But the car Mr. Marron usually drives is a Jeep. It has an oversize, reinforced front bumper. The officer concedes you could possibly hit someone with that bumper and not get a dent in it. But possibility isn't proof."

"What about the little blue suitcase?" she asked.

"No sign of that."

"Wint Marron could have retrieved it from the scene of the accident," she argued. "There might be blood on it. Though he could have washed it off—or burned the thing . . ."

"Miss Royce," Sergeant Evatt interrupted, "I've also mentioned this matter to the lieutenant. He doesn't seem to think that the kind of evidence you've offered us is really enough to ask for a search warrant. We don't have any real grounds for suspicion. You weren't exactly an eyewitness."

"So you're not going to do anything."

"There isn't anything we can do right now."

"You think that I'm a crackpot?"

"Nobody said that, Miss Royce. But we've followed it through as far as we can go—for now, anyway."

She confided at last in Alan, and Alan scoffed. No, he would not try to sneak into Wint Marron's garage to inspect his Jeep, or into Marron's house to look for a bloody blue suitcase. Perhaps she had received telepathic signals or vibrations from Marron, but if Marron had murdered his wife, that was the business of the police—not his or hers. She was furious.

That was one of the reasons why she left the city. Another reason was that she was frightened of Wint Marron.

She had no logical explanation for her fear. She had already communicated with the police, and Wint knew she had. Therefore, he wouldn't dare do anything violent to her. What could he do, then? Well, he could annoy her, threaten her. She was almost certain that he would. So she wanted to escape, get away, let time pass. Then perhaps she'd stop seeing into Wint Marron's mind. Perhaps then she could forget.

She begged leave of absence from the agency and drove away that afternoon. Nowhere in particular, not in any special direction. Just out of town. To somewhere different.

She ended up, toward sunset, at the Northway Motel in a small town, not more than a village, called Northway. The motel was a typical long building, with the rooms side by side, and space in front of each unit for the guest's car. A restaurant adjoined. She had a sandwich, and when she strolled back to her door, night had fallen and the stars were out. She checked her car again to make sure it was locked, then went inside.

Guessing that she would need them, she took two sleeping tablets, indulged in a long hot shower, propped herself up in bed on the motel's excellent pillows, and tried to read. It was a futile exercise.

Hours passed. She squirmed restlessly in the bed. The book did not interest her. She turned the light out finally, then stared into the darkness.

She couldn't get Wint Marron out of her mind. He knew that she knew—but did he know how much she knew? Surely her mind couldn't be a completely open book to him. Might he even be afraid that she knew more than she actually did? How he had disposed of the blue suitcase, for instance. Or the identity of Paula's companion in that cocktail lounge.

Since she didn't want to share any more of Wint Marron's guilty secrets, could she send him the message that he had nothing further to fear from her, that she was finished playing public-spirited citizen and informing on a murderer? But would he believe her, would he trust her . . . ?

In the darkness of that strange room she suddenly sat upright. He didn't trust her! Wint Marron was saying that to her, right at this moment.

She came near to panic. For she knew something else too. Whether it was telepathy this time, or a kind of animal instinct for the proximity of danger, or whether she had actually heard a small noise, she wasn't sure. But she knew! Wint Marron was there.

She eased out of the bed. In the front wall of her room near the door was a large window, heavily draped. She inched the drape aside to make a small peephole, found a venetian blind, bent down one of the slats.

At first she saw nothing outside. The driveway was fairly well lighted. Her car was there, a hulking lump of shadow.

Then she did hear a noise, this time unmistakable, the scrape of the sole of a shoe on the sidewalk close to her door. A dark shape passed the window, paused beside her car.

A man. Wint Marron. It could be no other. If she clung to any desperate doubt, however, that doubt was erased when the man walked around to the rear of the car and the light fell on his head and shoulders. Cheryl Royce saw Wint Marron's lean, dark, handsome face.

He had followed her. Quite easily, of course, because she had sent him the message. Northway, the Northway Motel.

Now he was interested in her car—making sure it was the right car, and since it was parked there, checking which was the right door, the right room. He was going to do something to the car, or try to enter her room . . . or perhaps simply wait for her to come out.

Panic overwhelmed judgment. She could phone the motel clerk, ask him to call the Northway police. But the police would never believe her. They hadn't before. They wouldn't now. Not until Wint Marron did something, and then it would be too late. Besides, the police were her enemies. Going to the police had caused Wint Marron to fear her, then to pursue her. Her only safety was in convincing Wint that she'd never go to the police again.

But right now, while he was still angry with her, she must escape. How: *Don't plan . . . don't plan,* some part of her brain warned her. *Wint can read your mind, don't you know that? If you plan where you're going, he'll be there waiting for you. So leave your mind blank . . . use instinct . . . act blindly . . . don't panic . . .*

She dressed quickly, feeling in the dark for her clothes. She refused to think. *I'm getting dressed . . . no, I must not even think that,* she reminded herself. *I must think neither about the future nor the present.*

She stood fully dressed now in the middle of the dark room. It was difficult, almost impossible, to keep her mind blank. The apparatus just isn't constructed that way. But she tried.

The room had a rear window also. She had to pull aside the drape and raise the blind. The window itself resisted for a moment, but finally moved upward. There was a small squeak and a groan as it did so, perhaps not audible on the front side of the building. Without hesitation, without considering the problem that she might be seen, avoiding concentration on the matter, Cheryl eased one leg through the opening, then her torso, then the other leg.

She was standing on a grassy lawn. *Where now?* No, she mustn't think. Just act, move.

She heard traffic noises from the highway, out front. Although she had been in bed for some time, the hour still wasn't late. There were people around, no need to be afraid.

She walked past the rear of the motel restaurant. Inside were a waitress and a customer or two, but the place appeared ready to close. No refuge there. Wint could follow her there anyway.

She walked on, trying not even to note her surroundings, trying not to reflect upon the sense images her eyes gathered. Something large loomed in her path: the rear of a truck. She walked around the more shadowed side of it. Not too long a truck. Not a trailer rig.

A man stood near the front end, smoking a cigarette. Maybe the driver. He heard her footsteps, turned to watch her approach. There was no light on his face, only the glowing tip of the cigarette. She stopped close to him.

"Is this your truck?"

Apparently startled, he didn't answer for a moment. "Yes," he said finally.

"Are you going somewhere or staying here?"

"I'm leaving," he said after another hesitation, "just as soon as I finish this cigarette."

"Will you give me a ride?"

The tip of the cigarette glowed more brightly as the truck driver took a long drag. "Where do you want to go?" he asked.

"It doesn't matter."

"Look, I'm going to . . ."

He stared at her, puzzled, but her face was as much in shadow as his. He dropped his cigarette butt on the gravel and didn't bother to grind it out. What he was thinking was as obvious as if he too were on her mental wavelength. He couldn't guess what kind of risk he might be taking, but the proposition was intriguing . . .

"Hop in," he said after a long moment, and opened the door for her.

I've never ridden in this large a truck before, she thought as she climbed into the cab. But then she told her mind to be still. *Don't think words . . . be quiet . . . go to sleep . . . yes, sleep . . . hypnotize yourself.*

The driver climbed in on his own side, started the engine, and the truck rolled out. Cheryl kept her eyes closed, but in trying so hard not to, she sensed that they had turned left onto the highway. Did Wint notice the truck's departure? Maybe not. Surely he couldn't read her every thought. He needn't know that she was in the truck.

"I don't know whether I should be doing this," the driver was saying. "You on drugs or something?"

"No, I'm not on drugs."

"You're not the other type. So you must be running away. Who from? Your husband?"

"No. I'm sorry. I can't explain."

"I may be doing something illegal."

"No, you're not. I guarantee you that."

They drove in silence for a while. Cheryl tried to keep her eyes closed, not to notice road signs. The driver glanced at her sideways now and then, she realized. But whatever he might be thinking, she had less to fear from him than from Wint Marron.

"Is there a car following us?" she asked suddenly.

She regretted the question instantly, because the driver became alarmed. He glanced at his mirror. "Nobody back there now. Look, who are you expecting to follow us?"

"Nobody."

"You might be running away from the police."

"I'm not."

"I don't want to get mixed up in anything."

"All you have to do is take me somewhere. Anywhere."

"I'm just going to Jackson Harbor."

She gave a little shriek, and put her fingers in her ears, but it was too late. The name of their destination pounded in her brain . . . *Jackson Harbor* . . . she couldn't stop it. And she knew, she knew absolutely, that the name was vibrating through the ether, straight back to Northway, back to Wint.

"What's the matter with you?"

"Let me out!" she screamed. "Just let me out!"

"Look, I said I'd take you—"

"Let me out, or I'll jump!" She poised with the door half open.

"Wait a minute. Wait a minute. Let me find a place where I can get off the pavement."

He'd put the brakes on, and the truck was slowing down, so she waited. He picked a place finally, and edged off onto the shoulder. But long before the truck had come to a dead stop, Cheryl had the door open, had climbed down to the running board. "Thanks," she called back to the man, and jumped.

She landed on her feet, stumbled, but didn't fall. Only then, when she was safe, did she look to see where she was. A road marker loomed in the bright headlights of the truck. Junction . . . K.

Wint will know exactly where I am, she thought. She shouted to the truck driver. She wanted to get back in, but already the engine was roaring and the big rear tires were spitting gravel at her. Before she could catch up with it, the big vehicle had turned back onto the highway. In a moment it had diminished to a pair of taillights, then it was gone completely.

She was left alone, afoot and in darkness, her exact location pinpointed to Wint Marron as the junction of Road "K" with the main highway.

Her first instinct was to try to hitch another ride, till she realized the possibility that the first car to stop for her might be Wint's. Or maybe he wouldn't stop. Wint had another method of dealing with female hitchhikers who had displeased him.

A pair of headlights came hurtling down the highway toward her. She dropped into the weeds at the side of the road. She lay there until the lights and the car flashed by.

This main road was dangerous: too many cars. She picked herself up out of the weeds and ran in the only direction left open, down Road K.

Wint knew where she was going, of course, for the moment. *Road K* pounded in her mind in the same rhythm as her feet pounded on the gravel. But she would get lost—lost, that was the answer to her problem. If she didn't know where she was, neither would Wint. She would find an even smaller road than this, a dirt road, and follow that. Or simply run across fields or through the woods.

But she hesitated to plunge off into the darkness. She had only a vague idea of the geography of this area. She knew approximately where Northway was. How far toward Jackson Harbor had they gotten? Jackson Harbor was on the lake, of course. But there were other bodies of water in between, as she recalled the map, a couple of small rivers . . . and weren't there marshes or swamps? Quicksand, maybe?

Was she doing the right thing, running away from civilization, running into a sparsely populated semi-wilderness? Maybe she should have stayed in the truck, stayed with people. But it was too late now.

It was a clear night, with moon and stars. She could see her way along the road. The woods would be dark, though. She couldn't bring herself to leave the road. She'd find that unmarked side road.

But she didn't. Panting, she had to slow to a walk. And then she stopped.

Where did you go, Cheryl?

It was as if the question had been spoken aloud, it was so clear, precise. But she was alone there on the road. She knew, however, exactly where the question had come from.

Wint Marron was standing by the open rear window of her room at the Northway Motel. That had been a mistake, hadn't it, to leave that window open? Wint stood there, and she was with him, looking at the window through Wint's eyes.

Then he climbed inside, and she accompanied him. A flashlight beam searched the room, glided over the walls, lingered for a moment on the empty, mussed bed.

We're communicating, aren't we, Cheryl? Like a voice, speaking to her from within her own brain. *You know I'm here.* There was a long pause. *And I know where you are.*

Was he lying? She closed her eyes and ground her teeth together in a desperate mental effort not to think about the lonely gravel road and the dark woods on either side.

Don't try to hide from me, Cheryl.

She pressed her lips together to smother a gasp.

You hitchhiked, didn't you?

He was groping, guessing. He didn't know as much as he pretended to. She went on trying to keep her mind blank.

You went to the police. I knew that, didn't I, Cheryl? And I found the Northway Motel, didn't I?

He was goading her, trying to panic her. If he succeeded, she would lose control and perhaps betray her whereabouts.

It's your own fault, you know, Cheryl. You butted into a private affair. It was a while before I realized you were butting in. I guess I should have been more careful, because I was the one who discovered that we could share our thoughts. I even mentioned to you that this telepathy thing could run in both directions. It's too bad, though, it turned out the way it did. You're a cute girl, Cheryl. I did want to kiss you that night we met. After I got rid of Paula, and things had settled down a little, I might have looked you up. Yes, it's your fault, Cheryl. Even after Paula, you didn't have to go to the police. You didn't have to turn against me. Not when you and I were so intimate. Couldn't you understand? Couldn't you sympathize? Haven't you ever been jealous? When I saw Paula with that Don Bruno . . .

She screamed, a short, choked, stifled scream. Don Bruno, not a very ordinary name. That detective had said that if she could identify the other man in the case the police would have something to go on. Now she knew who the other man was—but she didn't want to know!

Cheryl!

He must not have been aware that she hadn't known before. But now he surely realized the slip he had made. He had given her a weapon against him, and now he must disarm her, silence her.

She started running again, on the gravel road, Road K. Turn off into the woods? No, not now. Wint could run through the woods better than she could. No, she had to stay on the road, find somebody, find help, find a telephone. It had to be on this road. Going back to the highway would mean rushing to meet Wint. This was her only road. This road led somewhere. And when she found that telephone, she would call Sergeant Evatt, and she would shout to him, "The man's name is Don Bruno! Locate him! Make him admit that he was going to pick up Paula Marron who would be carrying a suitcase! Don Bruno can tell you enough so you can arrest Wint Marron for murder!"

She ran on. If the rough gravel hurt her feet through the thin soles of her shoes, she wasn't aware of it. She'd gotten her second wind now. She could make it. Wint was still miles behind her, getting into his car, consulting his map, searching for Road K.

She concentrated on not thinking, on not letting her surroundings impinge upon her senses. *Don't give Wint any clues. Don't give him any landmarks. Don't let him know if this road is going through woods or swamps, or by a stream or near a lake. Don't see any of those things. Just look for one thing. A light. A light that will mean human habitation.*

How much time passed? In her state of suspended awareness she didn't know. Minutes . . . miles . . . neither had meant anything.

Until two sensations came to her at exactly the same moment. One that she welcomed and one that she feared. One from the front and one from the rear. A sight and a sound.

Up ahead, still distant, she saw it, a mere pinhead of illumination amid the woodland foliage. And simultaneously, behind her, she heard the far-off growl of an automobile engine.

She raced that approaching sound. It was coming down Road K, she knew that, and as it drew nearer she even thought she recognized it. She'd heard it once before, the evening that Paula Marron was struck down by a hit-and-run driver. Wint was pursuing her in his Jeep, that Jeep with its reinforced front bumper which wouldn't dent when it smashed into a human body.

But the light grew closer too. The road curved and the light swung to a new position, almost straight ahead. A yellow light, growing larger and larger. A porch light? It didn't matter. Any kind of light meant people, safety.

The Jeep engine was loud in her ears now. She thought she could hear too the rasp of its tires on the gravel. But the light loomed brighter and closer too.

She saw other things now. A reflection of the light, a vertical gleaming bar of yellow. On water, a stream or a narrow inlet, and the light was on the far side.

For a dreadful moment she supposed that she was lost, isolated from that help on the other bank. But then the light illuminated—ever so slightly, and off a bit to the left where the road was curving again—*a bridge!*

Not much of a bridge. Wooden. Old. Rickety. But a bridge nevertheless, leading to the other side of the water and to the light.

Behind her—only yards—the roar of the engine and the scream of tires clawing gravel rose together into one deafening crescendo.

Her flying feet touched the first board of the bridge. Then the Jeep's headlights, swinging around that last little curve of the road suddenly illuminated the whole world . . . herself . . . the floor of the bridge . . . the darking shining water just ahead of her outstretched foot . . .

She couldn't stop. It was too late for that. Her foot leaped ahead of her out into space. There was nothing else beneath it, until the black surface of the water rose up to meet her.

Just as she sank into it, rubber tires hit the boards of the bridge and the hurtling Jeep found the same emptiness in front of it. It sailed over Cheryl's head, darkening the sky, just as her head went under water.

In the water then she felt the exploding pressure waves as the metal monster plunged in just beyond her. She bobbed to the surface.

There was nothing there. The sky was empty. The roar was silenced. Nothing but huge ripples, almost waves, spreading out from the spot where the Jeep had disappeared.

Wint!

She blurted his name, silently, inside her brain. But there was no answer, no communication. The connection was cut. The line was dead at the other end.

Yes, dead . . . or dying. She sensed that somehow. Wint Marron's head had hit something hard, like the windshield. Unconscious, helpless, wedged into his seat, he was drowning now.

She swam a stroke or two toward the source of those ripples. "Wint!" she called aloud.

A numbness seized her. A coldness. She became certain of an unalterable fact. Wint was dead.

So she swam back, toward the bridge . . .

Bridge? She looked at the wooden structure in the moonlight. Not a bridge at all. Only a pier.

She shivered then, not at the coldness of the water. She had killed him. She had killed Wint. Had he known differently, he might have been able to stop the Jeep. But her brain had sent him the wrong message. Not pier. Bridge . . .

ARTHUR PORGES

The Invisible Tomb

Captain Gregg, in common with some other normally hard-headed people, believed that related events tend to occur in triples. Having just struggled through two cases that involved tricky hiding places—first, one involving a ruby; second, a rare book—he was not altogether surprised to confront the problem of a missing body.

It was, naturally, the worst of the sequence. It's easy enough to hide small objects, but to dispose of roughly one hundred pounds of woman, and in a relatively limited space, is another matter; Gregg could hardly believe it. But unless the murderer had somehow carried the remains through twenty miles of suburban streets to what precious little open country—three-cow "ranches" and the like—existed in so densely populated an area, there to be buried in a shallow grave certain to be found, what alternatives were possible? No, Elsa Newman must be in the Newman basement, house, or yard. Only she wasn't, if Gregg knew anything about conducting a search.

In the other two cases, the criminals had found by brilliant ingenuity—one had to give them that much—how small items like a gem and a book could be hidden almost in plain sight, on the *Purloined Letter* principle, and baffle the most competent detective.

Certainly they had fooled Gregg, forcing him to get help, unorthodox, but effective, in order to solve the seemingly impossible puzzles presented by the talented crooks; and now, for the third time, Gregg was driven to seek out his peculiar consultant. He didn't enjoy having to do it, but knew when he was licked.

Julian Morse Trowbridge looked like a dissipated gnome badly hungover from too much fermented toadstool juice, or whatever the species imbibes when on a bender. His vast, pallid face, moist and unhealthy in its flabbiness, was set on a thready neck. As for his torso, that suggested the ultimate "Before" of the most exaggerated advertisement for a physical culture course. But inside the big, bullet-shaped head was a remarkable brain, packed with esoteric knowledge instantly available on call.

Trowbridge had graduated from Harvard at fourteen, and two years later had a PhD in mathematical physics, but his intellect was decades ahead of his emotional balance, so the boy had broken down and fled from the academic world. Now, at fifty, he lived in a ramshackle house full of books, where he acted as a kind of neighborhood Solomon, handing out free, and usually quite good, advice to all those who asked for it.

When Captain Gregg came for the third time in as many months, he found the gnome explaining patiently, in precise and pedantic terms, a theorem in calculus to a pimply boy whose one burning aim was to con the old creep into doing his homework for him.

"Continuity does *not* imply differentiability," Trowbridge assured the young seeker-after-truth. "Remember that, my boy, and all difficulties with this kind of problem will vanish," he added brusquely.

He politely ushered the student to the door and, sighing with relief, turned to Gregg.

"I take it you didn't do him much good," the detective said dryly.

"I fear you are right; the chap simply hasn't the brains for college. It's a dreadful thing to say, but I really think he does not fully grasp the idea of a function. However," with a twinkling glance at Gregg, "you've done fairly well under the same handicap. Your problem, I'm sure, is not mathematical."

"Things happen in threes," the detective said. "Twice I've been to you about stuff hidden where anybody should have been able to find it, and nobody could until Trowbridge showed the way. Well, this time it's a whole body—a woman; height, five-four; weight, ninety-eight. Missing two weeks now; presumed dead—by me—but no body, even though, incredibly, she ought to be hidden right in the house or the smallish yard. If it weren't for the last two cases, I wouldn't dream of her being that handy, but now—"

The gnome sank deeper in the enormous, sagging, musty armchair he favored.

"Ahhh," he sighed happily. Of all the problems brought to him, he most enjoyed puzzling crimes; they added glamor to his emotionally starved existence. Math was fascinating, but too bloodless. "Tell me about it. Who's your suspect, and why?"

"It's a simple case as to motive and probable killer. Leo Newman's the guy. He's big, ugly, bald, has a pot—and a pretty wife. Brought her back from Germany in 1949. She was only sixteen, and obviously wanted to get away from the mess there. Elsa Keller was her name; blonde, very cute, and flirtatious; the kind of wife who invites the mailman in for coffee—or the grocery boy; the phone installer; anything male that's handy. Newman fought with her often, and threatened to kill her. The neighbors heard them going at it.

"Well, two weeks ago she disappeared. People next door say she and Newman were battling again, that she stopped screaming at him very suddenly. Then it was quiet, and stayed that way.

"He claims she ran away, but nobody saw her leave. There's no evidence of her taking bus, train, or plane, and all her clothes are in the house except, possibly, what she was wearing at the time. Now I figure he lost his temper and killed her, maybe not intending to. Then he disposed of the body somehow. But where? There are square miles of tidy little lawns, and then more roomy suburbs, but no place a body could be buried and not found fast. His own house is an old one and quite big, with attics and plenty of crawl spaces; but, hell, Julian, no spot where we couldn't find a woman's corpse. He didn't chop her up, because that *always* leaves traces—blood, tissue, something—the crime lab boys are sure to find.

"That's really the whole bit. She's gone, but couldn't have run off; so she must be dead. But if so, where did he hide her?"

"That depends, I would say," Trowbridge said calmly, "on how ingenious Mr. Leo Newman is. Is he ingenious?"

"In a way. He's handy, that's certain. Has a big shed full of tools, drills, a lathe; welding, soldering, and brazing equipment; concrete mixes; boxes of bolts, nuts, pipes, chains. Obviously he could repair or make a lot of things, but that's not the same as inventing an invisible grave."

"She's not buried in the small yard, of course."

"You just bet not. We probed every square inch. The lawn hasn't been touched."

"How does he behave?"

"Like a guilty man, I'd say. Very uneasy, as if he weren't at all sure he'd fooled us. Insisted she ran off with one of her many lovers, but wasn't angry— just scared. After we'd searched the place for hours, the next day he moved out to a hotel. I wonder why. Why pay rent when you have your own house? I guessed at first he did have her stashed inside somehow, and knew that after a few days in this warm weather it would be . . . well . . . unpleasant and a dead giveaway. But we've been back twice, with warrants, sniffing around, and there's nothing. So you see—" Gregg shrugged.

"I would be inclined to agree," the gnome said, "that there must be some particular significance in his moving out, but without more data it would be foolish to speculate. May I have a dossier, the usual things, to work with?"

"You bet," the detective assured him. He put a large, scabrous briefcase on Trowbridge's desk, which seemed already sagging under dozens of dusty books, each fatter than the next. "You'll find everything inside: Newman's statements; pictures of him and Elsa; photos of house and grounds; miscellaneous information, like his cheapness," Gregg added bitterly. "He must have known we'd go over the house a few more times, so he had all the utilities shut off; no gas, water, or electricity. On a dark day, or at night, we have to use flashlights. If it was winter, we'd freeze. Naturally, our warrants don't entitle us to use Newman's utilities! I suppose it's the only way he can get back at us; can't keep us out, but he can make our work harder."

Trowbridge cocked his great head. "Spite?" he said softly. "I wonder. How very odd!"

"What are you getting at?" Gregg asked quickly. "Did I miss something again?"

"Nothing; nothing," was the hasty reply, "except that your big, burly, bullying kind doesn't usually get spiteful in so womanish a way. I'll have to think about it."

"Give me a ring, as usual, if you come up with an angle," the detective said.

"Of course," the gnome said, reproach in his voice, escorting Gregg to the door.

The call would probably come at three in the morning, the detective knew, but that couldn't be helped. Trowbridge had his own cycles of activity, more like those of some distant planet than of Earth.

Gregg was wrenched from his deepest sleep of the night at four a.m., as it happened. He fumbled for the phone, hopeful but justifiably querulous. Why couldn't Trowbridge have waited another two hours? Then he felt a pang of guilt; after all, the little guy was trying to help in his own way.

"It is I—Julian," the phone announced pedantically.

"That figures," the detective groaned. "Whatchu got?"

"Maybe nothing, but there's a logical inference," one of his pet phrases, "*provided* your conviction that the body wasn't removed from the premises is sound."

"I think it is," Gregg said, wide awake now. "Everything indicates Newman stuck close to the neighborhood up to the time of our search. Just went to his job, did some shopping, and came home. No long drives, judging from the odometer and what his garage says. So let's have your theory."

"I build on the matter of his moving out," the gnome said cautiously. "Did he have the utilities stopped because of leaving, or was his change to a hotel the excuse for cutting them off? That's the vital point."

"What's the point in having no service at the house? We still searched."

"If they were on, and he still living there, you might wonder why no hot water," was the cryptic reply.

"No hot water," Gregg repeated. Then he gulped. "Hey, are you suggesting— no, it can't be! She was small, but there isn't that much space in a heater! It's not all hollow, has a million pipes and fittings."

"Not really. The actual tank is almost big enough, but any pipes are easily burned out with a torch. You did say, and the dossier confirms, that he knows how to use one."

"Sure, but—"

"All right. He removes the top, cleans out the whole cylinder, which your photos of the house show is a biggish one. The few holes for pipes are quickly welded shut, but so that nothing shows on the outside. Not," he added maliciously, "that anybody took much of a look. Then he puts the body inside, welds the top back on, and has a hermetically sealed, metal tomb—in plain sight, but invisible psychologically. The pipes he adds to his junk piles, already full of such stuff. Oh, it's a wild gamble, but he's scared and desperate. If you once overlook the tank, he can wait you out for months until all surveillance stops. Hermetically sealed, remember, a perfect tomb. But no hot water! Hence the hotel. Make sense?"

There was a pregnant silence for some moments, then the detective managed, "Yes, but I won't believe it until we open the thing! Logic is fine, Julian, but so is sanity. Imagine the gall in stashing her right under our noses. That smarts!" He gave a short, barking laugh. "I'll never sleep now; I'm going to check right away."

When the invisible tomb was opened, two hours later, they found the crumpled remains of Elsa Keller Newman.

JAMES H. SCHMITZ

Just Curious

Roy Litton's apartment was on the eighteenth floor of the Torrell Arms. It was a pleasant place which cost him thirty-two thousand dollars a year. The living room had a wide veranda which served in season as a sun deck. Far below was a great park. Beyond the park, drawn back to a respectful distance from the Torrell Arms, was the rest of the city.

"May I inquire," Roy Litton said to his visitor, "from whom you learned about me?"

The visitor's name was Jean Merriam. She was a slender, expensive brunette, about twenty-seven. She took a card from her handbag and slid it across the table to Litton. "Will that serve as an introduction?" she asked.

Litton studied the words scribbled on the card and smiled. "Yes," he said, "that's quite satisfactory. I know the lady's handwriting well. In what way can I help you?"

"I represent an organization," Jean said, "which does discreet investigative work."

"You're detectives?"

She shrugged, smiled. "We don't refer to ourselves as detectives, but that's the general idea. Conceivably your talents could be very useful to us. I'm here to find out whether you're willing to put them at our disposal from time to time. If you are, I have a test assignment for you. You don't mind, do you?"

Litton rubbed his chin. "You've been told what my standard fee is?"

Jean Merriam opened the handbag again, took out a check and gave it to him. Litton read it carefully, nodded. "Yes," he said, and laid the check on the table beside him. "Ten thousand dollars. You're in the habit of paying such sums out of your personal account?"

"The sum was put in my account yesterday for this purpose."

"Then what do you, or your organization, want me to do?"

"I've been given a description of how you operate, Mr. Litton, but we don't know how accurate the description is. Before we retain you, I'd like you to tell me exactly what you do."

Litton smiled. "I'm willing to tell you as much as I know."

She nodded. "Very well, I'll decide on the basis of what you say whether or not your services might be worth ten thousand dollars to the organization. Once I offer you the assignment and you accept it, we're committed. The check will be yours when the assignment is completed."

"Who will judge when it has been completed?"

"You will," said Jean. "Naturally there will be no further assignments if we're not satisfied with the results of this one. As I said, this is a test. We're gambling. If you're as good as I've been assured you are, the gamble should pay off. Fair eno ןgh?"

Litton nodded. "Fair enough, Miss Merriam." He leaned back in his chair. "Well, then—I sometimes call myself a 'sensor' because the word describes my experiences better than any other word I can think of. I'm not specifically a mind reader. I can't predict the future. I don't have second sight. But under certain conditions, I turn into a long-range sensing device with a limited application. I have no theoretical explanation for it. I can only say what happens.

"I work through contact objects; that is, material items which have had a direct and extensive physical connection with the persons I investigate. A frequently worn garment is the obvious example. Eyeglasses would be excellent. I once was able to use an automobile which the subject had driven daily for about ten months. Through some object I seem to become, for a time which varies between approximately three and five minutes, the person in question." Litton smiled. "Naturally I remain here physically, but my awareness is elsewhere.

"Let me emphasize that during this contact period I *am*—or seem to be—the other person. I am not conscious of Roy Litton or of what Roy Litton is doing. I have never heard of him and know nothing of his sensing ability. I am the other person, aware only of what he is aware, doing what he is doing, thinking what he is thinking. If, meanwhile, you were to speak to the body sitting here, touch it, even cause it severe pain—which has been done experimentally—I wouldn't know it. When the time is up, the contact fades and I'm back. Then I know who I am and can recall my experience and report on it. Essentially, that's the process."

Jean Merriam asked, "To what extent do you control the process?"

"I can initiate it or not initiate it. I'm never drawn out of myself unless I intend to be drawn out of myself. That's the extent of my control. Once it begins, the process continues by itself and concludes itself. I have no way of affecting its course."

Jean said reflectively, "I don't wish to alarm you, Mr. Litton. But mightn't you be running the risk of remaining permanently lost in somebody else's personality . . . unable to return to your own?"

Litton laughed. "No. I know definitely that can't happen, though I don't know why. The process simply can't maintain itself for much more than five minutes. On the other hand, it's rarely terminated in less than three."

"You say that during the time of contact you think what the other person thinks and are aware of what he's aware?"

"That's correct."

"Only that? If we employed you to investigate someone in this manner, we usually would need quite specific information. Wouldn't we have to be extremely fortunate if the person happened to think of that particular matter in the short time you shared his mind?"

"No," said Litton. "Conscious thoughts quite normally have thousands of ramifications and shadings the thinker doesn't know about. When the contact dissolves, I retain his impressions and it is primarily these ramifications and shadings I then investigate. It is something like developing a vast number of photographic prints. Usually the information my clients want can be found in those impressions in sufficient detail."

"What if it can't be found?"

"Then I make a second contact. On only one occasion, so far, have I been obliged to make three separate contacts with a subject to satisfy the client's requirements. There is no fee for additional contacts."

Jean Merriam considered a moment. "Very well," she said. She brought a small box from the handbag, opened it, and took out a ring which she handed to Litton. "The person in whom the organization is interested," she said, "was wearing this ring until four weeks ago. Since then it's been in a safe. The safe was opened yesterday and the ring taken from it and placed in this box. Would you consider it a suitable contact object?"

Litton held the ring in his palm an instant before replying. "Eminently suitable!" he said then.

"You can tell by touching such objects?"

"As a rule. If I get no impression, it's a waste of time to proceed. If I get a negative impression, I refuse to proceed."

"A negative impression?"

Litton shrugged. "A feeling of something that repels me. I can't describe it more definitely."

"Does that mean that the personality connected with the object is a repellent one?"

"Not necessarily. I've merged with some quite definitely repellent personalities in the course of this work. That doesn't disturb me. The feeling I speak of is a different one."

"It frightens you?"

"Perhaps." He smiled. "However, in this case there is no such feeling. Have you decided to offer me the assignment?" he asked.

"Yes, I have," Jean Merriam said. "Now then, I've been told nothing about the person connected with the ring. Since very few men could get it on, and very few children would wear a ring of such value, I assume the owner is a woman—but I don't know even that. The reason I've been told nothing is to make sure I'll give you no clues, inadvertently or otherwise." She smiled. "Even if you were a mind reader, you see, you could get no significant information from me. We want to be certain of the authenticity of your talent."

"I understand," Litton said. "But you must know what kind of information your organization wants to gain from the contact?"

Jean nodded. "Yes, of course. We want you to identify the subject by name and tell us where she can be found. The description of the locality should be specific. We also want to learn as much as we can about the subject's background, her present activities and interests, and any people with whom she is closely involved. The more details you can give us about such people, the better. In general, that's it. Does it seem like too difficult an assignment?"

"Not at all," Litton said. "In fact, I'm surprised you want no more. Is that kind of information really worth ten thousand dollars to you?"

"I've been told," Jean said, "that if we get it within the next twenty-four hours, it will be worth a great deal more than ten thousand dollars."

"I see." Litton settled comfortably in the chair, placed his clasped hands around the ring on the table, enclosing it. "Then, if you like, Miss Merriam, I'll now make the contact."

"No special preparations?" she inquired, watching him.

"Not in this case." Litton nodded toward a heavily curtained alcove in the wall on his left. "That's what I call my withdrawal room. When I feel there's reason to expect difficulties in making a contact, I go in there. Observers can be disturbing under such circumstances. Otherwise, no preparations are necessary."

"What kind of difficulties could you encounter?" Jean asked.

"Mainly, the pull of personalities other than the one I want. A contact object may be valid, but contaminated by associations with other people. Then it's a matter of defining and following the strongest attraction, which is almost always that of the proper owner and our subject. Incidentally, it would be advantageous if you were prepared to record my report."

Jean tapped the handbag. "I'm recording our entire conversation, Mr. Litton."

He didn't seem surprised. "Very many of my clients do," he remarked. "Very well, then, let's begin . . ."

"How long did it take him to dream up this stuff?" Nick Garland asked.

"Four minutes and thirty-two seconds," Jean Merriam said.

Garland shook his head incredulously. He took the transcript she'd made of her recorded visit to Roy Litton's apartment from the desk and leafed through it again. Jean watched him, her face expressionless. Garland was a big gray-haired bear of a man, coldly irritable at present—potentially dangerous.

He laid the papers down, drummed his fingers on the desk. "I still don't want to believe it," he said, "but I guess I'll have to. He hangs on to Caryl Chase's ring for a few minutes, then he can tell you enough about her to fill five typed, single-spaced pages . . . That's what happened?"

Jean nodded. "Yes, that's what happened. He kept pouring out details about the woman as if he'd known her intimately half her life. He didn't hesitate about anything. My impression was that he wasn't guessing about anything. He seemed to know."

Garland grunted. "Max thinks he knew." He looked up at the man standing to the left of the desk. "Fill Jean in, Max. How accurate is Litton?"

Max Jewett said, "On every point we can check out, he's completely accurate."

"What are the points you can check out?" Jean asked.

"The ring belongs to Caryl Chase. She's thirty-two. She's Phil Chase's wife, currently estranged. She's registered at the Hotel Arve, Geneva, Switzerland, having an uneasy off-and-on affair with one William Haskell, British ski nut. He's jealous, and they fight a lot. Caryl suspects Phil has detectives looking for her, which he does. Her daughter Ellie is hidden away with friends of Caryl's parents in London. Litton's right about the ring. Caryl got it from her grandmother on her twenty-first birthday and wore it since. When she ran out on Phil last month, she took it off and left it in her room safe. Litton's statement, that leaving it was a symbolic break with her past life, makes sense." Jewett shrugged. "That's about it. Her psychoanalyst might be able to check out some of the rest of what you got on tape. We don't have that kind of information."

Garland growled, "We don't need it. We got enough for now."

Jean exchanged a glance with Jewett. "You feel Litton's genuine, Mr. Garland?"

"He's genuine. Only Max and I knew we were going to test him on Caryl. If he couldn't do what he says he does, you wouldn't have got the tape. There's no other way he could know those things about her." Garland's face twisted into a sour grimace. "I thought Max had lost his marbles when he told me it looked like Phleger had got his information from some kind of swami. But that's how it happened. Frank Phleger got Litton to tap my mind something like two or three months ago. He'd need that much time to get set to make his first move."

"How much have you lost?" Jean asked.

He grunted. "Four, five million. I can't say definitely yet. That's not what bothers me." His mouth clamped shut, a pinched angry line. His eyes shifted bleakly down to the desk, grew remote, lost focus.

Jean Merriam watched him silently. Inside that big skull was stored information which seemed sometimes equal to the intelligence files of a central bank. Nick Garland's brain was a strategic computer, a legal library. He was a multimillionaire, a brutal genius, a solitary and cunning king beast in the financial jungle—a jungle he allowed to become barely aware he existed. Behind his secretiveness he remained an unassailable shadow. In the six years Jean had been working for him she'd never before seen him suffer a setback; but if they were right about Litton, this was more than a setback. Garland's mind had been opened, his plans analyzed, his strengths and weaknesses assessed by another solitary king beast—a lesser one, but one who knew exactly how to make the greatest possible use of the information thus gained—and who had begun to do it. So Jean waited and wondered.

"Jean," Garland said at last. His gaze hadn't shifted from the desk.

"Yes?"

"Did Litton buy your story about representing something like a detective agency?"

"He didn't seem to question it," Jean said. "My impression was that he doesn't particularly care who employs him, or for what purpose."

"He'll look into anyone's mind for a price?" It was said like a bitter curse.

"Yes . . . his price. What are you going to do?"

Garland's shoulders shifted irritably. "Max is trying to get a line on Phleger."

Jean glanced questioningly at Jewett. Jewett told her, "Nobody seems to have any idea where Frank Phleger's been for the past three weeks. We assume he dropped out of sight to avoid possible repercussions. The indications are that we're getting rather close to him."

"I see," Jean said uncomfortably. The king beasts avoided rough play as a matter of policy, usually avoided conflict among themselves, but when they met in a duel there were no rules.

"Give that part of it three days," Garland's voice said. She looked around, found him watching her with a trace of what might be irony, back at any rate from whatever brooding trance he'd been sunk in. "Jean, call Litton sometime tomorrow."

"All right."

"Tell him the boss of your detective organization wants an appointment with him. Ten o'clock, three days from now."

She nodded, said carefully, "Litton could become extremely valuable to you, Mr. Garland."

"He could," Garland agreed. "Anyway, I want to watch the swami perform. We'll give him another assignment."

"Am I to accompany you?"

"You'll be there, Jean. So will Max."

"I keep having the most curiously definitive impression," Roy Litton observed, "that I've met you before."

"You have," Garland said amiably.

Litton frowned, shook his head. "It's odd I should have forgotten the occasion!"

"The name's Nick Garland," Garland told him.

Still frowning, Litton stared at him across the table. Then abruptly his face paled. Jean Merriam, watching from behind her employer, saw Litton's eyes shift to her, from her to Max Jewett, and return at last, hesitantly, to Garland's face. Garland nodded wryly.

"I was what you call one of your subjects, Mr. Litton," he said. "I can't give you the exact date, but it should have been between two and three months ago. You remember now?"

Litton shook his head. "No. After such an interval it would be impossible to be definite about it, in any case. I keep no notes and the details of a contact very quickly grow blurred to me." His voice was guarded; he kept his eyes on

Garland's. "Still, you seemed familiar to me at once as a person. And your name seems familiar. It's quite possible that you have been, in fact, a contact subject."

"I was," Garland said. "We know that. That's why we're here."

Litton cleared his throat. "Then the story Miss Merriam told me at her first visit wasn't true."

"Not entirely," Garland admitted. "She wasn't representing a detective outfit. She represented me. Otherwise, she told the truth. She was sent here to find out whether you could do what we'd heard you could do. We learned that you could. Mr. Litton, you've cost me a great deal of money. But I'm not too concerned about that now, because, with your assistance, I'll make it back. And I'll make a great deal more besides. You begin to get the picture?"

Relief and wariness mingled for an instant in Litton's expression. "Yes, I believe I do."

"You'll get paid your regular fees, of course," Garland told him. "The fact is, Mr. Litton, you don't charge enough. What you offer is worth more than ten thousand a shot. What you gave Frank Phleger was worth enormously more."

"Frank Phleger?" Litton said.

"The client who paid you to poke around in my mind. No doubt he wouldn't have used his real name. It doesn't matter. Let's get on to your first real assignment for me. Regular terms. This one isn't a test. It's to bring up information I don't have and couldn't get otherwise. All right?"

Litton nodded, smiled. "You have a suitable contact object?"

"We brought something that should do," Garland said. "Max, give Mr. Litton the belt."

Jean Merriam looked back toward Jewett. Garland hadn't told her what Litton's assignment was to be, had given her no specific instructions, but she'd already turned on the recorder in her handbag. Jewett was taking a large plastic envelope from the briefcase he'd laid beside his chair. He came over to the table, put the envelope before Litton, and returned to his place.

"Can you tell me specifically what you want to know concerning this subject?" Litton asked.

"To start with," Garland said, "just give us whatever you can get. I'm interested in general information."

Litton nodded, opened the plastic envelope and took out a man's leather belt with a broad silver buckle. Almost immediately an expression of distaste showed on his face. He put the belt on the table, looked over at Garland.

"Mr. Garland," he said, "Miss Merriam may have told you that on occasion I'm offered a contact object I can't use. Unfortunately, this belt is such an object."

"What do you mean?" Garland asked. "Why can't you use it?"

"I don't know. It may be something about the belt itself, and it may be the person connected with it." Litton brushed the belt with his finger. "I simply have a very unpleasant feeling about this object. It repels me." He smiled apologetically. "I'm afraid I must refuse to work with it."

"Well, now," Garland said, "I don't like to hear that. You've cost me a lot, you know. I'm willing to overlook it, but I do expect you to be cooperative in return."

Litton glanced at him, swallowed uneasily. "I understand—and I assure you you'll find me cooperative. If you'll give me some other assignment, I assure you—"

"No," Garland said. "No, right now I want information about this particular person, not somebody else. It's too bad if you don't much like to work with the belt, but that's your problem. We went to a lot of trouble to get the belt for you. Let me state this quite clearly, Mr. Litton. You owe me the information, and I think you'd better get it now."

His voice remained even, but the menace in the words was undisguised. The king beast was stepping out from cover; and Jean's palms were suddenly wet. She saw Litton's face whiten.

"I suppose I do owe it to you," Litton said after a moment. He hesitated again. "But this isn't going to be easy."

Garland snorted. "You're getting ten thousand dollars for a few minutes' work!"

"That isn't it. I . . ." Litton shook his head helplessly, got to his feet. He indicated the curtained alcove at the side of the room. "I'll go in there. At best, this will be a difficult contact to attempt. I can't be additionally distracted by knowing that three people are staring at me."

"You'll get the information?" Garland asked.

Litton looked at him, said sullenly, "I always get the information." He picked up the belt, went to the alcove, and disappeared through the curtains.

Garland turned toward Jean Merriam. "Start timing him," he said.

She nodded, checked her watch. The room went silent, and immediately Jean felt a heavy oppression settle on her. It was almost as if the air had begun to darken around them. Frightened, she thought, *Nick hates that freak . . . Has he decided to kill him?*

She pushed the question away and narrowed her attention to the almost inaudible ticking of the tiny expensive watch. After a while she realized that Garland was looking at her again. She met his eyes, whispered, "Three minutes and ten seconds." He nodded.

There was a sound from within the alcove. It was not particularly loud, but in the stillness it was startling enough to send a new gush of fright through Jean. She told herself some minor piece of furniture, a chair, a small side table, had fallen over, been knocked over on the carpeting. She was trying to think of some reason why Litton should have knocked over a chair in there when the curtains before the alcove were pushed apart. Litton moved slowly out into the room.

He stopped a few feet from the alcove. He appeared dazed, half-stunned, like a man who'd been slugged hard in the head and wasn't sure what had happened. His mouth worked silently, his lips writhing in slow, stiff contortions as if trying to shape words that couldn't be pronounced. Abruptly he started forward. Jean thought for a moment he was returning to the table, but he went past it, pace quickening, on past Garland and herself without glancing at either of them. By then he was almost running, swaying from side to side in long staggering steps, and she realized he was hurrying toward the French doors which stood open on the wide veranda overlooking the park. Neither Garland nor Jewett moved from their chairs, and Jean, unable to speak, twisted around to look after Litton as they were doing. She saw him run across the veranda, strike the hip high railing without checking, and go on over.

The limousine moved away from the Torrell Arms through the sunlit park, Jewett at the wheel, Garland and Jean Merriam in the back seat. There was no siren wail behind them, no indication of disturbance, nothing to suggest that anyone else was aware that a few minutes ago a man had dropped into the neatly trimmed park shrubbery from the eighteenth floor of the great apartment hotel.

"You could have made use of him," Jean said. "He could have been of more value to you than anyone else in the world. But you intended to kill him from the start, didn't you?"

Garland didn't reply for a moment. Then he said, "I could have made use of him, sure. So could anyone else with ten thousand dollars to spare, or some way to put pressure on him. I don't need somebody like Litton to stay on top. And I don't like the rules changed. When Phleger found Litton, he started changing them. It could happen again. Litton had to be taken out."

"Max could have handled that," Jean said. Her hands had begun to tremble again; she twisted them tightly together around the strap of the handbag. "What did you do to get Litton to kill himself?"

Garland shook his head. "I didn't intend him to kill himself. Max was to take care of him afterward."

"You did something to him."

Garland drew a long sighing breath. "I was just curious," he said. "There's something I wonder about now and then. I thought Litton might be able to tell me, so I gave him the assignment."

"What assignment? He became someone else for three minutes. What happened to him?"

Garland's head turned slowly toward her. She noticed for the first time that his face was almost colorless. "That was Frank Phleger's belt," he said. "Max's boys caught up with him last night. Phleger's been dead for the last eight hours."

HENRY SLESAR

The Girl Who Found Things

It was dark by the time Lucas stopped his taxi in the driveway of the Wheeler home and lumbered up the path to the front entrance. He still wore his heavy boots, despite the spring thaw; his mackinaw and knitted cap were reminders of the hard winter that had come and gone.

When Geraldine Wheeler opened the door, wearing her light-weight traveling suit, she shivered at the sight of him. "Come in," she said crisply. "My trunk is inside."

Lucas went through the foyer to the stairway, knowing his way around the house, accustomed to its rich, dark textures and somber furnishings; he was Medvale's only taxi driver. He found the heavy black trunk at the foot of the stairs, and hoisted it on his back. "That all the luggage, Miss Wheeler?"

"That's all, I've sent the rest ahead to the ship. Good heavens, Lucas, aren't you *hot* in that outfit?" She opened a drawer and rummaged through it. "I've probably forgotten a million things. Gas, electricity, phone . . . Fireplace! Lucas, would you check it for me, please?"

"Yes, Miss," Lucas said. He went into the living room, past the white-shrouded furniture. There were some glowing embers among the blackened stumps, and he snuffed them out with a poker.

A moment later the woman entered, pulling on long silken gloves. "All right," she said breathlessly. "I guess that's all. We can go now."

"Yes, Miss," Lucas said.

She turned her back and he came up behind her, still holding the poker. He made a noise, either a sob or a grunt, as he raised the ash-coated iron and struck her squarely in the back of the head. Her knees buckled, and she sank to the carpet in an ungraceful fall. Lucas never doubted that she had died instantly, because he had once killed an ailing shorthorn bull with a blow no greater. He tried to act as calmly now. He put the poker back into the fireplace, purifying it among the hot coals. Then he went to his victim and examined her wound. It was ugly, but there was no blood.

He picked up the light body without effort and went through the screen door of the kitchen and out into the back yard, straight to the thickly wooded acreage that surrounded the Wheeler estate. When he found an appropriate place for Geraldine Wheeler's grave, he went to the toolshed for a spade and shovel.

It was spring, but the ground was hard. He was stripped of mackinaw and cap when he was finished. For the first time in months, since the icy winter began, Lucas was warm.

April had lived up to its moist reputation; there was mud on the roads and pools of black water in the driveway. When the big white car came to a halt, its metal skirt was clotted with Medvale's red clay. Rowena, David Wheeler's wife, didn't leave the car, but waited with an impatient frown until her husband helped her out. She put her high heels into the mud, and clucked in vexation.

David smiled, smiled charmingly, forgiving the mud, the rain, and his wife's bad temper. "Come on, it's not so bad," he said. "Only a few steps." He heard the front door open, and saw his Aunt Faith waving to them. "There's the old gypsy now," he said happily. "Now remember what I told you, darling, when she starts talking about spooks and séances, you just keep a straight face."

"I'll try," Rowena said dryly.

There was affectionate collision between David and his aunt at the doorway; he put his arms around her sizable circumference and pressed his patrician nose to her plump cheek.

"David, my handsome boy! I'm so glad to see you!"

"It's wonderful seeing you, Aunt Faith!"

They were inside before David introduced the two women. David and Rowena had been married in Virginia two years ago, but Aunt Faith never stirred beyond the borders of Medvale County.

The old woman gave Rowena a glowing look of inspection. "Oh, my dear, you're beautiful," she said. "David, you beast, how could you keep her all to yourself?"

He laughed, and coats were shed, and they went into the living room together. There, the cheerfulness of the moment was dissipated. A man was standing by the fireplace smoking a cigarette in nervous puffs, and David was reminded of the grim purpose of the reunion.

"Lieutenant Reese," Aunt Faith said, "this is my nephew, David, and his wife."

Reese was a balding man, with blurred and melancholy features. He shook David's hand solemnly. "Sorry we have to meet this way," he said. "But then, I always seem to meet people when they're in trouble. Of course, I've known Mrs. Demerest for some time."

"Lieutenant Reese has been a wonderful help with my charity work," Aunt Faith said. "And he's been such a comfort since . . . this awful thing happened."

David looked around the room. "It's been years since I was here. Wonder if I remember where the liquor's kept?"

"I'm afraid there is none," Reese said. "There wasn't any when we came in to search the place some weeks ago, when Miss Wheeler first disappeared."

There was a moment's silence. David broke it with, "Well, I've got a bottle in the car."

"Not now, Mr. Wheeler. As a matter of fact, I'd appreciate it if you and I could have a word alone."

Aunt Faith went to Rowena's side. "I'll tell you what. Why don't you and I go upstairs, and I'll show you your room?"

"That would be fine," Rowena said.

"I can even show you the room where David was born, and his old nursery. Wouldn't you like that?"

"That would be lovely," Rowena said flatly.

When they were alone, Reese said, "How long have you been away from Medvale, Mr. Wheeler?"

"Oh, maybe ten years. I've been back here on visits, of course. Once when my father died, four years ago. As you know, our family's business is down south."

"Yes, I knew. You and your sister—"

"My half sister."

"Yes," Reese said. "You and your half sister, you were the only proprietors of the mill, weren't you?"

"That's right."

"But you did most of the managing, I gather. When your parents died, Miss Wheeler kept the estate, and you went to Virginia to manage the mill. That's how it was, right?"

"That's how it was," David said.

"Successfully, would you say?"

David sat in a wing chair, and stretched his long legs. "Lieutenant, I'm going to save you a great deal of time. Geraldine and I didn't get along. We saw as little of each other as both could arrange, and that was *very* little."

Reese cleared his throat. "Thank you for being frank."

"I can even guess your next question, Lieutenant. You'd like to know when I saw Geraldine last."

"When did you?"

"Three months ago, in Virginia. On her semiannual visit to the mill."

"But you were in Medvale after that, weren't you?"

"Yes. I came up to see Geraldine in March on a matter of some importance. As my aunt probably told you, Geraldine refused to see me at that time."

"What was the purpose of that visit?"

"Purely business. I wanted Geraldine to approve a bank loan I wished to make to purchase new equipment. She was against it, wouldn't even discuss it. So I left and returned to Virginia."

"And you never saw her again?"

"Never," David said. He smiled, smiled engagingly, and got to his feet. "I don't care if you're a teetotaler like my aunt, Lieutenant, I've *got* to have that drink."

He went toward the front hall, but paused at the doorway. "In case you're wondering," he said lightly, "I have no idea where Geraldine is, Lieutenant. No idea at all."

Rowena and Aunt Faith didn't come downstairs until an hour later, after the lieutenant had left. Aunt Faith looked like she had been sleeping; Rowena had changed into a sweater and gray skirt. In the living room, they found David, a half-empty bottle of Scotch, and a dying fire.

"Well?" Aunt Faith said. "Was he very bothersome?"

"Not at all," David said. "You look lovely, Rowena."

"I'd like a drink, David."

"Yes, of course." He made one for her, and teased Aunt Faith about her abstinence. She didn't seem to mind. She wanted to talk about Geraldine.

"I just can't understand it," she said. "Nobody can, not the police, not anybody. She was all set for that Caribbean trip, some of her bags were already on the ship. You remember Lucas, the cab driver? He came out here to pick her up and take her to the station, but she wasn't here. She wasn't anywhere."

"I suppose the police have checked the usual sources?"

"Everything. Hospitals, morgues, everywhere. Lieutenant Reese says almost anything could have happened to her. She might have been robbed and murdered; she might have lost her memory; she might even have—" Aunt Faith blushed. "Well, this I'd *never* believe, but Lieutenant Reese says she might have disappeared deliberately—with some *man*."

Rowena had been at the window, drinking quietly. "I know what happened," she said.

David looked at her sharply.

"She just left. She just walked out of this gloomy old house and this crawly little town. She was sick of living alone. Sick of a whole town waiting for her to get married. She was tired of worrying about looms and loans and debentures. She was sick of being herself. That's how a woman can get."

She reached for the bottle, and David held her wrist. "Don't," he said. "You haven't eaten all day."

"Let me go," Rowena said softly.

He smiled, and let her go.

"I think the lieutenant was right," Rowena said. "I think there was a man, Auntie. Some vulgar type. Maybe a coal digger or a truck driver, somebody without any *charm* at all." She raised her glass in David's direction. "No charm at all."

Aunt Faith stood up, her plump cheeks mottled. "David, I have an idea—about how we can find Geraldine, I mean. I'm certain of it."

"Really?"

"But you're not going to agree with me. You're going to give me that nice smile of yours and you're going to humor me. But whether you approve or not, David, I'm going to ask Iris Lloyd where Geraldine is."

David's eyebrows made an arc. "Ask who?"

"Iris Lloyd," Aunt Faith said firmly. "Now don't tell me you've never heard of that child. There was a story in the papers about her only two months ago, and heaven knows I've mentioned her in my letters a dozen times."

"I remember," Rowena said, coming forward. "She's the one who's . . . psychic or something. Some sort of orphan?"

"Iris is a ward of the state, a resident at the Medvale Home for Girls. I've been vice-chairman of the place for donkey's years, so I know all about it. She's sixteen and amazing, David, absolutely uncanny!"

"I see." He hid an amused smile behind his glass. "And what makes Iris such a phenomenon?"

"She's a seer, David, a genuine clairvoyant. I've told you about this Count Louis Hamon, the one who called himself Cheiro the Great? Of course, he's dead now, he died in 1936, but he was gifted in the same way Iris is. He could just *look* at a person's mark and know the most astounding things—"

"Wait a minute. You really think this foundling can tell us where Geraldine is? Through some kind of séance?"

"She's not a medium. I suppose you could call her a *finder*. She seems to have the ability to *find* things that are lost. People, too."

"How does she do it, Mrs. Demerest?" Rowena asked.

"I can't say. I'm not sure Iris can either. The gift hasn't made her happy, poor child—such talents rarely do. For a while, it seemed like nothing more than a parlor trick. There was a Sister Theresa at the Home, a rather befuddled old lady who was always misplacing her thimble or what-have-you, and each time Iris was able to find it—even in the unlikeliest places."

David chuckled. "Sometimes kids *hide* things in the unlikeliest places. Couldn't she be some sort of prankster?"

"But there was more," Aunt Faith said gravely. "One day, the Home had a picnic at Crompton Lake. They discovered that an eight-year-old girl named Dorothea was missing. They couldn't find her, until Iris Lloyd began screaming."

"Screaming . . .?" Rowena said.

"These insights cause her great pain. But she was able to describe the place where they would find Dorothea; a small natural cave, where Dorothea was found only half-alive from a bad fall she had taken."

Rowena shivered.

"You were right," David said pleasantly. "I can't agree with you, Auntie. I don't go along with this spirit business; let's leave it up to the police."

Aunt Faith sighed. "I knew you'd feel that way. But I have to do this, David. I've arranged with the Home to have Iris spend some time with us, to become acquainted with the . . . aura of Geraldine that's still in the house."

"Are you serious? You've asked that girl *here?*"

"I knew you wouldn't be pleased. But the police can't find Geraldine, they haven't turned up a clue. Iris can."

"I won't have it," he said tightly. "I'm sorry, Auntie, but the whole thing is ridiculous."

"You can't stop me. I was only hoping that you would cooperate." She looked at Rowena, her eyes softening. "You understand me, my dear. I know you do."

Rowena hesitated, then touched the old woman's hands. "I do, Mrs. Demerest." She looked at David with a curious smile. "And I'd like nothing better than to meet Iris."

Ivy failed to soften the Medvale Home's cold stone substance and ugly lines. It had been built in an era that equated orphanages with penal institutions, and its effect upon David was depressing.

The head of the institution, Sister Clothilde, entered her office, sat down briskly, and folded her hands. "I don't have to tell you that I'm against this, Mrs. Demerest," she said. "I think it's completely wrong to encourage Iris in these delusions of hers."

Aunt Faith seemed cowed by the woman; her reply was timid. "Delusions, Sister? It's a gift of God."

"If this . . . ability of Iris' has any spiritual origin, I'm afraid it's from quite another place. Not that I admit there *is* a gift."

David turned on his most charming smile, but Sister Clothilde seemed immune to it.

"I'm glad to see I have an ally," he said. "I've been telling my aunt that it's all nonsense—"

Sister Clothilde bristled. "It's true that Iris has done some remarkable things which we're at a loss to explain. But I'm hoping she'll outgrow this—whatever it is, and be just a normal, happy girl. As she is now—"

"Is she very unhappy?" Aunt Faith asked sadly.

"She's undisciplined, you might even say wild. In less than two years, when she's of legal age, we'll be forced to release her from the Home, and we'd very much like to send her away a better person than she is now."

"But you *are* letting us have her, Sister? She can come home with us?"

"Did you think my poor objections carried any weight, Mrs. Demerest?"

A moment later, Iris Lloyd was brought in.

She was a girl in the pony stage, long gawky arms and legs protruding from a smock dress that had been washed out of all color and starched out of all shape. Her stringy hair was either dirty blonde or just dirty; David guessed the latter. She had a flat-footed walk, and kept twisting her arms. She kept her eyes lowered as Sister Bertha brought her forward.

"Iris," Sister Clothilde said, "you know Mrs. Demerest. And this is her nephew, Mr. Wheeler."

Iris nodded. Then, in a flash almost too sudden to be observed, her eyes came up and stabbed them with such an intensity of either hostility or malice that David almost made his surprise audible. No one else, however, seemed to have noticed.

"You remember me, Iris," Aunt Faith said. "I've been coming here at least once a year to see all you girls."

"Yes, Mrs. Demerest," Iris whispered.

"The directors have been good enough to let us take you home with us for a while. We need your help, Iris. We want you to see if you can help us find someone who is lost."

"Yes, Mrs. Demerest," she answered serenely. "I'd like to come home with you. I'd like to help you find Miss Wheeler."

"Then you know about my poor niece, Iris?"

Sister Clothilde clucked. "The Secret Service couldn't have secrets here, Mrs. Demerest. You know how girls are."

David cleared his throat and stood up. "I guess we can get started any time. If Miss Lloyd has her bags ready . . ."

Iris gave him a quick smile at that, but Sister Clothilde wiped it off with, "Please call her Iris, Mr. Wheeler. Remember that you're still dealing with a child."

When Iris' bags were in the trunk compartment, she climbed between David and his aunt in the front seat, and watched with interest as David turned the key in the ignition.

"Say," she said, "you wouldn't have a cigarette, would you?"

"Why, Iris!" Aunt Faith gasped.

She grinned. "Never mind," she said lightly. "Just never mind." Then she closed her eyes, and began to hum. She hummed to herself all the way to the Wheeler house.

David drove into town that afternoon, carrying a long list of groceries and sundries that Aunt Faith deemed necessary for the care and feeding of a sixteen-year-old girl.

He was coming out of the Medvale Supermarket when he saw Lucas Mitchell's battered black taxicab rolling slowly down the back slope of the parking lot. He frowned and walked quickly to his own car, but as he put the groceries in the rear, he saw Lucas' cab stop beside him.

"Hello, Mr. Wheeler," Lucas said, leaning out the window.

"Hello, Lucas. How's business?"

"Could I talk to you a minute, Mr. Wheeler?"

"No," David said. He went around front and climbed into the driver's seat. He fumbled in his pocket for the key, and the sight of Lucas leaving his cab made it seem much more difficult to find.

"I've got to talk to you, Mr. Wheeler."

"Not here," David said. "Not here and not now, Lucas."

"It's important. I want to ask you something."

"For the love of Mike," David said, gritting his teeth. He found the key at last, and shoved it into the slit on the dashboard. "Get out of the way, Lucas, I can't stop now."

"That girl, Mr. Wheeler. Is it true about the girl?"

"What girl?"

"That Iris Lloyd. She does funny things, that one. I'm afraid of her, Mr. Wheeler, I'm afraid she'll find out what we did."

"Get out of the way!" David shouted. He turned the key, and stomped the accelerator to make the engine roar a threat. Lucas moved away, bewildered, and David backed the car out sharply and drove off.

He got home to find Rowena pacing the living room. Her agitation served to quiet his own. "What's wrong?" he said.

"I wouldn't know for sure. Better ask your aunt."

"Where is she?"

"In her room, lying down. All I know is she went up to see if dear little Iris was awake, and they had some kind of scene. I caught only a few of the words, but I'll tell you one thing, that girl has the vocabulary of a longshoreman."

David grunted. "Well, it'll knock some sense into Aunt Faith. I'll go up to see her, and tell her I'll take that little psychic delinquent back where she came from—"

"I wouldn't bother her now, she's not feeling well."

"Then I'll see the little monster. Where is she?"

"Next door to us, in Geraldine's room."

At the door, he lifted his hand to knock, but the door was flung open before his knuckles touched wood.

Iris looked out, her hair tumbled over one eye. Her mouth went from petulant to sultry, and she put her hands on the shapeless uniform where her hips should be.

"Hello, handsome," she said. "Auntie says you went shopping for me."

"What have you been up to?" He walked in and closed the door. "My aunt isn't a well woman, Iris, and we won't put up with any bad behavior. Now, what happened here?"

She shrugged, and walked back to the bed. "Nothing," she said sullenly. "I found a butt in an ash tray and was taking a drag when she walked in. You'd think I was burning the house down the way she yelled."

"I heard you did some fancy yelling yourself. Is that what the Sisters taught you?"

"They didn't teach me anything worthwhile."

Suddenly, Iris changed; face, posture, everything. In an astonishing transformation, she was a child again.

"I'm sorry," she whimpered. "I'm awfully sorry, Mr. Wheeler. I didn't mean to do anything wrong."

He stared at her, baffled, not knowing how to take the alteration of personality. Then he realized that the door had opened behind him, and that Aunt Faith had entered.

Iris fell on the bed and began to sob, and with four long strides, Aunt Faith crossed the room and put her plump arms around her in maternal sympathy.

"There, there," she crooned, "it's all right, Iris. I know you didn't mean what you said, it's the Gift that makes you this way. And don't worry about what I asked you to do. You take your time about Geraldine, take as long as you like."

"Oh, but I *want* to help!" Iris said fervently. "I really do, Aunt Faith." She stood up, her face animated. "I can *feel* your niece in this house. I can almost hear her—whispering to me—telling me where she is!"

"You can?" Aunt Faith said in awe. "Really and truly?"

"Almost, almost!" Iris said, spinning in an awkward dance. She twirled in front of a closet, and opened the door; there were still half a dozen hangers of clothing inside. "These are *her* clothes. Oh, they're so beautiful! She must have looked beautiful in them!"

David snorted. "Has Iris ever seen a photo of Geraldine?"

The girl took out a gold lamé evening gown and held it in her arms. "Oh, it's so lovely! I can *feel* her in this dress, I can just *feel* her!" She looked at Aunt Faith with wild happiness. "I just know I'm going to be able to help you!"

"Bless you," Aunt Faith said. Her eyes were damp.

Iris was on her best behavior for the rest of the day; her mood extended all the way through dinner. It was an uncomfortable meal for everyone except the girl. She asked to leave the table before coffee was served, and went upstairs.

When the maid cleared the dining table, they went to the living room, and David said, "Aunt Faith, I think this is a terrible mistake."

"Mistake, David? Explain that."

"This polite act of Iris'. Can't you see it's a pose?"

The woman stiffened. "You're wrong. You don't understand psychic personalities. It wasn't *her* swearing at me, David, it was this demon that possesses her. The same spirit that gives her the gift of insight."

Rowena laughed. "It's probably the spirit of an old sailor, judging from the language. Frankly, Aunt Faith, to me she seems like an ordinary little girl."

"You'll see," Aunt Faith said stubbornly. "You just wait and see how ordinary she is."

As if to prove Aunt Faith's contention, Iris came downstairs twenty minutes later wearing Geraldine Wheeler's gold lamé gown. Her face had been smeared with an overdose of makeup, and her stringy hair clumsily tied in an upsweep that refused to stay up. David and Rowena gawked at the spectacle, but Aunt Faith was only mildly perturbed.

"Iris, dear," she said, "What have you done?"

She minced into the center of the room. She hadn't changed her flat-heeled shoes, and the effect of her attempted gracefulness was almost comic; but David didn't laugh.

"Get upstairs and change," he said tightly. "You've no right to wear my sister's clothes."

Her face fell in disappointment and she looked at Aunt Faith. "Oh, Aunt Faith!" she wailed. "You know what I told you! I *have* to wear your niece's clothes, to feel her . . . aura!"

"Aura, my foot!" David said.

She stared at him, stunned. Then she fell into the wing chair by the fireplace and sobbed. Aunt Faith quickly repeated her ministrations of that afternoon, and chided David.

"You shouldn't have said that!" she said angrily. "The poor girl is trying to help us, David, and you're spoiling it!"

"Sorry," he said wryly. "I guess I'm just not a believer, Aunt Faith."

"You won't even give her a chance!"

Aunt Faith waited until Iris' sobs quieted, her face thoughtful. Then she leaned close to the girl's ear. "Iris, listen to me. You remember those things you did at the Home? The way you found things for Sister Theresa?"

Iris blinked away the remainder of her tears. "Yes."

"Do you think you could do that again, Iris? Right now, for us?"

"I—I don't know. I could try."

"Will you let her try, David?"

"I don't know what you mean."

"I want you to hide something, or name some object you've lost or misplaced, perhaps somewhere in this house."

"This is silly. It's a parlor game—"

"David!"

He frowned. "All right, have it your own way. How do we play this little game of hide-and-seek?"

Rowena said, "David, what about the cat?"

"The cat?"

"You remember. You once told me about a wool kitten you used to have as a child. You said you lost it somewhere in the house when you were five, and you were so unhappy about it that you wouldn't eat for days."

"That's preposterous. That's thirty years ago—"

"All the better," Aunt Faith said. "All the better, David." She turned to the girl. "Do you think you can find it, Iris? Could you find David's cloth kitten?"

"I'm not sure. I'm never sure, Aunt Faith."

"Just try, Iris. We won't blame you if you fail. It might have been thrown out ages ago, but try anyway."

The girl sat up, and put her face in her hands.

"David," Aunt Faith whispered, "put out the light."

David turned off the one table lamp that lit the room. The flames of the fireplace animated their shadows.

"Try, Iris," Aunt Faith encouraged.

The clock on the mantelpiece revealed its loud tick. Then Iris dropped her hands limply into her lap, and she leaned against the high back of the wing chair with a long, troubled sigh.

"It's a trance," Aunt Faith whispered. "You see it, David, you must see it. The girl is in a genuine trance."

"I wouldn't know," David said.

Iris' eyes were closed, and her lips were moving. There were drops of spittle at the corners of her mouth.

"What's she saying?" Rowena said. "I can't hear her."

"Wait! You must wait!" Aunt Faith cautioned.

Iris' voice became audible. "Hot," she said. "Oh, it's so hot . . . so hot . . ." She squirmed in the chair, and her fingers tugged at the neckline of the evening dress. "So hot back here!" she said loudly. "Oh, please! Oh, please! Kitty is hot! Kitty is hot!"

Then Iris screamed, and David jumped to his feet. Rowena came to his side and clutched his arm.

"It's nothing!" David said. "Can't you see it's an act?"

"Hush, please!" Aunt Faith said. "The girl is in pain!"

Iris moaned and thrashed in the chair. There were beads of perspiration on her forehead now, and her squirming, twisting body had all the aspects of a soul in hell-fire.

"Hot! Hot!" she shrieked. "Behind the stove! Oh please, oh please, oh please . . . so hot . . . kitty so hot . . ." Then she sagged in the chair and groaned.

Aunt Faith rushed to her side and picked up the thin wrists. She rubbed them vigorously, and said, "You heard her, David, you heard it for yourself. Can you doubt the girl now?"

"I didn't hear anything. A lot of screams and moans and gibberish about heat. What's it supposed to mean?"

"You *are* a stubborn fool! Why, the kitten's behind the stove, of course, where you probably stuffed it when you were a little brat of a boy!"

Rowena tugged his arm. "We could find out, couldn't we? Is the same stove still in the kitchen?"

"I suppose so. There's some kind of electronic oven, too, but they've never moved the old iron monster, far as I know."

"Let's look, David, please!" Rowena urged.

Iris was coming awake. She blinked and opened her eyes, and looked at their watching faces. "Is it there?" she said. "Is it where I said it was? Behind the stove in the kitchen?"

"We haven't looked yet," David said.

"Then look," Aunt Faith commanded.

They looked, Rowena and David, and it was there, a dust-covered cloth kitten, browned and almost destroyed by three decades of heat and decay; but it was there.

David clutched the old plaything in his fist, and his face went white. Rowena looked at him sadly, and thought he was suffering the pangs of nostalgia, but he wasn't. He was suffering from fear.

In the beginning of May, the rains vanished and were replaced by a succession of sunlit days. Iris Lloyd began to spend most of her time outdoors, communing with nature or her own cryptic thoughts.

That was where David found her one midweek afternoon, lying on the grass amid a tangle of daisies. She was dissecting one in an ancient ritual.

"Well," David said, "what's the answer?"

She smiled coyly, and threw the disfigured daisy away. "You tell me, Uncle David."

"Cut out the Uncle David stuff." He bent down to pick up the mutilated flower, and plucked off the remaining petals. "Loves me not," he said.

"Who? Your wife?" She smirked at him boldly. "You can't fool me, Uncle David. I know all about it."

He started to turn away, but she caught his ankle. "Don't go away. I want to talk."

He came back and squatted down to her level. "Look, what's the story with you, Iris? You've been here over a week and you haven't done anything about— well, you know what. This is just a great big picnic for you, isn't it?"

"Sure it is," she said. "You think I want to go back to that sticky Home? It's better here." She lay back on the grass. "No uniforms. No six a.m. prayers. None of that junk they call food . . ." She grinned. "And a lot nicer company."

"I suppose I should say thank you."

"There's nothing you can say I don't know already." She tittered. "Did you forget? I'm psychic."

"Is it really true, Iris," he said casually, "or is it some kind of trick? I mean, these things you do."

"I'll show you if it's a trick." She covered her eyes with both hands. "Your wife hates you," she said. "She thinks you're rotten. You weren't even married a year when you started running around with other women. You never even went to the mill, not more'n once or twice a month, that was how *you* ran the business. All *you* knew how to do was spend the money."

David's face had grown progressively paler during her recitation. Now he grabbed her thin forearm. "You little brat! You're not psychic! You're an eavesdropper!"

"Let go of my arm!"

"Your room is right next door. You've been listening!"

"All right!" she squealed. "You think I could help hearing you two arguing?"

He released her wrist. She rubbed it ruefully, and then laughed, deciding it was funny. Suddenly she flung herself at him and kissed him on the mouth, clutching him with her thin, strong fingers.

He pushed her away, amazed. "What do you think you're doing?" he said roughly. "You dumb kid!"

"I'm not a kid!" she said. "I'm almost seventeen!"

"You were sixteen three months ago!"

"I'm a woman!" Iris shrieked. "But you're not even a man!" She struck him a blow on the chest with a balled fist, and it knocked the breath out of him. Then she turned and ran down the hill toward the house.

He returned home through the back of the estate and entered the kitchen. Aunt Faith was giving Hattie some silverware-cleaning instructions at the kitchen table. She looked up and said, "Did you call for a taxi, David?"

"Taxi? No, why should I?"

"I don't know. But Lucas' cab is in the driveway; he said he was waiting for you."

Lucas climbed out of the cab at David's approach. He peeled off the knitted cap and pressed it against his stomach.

"What do you want, Lucas?"

"To talk, Mr. Wheeler, like I said last week."

David climbed into the rear seat. "All right," he said, "drive someplace. We can talk while you're driving."

"Yes, sir."

Lucas didn't speak again until they were out of sight of the estate; then he said, "I did what you told me, Mr. Wheeler, 'zactly like you said. I hit her clean, she didn't hurt a bit, no blood. Just like an old steer she went down, Mr. Wheeler."

"All right," David said harshly. "I don't want to hear about it anymore, Lucas, I'm satisfied. You should be, too. You got your money, now forget about it."

"I picked her up," Lucas said dreamily. "I took her out in the woods, like you said, and I dug deep, deep as I could. The ground was awful hard then, Mr. Wheeler, it was a lot of work. I smoothed it over real good, ain't nobody could guess what was there. Nobody . . . except—"

"Is it that girl? Is that what's bothering you?"

"I heard awful funny things about her, Mr. Wheeler. About her findin' things, findin' that little kid what fell near Crompton Lake. She's got funny eyes. Maybe she can see right into that woman's grave . . ."

"Stop the car, Lucas!"

Lucas put his heavy foot on the brake.

"Iris Lloyd won't find her," David said, teeth clenched. "Nobody will. You've got to stop worrying about it. The more you worry, the more you'll give yourself away."

"But she's right behind the house, Mr. Wheeler! She's so close, right in the woods . . ."

"You've got to forget it, Lucas, like it never happened. My sister's disappeared, and she's not coming back. As for the girl, let me worry about her."

He clapped Lucas' shoulder in what was meant to be reassurance, but his touch made Lucas stiffen.

"Now, take me home," David said.

He worried about Iris for another five days, but she seemed to have forgotten the purpose of her stay completely. She was a house guest, a replacement for the missing Geraldine, and Aunt Faith's patience seemed inexhaustible as she waited for the psychic miracle to happen.

The next Thursday night, in their bedroom, Rowena caught David's eye in the vanity mirror and started to say something about the mill.

"Shut up," he said pleasantly. "Don't say another word. I've found out that Iris can hear every nasty little quarrel in this room, so let's declare a truce."

"She doesn't have to eavesdrop, does she? Can't she read minds?" She swiveled around to face him. "Well, she's not the only clairvoyant around here. I can read her mind, too."

"Oh?"

"It's easy," Rowena said bitterly. "I can read every wicked thought in her head, every time she looks at you. I'm surprised you haven't noticed."

"She's a child, for heaven's sake."

"She's in love with you."

He snorted, and went to his bed.

"You're her Sir Galahad," she said mockingly. "You're going to rescue her from that evil castle where they're holding her prisoner. Didn't you know that . . .?"

"Go to sleep, Rowena."

"Of course, there's still one minor obstruction to her plans. A small matter of your wife. But then, I've never been much of a hindrance to your romances, have I?"

"I've asked you for a truce," he said.

She laughed. "You're a pacifist, David, that's part of your famous charm. That's why you came up here in March, wasn't it? To make a truce with Geraldine?"

"I came here on business."

"Yes, I know. To keep Geraldine from sending you to prison, wasn't that the business?"

"You don't know anything about it."

"I have eyes, David. Not like Iris Lloyd, but eyes. I know you were taking money from the mill, too much of it. Geraldine knew it, too. How much time did she give you to make up the loss?"

David thought of himself as a man without a temper, but he found one now, and lost it just as quickly. "Not another word, you hear? I don't want to hear another word!"

He lay awake for the next hour, his eyes staring sightlessly into the dark of the room.

He was still awake when he heard the shuffle of feet in the corridor outside. He sat up, listening, and heard the quiet click of a latching door.

He got out of bed and put on his robe and slippers. There was a patch of moonlight on his wife's pillow; Rowena was asleep. He went noiselessly to the door and opened it.

Iris Lloyd, in a nightdress, was walking slowly down the stairway to the ground floor, her blonde head rigid on her shoulders, moving with the mechanical grace of the somnambulist.

At the end of the hall, Aunt Faith opened her door and peered out, wide-eyed. "Is that you, David?"

"It's Iris," David said.

Aunt Faith came into the hallway, tying her housecoat around her middle, her hands shaking. David tried to restrain her from following the girl, but his aunt was stubborn.

They paused at the landing. Iris, her eyes open and unblinking, was moving frenetically around the front hall.

"What did I forget?" the girl mumbled. "What did I forget?"

Aunt Faith reached for David's arm.

"You're late," Iris said, facing the front door. "It's time we were going . . ." She whirled and seemed to be looking straight at her spectators, without seeing them.

"We have to be going!" she said, almost tearfully. "Oh, please get my luggage. I'm so nervous. I'm so afraid . . ."

"It's a trance," Aunt Faith whispered, squeezing his hand. "Oh, David, this may be it!"

"What did I forget?" Iris quavered. "Gas, electricity, phone, fireplace . . . Is the fireplace still lit? *Oh!*" She sobbed suddenly, and put her face in her hands.

David took a step toward her, and Aunt Faith said, "Don't! Don't waken her!"

Now Iris was walking, a phantom in the loose gown, toward the back of the house. She went to the kitchen, and opened the screen door.

"She's going outside!" David said. "We can't let her—"

"Leave her alone, David! Please, leave her alone!"

Iris stepped outside into the back yard, following a path of moonlight that trailed into the dark woods.

"Iris!" David shouted. "*Iris!*"

"No!" Aunt Faith cried. "Don't waken her! You mustn't!"

"You want that girl to catch pneumonia?" David said furiously. "Are you crazy? Iris!" he shouted again.

She stopped at the sound of her name, turned, and the eyes went from nothingness to bewilderment. Then, as David's arms enclosed her, she screamed and struck at him. He fought to drag her back to the house, pinning her arms to her side. She was sobbing bitterly by the time he had her indoors.

Aunt Faith fluttered about her with tearful cries. "Oh, how could you do that, David?" she groaned. "You know you shouldn't waken a sleepwalker, you know that!"

"I wasn't going to let that child catch her death of cold! That would be a fine thing to tell the Sisters, wouldn't it, Auntie? That we let their little girl die of pneumonia?"

Iris had quieted, her head still cradled in her arms. Now she looked up, and studied their strained faces. "Aunt Faith . . ."

"Are you all right, Iris?"

There was still a remnant of the sleepwalker's distant look in her round eyes. "Yes," she said. "Yes, I'm all right. I think I'm ready now, Aunt Faith. I can do it now."

"Do it now? You mean . . . tell us where Geraldine is?"

"I can try, Aunt Faith."

The old woman straightened up, her manner transformed. "We must call Lieutenant Reese, David. Right now. He'll want to hear anything Iris says."

"Reese? It's after two in the morning!"

"He'll come," Aunt Faith said grimly. "I know he will. I'll telephone him myself; you take Iris to her room."

David helped the girl up the stairs, frowning at the closeness with which she clung to his side. Her manner was meek. She fell on her bed, her eyes closed. Then the eyes opened, and she smiled at him. "You're scared," she said.

He swallowed hard, because it was true. "I'm sending you back," he said hoarsely. "I'm not letting you stay in this house another day. You're more trouble than you're worth, just like Sister Clothilde said."

"Is that the reason, David?"

She began to laugh. Her laughter angered him, and he sat beside her and clamped his hand over her mouth.

"Shut up!" he said. "Shut up, you little fool!"

She stopped laughing. Her eyes, over the fingers of his hand, penetrated his. He put his arm to his side.

Iris leaned toward him. "David," she said sensuously, "I won't give you away. Not if you don't want me to."

"You don't know what you're talking about," he said uncertainly. "You're a fraud."

"Am I? You don't believe that."

She leaned closer still. He grabbed her with brutal suddenness and kissed her mouth. She moved against him, moaning, her thin fingers plucking at the lapel of his robe.

When they parted, he wiped his mouth in disgust and said, "What part of hell did you come from, anyway?"

"David," she said dreamily, "you'll take me away from that place, won't you? You won't let me go back there, will you?"

"You're crazy! You know I'm married—"

"That doesn't matter. You can divorce that woman, David. You don't love her anyway, do you?"

The door opened. Rowena, imperious in her nightgown, looked at them with mixed anger and disdain.

"Get out of here!" Iris shrieked. "I don't want you in my room!"

"Rowena—" David turned to her.

His wife said, "I just came in to tell you something, David. You were right about the walls between these rooms."

"I hate you!" Iris shouted. "David hates you, too! Tell her, David, why don't you tell her?"

"Yes," Rowena said. "Why don't you, David? It's the only thing you haven't done so far."

He looked back and forth between them, the hot-eyed young girl in the heavy flannel nightdress; the cool-eyed woman in silk, waiting to be answered, asking for injury.

"Damn you both!" he muttered. Then he brushed past Rowena and went out.

Lieutenant Reese still seemed half-asleep; the stray hairs on his balding scalp were ruffled, and his clothes had the appearance of having been put on hastily.

Rowena, still in nightclothes, sat by the window, apparently disinterested. Aunt Faith was at the fireplace, coaxing the embers into flames.

Iris sat in the wing chair, her hands clasped in her lap, her expression enigmatic.

When the fire started, Aunt Faith said, "We can begin any time. David, would you turn out the lamp?"

David made himself a drink before he dimmed the lights, and then went over to the chair opposite Iris.

Aunt Faith said, "Are you ready, my child?"

Iris, white-lipped, nodded.

David caught her eyes before they shut in the beginning of the trance. They seemed to recognize his unspoken, plaintive question, but they gave no hint of a reply.

Then they were silent. The silence lasted for a hundred ticks of the mantelpiece clock.

Gradually Iris Lloyd began to rock from side to side in the chair, and her lips moved.

"It's starting," Aunt Faith whispered. "It's starting . . ."

Iris began to moan. She made sounds of torment, and twisted her young body in an ecstasy of anguish. Her mouth fell open, and she gasped; the spittle frothed at the corners and spilled onto her chin.

"You've got to stop this," David said, his voice shaking. "The girl's having a fit."

Lieutenant Reese looked alarmed. "Mrs. Demerest, don't you think—"

"Please!" Aunt Faith said. "It's only the trance. You've seen it before, David, you know—"

Iris cried out.

Reese stood. "Maybe Mr. Wheeler's right. The girl might do herself some harm, Mrs. Demerest—"

"No, no! You must wait!"

Then Iris screamed, in such a mounting cadence of terror that the glass of the room trembled in sympathetic vibration, and Rowena put her hands over her ears.

"*Aunt Faith! Aunt Faith!*" Iris shrieked. "I'm here! I'm here, Aunt Faith, come and find me! Help me, Aunt Faith, it's dark! So dark! Oh, won't somebody help me?"

"Where are you?" Aunt Faith cried, the tears flooding her cheeks. "Oh, Geraldine, my poor darling, where are you?"

"Oh, help me! Help, please!" Iris writhed and twisted in the chair. "It's so dark, I'm so afraid! Aunt Faith! Do you hear me? Do you hear me?"

"We hear you! We hear you, darling!" Aunt Faith sobbed. "Tell us where you are! Tell us!"

Iris lifted herself from the chair, screamed again, and fell back in a fit of weeping. A few moments later, the heaving of her breast subsided, and her eyes opened slowly.

David tried to go to her, but Lieutenant Reese intervened. "One moment, Mr. Wheeler."

Reese went to his knees, and put his thumb on the girl's pulse. With his other hand, he widened her right eye and stared at the pupil. "Can you hear me, Iris? Are you all right?"

"Yes, sir, everything."

"Do you know where Geraldine Wheeler is?"

She looked at the circle of faces, and then paused at David's.

His eyes pleaded.

"Yes," Iris whispered.

"Where is she, Iris?"

Iris' gaze went distant. "Someplace far away. A place with ships. The sun is shining there. I saw hills, and green trees . . . I heard bells ringing in the streets . . ."

Reese turned to the others, to match his own bewilderment with theirs.

"A place with ships . . . Does that mean anything to you?"

There was no reply.

"It's a city," Iris said. "It's far away . . ."

"Across the ocean, Iris? Is that where Geraldine is?"

"No! Not across the ocean. Someplace here, in America, where there are ships. I saw a bay, and a bridge and blue water . . ."

"San Francisco!" Rowena said. "I'm sure she means San Francisco, Lieutenant."

"Iris," Reese said sternly. "You've got to be certain of this, we can't chase all over the country. Was it San Francisco? Is that where you saw Geraldine?"

"Yes!" Iris said. "Now I know. There were trolleys in the streets, funny trolleys going uphill . . . It's San Francisco. She's in San Francisco!"

Reese got to his feet, and scratched the back of his neck. "Well, who knows?" he said. "It's as good a guess as I've heard. Has Geraldine ever been in San Francisco before?"

"Never," Aunt Faith said. "Why would she go there, David?"

"I don't know," David grinned. He went over to Iris and patted her shoulder. "But that's where Iris says she is, and I guess the spirits know what they're talking about. Right, Iris?"

She turned her head aside. "I want to go home," she said. "I want Mother Clothilde . . ." Then she began to cry, softly, like a child.

It was spring, but the day felt summery. When David and Aunt Faith returned from the Medvale Home for Girls, the old woman looked out of the car window, but the countryside charm failed to enliven her mood.

"Come on, you old gypsy," David laughed, "your little clairvoyant was a huge success. Now all the police have to do is find Geraldine in San Francisco—if she hasn't taken a boat to the South Seas by now."

"I don't understand it," Aunt Faith said. "It's not like Geraldine to run away without a word. Why did she do it?"

"I don't know," David replied.

Later that day he drove into town. When he saw Lucas standing at the depot beside his black taxi, he pulled up and climbed out, the smile wide on his face. "Hello, Lucas. How's the taxi business?"

"Could be better." Lucas searched his face. "You got any news for me, Mr. Wheeler?"

"Maybe I do. Suppose we step into your office."

He clapped his hand on Lucas' shoulder, and Lucas preceded him into the depot office. He closed the door carefully, and told the cabman to sit down.

"It's all over," David said. "I've just come from the Medvale Home for Girls. We took Iris Lloyd back."

Lucas released a sigh from deep in his burly chest. "Then she didn't know? She didn't know where the—that woman was?"

"She didn't know, Lucas."

The cabman leaned back, and squeezed the palms of his hands together. "Then I did the right thing. I knew it was the right thing, Mr. Wheeler, but I didn't want to tell you."

"Right thing? What do you mean?"

Lucas looked up with glowing eyes, narrowed by what he might have thought was cunning. "I figured that girl could tell if the body was buried right outside the house. But she'd never find it if it was someplace else. Ain't that right? Someplace far away?"

A spasm took David by the throat. He hurled himself at Lucas and grabbed the collar of his wool jacket.

"What are you talking about? What do you mean, someplace else?" Lucas was too frightened to answer. "What did you do?" David shouted.

"I was afraid you'd be sore," Lucas whimpered. "I didn't want to tell you. I went out in the woods one night last week and dug up that woman's body. I put it in that trunk of hers, Mr. Wheeler, and I sent it by train, far away as I could get it. Farthest place I know, Mr. Wheeler. That's why Iris Lloyd couldn't find it. It's too far away now."

"Where? Where, you moron? San Francisco?"

Lucas mumbled his terror, and then nodded his shaggy head.

The baggagemaster listened intently to the questions of the two plainclothesmen, shrugged when they showed him the photograph of the woman, and then led them to the Unclaimed Baggage room in the rear of the terminal. When he pointed to the trunk that bore the initials G.W., the two men exchanged looks, and then walked slowly toward it. They broke open the lock, and lifted the lid.

Three thousand miles away, Iris Lloyd sat up in the narrow dormitory bed and gasped into the darkness, wondering what strange dream had broken her untroubled sleep.

Death Trance

Gregory Zeno picked up the buzzing house phone. "Yes?"

"Mr. Zeno? There's a young lady down here, Miss Anne Thomas. She claims an appointment."

"Yes. Please send Miss Thomas right up."

Zeno was a slight, slender man of thirty-five, with hair white as sun-bleached bone, a round face as innocent as a cherub's, and eyes a pale gray with a sleepy look about them. He left the study, crossed down the long living room, and was at the door, waiting, when the bell rang.

The girl to whom he opened the door was tall, golden, with green eyes and a good figure, in her early twenties. She struck Zeno as a vital person, but at the moment she seemed to be under rigid control, a shadow of apprehension behind her eyes.

"Miss Thomas? Please come in."

She stepped inside, and Zeno closed the door. He saw her looking around with quickening interest, but he was accustomed to people being impressed by his apartment in the high-rise area of Westwood. It was expensively furnished, ultramodern with clean, stark lines and in simple, basic colors, except for a few pictures on the walls, like vivid splashes of paint.

Zeno knew that most people associated the occult with another century, expecting darkness and shadow, furniture decorated with cabalistic signs, perhaps even creaking doors and unswept cobwebs, and so were disconcerted when confronted with living quarters as modern as a space rocket's functional furnishings.

Her inspection finished, Anne Thomas gave him a single flashing glance, but said nothing.

Zeno motioned. "Shall we go into my study?"

The study was more in keeping. Three walls were lined with books on the occult, the psychic, the mysterious. There was even a crystal ball on a pedestal in one corner, a contemptuous gift from a medium Zeno had exposed for a fraud.

Zeno seated the girl across from his desk and asked, "A drink, Miss Thomas? Perhaps a glass of sherry?"

"No, Mr. Zeno, thank you."

Zeno sat behind his desk."What can I do for you?"

"Well, I ..." She hesitated, moistening her lips with her tongue, then blurted, "My stepfather is trying to get my mother to kill herself!"

Zeno frowned. "I'm sorry to hear that, of course, but why come to me? I'm not a private detective, not in the usual sense. I only take cases involving the occult."

"But you don't understand! This *is* in your field. My mother believes in mediums, spirits, things like that. My stepfather caters to this. He has brought a medium around who claims communication with my dead father's spirit, and this spirit wants Mother to join him on the other side. Now do you see?"

"Who is this medium?"

"A woman named Madame Tora. Do you know her?"

"No, but that doesn't mean anything."

"Well, she is something else! Mr. Zeno, are any of these mediums authentic?"

Zeno said cautiously, "Let's just say it hasn't been proved to my satisfaction either way. I've found several to be frauds, yet that doesn't mean there aren't any authentic mediums."

"This one must be a fake. She must be! There's something else, you see. My father was killed two years ago in a fall from the roof of our house. It was ruled an accident. But this voice that's supposed to be my father's says someone pushed him over, but he doesn't know who. Mother thinks she may have done it. Did you ever hear such nonsense?"

"It isn't nonsense if your mother believes it. Does she?"

"She's beginning to. But she wouldn't hurt a fly, much less push Dad off a roof. If anybody did it, it was my stepfather."

"Do you have any reason to suspect him?"

"Well, Dad left Mother well off and Darrin—that's my stepfather, Darrin Woods—was hanging around Mother before Dad was . . . before Dad died."

"It's not unusual for children to dislike stepfathers."

"Oh, I don't like him! Heavens, no! But I'm sure he married Mother for her money. If she kills herself, he'll have it all. If he can manage that, couldn't he have killed my father?"

"I'm hardly in a position to give an opinion."

"But if you take the case . . . *Will* you take the case?"

Zeno scrubbed a hand down across his face, then reached a sudden decision. "Yes, I'll see what I can do."

Anne's face lit up. Then she leaned forward to say tensely, "There's a . . . sitting at the house tonight. You can come, see what this Madame Tora is all about. I'm home from college for the summer. I'll tell them you're a . . . Oh, a college instructor interested in parapsychology."

"That sounds fine, Anne. What time?"

"The sitting starts at eight."

"I'll be there."

He escorted her out, then returned to stare somberly out the study window. He knew why he had taken on her problem. Of course it seemed an interesting case, the sort that always intrigued him, but that wasn't the whole of it. The similarity between her mother's situation and Zeno's own mother was uncanny, a little frightening.

Zeno had been ten when his father was killed in a hunting accident. For three years thereafter, his grieving mother went from medium to medium seeking contact with her dead husband. Finally she found one who helped her communicate. Either that, or the medium was an ingenious fraud, and the voice purported to be that of Zeno's father had begged his wife to join him on the other side until she had finally killed herself.

From that day forward, Zeno's interest in the occult mounted until, in the end, he became an investigator into psychic phenomena, always searching for concrete proof of the existence of spirits. So far, as he had told Anne, he had uncovered a number of fake mediums, yet he had not resolved the question to his own satisfaction. Until he did, he would never know whether or not his mother's suicide had been the result of a fraud practiced on her.

It was easy to see how Anne's father could have been killed by a fall from the roof. The house was in the Hollywood hills, up one of the old canyons, perched like a gray, medieval castle on the lip of a bluff, a straight drop of several hundred feet to the floor of the canyon.

"He fell from here," Anne said in a subdued voice, "or was pushed."

The roof of the building was flat, with a three-foot parapet around the edge. There was a sort of garden on the roof, with potted shrubs and trees, chairs and a table with an umbrella.

Zeno had been a little early and Anne, watching for him, had taken him up on the roof.

"I suppose it's possible to fall off but it wouldn't be easy," he said. "Not with that wall to fall over."

"Well, you see . . ." Anne shifted her feet uncomfortably, avoiding his gaze. Then she blurted, "Dad drank. He often sat up here alone at night, drinking—as he was that night. The autopsy showed he'd consumed quite a bit. It was decided he was drunk and stumbled over."

"One thing puzzles me, Anne. You said your mother is afraid she may have pushed him over. Doesn't she *know?*"

"She isn't sure, not positively." Again she looked away. "She drank too, you see. Then, I mean. They weren't getting along well. They'd been quarreling for some time. What about, I'm not sure. Maybe about Darrin hanging around Mother. She was supposed to be downstairs asleep at the time. But the thing is, she used to get up and wander around when she'd been drinking and not remember a thing later." She faced him defiantly. "I guess you think we're a weird family, Mr. Zeno."

"I never judge people, Anne," Zeno said gently. "At least, not until all the evidence is in."

His gaze went past her to a man who was striding briskly toward them. He was on the far side of fifty, slender, tanned, and had black hair with a distinguished peppering of gray. He was quite handsome and beautifully dressed.

Anne had turned at the sound of approaching footsteps. Her face became an expressionless mask.

"My dear, the sitting is about to begin," the newcomer said in a rich voice that matched his appearance.

"This is the instructor I told you about, Gregory Zeno. Mr. Zeno, this is my stepfather, Darrin Woods."

The man's handshake was firm. "We're always delighted to have someone join us who's truly interested in the occult."

"Oh, I'm interested," Zeno said. "Very interested."

"Then shall we go down?"

Woods extended his arm to Anne. She ignored it and strode on ahead.

The seance was held in a room on the first floor. Apparently it had once been a study. Now, it was bare of furniture except for a round dinette table and a half dozen chairs ringing it.

There were two women sitting at the table.

Helen Woods, Anne's mother, was in her late forties, with brown eyes and brown hair. There was an ethereal quality about her, her skin almost translucent, as though she already hovered on the threshold of the other world. She responded not at all when Anne introduced Zeno, and he doubted she was even aware of his presence. She reminded him of a drug addict waiting impatiently for a fix. From past experience with such situations, he knew this wasn't as fanciful as it seemed.

Madame Tora was somewhat of a surprise. Many mediums that Zeno had encountered were often physically unattractive, but not Madame Tora. She was about thirty, with a cloud of hair the color of rust, a provocative face, and she wore a green mini-dress to match her eyes. She eyed him closely, but accepted his presence without comment.

Zeno was seated at the table between Anne and Madame Tora. Woods dimmed the lights, blindfolded Madame Tora with a silk scarf, then sat directly across from Zeno. They linked hands all the way around the table.

Madame Tora tilted her head back. In a moment her breathing quickened, became a harsh, rasping sound in the room. Her head rolled on her neck. She grew more and more agitated. Then she said, "Fredrick? Are you there, Fredrick?"

"Fredrick is her spirit control," Anne whispered in Zeno's ear, "or so she claims."

Zeno nodded without taking his gaze from the medium.

Now a deep male voice issued from the medium's lips. "Yes, Madame Tora. This is Fredrick."

"Is someone with you, Fredrick? Someone who wishes to communicate?"

"Yes, someone who . . ."

As Zeno watched, the cords in Madame Tora's throat tautened like steel cables, and the male voice coming from her changed subtly. "Helen, are you there, darling? This is Keith."

Zeno saw a quiver go through Helen Woods, and she said hoarsely, "Yes, Keith, I'm here."

Zeno looked at her. She sat rigidly, eyes wide and staring at the medium. Zeno's glance moved on to Woods. He, also, was looking at the medium with a fixed stare.

The thought passed through Zeno's mind that they could both be in a state bordering on a hypnotic trance. That could mean that Woods was equally convinced of Madame Tora's authenticity. Or it could mean . . .

"Helen, have you decided?"

"No, Keith. Not yet. I—"

"There isn't a great deal of time, Helen. Soon I may move on to another plane. And if that happens, we will not be able to—" The voice began to fade.

"Keith! Don't go! Not yet!"

"Good-bye, Helen. Good-bye, my darling . . ." The voice faded and was gone.

"No!" Helen Woods tore her hand from Darrin's grasp and leaped to her feet. "Keith, wait! Please wait!"

Madame Tora slumped, arms hanging loosely at her sides, head bent over the chair back. Helen Woods collapsed, head in her hands on the table, sobbing wildly. Zeno stood up and went to her, but her husband jumped up, pushing Zeno aside. "Don't touch her! I'll take care of her."

The woman seemed only half-conscious as Woods helped her from the room. Zeno stared after them, a thought nudging his mind. Anne touched his arm, and he looked around. Madame Tora had roused and was briskly preparing to depart, ignoring them as though they didn't exist.

Anne started to leave and Zeno followed her, neither speaking on their way up to the roof. It was full dark now, the air refreshing.

Anne took out a cigarette and leaned back against the parapet. He struck a match for her.

She expelled smoke and said, "Well?"

"If you want to know if she's a fraud, I'm not prepared to answer that. She could be a ventriloquist. She could be a good voice mimic. She could be many things, even a true medium. But that's not the important thing."

"Then what is, for heaven's sake?"

"Your mother's guilt, real or imagined. Has she ever been hypnotized?"

Anne looked perplexed. "Mother? Hypnotized? Not that I know about. What does that have to do with anything?"

"I'm not sure." He stared thoughtfully down at the lights in the canyon below.

"I think they're having an affair, Darrin and that Madame Tora," Anne said with unexpected venom. "I think he's promised to marry her if Mother dies."

"People recall things under hypnosis, things they've forgotten ever doing, things their minds have blanked out for one reason or another," Zeno said, pointedly ignoring her remark. "Do you think your mother would consent?"

"He'll be opposed, I know, but I'm sure I can talk her into it. Do you think it will work?"

"It might, if she's a good hypnotic subject, and I think she is, from watching her tonight. But there's one thing you should take into consideration, Anne."

"What's that?"

"There's always the possibility she's guilty. If she is, it'll probably come out."

"I'm willing to take that chance and I'm sure Mother is, too."

The hypnotic session also took place in the former study. The hypnotist was one Zeno had used before. Zeno was himself a good amateur hypnotist, but he thought this too important to trust to amateurs. To be effective, a hypnotist must practice intense concentration and Zeno wanted his attention free for something else.

Madame Tora had asked to be present. Anne had balked at this, but it suited Zeno's purpose to have the medium there.

Zeno had given the hypnotist certain instructions. The chairs were arranged so that Woods and his wife were side by side, the others somewhat apart. When everyone was seated, the hypnotist took up a stance in front of them. He was a distinguished-looking man, with a shock of gray hair and a rich, resonant voice.

"Now I want you to relax completely, let every muscle go slack, and concentrate on the sound of my voice. Make your mind as blank as a clean sheet of paper and think of nothing but the sound of my voice . . ."

Zeno had warned Anne as to what to expect, had told her to think of something exciting that had recently happened to her, concentrate on anything but the hypnotist's voice. Zeno had a strong suspicion that Madame Tora didn't need any warning.

"Now you are completely relaxed," the hypnotist intoned. "Close your eyes. You are getting sleepy, very sleepy. You are thinking sleep . . ."

Zeno's surmise had been correct. Helen Woods was a good hypnotic subject. She was going under. But even more to Zeno's satisfaction, he noted that Woods also had his eyes closed, his head and hands hanging limply.

After a little, the hypnotist said in a sharper tone, "Helen, extend your arm straight out. That's fine. Not it is rigid as an iron bar. You cannot bend it. You *cannot* bend it! Now . . . try to bend it, Helen."

The woman's efforts to bend the arm were clearly visible, but try as she would, she couldn't lower it.

"Good, Helen. That's fine. You may lower it. Now, Helen, we are going back two years, back to the evening of your first husband's death. Do you remember that evening, Helen?"

A low, moaning sound came from Helen Woods. "Yes . . . I remember . . ."

"Were you with him on the roof at the time of his death?"

She was silent.

"Were you *with* him, Helen?"

"No . . . I was in bed. Asleep. I'd had too much to drink."

"You were *not* on the roof with him at the time?"

"No, no! In bed!"

"You didn't push him over the edge?" The hypnotist's voice curled at her like a lash.

"No, no . . . I was . . ." Helen Woods was laboring, her face shiny with sweat. "I was in bed . . . Asleep, asleep."

Anne stirred by Zeno's side, murmuring in protest. Zeno clamped his hand around her wrist and held her still.

"All right, Helen." The hypnotist's voice became gentler. "You will relax now. You will go deeper into sleep, deeper . . ."

The lines of strain left the woman's face, and she slumped down in the chair, limp as a rag doll.

The hypnotist turned to Woods, who was in a trance apparently as deep as his wife's. "Darrin, do you hear me?"

"Yes . . . I hear you."

The hypnotist picked up the man's right hand. "Your right hand is numb, Darrin. Do you understand? It is numb. You cannot feel a thing."

The hypnotist took a needle from his pocket and pricked Woods' thumb. He didn't flinch or cry out. A drop of blood oozed from the thumb. The hypnotist wiped away the blood and let the hand fall.

"Darrin, look toward the door."

Woods brought his head around and stared at the closed door.

"There is a man just entering. Do you see him?"

"I . . . Yes, I see him."

"He is a policeman, Darrin."

Woods became noticeably agitated. "A policeman?"

"Yes, Darrin, a plainclothes detective. He is here to question you about the death of Keith Thomas." The hypnotist made his voice stern. "You are to answer his questions truthfully."

A cry came from Madame Tora. "Darrin, don't be a fool! There's no one there! No cop, nobody!" She jumped up and ran toward Woods.

Zeno had been prepared. He stepped into her path and seized her arm. "Now, Madame, you don't want to interfere. And why should you be concerned if Mr. Woods thinks a policeman is present? Do you have something to hide?" He watched her closely.

She paled, eyes widening. "Of course not! I just don't like to see him made a fool of."

"But that's the name of the game, isn't it? The hypnotic subject doing and saying things he wouldn't otherwise?"

She recoiled from him as though he'd hissed at her like a venomous snake, and resumed her seat without another word.

"Darrin, were you on the roof the night Keith Thomas died?" the hypnotist asked.

Woods twitched, as though from a delayed reaction to the pin prick, but he didn't speak.

"Darrin, did you push him off the roof?"

"I . . ."

Another cry came from Madame Tora. This time she broke for the door. Again Zeno had anticipated her. He caught her three steps from the door.

"What's your hurry, Madame?"

"Let me go!" She tried to pull loose.

"Are you afraid of what he might tell us? Are you implicated in some way?"

"I'm implicated in nothing! If he tells you I am, he's lying! He pushed that man off the roof! I didn't know about it until long afterwards. He said . . ." The words spilled from her in a flood. "He said all I had to do was . . ." She broke down completely, hands over her face, shoulders heaving.

Zeno led her gently back to the chair. "Anne, you'd better call the police now."

As the police started to take Madame Tora away, Anne stopped them with a gesture. "Madame Tora, my father's voice . . . Was that . . . ?"

Madame Tora had recovered some of her aplomb. She said haughtily, "You dare ask that of *me*? Are you insinuating that I am a fraud?"

Gathering the shreds of her dignity around her like a tattered cloak, she swept from the room, leading the policemen instead of being led.

Zeno and Anne were left alone. Woods had been awakened from his trance and taken away earlier. Zeno had taped the session on a small recorder and had played it back for the police and Anne's mother, who had dissolved into hysterics and fled to her bedroom.

Anne shivered, hugging herself. She said violently, "I hate this place! I'm getting Mother out of here."

By unspoken agreement, they mounted the stairs to the roof.

"Mr. Zeno, did he push my father off the roof?"

"It appears quite likely, Anne."

"Will they convict him?"

"The odds are good, especially since Madame Tora let the cat out."

"But can they use what you taped?"

"Not in court, no. But by playing your stepfather against Madame Tora and using the tape, I think they'll get a confession."

"Would he have confessed if the hypnotist had kept on?"

Zeno shook his head. "Not likely. If that were so, the police would use hypnosis all the time. There are many misconceptions about hypnosis. It's almost impossible to force someone to do something against his will."

"But he seemed to believe there was a policeman in the room."

"A susceptible subject, which your stepfather is, can be made to believe many things but not *do* them against the dictates of the subconscious. For instance, there are cases on record of people jumping to their death while in a hypnotic trance by being told a ten-story window is the door to another room. Yet, if they were told the window *was* a window and ordered to step out, they wouldn't do it."

"Yet Madame Tora believed he was going to confess."

Zeno smiled. "That's what I had hoped."

Anne was silent for a moment before she said in a low voice, "Mr. Zeno, do you think . . .?" She shivered again. "We still don't know for sure if Madame Tora's a fraud, if my father's voice . . ."

Zeno said thoughtfully, "No, we don't know that for sure, do we?"

GEORGE C. CHESBRO

The Healer

The man waiting for me in my downtown office looked like a movie star who didn't want to be recognized. After he took off his hat, dark glasses and leather maxi-coat he still looked like a movie star. He also looked like a certain famous Southern senator.

"Dr. Frederickson," he said, extending a large, sinewy hand. "I've been doing so much reading about you in the past few days, I feel I already know you. I must say it's a distinct pleasure. I'm Bill Younger."

"Senator," I said, shaking the hand and motioning him toward the chair in front of my desk. I had a sudden, mad flash that the senator might be looking for a new campaign gimmick, like an endorsement from a dwarf criminologist-college professor-private detective. Those are the kinds of mad flashes you get when you're a dwarf criminologist-college professor-private detective. I went around to the other side of the desk. Younger, with his boyish, forty-five-year-old face and full head of brown, modishly-cut hair, looked good. Except for the fear in his eyes he might have been ready to step into a television studio. "Why the background check, Senator?"

He half-smiled. "I used to take my daughter to see you perform when you were with the circus."

"That was a long time ago, Senator." It was six years. It seemed a hundred.

The smile faded. "You're famous. I wanted to see if you were also discreet. My sources tell me your credentials are impeccable. You seem to have a penchant for unusual cases."

"Unusual cases seem to have a penchant for me. You'd be amazed how few people feel the need for a dwarf private detective."

Younger didn't seem to be listening. "You've heard of Esteban Morales?"

I said I hadn't. The senator seemed surprised. "I was away for the summer," I added.

The senator nodded absently, then rose and began to pace back and forth in front of the desk. The activity seemed to relax him. "Esteban is one of my constituents, so I'm quite familiar with his work. He's a healer.

"A doctor?"

"No, not a doctor. A psychic healer. He heals with his hands. His mind." He cast a quick look in my direction to gauge my reaction. He must have been satisfied with what he saw because he went on. "There are a number of good psychic healers in this country. Those who are familiar with this kind of phenomenon consider Esteban the best although his work does not receive much publicity. There are considerable . . . pressures."

"Why did you assume I'd heard of him?"

"He spent the past summer at the university where you teach. He'd agreed to participate in a research project."

"What kind of research project?"

"I'm not sure. It was something in microbiology. I think a Dr. Mason was heading the project."

I nodded. Janet Mason is a friend of mine.

"The project was never finished," Younger continued. "Esteban is now in jail awaiting trial for murder." He added almost parenthetically, "Your brother was the arresting officer."

I was beginning to get the notion that it was more than my natural dwarf charm that had attracted Senator Younger. "Who is this Esteban Morales accused of killing?"

"A physician by the name of Robert Edmonston."

"Why?"

The senator suddenly stopped pacing and planted his hands firmly on top of my desk. He seemed extremely agitated. "The papers reported that Edmonston filed a complaint against Esteban. Practicing medicine without a license. The police think Esteban killed him because of it."

"They'd need more than thoughts to book him."

"They . . . found Esteban in the office with the body. Edmonston had been dead only a few minutes. His throat had been cut with a knife they found dissolving in a vial of acid." The first words had come hard for Younger. The rest came easier. "If charges had been filed against Esteban, it wouldn't have been the first time. These are the things Esteban has to put up with. He's always taken the enmity of the medical establishment in stride. Esteban is not a killer—he's a healer. He couldn't kill anyone!" He suddenly straightened up, then slumped into the chair behind him. "I'm sorry," he said quietly. "I must seem overwrought."

"How do you feel I can help you, Senator?"

"You must clear Esteban," Younger said. His voice was steady but intense. "Either prove he didn't do it, or that someone else did."

I looked at him to see if he might, just possibly, be joking. He wasn't. "That's a pretty tall order, Senator. And it could get expensive. On the other hand, you've got the whole New York City Police Department set up to do that work for free."

The senator shook his head. "I want one man—you—to devote himself to nothing but this case. You work at the university. You have contacts. You may be able to find out something the police couldn't, or didn't care to look for. After all, the police have other things besides Esteban's case to occupy their attention."

"I wouldn't argue with that."

"This is *most* important to me, Dr. Frederickson," the senator said, jabbing his finger in the air for emphasis. "I will double your usual fee."

"That won't be nec—"

"At the least, I must have access to Esteban if you fail. Perhaps your brother could arrange that. I am willing to donate ten thousand dollars to any cause your brother deems worthy."

"Hold on, Senator. Overwrought or not, I wouldn't mention that kind of arrangement to Garth. He might interpret it as a bribe offer. Very embarrassing."

"It *will* be a bribe offer!"

I thought about that for a few seconds, then said, "You certainly do a lot for your constituents, Senator. I'm surprised you're not President."

I must have sounded snide. The flesh on the senator's face blanched bone-white, then filled with blood. His eyes flashed. Still, somewhere in their depths, the fear remained. His words came out in a forced whisper. "If Esteban Morales is not released, my daughter will die."

I felt a chill, and wasn't sure whether it was because I believed him or because of the possibility that a United States senator and presidential hopeful was a madman. I settled for something in between and tried to regulate my tone of voice accordingly. "I don't understand, Senator."

"Really? I thought I was making myself perfectly clear. My daughter's life is totally dependent on Esteban Morales." He took a deep breath. "My daughter Linda has cystic fibrosis, Dr. Frederickson. As you may know, medical doctors consider cystic fibrosis incurable. The normal pattern is for a sufferer to die in his or her early teens—usually from pulmonary complications. Esteban has been treating my daughter all her life, and she is now twenty-four. But Linda needs him again. Her lungs are filling with fluid."

I was beginning to understand how the medical establishment might get a little nervous at Esteban Morales' activities, and a psychic warning light was flashing in my brain. Senator or no, this didn't sound like the kind of case in which I liked to get involved. If Morales were a hoaxer—or a killer—I had no desire to be the bearer of bad tidings to a man with the senator's emotional investment.

"How does Morales treat your daughter? With drugs?"

Younger shook his head. "He just . . . *touches* her. He moves his hands up and down her body. Sometimes he looks like he's in a trance, but he isn't. It's . . . very hard to explain. You have to see him do it."

"How much does he charge for these treatments?"

The senator looked surprised. "Esteban doesn't charge anything. Most psychic healers—the real ones—won't take money. They feel it interferes with whatever it is they do." He laughed shortly, without humor. "Esteban prefers to live simply, off Social Security, a pension check and a few gifts—small ones—from his friends. He's a retired metal shop foreman."

Esteban Morales didn't exactly fit the mental picture I'd drawn of him, and my picture of the senator was still hazy. "Senator," I said, tapping my fingers lightly on the desk, "why don't you hold a press conference and describe what you feel Esteban Morales has done for your daughter? It could do you more good than hiring a private detective. Coming from you, I guarantee it will get the police moving."

Younger smiled thinly. "Or get me locked up in Bellevue. At the least I would be voted out of office, perhaps recalled. My state is in the so-called Bible Belt, and there would be a great deal of misunderstanding. Esteban is not a religious man in my constituents' sense of the word. He does not claim to receive his powers from God. Even if he did, it wouldn't make much difference." The smile got thinner. "I've found that most religious people prefer their miracles well-aged. You'll forgive me if I sound selfish, but I would like to try to save Linda's life without demolishing my career. If all else fails, I will hold a press conference. Will you take the job?"

I told him I'd see what I could find out.

It looked like a large, photographic negative. In its center was a dark outline of a hand with the fingers outstretched. The tips of the fingers were surrounded by waves of color, pink, red and violet, undulating outward to a distance of an inch or two from the hand itself. The effect was oddly beautiful and very mysterious.

"What the hell is it?"

"It's a Kirlian photograph," Dr. Janet Mason said. She seemed pleased with my reaction. "The technique is named after a Russian who invented it about thirty years ago. The Russians, by the way, are far ahead of us in this field."

I looked at her. Janet Mason is a handsome woman in her early fifties. Her shiny gray hair was drawn back into a severe bun, highlighting the fine features of her face. You didn't need a special technique to be aware of her sex appeal. She is a tough-minded scientist who, rumor has it, had gone through a long string of lab-assistant lovers. Her work left her little time for anything else. Janet Mason has been liberated a long time. I like her.

"Uh, what field?"

"Psychic research: healing, ESP, clairvoyance, that sort of thing. Kirlian photography, for example, purports to record what is known as the human *aura,* part of the energy that all living things radiate. The technique itself is quite simple. You put an individual into a circuit with an unexposed photographic plate and have the person touch the plate with some part of his body." She pointed to the print I was holding. "That's what you end up with."

"Morales'?"

"Mine. That's an 'average' aura, if you will." She reached into the drawer of her desk and took out another set of photographs. She looked through them, then handed one to me. "This is Esteban's."

I glanced at the print. It looked the same as the first one, and I told her so.

"That's Esteban at rest, you might say. He's not thinking about healing." She handed me another photograph. "Here he is with his batteries charged."

The print startled me. The bands of color were erupting out from the fingers, especially the index and middle fingers. The apogee of the waves was somewhere off the print; they looked like sun storms.

"You won't find that in the others," Janet continued. "With most people, thinking about healing makes very little difference."

"So what does it mean?"

She smiled disarmingly. "Mongo, I'm a scientist. I deal in facts. The fact of the matter is that Esteban Morales takes one hell of a Kirlian photograph. The implication is that he can literally radiate extra amounts of energy at will."

"Do you think he can actually heal people?"

She took a long time to answer. "There's no doubt in *my* mind that he can," she said at last. I considered it a rather startling confession. "And he's not dealing with psychosomatic disorders. Esteban has been involved in other research projects, at different universities. In one, a strip of skin was removed surgically from the backs of monkeys. The monkeys were divided into two groups. Esteban simply handled the monkeys in one group. Those monkeys healed twice as fast as the ones he didn't handle." She smiled wanly. "Plants are supposed to grow faster when he waters them."

"What did you have him working on?"

"Enzymes," Janet said with a hint of pride. "The perfect research model; no personalities involved. You see, enzymes are the basic chemicals of the body. If Esteban could heal, the reasoning went, he should be able to affect pure enzymes. He can."

"The results were good?"

She laughed lightly. "Spectacular. Irradiated—'injured'—enzymes break down at specific rates in certain chemical solutions. The less damaged they are, the slower their rate of breakdown. What we did was to take test tubes full of enzymes—supplied by a commercial lab—and irradiate them. Then we gave Esteban half of the samples to handle. The samples he handled broke down at a statistically significant *lesser* rate than the ones he didn't handle." She paused again, then said, "Ninety-nine and nine-tenths percent of the population can't affect the enzymes one way or the other. On the other hand, a very few people can make the enzymes break down *faster*."

"'Negative' healers?"

"Right. Pretty hairy, huh?"

I laughed. "It's incredible. Why haven't I heard anything about it? I mean, here's a man who may be able to heal people with his hands and nobody's heard of him. I would think Morales would make headlines in every newspaper in the country."

Janet gave me the kind of smile I suspected she normally reserved for some particularly naive student. "It's next to impossible just to get funding for this kind of research, what's more, publicity. Psychic healing is thought of as, well, *occult*."

"You mean like acupuncture?"

It was Janet's turn to laugh. "You make my point. You know how long it took Western scientists and doctors to get around to taking acupuncture seriously. Psychic healing just doesn't fit into the currently accepted pattern of scientific thinking. When you do get a study done, none of the journals want to publish it."

"I understand that Dr. Edmonston filed a complaint against Morales. Is that true?"

"That's what the police said. I have no reason to doubt it. Edmonston was never happy about his part in the project. Now I'm beginning to wonder about Dr. Johnson. I'm still waiting for his anecdotal reports."

"What project? What reports? What Dr. Johnson?"

Janet looked surprised. "You don't know about that?"

"I got all my information from my client. Obviously, he didn't know. Was there some kind of tie-in between Morales and Edmonston?"

"I would say so." She replaced the Kirlian photographs in her desk drawer. "We actually needed Esteban only about an hour or so a day, when he handled samples. The rest of the time we were involved in computer analysis. We decided it might be interesting to see what Esteban could do with some real patients, under medical supervision. We wanted to get a physician's point of view. We put some feelers out into the medical community and got a cold shoulder—except for Dr. Johnson, who incidentally happened to be Robert Edmonston's partner. I get the impression the two of them had a big argument over using Esteban, and Rolfe Johnson eventually won. We worked out a plan where Esteban would go to their offices after finishing here. They would refer certain patients—who volunteered—to him. These particular patients were in no immediate danger, but they would eventually require hospitalization. These patients would report how they felt to Edmonston and Johnson after their sessions with Esteban. The two doctors would then make up anecdotal reports. Not very scientific, but we thought it might make an interesting footnote to the main study."

"And you haven't seen these reports?"

"No. I think Dr. Johnson is stalling."

"Why would he do that after he agreed to participate in the project?"

"I don't know. Maybe he's had second thoughts after the murder. Or maybe he's simply afraid his colleagues will laugh at him."

I wondered. It still seemed a curious shift in attitude. It also occurred to me that I would like to see the list of patients that had been referred to Morales. It just might contain the name of someone with a motive to kill Edmonston—and try to pin it on Esteban Morales. "Tell me some more about Edmonston and Johnson," I said. "You mentioned the fact they were partners."

Janet took a cigarette from her purse and I supplied a match. She studied me through a cloud of smoke. "Is this confidential?"

"If you say so."

"Johnson and Edmonston were very much into the modern big-business aspect of medicine. It's what a lot of doctors are doing these days: labs, ancillary patient centers, private, profit-making hospitals. Dr. Johnson's skills seemed to be more in the area of administration of their enterprises. As a matter of fact, he'd be about the last person I'd expect to be interested in psychic healing. There were rumors to the effect they were going public in a few months."

"Doctors go public?"

"Sure. They build up a network of the types of facilities I mentioned, incorporate, then sell stocks."

"How'd they get along?"

"Who knows? I assume they got along as well as any other business partners. They were different, though."

"How so?"

"Edmonston was the older of the two men. I suspect he was attracted to Johnson because of Johnson's ideas in the areas I mentioned. Edmonston was rumored to be a good doctor, but he was brooding. No sense of humor. Johnson had a lighter, happy-go-lucky side. Obviously, he was also the more adventurous of the two."

"What was the basis of Edmonston's complaint?"

"Dr. Edmonston claimed that Esteban was giving his patients drugs."

I thought about that. It certainly didn't fit in with what the senator had told me. "Janet, doesn't it strike you as odd that two doctors like Johnson and Edmonston would agree to work with a psychic healer? Aside from philosophic differences, they sound like busy men."

"Oh, yes. I really can't explain Dr. Johnson's enthusiasm. As I told you, Dr. Edmonston was against the project from the beginning. He didn't want to waste his time on what he considered to be superstitious nonsense." She paused, then added, "He must have given off some bad vibrations."

"Why do you say that?"

"I'm not sure. Toward the end of the experiment something was affecting Esteban's concentration. He wasn't getting the same results he had earlier. And before you ask, I don't know why he was upset. I broached the subject once and he made it clear he didn't want to discuss it."

"Do you think he killed Edmonston?"

She laughed shortly, without humor. "Uh-uh, Mongo. That's your department. I deal in enzymes; they're much simpler than people."

"C'mon, Janet. You spent an entire summer working with him. He must have left some kind of impression. Do you think Esteban Morales is the kind of man who would slit somebody's throat?"

She looked at me a long time. Finally she said, "Esteban Morales is probably the gentlest, most loving person I've ever met. And that's all you're going to get from me. Except that I wish you luck."

I nodded my thanks, then rose and started for the door.

"Mongo?"

I turned with my hand on the doorknob. Janet was now sitting on the edge of her desk, exposing a generous portion of her very shapely legs. They were the best looking fifty-year-old legs I'd ever seen—and on a very pretty woman.

"You have to come and see me more often," she continued evenly. "I don't have that many dwarf colleagues."

I winked broadly. "See you, kid."

"Of course I was curious," Dr. Rolfe Johnson said. "That's why I was so anxious to participate in the project in the first place. I like to consider myself open-minded."

I studied Johnson. He was a boyish thirty-seven, outrageously good-looking, with Nordic blue eyes and a full head of blond hair. I was impressed by his enthusiasm, somewhat puzzled by his agreeing to see me within twenty minutes of my phone call. For a busy doctor-businessman he seemed very free with his time—or very anxious to nail the lid on Esteban Morales. He was just a little too eager to please me.

"Dr. Edmonston wasn't?"

Johnson cleared his throat. "Well, I didn't mean that. Robert was a . . . traditionalist. You will find that most doctors are just not that *curious*. He considered working with Mr. Morales an unnecessary drain on our time. I thought it was worth it."

"Why? What was in it for you?"

He looked slightly hurt. "I considered it a purely scientific inquiry. After all, no doctor ever actually *heals* anyone. Nor does any medicine. The body heals itself, and all any doctor can do is to try to stimulate the body to do its job. From his advance publicity, Esteban Morales was a man who could do that without benefit of drugs or scalpels. I wanted to see if it were true."

"Was it?"

Johnson snorted. "Of course not. It was all mumbo jumbo. Oh, he certainly had a psychosomatic effect on some people—but they had to believe in him. From what I could see, the effects of what he was doing were at most ephemeral, and extremely short-lived. I suppose that's why he panicked."

"Panicked?"

Johnson's eyebrows lifted. "The police haven't told you?"

"I'm running ahead of myself. I haven't talked to the police yet. I assume you're talking about the drugs Morales is supposed to have administered."

"Oh, not *supposed* to. I *saw* him, and it was reported to me by the patient."

"What patient?"

He clucked his tongue. "Surely you can appreciate the fact that I can't give out patients' names."

"Sure. You told Edmonston?"

"It was his patient. And he insisted on filing the complaint himself." He shook his head. "Dr. Mason would have been doing everyone a favor if she hadn't insisted on having the university bail him out."

"Uh-huh. Can you tell me what happened the night Dr. Edmonston died? What you know?"

He thought about it for a while. At least he looked like he was thinking about it. "Dr. Edmonston and I always met on Thursday nights. There were records to be kept, decisions to be made, and there just wasn't enough time during the week. On that night I was a few minutes late." He shook his head. "Those few minutes may have cost Robert his life."

"Maybe. What was Morales doing there?"

"I'm sure I don't know. Obviously, he was enraged with Robert. He must have found out about the Thursday night meeting while he was working with us, and decided that would be a good time to kill Dr. Edmonston."

"But if he knew about the meetings, he'd know you'd be there."

Johnson glanced impatiently at his watch. "I am not privy to what went on in Esteban Morales' mind. After all, as you must know, he is almost completely illiterate. A stupid man. Perhaps he simply wasn't thinking straight . . . if he ever does." He rose abruptly. "I'm afraid I've given you all the time I can afford. I've talked to you in the interests of obtaining justice for Dr. Edmonston. I hoped you would see that you were wasting your time investigating the matter."

The interview was obviously over.

Johnson's story stunk. The problem was how to get someone else to sniff around it. With a prime suspect like Morales in the net, the New York police weren't about to complicate matters for themselves before they had to, meaning before the senator either got Morales a good lawyer or laid his own career on the line. My job was to prevent that necessity, which meant, at the least, getting Morales out on bail. To do that I was going to have to start raising some doubts.

It was time to talk to Morales.

I stopped off at a drive-in for dinner, took out three hamburgers and a chocolate milk shake intended as a bribe for my outrageously oversized brother. The food wasn't enough. A half hour later, after threats, shouts and appeals to familial loyalty, I was transformed from a dwarf private detective to a dwarf lawyer and taken to see Esteban Morales. The guard assigned to me thought it was funny as hell.

Esteban Morales looked like an abandoned extra from *Viva Zapata*. He wore a battered, broad-brimmed straw hat to cover a full head of long, matted gray hair. He wore shapeless corduroy pants and a bulky, torn red sweater. Squatting down on the cell's dirty cot, his back to the wall, he looked forlorn and lonely. He looked up as I entered. His eyes were a deep, wet brown. Something moved in their depths as he looked at me. Whatever it was— curiosity, perhaps—quickly passed.

I went over to him and held out my hand. "Hello, Mr. Morales. My name is Bob Frederickson. My friends call me Mongo."

Morales shook my hand. For an old man, his grip was surprisingly firm. "Glad to meet you, Mr. Mongo," he said in a thickly accented voice. "You lawyer?"

"No. A private detective. I'd like to try to help you."

"Who hire you?"

"A friend of yours." I mouthed the word "senator" so the guard wouldn't hear me. Morales' eyes lit up. "Your friend feels that his daughter needs you. I'm going to try to get you out, at least on bail."

Morales lifted his large hands slowly and studied the palms. I remembered Janet Mason's Kirlian photographs; I wondered what mysterious force was in those hands, and what its source was. "I help Linda if I can get to see her," he said quietly. "I must touch." He suddenly looked up. "I no kill anybody, Mr. Mongo. I never hurt anybody."

"What happened that night?"

The hands pressed together, dropped between his knees. "Dr. Edmonston no like me. I can tell that. He think I phony. Still he let me help his patients, and I grateful to him for that."

"Do you think you actually helped any of them?"

Morales smiled disarmingly, like a child who has done something of which he is proud. "I know I did. And the patients, they know. They tell me, and they tell Dr. Edmonston and Dr. Johnson."

"Did you give drugs to anybody?"

"No, Mr. Mongo." He lifted his hands. "My power is here, in my hands. All drugs bad for body."

"Why do you think Dr. Edmonston said you did?"

He shook his head in obvious bewilderment. "One day the police pick me up at university. They say I under arrest for pretending to be doctor. I no understand. Dr. Mason get me out. Then I get message same day—"

"A Thursday?"

"I think so. The message say that Dr. Edmonston want to see me that night at 7:30. I want to know why he mad at me so I decide to go. I come in and find him dead. Somebody cut throat. Dr. Johnson come in a few minutes later. He think I do it. He call police . . ." His voice trailed off, punctuated by a gesture that included the cell, and the unseen world outside. It was an elegant gesture.

"How did you get into the office, Esteban?"

"The lights are on and door open. When nobody answer knock I walk in."

I nodded. Esteban Morales was either a monumental acting talent or a man impossible not to believe. "Do you have any idea why Dr. Edmonston wanted to talk to you?"

"No, Mr. Mongo. I thought maybe he sorry he call police."

"How do you do what you do, Esteban?" The question was meant to surprise him. It didn't. He simply smiled.

"You think I play tricks, Mr. Mongo?"

"What I think doesn't matter."

"Then why you ask?"

"I'm curious."

"Then I answer." Again he lifted his hands, stared at them. "The body make music, Mr. Mongo. A healthy body make good music. I can hear through my hands. A sick body make bad music. My hands . . . I can make music good, make it sound like I know it should." He paused, shook his head. "Not easy to explain, Mr. Mongo."

"Why were you upset near the end of the project, Esteban?"

"Who told you I upset?"

"Dr. Mason. She said you were having a difficult time affecting the enzymes."

He took a long time to answer. "I don't think it right to talk about it."

"Talk about what, Esteban? How can I help you if you won't level with me?"

"I know many things about people, but I don't speak about them," he said almost to himself. "What make me unhappy have nothing to do with my trouble."

"Why don't you let me decide that?"

Again, it took him a long time to answer. "I guess it no make difference any longer."

"*What* doesn't make a difference any longer, Esteban?"

He looked up at me. "Dr. Edmonston was dying. Of cancer."

"Dr. Edmonston told you that?"

"Oh, no. Dr. Edmonston no tell anyone. He not want anyone to know. But I know."

"How, Esteban? How did you know?"

He pointed to his eyes. "I see, Mr. Mongo. I see the aura. Dr. Edmonston's aura brown-black. Flicker. He dying of cancer. I know he have five, maybe six more months to live." He lowered his eyes and shook his head. "I tell him I know. I tell him I want to help. He get very mad at me. He tell me to mind my own business. That upset me. It upset me to be around people in pain who no want my help."

My mouth was suddenly very dry. I swallowed hard. "You say you *saw* this aura?" I remembered the Kirlian photographs Janet Mason had shown me and I could feel a prickling at the back of my neck.

"Yes," Morales said simply. "I see aura."

"Can you see *anybody's* aura?" I had raised my voice a few notches so that the guard could hear. I shot a quick glance in his direction. He was smirking, which meant we were coming in loud and clear. That was good . . . maybe.

"Usually. Mostly I see sick people's aura, because that what I look for."

"Can you see mine?" I asked.

His eyes slowly came up and met mine. They held. It was a moment of unexpected, embarrassing intimacy, and I knew what he was going to say before he said it.

Esteban Morales didn't smile. "I can see yours, Mr. Mongo," he said softly.

He was going to say something else but I cut him off. I was feeling a little light-headed and I wanted to get the next part of the production over as quickly as possible. I could sympathize with Dr. Edmonston.

I pressed the guard and he reluctantly admitted he'd overheard the last part of our conversation. Then I asked him to get Garth.

Garth arrived looking suspicious. Garth always looks suspicious when I send for him. He nodded briefly at Esteban, then looked at me. "What's up, Mongo?"

"I just want you to sit here for a minute and listen to something."

"Mongo, I've got *reports!*"

I ignored him and he leaned back against the bars of the cell and began to tap his foot impatiently. I turned to Esteban Morales. "Esteban," I said quietly, "will you tell my brother what an aura is?"

Morales described the human aura and I followed up by describing the Kirlian photographs Janet Mason had shown me: what they were, and what they purported to show. Garth's foot continued its monotonous tapping. Once he glanced at his watch.

"Esteban," I said, "how does my brother look? I mean his aura."

"Oh, he fine," Esteban said, puzzled. "Aura a good, healthy pink."

"What about me?"

Morales dropped his eyes and shook his head mutely.

The foot-tapping in the corner had stopped. Suddenly Garth was beside me, gripping my arm. "Mongo, what the hell is this all about?"

"Just listen, Garth. I need a witness." I took a deep breath, then started in again on Morales. "Esteban," I whispered, "I asked you a question. Can you see my aura? Damn it, if you can, say so! I may be able to help you. If you can see my aura you have to say so!"

Esteban Morales slowly lifted his head. His eyes were filled with pain. "I cannot help you, Mr. Mongo."

Garth gripped my arm even tighter. "Mongo—"

"I'm all right, Garth. Esteban, tell me what it is you see."

The healer took a long, shuddering breath. "You are dying, Mr. Mongo. Your mind is sharp, but your body is—" He gestured toward me. "Your body is the way it is. It is the same inside. I cannot change that. I cannot help. I am sorry."

"Don't be," I said. I was caught between conflicting emotions, exultation at coming up a winner and bitterness at what Morales' statement was costing me. I decided to spin the wheel again. "Can you tell about how many years I have left, Esteban?"

"Five," Morales said in a choked voice, "Maybe six or seven. Why you make me say these things?"

I spun on Garth. I hoped I had my smile on straight. "Well, brother, how does Esteban's opinion compare with the medical authorities'?"

Garth shook his head. His voice was hollow. "Your clients get a lot for their money, Mongo."

"How about getting hold of a lawyer and arranging a bail hearing for Esteban. Like tomorrow?"

"I can get a public defender in here, Mongo," Garth said in the same tone. "But you haven't proved anything."

"Was there an autopsy done on Edmonston?"

"Yeah. The report is probably filed away by now. What about it?"

"Well, that autopsy will show that Edmonston was dying of cancer, and I can prove that Esteban knew it. I just gave you a demonstration of what he can do."

"It still doesn't prove anything," Garth said tightly. "Mongo, I wish it did."

"All I want is Esteban out on bail—and the cops dusting a few more corners. All I want to show is that Esteban knew Edmonston was dying, fast. It wouldn't have made any sense for Esteban to kill him. And I think I can bring in a surprise character witness. A heavy. Will you talk to the judge?"

"Yeah, I'll talk to the judge." Again, Garth gripped my arm. "You sure you're all right? You're white as chalk."

"I'm all right. Hell, we're all dying, aren't we?" My laugh turned short and bitter. "When you've been dying as long as I have, you get used to it. I need a phone."

I didn't wait for an answer. I walked quickly out of the cell and used the first phone I found to call the senator. Then I hurried outside and lit a cigarette. It tasted lousy.

Two days later Garth popped his head into my office. "He confessed. I thought you'd want to know."

I pushed aside the criminology lecture on which I'd been working. "Who confessed?"

Garth came in and closed the door. "Johnson, of course. He came into his office this morning and found us searching through his records. He just managed to ask to see the warrant before he folded. Told the whole story twice, once for us and once for the DA. What an amateur!"

I was vaguely surprised to find myself monumentally disinterested. My job had been finished the day before when the senator and I had walked in a back door of the courthouse to meet with Garth and the sitting judge. Forty-five minutes later Esteban Morales had been out on bail and on his way to meet with Linda Younger. Rolfe Johnson had been my prime suspect five minutes after I'd begun to talk to him, and there'd been no doubt in my mind that the police would nail him, once they decided to go to the bother.

"What was his motive?" I asked.

"Johnson's forte was business. No question about it. He just couldn't cut it as a murderer . . . or a doctor. He had at least a dozen malpractice suits filed against him. Edmonston was getting tired of having a flunky as a partner. Johnson was becoming an increasing embarrassment and was hurting the medical side of the business. Patients, after all, are the bottom line. Edmonston had the original practice and a controlling interest in their corporation. He was going to cut Johnson adrift, and Johnson found out about it.

"Johnson, with all his troubles, knew that he was finished if Edmonston dissolved the partnership. When Dr. Mason told him about Morales, Johnson had a notion that he just might be able to use the situation to his own advantage. After all, what better patsy than an illiterate psychic healer?"

"Johnson sent the message to Esteban, didn't he?"

"Sure. First, he admitted lying to Edmonston about Esteban giving drugs to one of Edmonston's patients, then he told how he maneuvered Edmonston into filing a complaint. He figured the university would bail Esteban out, and a motive would have been established. It wasn't much, but Johnson didn't figure he needed much. After all, he assumed Esteban was crazy and that any jury would know he was crazy. He picked his day, then left a message in the name of Edmonston for Esteban to come to the offices that night. He asked Edmonston to come forty-five minutes early, and he killed him, then waited for Esteban to show up to take the rap. Pretty crude, but then Johnson isn't that imaginative."

"Didn't the feedback from the patients give him any pause?"

Garth laughed. "From what I can gather from his statement, Johnson never paid any attention to the reports. Edmonston did most of the interviewing."

"There seems to be a touch of irony there," I said dryly.

"There seems to be. Well, I've got a car running downstairs. Like I said, I thought you'd want to know."

"Thanks, Garth."

He paused with his hand on the knob and looked at me for a long time. I knew we were thinking about the same thing, words spoken in a jail cell, a very private family secret shared by two brothers. For a moment I was afraid he was going to say something that would embarrass both of us. He didn't.

"See you," Garth said.

"See you."

PATRICK O'KEEFFE

Murder by Dream

My cousin Janice first told me about her strange flower dreams one afternoon on our way home from high school. As we passed the florist next to Sitwell's drug store, she remarked dolefully, "I'm going to hear of a death in the family."

"What makes you say that?"

"I dreamed of flowers last night, and every time I dream of them I always get news of a death in the family soon afterward, on one side or the other."

"Maybe a coincidence or two," I suggested.

"It's been happening for the past few years. I've never known it to be wrong."

Next day a telegram brought word from San Francisco that Grandma Barrow had passed away. Six months later my father died of a heart attack, and Janice told me that she had dreamed of flowers the night before.

His untimely death was the cause of my going to sea. Mother was a semi-invalid, and I had neither the competence nor the desire to take over my father's wholesale paint business. My ambitions lay in radio, and if father had lived I would have gone to college and studied radio engineering. The business was sold and, putting my few years of amateur-radio experience to professional use, I passed for a radio-telegraph operator's license and took the first opening aboard ship. On my salary I managed to keep mother in our home and put a little aside for future college fees.

I used to see Janice between voyages, since she lived only a few blocks away, and during that seagoing period I happened to be at home prior to the deaths of Uncle Charlie, Aunt Laura, and cousin Joe's wife, who was killed in a plane collision. On each occasion Janice told me that she had had her usual flowers dream. I was at sea when Grandpa Barrow died, and also when cousin George drowned, but Janice mentioned in her letters that she had dreamed of flowers preceding the news of each death.

Until Janice met Bob, I think I was the only one in whom she confided about her flower dreams, for we were like brother and sister, each of us being an only child. She was reluctant to tell anyone else in or connected with the family, for fear of creating anxiety when she had the dream, especially if some member happened to be sick. The only person I mentioned them to was a Jesuit missionary we once had as an intransit passenger to Panama. I told him about the dreams during a chat on preternatural and supernatural phenomena and manifestations.

"Do you think Janice's dreams have any meaning or purpose?" I asked.

He was a large, elderly man with a venerable brown beard that swept a wide chest as he shook his head dubiously.

"If they were of divine origin their meaning or design would perhaps be less obscure, more easily interpreted. I see none in your cousin's dreams. We must never forget, though, that dreams may be of evil origin. Satan seeks souls in ways other than by pact. As long as we don't allow dreams to influence us, don't make a superstition of them, they are powerless to harm us."

When I repeated the Jesuit's words to Janice, she said, "I'm naturally upset each time I have the dream, waiting to see who has died. I can't help being affected like that."

"You believe in the dream, so that amounts to making a superstition of it," I said.

"But Phil, it's never been wrong. I can't help but believe in it. I don't see how just believing it will come true can harm me."

"I don't either," I said. Nevertheless, I had an uneasy feeling about her dreams. There was something unnatural in them. I wished she did not have them.

It was about a year later that Janice and Bob made their honeymoon cruise. Janice had met Bob when the firm he worked for audited the books at the bank soon after Janice had taken a job in the Trust Department. Janice brought him home for supper that same weekend, so rapidly had they discovered each other, and within a year they were married. They agreed on a summer honeymoon cruise, and Janice wanted it to be with me. I was then chief radio officer of the new Crescent liner running to Bermuda, the Leeward Islands and down to Trinidad.

Southbound, we had a full passenger list, roughly a hundred and fifty. Janice and Bob would have been no less happy if the ship had been empty, for all they wanted was each other's company. However, they did not act the inseparable newlyweds, but gave more than their share of time toward helping others to enjoy the cruise by taking part in all the games and competitions. Bob, who was something of an acrobat and liked to show off his talent, won first prize on amateur night; Janice placed second in the bridge tournament. To all on board they were Janice and Bob rather than Mr. and Mrs. Blake. Scarcely anyone could fail to be charmed by Janice on sight, with her friendly round face and warm dark eyes; and no one glancing from her to Bob's cheerful smooth-skinned face and head of tossed light hair ever needed to wonder what she saw in him.

Nothing happened to mar Janice's enjoyment of the cruise until it was more than half over and we were returning north among the islands. Janice and Bob used to take part in the usual evening dancing for a while, and then Janice would help to make up a foursome at bridge. Bob was a rabid poker fan, with little taste for bridge, and southbound he had managed to get up an odd game or two with husbands whose wives had not already drafted them for the bridge tables. In Trinidad, however, a number of oilmen from the Venezuelan fields joined the ship as passengers to New York. Flush with vacation pay, and poker their chief evening pastime, they were exactly what Bob would have ordered.

The bridge games generally ended in the lounge toward midnight, but the poker sessions in the smoking-room sometimes lasted until the early hours of the morning, although Bob usually quit soon after Janice had looked in on her way to their cabin. Once, it was almost two o'clock before he appeared, saying that he was well ahead and didn't like to quit without giving the others a chance to win some of it back. Janice laughingly told him that the next time he came home late, she would be the outraged wife and lock him out.

The next night, when it was almost two-thirty and Bob had not yet come in, Janice got out of bed and bolted the door, and then lay down again and resumed reading a ship's library novel in anticipation of some fun at Bob's expense when he found himself locked out.

Bob, however, was long in coming, and Janice fell asleep with the book in her hands and the bed light on. It was after seven when she awoke. Her first thought was of Bob. She was puzzled that he had not aroused her. Although she was a sound sleeper, a knock or two on the door would have wakened her. She concluded that Bob, finding the door locked and her apparently asleep, had chosen not to disturb her and had perhaps gone to one of the oilmen's cabins to sleep on a settee.

Then suddenly she was terror-stricken. During the night she had dreamed of flowers. She had seen them in a vase in a window. She turned out at once and dressed, frantically hoping that Bob would come in any minute and start washing and shaving for breakfast. By the time the first gong sounded, he was still absent. Janice hurried out on deck, clinging to a hope that Bob was sleeping late in one of the poker players' cabins. She saw a group of the oilmen chatting by the rails on the promenade deck. She rushed up to them and asked where Bob was. They did not know, nor had he slept in any of their cabins.

Janice turned to other passengers. None had seen Bob that morning. Janice came running up to the radio room in stark panic.

"Something's happened to Bob," she moaned.

I got her calmed down, and she told me about her dream and that Bob was missing.

"He's probably keeping out of sight somewhere to pay you back for locking him out," I said.

That was really wishful thinking, but it wasn't without good grounds. Janice and Bob had played pranks on each other during the cruise, as when Bob put sand in Janice's bed and she had responded by getting the bedroom steward to shut off the water when Bob was soaped up under the shower.

"He'll have to show his face this forenoon," I said. "There's a boat and fire drill at ten o'clock."

Bob was missing from boat drill. Janice came running to the radio room again, almost hysterical.

"He must have fallen overboard," she wailed.

"Not a chance in this weather," I told her. "He's hiding somewhere. Wait here till I come back."

I left her with the third radio officer and went straight to the captain's quarters, desperately hoping I was right about Bob. Old Blagdon decided that if it was all a joke on Bob's part, it was more than time to end it. He had Bob paged over the loudspeakers. There was no response. The captain ordered the chief officer to make a quick search of the ship. He summoned one of the oilmen to his office. The oilman told us that the poker game had ended soon after four o'clock, but that Bob had dropped out around three-thirty and gone to his cabin.

"He didn't sleep in it," the captain said. "He's missing."

The oilman, a skinny, sunbrowned Oklahoman in khaki shorts, looked concerned. After a moment's thought, he asked, "Do you know if his wife locked him out of their cabin last night?"

I answered him. "Yes. She did it in fun."

"Then maybe that's it. He told us she'd said she would next time he stayed out late, but he said he knew a way to fool her. His idea was to lower himself down the ship's side from the rails and slide feet first through the bathroom porthole. He said he'd already given it half a try when she wasn't around and had found it easy enough. He meant to walk in on her, leaving her to wonder how he'd managed it. We thought it a pretty risky stunt, even for a double-jointed guy like him. I guess he must have slipped, or something."

If the oilman's guess was correct, then Bob had been overboard for nearly eight hours up to that moment. Yet he was a powerful swimmer, and if he conserved his strength, he could keep afloat in that warm, calm sea for many hours to come. On the dark side were the possibilities that he might have injured himself against the hull as he slipped, or perhaps he had got foul of the propellers. Sharks prowled those waters too.

Captain Blagdon decided that the prospects of finding Bob still afloat were good enough to warrant turning the ship back. He was a hardheaded old seagull in some ways, but he had a human streak running through him like a blue strand in a manilla rope. I believe he would have put the ship about solely out of sympathy for Janice, even if he had felt there was no hope of finding Bob. He did not even wait for the chief officer's report on the ship search, which proved negative.

I hurried back to the radio room, where Janice sat waiting for me in her gay cruise blouse and pink shorts but with anguish in her dark eyes. When I broke the news to her, she moaned, "My dream!" and collapsed.

I sent for the ship's doctor and a stewardess, and when Janice recovered I went below with them to her cabin. Before he left, the doctor gave her a tranquilizer. After he'd gone, Janice cried piteously to me:

"It's all my fault. I'll never see Bob again."

It was Bob I blamed to myself. The row of portholes to Section "C" cabins was just below the rails on the port side. To worm in through one of them a man merely had to climb over the rails, grasp the lowest one, and lower his legs to the opening, thrust them in and slide through feet first, shifting his hand grip from the rail down to the edge of the fishplate and letting go as soon as his shoulders were safely inside. The ship not being air-conditioned, the ports were kept open in tropical waters.

I had known of more than one steward to slip into a cabin that way for some passenger who had lost his key when another one was not immediately available, but only in port and on the offshore side where nothing worse than a ducking was risked, and never at sea, during darkness and with the ship under way. Bob must have been crazy.

It was still light when we approached the vicinity of what was estimated to have been the ship's position at the time that Bob dropped overboard. There was no shortage of lookouts. Passengers in all kinds of bright cruise regalia lined the rails on both sides, although the merriment had been suspended when the orchestra had put aside the instruments with the first word that Bob was missing overboard. I posted myself high up on the radar mast.

The conditions for sighting a man in the water were favorable. The sea was unrippled, as if glassed over, gray at that late hour of the day. Yet while a man's head would stand out like a dark polka dot at close hand, from even a short distance it could be as inconspicuous as a bubble.

With the approximate position of Bob's likely whereabouts as a center, Captain Blagdon cruised in widening circles until long after dark, with searchlights and spotlights waving beams from the bridge like the feelers of some lost marine monster. Not so much as a piece of driftwood or ship garbage was sighted. Gloom spread over the entire ship, and when Captain Blagdon swung her back to her original course, even the most carping among the passengers would have conceded that the captain had done his utmost. It was like turning away from a new grave.

Captain Blagdon, however, was not without hope, and he went below with me to Janice's cabin to try to instill it in Janice. She had not stirred out on deck during the search, convinced that her dream had arisen from Bob's death. She had changed into a dark dress with a black belt.

"You mustn't give up hope for a long while yet," the captain said. "Bob may very well have been picked up by some vessel. If it's a small one with no radio, you won't hear from Bob until she calls at her next port, and that may be halfway round the world."

But Janice only wept, and when the captain had gone, she sobbed to me, "I could have told him about my dream, but he wouldn't have understood it as you and I do."

"I don't understand it your way, Janice. It could mean someone else in the family and not Bob. It could be wrong, too, and not mean a death, not anyone's death."

"Phil, in your heart you don't mean that. You're trying to be kind, like everyone else, trying to pacify me with false hope."

"I do mean it, and it's not false hope. You can't see it because you're making a superstition of your dream. It's harming you, blinding you to reason."

"I can't suffer any worse harm."

I could make no impression on Janice. She mourned Bob as dead. She kept to her cabin all next day, scarcely touching the tempting trays brought by the stewardesses, refusing to let in passengers wishing to show their sympathy and express their hopes for Bob's safety. I spent most of my spare time with her. Between fits of weeping she lay motionless on the bed or sat in a chair and gazed fixedly at the bolt on the closed door. At intervals she would moan, "Why did I do it? Why couldn't I have seen what would happen to him?"

Before I turned in late that evening, I went down to Janice's cabin again. There was a tray of untouched food on the dresser, the coffee now cold. I had hardly closed the door before Janice cried:

"Oh, Phil, I can't go on living without Bob."

I had no fear that Janice, as a devout Catholic, would damn her soul for all eternity by taking her own life. "Janice," I pleaded, "don't go on brooding and starving yourself. You'll bring on a nervous breakdown, and wouldn't that be a fine state for Bob to find you in?"

"Please don't torture me, Phil. I'll never see Bob again in this world. Phil, I'm losing my mind."

There was a strange look in Janice's sunken and red-rimmed eyes, and it frightened me. Perhaps she was really going out of her mind. I felt desperate, helpless. The faintest hope that Bob was still alive might help to keep her mind in balance until the first shock had passed, even though the hope turned out to be false; but it was impossible to force it past the barrier of her dream. It seemed to me that the only thing able to save Janice's sanity would be word that Bob had been picked up, and it would have to come soon.

Before I left I said, "Janice, try to get a good night's sleep. You need it badly. There may be good news for you tomorrow."

She lay on the bed, staring up at the deckhead, and did not seem to hear me, but she answered my "Good night, Janice," as I closed the door.

About seven o'clock the next morning I received a radiogram that threw me into wild joy. It was from Bob. He had been picked up by an auxiliary trading schooner, without radio. He had been unable to get word to us until the vessel had berthed in San Juan.

I did not stop to ring for the bellboy. I rushed below to deliver the message myself. I knocked on Janice's door. I knocked again, louder. There was no response. Thinking that Janice might finally have fallen into heavy sleep, I opened the door and peered inside.

There was no sign of Janice. The bathroom door was open; I called out, but there was no response. Thinking hopefully that Janice was at last beginning to recover from her crushing grief and had gone up on deck, I was about to withdraw when I spotted the envelope. It was wedged between the mirror above the little dressing-table and the bulkhead. The sight of it chilled the joy in my heart—Janice missing, a note left behind. I stepped inside and read the name on the envelope, ship stationery. It was mine. I was stricken with anguish by the note inside.

"Good-bye, dear Phil. I've gone to join Bob. Lovingly, Janice."

Janice had placed a chair under the bathroom porthole to stand on. She had not only set out to join Bob, but had also chosen the same point of departure. I knew it would be futile to have the ship turned back a second time. Janice could not swim.

Possibly a Satanic chuckle followed Janice as she started on her last journey. Her dream had not foreshadowed news of Bob's death but of her own, and in diabolical fashion had brought it about. I prayed that the Recording Angel would mercifully be able to write, "While of unsound mind." To me, no less than if Janice had been driven by human agency into committing her last act, it was murder.